www.sevenstonesofpower.com

THE SAPPHIRE RING

ANDY STONE

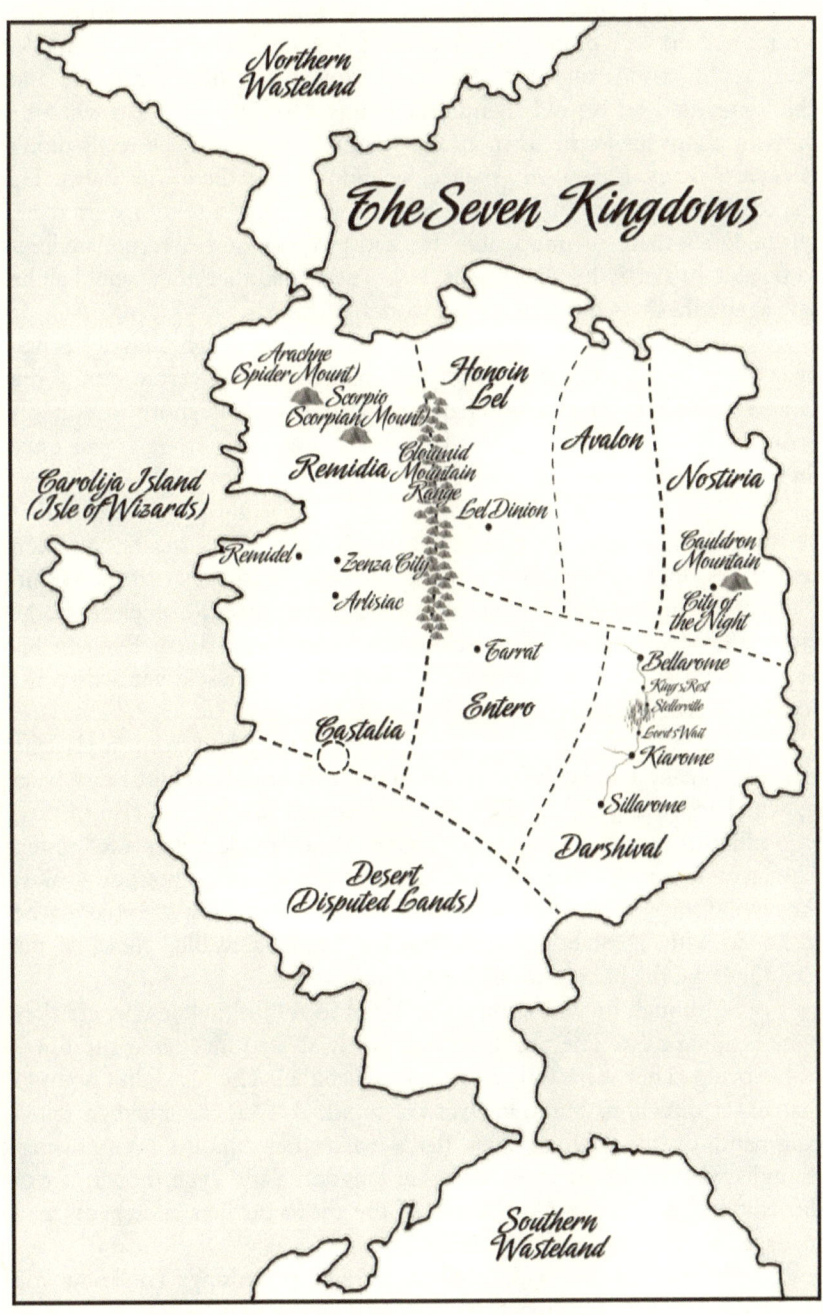

The Seven Kingdoms

Prologue: Light of a New Day

The light shone through Bern's bedroom window. It had been a week since the new moon had come and gone. He had watched the moon every night, wondering what Alaric was doing. The life of his wife and children rested on his old friend's shoulders. He always felt sad when he thought about his home town and his family. As much as he really didn't have too many friends in Arsiliac he didn't wish them any harm. He wanted nothing more than to return home and make sure they were okay, but he knew that was impossible. He had too many other responsibilities to be able to satisfy his own needs. If he succeeded then they would all be safe again; that was the goal he was working towards.

Bern rubbed his freshly shaved chin. The rough shaves he had been given in the army were nothing compared those given to him in the Grand Cathedral. His brown hair had also been cut short to suit his position. It was a luxury he wasn't sure he was going to get again once they left Castalia.

There were other perks to being the General of the Alliance that he hadn't had time to appreciate before. A team of masseuses had been sent to his private chambers on his second day of residence in the Grand Cathedral. They worked out all the knots and strains in his thick set body. He couldn't remember his muscles ever feeling so relaxed. Even in his previous life as a farmer he would go to bed with muscle pains that just seemed to sort themselves out by morning.

He was starting to get nervous again. They had been in Castalia too long but he had achieved everything that he needed. Linus had been crowned and was officially the new High Chancellor. He had also offered a good number of soldiers to the Alliance which made things a lot easier. The army had more than doubled in size from that which stood against the Evil One's fake army in Avalon. They were now a force to be reckoned with. Bern hoped now that his numbers rivalled those of the Evil One, the final battle would be coming soon.

Although he was waiting for Alaric to return he knew where they were heading next. The prophecy had gently started tugging at the fibres of his being. They were to head north to Remidel. The tug didn't point in that exact direction, but Bern wasn't stupid. A Dark Knight had taken command of the city, at least that's what the rumours were saying. Remidia was closed off from the other kingdoms and even though it was difficult to pass the borders some of the more devious merchants had managed to find their way through.

The words he had received weren't promising. He knew the dwarf Gilgi was in fact the Dark Knight Dargoz and he wished he had known that before they had left Avalon. If he did then there was a good chance he could have avoided his next mission. Although the thought was in his head, he that it wasn't true. There was nothing he could have done to avoid the next stage of his journey. All he had to do was to wait for Alaric to arrive. He could only hope that it was soon. He didn't know how long he could keep the army in Castalia. It was good that the soldiers had a chance to rest, but it would only be a matter of time before they started getting into mischief. It seemed to be a recurring problem he had to find a solution for.

As if by pure will alone Alaric suddenly appeared in his room. Bern should have been surprised, but not much took him by surprise anymore. He had seen too many things to be shocked by a mere sudden arrival. He had a feeling Alaric would be arriving, that was a bonus for being tied into his fate.

There was something very different about the man standing before him and not in appearance. His blonde hair was still cut short and he wore the same black leather coat, jerkin and trousers from when he had last seen him. Although his eyes looked green Bern thought he could see a strange tinge around them.

It was his demeanour that had changed. There was a power in his presence that had only been on the verge of existing before. Bern wasn't sure what had happened since Alaric had left Jarrat, but it was definitely something life-changing.

"Hello Bern!" his voice was cold, not like his friend at all, reconfirming that something had indeed changed inside him.

"Hello Alaric. Have a seat, it seems as though we have much to discuss." Bern offered him a chair by the window.

A cool breeze blew in which did little to affect the heat of the day. For the moment Bern was happy with small mercies. He really didn't like the intense heat of Castalia and was glad for the relief. Alaric didn't seem to notice the heat or the freshness of the breeze. He seemed focused on something in the distance, but when Bern looked he couldn't see anything interesting.

Bern though it was going to be a good day when he woke up with the sun, now he wasn't so sure. There was definitely something wrong with Alaric and he didn't know if he had the courage to find out what it was.

"I am glad to see you arrived back here safely." Bern continued when Alaric didn't speak. "I trust all went well on the mountain."

"That is a very long story. The short version is that we made our time restraint and we now have the Opal stone. There will be time to regale you with the story, but now isn't that time." His voice was still emotionless.

"What is it I can do for you?" Bern asked.

That was a tough question. For the moment Bern could do nothing for him. Alaric needed to speak with Heryion or at least the entity of the strange little man who resided inside Bern. He doubted Heryion was its real name. He was sure there had been many names in the past as it crossed from vessel to vessel. The problem was that it only appeared when it was good and ready. There didn't seem to be any way to summon it. Even Alaric had no idea how he could bring the entity out.

"Don't worry Alaric, I'm still here." Bern's voice had changed and Alaric knew it was Heryion.

"What is your real name?" the coldness had left his voice. It wasn't the original question he wanted to ask, but the words had forced their way out of his mouth.

"That isn't the question that you really wanted to ask, is it?" Heryion wasn't going to give that away. "Let's focus on what's important. Bern is getting strong. I won't be able to control him for much longer. He is starting to merge with my presence. He can remember some of the things I did in the past. In fact he is remembering more and more each day. I have never experienced anything like this before. Normally by now I have overcome the vessel and completely taken over, but I digress. What is it you need from me?"

"Kahn is still alive. I need to know where he is." Alaric got straight to the point. "You were the last one to see him alive."

"The last time I saw him he was flying above the Mountain Chest peak. I used him to destroy the Orb of Hazyra. I'm pretty sure I have told you this story?"

The memory returned to Alaric. He remembered the story Heryion had told him outside the City of Night. He also recalled that Heryion had told him Kahn was the last of the Black Dragon Clan, but that was not the case. He thought about saying something, but then decided to save his breath. Now Kahn was not only the last of the Black Dragon clan, but the last of the dragons.

"So you think he is still there?" Alaric asked.

"That's where his lair is, so that's where I would start looking for him."

Alaric silently cursed. The path he had set Eldred and the others on would lead them very close to Khan's lair. There was nothing he could do about. That was the path the prophecy wanted them to take and they would have to fend for themselves. There was a good chance that Kahn would be hibernating after his ordeal with Heryion.

"Now that really isn't the question you came here to ask me. You better get to the point soon or lose this opportunity."

"You're right." Alaric still sounded cold. There was no emotion to his voice. "I don't really know how to explain this, but I'm looking for something or someone."

"So what do you need me to do?" Heryion didn't like what he was hearing.

"They're not in the plain of existence; I guess that is the best way to explain it. I have been trying for the past few days to reach this place, but I can't. It is like when you enter someone else's consciousness."

Heryion thought for a moment. He was intrigued with what Alaric was saying. He had indeed thought of the theory before, but he didn't think it was possible.

"I can't help you with that one." Heryion admitted. Alaric's face dropped and Heryion wasn't sure if he was sad or angry. Something had definitely changed within him, Heryion knew that. The Opal stone had unlocked something inside his head. He wasn't sure if it was a good thing or a bad thing. Things weren't quite working out the way he expected. "There is someone who might be able to help you."

"Where do I find them?" Alaric asked quickly.

"There is a small island on the other side of the world. It is sparsely populated, nothing like our world. On the island there is an old man by the name of Mesula. If anyone is able to help you he will. The only problem you have is getting there. On the off chance you can find someone to captain a boat, it'll take you half a year at best to get there." Heryion explained.

"Don't worry about that. I'll be able to make it in good time. If you get a chance, say goodbye to Bern for me." And with that Alaric disappeared again.

At least it seemed as though Alaric knew what he was doing. It had been a long time since he had seen such purpose in his eyes. It could only be a good thing. His shortness and coldness, however, was a different story altogether. It was that thought that was thick in his mind as Heryion faded into the background.

Bern looked around in surprise. He was sure he was just talking to Alaric. The man had appeared in such a hurry there was no reason why he shouldn't have left in much the same way, but it was strange that he didn't say goodbye. He felt as though there was a conversation missing. It was like he was looking into a thick mist. He knew there was something on the other side, but it was too obscured for him to make out. He had a sneaky suspicion the entity that resided inside his body had made an appearance. Before too much longer Bern was going to have to summon the entity and work out exactly who or what it was. For the meantime he had his own mission to work on.

It was time for the army to move north. He was excited at the prospect of returning to his homeland. To add to his excitement he would be able to bring the army close to Arsiliac on their way to Remidel. Given the chance he was going to make a detour to see his family. That was something he had been dreaming of for a long time.

There were still a few things left to do in Castalia and as soon as they were finished the army would be on the move again. That was enough motivation for Bern to forget about Alaric and concentrate on the job in front of him.

***

"What do you mean that we need to shut down the outer towns?" Hawthorne didn't like what he was hearing.

The prince had thought Gilgi was supporting his cause when he moved the army of dwarves back to Remidel with him, but now he wasn't so sure. He had showed deference all the way until they reached the capital. Once he had met with the king he didn't really seem to care about Hawthorne. As much as the prince was used that sort of behaviour he found it quite disturbing. More disturbing was that Faxon was listening to everything Gilgi said. It was almost like the dwarf was now running the kingdom and that wasn't right at all.

"We need to bring all our soldiers towards the capital." Gilgi spoke on Faxon's behalf.

Each time the Dwarf answered a question for his father it made his blood boil. He wanted nothing more than to reach across the table and throttle him, but that wasn't an option. His father supported Gilgi and for the moment Hawthorne would have to bite his lip and bide his time.

"The families won't want to leave their homes. We can't make them just pack up and leave." Hawthorne did his best to protest his peoples' cause.

"The families can stay where they are for all that I care. All I want are the solders and any men able to swing a sword or shoot an arrow." Gilgi smiled an evil smile. He knew he was provoking Hawthorne and he liked it.

"You can't expect the men to leave their families and their homes. What are you trying to gain?" Hawthorne couldn't believe what he was hearing.

"Have you not heard the rumours? There is an army amassing in Castalia and it marches on Remidia. If we are going to survive then we need to fortify our position and the strongest position we have is the capital. Now if we have to sacrifice some of the outer town and villages then so be it."

Hawthorne had to admit that he did have a point. In fact if it wasn't Gilgi offering the idea then he might have gone along with the plan, but that wasn't going to happen. He would fight Gilgi as much as he could. He knew his father would side with the Dwarf and there was nothing he could do to change his mind. The only thing he gained by arguing was time. Each second he stole from Gilgi was a second he gained in returning control of the Kingdom to his father.

"They are just rumours. There is no reason for us to fear the Alliance. They are not coming to invade. Sure we left them at Avalon, but that doesn't mean they have forsaken us. If the army is indeed marching into Remidia then it's for completely different reasons." Hawthorne wasn't going to give up.

Gilgi was happy enough with the argument the way it was going. For the moment the prince seemed to have the advantage, at least that is the way the other nobles in the room would see it, but when it was said and done Gilgi would win. That would prove more to the others than just having another victory. Once Faxon decreed that the soldiers were to be brought to the capital then they would know who was in favour.

"Oh, how nice it would be to live in ignorance?" Hawthorne couldn't believe what he was hearing and that fact that his father was still saying nothing. "They are no mere rumours. The Alliance has taken Castalia and it'll only be a matter of time before they march on Remidel. We need to protect ourselves now and that's exactly what I'm going to do." Gilgi's voice had remained calm but now he started to raise it.

Hawthorne wanted nothing more than to stand from the table, walk to where Gilgi was sitting next to his father and strike the dwarf. He wanted to keep striking him until he ran out of energy. Something was not right and had not been for a long time.

Gilgi sat in his rightful seat by Faxon's side. Surely there were others in the room that also noticed the change in their king. It was enough to enrage Hawthorne, but he kept his anger under control. He took a deep breath before he spoke again.

"What about the stories coming in from the outposts where there have been attacks from the Evil One's minions." Hawthorn wasn't watching Gilgi as he spoke. If he had he would have noticed the Dwarf cringe at the mention of the 'Evil One'. "We can't pull the soldiers out of these areas."

Gilgi slammed his fist down on the table. He was sick of the conversation. He was happy to belittle the prince in front of the council members present, but now he risked losing his edge. Hawthorne made a very good point and as much as the king was on Gilgi's side there was a chance for a revolt if Hawthorne could gain enough support. It was better for him to end the conversation than risk losing face.

"We are finished here. The king has made his decision. This is just so you know what we're doing. It isn't up for debate." Gilgi ended the meeting.

Hawthorne wanted to continue, but he knew there wasn't any point. His father had not said a word since the meeting had started. He was no longer the man Hawthorne remembered and there was nothing he could do to get through. In the end he decided that he would have to take a different approach. The scouts had reported that Bern was now in command of the army, but Hawthorne wasn't sure he believed it. By all accounts Jarwe was still alive and he couldn't believe the general would relinquish his command. Either way he needed to get word to the Alliance and explain the situation in Remidia, and he needed to do it quickly.

"I accept your command," he looked at his father as he spoke. "I will go and let the barracks know there will be an influx of soldiers coming."

Without waiting for a response Hawthorne stood and left the room. He wanted to have the last word and didn't want to give Gilgi another chance to undermine him. There was much he had to do. Time was running short and he needed to get word to the Alliance. He would have to send his most trusted messenger if he was going to succeed. There were many who were now on Gilgi's side, but he still had men he trusted.

Hawthorne rushed through the halls of the palace deep in thought. He ignored the functionaries moving around him. He had to find Galt, the only man he could trust to take his message to Bern. The two had not left on great terms, but Hawthorne was sure if Bern was now the general he would do the right thing. He couldn't leave his homeland to ruin, regardless of what had happened in the past.

It was that thought that raced through his mind. He had been so sure that he was doing the right thing bringing the army back to Remidel. If it was indeed to be the ruin of his father's kingdom and his beloved homeland then there was no one to blame but himself. There was no way he was going to let that happen. He still had people loyal to him within the palace and there had to be a way to delay the message from reaching the outlying towns. There was so much for him to do and very little time.

***

Galt didn't want long after Hawthorne left his offices before he made his way to the stables. This was a job he would take care of personally. If Hawthorne felt it was important enough to make the request in person then it was important enough for Galt to undertake the task himself. He had been instructed not to open the letter, which had the royal seal, and that was exactly what he was not going to do. He knew well enough that if Hawthorne told him not to read it than he shouldn't. He wasn't in the habit of reading his client's notes, but sometimes curiosity and commonsense got the better of him. Usually he had to make sure the message or package he was transporting wouldn't put his men in danger. At least that was the excuse he used whenever he opened something.

What he was transporting was the least of his troubles. The first thing he had to do was to exit the city. The city had been locked down by order of the king. Normally he would have just used the prince's seal to leave, but he knew that wasn't an option. Of course there were ways out of the city without having to use the main gates, but they were becoming few and fair between. Those which hadn't already been shut down by the Royal Guards were controlled by thugs and thieves. A pouchful of gold was always persuasive, but that also wasn't an option. The money he would be paid for delivering the letter wouldn't cover the charge of exiting the city, let alone for his return.

He only had one option to escape. There was a stable towards the northern side of the city and at the back of the stable was a hole in the outer wall. This led to a small building on the outside of the city. The owner owed Galt a favour and now it was time to call it in. All he could hope was that the king had not already found it.

As he casually led his horse towards the stable he wanted nothing more than to open the letter. He craved to find out what was written. He knew that something wasn't right with the city and he was sure the answers were inside. He kept his head down has he walked, his horse limping behind him. The horse had been trained to walk with a limp, a skill that came in very handy.

The stable he was looking for was renowned for having the best farrier in town. If Galt was leading a lame horse there then no one would ask any questions. It might have been over kill, but he didn't want to take any chances. If someone recognised him then they might start asking questions and the last thing he needed was people spreading rumours about the stable. After all he did need to return to the city once he had delivered the message.

"Hello there Farrar!" Galt greeted when he arrived at the stable. "It seems as though the old mare has thrown a shoe again," it was a pretence for those who were within earshot.

"Well you better bring her inside then." Farrar returned.

It wasn't the first time Galt had brought the mare to him and he knew that there was nothing wrong with her. He wasn't overly happy with what it meant, but it wasn't a conversation he wanted to have on the street. The more people who came to use his little exit the greater chance he had of being caught and that meant a death sentence.

"The old mare looks fine Galt," Farrar said as he made a show of checking the mares hoof. "The shoe is still firmly in place." Instead of asking the question he shot Galt a look.

The gaze made Galt blush slightly. He was embarrassed at being caught out in his ruse. It was strange that Farrar didn't play along. Normally it was quite obvious why Galt brought the mare to his stable. That did nothing to instil any confidence in the old messenger.

"I need to get out of the city." Galt came straight to the point.

"Then why don't you go to the main gate. That is the best way to leave the city." He felt Farrar was being deliberately obtuse.

"You know that no one can get out through the main gates. I wouldn't be here if it wasn't an emergency."

"Keep quiet," Farrar looked around nervously. "Now I don't know what you're insinuating, but there is nothing for you here." He kept his voice low.

"I know you have a way out of the city, I have used it before and you know that. Now if you can let me through I'll be out of your way."

"Keep your voice down. There are spies everywhere. The soldiers are offering large rewards to any information on the secret gaps in the wall. I can't use it at the moment. People are watching me."

"I need to get out of the city and you are my only hope. I have a... an important message," he couldn't let anyone know who he was carrying it for. "I need to get out now and you owe me." He had hoped not to use his wildcard, but it seemed as though he didn't have a choice.

"I know what you did for me, but that is in the past. If I get caught then I'll end up on the hangman's gibbet. Now, please, you have to go," again he looked around nervously.

"I could have ended up on the gibbet too, but I didn't reveal your name. It would have been much easier for me to let them know your involvement, but I didn't. Now it is time for you to pay back the favour," Galt was starting to reflect Farrar's nervousness.

Suddenly there was a crashing sound that came from the front of the stable. The noise made both men jump, which in turn unsettled the mare. After their last conversation there could be no doubt who it was.

"The soldiers are already here. You have to let me go. I have to get my message through. It'll be better for you if you're alone. No one saw me come in here, so no one will know if I leave." There was little time left.

Farrar agonised over the decision for the split second that he had and then agreed to his request. There was no point in two of them joining the hangman and it seemed as though Farrar's cast had already been set. Galt had made a valid point, it would be less suspicious if he was alone.

There was another horse in the stable that needed shoeing, so he had an excuse for being there.

"Go and don't let me see you again. We are even and that is the end of it," Farrar waved him away as he moved towards the front of the stables.

Galt smiled before quickly moving towards the back of the stable to a room that contained a lot of tools and equipment. There was a large group of shelves in the middle of the back wall covered with heavy looking tools. It was the perfect guise for hiding the hole which led to the outside of the city. An ordinary looking hammer was the lever that set the wheels in motion. When he moved the hammer he heard the sound of cogs grinding and then the shelves started to slide across, revealing a gaping hole in the wall. He quickly ushered the mare through and then followed himself before the shelves started to slowly move back into place. He could only hope that they were back in place before the soldiers reached the back room. Farrar would see that they didn't, he was sure of that.

There was a small tunnel on the other side that was in complete darkness. If Galt hadn't been there before he wouldn't have known what he was looking for. There was a lever on the wall opposite the shelves which opened another seemingly innocent set of work shelves on the other side. Again the cogs started to grind when he pulled on the lever.

The mare was glad to be out of the darkness almost as much as Galt. They were now in a small room in another stable on the outside of the city. This stable had been abandoned for over a decade. When Farrar had discovered what he had at the back of his stable he had bought the stable on the other side. The last thing he wanted was to allow access to anyone. The owner didn't know what he had and was happy to sell for the inflated price that Farrar was offering. The farrier had recovered his cost and then some by smuggling people and goods into and out of the city. His price was much cheaper than the Royal Duties when it came to sensitive items, but his contraband prices were much more expensive.

Galt breathed a sigh of relief when the shelf locked back into place. He had made it. Now all he had to do was race towards Castalia and deliver the message. As much as it was a long and treacherous road he felt as though he had passed the hardest test. He smiled to himself as he lef his mare out of the front door.

The relief he felt quickly dissipated when he saw a group of six soldiers on horseback. It looked as though they had just arrived and Galt couldn't believe his luck. His mind raced with different excuses on how he could explain his appearance.

"Who are you?" the head soldier asked in a gruff voice.

There was something different about these soldiers, something that Galt couldn't quite put his finger on. They wore the armour of the city guard, but something wasn't quite right. It was as if they were colder than the other soldiers he met. For a moment a shot of terror passed through his body. He didn't think there was any excuse that could keep him alive. All he could do now was attempt to hide whatever secrets the letter contained.

"I am a traveller. I tried to gain entrance to the city yesterday, but was turned away at the gates. This was the first place I could find shelter." The lie was weak.

"There are inns closer to the gate." The soldier was trying to work out what he had been told. He knew that it didn't make sense. He didn't look like a man who had spent the night in an abandoned stable.

"I had my money pouch stolen from me. The outer city is in disarray," he had heard the rumours of the outer city and thought it would be a passable lie.

"I think you should empty your pockets," the soldier dismounted from his horse and drew his sword. He wasn't pleased with what he was hearing. "Let's see if your story checks out."

That wasn't what Galt wanted to hear. His gold pouch was safely tucked away in his chest pocket, soon to be revealed. Galt did his best to make a show of searching his pockets. In a moment of desperation he jumped on his horse and tried to make a dash for it. The mare only took a few steps before Galt was knocked from his horse by one of the soldiers. The mare took the opportunity to make a bolt for freedom. No one really cared about her, their concern was for the man gasping for air and writhing on the ground before them.

The lead soldier placed his foot on Galt's chest and pushed down. "Now let's try this again. What are you doing here?"

"Nothing. I told you already. I just stayed the night and now I'm going to move on." He knew there was no point telling the truth. His life had been forfeited the moment he had jumped on the horse, if not earlier. He wondered if he was doomed ever since he got out of bed that morning. He wished he had been able to say goodbye to his wife and children, but he rushed away once he received Hawthorne's message. All he did was send a message that he'd be away for a few weeks. That would be the last thing his family heard from him. It was best that he kept them out of it.

"Very well, we shall do this the hard way then." The other soldiers dismounted.

Two men grabbed Galt by the arms and dragged him to his feet. His head swam, still dazed from the fall. They pushed him up against the stable wall whilst another soldier stuck his sword into Galt's shoulder, effectively pinning him to the wall. Galt cried out in pain. He hoped that there would be someone nearby to help him, but he knew that wouldn't be the case.

"Now let's try this one more time?"

"I've told you everything, now please, let me be on my way." Even has he spoke a soldier started going through his pockets. First he came across the money pouch and then the letter with the royal seal.

"Look at this sir!" the soldier passed him both the letter and the pouch.

The lead soldier looked at the letter and then thought for a moment. Slowly he drew his dagger and slid it along the seal.

"No!" Galt cried out as the soldier read the letter.

"Well it seems as though we have a traitor in our midst. Who would have thought it was the prince himself? Well I guess Gilgi will be interested in reading this and I'm sure Faxon will have his son imprisoned," there was an evil sneer on his face.

"So this is the way it is? You have betrayed everything and everyone!" Galt coughed up blood as he tried to have some impact.

"Kill him!" the lead soldier turned away, still looking at the letter.

Galt's screams only lasted a moment as the soldiers plunged their swords into him. His last thoughts were of his family and he hoped they survived the storm.

Chapter 1: Unusual

Alaric had left in such a hurry the night before that no one really knew what to make of it. Something had changed in him; that was obvious to everyone, but no one knew what. No one spoke as they ate a small meal before going to sleep. It had been a strange old night and everyone much preferred it to be over than to prolong it with questions no one could answer. Viper was taking the death of the two dragons harder than everyone had expected. He sat as far away from the campfire as he could without losing the heat. As much as he could regulate his temperature he was still cold blooded. He couldn't let the others see that he was starting to weaken.

In the morning they were woken by a light drizzle in the sky. The trees kept most of the rain at bay, but they couldn't keep it all from reaching the ground. The weather did nothing to lift their sullen mood. No one would be surprised if the rain was simply mirroring their temperament. No one felt like moving on as they ate a small breakfast.

"What do we do now?" Alena finally asked as she finished her last mouthful.

There was a moment of silence as the question sunk in. They had all been thinking it, but no one had been prepared to give voice to it. They had relied on Alaric to make their decisions for so long that they were unsure who was now in control. It had been Eldred in the past so he was the logical decision.

Alena wore a simple brown cotton riding dress with green stockings. She felt good to be back inside a forest, even if it was nearing snow season. As an elf she had an affinity with the trees and felt uncomfortable if she was away from them for too long. Her time in the dungeons of Jarrat had been the worst in her life. She had brushed her long, blonde hair before she sat down to eat. For some reason that was important to her, more so that morning. If Alaric suddenly returned she wanted to make sure she looked her best. It was a silly fancy, but it was one she would continue until his return.

"I suppose we should follow Alaric's instructions. We need to travel to Lel Dinion." Eldred made no move to rise.

The elderly wizard looked especially aged that morning. He could have easily changed his appearance to that of a younger man, but he didn't want to waste the energy. With Alaric gone there was no telling what strains he would be forced to face. In his current state he wasn't sure he would even be able to defeat Viper if the serpentant decided to attack.

"Do we make straight for Lel Dinion or follow the path that Alaric set out for us? I know for one which way I want to go," Richmond added.

Again the question was met by silence. Alaric had told them to make for Lel Dinion via Haskar peak, a trail known in the past as Dragon's pass, but only Eldred knew that name and he wasn't about to reveal that to anyone. He had never liked the idea when it had been suggested, it was a dangerous route, even if the creatures it was named after no longer controlled the pass. Crossing the Cloumid's was precarious at the best of times and the reason why the trade routes all veered to the south, but the Dragon's pass was the worst. It was not an easy decision to make. To take the easy road would keep them safe, but it would also be disobeying Alaric. Each option had its pluses and its minuses. He wished that he didn't have to make the decision.

"As much as it pains me, I feel as though we have to do what Alaric has instructed." He could feel the subtle tug of the prophecy and it was urging him to the north. No matter what he thought there could be no doubt in which direction they should be travelling. "We will have to brave the Zmaj pass." That was the official name for the pass, Zmaj being an ancient word for dragon.

"Then I suppose we should keep moving. It doesn't look like this rain is going to ease up anytime soon." Richmond commented as his stood.

Richmond scratched at the side of his face. He had not had a chance to shave since leaving the seaside town of Shoretown. When he was Lord of Bellarome in the Kingdom of Kiarome, a position he may still hold, he wouldn't have gone more than two days without shaving. He had also managed to get his brown hair cut in Shoretown, although there had been little time for it to grow he knew it wouldn't be long before it became a bushy mess. Like Eldred, he was starting to show more signs of aging than was natural, but the strength still remained in his body.

"Let's hope it doesn't start to snow." It was the first thing Viper had said all day and his words were brushed aside as simple nonsense.

Alena almost sobbed as she stood. Somewhere, deep inside her, she had hoped that Alaric would return before they left. She couldn't believe he had just upped and left her. When he had rescued her from Jarrat she thought they would be together forever. It was a silly childhood dream, and she was much older than that, but the thought of romance was still thick in her mind. She cringed as she thought about the prison and the treatment from the Dark Knight. It was a time she hoped she would never remember. When Alaric returned she would have to get him to erase that part of her mind. She was sure with the aid of the Opal stone it was something he'd be able to do. Then she thought of the stones and wondered if Eldred would be able to help her. She would wait for an opportunity to speak to him in private.

Richmond was the only one who looked like he was keen to be on the move. As much as he didn't want to be away from the warmth of the fire he was excited to be going. The mood of the group had been so depressing, not to mention the gentle rain. He figured that once they were on the road again it would lift their spirits and that could only be a good thing. There had also been too much sadness in his life. He had felt that way ever since his best friend, Tancred, had died. There had been no time to grieve for his loss and he really didn't think the forest was the most appropriate place for it. Sitting around the campfire in silence did nothing to help. At least now they had a goal, something to aim for. That would be enough to keep his mind busy.

Eldred looked around the campsite, just to make sure they weren't leaving anything behind. He had a bad feeling that someone was following them and he didn't want to leave a trail. The fire would prove that someone had been there, but it wouldn't say who. Before he had not wanted to move, but now he couldn't get away quickly enough. He had a bad feeling that if they lingered they would be in trouble.

"Let's get moving. There's no point remaining here any longer." Eldred barked.

Viper was the last to leave. He could hardly believe the events of the night before. For a long time he had dreamed of seeing one of the Great Dragons again, but the result had not been what he had in mind. He couldn't believe they had killed each other. He knew there had been animosity between the clans in the past, but that was a long time ago. With such few numbers he would have hoped the two creatures could have put aside their differences for the greater good of their species. Now there was only one left alive and no chance for reproduction. Kahn was the last of the great dragons and that was indeed a sad thought. Things had not turned out like he had expected, not that he really knew what to expect. He couldn't believe that his brother, Adder, had lured them to the mountain for such a result. There had to be another reason, but it eluded him. He wouldn't rest until he knew what it was. Once he was done he planned on hunting down his brother and torturing the answer from him if necessary. In fact he might just torture Adder for the fun of it.

Before they left, Viper tried to mount Adelanta. At first he managed to sit in the saddle for a second before the white stallion bucked him to the ground. He stamped his front hoof in disapproval. The elven horse had become accustomed to the feel of Alaric on his back and didn't appreciate the serpentant. The brown mare he had been given was a suitable horse, but nothing compared to the white elven horses.

Eldred slowly patted Tormenta's neck. His elven stallion didn't like Adelanta's reaction to Viper.

Richmond was happy with his mare. As much as he thought it would be nice to ride Adelanta he wasn't about to make the same mistake as Viper.

Alena would ride her own elven mare, Lluvia. She had known that horse since she was a foal, but had not taken her with her when she left her home of Eljhem. It wasn't until she had met her father outside of Jarrat before she was reunited with her.

Eldred started leading them to the north. He didn't really know why, but it felt like the right path to take. He wasn't about to go against his feelings. If the prophecy wanted to make their path then he wasn't going to argue. The path Alaric had told them to take wasn't one he would have chosen for them. In fact short of travelling into the Northern Wasteland itself he would have picked any other route to Lel Dinion. For the moment he was happy to be at peace within himself and fighting the urge to travel north would promptly stop that.

The rain continued to fall during the morning and into the afternoon. No one felt the urge to stop for the midday meal. The dismal weather only proved to increase their morose moods. The only plus was that it was a light drizzle and not pouring rain. Regardless, by the time they decided to stop for the night they were all soaking wet. Even the magic wheelers had given up trying to remain dry. As there was nowhere completely sheltered for them to camp for the night the best they could do was find a small cluster of trees.

Eldred did his best to light a fire with the limited amount of dry wood they could find. In the end he piled on more wet wood and then used a simple spell to get a roaring fire started. He needed to get it hot enough to burn with the drops of rain making its way through the trees. The last thing they wanted was the fire to go out during the night. It was cold enough as it was.

"Why do you think Alaric left us?" Richmond asked as they ate. There had been no conversation since they had stopped and Richmond hated the silence. The weather was depressing enough as it was without sitting and staying quiet.

"I'm sure he had a very good reason," Eldred responded, not interested in conversation.

Richmond recognised the tone, but he wasn't going to give up so easily. "I know that, but it's the reason that has me perplexed. Something has changed in him. He seemed a lot harder than before. Another thing!" The thought just came to him. "Why would he leave the stones with us?"

Eldred almost snapped when he heard Richmond's last question. It had been one that he had put safely into the back of his mind. The stones were safely tucked away at the back of his pack and he much preferred not to think about them. The power they held was tempting, but Eldred knew it would be too much for him. He wasn't strong enough to control them. It was safer for him to leave them where they were.

"I wish I had some answers for you Richmond, but this is just as much of a shock to me as it is to you. There was a time when I thought I had all the answers. Now it seems as though I am lost. Even the prophecy doesn't seem to have any answers anymore."

"What does that mean?" Richmond pushed.

Eldred let out a sigh. He really wanted to end the conversation. It was something he really didn't want Viper to know. They had all become used to his presence which was a dangerous thing. Complacency would mean sensitive information being passed to the serpentant. That could easily mean disaster for them all.

"From what I can gather it means that our future is not as set as it once was. There has been in a shift in the Seven Kingdoms. I don't know what it was or when it happened, but it surely did. We need to be very careful. Without an idea of what is before us we could very easily be walking into a trap," Eldred explained.

"I have noticed it too." Viper had been listening carefully, remaining silent so not to draw any attention to himself. When he realised Eldred was still wary of him he figured there was little point in remaining anonymous. "A while back there was a change in the energy around us. It was very subtle at first, so subtle I didn't really take much notice of it. The more that time went on the more I noticed. I can't put my finger on what it is, but I know it's there."

"You should all try and get some sleep. It'll be another long day in the saddle tomorrow," Eldred suggested, with all the talk he wanted to spend some time reading the prophecy. He hoped there was still something for him to find.

Alena and Richmond were happy with the suggestion. It would be hard to find a dry place to sleep, but it was worth a try. Viper wasn't happy with being brushed aside. Like Eldred he could spend days awake without needing sleep. It was a process that increased with the use of magic. The cold weather was making him sluggish and he did feel he should rest, but that wasn't the point. If he was going to complete his mission he needed their trust. He felt as though he'd been close with Alaric, but now he was gone he was going to have to start again with Eldred. He doubted it was going to be as easy.

Eldred flicked through the pages with the aid of the firelight. He seemed to ignore the fact that Viper was watching him from the other side. There was something for him to find in the prophecy, he was sure of that. The only problem, as always, was knowing where to look. He had come to accept the fact that the prophecy would change at will. It had been a revelation that Alaric had discovered and a disturbing one at that. If the prophecy could change then it meant that its words weren't set in stone. It was that thought that stuck in his mind as he scoured the pages for information. Even if he found what he was looking for it didn't mean it would come to pass. That was a frustrating thought indeed.

The night passed without incident or discovery. The rain continued to fall, but they managed to get some sleep, all except for Eldred. He refused to put the great tome down. With each passing page he felt he was closer to finding the answer he so desperately needed.

The rain eased when they woke and the sun threatened to peek through the clouds, but the mood of the group reflected Eldred's moroseness. He didn't like the fact that they were starting the day with no real idea of what was ahead of them. It was with great despair that he tucked the prophecy back into his pack.

"How goes our supplies?" Richmond asked when they finished their morning meal.

That was a question Eldred had wished he had not been asked. They had brought enough supplies to get them to the mountain and back to Remidel. Alaric's plans for them had not been expected and they only had enough food for another five or six days. The forest was filled with game, but they had yet to see any.

"We have enough for the week, but we'll need to get some more soon. There should be deer aplenty in these woods." Eldred explained.

"I haven't seen any game since we arrived," Alena added. "There have been no track signs either."

That was indeed a worrying sign. They were far enough away from the mountain now that the dragon wouldn't be an issue. There were no good reasons why there shouldn't be any animals in the forest. For the first time Eldred realised, besides the rain, that there was no movement within the forest around them. No birds, no animals, even the trees didn't move in the slight breeze that was blowing.

"There is something very unnatural about this place. I think we should keep moving," Eldred suggested.

"I think that's a very good idea," Alena replied, also sensing the strangeness about the forest.

Eldred loaded the packs onto Adelanta. The stallion wasn't prepared for anyone else to ride on his back, but he was happy to take the extra load in baggage. It would make life easier for the other horses and he was happy to help out. He would have let Alena on his back, as he knew the relationship between her and Alaric, but she was happy to ride Lluvia.

Viper was the last to saddle and leave. He had not paid much attention to his surroundings until the others started talking. He knew Nyrra would have creatures lurking in the forest, that was something he had always suspected. He was surprised at the fact it was Raheem waiting for them at the Scorpion Mountain and not a trap set by Nyrra. Now he listened and pushed out with his senses. There was something there, he was sure of it, but he couldn't figure out exactly what it was. He would certainly fail in his task if he let them become captured. Then his own life would be at risk. He didn't think Nyrra's agents would be able to decipher between friend and foe.

As the day wore on the rain finally dissipated. The ground was still soft underfoot and water still dripped from the pine needles. It still did nothing to lift their moods. The feeling of impending doom only strengthened. Throughout the day there was still no sign of animal life. It didn't bode well for their food supplies. When they stopped for the night there was much to be discussed.

"I can't shake the feeling the something is watching us. It came across me late this afternoon and has been progressively getting worse." Alena was the first to speak.

"I know what you mean. It's very discerning," Richmond agreed.

"There's something more to it. There's a feeling… a feeling of dread in the air. I think we would be wise to post a watch for tonight," Eldred suggested.

He would normally suggest that he take the watch, but since he had not slept the night before he needed some sleep. He felt as though he was getting old. A few years back he would have been able to stay awake for weeks on end. Now one night without sleep and he was starting to feel the strain. Helping Viper transport them to the Scorpion Mountain also had taken a lot of energy out of him.

"I can take the watch if you like?" Viper was almost too afraid to make the offer. "I got plenty of sleep last night and don't mind missing a night every now and then."

Although it was Viper making the offer no one really wanted to complain. Both Alena and Richmond were tired from the day's ride. There was no respite from sitting in the saddle all day and the stress of the situation was also getting to them. Eldred wasn't overly happy, but it was the best of a bad situation.

"Thank you Viper." It wasn't the first thing that came to his mind, but they were the first words to come out. "Now I trust that you won't try anything." Eldred wasn't going to leave anything to chance. Even as he spoke he was in the process of weaving a warding spell to stop anyone from opening his pack. The contents were far too valuable. Eldred didn't want to think of the repercussions if the serpentant managed to get hold of even one of the stones.

That was the last thing on Viper's mind, but he didn't take offence to Eldred's suggestion. All he wanted to do was prove his trustworthiness and it seemed to be the perfect opportunity. If he could keep watch the entire night without fault then they would have to trust him. Whether or not that would be the case in the morning it was worth a shot.

"I wouldn't think of it Eldred." That was the truth. "Now don't waste this opportunity. We rode hard today and the night is wearing fast. It'll be morning soon."

Eldred wasn't sure if he trusted Viper, but the spell was set and there was nothing he could do to steal either the stones or the *Prophecy of the Stones*. He could only hope that they all woke in the morning, but he really didn't think Viper was planning on murdering them in their sleep. He was up to something, there was no doubt about that, but Eldred was sure that killing them wasn't it.

Before either of them could ponder their suspicions they were all fast asleep. Viper remained close to the fire. The warmth filled him and made him stronger. He didn't like the cold. It bit at him and took his strength. He longed to be back in a warm climate. He really should be safely tucked away in a cave somewhere sleeping away the cold weather. It was going to snow soon, he could feel it in the air and it was making him uncomfortable. There was something else though, something that everyone felt. Part of the reason he had offered to stand watch was the opportunity for quiet reflection. It wasn't a new feeling for him, but one he had not felt for a long time. There was a presence in the air and he needed to figure out what it was before the answer was thrust upon them.

The uncanny feeling didn't leave Viper throughout the night, but they were left unhindered. It seemed as though whatever was out there was quite happy to sit and watch. Viper didn't know if it was a good thing or a bad thing, but was leaning towards the latter. Not knowing was really starting to get to him. Not knowing was becoming a common part of his life and he didn't like at all.

Eldred was happy to wake in the morning and find the campsite in much the same condition as the night before. Despite his fears of Viper being left unattended he had a good night's sleep and without the constant rain it was much more comfortable. The relief was clear on all their faces when they woke in the morning.

"I've been trying to tell you that I am on your side." Viper knew he should have kept his mouth shut, but he couldn't help himself. "Now I hope you will all see that it's true."

His words did little to settle their nerves. If he hadn't spoken they might have started to believe what he was trying to tell them.

"I don't think so Viper. It'll take a lot more than that for us to put any serious trust in you," Eldred snapped.

Along with the distrust the feeling that someone was watching them also returned. There had been some respite whilst they were sleeping, but now everyone felt it and it made their skin crawl.

"Let's keep moving. I don't really feel like staying here any longer. We can stop later for something to eat." Eldred suggested and no one objected.

Viper didn't object either. He was quite happy to try and ignore his little faux pas and moving on was the best way to go about it.

It was much easier to ignore the feeling when they were riding. There was that, but Viper figured the further they travelled the closer they were to finding out who or what was watching them. The feeling of familiarity was annoying him more than the fear of a trap.

Almost as soon as they started out the rain started to fall. It was gentle at first, but as the morning progressed it strengthened. That made the decision easy to keep riding instead of stopping to eat. Although they were hungry there would be no solace in eating in the rain. It wasn't until after midday before the hunger became too unbearable and they stopped. The thick pines weren't enough to keep the rain from falling on them, although they did provide some shelter.

When they stopped the feeling of being watched became more than a background annoyance.

"What is it?" Alena asked, frustrated.

"I don't know, but I have a bad feeling that we are going to find out soon enough. There is a magical aura in the air. I've felt it growing ever since we started out this morning," Eldred explained. "It has been with us for a long time, but it was too subtle for me to realise."

Viper had to agree, albeit silently to himself. He had suspected the same thing, but wasn't as tuned in as Eldred. He was loathed to be the first one to suggest such a thing. He knew it was better to keep things to himself for a while. Building up their trust was proving to be much tougher than he had expected. He didn't want to do anything to bring attention to himself. There would be time for revelations, but now was not one of them. For the moment he was happy to listen and try and conserve as much energy as possible. The rain had dropped the temperature again and he figured it was getting close to freezing.

"What does that mean?" Richmond asked.

"I fear that it means we are riding into a trap." Eldred kept his head down as he spoke, just as much to keep the rain from his face as to hide his expressions from the others.

"Then we should find another course?" Richmond suggested.

"I fear that it's already too late."

"Alaric set us on this course. Surely he wouldn't lead us into a trap. There has to be another explanation," Alena retorted.

"I hope you're right. I hope you're right." Was all Eldred could say.

That was enough to end the conversation. No one wanted to ponder the thought any further. What would be would be and there was nothing they could do about it. All they could do was keep their wits about them and be prepared for an attack. They had been through a lot together and this would just be another challenge they would need to overcome.

Once they had eaten they were back in the saddle. No one wanted to sit in the rain any longer than they had to. Given half a chance they would have eaten while riding, but they needed to give the horses a chance to rest. It had been just as tough on them and the soft ground under hoof didn't make it any easier.

Suddenly the rain stopped around mid-afternoon and the temperature increased considerably. The sudden change in the weather was enough to make them stop and take note of their surroundings. It was clearly unnatural and that meant they were nearing an answer.

"Where are we?" Alena asked. "There is something very familiar about this place."

"I'm not sure, but I think we're about to find out." Eldred pointed to a figure up in the trees not too far ahead. He wore a green robe with the hood hiding his face.

"What brings you to these parts?" the voice was a lot closer than the figure they could see. "These are protected lands. Speak quickly or feel the pain of an arrow through your hearts."

"We are simple travellers and mean you no harm." Eldred kept his head straight not bothering to search for the owner of the voice who he knew would be hidden. "Please let us pass and be on our way."

There was a moment of silence. Alena thought she could hear voices speaking softly, but she wasn't sure. She wanted to look around to see if she could see anyone else, but she followed Eldred's lead and stared straight ahead.

"A likely story, what business does a wizard, an elf, a man and a serpent have in these parts?"

Hearing the words Viper cursed himself for not having his hood drawn. In the rain it seemed like it would be logical to have it protecting his head, but it had remained down for the day. He figured that it wouldn't have mattered anyway. The voice seemed to know more than just what his eyes saw.

"Who are you? We might be inclined to be more forthright with you if we knew who you are?" Eldred wasn't going to be talked down, but he knew he needed to tread lightly.

"That is the least of your concerns. For the moment you should be concerned with keeping your heads on top of your necks." There was no sarcasm in his voice.

"We are simple travellers. We are on our way to Lel Dinion. We mean you no harm," Eldred explained slowly.

"I'll give you one more chance to rethink your story," there was no humour in the voice.

Eldred let his shoulders drop. He had told the truth, well at least part of the truth and that had got him nowhere. He couldn't reveal anything else until he knew who he was talking to. As much as he didn't think they were agents of the Evil One he couldn't take the risk.

"Well it looks like you've made your choice. We'll let the magistrate get to the bottom of things."

When he finished there was a subtle sound of whistling in the air. Before any of them could react they all felt a sharp needle pierce them in the back of the neck. Within a few seconds everything went dark and they all collapsed to the ground.

Chapter 2: Friend or Foe?

Slowly Eldred started to wake. His first sense was a splitting headache. At first he couldn't remember what had happened. His head was swimming and the last thing he could remember was leaving the campsite that morning. Slowly the recollections returned to him and with that came a moment of panic. Instantly he tried to draw in some energy, but quickly realised that he couldn't. Whoever it was who had captured them had managed to block him from creating magic. The warning bells started to ring.

Once his panic started to subside Eldred had a look around at his surroundings. The other three were lying on the floor next to him, still unconscious and it seemed as though they were in a small wooden room. When he saw the metal bars on the door and no windows he realised it was a prison cell. A small amount of light peeked through the gaps in the bars, although it didn't look natural.

Holding his head to give it support, Eldred lifted himself from the ground with his free hand. It took him a moment to settle himself before he was able to take his first step. Whatever poison had been used to knock him out was obviously still in his system. Slowly he made his way across to the door, trying his best to keep whatever was left in his stomach from rising. Just before he reached the door he failed in his task. He retched three times bringing up a green and brown liquid along with a foul stench. No matter what he tried he couldn't keep it down. Once he had emptied his stomach he felt a lot better, besides the incessant ringing in his head.

On the other side of the door Eldred could see a small lantern hanging out the front of the cell. The only other thing he could see was thick pine foliage. It was at that moment he could feel the cell swaying. Wherever they were he knew they were up in a pine tree.

Slowly Alena and Richmond started to stir which brought Eldred's attention back to the cell. They looked as bad as he had when they awoke. He knew it was only a matter of time before they lost the contents of their stomachs as well. As soon as the thought came to him they turned their heads and vomited. The smell was almost enough to make him retch again, but he controlled himself. Both Alena and Richmond slowly stood and moved away from their mess.

Viper was the only one left on the floor and they all watched and waited for him to wake, but he didn't stir.

"Where are we?" Richmond finally asked when nothing happened. He held his arm over his nose in an attempt to block the smell.

"I don't know, but it seems as though we've been imprisoned. Whatever they drugged us with seems to leave us without the contents of our stomachs. Hopefully that's all the side effect of it," Eldred replied.

"I don't think Viper is recovering." Alena pointed to where was lying. "He hasn't moved at all."

As much as Eldred didn't want to touch the snake he was the only one who could tell if he was still alive. He carefully made his way over and knelt down beside him. Slowly he put his ear next to Viper's nose to see if he was still breathing. There were slow, laboured breaths. Eldred wasn't completely sure, but it didn't sound right.

"I think the drug might have a more severe effect on serpentants." Eldred suggested when he returned to where they were standing.

"Then we should get help for him?" it was more of a statement than question from Alena.

Eldred thought for a moment. It was a good chance for them to be rid of the serpentant, but in the end he couldn't bring himself to let him die. In the back of his mind he could feel the prophecy pushing him towards the door to get assistance.

"Help, we need some help!" Eldred called through the bars, desperately looking to see if there was someone on the other side.

"What do you want?" the voice was gruff from outside. Eldred strained to try and see who it was, but he was well hidden.

"One of our companions has not woken up from the drug. We fear that he is in need of assistance."

"The drug, as you so eloquently put it, affects people differently. He will wake in his own time. It has never been fatal before." The voice scoffed.

Alena thought there was something very familiar about the way he spoke. His voice was hash, but still familiar. She knew it was going to annoy her until she found out.

"That would be all well and good if he was a man, but that isn't the case. Our companion is of a different kind and he needs help." Eldred tried his best to explain without giving away any pertinent information.

"We know he is a serpentant and that is exactly the reason why you are all in the cell. I have been instructed to leave you there until the magistrate is ready to see you."

Eldred's shoulders dropped. He was getting nowhere fast, but the prophecy wasn't going to let him give up.

"At least tell me who it is that is keeping me prisoner."

"That is not for me to tell. All I am here to do is make sure you don't escape."

"At least give us some water to clean the mess that your drug has caused."

"Unless you are ready to tell us why you're here then you can just deal with it." There was a smugness to his voice.

That was all Eldred had. He wasn't prepared to say anymore. If they wouldn't accept the truth then there wasn't much more he could do.

"Surely this has gone on for too long. There has to be something we can tell them to let us out," Richmond said, keeping his voice low so no one outside could hear him.

"We can't tell them why we're travelling to Lel Dinion and we certainly can't tell them why we're here. For the most part it's because I have no idea why we're here. What would you have me do?" Eldred spoke louder than he should.

That brought silence from the others. No one knew what they should say. The stench coming from the vomit did nothing to help their train of thought and their throbbing heads made it worse.

"Well we can't stay here much longer," Alena replied.

"I'm sure things will play out soon enough." Eldred didn't sound too optimistic.

They waited in silence for what seemed an eternity before suddenly they heard a bolt sliding on the other side of the door. They backed away and waited to see who it was. Two tall, slender, robed and hooded figures entered the cell. Their robes were a rich green and they held slender wooden pikes with sharp metal spikes on the ends. Eldred didn't think they looked too menacing, but he couldn't be completely sure.

"The magistrate will see you now and think yourselves lucky that he's seeing you at this late hour."

"What about our companion?" Eldred asked before he moved.

"The snake is not welcome in our land. He will remain here until we decide what to do with you."

"That isn't right. He could die when we are out," Alena said.

"And what would an elf care about a snake?" there was disgust in his voice.

"Our business is our own and you should respect that," Alena was starting to get annoyed. "Let us be on our way, we mean you no harm." Alena couldn't shake the feeling that there was something very familiar about the hooded figure. "You're not from around here are you?" It was a strange question.

"It isn't your place to ask questions. The magistrate will get the answers, not you." The second robed figure spoke for the first time.

"Of course, I forget myself. It's time to go."

There was no point trying to convince the two before them. It was obvious they weren't the ones able to make any decisions. If they were going to get out it would be the magistrate they would have to convince.

Eldred led Alena and Richmond out of the cell. The two armed figures waited for them to leave before following.

"Watch your step, we are high above the ground." The warning came just in time as Eldred was about to step off the small ledge outside the prison cell.

"How are we supposed to get down?" Even when Eldred asked the question he knew what the response would be.

"Just wait!"

The sound of cogs moving into action could be heard from somewhere above. Now they could see four ropes hidden in the foliage before them. Slowly a wooden lift was hoisted until it was level with the platform. Eldred wasn't sure if the lift looked completely steady, but he was sure it was the way the got up so it had to be safe.

"We'll take you down one at a time. Wizard, you go first." It wasn't unnecessary, but the guard gave Eldred a gentle push with the butt of his pike.

Moving carefully Eldred walked onto the platform. It swayed slightly, but it seemed sturdy enough. He was followed closely by the first guard. When they were both safely on board the guard pulled a lever and the platform slowly started to lower.

There was little to see through the thick pine needles until they reached the ground. Once they were there Eldred hoped to be able to get a better understanding of where they were. Unfortunately there was nothing really for him to see. The trees were tightly packed together and the floor was blanketed with pine needles.

One by one the others were brought to the forest floor. Eldred thought about investigating further, but then decided against it. He couldn't risk everyone's lives for a little information so he just waited patiently.

"Let's go."

The first guard led the way whilst the other kept the rear. After a short walk they came upon the village. The pine trees started to thin out and around the bases of the trees were rudimentary huts. They looked to be of poor quality and put together in a hurry. Eldred didn't think that boded well for them. The buildings were built from a mixture of wood and mud. They were definitely makeshift and not built to last. Whoever it was hadn't been there long and didn't look like they were planning to stay. That could only mean they were part of Nyrra's army. Eldred quickly looked around for a chance to escape, although he doubted there was going to be one. Although he couldn't see anyone else he was sure there would be archers somewhere in the trees.

Slowly, as they progressed through the temporary village, more robed figures could be seen moving around. When they saw the prisoners they quickly disappeared again. They were completely covered making it impossible to tell who they were. That made things even more frustrating and in the end he decided to wait until they reached the magistrate. There weren't going to be any answers until then.

The guards led them to what Eldred assumed was the centre of the village. There was a large clearing on the ground and the area was lit by a multitude of lanterns and candles giving it quite a surreal feel. At the far end of the clearing was another platform. It was obvious that the magistrate's building was somewhere in the canopy and Eldred thought it seemed quite odd. With the state of the rest of the village there didn't seem to have been any time to build any major infrastructure in the trees. Eldred couldn't imagine someone who was as seemingly important as the magistrate having an unsuitable building to conduct his business. At least this time the lift looked much sturdier and was capable of transporting all five of them at once.

The first guard stepped onto the platform and indicated for the others to do the same. Once they were all on he pulled a lever and the platform started to slowly rise. It didn't take long before they were back in the thick pine needles. Their view outside the lift was completely obscured for about five minutes before things opened up again. There was no telling how high they had travelled.

What waited for them at the end of the journey was not at all what they expected. The branches of the pine trees stopped growing for about fifteen feet from where the platform landed. They hadn't been chopped down they had simply just stopped growing. That wasn't nearly the strangest thing about the way the trees had grown. From the base of the lift the branches had grown and intertwined together make a perfect floor. The same had happened at the top, creating a perfect ceiling above them that looked like it would remain dry even under the worst storm.

The focal point of the phenomenon was the building across from the lift. It was intricately designed, unlike the rudimentary huts around the base of the trees and designed with style and dignity. The face was built from timber, but not pine. Eldred wasn't sure exactly what timber had been used, but he was sure it wasn't local. It was built to the ceiling where the branches acted as the roof. The front was painted a multitude of bright colours with intricate runes painted in black. The sight gave Eldred a glimmer of hope. He could guess who had built such a place and only hoped they still resided there.

Standing out of the front of the building were half a dozen robed guards. Their robes were a deep brown and again covered their bodies completely. They stood still and didn't seem to notice the newcomers.

The guards led Eldred and the others towards the building.

"Do you have any idea who they are?" Richmond asked.

"Keep quiet. No talking until the magistrate speaks to you," the guard kept his voice low. He almost sounded afraid to speak himself.

Eldred was grateful for the response. He didn't want to voice a guess on the chance he was wrong. If he was able to use magic he could have easily discovered who their captors were, but that wasn't the case. All he could do was wait, just like the others.

The first guard opened the door and waited for the three to enter. The six standing guard outside didn't move as the group approached and entered the building. Richmond wasn't sure if they were alive or just statues.

Inside was a small entrance room which had a long hallway on the other side. The three waited for the guards before they were led down the hallway. There were doors on either side, but it was the large double doors at the end that they were heading for. Their nerves started to set in.

One of the guards opened the door and indicated that they should enter. Neither of the guards entered the room, they just shut the doors behind them.

The room they were in took up half the building. It was painted completely white. A globe of light floated just under the ceiling in the middle. It was more than enough to illuminate the entire room. Opposite the doors was a small dais with a larger, higher one behind. On the front dais was a small rectangular table with a high backed chair behind it. Sitting on the chair was a figure dressed in a white robe, similar in design to the others being worn. On the second dais there were twelve thrones. The two in the middle were larger than the others. They were carved from mahogany and had intricate runes engraved around the frame. The two middle thrones also had robed figures seated on them. The one on the left wore a red robe and the one on the right wore blue.

Eldred walked into the middle of the room and knelt in front of the dais. He was confident he was right in his assumption and he was doing the appropriate thing.

"Stand Eldred, we appreciate you deference, but in these times it is completely unnecessary." The magistrate, dressed in white, spoke.

"Thank you magistrate," Eldred responded as he rose.

Richmond and Alena both wanted to speak, but knew it wasn't appropriate. They were somewhat relieved to see that Eldred seemed to know who he was talking to.

"And we are curious as to your travelling companions. A she-elf, but by the looks of her not from these areas, a human and a lord as we are led to believe, but it is the snake we are most interested in. I don't think we have ever heard tales of one of the Council of Wizards befriending a serpentant, unless he is a prisoner of yours?" the magistrate continued.

"As you know we are on a quest to defeat the Evil One. That is why we must all travel together. I can assure you it isn't by choice," Eldred explained.

"Yes, we know of your journey." A male voice came from the figure in red. "And pray tell how is our son?"

"Your Majesty, I regret to inform you that Palentonal is dead. He was poisoned in a battle with the Evil One's minions and died a few days later. He fought bravely and died with honour protecting the Chosen One's destiny."

"And was that destiny not supposed to be fulfilled on the Cauldron Mountain. I take it that has not come to pass?" the voice was harsh.

Eldred had dreaded this day. He knew that it would come around eventually, but he'd hoped that everything would be finished by the time he returned. In the back of his mind he wondered if this had been the reason why Alaric had sent them on this path. It was those thoughts that could turn a person mad and he quickly brushed them aside. There would be time for pondering later.

"That is what we believed, but it seems as though that wasn't the case. Alaric went to the mountain, but it wasn't the battle we expected. The battle continues as does our mission," Eldred explained as best he could.

"Then the council was right in its decision. Palentonal should never have left with you. Even when he left we knew we would never see him again. We have mourned for the loss of our son and he would have been a valuable member of the council. Who knows, if he had been here the disaster may not have befallen us?"

At that moment the three pulled their hoods back. Now that Eldred knew who they were there seemed little point in secrecy. Their features were clearly those of elvish kind which caused Alena and Richmond to visibly relax. They had not been caught in a trap, or at least Nyrra's followers weren't behind it. The only question now was what the elves were planning on doing with them. They didn't seem to be in any hurry to let them leave.

An elf and a she-elf sat in the seats behind the magistrate. They still held the youthful features that were synonymous with elvish kind, but there was also a clear sign of age on their faces. Both had dark black hair with flecks of grey. Nether of them looked pleased with the newcomers.

The magistrate had the appearance of age, but with no sign of aging on his face. It was a hard façade to grasp. His hair was blonde and tied back in a tail. There was a stern expression on his face and it was clear he wasn't in the mood for mischief.

"What was the disaster? Why are you here?" Eldred asked.

"I will be the one asking the questions," the magistrate's voice was hard.

Eldred was about to speak, but thought better of it. He could feel the tension in the room. The last time Eldred visited the Northern Elves he had taken their son away against the wishes of the council. He could only hope they wouldn't be vengeful for the loss of Palentonal. He had served for the good of all including his family, but Eldred didn't think they would understand.

"Now tell me why you are travelling with a serpentant?" the magistrate re-asked the question.

"To answer that question honestly... I really don't know. He found us on his travels and explained that he was there to help. I was extremely suspicious, but Alaric allowed him to travel with us. I am sure that he has a secret agenda, but it seems as though the prophecy wants him to continue with us. I don't think we could leave him even if we wanted to and believe me the thought has crossed my mind on more than one occasion. He has been with us for over a month and to date he has been nothing but true to his word. I can't say that I like the situation, but he has proven his worth," Eldred wasn't sure if he was trying to convince the magistrate or himself. "I'm sorry if that is somewhat vague, but that is the best I can give you."

There was a moment of silence as the magistrate thought on the information. There was no expression on his face that any of them could read. Eldred could only hope that telling the truth was going to get them the result they wanted.

"And what about you she-elf? Where do you come into the mix?" The magistrate seemed to ignore Eldred's response. In fact he was unsure what to make of things and was hoping for assistance from the council members behind him.

"I am Alena, daughter of Orric of Elhjem. I have been tied in with the prophecy from the date of my birth. I was destined to travel with the Chosen One and help him defeat the Evil One." Alena had prepared her speech and was ready for the question.

Again the magistrate had to pause. He wasn't expecting such a response. As much as the Northern Elves liked to keep to themselves they did have relations with their cousins. They all had a great respect for Orric, one of the eldest and most respected elves still alive. There were instantly many more questions the magistrate wanted to ask, but they weren't pertinent to the interrogation.

"And you, lord from Darshival, what is your connection to this strange group?"

"I am Richmond, Lord of Bellarome, although that life seems to be a lifetime away. I, like the others, am a slave to the prophecy. Looking back now I somehow always knew that I would be leaving Bellarome, but it wasn't until Alaric arrived did I know where I was going, or at least who I was supposed to follow. I lost a great friend not long ago to this quest and for his sake I would like to see it out to the end." Richmond spoke confidently even though he was still very nervous.

"I see. Well they are some very interesting tales you have told. We will need time to discuss how we proceed from here. You can wait in the alcove room." The magistrate pointed to a door at the far end of the room.

Eldred wanted to ask more questions, but it seemed as though he wouldn't get the chance. Again all he could do was what the magistrate had instructed. He led the other two through the door and into the alcove room.

"What's going on?" Richmond asked.

"I'm not sure. They are the Northern Elves, but this isn't their home. We are still too far south to have entered their territory."

"So where do you think we are?" Alena asked.

"I have no idea. I was going to ask you the same question. With your relationship with the Northern Elves I thought you might know," Eldred replied.

"It has been over a century since the last envoy was sent from the Northern Elves and we hadn't sent one for many years prior to that. I am afraid that our relationship has waned over the years. Maybe that is why they weren't so keen to help in our struggle against Nyrra. It seems as though they were happy in the protection of their woods and didn't care for the outside world."

"Then I guess we'll just have to wait." Eldred resigned.

"Surely they will let us go. They aren't agents of the Evil One. They will have to support our cause?" Richmond hoped.

"I wouldn't put all your gold on that one Richmond. I don't have a good relationship with these elves. I'm sure that they haven't forgiven me for taking their son away. Those were his parents sitting on the council behind the magistrate."

"The Northern Elves took themselves away from the rest of the Seven Kingdoms a long time ago. They didn't care for men and I'm sure that hasn't changed. They have no love for Nyrra, but I don't think they would weep if every Kingdom fell to his sword," Alena explained. "I don't think they will do us any favours."

That wasn't what anyone wanted to hear. It had been such a relief when they realised it was elves who held them captive and not Nyrra, but that relief had only lasted for a short time. Now they weren't sure if they were going to be able to leave any time soon.

They sat in silence for what seemed an eternity before the door was opened. The magistrate stood on the other side with a grave expression on his face.

"You may return," was all he said.

Slowly they made their way back into the main room. The magistrate took his seat and the two seated behind him had stern expressions on their faces. Alena didn't think it boded well for their chances.

"As you know we have long been dubious of this prophecy you follow." It was the she-elf who spoke, not the magistrate as they had expected. "We have not seen anything to prove that there is a force controlling our destiny." Their hearts sank. "You took our son and caused us much pain and now it seems that his life was lost for nothing." Eldred wanted nothing more than to defend his decision and Palentonal's choice, but he knew that would do more harm than good. "You bring evil into our land and you tell us lies and half-truths. However in light of recent circumstances we need to have a little faith. There is a threat to our land and that is something we can't simply ignore. With that in mind we are willing to let you leave."

No one knew what to say. It wasn't the response they had expected, but it was gratefully received. Alaric had not given them a time frame to reach Lel Dinion, but they all knew every day was pertinent.

"Thank you for you graciousness. I only ask one thing. Our supplies are low and it would be greatly appreciated if we could restock for our journey."

"We will give you food and water, but the snake is not welcome in our land. We still remember the carnage they caused us in the past." Palentonal's father said.

That was fair enough. Eldred had read the story of when the serpentants were more than just legend. When their queen was still alive they had murdered many elves in their quest for power. The evils of the past would be a lot harder for them to forgive.

The three elves remained seated while they left the building. There were many questions Eldred had, but it seemed as though they would remain unasked. He doubted the guards, who he was sure would be waiting to take them back to Viper, would give him any answers.

Again there was little life around the makeshift village as they walked back to the prison cell. It seemed as though the elves were afraid of the newcomers. Whatever had happened had made them very timid. That only added to the questions Eldred wanted answers to. Something either was or had gone very wrong.

"What's happening around here?" even though he knew he wouldn't get a response he thought it was worth asking the question.

"If the magistrate didn't give you the information then I can only assume he doesn't want you to know. I don't know what you spoke about and I don't really care. I have been instructed to escort you back to the snake and then to the border and that is exactly what I'm going to do." The guard responded.

The guards kept the hoods over their faces, even though they knew they were all elves. There didn't seem much point in secrecy, but that was the way they continued.

"I'll take one of you up to get your friend," the guard stated when they reached the lift.

"I'll go," Eldred said.

It wasn't as smooth a ride as it had been travelling up to see the magistrate. The platform rocked more than Eldred had remembered on the way down. There was another guard waiting for them at the top.

"Has the prisoner caused you any trouble?" the first guard asked.

"Haven't heard a peep," was the response.

Eldred didn't think it was a good sign. Viper didn't look well when they left and it seemed as though he was still unconscious. His fears were proven as they walked into the prison cell. The vomit had not been cleaned up and Eldred had to cover his nose to stop himself from retching. Viper still lay in the same spot where they had left him.

"This isn't right!" Eldred snapped. "You are elves, you are better than this. You should never treat a prisoner this way."

The guard didn't know what to say. He had not expected such a commanding comment from Eldred. There was truth to his words, but times had changed and they had to change with them.

"I know the serpentants have wronged you in the past, but have you not yourselves wronged others. There was a time when the elves subjugated men and dwarves alike." Eldred was grasping at straws.

"And we still pay for those mistakes." The guard didn't sound confident.

"You hide in the forest by choice, not by necessity," Eldred returned.

"We *live* in the forest because the rest of the world has been taken over by men. There is no choice in the matter."

"Be that as it may but Viper will die is he doesn't receive medical assistance. He is vital to our cause and therefore everyone's livelihood. If he dies then you risk handing the world over to Nyrra." There was no lie in Eldred's words.

"Very well, we will have him moved to better quarters and get someone to look at him. I wouldn't get my hopes up though. Herbs and medicine are hard to come by. I don't know if the magistrate would like wasting any on the likes of that." The guard followed Eldred out of the cell.

There was no point in remaining in the filth while they waited for assistance. Eldred went down with the guard to join the others. He figured they would like to know the status of Viper's condition.

"It doesn't look good. He hasn't moved since we left," Eldred explained. "We are going to have him moved and get someone look at him."

It wasn't long before half a dozen armed elves returned. They were dressed in the same green robes as the other guards. There could be no doubt that even in his current state they still didn't trust Viper. They brought him down as carefully as they could. Even without being able to see their faces it was obvious they didn't want to touch him. Once they were down they carried him to one of the huts.

"We need this hut," the guard spoke to a young looking she-elf when they arrived.

At first she looked surprised when the guards came in. She was dressed in a brown robe with the hood down. When she saw the others a look of horror crossed her face, even before she realised who was being carried into her makeshift home.

"What's happening? I have already lost my home, why am I being kicked out of here?" she didn't sound happy.

"Now Bryanne you know these times are tough and we must all do what we can. The magistrate has instructed me to use your hut to house the visitors. You can stay with Dierdre until they leave." The guard instructed.

She still didn't look happy, but she took what she could hold, pulled the hood over her face and left.

Inside, the hut didn't look like it was large enough to house all four of them. There was one small bed in the corner, a small chest of drawers a table and two chairs. There was only just enough space on the floor if they lay next to each other. If this was where they had to stay then it would have to do. He didn't think the elves would be happy if they just slept outside.

"The läkaren will be here shortly. Be thankful that we still have one around. Wait here and don't go anywhere."

"What is a läkaren?" Richmond asked.

"It's basically the elven word for a physician. It's meaning is a little broader than that, but essentially that's what it means."

"So what do we do now?" Alena asked. "Surely we can leave Viper and keep moving. This is the out that we have been looking for?"

"I can't say that the thought hasn't crossed my mind, but I don't think that's possible. He is tied to us now, whether by the prophecy or by Alaric's design we need to keep him with us," Eldred replied.

That wasn't the answer they were looking for. Neither Alena nor Richmond would mind if he just died where he lay. Even though that's how they felt they knew that Eldred was right. For whatever reason Viper was now part of their group whether they liked it or not.

Before long the läkaren returned. He was dressed in a deep purple robe and unlike the others his hood was down. His facial features were aged. Many wrinkles covered his face and his hair was bright white. They could only marvel at how old he must be to show such signs.

"What seems to be the problem here?" the läkaren asked.

"The drug your soldiers used to knock us out is having an adverse effect on the serpentant. He hasn't woken up yet and he doesn't look like he will anytime soon," Eldred explained.

The läkaren slowly moved to where Viper was lying. He didn't seem as nervous as the other elves to touch the serpentant. It was more that he wanted to survey the situation first. Once he had checked over Viper he took some vital signs, at least as best he could. Once he was done he took a step back and rubbed his chin, not taking his eyes from the patient. When he was satisfied with his diagnosis he turned to the others.

"This is something I haven't seen before. The herb we use is not lethal. I can't understand why it's had such a reaction. There is something I can give him, but whether it will work or not I don't know." With that the läkaren left the hut.

"You must remain here until he has recovered or died." The guard didn't seem to care either way.

"What about our possessions?" Eldred asked just before the guard left the hut.

"The magistrate will decide what to do with them in the morning. Your horses are fine. They are being cared for."

"I would like our things now!" Eldred snapped. The stones and the prophecy would be safe in his bag. The ward he created would still be in place, but he would feel happier if he had them.

"The council will be sleeping now. There is nothing I can do for you. Get some sleep and I'm sure the magistrate will be happy to see you when he wakes." The guard didn't wait for a response.

There was nothing else they could do. The floor of the hut didn't look too appealing, but that was all they had.

Chapter 3: Death and Destruction

The läkaren returned before morning and applied a salve to Viper. Along with the medicine came a rank smell which did nothing to aid the sleep of the others. He left without saying a word giving them no indication on how long it might take for Viper to recover, if at all.

It was mid-morning before the guard returned to take them to see the magistrate. The smell had slowly faded during the morning and they were able to get some sleep. There didn't seem to be any change to Viper's condition, so it didn't look like they would be leaving anytime soon. Everyone was starting to get claustrophobic in the small hut. When the guard entered the gust of fresh air that blew in was a welcome change.

"The magistrate will see you now," was all the guard said before he left the hut again.

It didn't take long for the three to follow him. They had been cooped up and were keen for more fresh air. Outside it was brighter than they expected under the thick foliage. Eldred was sure that only part of the light was natural, although he didn't have time to investigate further. He had never known of the small village they were in and that piqued his interest.

The magistrate and the two council members met them at the bottom of the lift. The guard simply left them when they arrived and they all went up to the building together. This time they entered a room along the hallway where a large table was set in the middle with chairs around. A large platter of fruit, breads, cheeses and meats was in the centre. No one questioned where the food had come from. They had seen no fruit bushes, animals or anything to make bread since they had arrived.

"We would like our possessions back," Eldred started the conversation as soon as they were all seated.

"First I think we should introduce ourselves." The magistrate ignored the request. "I am Torrin, magistrate of the Northern Elves. This is Palen, Lord of the High Council and his wife Kyrene, second of the High Council." Torrin introduced.

"What happened here?" Eldred asked.

"That is a long story, but for now eat. I'm sure you are all hungry," Kyrene offered.

As much as Eldred wanted answers he was very hungry. They had not been given food the night before so they didn't need to be asked twice before they started filling their plates.

"How is the snake this morning?" Torrin asked.

"There has been no change to his condition. The läkaren gave him something last night, but it doesn't seem to be working," Eldred explained.

"You can stay one more night, but then you must be on your way," Torrin snapped.

"We cannot leave without him. For whatever reason he is tied to us now," Eldred replied quickly.

"Then you better hope he is fit to ride in the morning." Torrin would not be swayed.

Eldred thought for a moment before deciding it wasn't worth pushing any further. It was a bridge they would have to cross if and when they reached it. Hopefully the medicine would do its job and Viper was up and about before the morning.

"Please tell me what has happened and why you are here?" Eldred changed the subject. "What has happened to Nordligträ?"

Torrin looked at Palen and Kyrene who in turn nodded. He didn't look happy, but he continued nevertheless.

"It was about a month ago. We were attacked without warning. The Evil One's orglin came from the woods. We don't know how they broke through our wards, but that is just semantics."

That in itself was a worrying sign. Nordligträ, the home of the Northern Elves, was supposed to be impregnable. That was one of the reasons why they didn't want to take part in the war. They had believed that they were safe in their home and couldn't be touched by the Evil One. Eldred had his suspicions that Nyrra himself had been involved in the attack. He was sure the Dark Knights had all been busy elsewhere and Nyrra was the only other one powerful enough to instigate such a thing. It had been the first time that Eldred had suspected Nyrra being involved with any of the assaults. This could only mean that he was growing in strength and the final battle would be taking place soon. He wanted nothing more than to check the prophecy for clues of what might have actually happened. It also meant that they would need to leave very soon. Time was running out and they might just have to leave in the morning with or without Viper. Again it wasn't worth thinking about until it came to pass.

"We fought bravely, but there was nothing we could do. Wave after wave of orglin crashed through our defences. It seemed as though after we killed one another ten would take its place. In the end we had to retreat here, Akastiere, our safe haven. It has been over five hundred years since we have needed to use this place, as I'm sure you have guessed by the rudimentary huts we're now forced to use. We have yet to be attacked from the orglin again. This place should be safe for us, but we also thought that about Nordligträ. Now we don't know what to think. The remaining elves are afraid to leave their huts. This is no way for us to live."

"That is terrible news," Eldred was genuine. "This is the last bastion of the elves to fall. Eljhem was taken a while ago. Orric and his elves now march with the Alliance."

"Then all is lost. We have no chance for recourse." Palen sounded resigned.

"You can follow Orric's lead and join the Alliance. They will need all the help they can get when it comes time for the final battle against Nyrra's army," Eldred added.

"And what of our home? What of Nordligträ? What of the *Tree of Life*? Remember that the sacred relic of the old world resides there. We can only imagine what the orglin are doing to it now. If they cut it down then the forest will die and this will become a wasteland," Torrin explained.

Eldred had forgotten about the *Tree of Life*, the final place of Emerald. Like the others it was an extremely magical place and an intricate part to the balance of the world. There was no telling what Nyrra had planned for it, but cutting it down would be the place to start. If he succeeded then all the vegetation in the Seven Kingdoms would shrivel and die. That was something they couldn't let him achieve.

Alena had heard stories of the tree, many years ago. All elvish children were taught the importance of the *Tree of Life*. For a long time she had thought it just a tale to tell children, although the teachers always stressed that it was true.

"Go to the Alliance. They march on Remidel to free it from subjugation. Help them and they will help you. Let the council vote. Where are the other members?" Eldred pushed his idea.

"They are all dead. Kyrene and I are all who remain," Palen explained. "We are the last of the council."

An expression of pure horror crossed Eldred's face. Although his relationship with the Northern Elves had been strained over the years he still had a soft spot for them. In his younger years he had spent time with the elves and had known some of the older members of the council quite well. They had been good friends for a time and even though things had changed he still remembered those days.

"They will be sorely lost. I am truly sorry to hear that," Eldred responded after a moment of reflection.

"We have come to terms with their deaths. Loss of life is never easy, but we have to move on. There has been more death in the last few months than there has been in the last hundred years. It is not those deaths that we are here to discuss. It's the future that is our concern." There was no emotion to Palen's voice.

Eldred didn't know how to respond to that statement. It was harsh, but true. He had never known the elves to be so emotionless regarding death. Normally the period of mourning took a month for just one death. It seemed as though that was a thing of the past. He had to admit that Orric did get straight down to business after Elhjem had been attacked, but that was different. He knew what was coming. The attack on Nordligträ had come as a complete surprise.

"Nevertheless we feel for your pain, but as you said it is time to move on. Now it is time for you to join the battle against the Evil One. The Alliance needs all the help it can get if it's going to succeed." Eldred pushed forward.

"We are in no position to got to war!" Torrin spoke louder than he had intended. He didn't appreciated what Eldred was suggesting. "We have been through a great ordeal and it will take us a long time to recover from our loses."

"But Palen said you have moved on?" Alena instantly wished she hadn't spoken.

"We have come to terms with the fact that we have lost a lot of elves, but that does not mean we have recovered. We need to move on, but that doesn't mean leaving our safe haven." Torrin spoke calmer this time. "We need to regroup and take our land back. If the *Tree of Life* falls then the Seven Kingdoms will become a barren wasteland."

Eldred silently cursed himself for not seeing it sooner. If he had then he could have planned for the attack, or at least that was the thought that kept racing through his mind. It made perfect sense to him now. If Nyrra was able to destroy the *Tree of Life* then he could destroy all vegetation in the Seven Kingdoms with one blow. The reason Eldred had never thought of the strategy, was that he wouldn't have thought it was possible.

The *Tree of Life*, as with the other relics of the God Kings, contained immense amounts of magic. As would be expected it was the elves who were first drawn to it, as creatures of the forest it was a natural calling. They harness the power of the trees to create their home and with it a protective barrier to ward off evil. This was what was most disturbing about Nyrra's attack. Something had happened to allow creatures of evil past the outskirts of Nordligträ.

"How was it that the orglin were able to pass through your barriers?" Eldred needed more information before he made his judgement.

The three elves looked at each before they answered. Something passed between them before they returned to the others. It was Torrin who had been chosen to speak.

"We've noticed a change in the world. It was around the time we assume Nyrra broke free from his prison to the north. There was a subtle change in the air, I don't know how else to explain it." Torrin was struggling for words. "Every now and then there was a subtle scent to air, like rancid meat, something that has never reached us in Nordligträ." This was the type of information that Eldred was looking for. "Some of the pines were starting to turn yellow and fall to the ground," he turned to Richmond, "which is something that never happens."

"At first it was barely noticeable, but eventually it became apparent to all of us. Even the *Tree of Life* was starting to show signs of age. A mighty oak in the middle of a pine forest, it is easy enough to notice the changes. At first the leaves started to turn orange and red."

"But surely this time of year that would be normal for an oak tree?" Richmond couldn't help himself.

"This is no normal oak tree, this is the *Tree of Life*." Palen almost sounded offended as he made the comparison.

"As Palen said, it is the *Tree of Life*. Its leaves remain green all year round and its bark never ages. It is the source of life for everything in the Seven Kingdoms, one way or another. In the history of our lives there has never been any record of the *Tree of Life* ever showing signs of age."

"I feel that there is more to this than just leaves changing colour?" Eldred mused.

"It was a few months after the leaves started to change. Slowly strips of bark started to peel from the trunk. Every so often twigs would fall from the canopy. It was like the tree itself was dying." Torrin didn't know what else to say.

"Was it like the tree itself was being attacked?" Alena asked.

"That's what we though too, at first. But if someone was attacking the tree we would have felt their presence." Kyrene spoke for the first time, her voice was oddly cold. They were all expecting more emotion from her. "The council, more so than the other elves, are in tune with the *Tree of Life*. We can feel her life cycles, even if she doesn't show any outward signs. We feel her life energy flowing through us."

"It is a wondrous feeling," Palen added.

"Yes, my love. But that also started to change. It was almost like the *Tree of Life* was becoming sick," Kyrene continued.

"But this was a long time before the attack. Nyrra was moving towards Nostiria. He couldn't have been the one behind it," Eldred argued. "It must have been someone else."

"Maybe one of the Dark Knights? It wasn't until recently that they were all accounted for," Alena added.

It seemed like a reasonable response, but Kyrene didn't look pleased.

"They wouldn't have the power to do what is necessary to make such a change to the tree. She is much stronger than that." She returned.

"What if some of the Dark Knights were working together? Surely that would be enough to make a start." Alena added.

"You and your kind have been away for too long. You forget the power that is held within her arms. She has the power of the forest around her. That is not something that can be taken away lightly. No, we don't believe the Dark Knights were involved."

"Then you suspect it was Nyrra himself?" Eldred asked.

"That is what we suspect."

"But why would he leave the orglin to finish the job?" Richmond was trying to figure it out and their theory seemed to have too many flaws. "If he was able to break through the defences why wouldn't he have destroyed the tree himself? That would be the way I'd do it."

"That's what we thought at first, but nothing else makes sense. There could be many reasons why he didn't continue the assault," Torrin returned.

"There is a very good chance that he wasn't strong enough to finish the job," Palen added.

"We do believe that he has been in a weakened start since breaking out of the Northern Wasteland. It would have taken a lot of his power to accomplish such an act," Eldred mused.

"We also believe that is why it took him so long to make his move. He has been a disease on this land ever since he broke through, but he has been gradually gaining strength," Torrin continued.

"That still doesn't explain why he couldn't have destroyed the tree. Surely breaking through the defences around Nordligträ was the tricky part. How hard would it be to cut down a tree?" Richmond asked.

"You obviously have no idea what you are talking about," Palen snapped.

"Please, this is not time for harsh words," Kyrene cooed. "He is not to know better."

"The tree is strong. She is quite capable of defending herself and striking back. If the Evil One was weakened it would be quite possible for the *Tree of Life* to kill him. Now you see why he couldn't finish the job, if in fact it was him," Torrin explained.

That all made sense, except for the part about the tree fighting back. Richmond had no idea how a tree could fight, but then again there was a lot about his current situation that he didn't understand. It seemed everyday he was sinking further and further behind everyone else, no matter how much he was learning. Sometimes he had to wonder what he was doing in the small group, what did he really have to offer?

"Then what are the orglin doing?" Eldred quickly moved on. "If the tree could kill Nyrra then it should have no problems fighting off the orglin?"

"Now if that was true we wouldn't be here now would we?" Palen scoffed.

"I don't know about anyone else, but this isn't making any sense to me," Richmond replied.

"It's a complicated matter and one that even we don't understand completely." Torrin explained as best his could. "As much as we are one with the *Tree of Life* there is still much that we don't understand. The orglin came in great numbers and we fought as best we could, but in the end there was nothing we could do. We had to retreat and we couldn't stay to see what she was doing to fight back."

Eldred was sure in the end the information would be important, but for the moment he couldn't work it out. He had studied the seven artefacts when he was young, but there had been limited information on them. It was no surprise that if the elves who lived around one such artefact their entire lives didn't fully understand it then the books wouldn't have much information.

"So that brings me back to my original suggestion. You need to meet the Alliance. They will help you if you help them." Eldred saw another opening.

No one could deny Eldred's words. They made sense and it seemed as though it was the only way the elves could return home. There was a chance that the *Tree of Life* was killing the orglin attacking it, but no one really thought that was plausible. All the tree could do was survive long enough for rescue to arrive. That was the most logical and realistic thought. It still did nothing to help Eldred with his cause and he was sure it did nothing to help the elves. He couldn't understand why they couldn't see he was trying to help them.

"As I told you before, we will remain here. Once we have regrouped we will need to mount our own attack," Palen spoke the revelation. Both Torrin and Kyrene looked somewhat shocked with his announcement. "We can't hope and wait for help from the Alliance. By the time it comes it may already be too late."

Eldred couldn't argue with that, as much as he wanted to. Everything within him was telling him that they had to join the Alliance, everything except for a small voice inside his head. There didn't seem to be anything they could do though, not against a hoard of orglin. They would need an army to accomplish such a feat. It was frustrating that either option seemed to be leading towards the death of the *Tree of Life* and Nyrra's success.

"I'd like to take a look for myself," Eldred said after a long pause. "Things don't really seem to be making sense and seeing things with my own eyes will shed some light on the best course of action."

There was another pause as the two remaining council members and the magistrate thought on Eldred's suggestion. At least it sounded like a suggestion to them.

"I think that sounds like a good idea. We need to know what the situation is before we make our next move,' Torrin finally spoke. "Let us hope that she still stands tall."

"We would know is she has fallen and let's hope that doesn't happen," Kyrene added.

"We shall send scouts with you Eldred. Then you can report back what you have found," Palen ended.

Eldred wasn't planning on scouting and returning. With a little luck Viper would be ready to move when they had finished with the council. His plan was to get a look at the tree and then continue with his own mission, but it didn't seem as though that would be the case. He had to admit though, that he would like the assistance of trained elvish scouts. There was less chance of getting caught that way and there was no telling what the *Tree of Life* was thinking. She could easily mistake him for the enemy.

"I think you should leave right away. There is no time to waste," Kyrene suggested.

Eldred had many more questions, but he knew he had already pushed his luck too far. For the moment he would have to be satisfied with the answers he had received. He had to admit he really did want to see the *Tree of Life*. In all his times in Nordligträ he had never seen the tree, nor known of its whereabouts. That was one thing he found odd. In all his studies none of the texts revealed its location.

"Very well. You need to check on Viper. Hopefully he should be awake by now," Eldred spoke to both Richmond and Alena, although he didn't really believe his words.

"I'm coming with you!" Alena stated as they left the building.

"I would prefer it if you stayed here." Kyrene spoke. "Our scouts should be enough to get Eldred there and back safely."

"I am quite capable of looking after myself. I have always heard stories of the *Tree of Life* when I was younger. Now that I have an opportunity to see her for myself I am not going to give up that chance. With all due respect." She lowered her head slightly. Their candour had made Alena complacent and she quickly remembered they were still somewhat prisoners.

"Very well Alena, I would hate to be the one who prevented you from reaching such a goal. We will send Ewan and Mahon with you. They are our best trackers…" everyone knew Palen meant the best still alive even though he didn't continue with his thought. "They will be able to show the way."

Eldred had to admit that would make the mission go a lot quicker. He really didn't know exactly where they were, which would make it hard to find where they were going. He scolded himself for not thinking about that earlier.

"Richmond, you check on Viper. We'll be back as soon as we can." Eldred spoke as they left the platform.

As much as Richmond didn't want to be left behind he knew there was little point in arguing. In the end he figured that he would only slow them down and if the orglin noticed them it wouldn't be good. The thought of staying in the small room with Viper did nothing to settle his nerves.

"You can move freely whilst you're here," Torrin offered. "Please be careful around the others. They are rightfully sceptical of strangers and the serpent.

That made Richmond a little happier. At least he was going to be able to spend his time in the open air. Being cooped up in the small hut with Viper wasn't appealing and if he was still unconscious then it would be even more tedious.

"Thank you," he responded, trying his best to keep the smile from his face.

The guards returned to escort Richmond back to the hut. He thought it was odd that he had just been given free range, but he wasn't about to complain. Every hut looked the same and he didn't think that he would be able to pick the one they had been imprisoned in.

There were no other elves wandering the forest floor. It seemed as though they were still nervous about the newcomers. He wasn't sure if that would change before they left. It was a shame that such a community should know such fear. Although he had little to do with elves he had read stories when he was younger, not to mention the time he had spent with Alena, and he felt for their plight. They were supposed to be majestical creatures and they weren't supposed to be hiding in fear.

When they reached the hut Richmond was hit by a foul stench when he opened the door. Before he could see if Viper was awake he had to leave the hut.

"What's wrong?" the guard asked.

"Something has happened, I think you should get the läkaren," Richmond suggested.

The sound of his voice was enough to get the guard moving. He wasn't sure what Richmond had seen and he wasn't sure he wanted to. The waft of bad odour drifting in his direction was enough.

It wasn't long before the guard returned with the läkaren. He had a large leaf covering his nose and mouth. Richmond wasn't sure what plant it had come from. He had never seen anything like it before in his life. The läkaren carried another leaf in his hand for Richmond.

"This will cover the smell and help you breathe," he offered.

Richmond hesitated at first before taking it. There were two straps to go around his ears. When he had the leaf in place he noticed that there was a minty smell to it. He had to admit that it was quite pleasant and not at all what he was expecting.

Inside the hut was a completely different story. The läkaren stepped inside first before motioning for Richmond to follow.

What was waiting for them inside wasn't at all what Richmond had been expecting, not that he really knew what he was expecting. In front of the bed in the middle of the room was a pile of dead skin. Richmond could only guess that was the cause of the stench, but the leaf did its job and kept the odour at bay. Lying on the bed was the still form of Viper, but Richmond was sure that he had moved since they left him.

"Did you move him at all?" the läkaren asked confirming his suspicions.

"No, we didn't touch him."

"Then it is as I expected, the medicine worked."

Richmond had no idea what he was talking about. Sure it looked as though Viper had moved and he didn't think that any of the other elves would have done such a thing, but that didn't mean that he was well. The serpentant was still unconscious and by the looks of things he was missing his skin.

"How can you say the medicine is working? If anything he looks worse than he did this morning?" Richmond asked.

"You don't know much about serpentant physiology, do you?" Richmond simply shook his head. He remained close to the door, not waiting to move any further into the hut. "Snakes shed their skin when they need to grow. Serpentants are similar in the sense that they will also shed their skin from time-to-time. One of those times is when they are suffering from a terrible illness. They shed their skin to get rid of the disease. I can only assume that the medicine helped to dispel the poison through his skin."

That made sense to Richmond although he still wasn't completely sure that was the case. The läkaren checked over Viper despite his diagnosis. One thing Richmond noticed was that he didn't touch the serpentant. He did his inspections as closely as he could without touching him. When he was comfortable with his diagnosis he led Richmond from the hut. Neither of them wanted to spend any more time in there than they had to.

Once they were outside the läkaren took his leaf mask off. Richmond quickly followed suit. Despite the minty smell it was nothing compared to the fresh air of the forest. He took a deep breath and felt much better.

"So if shedding his skin makes him better, why is he still unconscious?" It didn't make sense to Richmond. "How do I know you just haven't made things worse?" He instantly wished he hadn't made the last comment, but there was nothing he could do about it.

"I won't lie to you. It would bring me great pleasure to drive a blade into its black heart, but the council have given us strict instructions that it is not to be touched and I for one am taking that very seriously," and very literally Richmond thought.

"That still doesn't explain why he is still unconscious," Richmond was a lot softer this time.

The läkaren sighed before answering. "When they shed their skin they are weakened for a while afterwards. I have no idea how long that weakness will last, but when it passes they become very strong. I guess it is their cycle of life. They are at their strongest once they have shed. Now, as much as I love a good lesson, it is time for me to be leaving. As I understand it you are free to come and go as you please, but you need to be careful of the other elves. They are still not used to your presence and I doubt they will ever be. Just be mindful of that."

Richmond nodded his head without answering. The läkaren was happy with that response and didn't waste any time in leaving. Richmond was glad to be rid of him. There was something very unnerving about the elf's attitude. He wondered at whether his comment about not killing Viper was true. For a moment he thought about remaining with the serpentant, but the thought of returning to the room with the dead skin quickly changed his mind.

Slowly Richmond started to make his way around the makeshift village. There was no one else on the forest floor around him. It seemed as though the elves would remain inside until they left, regardless of the fact that they now have been approved by the council. Richmond wasn't going to let that thought ruin his afternoon. He would take the opportunity to enjoy the peace and try his best to relax.

Chapter 4: Tree of Life

The two elves led the way towards the *Tree of Life* at a swift pace. They moved effortlessly through the thick undergrowth. A multitude of ferns and other plants grew around the trees now they had left the makeshift village. Alena had no problems keeping up with them, but Eldred was falling behind. The wizard, albeit it being in great shape for his age, wasn't able to keep up.

Mahon popped out through the trees to check on him. Eldred took the opportunity to rest, putting his hands on his knees as he panted for breath.

"You need to move more carefully." There was a harshness to Mahon's voice that surprised him. "There is no telling where the orglin are hiding. If you give away our position then we are all dead. Just think about that."

Mahon didn't wait for a response before he disappeared back into the trees. Eldred shook his head. If he could use the power surrounding him then they wouldn't have had that conversation. He knew that he wouldn't be able to move like the trackers, but he would be able to do a lot better than he currently was.

"Don't worry about them Eldred." Alena appeared out of the trees and it took all of Eldred's willpower not to jump in surprise. It seemed as though she was enjoying running with the trackers. "If you need to rest then we can." Although she didn't mean to sound condescending her words ended up that way.

"No, I'll be fine." Eldred, in turn, tried his best not to sound offended. "Do you have any idea how long it will be before I can use magic again?" He asked the question, although he didn't believe she would know the answer.

"I can find out for you," Alena offered.

"That's alright, it'll happen when it happens. Now we best be on our way."

Eldred waited for Alena to disappear again before he started. He had to admit that Mahon was right. Stealth was more important than speed. If they were discovered by the orglin then they would all be either dead or captured and he didn't think there was much chance of the latter.

Keeping quiet was a lot easier said than done. The undergrowth was thick and didn't allow for easy movement. Eldred struggled to find a path that would ease his journey. When he found a clear one it quickly ended in thick ferns and bracken. He knew nothing was going to change until he could use magic again.

They had been travelling for another hour before Eldred finally ran into the three elves again. They were waiting for him at a small clearing. Eldred was glad for another chance to rest. The going had been tough and he was already far behind the others.

"We are getting close now. There is a small group of orglin ahead of us," Ewan kept his voice low, even though the orglin were well out of earshot.

"How far are we from the *Tree of Life*?" Eldred asked.

"No more than half an hour, if we were free of enemies. Depending on where the orglin are positioned I would be expect it to take twice as long," Mahon replied. "You should be able to feel her majesty now."

Eldred closed his eyes and reached out. As with every other time he had tried he expected to be blocked straight away. All of a sudden he could embrace the power around him and it was wonderful. There was nothing like it in the world. He had completely forgotten the pure majesty of the *Tree of Life*, but there was also something wrong, there was an evil in the air. Eldred knew that it wasn't supposed to be there. It was Nyrra's taint, there could be no doubt about it. On the plus side it wasn't strong enough to bring down the tree.

Now that Eldred could use magic again he would be able to keep up with the elves. Not only that, but he would be able to mask their movements.

"We'll rest now. Once we get moving there will be no time to stop and if we get seen then we'll need to run for our lives," Ewan explained.

As much as Eldred wanted to keep going he wasn't sure if they were just being nice to him or whether they needed a rest themselves. With the power of the *Tree of Life* inside him he felt like he could walk for days, but he didn't want the others to know.

"I can feel something evil in the air," Alena changed the subject when no one responded to Ewan. "I do hope the *Tree of Life* is still alright."

"You would know if she was dead. You would feel it in the air," Mahon explained.

After a short break they were off again. This time the trackers didn't disappear from sight. They waited to make sure Eldred was able to stay with them. With the orglin so close it was too dangerous for them to travel the way they had been. Eldred didn't bother to explain that he was able to keep up with their pace. He was happy just to follow on behind.

They didn't continue for long before Ewan raised his hand causing them all to stop. He waited for Eldred to reach whispering distance before he spoke.

"There is a small group of orglin ahead of us. We could try and kill them all, but I think it would be safer to skirt around them." Ewan kept his voice low.

"I don't think it's worth risking the bloodshed. If there are more nearby then the ruckus will alert them to our presence. It might take a little longer, but I think it's worth it," Eldred replied.

No one argued with them. As much as they could have taken care of the small group of orglin it wasn't worth the risk. If they alerted the rest of the hoard then their lives would be over.

As they discussed their next move the subtle scent of burning wood drifted across them. Suddenly a horror filled their hearts.

"They are burning the *Tree of Life*!" Alena gasped, almost forgetting to keep her voice low.

"Let's not jump to conclusions. We don't know that," there was little confidence in Eldred's voice.

"Then we should get there quickly!" Ewan jumped up, but was quickly pulled down by Mahon.

"Getting killed will do nothing for her," Alena said.

Mahon remained calm although he too was obviously keen to keep moving.

"We need to stick with the original plan. The only way we're going to help her is by getting information back to the council," Alena continued

"Let's keep moving. We need to be very careful. Whatever we find when we reach the *Tree of Life* we have to keep our emotions in check." Eldred hoped he could stand by his own words. Although he didn't have a history like the elves he certainly knew what the tree meant to the Seven Kingdoms.

There was no more discussion as they made their way on the last leg of their journey. Mahon led the way with Ewan taking the rear. They wanted to make sure that Eldred was able to keep up. No one realised that with his ability to use magic again he had no problems in keeping the pace. Alena tracked closely behind Mahon. She was very keen to reach the *Tree of Life*.

Mahon kept a brisk pace when he could sense that the orglin weren't close by, but he was forced to stop and listen often. Most of the time there was nothing for him to hear, but he figured it was better to stop and find nothing than walk into a trap. In the end the brisk pace and the constant stopping did nothing to save them time.

The further they travelled the thicker the smell of burning wood became. Wisps of grey smoke flicked through the trees and ash started to fall like snowflakes. Mahon suddenly brought them to another halt as he looked at the ash falling around him.

"She is just through those trees ahead. There is too much ash and smoke for the *Tree of Life* to be the only tree burning. I feel that the orglin are trying to burn the entire forest down."

"If that's the case then we need to be extra careful. The last thing we want is to be burned alive," Ewan added.

The words didn't need to be said. The thoughts were going through everyone's minds. As much as they wanted to see what was happening ahead of them they knew they had to be even more careful. The closer they came to the tree the thicker the clouds of smoke became.

Reaching a place where they could view the *Tree of Life* was harder than they thought. Each time Mahon thought he had found them a safe passage they ran into another group of orglin. On more than one occasion they nearly literally ran into them. If it wasn't for Eldred's subtle spell then they would have been detected. Each time they had to back track further and further. It seemed as though they weren't getting any closer to their destination.

It took over a dozen different routes before they finally reached a vantage point. The sight before them wasn't nearly as bad as they had expected, but it was still a shock. Bodies of orglin were scattered around the base of the tree. It seemed as though the *Tree of Life* wasn't as defenceless as they thought. Even when Palen had told them she was able to defend herself Eldred didn't completely believe him.

The orglin kept their distance and hurled lit branches and large sticks at the tree. Each time the fire bombs were stopped by an invisible barrier as they were about to strike. They were then left to fizzle out on the ground. Alena had to smile to herself, although the sight before her was horrific, at the way the *Tree of Life* was protecting herself. She had to admit that the situation was better than she expected.

Stray projectiles that hit trees near the *Tree of Life* were soon extinguished by random bursts of rainfall. No one could doubt that it was the *Tree of Life* that was creating the rain. Both Mahon and Ewan both held the hilts of their swords. They wanted nothing more than to charge out into the open and start slaying the orglin, but they both knew that would only get them killed. For the moment it seemed as though the *Tree of Life* was capable of defending herself.

"What do we do now?" Alena spoke as softly as she could. She wasn't even sure if anyone heard her. After a few seconds had passed she was about to re-ask the question when Ewan answered.

"We need to get this information back to the others, although I'm not really sure what to make of it."

"I'm not so sure I'm satisfied," Mahon added. "As much as it seems the she is taking care of her attackers I'm not completely sure. I think we should watch a little longer."

"The longer we stay here the greater the chance of being found and if that happens it won't matter what we've discovered. No, we need to leave now."

"Ewan is right," Eldred spoke for the first time. "I'll explain further once we are away from the orglin." As much as his words were mysterious there could be no doubt in them. It was time for them to leave.

Even though Mahon wanted to stay and make sure the *Tree of Life* was indeed safe, or at least capable of looking after herself, he was glad to be on the move again. No one wanted to stay around the orglin. The creatures radiated evil. It contaminated the forest around them and they could all feel the effects.

The journey back towards the council felt as though it had taken a lifetime before Eldred finally called them to a halt. "We are now free of the orglin."

"What is it that you need to tell us?" Mahon didn't wait for Eldred to offer the information.

"The tree is still strong. There is a great deal of strength within."

"That is a good thing?" Alena was trying to work out why Eldred's words were so sombre.

"It is strong now, but it won't last forever. The orglin are having their effect."

"Then we need to act now!" Mahon stood as he spoke.

"How long do we have?" Ewan spoke in a calmer tone.

As much as Eldred had hoped he wouldn't be asked, he knew the question was coming. There was no way he could give an honest response. He had no idea what the truth was, but it did give him a chance to convince the elves to do what he wanted. That in itself could be invaluable.

"There is still time, but it is quickly running out." Eldred explained, trying his best to keep a straight face. No one was really looking at him and therefore didn't see the wry grin slowly appear. Eldred silently cursed himself for not being able to control his emotions.

"Then we need to keep moving. We have to get this information back to the others. The council will need know what is happening." Mahon's nerves were still on edge.

"I'll rush back and explain it to them. You can lead these two back to the village," Ewan knew that whomever returned needed to have a calm head and that definitely wasn't going to be Mahon. He was already so worked up there was no telling what state he would be in when he finally arrived.

"I think it would be better if I brought the news to the council." There was no real reason behind Mahon's statement.

"You two go on ahead. I know the way back for the moment." They both gave Alena a strange look, before they quickly realised that she too was an elf. "It's more important that you explain the situation."

"But..." Eldred spoke as Ewan jumped to his feet. "Be careful what you tell them. There is more to this than you know."

With Eldred's warning in their ears the two trackers started off back to the makeshift village. Ewan was split between asking Eldred what he meant and getting back before Mahon. The fact that Mahon had ignored Eldred's words and had already left made Ewan's decision easy. As much as he regretted not pushing Eldred further he knew that he had to get back to the village.

Alena also stood, but Eldred remained seated. It seemed as though he wasn't quite ready to leave. He liked to tell himself it was because he just wanted to speak with Alena in private, but his fatigue was also playing its part.

"What is it Eldred?" Alena asked when he didn't offer any information.

"We need to get the elves to seek the help of the Alliance and in turn help the Alliance retake Remidel." It wasn't the first time Eldred had mentioned that direction for the Alliance, but he had yet to explain how he knew. For the moment that was in essence irrelevant to the conversation.

"That sounds reasonable enough, but I don't see why you couldn't have said that in front of the others. We'd probably have a better chance of that happening if Mahon and Ewan also gave that point-of-view."

"The problem I have is that I'm not sure the *Tree of Life* has that much time left. She is fighting hard, but I could sense a weakness as well. The orglin attack is relentless."

"Then you should tell the council that!" Alena sounded shocked.

"If I was to tell them that they would rush in to help. I'm sure they will all end up dead and the tree will be just as doomed."

Alena was starting to see the conundrum. There was a very good chance all the elves would die if they tried to attack the orglin. There were just too many of them. Sheer weight of numbers would sway the battle in the orglin's favour. Although Alena had to admit, with the strength of the *Tree of Life* and their skill fighting in the forest, there was a chance the elves would survive. She was grasping at straws, but it was all she had.

"I know, deep down, that the elves have to help the Alliance, but there is also something telling me that we shouldn't leave the tree." Eldred looked off into the distance, as if he wasn't really speaking with Alena.

"Well I guess in the end you can leave the decision to the council." Alena thought it made sense. "Now let's get going. We'll need to make up ground if you want to be part of the decision making process, otherwise they could be done before we make it."

As much as Eldred would have been happy to remain seated for a while he knew Alena was right. Ewan would remain calm, but it was Mahon they had to worry about. There was no doubt he would try and get the elves to mobilise. That in itself could be enough to sway them. Eldred had to remain stalwart in his decision to push them towards Remidel. At least then the council could make an informed decision, even if he was planning on withholding information.

Eldred thought he heard his bones creak as he lifted himself from the ground. Looking at Alena he realised that she hadn't heard anything and figured he was just being silly. There was no doubt in his mind that he would be happy once they had left the magic-free zone. He felt as though he had aged a lifetime in the last few hours, opposed to the many lifetimes he had already lived.

It was on dusk when the pair finally made it back to the village. Eldred had tried to move faster and keep up with Alena, but he just couldn't do it. He had a great empathy for those he travelled with and pushed hard. Once everything was done he was looking forward to returning to his home on the Wizard's Isle. He wanted nothing more than to roll into bed and go to sleep.

As they approached the village they were met by some guards. Any thought of rest was now completely gone. They could only hope that they hadn't taken too much time in returning. The two trackers had returned an hour before them and there was no telling what story they had given the council. On the plus side it didn't look like the elves were mobilising for an attack.

"The council wishes to see you," was all the guard said.

Nothing more needed to be said. Although they knew the way the guards escorted them anyway.

"So this is disturbing news indeed." Kyrene didn't wait for greetings. "Is what Mahon says true or should we trust Ewan?"

Eldred felt as though it was a loaded question. There was no right answer without knowing what each elf had already said. All he could do was explain his own point-of-view. It wasn't going to be an easy task.

"The tree is strong. She," Eldred thought it would be better to refer to the tree as she and not it "has defences that seem to be keeping the orglin at bay." Eldred spoke slowly and carefully.

"We have been told as much. Tell us something we don't know." Kyrene's tone was bordering on rudeness. Eldred didn't think that was a good sign.

Again Eldred would have loved to have been able to use magic. It would have washed away the fatigue and given him the strength to continue. Now it was just pure willpower that kept him from losing consciousness.

"The tree will fall, eventually, if she doesn't receive any help."

"See, that's what I told you." Mahon didn't give Eldred a chance to continue. "We need to attack now before it is too late."

"Quiet Mahon!" Palen boomed. "You were told to remain quiet until asked to speak and that is what you shall do." The sudden outburst came as a surprise to everyone.

Eldred waited for a moment before he continued. "But now is not the time to rush in. She is holding her own for the moment and there aren't enough elves to defeat the orglin." Eldred paused for a response.

When none came Palen looked towards Mahon and Ewan. It seemed as though he was looking for a response from his scouts. Neither of them wanted to speak out of turn, not knowing who had been given permission to speak.

"What do you think Mahon?" Palen finally asked.

"Now is the time to attack. Now is when the *Tree of Life* is still strong. We can attack whilst she keeps them distracted." Mahon seemed very proud of his revelation.

"These words sound wise, what say you Ewan?" Palen asked the question before Eldred had a chance to respond.

"If what Mahon says is true then it would make sense, but I'm not sure he's correct. We don't know how many orglin there are attacking the tree. We didn't think it wise to linger too long, for fear we'd be caught." Ewan responded.

"What about the *Tree of Life*? Do you think she can remain much longer?" Palen pushed.

Ewan looked uncomfortable. Eldred was sure they had already spoken of such matters, but he asked the question anyway. Eldred had a bad feeling that he already knew what the answer was going to be and it wasn't the one he was looking for.

"From what I saw it will only be a matter of time before she falls." Ewan kept his eyes low as he spoke.

"Well, what do you have to say about that?" Palen almost made an accusation with his question.

"What they say is true. Without support the *Tree of Life* will fall, but there is still time. If you send your elves into battle now they will all die." Eldred continued.

"But the *Tree of Life* will protect us. You have seen it with your own eyes. We have heard the testimonies of Ewan and Mahon." Palen interrupted again.

"Please Palen, let him finish. If you don't want to hear his answers then don't ask the questions." Kyrene tried to be as diplomatic as possible. She knew her husband was starting to become enraged.

"Of course, my love, please continue."

Eldred breathed a sigh of relief. He wasn't sure how that was going to end up, but it seemed to be in his favour.

"It is true, the *Tree of Life* will give you some protection, but I doubt it will be enough to save you. If it was the Evil One's plan to destroy the *Tree of Life* then he wouldn't have left the orglin short. There will be many more than we could see, that I would put my life on." Eldred paused as he let the information sink in. "I can't speak as to how long the *Tree of Life* will survive, but I know she is strong and she won't give up lightly. The only way I can see her surviving is if you gain the assistance from the Alliance." The more Eldred had thought on the matter, the more he agreed with it.

"And you Alena. What is your opinion on the matter?" Palen asked when it was clear that Eldred had finished speaking.

Alena looked at Eldred before she spoke. She had been hoping that she would not be called to answer anything. It had crossed her mind to return to their hut to rest, but the thought of returning to the small space didn't appeal to her.

"I think Eldred is right," she finally spoke. "If you send in your elves you will surely die and the *Tree of Life* will be doomed anyway. Now I can't say you won't be too late waiting for the Alliance, but it is the only option I can see."

"Thank you for your candour." Kyrene spoke before Palen had a chance to. "I think we need to think on things and make our decision in the morning. You are free to stay here tonight, but tomorrow may be a different story."

It was clear that Palen wanted to keep talking, but he deferred to his wife. It was time for them to discuss matters in private. He wished for nothing else than for the other council members to still be alive. The decision was too big for the two of them to make on their own, but they were all that was left.

Eldred and Alena were just as happy to be leaving. There was much more that could be said, but neither of them wanted to speak for fear of saying the wrong thing. At least the council seemed prepared to discuss the matter, which was more than Eldred had thought would happen.

"I think that went well," Alena started when they left the building.

It seemed as though they were to be trusted by the elves as there were no guards waiting for them when the platform touched the ground. It freed up their conversation.

"Only time will tell." Eldred wasn't so sure, but he didn't want to share his opinion. "Now I'm more concerned about Viper's condition. I really hoped we could have been on the move before nightfall." That wasn't exactly a lie. If he wasn't feeling deathly tired he would have wanted them to be on their way. "Either way we are going to have to wait until the morning to see what the elves are going to do."

Alena didn't respond. She knew she had said what Eldred had wanted, but she wasn't completely sure she had made the right decision. There was something inside of her that wanted to protect the tree at all costs. Something had touched her deep inside seeing such magical beauty. She had felt the glory of the *Tree of Life* and she didn't want to let it go.

"Are you sure there isn't anything you can do?" Alena asked, changing the subject. "You do have the Emerald stone. Surely that can do something to help."

The thought had also crossed Eldred's mind, but it was not something he was prepared to do. There was no telling what would happen if the Emerald stone came so close to the *Tree of Life*. The two forces could be enough to rip the world apart and that wasn't a risk Eldred was prepared to take.

"I don't know what would happen if we brought the two together. I know that it seems as though the two are connected, but it's not as simple as that." Eldred tried his best to explain something he really wasn't sure about himself. "No, this is the best plan to save the tree. They need to join the Alliance and bring them here."

"I'm not sure they will like bringing strangers to their sacred land. I remember they were dubious allowing my father's emissaries," Alena explained.

"I think when it comes to the *Tree of Life* they will do whatever it takes to keep it alive." There was no doubt in Eldred's words. "Anyway, there is nothing we can do about it now. We have to get ready to leave."

When they returned to their miserly accommodation they found Richmond standing outside. He had a small bowl in his hand and it looked as though he was just finishing eating. Eldred didn't think it looked like a good sign.

"How is Viper?" Eldred asked without greeting him.

Richmond explained what had happened in their absence. He did not have the stomach to risk the stench to see if Viper was awake. He figured that the serpentant would surface when he was ready.

"I'm sure it's not that bad," Alena pushed her way past Richmond.

Eldred knew what Richmond said was true, but his need to find out if Viper was conscious outweighed his common sense. Alena only just managed to get the door open before she returned. She gagged a few times before she was able to compose herself.

"I told you," Richmond had a broad smile on his face and Eldred had to chuckle.

"What did you see inside?" Eldred asked.

"I saw Viper sitting on his bed," Alena cringed at the thought of the stench. "It seems as though he's going to be alright."

Slowly the door opened and Viper poked his hooded head.

"Is it safe to come out?" his voice sounded weak.

"I think you should be fine. I haven't seen any elves around," Eldred replied, taking a quick look around.

Viper slowly stepped outside. He looked shaky on his feet. Richmond had to believe what the läkaren had told him. It seemed as though Viper was going to be in a weakened state for a while. It would be a perfect time to do away with him, if only that was an option.

"Where are we? What's happened?" Viper asked.

"We were drugged. It seems as though you had an adverse reaction to it. You have been unconscious for a couple of days. The läkaren gave you something that made you shed your skin and now it seems as though you are fine, if not a little groggy." Eldred continued to explain about the elves and their situation, without mentioning the *Tree of Life*.

Viper rolled the sleeves up on the robe and looked at his skin. Before the change his skin was a dark, almost sickly, green. Now it was a fresh green-yellow colour. He studied his arm for a moment before sliding the sleeves back over his hands. Although no one could see his face they could tell by his body language that something was wrong.

"What is it?" Alena eventually asked.

"This wasn't supposed to happen."

"What wasn't supposed to happen?"

"I wasn't due to shed my skin again for another hundred years or so. It wasn't that long ago since I last shed. This isn't a good sign." There was concern in his voice, or at least as best they could tell.

"What are you talking about?" They were all surprised when Eldred spoke.

Viper thought for a moment, he really wasn't sure if he should divulge his secrets, but in the end he decided he needed them to know if he was going to survive the next stage of their journey.

"We serpentants regenerate by shedding our skin. We do this every hundred years or so. This is something we were told to do by the queen when she was still with us." Viper paused.

"But after you shed don't you become more powerful?" Richmond asked.

"Yes, that is true. We are at our most powerful a few days after we shed, but it is that power that we need to use until we shed again. It was less than a year since my last shed. There is no telling what will happen now."

"So what does that mean?" Richmond asked.

"Normally it takes about a week to fully recover from shedding. That is after one hundred years. After such a short period of time there is no telling how long it will take for me to gain my strength back." When he finished speaking his legs crumbled underneath him. He sat upright and leant against the wall of the hut. Gasping for breath was the only way he could suck air into his lungs. They were all slowly starting to see the result of the premature shedding.

"Don't worry about me." There was a touch of sarcasm to his voice when no one came to his aid. "I will be able to travel. I assume since you are all here we'll be leaving soon. I doubt the elves want me around now that I am conscious again. By the sounds of things I am not sure they were that keen to have me here when I was unconscious." Viper was starting to sound sorry for himself.

"We are allowed to stay here until morning. They are making a decision on something important and I want to be around to see what it is. You should go back to the hut and get some rest. You will need all the strength you can muster for the morning." Eldred advised.

It was clear that Eldred wasn't going to divulge any more information and Viper didn't have the energy to push any further. It took all of his remaining energy to push himself to his feet and return inside the hut.

Just after Viper had returned inside a familiar looking elf arrived. They recognised him as one of the guards who had escorted them, but no one knew his name. He had a smile on his face, which seemed like a good sign.

"I have been informed of the state of your lodgings." He paused for a brief moment. "The council have generously offered you another home to stay in for your last night here." For some reason he didn't sound happy with the good news. It seemed as though the smile was forced.

As much as they didn't want to put another elf out of their home there was no way they could sleep in the stench. Instead they simply accepted the offer. Eldred didn't know how long he would be able to remain standing and the thought of a bed was almost overwhelming. The other two were simply happy to go along with Eldred. They all wanted a good night sleep before they were on the road again.

Chapter 5: Time to Rest?

They were woken in the morning by a knock on the door. All three had been given a bed for the night and none of them wanted to leave it. If it wasn't for the persistent knocking they would have been happy to spend the rest of the day in bed. In the end it was Eldred who dragged himself out first. He was met by the same guard as the one who had met them the night before. At the time Eldred wished that he had learnt the elf's name, but it seemed as though he was happy enough to forgo the pleasantries and get straight down to business.

"The council is ready to see you. They have made their decision." He didn't wait for a response before turning and leaving.

Alena and Richmond had to rush out of bed to catch up with them. As much as Eldred needed to rest there was no point in wasting time. Once they had their answer from the council, regardless of what that answer was, they would be on their way. Eldred had to keep telling himself that. Even if the council decided to throw themselves against the orglin then he would just have to accept it, no matter how bad an idea it was.

They were met at the foot of the tree which held the council building. Along with Kyrene, Palen and the magistrate were their horses and their packs. Eldred didn't know whether to be worried or relieved. Either way it seemed as though it wouldn't be long before they were on their way, although there was still no sign of Viper. It seemed as though he wasn't invited to their meeting.

"The serpent will be released once we are done here." Palen pre-empted the question.

"What have you decided?" Eldred changed the subject.

There was an uncomfortable silence as the three elves looked at each other. Although they called the meeting it seemed as though none of them wanted to speak. In the end it was up to the magistrate.

"As much as it pains us that such a decision has been left to the two remaining council members, it has been made. There is no time to bring more members into the council, although there are many still alive who deserve the position." No one was really sure where Torrin was going with his speech. "These are indeed dark times that we live in and we need to make tough decisions to ensure the survival of our race."

"Enough Torrin," Kyrene interrupted. "We have decided that we will leave the safety of our sanctuary and seek the army of men." Eldred let out an audible sigh of relief. It was only at that moment that he realised he had been holding his breath.

"It's not something we are happy about." Palen continued for his wife. "It has been longer than I can remember since last we left our home, if it has ever been done before. We have decided that this is our only course of action if we are going to save not only our home, but our entire way of life. We cannot let the *Tree of Life* fall or else all is lost."

Eldred had to admit he was happy with the result. When he went to sleep he had not expected to them to agree with him. He was sure they were going to go to their deaths in an act of futility to protect the tree. Now he could leave with the confidence that they were doing the right thing. Not only that, but the Alliance was getting a boost to their ranks, if only for a short period.

"So the only question we have now is where do we go?" Torrin asked.

"You must head for Remidel. That is where you'll meet the Alliance." Eldred wished he had a chance to consult the prophecy to confirm his theory, but time was against him. "I'm sure if you help them to retake Remidel they will help you defeat the orglin. Orric will be on your side and I'm sure you'll have no problems in convincing the army to save the *Tree of Life*."

"All your possessions are here and untouched." Kyrene changed the subject, clearly not interested in continuing their current conversation. "We have given you all the supplies we can spare. It's not much, but it should keep you going for a while. I suggest you do some hunting before you reach the mountains," her last comment was directed at Alena, "if you want to survive the pass."

"Thank you," Alena responded.

"I guess we should be leaving now." Eldred figured the meeting was as good as over.

"Fair thee well and I hope we meet again one day," Palen spoke to the group, although Eldred wasn't sure he truly meant it.

The farewell was brief. Once Palen had spoken the three elves returned to the building in the trees. They didn't wait to watch the group leave. There were obviously more important things they needed to do. It wouldn't be easy giving the news to the rest of the elves that they would be leaving the safety of their sanctuary. Not only that, but they were to leave the forest altogether and help those who they had always come to fear and loathe. Eldred didn't envy them.

They found Viper waiting for them out the front of the hut. He didn't look too steady on his feet, but at least he was upright and seemed eager to leave. That in itself was a promising sign.

"How are you feeling today?" Eldred asked.

"I'll be alright to ride. You don't have to worry about me." He sounded a little over-defensive in his response.

That was enough for Eldred. It was well past the time they needed to be on their way. The fact they would have to ride slowly to compensate for Viper's condition didn't make it any better. Now he had resigned himself to the fact that the serpentant was coming with them he couldn't risk leaving him behind. That's what frustrated Eldred the most. All he could do was hope and wait that Viper's part in their tale would soon be over.

"Let's get going then," Eldred replied.

They all mounted except for Eldred. He wanted to check his packs before they left. If any of the stones or the prophecy were missing he wanted to know. He found the prophecy sitting on top of his clothes, where he had left it, but the small chest containing the stones was missing. His heart instantly started pumping hard. If the elves had taken the stones then there was no telling what they would do with them. He relaxed when he came to his last pack. He found the chest mixed in with a variety of fruits and vegetables. It didn't look as though it had been opened.

"Are you coming?" Alena looked back towards him.

"I just had to check to make sure everything was still here."

Alena lead the way out of the village. Adelanta seemed to be somewhat disappointed to be leaving, but if they were to be on the move he wanted to get going. He missed having Alaric on his back, but he wasn't prepared to let anyone else ride him. He was happier to be used as one of the pack horses.

They rode of out the makeshift village in silence. There was still no sign of any other elves. That made Alena sad. She was almost ashamed at how timid her brethren had become, but the overwhelming feeling of sorrow overpowered it. It was a bad sign. Things were coming to a head and it seemed as though they were still far away from their destination. If the Evil One was close then their entire mission might be just a futile exercise. She had to try and shake that feeling. Depression was sinking in and it would be difficult to get rid of.

It wasn't until they were clear of the village did anyone speak. Richmond was the first the break the silence. He could feel the tension throughout the group and thought it was a good idea to try and break it.

"So what is our path now?" It was a fairly innocuous question.

"We head for Dragon's Pass and then on to Lel Dinion," Eldred seemed deep in thought and he mindlessly answered the question.

"Are you sure that is the right path for us to take. Zmaj Pass is not renowned to be the safest of routes. There are many other, safer, routes we could take?" Richmond didn't really think they would change direction, even though he really wanted to, it was more to keep the conversation going. He felt better hearing voices opposed to the incessant beating of hooves.

Eldred reined in his horse. The others followed suit.

"What did you say?" The question was genuine as he had not been listening. He had not been expecting any follow up to his answer.

"Ah, I just wondered why we don't take an easier route to Lel Dinion?" Richmond sounded a little concerned.

Eldred looked up and around before taking a deep breath. It seemed like a strange ritual and everyone waited to see what the result was going to be. Eventually he turned to the others, with a broad smile on his face.

"You don't feel it in the air?" Eldred asked, mysteriously.

The others looked around and tried to imitate Eldred's ceremony, but none of them realised what he was talking about. They knew Eldred had been acting strange ever since Alaric had left them, now they weren't sure if he was holding it together. Alena and Viper both knew they couldn't use magic and wondered if that was having an effect on him.

"You really can't feel that?" The question hung on the air for a moment before Eldred continued. "We have no choice in the direction we take. If you really feel deep down inside yourselves you will feel a tug to the north. We will be lead to Dragon's Pass regardless of what we want. I dare say it wouldn't be too hard to get turned around this deep in the forest."

"I'm sure you know what you're talking about, but an elf doesn't get turned around in a forest. That is one thing I can guarantee you," Alena replied.

"I have no doubt in your abilities, but let me ask you this. What direction have we been travelling in since we left the village?" Eldred's smile grew broader.

"That's easy. We left heading due west and our course hasn't changed, give or take missing a few trees." Alena sounded sure of herself.

"Would anyone else like to hazard a guess?" Eldred asked.

"We have been travelling north-west since about an hour ago," Viper's voice sounded weak.

"He's right. I wanted to lead us closer to the mountain range before we pushed north, but it seems as though the prophecy has different ideas for us," Eldred explained.

Alena surveyed her surroundings for a moment. Without being able to see the sun it was impossible to tell exactly where they were, but she now felt what Eldred was talking about. There was a tug to the north-west and it had been slowly dragging them off course.

"I guess you're right. We don't have any choice anymore," Alena didn't sound happy with the revelation.

"We should keep moving. There's no telling how long it will be before Viper needs to rest. We need to get as many leagues done as we can," Eldred kept his voice level, trying his best not to sound condescending.

"I will be fine. We ride until everyone is ready to stop. Don't make any exceptions for me," Viper tried to sound resilient even though his voice was still very weak.

The truth was that Eldred really didn't care about Viper. He was more concerned with himself. Until he was able to use magic again his body would struggle. Something had changed in the Northern Forest. It hadn't taken long when they were moving towards the *Tree of Life* before he could use magic again. In all the time he had visited the elves he had never experienced such a void in magic. The thought had plagued him when they were staying in Akastiere and had only increased since they had left.

As they continued he only thought he had another hour in him before he would need to rest. It was getting close to midday, so he figured they would need to eat. It was a good enough excuse to stop.

They stopped after another hour as per Eldred's instructions. Everyone was hungry so no one complained when he used Viper for an excuse. In truth Eldred was the one who needed the rest more than the others, but he couldn't let them know that. He knew that it couldn't be long before whatever it was that was shielding him would be gone.

"There is a strange feeling to the forest," Alena spoke whilst they were eating.

"What do you mean?" Eldred replied.

"I'm not sure. Something just feels wrong."

"Do you think it has anything to do with the attack on the *Tree of Life*?" Richmond asked.

Eldred kept a close eye on Viper. Although the serpentant didn't seem to be taking any notice of the conversation it was hard to tell with his hood drawn. Eldred didn't really want him to know about the *Tree of Life*, but there was no way to keep it from him. He could now only hope that Alena didn't reveal too much information.

"The forest does seem... wrong... maybe sick is a better word. It might have something to do with the attack on the *Tree of Life*. She is connected to every tree, every flower, every blade of grass in the Seven Kingdoms." Alena mused, just coming to the conclusion.

"You never told me what was happening there." It seemed as though Richmond was just making conversation.

"The situation was under control." Eldred cut in before Alena could answer. "The tree is a lot stronger than everyone gives it credit. It will survive until help arrives."

Richmond suddenly realised why Eldred had been so obtuse and stopped asking questions. The group went quiet again, which was, albeit somewhat depressing, what Eldred wanted. He didn't know what Viper could do with the information, but he wasn't going to take the risk.

"What about the magic Eldred?" Alena asked when they had finished eating. "I still can't feel anything. Maybe that is what is off about the forest?"

As much as Eldred didn't want to discuss the topic, he did want to get a response from Viper. He was hoping that the serpentant was also unable to use magic. If that wasn't the case then he was about to put them in a very dangerous situation.

"Still nothing. I would have thought that whatever it was that was blocking us would have worn off by now." Eldred watched Viper as he spoke. When there was no response he asked him. "What about you Viper?"

"It's a relief to me." Viper still sounded weak and his words forced. "I thought it was a side-effect of my recent shedding. It's good to know that I'm not the only one who can't use magic. At least that's something." Viper slumped a little more when he finished speaking.

"Well I guess we should be on our way again." As much as Eldred wanted nothing more than to continue resting he knew once they were away from the block he would start to feel better again.

Viper was the only one who didn't seem keen to be back in the saddle and was the last to mount. No one waited for him. In truth they were hoping he would just remain behind. Although they all knew that wouldn't happen they weren't going to make life easy for him.

They travelled for the rest of the day until the light faded and they could no longer see in the dark. Even though the sun had only just set it had already become cold. Eldred didn't like the crispness in the air. He knew it was only a matter of time before it started snowing. That wouldn't make their lives any easier. The elves had provided them with some thick deer-skin coats, but that would only protect them so much. Richmond and Alena were his main concern and even Viper, in his weakened state, worried him. For the moment he would be happy when a fire was burning brightly.

Without the ability to use magic Eldred huddled by the fire with the others. He wanted nothing more than to start reading through the *Prophecy of the Stone* again, but it seemed as though he would have to settle for a good night sleep. He didn't want to risk the others reading over his shoulder. There was a lot of sacred information contained in the text and he didn't want the others reading something they shouldn't.

When they woke there was a layer of frost on the ground. The fire had burned through the night and prevented any of them from getting wet, but it was still an uncomfortable morning. No one complained when Eldred suggested they get moving again after they had all eaten breakfast.

As they day progressed their course slowly started to bend around to the north-west again, but no one noticed. After Eldred's revelation they had resigned themselves to the fact that the prophecy would pull them in whichever direction it desired. In the end they would end up where they needed to be and that was all that mattered. Eldred didn't like not being in control of his own destiny, but when it was said and done the only difference was that he knew the choice had been taken from him. He was sure that at least for the last few years, if not his entire life, the prophecy had been leading him around as if he were on a leash.

They stopped for the night before the light had completely failed. So far they hadn't seen a sign of rain, which was promising. Without rain there was little chance of snow even though the temperature was dropping quickly.

In the distance they could see the peaks of the Cloumid Mountain range. A white tipped mountain could be seen over the tree tops. The sight was both ominous and exhilarating. There was something mysterious and dangerous about it.

Eldred stared at the peaks as the others set up camp. He had a bad feeling another disaster was awaiting them. The last time he had taken Dragons Pass it had not ended well. He had a run in with its namesake and was lucky to get out alive. There was a feeling that something very similar was waiting for them and there was nothing he could do to prevent it. If Khan was indeed residing inside the pass then there was a good chance at least one of them wouldn't make it to the other side.

"Come and eat?" Alena's voice broke him from his reverie.

Again the coldness in the air forced them all to sit close around the campfire, not giving Eldred an opportunity to read the prophecy. There was a chance he could wait for them all to sleep before he read the great tome, but he also wanted to take the opportunity to rest.

Viper was suffering the most from the cold. Serpentants, like other reptiles, were cold-blooded. They relied on the heat of the sun to keep them going. As much as they didn't need to hibernate like their relatives, they didn't like the cold and avoided it at all costs. In Viper's weakened condition he needed heat to heal himself. One thing he knew was that he was never to shed in winter. Regenerating was supposed to happen in summer when he would heal quicker and become stronger. Heading towards snow-capped mountains was about the worst thing he could do, but he had no choice. In his current condition he didn't have the energy to regulate his body temperature.

"So how long do you think it will take for us to reach Zmaj Pass?" Richmond asked when they finished eating. No one had spoken since they had started and Richmond thought it was a good way to reduce their morose feelings.

"That's hard to say," Eldred responded. He had been lost in thought and not expected the question.

"Why do you say that?" Richmond asked.

Eldred looked at Viper before speaking again. The serpentant didn't look interested in their conversation. He looked as though he was sleeping where he sat. Eldred figured that it was safe enough to speak in front of him.

"It seems as though the prophecy is messing with time again. I can't really tell where we are exactly, at least until we get closer to the mountain. It's too hard to tell just by the very tips of some of them." Eldred paused for a moment. "I do feel as though we will be at the pass in the next couple of days, at least if we keep up our current rate of travel."

There was a moment of silence as they all thought on the revelation. It should have taken them at least two weeks to reach the pass. The time saving would more than make up for the time they had lost with the elves. Alena came to the realisation before the others.

"So it seems as though the prophecy will get us to where it wants us to be when it wants us to be there." Alena revealed. "I'm not sure if it's a good thing or a bad thing."

"I hope it's a good thing, but I feel as though it's just the way it is, neither good nor bad." Eldred returned.

"So what are we supposed to make of that?" Richmond asked.

"Don't try and make anything of it. There won't be any answers, at least not tonight. For the moment we should be grateful that we know we are heading in the right direction at the right time. Whatever that means."

Eldred setup his bedroll when he finished speaking. He was tired of the conversation and figured if he made his preparations for sleep the others would follow suit. That wasn't the case. No one spoke until he had finished, but that all changed when he returned to the fire.

"What is it you're not telling us?" Alena pushed.

"Nothing!" Eldred wasn't expecting the question. "There is nothing that I know that I haven't revealed to you."

It wasn't exactly true, but under their current circumstances it would have to do. There was nothing really important he was keeping from them, or at least nothing he was certain about. That was the reason he wanted to read the *Prophecy of the Stone*. There was something off about their situation and he really wanted to know what it was. Only pouring through its many pages would he find the answers they were all looking for.

"I think it would be advantageous if we got some sleep now." Even as the words left his mouth he knew how futile they were.

"It doesn't make any difference. We could sleep in until midday and the prophecy would still see us at our destination by nightfall," Alena wasn't finished.

"That's if your theory is correct. If it's not then we could be wasting valuable time." Eldred retorted.

"Of course I'm not suggesting that we sleep the day away. All I'm saying is there is no real reason why we have to go to sleep so early." Alena replied, somewhat defensively.

"I can think of one good reason and that's because I'm tired from the day's ride. That's good enough for me and it should be good enough for the rest of you," Eldred didn't sound happy. It had been the first time that someone in the group had openly challenged him and he didn't like it. He was losing control and that wasn't a good sign. It was one thing for Alaric to challenge his authority, but Alena was completely different. There was nothing wrong with the other's thinking for themselves, they just needed to know when to trust him and when to question him.

Alena shot Richmond a look. At first he shrugged his shoulders before he realised that she wanted him to speak. He had been quite happy letting her go, but it seemed as though it was his turn. He wasn't so sure about questioning the old wizard. He could sense Eldred's annoyance and wasn't sure if he wanted to push any further.

"Good night then, I doubt we will be far behind you." Was all he could say.

Alena huffed before standing and leaving the fire.

"Be careful not to wander off too far. The nights are getting deathly cold." Eldred called from his bedroll.

She couldn't believe Richmond had backed down. There was no real reason why she should be challenging Eldred, it was just that something was bothering her and she couldn't put her finger on it. It was possible that it was the sensation she was receiving from the forest around her, but she really didn't think that was it. There was something else, something more personal. In the end she decided she didn't what to know what it was, especially since it was having such a profound effect on her and especially if it had something to do with Alaric. She had been sad when he had left. The time they had spent on the Wizards' Isle had been priceless. Even though she knew that they needed to continue their mission she just wanted to be with him.

The first time they had been separated she thought she was going to die and she very nearly did. When he came to save her she swore to herself that she would never let them be separated again. That choice had been taken out of her hands the day he had retrieved the Opal stone. She saw it in his eyes. Something had changed inside him and he didn't even stay long enough for her to ask him what. Now she didn't even know if he was the same person she had fallen in love with. She quickly banished that thought from her mind. It was thoughts like that which would lead to despair and that was more dangerous than the evil they fought. She had to hold onto the idea that one day they would meet again.

When she came out of her reverie she realised that she had completely wandered away from the campsite. She wished she had taken Eldred's advice and stayed close to the fire. The night air was close to freezing and Alena had not put on any additional clothes. She looked around, but the night was dark. Clouds covered the moon and the trees blocked out the slim light that crept through. It was at that moment that she realised she had no idea where she was or how to get back to the camp. Panic filled her body. She knew if she didn't get back to the warmth of the fire soon she wouldn't last the night. She also knew if she took the wrong path she would only travel further away from safety and the last thing she wanted to do was to yell out. There was no telling what evil creatures were lurking in the dark.

The only chance Alena had was to climb a nearby tree and try to gauge the direction by the stars. Not that she knew where she was or where she had come from, but she had to do something. Slowly she was starting to shiver and that in itself was a sign she had to do something. The next problem she had was attempting to climb a tree in the dark. The thick pine trees would be almost impossible to navigate without some light. As soon as Alena put her hand on the lowest branch of the nearest tree she knew that it was a pointless exercise. Instead of lifting herself into the tree she let herself drop to the ground.

In an attempt to warm her hands she blew hot breath on them. It was also a futile effort, but it was better than nothing. She looked around, but again it was too dark to see, even with her elven eyes. If anything it had become darker than before. For a moment she wondered how she managed to get so far without being able to see. Something wasn't adding up. She felt as though she had been lead to her current location.

All of a sudden a bright light shone a few paces in front of her. The light was so bright that Alena and to lower her head and cover her eyes. Before she had a chance to turn away Alena thought she saw a dark figure in the centre of the light. A sudden wave of horror washed over her. Whatever it was she didn't think it was friendly.

Chapter 6: Wood Sprite

"Stand my child," the voice from the light was deep and soothing. "I mean you no harm."

Alena slowly stood from her crouched position. She opened her hand slightly and saw that the intense light was starting to dissipate. Carefully she pulled her fingers away from her eyes and peeked at the sight before her. She had to blink a number of times before she could focus. The sight was not at all what she had been expecting.

The light dulled enough for Alena to see who was standing before her. It was an elderly looking man with long white hair. His face was lined with age, but it still looked as though it had the strength of youth. He was dressed in a thin green tunic trimmed with yellow stitching. It looked as though he should have frozen to death in the chill of the night and yet he didn't show any sign of the cold.

Alena waited patiently for the man to speak. She assumed he was some kind of sorcerer or wizard, although she couldn't say which side he was on. Although he looked harmless enough and his voice was calming, that wasn't necessarily a good sign. The only promising thing so far was that he had not made any move to attack her.

"Who are you and what do you want?" Alena's teeth chattered as she spoke.

"It has been a long time since I have seen an elf this far to the west, but there is something different about you," slight concern entered his voice. "You're not of the Northern Elves are you?" He let the question rest, but didn't wait for Alena to answer. "No, you are something different. I don't know if this is a good sign or an ominous one." He made a sign of thinking for a moment. "I choose to see it as a good sign and therefore that's what it shall be." His voice sounded melodical as he made his revelation.

Alena relaxed a little at his words, at least as much as she could in the freezing cold. She didn't know how much longer she could remain there. The longer the conversation took the greater the chance she would freeze to death. On the other hand if this was indeed an enemy she wasn't sure if she wanted to lead him to the others.

"I ask you again, who are you?" Alena's chattering teeth became even worse.

"I'm sorry child, how rude of me. I didn't notice that you must be deathly cold. Let me warm you up." He waved his hands in front of himself and the light glowed brighter.

A moment later Alena felt a warm sensation inside her chest. The feeling was so sudden that she gasped for breath. As the air hit her lungs the feeling of heat moved down her arms and legs and finally up through her head. When it finished moving it settled. Even the cold from around her couldn't penetrate the new shield of warmth. Alena couldn't help but smile. Whoever it was before her had just assured that she wouldn't die, at least for a while. All she had to do now was find her way back to the others, but she couldn't until she had more information about her saviour.

"Thank you, but..."

"That is perfectly fine. I couldn't have you dying on me, now could I?" It was a rhetorical question, although when Alena was about to respond he kept talking. "Now I am curious as to what you are doing all the way out here and where you have come from."

Alena let her shoulders drop. It seemed as though he wouldn't reveal who he was until she had given him more information. For the moment he seemed safe enough, so she didn't think there'd be any problem in giving him some information.

"I am travelling to Lel Dinion. I am from Elhjem." She kept her answers short.

"This is not the way to Lel Dinion from Elhjem. There is something not quite right with your tale." A scowl appeared on his face and his words lost some of their pleasantness.

Alena really didn't want to reveal any more information, but it didn't seem as though she had a choice. He knew more than she had expected. Now that she had spent some time with the strange glowing creature Alena wasn't so afraid. She felt there was something very familiar about him and that changed her original opinion that he was a sorcerer or a wizard. He was something else again.

"It has been a long time since I left Elhjem," Alena revealed a little more.

"Hmm. That would make some sense I suppose." He seemed happy with her answer. "You would know Orric then? It has been many years since I have seen him, mores the pity. I used enjoy my conversations with him."

The plot was thickening, now Alena really didn't know what to think.

"Orric is my father!"

The forest went deathly quiet and his light started to fade. It was clear that the figure in the light was stunned by the revelation. It looked as though he wasn't sure if Alena was telling the truth. There was an uncomfortable silence as he stared at her, as if he was trying to find something inside her. Alena didn't know what to do or say, so she remained still and waited for his response. Slowly a broad grin appeared on his face.

"Little Alena? Is that really you?"

Now it was Alena's turn to be surprised. How could he know her name?

"Who are you?" Alena asked breathlessly.

"I am sorry, I am getting old and sometimes I forget myself. My name is Gaius. We have met before, but I guess you were too young to remember." His voice had returned to its kindly tone.

The name did sound familiar, but she couldn't place from where she had heard it. The feeling that he was familiar was almost overwhelming. Even so she still had no idea who he was. And then suddenly it came to her, although she wasn't sure if her memory was serving her correctly.

"You're the Wood Sprite Gaius?" she asked in surprise.

"Yes, I suppose that is what you could call me. Yes, it has been a long time since I've gone under that name, but you can call me a Wood Sprite." Alena was lost. She didn't really understand what he was getting at.

"I thought all the Wood Sprites had died, many, many years ago?" Alena asked.

"Who told you that?" Gaius sounded genuinely upset.

Alena had to think back to her childhood. It was a lot further back than she was willing to admit. When she realised who had told her, she wished she'd had kept her mouth shut.

"It was my father," she spoke softly with the hope that he didn't fully hear her.

"Hmm..." The light waned again as he thought. "Yes, I do believe that you are right. That would make perfect sense."

Alena was getting frustrated with the half finished thoughts and sentences. He had just come up with a revelation that concerned her father and she had no idea what it was. It had been a long time since Orric had told her tales of Wood Sprites and it was hard for her to remember. Sometimes they were good stories and sometimes the Wood Sprites were made out to be evil creatures. That was one of the reasons she believed they were just stories to entertain young elves.

"What makes sense?" Alena asked when he didn't elaborate.

Gaius was looking off into the middle-distance, deep in thought. Alena wasn't even sure if he heard the question, but she wasn't about to re-ask it. He would either answer her or he wouldn't and the longer he waited the more Alena wasn't sure she wanted to hear the answer.

"Yes, sorry, I'm not surprised Orric didn't tell you the tale."

Before he could get any further with his story a light appeared in the forest behind her. She spun around to see what Gaius was looking at. It didn't take long before Eldred appeared with a makeshift torch. When he came into sight she realised that Gaius had disappeared, leaving her alone in the dark until Eldred arrived.

"What are you doing out here?" Eldred asked, doing his best to keep his voice low.

"Ah... I was just walking and thinking." She wasn't sure why she didn't mention Gaius, but there had to be a reason why he didn't wait for Eldred to arrive.

The cold quickly returned once Gaius left. She still held some of the heat he had given her, but she knew it wouldn't last long. She needed to get back to the campfire more than ever.

"What time is it?" Alena asked.

"It's well past midnight." Eldred replied, looking around as if he was trying to find something. "Richmond woke me up when he said you hadn't returned. I must admit I am thankful to find you in such a condition. When he woke me I feared for your life." Alena was already starting to shiver again.

"Speaking of which I think we should return to the camp. It definitely isn't getting any warmer."

Eldred took another quick look around before he led the way back to the campsite. He felt as though he was missing something. He couldn't put his finger on it, but things just didn't add up. What was Alena doing standing in the dark? And more to the point how was she still alive? It seemed as though she was only just starting to feel the cold and that really didn't make any sense.

It seemed to Alena that Eldred hadn't noticed the Wood Sprite or the bright light. That in itself made Alena wonder if it was just a dream. The thought didn't stay long as the freezing cold took over. Thankfully they too far away from the camp.

"Thank the Gods you're alright," Richmond jumped from where he sat and embraced Alena. She was somewhat surprised by his reaction, but did nothing to resist.

"Do you want to tell us what you were really doing out there for so long?" Eldred asked, even he had to admit he was grateful to be around the warmth of the fire again.

"Not tonight." Alena yawned, suddenly feeling the strain of the day. "I think sleep is in order now."

Eldred wasn't going to argue. It was going to be hard for him to get back to sleep now that he was up again, but he didn't want to keep the others up. With all the talk earlier about sleeping in late in the morning he didn't want to take the risk. Richmond had already returned to his bedroll and was sleeping soundly. There would be plenty of time to talk in the morning.

When he was sure Alena was sleeping and no one else was awake Eldred took the opportunity to scour through the prophecy. He felt rested enough to miss a little sleep again. As long as he didn't miss any full nights he figured that he'd be alright. He only managed an hour of reading, before he fell asleep by the firelight.

Eldred woke with a start at first light. He found the prophecy sitting face down on his lap. His first reaction was to make sure that no one had read anything, not that he could be sure what page he had finished on. When he looked around and saw that the others were still asleep that was enough to reassure him. He quickly returned the prophecy to his pack. For some reason he didn't want the others to know he was reading it. When it was safely tucked away, he realised it was a stupid way to feel.

"I'm glad the night is over." Richmond was the first to wake. "I didn't like Alena's chances of returning to us after being gone for so long. Do you know what she was doing?"

"I didn't get any information out of her."

"What happened?" Viper asked as he woke.

That quickly put an end to the conversation.

"Nothing exciting," Richmond replied.

"Something strange happened last night," Viper didn't seem perturbed by Richmond's short response as he quickly brought the fire back up to full strength. It had almost burnt out during the night, even with Eldred refuelling it, and the morning air was crisp. "I felt something last night. It's hard to explain, but I felt a... presence in the forest." Viper continued. Once the fire was burning again he rifled through his packs for something to eat. He didn't seem overly excited about continuing the conversation.

Eldred listened to his words carefully. There had been something very strange about the night's events. Alena had spent a lot of time in the forest by herself or at least that was the story she had told. There had definitely been something off about it, he knew that for sure. Viper's comments only strengthened his beliefs.

"Do you know anything about that?' Eldred asked Alena, figuring there was no point in trying to keep the conversation secret. There might be some important information he could gleam from the serpentant.

"Sorry, I wasn't paying attention," Alena spoke after taking a bite of an apple.

That was a lie, she knew where the conversation was heading and she was expecting the question. She didn't know what her position was. In the dim light of morning she wasn't even sure if what she remembered from the night before was real or had been just a dream. It seemed so surreal. For the moment she didn't want to share any information with the others.

"What were you doing out in the forest last night?" Eldred re-asked the question.

"Just walking and thinking." Alena wasn't sure if it was a lie or not.

"Something else must have happened. You were gone for a long time." Richmond added. "I was worried that you had died of exposure. It was deathly cold away from the fire."

"That is another thing," Eldred added "when I found you it didn't seem as though you were being affected by the cold. It wasn't until we started talking did you start suffering. Can you tell me how that makes any sense?"

Alena didn't know how to respond. They knew there were holes in her story, but she still didn't want to tell them about Gaius. At least not until she was sure he was real.

"I can't answer that. I didn't realise I was out for so long and I do apologise that I worried you so. I'm afraid that is all I can tell you. Now unless we want to truly test my theory about the prophecy I suggest that we finish our breakfast and be on the move again. We'll need to find some fresh water for the horses soon too," Alena attempted to change the subject.

It seemed as though her suggestions worked. As much as Eldred wasn't happy with her response, he had to admit that she was right. They did need to keep on the move. They couldn't rely on the prophecy to speed their travel and the horses did need fresh water. They couldn't keep watering them from their own supplies and it couldn't hurt to fill their water pouches before they reached the Dragon's Pass.

Alena felt much better when she was back in the saddle. It would give her some time to think before she had to answer more questions. She made sure that she kept Viper between herself and Eldred. She figured that he was less likely to question her if he had to speak through the serpentant. There was more information deep down in her memory that she needed to recall about Wood Sprites. Orric had told her tales when she was young, although he wasn't completely sure if they were true.

Slowly the stories started coming back to her...

***

"Have I told you the story about the wicked Wood Sprite?" Orric cooed at his daughter.

Alena was seven, maybe eight years old. It had been a long night and she was doing her best not to fall asleep. Orric did his best not to get upset, not that he really had anything else to do.

"Yes, father, please tell me that story," Alena sat up in her bed as she spoke.

"I will tell you if you lay down," Orric's voice had a fake sternness to it. Alena quickly obeyed in anticipation of the story. "Good, now let me think." Orric made a sign of thinking, only partly for show. "This happened a long time ago, or so the legend goes. A young Elven Prince was walking through the forest one day when he came across a rare flower with pink petals and a pale blue disk of seeds in the centre. The prince had never seen such a flower like it before, but he had heard stories. It was a magical okteb flower."

"No, that flower doesn't exist. It's just made up." Alena disputed.

"Now who is telling this story? I assure you the flower does exist, although where is grows now is a mystery even to me. Now would you like me to get back to the story?" When there was no answer he continued the tale. "There was only one solitary flower, but the prince knew that he could grow more. The flower was reputed to be the source of all flowers and a symbol of purity. He knew if he could grow more okteb flowers then his clan would thrive and the forest would be more beautiful beyond belief.

The only problem he had was the only way for an okteb flower to reproduce was with the aid of a Wood Sprite. Luckily for the prince he knew there was a Wood Sprite residing in the forest near to his village. Very carefully he pulled the plant from the ground, making sure he preserved the roots. He took the flower back to his village and ordered his scouts to find the Wood Sprite.

When the Wood Sprite returned the prince told him about the okteb flower he had found. The Wood Sprite was very excited to see the flower and promised the prince that if he gave him the flower he would see that it blossomed anew. The prince believed the sprite, but he didn't know there was an ulterior motive.

The Wood Sprite took the flower and disappeared one night. It wasn't until morning that the prince realised that both the flower and the Wood Sprite was missing."

***

That was all Alena could remember. She was sure there was more to the story, but she figured that she must have fallen asleep. It seemed like a strange story for her to remember. It painted a picture that Wood Sprites could not be trusted. She was sure there were other stories about

Wood Sprites that she had heard, but that was the only one she could remember. There was something about the way Orric had told that story; it was as if he was remembering actual events. She assumed that's why it stuck in her mind more than the others.

Even though she remembered the story she was not convinced that Wood Sprites were evil. Mischievous might be a better word, but it didn't explain why one would have betrayed the prince. She needed more information and the only way she was going to get it was through Eldred. She just had to work out a way of getting what she needed without revealing too much. She decided that the best time to talk was during lunch. As much as she didn't want the others to know there was a chance they could have some information as well.

"Do you know much about Wood Sprites?" Alena tried to make the question as casual a possible, but it didn't work. The other two quickly turned to Eldred for his response.

"This is somewhat unexpected, what makes you ask that?" Eldred sounded suspicious.

"Nothing really, I was just thinking about something my father told me many years ago. I thought you would know something about them."

"Well, to tell the truth I don't know much about them. That's more of a topic for Brielle. I'm sure she could regale you for hours on the subject, but I will try and give you my insight." He quickly added the last when he noticed Alena's face drop. "It's my understanding that Wood Sprites are a distant relative to elves and dryads, although much closer to dryads. They are creatures of the forest, if the name didn't already give that away. Some say they were the first worshippers of the God King Emerald. Others say they are direct decedents, I wouldn't be surprised if they are somewhere in-between."

"So they aren't evil?" Alena sounded relieved.

"I don't think so, well not that I have ever heard." Eldred wasn't much help. "I guess there's nothing stopping one of them from turning evil. This is a strange line of questioning Alena. What is this all about?" Eldred didn't believe her original excuse.

Alena was no closer to finding the answers she was after. She still didn't want to reveal anything until she was sure. Gaius had disappeared when Eldred arrived and there had to be a reason behind it. Until she knew if Gaius had evil intentions or not she'd keep him secret.

"Just making conversation. Now it seems as though we should be on the move again." Alena finished what she was eating and stood up.

Eldred noticed that her timing was impeccable again to avoid his question. There was no denying her. They had yet to find a stream or river to water the horses and he was loathed to empty their water pouches. It had been a long time since he had been in these parts of the Northern Forest, but he was sure there would be a water source nearby.

"This isn't the end of the conversation. We'll carry on when we stop tonight." It was almost a threat and if Alena didn't know any better she would have been offended.

As they travelled they kept the mountain range just out of view to the east, making it almost impossible to work out where they were. Whenever Eldred tried to swing their route around they always seemed to end up on the same path. There was nothing he could do to get a better idea of their location.

An hour before dusk they managed to come across a small brook. It was a little too convenient, but they decided that they would camp there regardless. The horses could drink their fill and then drink again before they left in the morning.

"So I think it's time you tell me why you're asking questions about Wood Sprites?" Eldred had sent Viper and Richmond to find firewood to give them a chance to speak in private. As the temperature was already starting to drop neither of them complained, although they probably would if they knew his ulterior motives.

Alena didn't want to answer the question, but she was running out of deflections. She still couldn't bring herself to tell him the truth. Although there was no way for her to find Gaius she knew that she'd meet him again. All she had to do was wait for him to find her.

"Just a theory I'm working on." She replied mysteriously.

Eldred shook his head. It wasn't the response he was looking for, but he didn't push any further. He knew there was more to Alena's question, but it seemed as though he would have to wait for answers. It was frustrating, but there were other things for him to do. With the others away and still some light he would take the opportunity to flick through the prophecy.

Alena was happy to sit and try and gather her thoughts. She had no idea what to make of the situation. Gaius was out there somewhere, she was sure she could feel him. She was sure that she felt his presence ever since they had started travelling again after lunch. There had been a small itch in the back of her mind trying to get her to move off course. She pushed it away. There was no way she was chasing the feeling whilst the others were around.

As the light started to fade Viper and Richmond returned with the wood. Alena was happy for the distraction. As much as Eldred was busy reading the prophecy the silence was still uncomfortable. Neither Richmond nor Viper looked as though they wanted to speak, but Alena felt better anyway. As she watched Viper stack wood in the centre of their camp she noticed that his legs were wobbling. It was the perfect way to start a conversation and break the silence.

"I think you should sit down Viper, before you fall down." Alena sounded like she was scolding a naughty child.

"I told you all before, I can carry my own weight. I won't be a burden. If there is wood to be collected then I'll collect it. If we need to get food then I will get it," although his words were strong his voice was weak.

"There's no need to put on a false bravado. If you are feeling weak then rest. You are bound to us now and until that changes there is nothing we can do to get rid of you, so you may as well do as you're told and sit down." Alena pointed to the ground.

Eldred's ears pricked up when he heard Alena's words. He knew there was no getting rid of Viper, but he wished she hadn't made it known. Even if Viper already knew the fact it didn't need to be spoken. Now there could be no doubt and in Eldred's mind that made Viper twice as dangerous. There was nothing he could do about it, but it seemed a good time to return the prophecy to his pack. There had been no new revelations of what lay ahead for them.

Surprising everyone, Viper did as he was told. His energy was all but drained and there was enough wood on the pile to keep the fire burning for a good few hours. It would need restocking before they went to sleep, but that would always be the case. He was grateful to be off his feet again. Richmond took care of lighting the fire. It was a useful skill to have and one that eluded those who were used to using magic.

When they had finished eating they all retired for the night. The long days ridings were starting to become weary. No one wanted to stay up and talk. They were all happy to get some sleep.

Alena woke in the middle of the night with a start. For a moment a feeling of panic came over her until she realised that nothing had happened. The fire still burnt strongly and the others were all sleeping soundly, yet she knew something was wrong. There was something in forest and it was calling out to her. She resisted for a few moments, but eventually she succumbed to the silent call. This time she made sure she wrapped herself as warmly as she could before setting off again.

As with the previous night Alena wandered with no real direction. The night was pitch black and yet she didn't run into anything. If her mind wasn't clouded then it would have seemed strange to her, but nothing seemed out of the ordinary. She could have been walking through the forest on a fine summer's morning.

It wasn't long before she came across the same light as the night before. Instantly she shielded her eyes when it came into sight. Slowly the light faded when Gaius realised it was in fact Alena standing before him.

When the light was back to a suitable level Alena looked up. She was relieved to see Gaius standing before her, although she knew that it could be no one else.

"Thank you for coming Alena," Gaius started.

"I'm not sure I really had a choice," Alena replied.

"You always have a choice my dear, but I have to admit I can be very persuasive when I want to be."

The spell that Gaius had over Alena to draw her to their meeting place had disappeared and Alena now knew exactly what was happening. The memories of her father's tale came rushing back. She wasn't going to let this Wood Sprite get the better of her.

"Tell me what it is that you want from me?" Alena snapped.

Gaius was taken aback by the harsh words. He wasn't expecting such a response. He looked at Alena carefully, now he wasn't so sure she was the same elf from the night before. He had been on his own for a long time and wasn't sure he could trust his eyes. After a quick once over he reassured himself that it was indeed Alena.

"You sound angry. Is there something I've missed?" Gaius' voice was solemn.

"I just don't like being dragged out into the cold in the middle of the night." It was surprisingly hard to keep the whole truth from him. The last thing she wanted to do was to let him know her real concerns. For the moment that small truth would be enough.

That answer seemed to be enough to appease the Wood Sprite. It seemed like a legitimate excuse and he was happy to let it slide.

"Tell me what you are doing in my forest." Gaius came straight to the point. "It has been many years since anyone has ventured this deep into the forest. The last group to cross my path didn't make it out again."

Now it was Alena's turn to be taken aback. It was the last comment she had been expecting. His tone hadn't changed much, but there was no doubt the threat was real.

"We don't mean you any harm. We are just passing through." Alena was suddenly defensive.

"I saw your group today and it's not what I'd call a common group of travellers. You are the only elf. There is a man and a wizard and something I couldn't quite put my finger on. Who and what is the snake-like creature. I get a bad feeling from him."

Alena sighed. Every fibre in her body wanted to leave. She suddenly had a bad feeling that Wood Sprites were as bad as her father had told her. That wasn't the feeling she had received the night before, but it definitely was now. Despite the feeling to flee she remained where she was.

"He is a serpentant and he is bound to us. I can assure you that we aren't happy about it either, but there is nothing we can do about it. He is imperative to our mission." Alena spoke quickly, feeling more and more uncomfortable.

There was a moment of silence as Gaius thought on what he had been told. The serpentants did jog something in his memory, but he couldn't quite grasp it. Then suddenly there was an expression of understanding on his face.

"Ah yes, the queen's creatures. It was my understanding that they were gentle creatures, that's not the feeling I sensed from him. There was something deep inside, that wasn't... quite right." Gaius mused.

"I don't know much about that," Alena replied. "Now what is it that you want with me?"

"I think it's time you go now. Be careful where you travel. I'll be watching you."

And with that the light suddenly blinked out and Alena was left standing in the dark. With the light gone the blackness was even more intense. There was no way Alena was going to attempt moving until she was able to at least make out some subtle outlines. The sky wasn't as dark as the previous night and once her eyes adjusted she would be able to make her way back. This time she had made sure she would remember how to return. The night was just as cold and even with the extra layers on she still felt the effects. Now she wanted nothing more than to return to the relative safety of their camp.

In the morning Alena was the first to wake. She had struggled to sleep once she had returned. There had been something very disturbing about her meeting with the Wood Sprite. She was glad that at least the sun had risen, she didn't think Gaius would try anything during the day.

She busied herself building the fire and trying to remove the chill of the night whilst the others slowly woke. She had made a decision that she would have to open up to Eldred about Gaius. She didn't want Viper and Richmond to hear the story, so she would wait until they were in the saddle again.

"Do you get the feeling that we aren't making as much ground as we have the last couple of days?" Eldred asked Alena as they rode.

Alena thought for a moment. She had to admit that she hadn't thought about it, but when she looked around the area it did look somewhat familiar. Again there was nothing really to gauge where they were, so it was impossible to tell. It did seem as though they had not made much ground the previous day. Alena had to wonder if the Wood Sprite had anything to do with it.

"I'm not sure, but I think you're right." Alena was about to elaborate on her concerns, but then stopped.

"Do you have any ideas why that might be the case?" Eldred sounded suspicious.

"No." Alena decided it wasn't the time to discuss the Wood Sprite.

Eldred didn't push any further. He wasn't sure exactly what Alena was up to, but he knew that she was hiding something. Until he was sure what it was he would wait and watch. It would only be a matter of time before Alena revealed herself.

In the end Alena decided it was best to tell the truth whilst they stopped for lunch. She had not wanted the others to know, but it seemed more appropriate than talking on horseback. She would be able to get a better read from Eldred's face if he was sitting down.

"The last few nights I have been speaking with a Wood Sprite named Gaius." Alena let the words pour out of her mouth.

There was silence for a moment as everyone let her words settle. It was a shock at first, but then it all started to make sense to Eldred. The others didn't really understand, but they were interested nonetheless. Alena waited for a response, but when none came she felt as though she should continue.

"I don't know how I came to find him. I was wandering in the forest, lost in thought, and I just... found him. Or it is probably more accurate to say he found me." Alena continued.

"Why didn't you just tell me this from the start?" Eldred kept his voice level.

Alena blushed slightly. "I wanted more information about the Wood Sprite before I mentioned that I had met one. I wasn't even sure if I would see it again, at least not until I did last night. It seems as though it's concerned about our presence in these woods."

Eldred thought for a moment. He had met a Wood Sprite many years before, but the name Gaius didn't mean anything to him. He was sure that they weren't evil creatures, as Alena had suggested, but he couldn't be sure. They were born and bred of the forest and whether they were interested in men was another story. Alena, being an elf, was a child of the forest and Eldred was sure that she would be safe from harm, the rest of the group he was not so sure. Now he really did need more information.

"What kind of feeling do you get from him?" Eldred asked.

"I'm not sure what you mean?"

"The questions you've been asking me, there has to be a reason behind them. What is it that has brought these concerns about the Wood Sprite and I don't believe they are tales your father used to tell you." Eldred was gentle yet firm.

Alena had to think for a moment. There was something in Eldred's words that made sense to her. There had been something off about the Wood Sprite that raised her concerns in the first place. Now she just had to remember what they were.

"You're right. There was something, somewhat disturbing about Gaius. It's hard to say. At first he seemed dazed and confused. Then he seemed angry. The greatest feeling of unrest I gained from him was last night when we were talking about you three; although now that I think on it, there was always a feeling of uncertainty about him. It was almost like there was an edge of sickness to him." Alena's words came out of her mouth as soon as they came into her mind.

"That is what I thought." Eldred paused for a moment as the others waited breathlessly for him to speak. "Gaius is connected to the Northern Forest and therefore more closely tied to the *Tree of Life*. I'm sure that feeling you've been getting from him is related. I have little doubt that Gaius is suffering from the attack on the tree. I would also assume that he doesn't know what is causing his unrest."

"So what does that mean for us?" Richmond asked.

"I'm not sure. Hopefully nothing. Hopefully we'll be at the mountains soon and out of his jurisdiction. For now I think we have stayed here long enough."

Eldred stood, but that was all he could do. He found that he could move no further. The others remained seated, also unable to move. A sudden panic filled their bodies, but there was nothing they could do, but wait.

Chapter 7: Hard Truths

"Well it seems as though you know who I am. Now it is time to return the favour." The Wood Sprite stepped into the clearing. He looked different to how Alena remembered him. His hair was dark and short and this time he wore a light brown tunic was green tips. Alena thought that he looked like one of the trees. His face had lost its whimsical feel and it was now hard. She was starting to think that her original fears were true.

"What do you want with us?" Eldred asked, keeping any fear out of his voice. He didn't want Gaius to know he had caught them by surprise.

"I want answers. I have spoken with Alena and I do not like what she told me. I had hoped to keep my identity secret, but it seems as though that didn't work. It does seem as though my powers have waned over the years, but I still have a few tricks up my sleeve." Gaius didn't give anything away.

"If you want answers then you are going to have to ask a question." Eldred responded when Gaius didn't elaborate.

"What are you doing in my forest?"

"As I am sure Alena has already explained to you, we are just passing through." Eldred wasn't going to give away too much information, at least without knowing what Alena had already told him.

"And where are you travelling to?" Gaius wasn't going to be easily satisfied.

Alena tried to speak, but no words came out. She wanted to assure Eldred that she had already told him the truth. She could only hope that he didn't try and deceive the wood sprite.

"We are travelling to Lel Dinion," Eldred felt compelled to speak.

He suddenly realised that there was magic in the air. It was subtle and not too common, which was the reason why he hadn't noticed it sooner. The feeling of elation filled his body as he created a quick spell of his own to counter the one Gaius was using. He could only hope that Gaius didn't realise. "That's all we're doing."

Gaius made a sign of thinking, Eldred hoped he wasn't delving for his spell. No one spoke for almost a minute before he spoke again.

"There is something wrong with the forest. I noticed it ever since you arrived. What is the story with the snake? I can sense something is off about him." He almost sneered at Viper.

Eldred had been hoping the question wouldn't be asked. As much as he wasn't under the spell any more he had to tell the truth. "It is not Viper you are sensing. As much as there is now kinship between us and the serpentant I can still vouch for him." Eldred paused for a moment as he considered his next words. "The *Tree of Life* is in danger. There is a hoard of orglin attacking it even as we speak."

Suddenly the firelight seemed to diminish and there was a feeling of horror in the air. Although Gaius' facade didn't change they all knew the sudden change was coming from him. No one wanted to say anything for fear of enraging him further. All they could do was wait for his response.

"Then it is worse than I feared. The battle has begun and I am alone." Gaius spoke aloud although it seemed as though he was talking to himself.

"What are you talking about?" Alena's words brought Gaius' attention back to the group.

"A few days ago when you entered my forest I felt an evil presence. It is like a sickness to the forest. I thought it was you. That was the only different thing that I could see. Now that I have met you I see that I was wrong, although I am still a little unsure about the snake." He started to drift off again.

Eldred was somewhat relieved at Gaius' response. There had been a feeling of unease that had been growing ever since the Wood Sprite had arrived. He could now see Alena's concerns. There was something about him didn't seem right. It wasn't evil, Eldred knew that for sure, but there was something definitely hostile about him. He couldn't be certain if it was directed at them, at least not anymore.

"Is there anything you can do to help?" Alena asked before Eldred had a chance to speak, not that he knew what to say.

There was a moment of silence again as Gaius thought on the question. A weird expression crossed his face and then it looked as though the answer finally dawned on him.

"What exactly are they doing? I can now feel her pain, but I don't know what they are doing. I need more information." It wasn't quite what they were expecting.

"The orglin have been trying to burn the *Tree of Life* to the ground, or at least they were when we saw them." Eldred suddenly wished that he hadn't mentioned the last part. He quickly continued in the hope that Gaius would miss it. "The *Tree of Life* was coping well enough extinguishing the fires and killing the odd orglin." Eldred stopped suddenly.

"So if you were there then why did you do nothing to stop the evil creatures?"

"There were only four of us and there are thousands of them. There was nothing we could do about it. All we were there to do was report back the Council of the Northern Elves." Again Eldred had revealed too much information. There was something about the Wood

Sprite that made him very uncomfortable and it wasn't the spell that had already been countered. No matter how careful he tried to be it seemed as though his mouth had different ideas.

"So what are the 'Northern' Elves doing to stop the attack?" Gaius asked, suspicion thick in voice.

"They are going to gain assistance. Their numbers have already been depleted by the orglin force. They sacked their village and the elves are now living in a makeshift village. They have left to try and get the Alliance army to help them defeat the orglin. It was that only option they had. If they fought without help then they would be doomed and the tree will die." Eldred explained as quickly as he could. Each word couldn't get out of his mouth fast enough.

Again there was silence as Gaius pondered on what he had been told. All the others could to do was wait for him to respond.

"I don't know why they didn't come to me. The *Tree of Life* might not be in my forest, but that doesn't mean that I can't help." Gaius almost sounded hurt.

Richmond didn't really know what he was talking about. The Northern Forest was the greatest forest in the Seven Kingdoms. One moment he said it was his forest and then he said it wasn't. As much as he wanted to ask the question he knew it was better if he kept his mouth shut. In the end it was Alena who asked it.

"You said you felt us when we set foot in your forest, but now you're saying the forest is someone else's? It doesn't make any sense." Alena responded, getting somewhat off topic.

Eldred was glad for the distraction.

"What you call the 'Great Northern Forest' is in fact a number of different forests. It seems that over the years those who should have remembered have forgotten." Gaius' accusatory tone was directed at Alena. "We are in my forest. It was once known as Gaiuslas. Arwan is the Wood Sprite who looks over Arwanlas where the elves and the *Tree of Life* call home. He should be the one who protects his land."

"What does that even mean?" Alena snapped.

"It is a shame that Orric banished Trynt from his rightful land. If he had not I'm sure you'd have a greater understanding of your history." Gaius shook his head. "I guess it's time for a history lesson. You may as well make yourselves comfortable."

Gaius joined them around the fire. Although he didn't need the heat he thought it was more sociable. He waited for the others to be seated before he sat down himself. When he was sure they were ready he started his tale.

"Wood Sprites were created around the dawn of time. Emerald created us to protect the forests from whatever the other God Kings might have created or what they were planning on creating. Emerald knew that what she had created..."

"What do you mean she?" Richmond asked in shock. "I thought Emerald was one of the God Kings? Wouldn't that mean that she is a he?" It was an insignificant slip of the tongue, but Richmond was interested in all the facts.

"The God Kings are neither male nor female, I thought even you men were taught that. Emerald chose to take the form of a female when she transcended, but again that doesn't make her female." Gaius sounded annoyed at having to repeat something so elementary. "So if you are referring to Emerald I feel as though she wants to be referred to in the feminine."

Gaius threw a log on the fire and small sparks flew into the night sky. The fire was burning strongly making it a useless exercise, but no one commented. When no one spoke Gaius continued.

"Emerald knew that what she had created would be in danger if she didn't create something to protect them. Trees, plants and flowers would have a difficult time defending themselves. Then men came along and started to chop down the trees to make their lodgings."

"Elves also used wood to build their houses!" Richmond protested the obvious attack.

"Yes, but elves are one with the forest and the forest is happy to give shelter to them. Now if you interrupt me again I'm going to get very upset." There was no humour in his voice. "Men raped the forest for their own greed. That's when Wood Sprites came into their own. When we felt men were taking too much we would take one of theirs." Richmond remembered stories he was told as a child about mischievous children being taken in the forest. He had always thought they were just tales, but now he wasn't so sure. In the end he was glad that he didn't test the theory. "We are creatures of the forest, creatures to be feared, but something got lost along the way and we faded into legend." Gaius stared into the fire as he spoke, clearly lost in memory. "My brothers and sisters have disappeared. It has been a long time since I have seen them. I know they are still alive, I can still feel that much, but where they are I do not know."

"What does all this mean?" Eldred asked. As much as he was enjoying the history lesson there was little time for it.

"We all have dominion over certain forests. This is my forest and spans all the way to the Cloumid Mountains. It doesn't run the full length though. It runs about half way through the middle. If I wish it then I could remove you from this land. I could remove you from my forest without much thought. Even with the two powerful magic users there is nothing you can do to stop me. That is the power I have in my forest. That is the power that was bestowed upon me by Emerald."

"So then you can kill the orglin?" Alena asked.

"Did you not listen to what I just said?" Gaius sounded as though his patience was running out. "I am in command of Gaiuslas, but that does not stretch as far the *Tree of Life*. She is in Lynethlas the forest controlled by Lyneth. I don't have that kind of power in her domain." Gaius paused in hope that the information would sink in.

"Surely there is something you can do?" Eldred asked.

"Well, it's not that I have no power outside of my forest, but it is greatly reduced."

"The *Tree of Life* has a great deal of power, can you somehow use that?" Alena asked, almost too afraid to speak.

"Hmm, yes, it does seem as though you haven't completely lost all of your heritage. There are two options before me. I can attempt to find Lyneth and have her destroy the orglin horde or I can attempt to do it myself. Now the first option would be the best. There is no doubt that Lyneth and the *Tree of Life* could wipe them from the face of the forest, but unfortunately I don't know how long it would take for me to find her. I can only just feel her on the edge of my senses. I couldn't even guarantee that she is still in the land you call the Seven Kingdoms."

"Surely, from what you have told us, she is linked to the forest and the *Tree of Life*. Wouldn't she already now that her land is in danger?" Eldred asked.

"That is the most disturbing thing about her absence. Yes you're right Eldred, this is something that should have woken her from her slumber and enraged her to her soul. This is obviously not the case." Gaius suddenly looked off into the night. There was a long silence before he returned to the others. "She is not getting any closer. I doubt she knows what is happening."

"How can that be?" Eldred pushed.

"She has been away for too long but I don't know for sure. I have never spent that long away from my home. Whenever I felt myself losing the connection with the forest I have always returned. I can only imagine what it must have taken for Lyneth to stay away."

"Maybe she was taken against her will." Everyone was surprised to hear Viper speak for the first time.

"That doesn't bare thinking about. If there is someone powerful enough to trap Wood Sprites then all the forests will burn." Gaius surmised.

Eldred wanted to tell him that Nyrra was powerful enough to kidnap the Wood Sprites, but there was little point. For the timeframe Gaius was talking about, it couldn't have been Nyrra anyway. That in itself was a concerning thought. If there was something else with that kind of power out there doing evil deeds then Eldred needed to know who it was. The fact that he had no idea who it was worried him. There were so many things that were disturbing about their situation and so many questions that had been left unanswered. Who was it that had been kidnapping Wood Sprites over the years? Why were they kidnapping them? What was their end game? Those were just a few that were rattling around in Eldred's mind. He didn't think he could handle it if there was another enemy just as powerful as Nyrra, if not more powerful, out there.

"Let's hope that is not the case," Eldred added.

"It looks like it rests on me to save the *Tree of Life*." Gaius didn't sound overly confident. "I have no idea how I'm going to be able to defeat over a thousand orglin. To be honest I'm not even sure how I'm going to beat one of them. It has been a long time since I have left my forest."

There was another moment of silence as everyone let the information sink in. It seemed as though Gaius was in trouble no matter which way he went. In the end Eldred came up with an idea.

"You don't need to kill any of the orglin," everyone was surprised to hear Eldred's words. He continued before anyone had a chance to question him. "The elves will bring back support from the Alliance. The army will crush the orglin. All you have to do is add your strength to that of the *Tree of Life*. You have to keep it alive long enough for help to come."

Gaius had to admit that was a much better solution. He wished there was some way he could contact Lyneth. There was no doubt she would know what to do. He couldn't understand how she could leave. He would give anything to have the *Tree of Life* in his forest, but that was not the case. Now he had to travel to another Wood Sprite's domain to attack an evil force. That was not something he was looking forward to, but at least now he had a plan. There was now hope that both he and the *Tree of Life* would survive. In the end he knew that the tree was the most important life-force in the world. If she died then it would only be a matter of time before all vegetation would die and that was something he couldn't let happen. It seemed as though the survival of his kind was left solely up to him. That in itself was an uplifting thought.

"Very well. That is a promising idea." Gaius paused yet again. "You will be safe whilst you are travelling through my forest, but be warned. Do not attempt to take any wood from any tree. Do not try to kill any of my animals for food. Stay by these rules and nothing will hinder your movements." There was something very serious about his warning, which made them all believe him. "I will do as you suggest, I will do my best to make sure the *Tree of Life* doesn't fall."

Gaius didn't wait around for further conversation. A few moments later no one knew whether he upped and left or whether he simply disappeared. From the time he stopped talking to the time they realised he was gone there was a gap in their memories.

"Well I think that could have been a lot worse." Viper was the first to speak.

"I really don't see how this is time for a joke!" Eldred snapped.

"It was no joke." Viper responded, defensively. "You heard what the Wood Sprite said. If he didn't like us then we would have been dead, or at least something to that affect."

"I'm sure it was just a mindless threat," Alena responded. "Something tied so closely to the forest wouldn't randomly kill."

"Random or not, he is more than capable of causing death. I came up against a Wood Sprite many, many years ago and it was by sheer luck that I escaped the encounter alive. Don't be fooled by their hayseed appearance. They are both sophisticated and capable of destruction." Viper warned, although it did seem as though he was just trying to make conversation. He seemed somewhat uncomfortable about the meeting with Gaius.

Eldred shook his head, but didn't make any further comment. The more he thought on it the more he thought that Viper was right. He had completely forgotten about the Wood Sprites. They would have been a valuable ally if he was able to convince them to join his cause, but now it seemed as though someone had taken them all from the Seven Kingdoms. That in itself was a very disturbing thought and one that he had to put out of his mind. There was nothing he could do about it now. He had to focus on the task ahead of him.

"I think we should get some sleep. Now that meeting is over I feel that it'll only be a day or two before we reach the pass." Eldred changed the subject.

As much as Viper didn't want silence he didn't argue. He had felt uncomfortable ever since Gaius arrived and that hadn't changed since he had left. His skin crawled and there was nothing he could do to change it. The conversation helped, but only a little. All he could do was try to sleep and hope in the morning the feeling was gone.

It wasn't until they were back in the saddle before the feeling of unrest started to pass. They were all grateful to be away from the campsite. Although Viper bore the worst of it the others also felt it. Something had been very off about the Wood Sprite and it reflected on all of them.

"I really wish you had been honest with me from the start," Eldred spoke to Alena as they rode. "There were questions I could have prepared if I had known the Wood Sprite had been talking to you."

Alena thought for a moment before she responded.

"I don't think I could have told you. I did think about it, but each time I did I thought it was wrong. I think the Wood Sprite twisted my mind." It was hard for Alena to admit.

Eldred had to admit that it made sense. There would be no other reason for her to keep her meeting a secret. Viper was right. The Wood Sprite was more powerful that he had originally thought. He really wished he had time to consult with Brielle on the history of the Wood Sprites. She would have much more information and might even possibly know where they had all gone.

Although her defence deserved a response Eldred didn't give her one. He was too lost in thought to think of something to say. Alena didn't mind. She was quite happy to let the conversation end there. The fog in her mind had started to lift and she started to remember the conversations she'd had with Gaius. At the time she had felt uncomfortable, but now she was feeling much better. There was something euphoric about the meeting that she was only just starting to experience. All of a sudden she couldn't believe that they were anything except wonderful. It was the true effect a Wood Sprite had on elves, it had just got lost somewhere.

They found another stream to camp by that night. It was just on dusk when they stopped and for the first time Eldred noticed how close they were to the mountain range. There was no doubt in his mind that the Wood Sprite had been affecting their course. It seemed as though he wasn't going to let them go until he knew they weren't evil. For the first time in a long time Eldred was able to place their location.

"If I'm right then we are about half a day's ride to the start of the pass." Eldred said as they sat around the campfire.

"What makes you say that?" Richmond didn't know why the question came out, but it was too late.

"The peak you can see to the east is the Zmija Vrh. It is the highest peak in the Cloumid Mountain range and means we are very close to the pass." Eldred seemed happy to give the geography lesson.

Viper stared off into the darkness at the peak. It felt like home.

"It is rumoured that somewhere in the Zmija Vrh is the home of the Queen of the Serpents." Eldred continued his lesson. "It is said to be the place where Nyrra tricked her into servitude." It seemed as though Eldred had forgotten that Viper was listening. "There is also a rumour that her body is still trapped there, waiting for someone to free her."

"That is not a rumour." Viper's voice was cold. "Nyrra betrayed her and now she is trapped. Her palace is high on the eastern side of the peak and that is where she resides."

"If you know she is trapped there then why don't you and the other serpentants rescue her?" It seemed logical enough to Richmond.

"What? Do you think we haven't already thought on that? Do you think if that was even possible we wouldn't have already done it?" Viper's voice became even colder.

"Easy Viper. The history of snakes isn't readily learned in the world of men. Richmond is not to know," Eldred chided.

"That's alright Eldred. Viper is right. That was a stupid question." Richmond knew Viper's words were warranted.

There was a moment of silence before Viper realised they were all waiting for him to speak. They were actually interested in his story. It was the first time they had ever really taken any notice of him, besides distrusting him.

"The Goddess is trapped by powerful magic. Nyrra has shrouded her palace. Even though I have been there before, many times, many years ago, I couldn't find it and believe me we have tried. Every time we thought we were getting close the land around us suddenly changed." Viper explained.

"I don't understand," Alena spoke when Viper paused. "Serpentants, like all reptiles, dislike the cold. Why would she build her palace in one of the coldest places in the Seven Kingdoms?"

"It wasn't always as cold is it is now. That is part of Nyrra's spell. The Goddess's palace was warm all year around. It didn't matter what the temperature was in the rest of the mountain range. It was a paradise, a place of beauty and he destroyed it. The Goddess is now trapped in a crystal ice prison. I'm sure the paradise is now under a thick covering of snow. Nyrra proceeded to force us into servitude. He threatened us with the fact that if we didn't do what he said he would kill the Goddess. We weren't sure if that was even possible, but we couldn't take that risk. That is why the serpentants have the reputation we have. Nyrra has twisted our paths to suit his own whims." Viper's voice was a mixture of sadness and disgust.

"If you are Nyrra's slaves then what are you doing with us." Richmond had a bad feeling that he already knew the answer. He didn't wait for Viper to respond before he continued. "It doesn't make any sense for you to help us. If your sole purpose is to save the Goddess then you should still be working for Nyrra. If that is the case then you are our enemy and should be dealt with accordingly." Although his words were threatening, Richmond made no move for his weapon.

"I guess I should have been expecting that." Viper didn't sound angry with the accusations. "That would have been true for more years than I'd care to admit, but not anymore. Nyrra promised that if we did his bidding he would let the Goddess free. At first we all believed it, but now some of us aren't so sure. Some of us aren't even sure if the Goddess is still alive, although that is not something we talk about. Anyway, the point of the story is that I now know that Nyrra will never let us or her free. We are too invaluable to him. Some of my brothers feel the same way. We now know the only way for us to be free is to kill him. Unfortunately not everyone shares our point of view. I can't tell you how disappointing it is to know that there are still some of th serpentants who believe Nyrra will one day release the Goddess. They are still working for him and are extremely dangerous."

"Who are they?" Eldred asked.

"I know that Python, and Rattle share the same thoughts as me. As far as the others go I can't be sure, but I believe that are still on the side of the enemy. I haven't spoken to any of my brothers in over a century, so a lot could have changed since then." Viper shrugged his shoulders.

"How do you know that they are still your allies?" Eldred didn't sound convinced.

"When you come to the realisation that you have been subjugated for centuries it's not something you easily forget. It's just a shame the others haven't come to the realisation." Viper continued.

The fire had started to die down and as much as he didn't want to break the conversation Richmond had to refuel it. The cold was starting to bite and he didn't want to risk the flames burning out. As quick as he could he placed three more logs on the fire and then returned to his seat.

"If you haven't spoken to them in over a century how do you know that they still follow Nyrra?" Alena asked when Richmond had resettled.

"I can't say for sure. All I know is that I was the first to come to the realisation. I knew that I couldn't share my theory with my brothers. If they didn't agree with me and they told Nyrra then my life would be over, and so would the Goddesses. I'm sure you can appreciate my dilemma. I know I'm right, but I can't even try and convince my brothers. I've had to wait for them to come upon the realisation themselves and then, without fail, they come and find me. I don't know what it is, but it seems as though when my brothers find out they know to seek me out."

If it wasn't for everything that had happened they might not have believed him, but there were so many unexplained events that they had to. So many things had happened that they couldn't explain and one more wasn't a big stretch.

"So we have two more allies out there somewhere. If you three are all working against Nyrra why aren't you working together? Wouldn't it be easier that way?" Alena asked.

"Nyrra made sure he gave us tasks that kept us away from each other. I guess he figured if we had time to speak together we would come up with the realisation a lot quicker. Either way it was dangerous enough for Rattle and Python to search me out." Viper's voice sounded weak as he continued. It was obvious that his strength had yet to return, although he did seem better than when they left the makeshift village.

"And what is your task that the Evil One set out for you," Richmond wasn't the only one who picked up on Viper's words, but he was the first to ask the question.

"I don't think that's something you want to know. All that you need to know is that I am here to help." Viper tried his best to deflect the question.

"I think we need to know what you agenda is Viper." Eldred's tone was severe. "If you have a mission from Nyrra then you have to share it with us."

"You're not going to like it and it's not going to change the fact that I am here to help you." Viper sounded worried.

"You're not making things any easier on yourself Viper. You can either tell us what Nyrra has told you to do or you can leave. I don't care what the prophecy wants. If I have to kill you to get rid of you then that's what I'll do." There was no doubt that in Viper's weakened state he'd be easy to kill.

"Okay." Viper sighed as he looked for the right words. He knew they wouldn't be happy either way, but he needed to make it sound as innocent as possible. In the end he just had to blurt the words out as Eldred made a show of getting up. "Nyrra instructed me to escort you through Dragon's Pass to Lel Dinion."

"That's it?" Richmond asked.

"I doubt that is it," Eldred responded. "What is it you're not telling us?"

"Nothing. He briefly came to me in a vision after I had left Jarrat. He was only there for a moment before he left again." There was no lie in his voice, but Eldred still thought there was something missing.

It was getting late and Eldred knew they would be at the pass before nightfall and if time moved slower then they could be there sometime during the day. As much as he wanted to question Viper further he knew that it was better they get some sleep. The serpentant looked as though he was exhausted. There would be time to question him further before they reached Lel Dinion.

Chapter 8: Zamj Pass

There was little conversation in the morning before they took to the road again and no one spoke of Viper's tale. It was the road ahead that filled their minds. Eldred had a bad feeling that there was something waiting for them in the pass, although he wasn't sure if it was good or evil. If he had to take a guess he would have said evil. He couldn't imagine there could be an ally waiting for them. Either way, sitting around was doing nothing to help.

They rode on in silence for the entire morning. The most disturbing thought about Viper's story was not that he had a job to do for Nyrra, or that it was exactly what he was doing, it was the fact that Nyrra seemed to know exactly what they had planned. If Nyrra knew what they were doing and where they were headed, then it meant there was something waiting for them at their destination. Every fibre in their bodies was telling them to turn around and kick their horses into a run, but they also knew they couldn't. The prophecy wanted them to ride to Lel Dinion and that was exactly what they were going to do, whether they liked it or not.

Eldred had a few more concerns that the others hadn't realised. Either one of two things could have happened. The first, and Eldred wasn't too sure on this one, was that Viper had been in contact with Nyrra since they had chosen their new course. The second thought, and the one which was both the most disturbing and the one he believed to be true, was that Viper had been given this task many years ago, which meant Nyrra knew their every move. Eldred had heard rumours that there was another prophecy, one that Nyrra had, one that told of a different story. Viper had mentioned it before, but he had not taken him seriously. If it was in fact real then he wasn't even sure if the *Prophecy of the Stone* was in fact the true prophecy. He needed more information from Viper, but he would wait until they stopped for the midday meal.

When they finally stopped to eat they were still not in sight of the opening to the pass. It was two hours past noon and as much as Eldred wanted to reach the pass that day he didn't want to push them too hard. There was a small stream that would allow them to water their horses and refill their pouches. Although there were mountain streams along the pass Eldred didn't want to leave anything to chance. There was a good chance some, if not all, of the streams would be frozen over.

"What you told us last night was disturbing," Eldred's words were so sudden that it surprised everyone as they sat and ate. The only words that had been spoken since leaving in the morning was Eldred stating they should stop to eat. "I need to know when it was that Nyrra gave you your instructions."

"I'm not really sure," Viper replied a little defensively.

"It's alright Viper, for the moment let us just assume that I believe your intentions. This is important information. If we are walking into a trap I need every advantage I can get."

Viper paused and thought for a moment. Eldred found that to be a disturbing sign. He knew his fears were going to be true.

"The last time I had contact with Nyrra was through his Dark Knight Argoz. The little worm came to me one night with the instructions from his master. Now how he managed to get the instructions from the Northern Wasteland I do not know and I didn't care to ask. There is something about Argoz that I really don't like and I didn't want to spend more time with him than I had to." Viper continued to explain. "The note he gave me outlined what he wanted me to do and the rest is history."

"It seems you have been tangled in our business for a long time now. What about your brothers? So far we've only heard from Adder. What are the rest of them doing? If they are working for Nyrra then why haven't we seen them?"

"I can't help you with that. As I told you before Nyrra doesn't like having us close to each other. I haven't spoken with the others in over a century. Whatever Nyrra set for them is a mystery to me."

"There is something missing. If this was always your mission then what were you doing with Count Kerwin? If I recall correctly you were part of the group who kidnapped our friends at Bordertown and then you were involved in the kidnapping of Eldred and myself with Ra'naroz. For someone who doesn't like Nyrra and his cronies you sure are spending a lot of time with them." Alena was furious.

"I needed to be sure of who you were before I contacted you. If you were indeed agents of Nyrra then I would reveal myself and cause my own death."

"We were needlessly tortured by Ra'naroz and yourself in the dungeons of Jarrat. You could have saved us at any time." Alena didn't sound impressed as the memories returned.

"There are a lot of things that I'm not proud of. I have my own agenda and that involves rescuing the Goddess and saving my kind. I don't care for your battle with Nyrra, but since our paths have crossed I am here to help. If I saved you then I would have shown Nyrra my true intentions. What happened in the past was unfortunate, but there is nothing I can do about it now."

There was silence. No one had expected such an outburst from Viper. At first anger rushed through Alena's body and she wanted to berate him, but before she did she realised he was right. His words did make sense. For good or for evil his life had been thrown into a battle that wasn't his. If what he said was true then he and his kind were hated by everyone, and not only that they were fighting on different sides. Alena couldn't imagine how hard that would be. She also couldn't believe she was finally starting to feel some empathy towards the creature. Befriending a serpentant wasn't something she ever thought she would do not that they were quite at friendship yet, but they were one step closer. No one else wanted to speak before Alena gave her opinion.

"I won't try and understand what you have been through. We have all been through tough times and if we are going to succeed then we need to move on. I don't think we need to speak of this again." It was more that she didn't want to speak of her time in the dungeon in Jarrat. It was the darkest time of her life and one where she wished she could have died, over and over again. It was a time that she wished could be completely wiped from her memory.

Eldred wasn't exactly pleased with that memory being brought up again. He could taste the vile liquid they poured down his throat to stop him from using magic. He also felt the pain of the torture again. It was for that reason he didn't get involved in the conversation. Talking about it would only make the sensations worse.

"I think we are forgetting the real question," Richmond spoke. "Why has both Nyrra and Alaric told us to go to Lel Dinion via Zmaj Pass?" Richmond let the question settle before he spoke again. "This has been troubling me ever since Viper brought it up. We know what is waiting for us in Lel Dinion, that hasn't changed and that is a good enough reason for both sides to send us there, but there is something else. Why have they both specifically told us to take Zmaj Pass? The only reason I can think of is that there must be something waiting there for us."

"But why would Alaric send us into danger?" Alena knew what he was getting at. "That doesn't make any sense."

"There has to be something that Nyrra knows that we don't. If it was just a case of getting to Lel Dinion then he wouldn't specify the path. I can't believe that it's just a coincidence." Eldred spoke with his head down.

"There may be something." Viper wasn't sure he should speak, but he thought it would only be a matter of time before someone asked him the question.

"What is it Viper?" Eldred sounded annoyed.

"It is rumoured that Kahn, now the last of the Great Dragons, has his home somewhere along the pass."

Everyone thought on his words. No one wanted to ask the question that was on everyone's minds and in the end Viper volunteered the information.

"I believe the rumours to be quite true. It is said that not too long ago there was a great explosion over the peaks of the pass. No one knows what caused it, but it is believed that Kahn was involved and I tend to agree."

"So what do we do?" Alena asked.

"We carry on and be very careful," Eldred returned.

That promptly ended the conversation. He felt they had already been sitting around for too long. The day was starting to fade and the entrance to the pass still wasn't in sight. As much as Eldred had wanted to make a start into the pass before nightfall he didn't think that was going to happen. If Kahn was guarding the pass then they'd be better to camp at the base of the mountain range and brave it in the morning. There was no telling how long it would take to get through and the least amount of time spent in the dark the better.

The tension was thick within the group for the rest of the afternoon. The threat of the great dragon loomed over them and even Viper seemed nervous. It was just on dusk when they finally reached the base of the Cloumid Mountain range. Two great stone columns stood on either side of the entrance to the pass. They were four feet thick and thirty feet tall. On the top of the columns were two carefully crafted dragons; their wings were spread as if they were about to take off. They looked out over the forest, daring anyone to pass. It now made sense why it was somewhere Kahn would make his home. As much as Eldred had been through the pass before he had completely forgotten the pillars.

"I think we would be best to camp in the forest tonight." There were no objections to his statement.

There was something very unsettling about the columns and no one wanted to camp within view of them. They rode for five minutes back into the forest before they were comfortable. The light had all but faded when they finally stopped for the night.

"Remember what Gaius told us. Just take wood from the ground. Don't take any from the trees." Alena warned as they went to collect the firewood, only Viper remained behind. He didn't have the energy to move any further.

The task wasn't as easy as it sounded. As the sun set the temperature had dropped from what had already been a cold day. There didn't seem to be as much wood on the ground as there had been in other parts of the forest. The trees were sparse around the entrance to Zmaj pass. It was as if they were too afraid to grow so close.

"We'll have to burn it sparingly," Eldred stated when they returned.

There was only a miserly looking pile of fire wood when they all finally gave up searching. To make matters worse the failing light made it almost impossible for Richmond to find anything decent. Alena was able to see better with her elven eyes and Eldred had created himself a small globe of light.

"Let's hope that it's enough to keep us from freezing to death." Richmond's teeth chattered as he spoke.

"I'll do what I can to make sure it doesn't burn too fast. I still have a few tricks up my sleeve."

When the fire was lit they realised for the first time that Viper was asleep. The serpentant still didn't look like he had recovered from his shedding. That was both a good sign and a bad one. It was good that he couldn't do anything to hurt them, but if he was indeed true to his word then they would need him at full strength to help them with whatever trial lay before them.

"What are we going to do about him?" Alena asked, only a hint of concern in her voice.

"What do you mean?" Eldred asked.

"He doesn't seem to be getting any better. It's going to be a tough ride through the mountain pass, much tougher than the ride through the forest," Alena returned.

Eldred had to laugh. He had no idea how long it had been since he had laughed. It felt strange, but nice. "I know it has been a long time since I have travelled the pass, but I don't think there is going to be much riding. The pass is treacherous in parts and for the most part it is rocky and unsafe for the horses. There is a great risk of them breaking an ankle. No, for much of the journey we will be on foot."

That wasn't the response Alena was looking for. That would make things even worse for Viper, not to mention make the travelling much slower, but for the moment that wasn't what concerned her the most. As much as the serpentant claimed he wouldn't be a burden he already looked worse for the travelling. Without a chance to recuperate properly she could only imagine that he was going to deteriorate.

"So that makes matters even worse," she spoke after a moment of reflection. "Is there nothing you can do to help him?"

Richmond listened to the conversation and wondered at the sudden change in Alena since the midday meal. She had brought up all the bad things Viper had done to her and now she was trying to help him, but he had to admit that he felt the same way. As much as Viper had wronged them in the past he did genuinely seem to be on their side now and if that was true then they needed him to be at his strongest.

"I know very little about the inner workings of serpentants, at least to the point of healing them with magic. My concern would be making him worse instead of better. By the sounds of things this has never happened to Viper before, so I can't even ask him for advice. I really don't think there is anything we can do. We just have to wait and hope that he recovers soon."

Alena wasn't happy with the response, but she understood. It seemed as though they were between a rock and a hard place. To make matters worse the freezing weather was doing nothing to help Viper's recovery. If the wood didn't last the night she wouldn't be surprised if he didn't wake up in the morning.

When the fire was fully lit and burning strongly Eldred stopped the conversation. He needed to create his spell before the fire ate up too much wood. Even with his spell it would be dubious whether the fire would last the night. It was tempting to chop some branches off the nearby trees, he wasn't sure if they were still in Gaius' forest, but it wasn't worth the risk. There was something very ominous about the Wood Sprite and he didn't want to anger him.

Instantly the flame grew larger and they could feel the heat intensify. Although the fire had strengthened, the wood seemed to burn slower. With a little luck the fire would keep them warm throughout the night.

"Now let's have something to eat and then get some rest. It's going to be a long journey over the mountain range and we'll need all of our energy."

Richmond and Alena shared a meal with Eldred before taking his advice and going to sleep. Eldred didn't go to sleep, he wanted to have another look at the prophecy. He needed to find the passage about them using the pass. Although he had read it cover to cover a number of times he had not read anything about Zmaj pass, but he knew it had to be there. If he was able to find it then there was a chance he could find what they were up against.

It was late in the night when he finally came across the passage he was looking for.

The strange little group has a path that's set,
both sides agree on the pass they should take.
There is more to this tale than meets the eye,
for who decides on what is true.
But for right or for wrong,
who's to know the truth.
What is waiting on the trail is known to none,

yet something there is they all now to be true.
One side sets a trap,
the other a plan.
Little more can be told
'till the journey be done
Watch to the sky,
and hide when its took.

There was little help in the passage and very little to be read into it. All he could gather for sure was that there was something to be done whilst they were on the pass, but it was unknown if it was for good or for evil. At least Eldred knew they were walking into a trap, that was a good sign. Whatever the reason Nyrra and Alaric had set them on their path no one was certain was the result would be. It wasn't the answers he was looking for, but at least it was something and enough to let him get some sleep. Before he settled for the night he threw the rest of the wood on the fire and restrengthened the spell.

The morning came around all too quickly. The fire just burned out before Eldred woke. He had set a small spell to let him know when the previous spell was extinguished. The others still looked comfortable enough and Eldred wasn't about to wake them. He busied himself collecting what little wood he could find. When he returned he found Richmond and Alena awake, but Viper still asleep.

"Is he even still alive?" Eldred asked as he started to light the fire.

"We saw him breathing before. He doesn't look well, but we're pretty sure he's still alive," Richmond replied, his teeth starting to chatter.

That was the only indication that Eldred had of how cold it was. Since speaking with Gaius he was able to comfortably regulate his own temperature again. Even though the fire burned through the night its heat would have waned in the last few hours. The intense cold would be doing Viper no favours. Eldred could only hope with a strong fire it might be enough to bring him around.

It wasn't until they had finished eating breakfast that Viper finally roused himself. The fire was burning strongly, and with Eldred's aid, radiating a lot of heat. He moved slowly and at first didn't look as though he knew where he was.

"How are you feeling?" Alena eventually asked.

"This cold isn't helping me at all." Viper struggled for words. "Normally I can control my temperature in the cold, but since my shedding I just don't have the strength."

That gave them another dilemma. Just when they had finally decided that Viper was on their side, or at least they were less suspicious of his motives, they weren't sure if they should take him on the dangerous route over the mountains. Once they started to climb the temperature would drop even lower and that could kill him.

"I think you might have to remain behind." Richmond suggested what the other two were thinking. "If you are feeling this way now then you aren't going to get any better climbing into the cold."

Viper coughed something that sounded like a laugh, but the others couldn't be sure. It was a little too guttural to be certain.

"It's good to know that you care, but as you know none of us have a choice in the matter." They knew he was right. "I will be alright. I have lived a long time and I don't plan on dying anytime soon. I will see the Goddess freed before I do." There was defiance in his voice.

There was no denying his logic. Even as the words came out of Richmond's mouth he knew it wasn't going to happen. Viper was coming with them and there would be nothing they could do to prevent it.

"Well, I guess we should get going," Richmond didn't sound overly confident.

No one argued with him, although Viper didn't look happy with the comment. He moved slowly and was the last to mount.

Grey clouds met them when they reached the pillars. There was little doubt that there would be snow before the day was done, just to make things more difficult. They stopped and stared at the structure for a moment. There was something very ominous about the stone dragons sitting on top of the columns and they seemed to loom in the gloom of the morning. Eldred took a deep breath before he led the way through.

The trail started to slope gently upwards at first and it was easy enough for them to remain on their horses. They hadn't been travelling for long before the first snowflake fell from the sky. It was the sign they had all been dreading. The snow was starting to fall and there was no guarantee it was going to stop.

A short time after Eldred decided that it would be safer if they started to walk the horses. The snow had only just started to cover the ground, but it was already getting hard to pick out the small rocks that littered the floor of the pass. It would obviously slow their journey, but he thought it was better than risking one of the horse's ankles. The only other problem was that Viper didn't look too sure on his feet. Eldred thought of telling him to mount again, but then thought better of it. If Viper wanted to tag along then he would just have to deal with it.

For the most part of the morning the journey was relatively easy. The snow was falling slowly and didn't cause them any problems, other than the fact that it was freezing cold.

They stopped to eat not long after midday. They found a small patch of trees off to the side of the pass. It had been the only time in the past few hours that they had found wood for a fire. Ideally they would have liked a cave to get out of the snow, but the shelter of the trees would have to do.

"Do you think it is wise to cut branches from a tree?" Alena asked as Eldred pulled an axe out from one of the packs.

"I'm pretty sure the pass is not in Gaius's domain and if it is then he's just going to have to deal with it. Without wood we aren't going to survive very long anyway. Viper looks like he's ready to die." Eldred nodded at the serpentant who had collapsed against a nearby aspen.

Eldred started chopping down branches when Richmond came to take over. As much as Eldred was still strong Richmond felt it was his duty to cut the firewood. It wasn't just that, but he didn't want to sit around in the cold. The heat from trekking was quickly starting to wear off.

Alena also did her best to busy herself. There were a number of small branches and twigs amongst the grove and she collected enough to at least get the fire started. Eldred was more than happy to create the spell required to get the wood burning.

Richmond had a thick layer of sweat when he joined them. There was enough wood for the fire, but there was now a lot more to stock up with for the rest of their trip. Eldred was sure there would be other trees, but they didn't have the time to stop and cut wood at each one. It was almost dusk when they finally had enough wood and in the end they decided that it would be better if they remained under the trees for the night as Viper was already sleeping.

"I think that we need to make the most of shelter when we find it during the night." Eldred's voice was sombre. There was something ominous in his tone that made the other two feel uncomfortable, but there were no arguments.

As soon as the sun disappeared a feeling of dread came over the group. Each time they looked towards the sky they were glad to see the cover of the trees. There was a feeling that there was something above the canopy trying to search them out, but no one was willing to leave the safety of the trees to check. They were quite happy to spend the night in blissful ignorance. The snow had all but dissipated by the time they were ready to sleep. They all hoped it was a sign that things would be warmer in the morning.

In the morning they all woke with the sun except for Viper. This time they didn't give him an opportunity to sleep in. They needed to eat and be on their way. Viper had to eat something if he was going to keep his strength up.

The snow had started to fall again in the early hours of the morning. Even with the protection of the trees they still woke to a gentle covering over everything. No one waited to remain seated for any longer than they had to. Even Viper didn't complain when Eldred suggested they keep moving.

Around mid-morning the incline of the path became steeper. More rubble covered the path and they were starting to have problems getting the horses to negotiate the treacherous trail. Adelanta did his best to spur the others onward, leading the way up the path, but they still had their reservations. To make matters worse the shelf on the right-hand-side fell away down into a deep chasm. If anyone or any of the horses lost their footing there was a good chance they would fall to their deaths. This did nothing to calm the nerves of the animals.

As the day wore on the snow increased its intensity until eventually they couldn't continue. They were lucky enough to find a small cave, large enough to house them and the animals for the night. It was a little crowded, but much better than the alternative. There was little chance of survival if they were to spend the night out in the open.

"At this rate this is going to take forever," Richmond complained as they ate.

"There isn't anything we can do about it. I can't change the weather," Eldred snapped, they were all tired and grumpy.

"We can always go back. It's got to be quicker going around to the north of the mountain range than continuing like this." Richmond sounded frustrated. He knew what he suggested wasn't an option.

No one bothered to respond to his suggestion. They all knew the answer. Travelling around the mountain range would be the easy option and one they'd all take in a heartbeat, but that wasn't possible. They had to make it over the mountain and there was nothing they could do about it.

"What are we going to do about him?" Alena changed the subject. Viper had again curled up and gone to sleep.

"I don't think there is anything we can do. He will recover when he recovers. All I know is that he is important to us and hopefully that will become apparent sooner rather than later."

That was the last of the conversation for the night. The strain of the day was wearing on them and they needed to sleep. Even Eldred chose sleep over reading through the prophecy. He had hoped he might be able to find some real answers, but fatigue got the better of him.

Chapter 9: Death from Above

It took another four days before they reached the peak of the trail and the true entrance to Zmaj Pass. A rocky corridor was cut into the mountain stretching for almost a mile. Two great columns rose up on either side with the same dragons on the top as at the foot of the mountain. The ones standing in front of them were much larger and grander. These were the original statues in reverence to the dragons. There were another two on the other end of the pass as well. To the left of the entrance a cave had been cut into the mountain wall. It was clearly man made.

"I think we should camp here for the night and make the pass in the morning." Eldred suggested.

"Is there not another cave on the other side that we could camp in? There is still enough light for us to get to the other side. We can camp there?" Richmond was keen to take the pass. There was something about the stretch in front of him that had him excited. He had heard of the pass when he was young, although he could never make out if it was true or just a legend. Now, standing in front of one setof the dragon pillars, there was something exhilarating about it. "We can even ride the pass since it is flat and there are walls on either side."

"There is a reason why the caves were made. There is more to the pass than meets the eye. We should camp here and journey through in the morning." Eldred did his best to explain.

"Eldred is right. If Kahn is somewhere nearby then he'll be able to sense us taking the pass, more so at night time." Viper backed up Eldred's decision. "As much as I'd love the see the great dragon I don't think it's in our best interest tonight."

Richmond still wasn't sure. There was something very compelling about the pass. The words made sense, but he still wanted to make the journey. As the others made their way into the cave Richmond stayed and stared along the pass. He wanted nothing more than to step through the columns, but he held himself back. If Viper was giving him a warning then he'd be a fool not to listen. He would have to wait until morning before he knew what was waiting for him on the other side.

"You're looking a little better," Alena spoke to Viper when she realised he was still awake.

"It seems as though the mountain air is doing me good." Alena wasn't sure if he was being sarcastic or not.

The air was very thin at the top of the mountains, which had made the day's journey more difficult. There was something else in the air though. Alena noticed it when they reached the entrance to Zmaj Pass.

She couldn't quite put her finger on it, but she knew it was there nevertheless.

The cave was larger than any of them had thought. There was even a makeshift stable at the back. It was obvious that it was manmade and had been added to over the years. It looked as though stonemasons had been brought in to work on the cave. In some places there were smooth stones which had clearly been deliberately fashioned. In other places rudimentary scratches remained by those who merely wanted to make the cave larger. It was the most homely place they had camped in since leaving the elven make-shift village.

The snow had fallen constantly for the last four days. It slowly covered the trail making their travelling slower and more treacherous. Another disturbing feature about the Zmaj Pass was there was no snow covering it at all.

"The snow has never fallen on the pass," Eldred explained. "I have no idea why. It's not something that has been studied by the council, or at least not to my knowledge. I guess that it's just a phenomenon of this world."

"Hardly," Viper scoffed.

"Do you have something to add to the conversation?" Eldred didn't sound happy with the interruption.

Viper sighed, he had not wanted to continue, but he knew they wouldn't let up if he didn't. He should have just kept his mouth shut although it was another opportunity to prove his worth.

"Zmaj pass, known in the common tongue as Dragon's Pass, was designed for that specific purpose."

"That doesn't make any sense," Richmond interrupted. "Dragon's can fly. Why would they need to build a pass across the mountains?"

Viper shook his head. "Well I guess we have time for another history lesson. Years ago, when the Goddess still walked the world, she had more followers than just the serpentants. The pass was built by men as a temple to the Goddess' greatest creatures, or at least what they saw as her greatest creatures, the dragons. We were happy enough to let that happen. As a rule, serpentants can't stand men, but I make an exception for you Lord Richmond," Viper added before Richmond could speak. "Anyway, obviously at one point in the construction of the temple they realised that if they were building a temple to worship the dragons it would be silly to put a roof on it. As dragons were more commonplace at this time they figured they could watch the great creatures flying through the sky whilst they were prostrating. That is how Zmaj temple became Zmaj pass. Half way along the pass there is a temple cut into the northern side of the mountain and a marble sacrifice table. The worshippers of the great dragons, or Dragonians as they referred to themselves, would bring sacrifices up the mountain. Once a year they would sacrifice a virgin girl to the great dragons to appease them."

"Why would the dragons want a sacrifice of a virgin?" Eldred was listening intently, but the last statement didn't make any sense. "I have never heard of dragons liking virgins and I have known a few in my time. In fact I have never heard of dragon's needing sacrifices to appease them, although nothing would surprise me with Kahn these days."

"Well, there might have been an outside influence involved in that one. Adder, I think it was, started the rumour that would keep the dragons from burning their villages. I know it was a little childish, but it seemed like a good idea at the time. I don't believe he mentioned virgins though, I believe the villagers came up with that part. The tracks we have been taking have been worn away over the years by those who have taken the pilgrimage to the shrine, so in a way I guess we should be grateful. It would have been much harder if we had to make our own way and I doubt we could have brought the horses." Viper was becoming somewhat defensive.

"So that doesn't explain why the snow doesn't fall on the pass or the 'shrine' as you call it." Eldred sounded grumpy.

"The shrine has been blessed by the Goddess. As you know reptiles, dragons included, dislike the cold. It was one of the last gifts she bestowed upon the Seven Kingdoms before she was betrayed by Nyrra. She created a space around the shrine that would never get cold. You will notice a sharp rise in the temperature when we step into the shrine tomorrow." Viper paused. "This is the last remnant of the Goddess and all we have left now. It had been too long since I have been here. Needless to say I didn't have to act too much when Nyrra gave me my assignment. If anything I had to dampen my eagerness."

"So if you are that keen to enter the pass, then what are you doing in here with us?" Richmond sounded suspicious.

"Believe me when I say it was more than tempting, but like anything else I do, I figured if I went on alone you would be suspicious of my motives. There is nothing untoward ahead, but I don't want to make you any more suspicious than you already are," Viper replied.

"Can you be sure there is nothing untoward waiting for us?" Alena had a bad feeling something bad was going to happen. There was something drawing her in and she knew it couldn't be a good sign.

"No, I can't be sure. All I know is that if there is something waiting for us then it's going to be as much a surprise to me as to the rest of us." Viper hoped his truthfulness was working.

Alena wasn't overly happy with his response. She would have much preferred it if he had just told them there was nothing waiting for them, although she wasn't sure she would have believed him anyway. There was something evil waiting for them, she knew that was true.

"What are we going to do for dinner?" Richmond asked, deliberately changing the subject. Whatever it was that was waiting for them could wait until morning.

The conversation remained light for the rest of the evening. No one really wanted to contemplate the next day. They were all quite happy with the change of topic. It wasn't too long after the sun had set before they were all sound asleep.

Alena was awoken suddenly in the middle of the night by a great screech. The fire was had almost burnt out, but there was still enough light for her to see that the others were still sound asleep. She let out a deep breath as she realised that it must have been a dream that woke her and her heart rate started to slow. To help calm herself she tossed a couple of logs onto the fire.

Just as she settled down to try and sleep again Alena thought she heard something outside the cave. It was enough to get her heart racing again. As much as she wanted to sleep the feeling was overwhelming. Eventually she had to rise and see what it was.

Alena slowly made her way out of the cave. The moon was bright in a cloudless sky. It was the first time in a long time that the moon wasn't covered by clouds. Alena instantly thought it was strange, but then scolded herself for being silly. For some reason she felt as though the noise had come from the sky, although it was impossible to truly tell.

After what seemed like an eternity Alena finally blinked. There was nothing in the sky and nothing around that could have made the noise. Even though she wasn't satisfied she wasn't going to spend all night watching the skies. As she turned to walk back into the cave she thought she saw something pass over the moon in her peripheral vision. The sight was enough to get her heart racing again, although she couldn't be sure what it was. Something was urging her towards the shrine. The feeling had been there before, but now it was much stronger. Before she knew it she had moved from where she was standing to the front of the two columns.

The urge to step over the line and enter the pass was almost overwhelming, but she held herself back. The moonlight seemed brighter towards the middle of the pass. Alena knew that was where the sacrificial altar was and the place she was being drawn to. It didn't make any sense to her. She was neither a woman nor a virgin and yet it seemed to be calling to her.

"What are you doing out here?" Richmond voice's sounded sleepy and his voice made Alena jump.

"There's something out here." Even though she hadn't seen anything she knew her statement was true.

"Then all the more reason for us to be inside. There is nothing for us out here. Come, before you get too cold."

Richmond took Alena by the arm. At first she didn't want to leave, but eventually his gentle tugging compelled her to move. A wave of relief washed over her body when she was back in the safety of the cave. There was still something calling to her, but it was more subtle now. She felt as though she could ignore it long enough to return to sleep.

No one was happier to see the morning than Alena. As much as she wasn't woken again her sleep was restless. The urge to leave the cave had gone and that could only be a good sign.

"What were you doing by the pass last night?" Richmond asked as they ate breakfast.

Alena had hoped Richmond would keep that to himself. She didn't really know how to answer.

"I don't know. I was woken by a strange sound and I just wanted to see what it was." That was the best she could do.

"How could you even think to go out at night?" Eldred sounded shocked. "You know there is a good chance Kahn is out there. If you came across him there is nothing you could do to protect yourself."

"I know." Alena had already scolded herself. "But there was something compelling me. It wanted me to cross the threshold of the pass, but I didn't. Whatever it was its gone now, so I don't think that we really need to discuss it any further."

The answer wasn't at all what they wanted, but they didn't push. Only Viper seeemed excited about crossing the pass. Any information on what was out there would have been helpful, but if Alena didn't know then there was no point in interrogating her anymore.

Outside the cave the snow had started to fall again. A thick layer covered the mountain floor and as expected no snow fell on the pass. They stopped at the entrance again. There was nothing on the other side, but no one wanted to pass.

"If it helps I can go first to show you there is nothing to be afraid of." Viper offered.

Eldred doubted that it would do anything to calm their nerves, but it wasn't going to hurt. Eldred gave Viper a nod of agreement.

Surprisingly the serpentant paused before taking a step onto the pass. Alena wasn't sure if he was nervous or saying a prayer to his Goddess. She thought she saw him speak under his breath, but she couldn't be completely sure.

The others waited before crossing onto the pass. Viper took a number of paces before he stopped and turned around. When he didn't burst into flame and get struck down by lightning they figured it was safe enough.

Eldred was the first to step onto the pass. The first thing he felt was a great warmth fill his body. He had been somewhat dubious with Viper's explanation the night before, but now he knew it was true. There was a massive field of magic around him and it was wonderful. He thought, if what Viper said was right, there would be a sickness to the place, but there wasn't. The magic was pure. Without thinking Eldred took his heavy robe off before taking another step forward.

The walls were amazing and Eldred stared at them in awe. They had been shaped and polished perfectly before being covered with carefully carved runes. The writing was in a language Eldred had never seen before. He guessed it was the language of the snakes, a long forgotten and much debated language. If he had not seen it himself he would have never believed it.

Richmond was the next to step into the shrine. He also felt the warmth and removed his robe. Although he couldn't feel the magic as Eldred did, he did feel something. It was as if the fatigue of the previous days trekking had been washed away. He moved past Eldred who was still marvelling at the walls.

Alena was the last to enter. The tug trying to pull her in was stronger than ever and that was disturbing. She knew that she had no choice, but she still couldn't bring herself to move. Taking a deep breath she forced her legs up and down. As soon as she was over the threshold her body suddenly froze. A great pain ripped through her body, but she was unable to scream. She couldn't move at all. She looked at the others, but they were engrossed in their own experiences and didn't notice.

The pain ripped through Alena in waves whilst the others basked in euphoria. They seemed happy in their own little worlds whilst she suffered. She had no idea why she had been singled out.

Suddenly there was a great gust of air and the sound of beating wings. It was enough to pull them out of their reverie. Alena could only move her eyes and couldn't see what it was, but the others had no problems seeing what was coming. A great black beast was hovering in the air above them. Their fears had come true, Kahn was about to join them.

The last of the great dragons and master of the Black Dragon Clan slowly lowered himself until he landed in the middle of the pass. He made no move to kill or attack and in turn no one else made a move, even Viper was waiting to see what Kahn was about to do. The great dragon watched the four of them closely. There seemed to be a look of confusion on his face, although it was hard to tell.

"It has been a long time since anyone has brought a sacrifice to me." Kahn's voice was deep and gruff. "And what a sacrifice you have brought. I can feel power in her. She is special." Kahn's forked tongue flashed out and flicked the air around it. Once his tongue was back in his mouth Kahn took a tentative step forward, re-adjusting his position so he could get a better view of the group before him. "This does seem like an odd group though, why is it you have brought me this sacrifice?"

"We haven't brought..." Richmond started to speak, but was suddenly silenced by an unseen force.

"She is not a sacrifice, oh great dragon." Viper stepped forward as he pulled his hood down.

The reaction on Kahn's face was hard to gauge. He was either surprised or angry, but no one knew which. They hoped it was surprise at seeing a serpentant.

"Tell me your name?" Kahn demanded.

"My name is Viper and I am one of the Goddess' chosen few." Viper's voice was commanding, but there was a hint of fear. The other's hoped that Kahn didn't notice.

The pain still ripped through Alena, although the waves had grown further apart since Kahn and Viper had started talking. She wanted to call out, but she still couldn't move. After listening to the conversation she believed that Kahn had done something to her, assuming that she was a present for him. Even though Viper had explained that she wasn't he still hadn't released her. She could see that both Richmond and Eldred were too fixated on the dragon to notice her. All she could do was suffer in silence and hope it would end soon.

"It has been a long time since I have seen one of your kind and now you tell me that you haven't brought a sacrifice to sate my hunger?" Kahn sounded angry.

"You forget yourself Kahn. The Goddess bestowed power upon me and my kind. You are here to serve me, not the other way around." There was definite nervousness in his voice.

In a fair fight Viper would have been much stronger than the dragon, but in his weakened state he knew that he wouldn't stand a chance. Kahn was the strongest of the Great Dragons and Viper didn't even think he could take down a dragonling. His only hope was to bluff and hope that Kahn didn't see through him.

"The Goddess left the Great Dragons in command. That is why she created this shrine for us. You may have been favoured at one place in time, but not anymore. If you haven't brought me a sacrifice then I can only assume you came here to die," Kahn's voice grew in intensity as he spoke and he took a menacing step forward.

"We are not here to fight you," Eldred thought it was time to speak.

"One of the Council of Wizards?" the question was rhetorical. "It has been a long time since one of you has come to visit here. Drake, I believe his name was, was lucky to leave with his life. He thought he would come and entreat with me. He was sadly mistaken. Let's see if you are any better."

When he finished his threats, Kahn beat his massive wings and took to the sky. The pass was just wide enough for him to spread his wings without touching the sides. As he lifted himself from the ground the spell that was holding Alena was suddenly released. She crumbled to the ground and cried out in pain. No one turned to see if she was alright. They were fixated on the dragon lifting himself into the sky.

"What do we do now?" Eldred asked Viper.

"Get prepared to defend yourself!"

There was nothing Richmond could do to help. It was up to the magic wielders to protect them. Seeing Alena on the ground he rushed to her side.

"Are you alright?" he asked.

"No!" her voice was weak. It was the only word she could get out.

Richmond made an effort to move her outside of the pass, but she was too heavy. That should have seemed odd to him, but even as he attempted to move her he knew it would be impossible. Whatever was coming they would have to be there for it.

Kahn lifted himself further into the sky before he took off. The black creature circled around the shrine once before coming in low at the far end. When he was half way along he let out a great breath of fire engulfing the pass. If he had not given them forewarning he would have roasted them alive. Eldred and Viper had a chance to put up a defensive shield. The fire spurted off it protecting all who were underneath. Once Kahn had passed over he soared high into the air again. He wasn't finished.

"So this is what you call 'nothing waiting for us' do you?" There was no humour in Eldred's voice.

"If you hadn't noticed he's trying to fry me as well. I think you'd do better to concentrate on the job at hand."

There was no more time for conversation as Kahn swooped down to make his second pass. The flames started at the same spot and again Viper and Eldred created a shield to protect themselves. The flame was more intense this time, but the shield stayed strong. Again Kahn soared into the sky once he was done.

Viper's legs started to wobble as he let the spell go. Despite the added strength he received from the magic surrounding the shine he was still weak from his shedding. It took all his willpower to remain on his feet and prepare for another attack.

"I don't know how long I can keep this up," Viper breathed hard. "This place has given me some of my power back, but it is waning fast."

"You keep going until your life runs out," Eldred spoke between clenched teeth. "We have to hold out."

The great dragon soared even higher in the sky before returning. He swooped low, but instead of blowing another burst of flame he pulled up short and landed with a thud. Eldred had already created the shield and was loathed to let it go until he knew what Kahn was about to do. The dragon took a step forward before lying on his stomach. He lowered his head and let it rest on the floor of his shrine.

"Why is a serpentant travelling with a wizard, a man and a rather delicious looking elf?" There was a quizzical look on the dragon's face, or at least that's what they thought it was.

Everyone was confused by the question. The attack had come so suddenly that they didn't expect it to end so soon. It seemed as though at some point in his flight pattern he had realised that something wasn't right. He needed more information before he killed those before him. The last time he had taken things for granted he had nearly died. The thought of the little man goading him to attack only to use the strength of his fire still weighed heavily in his mind. This time he would be smarter.

"We are on a mission to stop Nyrra and the tyranny he holds over the Goddess." Viper came straight to the point.

There was a grumble somewhere deep inside the dragon. It didn't sound as though he liked the response. They all waited nervously to hear what he would say next.

"Nyrra has always aided the Black Dragon Clan in our battle for supremacy. The other clans betrayed the Goddess to her detriment. We have fought side-by-side with Nyrra in defiance of those who saw to her demise. It is vengeance that has kept me going all these years and now the battle is almost over. There is only one more dragon left and I will see him dead."

"Cain is dead. He died in a battle with Raheem." Viper explained and Khan lifted his head up.

Eldred wasn't sure about the casual banter. It seemed dangerous to him, but at least it gave him time to try and think of a plan. If Kahn decided to attack again he wasn't sure how long they would be able to hold him back. Viper's strength wouldn't last much longer and Eldred could only do so much against the great dragon.

"I felt the death of my brother. Raheem was a good friend. I didn't realise that Cain was dead as well. It seems as though I am now the last of the dragons. Good. Now the Goddess has been avenged."

There was a moment of silence. Viper wasn't sure what to say next. He needed Kahn to know the truth about Nyrra and the Goddess, but it would be hard to change centuries of misinformation, especially as Kahn had built his life around those lies. The silence also gave the dragon a chance to soak in the information. He was the last of the dragons, something he always knew would happen. He had known for a long time that he would be the last, but he never really thought the day would come.

"Nyrra has lied to you. He's lied to all of us. It was Nyrra who imprisoned the Goddess and enslaved us all."

Kahn stood and took a step back when he heard Viper's words. No one could tell what the expression on his face meant.

"Nyrra told us that the other clan betrayed and murdered the Goddess. It was our duty to destroy them all." Kahn didn't sound certain of himself.

"That was a lie. Nyrra knew that you and the rest of the Black Dragon Clan wanted power. You craved the power that the other clans possessed and he knew that. It didn't take much to convince you to hunt down and kill the other clans." There was a lot more confidence in Viper's voice now. "Nyrra has betrayed you like he has betrayed all of us. It took me a long time to realise it. He's imprisoned the Goddess, if he hasn't already killed her. He has subjugated me and the other serpentants with threats and lies. Now we need to work together to kill Nyrra and free her."

Again there was a moment of silence as the information sunk in. This was not at all what Kahn had been expecting. At first there was good news that he had completed his task and then the news that it had all been a lie. Now he didn't know what to think. He knew there was no reason for Viper to lie to him. He remembered at one stage in his life the dragons had all deferred to the serpentants. They were the most favoured of the Goddess, but Nyrra had told him that things had changed. The Goddess no longer favoured the serpentants, but instead the dragons. Now he wasn't so sure. If Viper was telling the truth then he couldn't believe anything Nyrra had told him. Then again there was a chance Viper was only telling him this to stop them from being burnt to a crisp.

"So is that why you are here?" Kahn asked. "To tell me my life has been a lie."

"I don't know why we are here. We have been sent on this journey by both sides."

"So you do still work for Nyrra?" Kahn took a threatening step forward.

"No, but he still thinks I do. I can't risk him killing the Goddess, if she is in fact still alive. I have to pretend that I am doing what he wants, but that is as far as it goes. I will see him dead before I see his plans fulfilled." Viper spoke more passionately.

No one noticed the subtle spell Viper had created to make Kahn more malleable. It was risky for two reasons. If Kahn decided to attack Viper then he wouldn't have the energy to defend himself. The second, and most important, if Kahn realised what he was doing then that would seal their fate. There is no way the dragon would believe him if he realised he was being tampered with.

"I guess that is making sense." Kahn shook his head. It was as if he didn't believe what he was saying or thinking. "So why did you come to me?"

"We need your help." Suddenly it was dawning on Viper why both sides had told him to take this path. He needed to recruit Kahn into battle. Nyrra would think that he would convince Kahn to fight on his side, but that was not something he would even consider. "There is a battle brewing and your assistance is greatly needed."

"Why? Why should I fight on your side? Why should I fight at all? My battle is over. My war has been fought and won." Kahn was fighting with the spell inside his head.

"This battle is not over yet. You know, as the last of the great dragons, it is your destiny to take part in this. That isn't the decision that you have to make. The question is which side you will be fighting on?"

Kahn suddenly lifted himself into the sky without responding to the question.

"I don't think that went too well," Eldred commented.

"We'll see. If he attacks we know we've failed. If not, then I think he'll be on our side." Viper didn't give away anything with his tone.

As they watched the sky Kahn disappeared into the distance. Eldred could only imagine how high he must be to be out of sight.

"Alena needs help." Richmond figured it was time to speak up. It would be at least another minute or two before Kahn returned.

"What happened?" Eldred rushed to her side.

"Kahn assumed she was his sacrifice," Viper said. "From memory he likes to paralyse his victims and cause them pain. I can only assume that's what he has done to Alena."

Eldred kept his gaze on her as Alena nodded her agreement. She felt exhausted from the strain. Eldred tried to move her, but the spell still remained that kept her in the same spot. She could move on her own, but she didn't have the energy to stand.

"There's nothing I can do to help now. There is magic at play, but if Kahn attacks again I'll need all my strength to defend against him." Eldred stood as he spoke.

"I wouldn't worry too much about that," Viper spoke as he stared at the sky. "If Kahn decides to attack again then I don't think there is anything we can do to stop him."

Suddenly Kahn returned to view as he headed back towards his shrine. Eldred thought he was travelling too fast for landing and prepared himself for another attack. He wasn't sure if his shield alone would protect them all, but he wasn't about to give up.

As Kahn flew in closer he reduced his speed and came to a stop a few paces away from the group. Eldred's heart was racing as adrenaline pumped through his body. He really believed Kahn was going to attack them again, but it seemed as though Viper's words had worked.

"I don't know what to think. Something isn't right here, I know that much, but I don't know if you are trying to play me. It is hard to suddenly change how you think after many centuries, but something is telling me you are truthful. Either way I need time to think," Kahn started.

"So what does that mean for us?" Viper asked.

"It means that I am prepared to let you leave." Kahn sounded somewhat disappointed. "As far as Nyrra and your war goes I will need time to think on it. I'm assuming that the final battle isn't going to start tomorrow?"

"No, there is time before the final battle starts, but the war does rage on. Don't wait too long. The more time that passes the worse things are going to get. I'm sure the Alliance would love the assistance of a dragon," Viper warned.

Kahn snorted two puffs of smoke out of his noise. Eldred didn't think that was a good sign. He wanted to tell Viper to calm down, but he couldn't undermine him in front of Kahn. All he could do was hope that he didn't provoke the dragon to attack.

"I think it is time for you to leave before I lose my patience." There was no humour in Kahn's threat.

"There are two more things that I need from you." Eldred could have hit Viper for pushing his luck. Surely it was more important that they just leave with their skin intact.

"Make it quick, you have already tested my patience to the limit. Pray that you don't upset me further." Kahn took a menacing step forward and moved his head until it was almost touching Viper's. The move should have made the serpentant extremely nervous, but he didn't flinch.

"Firstly Alena, the elf who you thought was your sacrifice."

"What of her?"

"She is stuck to the ground. You need to release her." Viper thought about asking him to reverse the pain, but he didn't want to push his luck. What he had to ask next was much more important.

"It is done. Now you said there were two things you needed?" Kahn didn't sound impressed.

"Not long ago I was poisoned and as part of the healing process I had to shed my skin. Since then I have not been able to recuperate and I need all my strength to survive the upcoming trials. I've heard a rumour that dragons can heal serpentants with their magic. Some of my brothers have told me they have been healed this way. I was hoping that you could help me?"

Kahn thought for a moment. This wasn't at all what he was expecting. When he first saw the group trekking their way up the mountain he thought it was another sacrifice. He should have known better, since it had been such a long time since the last one. Now his life had been turned around and he didn't know what to think. All he wanted to do was get them out of his shrine and off his mountain. The quickest way to do that would be to acquiesce and that's exactly what he was going to do.

"Fine. I will do what I can to help, but I can't guarantee that it will work."

Without warning Kahn opened his mouth and breathed out a flame. The fire shot out towards Viper and completely engulfed him before Eldred had a chance to react. He thought about creating a shield, but when the flame didn't continue from the serpentant he held back. It was too late to save Viper and it didn't seem as though Kahn was about to attack the others.

It was over a minute before Kahn let the fire die out. When the flames dissipated they were all surprised to see Viper still standing there and he wasn't even smouldering. He looked as though he hadn't been touched by the flames at all. And then they noticed that his scaly skin had darkened in colour and he seemed to be standing straighter. Whatever Kahn had done it looked as though it had worked.

"Now you can leave," Kahn boomed the words before lifting himself from the ground. He hovered above the walls of the shrine for a moment. "If you linger then I'll be back!" The words resonated throughout the pass. There was no doubt that it wasn't an empty threat. He left them with those words and lifted himself further into the sky before flying off to the north.

Adelanta started by leading the other horses along the pass. The elven horses kept the other horses from bolting at the first sign of the dragon. Although they knew the dragon wasn't coming back it took them a moment to convince the others to keep moving.

The others waited until Kahn disappeared behind a mountain peak before they started for the other side. Alena still needed assistance from Richmond, although she was starting to feel much better since she had been released.

"Well that went rather well!" Viper spoke casually as they started for the other side, he sounded much stronger.

"We'll see about that. We still have to get to Lel Dinion." Eldred didn't sound as pleased with the turn of events.

Chapter 10: High and Low

Alaric finally landed on a sandy beach. He hoped this was the island he had been searching for. His first four jumps had landed him in the ocean. The first two times he had dried himself as he jumped, but then decided it wasn't worth the effort. Preparing for another dump in the water he landed face down on the sand. When he realised he was on dry land he quickly created the spell to dry himself and once that was done he patted the sand from his clothes.

After such a journey he should have been feeling exhausted, but he felt as fresh as if he'd had a really good sleep. The Opal stone had unlocked something inside of him, some of it good, some of it bad. Now he knew more than he could have learned in ten lifetimes. Now he had to put all the pieces together if he was going to defeat Nyrra.

The island was small and half way around the world from the Seven Kingdoms. The sun beat down hard and he would have been dry in a few minutes if he hadn't already done the job. Without thinking he adjusted his body temperature just before the first bead of sweat appeared on his brow. He wore the same long black leather coat with trousers and black leather jerkin that had become so comfortable. Under normal circumstances he would be sweating profusely.

His sword hung from his waist, the only possession he carried. He found that he could go days without food and still not feel hungry. His clothes never got dirty either, another perk of his new abilities, he was able to remove all dirt and grime without having to think about it.

On any other occasion Alaric would have looked around and noticed the beauty of the island. The beach had white sand with crystal aqua water lapping the shores. The foreshore sloped up to a grove of palm trees and soft grass. Alaric walked up the beach and didn't notice or smell the multitude of flowers. He was on a mission and that's all that mattered. The world seemed dull to him now. If he knew what he was missing then he might have been remorseful, but all he could see was his end goal, the destruction of Nyrra.

There was something not right about the island. As much as Alaric was sure it wasn't the place he was looking for he had to investigate further. There was a reason why he was there and he couldn't leave until he knew what it was. He laughed softly to himself as he walked through the palms. Even on the other side of the world the prophecy still tugged at him. It seemed as though he couldn't escape from his destiny until the job was done.

The trees started to became denser the further he walked. Large ferns slowed his journey and it wasn't long before he had to hack at the undergrowth with his sword. Even the strain didn't bring any sweat to his brow. Although it seemed as though he was wandering aimlessly he knew he was going in the right direction. Occasionally he would have to bypass the especially rocky terrain or a large lagoons, but it didn't take him long to get back on the right track.

A shiver ran down Alaric's spine as he suddenly got a bad feeling. There was something evil ahead, but there was also something good. He couldn't wait any longer. The destination finally landed in his mind and he blinked out of existence. When he returned he was standing in a small grove of palm trees. Short grass was mixed in with the soft sandy ground, but that was the last thing on Alaric's mind. What concerned him were the many cages hanging from the trees.

He walked a few paces and came out into a small clearing. He saw a man standing with his back to him. He was plump and wearing a simple singlet and shorts. The fat from his stomach and lower back hung over the sides of his waistband. His head was completely bald. Although it looked as though the man had spent most of his time in the sun his skin was almost pure white. This was not at all what Alaric was expecting.

"You may as well step out of the trees," the man slurped and licked his lips as he spoke. "I sensed your arrival when you landed on my island. As much as I was expecting someone, I can't say it was you, but by the aura I'm sensing you are going to be much tastier."

Alaric stepped forward as the man suggested. He figured there was little reason to remain hidden, not that he was truly hidden anyway. A strange feeling came over him as he stepped out into the sun. There was magic at play, but not any he had ever felt before. He knew this wasn't the man he was looking for. He had deliberately not looked too closely at the cages, if he didn't know who was inside them then he couldn't feel bad about leaving them there.

Time was against him and there were more important places for him to be. Without responding or waiting for the man to continue Alaric blinked himself out of existence, only something was wrong. The spell was second nature to him, but this time it didn't work. He remained in the clearing looking at the man's chubby back.

"Where is Mesula?" Alaric asked.

The man was taken aback at the question. It took him a moment before he answered. "Long gone. This is my island now."

"Who are you?"

"My name is Yzukio and this is my island. You can leave when I say you can leave." He seemed to know that Alaric had already tried. "For now you are my guest." On that statement Yzukio turned around. His face was not at all what Alaric was expecting. It looked as though he was only in his teens, but Alaric knew that wasn't possible. With each passing moment the feeling of unrest increased inside him.

"My name is Alaric." He thought he should return the favour. "What is it you do on this island?"

"I'll be the one who asks the questions. Although you are not yet my prisoner that can easily change." There was no humour in his threat.

Alaric wasn't completely sure if those words were right, but for the moment he wasn't going to test the theory. Touching the Opal stone had unlocked a lot in his mind, but it seemed as though he didn't know everything. He had no idea where he was or who he was up against so he needed to tread lightly. Something was stopping him from continuing his journey and that had to be some powerful magic. He didn't have time to be taken prisoner so he would have to placate Yzukio.

"Okay, then you should ask a question. I have little time for games." Alaric was harsher than he had planned, but he was starting to get annoyed.

"There is fire in you, that is plain to see. You are defiant even though you have already been caught in my trap. I have to admit this is something I haven't experienced before." Yzukio sounded amused. "What are you doing here?"

"I am looking for someone, but I don't know why I have landed here. The person I am looking for is not here." Alaric did his best to explain, but it was hard when he really didn't know himself.

"Who is it you're looking for? It's a big island, they could be here somewhere." He giggled when he finished. The noise sounded strange coming from the fat man.

"There is no one else on this island," Alaric replied. "Besides those in your cages of course."

"How do you know the person you're looking for isn't in one of these cages?" Yzukio licked his lips again.

There was something about Yzukio that made Alaric uncomfortable. There was something about the entire situation that made him very uncomfortable. He knew that he would need to show his dominance very soon. There was little chance of leaving without a fight, but he needed more information of who he was up against.

Since Yzukio had mentioned the cages Alaric started to take notice of them. He realised they were all filled, except for one. He couldn't see who was inside each of them, but he could feel their presence. There was a waning strength to each one as if the occupants had all been slowly tortured over many years. He didn't think that was too far from the truth.

"How do you know to breathe? How do you know to eat and drink? I can't explain it, but I know he's not there." Alaric again did his best to explain. He knew Yzukio was using a spell to try and squeeze the truth out of him. It was simple enough to block the spell without the fat man realising. To keep the ruse going he had to seem as though he was telling the truth, which he was, but that could easily change.

Alaric couldn't be sure, but he thought Yzukio had suddenly lost some weight. It wasn't much, but he could swear there was less fat hanging over his shorts. Things were getting stranger and Alaric had a sudden urge to flee. He was sure he could still leave by foot, but now he couldn't leave those who had been caged. If Yzukio was indeed evil then he couldn't just leave his prisoners to rot.

"You are a mystery, that's for sure." Yzukio slurped.

"What are you doing on this island?" Alaric turned the questioning around. He couldn't let the fat man control the conversation. It was time to show his dominance. "It is a long way from anywhere. It seems like a strange place to call home."

"You are powerful, I'll give you that much." Yzukio said as he licked his lips. "The air is palpable."

Yzukio slurped again and Alaric suddenly felt weak in the knees. His legs started to shake for a moment before he settled himself. The action was disturbing, but Alaric put it to the back of his mind. He needed to work out what Yzukio was all about.

"It's time you start to answer my questions. I can feel your energy around me and I know you are also strong, but don't underestimate my power," Yzukio said.

Alaric was really starting to get nervous. Something was seriously wrong. The longer he stayed the more danger he put himself in, but he couldn't leave until he worked out what was happening.

"Very well." Yzukio continued when Alaric didn't respond. "I have different tastes to those in your Seven Kingdoms. I tried living there once, but it was too... what's the word I'm looking for? Cluttered, I think that's it." Yzukio looked as though he was about to lick his lips again, but he stopped when he realised what he was doing. "It is much more pleasant for me to remain here, especially since I can get my food to come to me."

Alaric took a step backwards. It seemed the cages were filled with animals, but he hadn't seen a single one on the island. It might have been because they were all trapped, but Alaric didn't think that was the case. There was more to the fat man than met the eye. He was definitely more dangerous than he had first given him credit for.

"What is it exactly that you eat?" Alaric wasn't sure he wanted to know the answer.

Yzukio thought for a moment. It was a question he had not wanted to answer, but it was also one he had not wanted to be asked. His own power was growing, he knew that. Alaric was the most powerful creature on the island. As he basked in that power it started to corrupt his mind. Slowly he licked his lips again and followed it with a deep slurp. This time Alaric started to feel dizzy and his stomach churned and as he looked up he could have sworn he saw Yzukio become fatter. It took him over a minute to recover and as he did Yzukio just watched and smiled.

Suddenly it dawned on Alaric what the fat man fed on. He ate energy and drew on the power of others. Each time he had been making the slurping sound he had been slurping up Alaric's energy. Silently he cursed himself for not realising earlier, but he had never heard of anyone like him before. The only way he could successfully stop the man was to kill him. Now he wasn't even sure if he would be able to manage that.

"I wouldn't advise doing that again," Alaric spoke through clenched teeth. He wanted to hide both his anger and his weakness.

"Ha! I have to admit this is the first time my food has tried to stand up to me, but then again it's the first time my food has realised its food before being caged. Now you give me a dilemma that I have never faced before. As much as you aren't my normal food you are very tasty. I don't think I can let you leave now that I have had a taste." Yzukio sneered as he spoke and suppressed the urge to lick his lips.

The fat man knew if he fed too quickly there was a chance he could explode. He wished he hadn't already fed for the day so he could feast on Alaric. His prisoners had almost no flavour left and this new one was so delicious.

"I have no issues with you Yzukio." It was the truth as far as Alaric was concerned, although he was starting to doubt it. "I have to keep moving." Alaric tried to take a step backwards, but found his feet were stuck to the ground. "Let me go."

"I can't do that." Yzukio took a step forward. Even with small amount already drained from Alaric there was still more strength inside him than he could fathom. If the power hadn't already started to manifest itself within his brain he would have had the sense to let Alaric go.. "You will stay here and feed me until the end of time."

Alaric had to laugh. Even though he was stuck to the ground he had already worked out the spell to release himself. The advantage was his and he wanted it to remain that way. Before he had been quite happy to leave Yzukio be, but now he wanted to free the prisoners and kill the fat man. In the end there couldn't have been any other result. He had been brought to the island for a reason and that was the only one he could think of.

"You followed the trail I left for someone else and that is unfortunate, but that is the way it has played out." Yzukio slurped and licked his lips, but this time he was left with a confused expression on his face. "What have you done?"

"I warned you that I'm a lot stronger than anyone you have met before. You had your chance to set me free and you didn't take it. Now it is time for your doom," Alaric kept his voice level.

Yzukio wasn't happy with his meal being cut short, but he was by no means defenceless. The trail he used to bring his victims to the island and his ability to keep them locked up was just a small amount of what he could do. He took two steps backwards until he was standing in the centre of the clearing. Alaric remained, where he was, this was something he had been expecting. He wanted the fat man to show what he was capable of and was well prepared to defend himself.

The wind started to pick up and blow through the palms. Grains of sand flicked up against Alaric's boots. Whatever Yzukio was planning it was about to come to fruition. Alaric had already set his spell. The invisible barrier around him was impenetrable. The only downfall was he could neither move, nor create another spell. The advantage was that he could see how strong Yzukio was without risking his life.

The ground started to shake around him and the barrier was hit by an invisible force. The force pounded against the shield from all angles with no effect. Alaric could feel the barrier being attacked and was almost knocked to the ground on more than one occasion. Yzukio was starting to go red in the face with the strain. He was throwing everything he had at Alaric. The barrage went on for five minutes before he finally realised it wasn't having any effect.

Alaric noticed that Yzukio had lost a lot of weight. Now it was all starting to make sense. Yzukio fed on the energy of others and then used it for his own. It seemed as though the spells were draining his reserves. The fat rolls still poured over the sides of his shorts, but he had definitely shed some pounds.

"Is that all you've got." That would be the easiest way for Alaric to win. He needed to get Yzukio to keep attacking until he ran out of energy. "I could have done that in my sleep."

Yzukio didn't realise what Alaric was doing and had already prepared his next attack. He figured that the first attack was too weak. If he wanted to attack Alaric then it would have to be a stronger spell. What he didn't realise was there was no way to magically break Alaric's barrier. A physical attack, on the other hand, he was completely vulnerable to.

Suddenly the sand was swept up in a whirlwind. At first Alaric thought that Yzukio had gone with a weaker spell as the grains of sand slow circled his barrier. As the spell continued more and more sand gathered in the mini tornado. In less than a minute Alaric's barrier was completely covered with wildly swirling sand. It looked like he was encased in a glass egg. The scene before him was madness, but Alaric remained safe in his shell.

What happened next was a shock to Alaric. A single grain of sand penetrated his shield and slashed him across the cheek. It wasn't the shock of the sudden pain that worried him, it was the fact that Yzukio had managed to break through. As much as he had never tried it before he knew that the spell was supposed to be impregnable. He knew it in every fibre of his body, but it seemed as though that wasn't true. That changed everything he knew, or thought he knew, but it wasn't the time to be retrospective. He could reflect all he wanted once he had disposed with the ever reducing fat man.

Alaric could feel the spell around him grow in power. Occasionally another grain of sand would penetrate the shield and slash at his face, his coat and his pants. The longer the spell progressed the more sand got through his defences. It was only a matter of time before the shield and Alaric were both cut to shreds. He needed to think of a different plan and he needed to do it quickly.

The timing had to be perfect. There would be less than a second between the time of Alaric releasing the shield and being cut to ribbons. The spell also needed to be quick and powerful enough to diffuse whatever Yzukio had created. The whirling vortex of sand prevented Alaric from seeing how the spell was made. There was no chance of unravelling it, even if there was time he didn't think it was possible.

Alaric took a deep breath before releasing the spell that created the shield. Instantly the sand rushed in to rip Alaric to sheds. Only two grains touched him before the entire vortex exploded outwards. The sand few out into the air before suddenly dropping to the ground. Not a single grain touched Yzukio.

When the sand settled Alaric saw that Yzukio had almost lost almost all of his weight. There were a couple of small rolls of fat left, but all in all he looked very fit. It was the perfect time for Alaric to attack himself, but he still wanted to wait and see what Yzukio would do next.

"It seems as though I have underestimated you," Yzukio's voice remained strong even though it was obvious he was weakening. "I will let you go. You can be on your way and I won't do anything to stop you."

Alaric had to laugh. It was only now that he was defeated that he could see the error in his ways. He hoped that he would be able bluff his way out of his current predicament, although without a new source of food he didn't think he would survive for much longer. Even if he drained those who remained in the cages it would only sustain him for another week or two.

"You know there is no way I am going to leave you here with your prisoners. It is time to set them free." Alaric made no move to the cages. Again he wanted to see Yzukio's reaction.

"No, you can't. They are my food. Without them I will die." Yzukio pleaded. He knew his threats wouldn't work. His only way out was to beg for his life.

"Who do you have inside these cages?" Alaric asked.

"No one of any significance. No one you would be interested in," Yzukio whimpered.

"That's no answer at all. If you lured them to your island then there has to be some reason. Now, tell me who they are." Alaric's voice was hard as steel. He was a second away from destroying him.

"They are ki'yousei, nothing you should worry yourself about. Simply leave and we'll leave it at that."

Although Yzukio used a language Alaric had never heard before he knew exactly what he said. His prisoners were Wood Sprites and that suddenly made a lot of sense to him. Although he had never met a Wood Sprite he knew they were powerful creatures. He also knew it had been a long time since anyone had seen a Wood Sprite, or at least anyone he knew.

The Wood Sprites had been slowly lured to Yzukio's island over the years where he had been feeding on their power. Alaric had to admit it was the perfect crime. Wood Sprites were solitary creatures at the best of times. They preferred to spend their time alone in their forests. No one would notice if they went missing and it seemed as though no one had.

"Let the Wood Sprites go and swear not to lure them back and I might just consider letting you live," he didn't think the threat was going to work. Even as the words came out of his mouth he knew he was going to have to kill Yzukio.

"If you take my food then I will die." If he was surprised that Alaric knew who the prisoners were he didn't show it. As he spoke Yzukio came to the realisation that there was only one way this would end. "I guess we know what needs to happen."

Before Yzukio was able to create his last spell Alaric wrapped him up in threads of air. He squeezed tightly causing Yzukio to gasp. Yzukio tried to reach for the spell he was hoping would kill Alaric, but he couldn't find it. Whatever Alaric was doing it was stopping him. He wanted to cry out in anguish, but he couldn't speak.

"I guess it was always going to come to this, it's just a shame really. I have a lot of killing ahead of me and I was hoping that wouldn't start again before I returned to the Seven Kingdoms. I guess that was just wishful thinking. I don't know why I thought you'd be any different." Slowly Yzukio was raised until he was floating a foot above the ground.

Alaric had already decided the former fat man's fate. The vortex that Yzukio had thrown at Alaric had given him the idea. Slowly a pin hole appeared on the ground underneath the floating man. At first it was so small that Yzukio didn't notice it. It wasn't until it was a foot wide before he realised what was happening. At first he thought Alaric was going to bury him alive. He wanted to plead for mercy, but Alaric kept the gag on him. One thing Alaric couldn't allow was for Yzukio's pleas to weaken his resolve. There would be enough memories of people screaming to keep him awake for a lifetime and he didn't need one more. At the very least Yzukio's death would be silent, although it was going to be extremely painful. Alaric wasn't about to let him off for all the pain he had caused the Wood Sprites.

When the hole was three paces wide and twice as deep the sand started to swirl like the vortex Yzukio had created. When Alaric was happy with the speed he slowly started to lower Yzukio further into the pit. He stopped when Yzukio's head was just below ground level. There was still plenty of room between Yzukio and the spinning sand, but that didn't stop the look of pure horror appearing on his face. If he had been able to speak he would have been screaming at the top of his lungs. It was the first time in his life that he had ever felt fear.

There was always the rush when Yzukio tempted another Wood Sprite to the island, but that was different. Deep down he knew he was strong enough to defeat a Wood Sprite even if it realised what he was doing, but it had always been too late. Now he was trapped and was about to die. It was something he never thought he would experience.

Yzukio remained in the middle of the hole as the sand started to close in. It swirled fast and faster as it became closer. At first it ripped the clothes from his body, but it didn't stop there. Slowly it started to shred his skin. He opened his mouth but nothing came out. His felt as though he was going to rip apart with the strain of trying to scream. The pain was unbearable, but he couldn't drift away, Alaric made sure of that. He was going to keep Yzukio conscious for the entire experience. It was all he deserved.

Blood and shredded skin spun out from the vortex, but none of it stuck to him. He could only imagine the pain Yzukio was experiencing and he suppressed the urge to smile. One thing he didn't want to do was start enjoying the pain he was causing. That was one step closer to him becoming the thing he was trying to destroy. With that thought in his mind he let the hole fill and swallow up what was left of Yzukio's body.

Alaric breathed a sigh of relief when it was over. This was not at all what he had been expecting. The Opal Stone had unlocked a lot of missing information from within his mind, but it seemed as though there were still things he didn't know. It was a good warning that he didn't know everything and he still needed to be careful. Now it was time to release Yzukio's prisoners. He was excited to meet a Wood Sprite.

Alaric stood in the middle of the clearing and raised his arms above his head. Slowly he wiggled his fingers. After a moment the locks on the cages broke off and fell to the ground.

"You can come out now. Your captor is dead and you are free." Alaric boomed.

There was no movement from the cages. Alaric didn't think it was a good sign. Yzukio had been quite large when he arrived which meant he had fed recently. As much as he didn't want to believe they were all dead it had to be a possibility but however he didn't think Yzukio would be stupid enough to kill all his food. "It's alright, you're safe now." Alaric tried to reassure them.

Slowly the door to one of the cages opened and what looked to be a young girl stepped out. Her clothes, her face and her hair were marred with dirt, although Alaric couldn't for the life of him work out where it had come from. He had only seen sand since arriving on the island.

"Who are you?" her voice was sweet and innocent. "Are you here to save us?"

"I came here by accident, but it seemed as though that's why I am here. Yuzkio is dead and you are free to return to your forests."

"Come out everyone, we are free!" her voice was weak, but somewhat vibrant.

Slowly the doors to the other cages opened and the rest of the Wood Sprites entered the clearing. They looked in the same condition as the little girl Wood Sprite. They were all dishevelled and yet there was a strength to them that was undoubtable. Alaric couldn't imagine what they had been through or how long they had been imprisoned.

"What is your name?" the Wood Sprite looked like an aged man, although he showed none of the frailties.

"My name is Alaric and you are all safe now."

"Thank you Alaric. My name is Rhett." He introduced himself.

"What are we to do now?" the young girl asked.

"Be calm Mabyn, I'm sure Alaric has a plan for us?"

Alaric hadn't thought what he'd do with the Wood Sprites once he had freed them. He had assumed they would know what to do. They had managed to make their way to the island so he figured they'd know how to get home. As he looked around the strange little group he realised there were only twelve Wood Sprites standing before him and his heart sank.

"I see only twelve of you. Did one of you die?" Alaric came straight to the point. Tact wasn't something he had time for anymore.

"One of us didn't make it, but it's not what you're thinking." Mabyn chose to speak. Although she looked the youngest Alaric didn't think that was the case. There was a presence about her that the others didn't have and that was saying something. "Gaius never arrived. I can only assume he is still home. It seems as though he was stronger than all of us in resisting Yzukio's call."

Without warning Alaric's eyes rolled back into his head and he started to convulse. It only lasted for a second but it was unmistakable. When it was finished Alaric gasped for breath and had to support himself against a nearby tree. He had not become used to the sudden flashes that he had been having ever since touching the Opal Stone.

"Are you alright?" Mabyn asked.

"Yes, sorry, it's something that happens from time to time." Alaric wasn't apologising for the spasm, but more for the vision that was now implanted in his brain. Some of the memories were his and some were not, but the result was still the same. Now that he had rescued the Wood Sprites he needed to set them a task. "There is trouble in the Seven Kingdoms."

"There has always been trouble in the Seven Kingdoms that is one of the reasons why we all left. No one cares for the old ways. Only the elves care for the forest and they only seem concerned with their own backyards. Why should we care about the troubles of our old lives?"

Alaric could hardly believe what he was hearing. He thought the Wood Sprites would be crawling over themselves to return to their homeland.

"Does Mabyn speak for all of you?" Alaric now knew that Mabynlas, Mabyn's forest, consisted of the woodland to the north of Jarrat. It was populated with animals and Alaric hoped those who had elves in their land would have different views. "What about you Rhett?" Rhett's land consisted of the forest in and around Elhjem." Alaric now knew all the names of the Wood Sprites around him. That was a definite advantage to his small seizures. The knowledge he was gaining was going to be invaluable to his survival.

"What she speaks is true. When we left who came to rescue us. Even the elves have forgotten what we have done for the forests." There was a bitterness to his voice.

"Rhett is right. We have suffered many years of torture and torment at the hands of Yzukio. No one came to rescue us. Why should we help them?" Trynt, the youngest looking of the male Wood Sprites spoke.

"Hear me out and if you wish to leave those who you serve and protect to die at the hands of evil then so be it." Alaric wasn't going to pander to them. He could see the usefulness of the Wood Sprites, but he didn't have time to waste. He needed to say his piece and then move on. "Where is Blodwyn? Ah there she is? It is Blodwynlas which is the last home of the dryads. Can you tell me that you no longer care about them?" Alaric had remembered the promise he had made to Xynate, Queen of the Dryads, and he figured this was a better way to fulfil it.

A middle aged looking woman stepped forward. She had short cut brown hair and a pointed nose. Alaric noticed that her skin was already starting to lose the grime, which made him wonder even more where it had come from. She was slightly plump, which was different to all the other Wood Sprites, and she had a homely look about her. If Alaric didn't know better he would have figured she was the mother figure of the group

"I do, but what the others say does make sense. They all left us here to rot," Blodwyn didn't sound as sure as the other two.

"You know they couldn't leave Blodwynlas. And you say that they all left you here to rot, but did you tell anyone where you were going? I only came here by accident. You can't hide yourself away from the world and then wonder why the world doesn't notice when you disappear. No, now it is time for you to fight for the lands you have forsaken. The forests that you love the most are in danger of destruction. The Morel have besieged the Dryads for years and their battle is almost won." His words were met with stunned silence. They were starting to understand what he was saying. "And that isn't even the most disturbing news. Arawn!" Arawn was a strong, male. His physical appearance was the strongest of them all, although physical strength meant nothing to them. "Arawnlas is home to the *Tree of Life*."

"I know where my land is and what it contains," Arawn's voice was gruff. He wasn't sure where Alaric was going, but he figured there was an accusation in there somewhere. "What is your point?"

"Even as we speak Nyrra's orglin are besieging her and with each passing day they come one step closer to succeeding." Alaric remained calm.

"That is impossible. Not even Nyrra could be that stupid to attack the *Tree of Life*. Killing her would eventually destroy all the vegetation in the Seven Kingdoms. He knows that and wouldn't risk it," Arawn retorted. He couldn't believe what he was hearing.

"That is exactly what Nyrra wants. He wants to rid the word of anything that could be considered beautiful. He wants to rid the world of life and there is no better place to start."

"What are the elves doing? They should be there defending her?" Mabyn almost snarled as she asked the question.

"The elves in Nordligträ have all but been destroyed. I fear without your help the orglin will finish off the job soon enough," Alaric explained as best he could without completely understanding the situation. He could only hope that the information he received was true. Deep down he knew it was.

"What about the others. Surely there are other tribes that can help and what about the others like you? Isn't there supposed to be armies of men? Couldn't they help?" Arawn didn't sound quite so sure of himself.

"The Alliance Army is busy fighting Nyrra elsewhere and they don't know the *Tree of Life* is in danger. If they did I'm sure they will help, but I don't think the elves are going to ask for it. If they go up against the orglin alone then both they and the tree are doomed. You are the only hope and even now it may be too late to do anything, but you must try."

"Then we must go!" Arawn made his decision and hoped the others agreed with him. He had an affinity with the *Tree of Life* over that of the other sprites and he wasn't going to let her die.

"I agree." Blodwyn was also keen to save her dryads.

The others weren't as quick to respond. They were debating whether Alaric spoke the truth. After some persuading from both Arawn and Blodwyn they all decided to return to the Seven Kingdoms. Alaric watched and waited as they all disappeared. They all seemed to know how to return, which was something that had eluded Alaric. Now it was time for him to continue his journey. Time was slipping away, but he was sure that his little stopover had been necessary.

When all the Wood Sprites had left the island Alaric suddenly felt very tired. It had been the first time he had felt any kind of fatigue since touching the Opal Stone. With a simple thought the feeling disappeared and he felt numb again. He would have loved a chance to sleep, but there just wasn't time for it. He doubted he would get a chance to sleep again, at least not while Nyrra still lived. That was enough motivation to keep him going. It was that thought that was thick in his mind when he disappeared. He could only hope that his next landing would be at the destination he was looking for.

Chapter 11: Coronation

Bern woke in the Grand Cathedral. He had been given a share of the High Chancellor's apartment. It had been a busy few days, but he had still managed to catch up on some sleep. It had been a while since he had been able to sleep in such luxury. As much as it was nice he didn't want to get too used to it. Before too long they would be back on the road and he would be back sleeping on a bedroll on the cold dirt.

Bern wanted nothing more than to pull on his riding leathers over his thick upper body and muscular legs, but he needed to wear something more appropriate for his time in the Grand Cathedral. He quickly brushed his short brown hair and rubbed his face. There was three days growth and he knew he would need to shave before he left.

It was another big day. It was time for Linus' coronation. Things had moved faster than they should have and not quite to tradition. Bern saw Augustus stripped of his position as soon as he had returned from the army, but the High Chancellor had not gone easily. At first he refused to give up the position. He had called his special guard, but they didn't come. Bern had already taken temporary control of the city and all of the soldiers. It wasn't something that he wanted to do, but it was the only way to stop the city from descending into civil war. When Augustus realised there was no help coming, he pleaded with Bern to keep his position, but there was no chance Bern was going to back down. He had seen firsthand what the High Chancellor had done in his time of reign and there was no chance for forgiveness. He would pay for his crimes of the past, but it wasn't up to Bern to dish out the punishment. That was a job for the new High Chancellor and that would be the first thing on his agenda.

There was a gentle knock on the door and a serving girl walked into the room. She wore a loosely fitted silk dress. Bern estimated that she could be no more than eighteen. Her long brown hair hung half way down her back. All in all Bern thought she was quite attractive. That was one thing that always amazed him. His whole life he had always envisaged the Grand Cathedral as a place of piety and quiet contemplation and as much as half of that was true it wasn't entirely. The serving girls were all young, beautiful and very willing. If Bern wasn't married he could have become used to the life, but it was a life that would never exist. The thought of his wife and children made him worry. He knew their next path would lead them into Remidia and towards Arsiliac. He wanted nothing more than to see if his family was alright. He had to believe that they were. He figured he'd know if anything happened to them, the prophecy owed him that much.

The serving girl left a platter of food on a nearby table. Before she left she smiled and winked at Bern. A short while ago that would have made him blush and feel uncomfortable now he just smiled back and let her leave. They all knew that he was married and wasn't interested in playing around. Enough had tried over the past few days for the rumours to spread, but it didn't stop them trying.

Bern laughed to himself. He had to laugh. It was either that or cry. There was still much to be done before they left the city, but for the moment he had time to relax. The city was in preparations for the party of a lifetime. No one really knew why there was to be a change in the High Chancellor and no one really cared, not the regular populous of Castalia anyway. The coronation was an excuse for a week long party. Those who had to work would be properly compensated.

The coronation was a double edged sword in Bern's mind. It meant they couldn't leave the city for at least five days. The soldiers would want to join in the festivities and Bern wasn't going to begrudge them that. The army would have to be on its best behaviour. Anyone caught brawling or causing trouble would spend the rest of the time in stocks. That would be enough to stop most of them causing trouble, but he knew he couldn't stop them all. Soldiers, alcohol, women and a weeklong party were not a good mix.

The extra time gave Bern an opportunity to clean up all the loose ends in Castalia, there was still much to be done. Hulkan had been in talks with his father and the Western Dwarves Guild. Their alliance would be invaluable. Not all the dwarves had left with Gilgi and Prince Hawthorne. There were some blacksmiths with the army, but nothing compared to what the dwarves were capable of. The dwarves wouldn't be taking part in the celebration. Their deity, Horinga, had no connections with the Grand Cathedral or the High Chancellor. They would take part in the drinking at night, that was for sure, but they would go to work during the day as normal. Bern would use this time to his advantage and try and meet with Brac. Hulkan had been meeting with his father, Ilar, each day, but had yet to get a meeting with the temporary leader of the guild. After the coronation he would meet with Ilar himself and reiterate the urgency of his meeting. If that didn't work then he would try a more persuasive tact.

For the moment he had to concentrate on the coronation. He wasn't sure how it happened, but he was to be involved. He only had a small part, but that was enough. The High Priest of Sapphire would coronate Linus and he would become the second High Chancellor of Sapphire. The High Priest would then ask seven questions and Bern was the one who had to answer 'I know this man to be good and faithful in his service to the God King Sapphire.' Seven men had to act as witnesses for the Seven God Kings and Bern would be the final one. It was a small role, but it still made him nervous. He still couldn't work out how he had been chosen amongst the other highly religious figures, but it wasn't something he could refuse.

He sat and ate his breakfast in his underclothes as he had been advised. It wouldn't be long before four young serving women came to dress him.

It was the most ridiculous thing he had heard. He could easily dress himself and did so on a daily basis. Even as General of the Alliance the other commanders had suggested he get a group of servants, but he had denied all but those he considered necessary. This was also something he couldn't refuse. The ceremony had to be followed to the letter and that meant that his blue robes would be dressed on him.

Just as he placed his knife and fork down on his plate there was a tentative knock on the door. Before Bern had a chance to respond the door was slowly pushed open. He didn't really know what to expect, except for the brief description of his role and things he couldn't get wrong, so if there were things that he found odd he would just have to let it pass. Four young girls stepped into the room. Bern thought they couldn't be older than fourteen. They all wore sheer white, lace dresses, that revealed more than what Bern thought was appropriate. The tradition baffled him and he could only cringe at how it started.

The girls kept their faces down, but it was more from deference than embarrassment. That again made Bern wonder, but there were more important matters to take up his mind. Now it was time for him to be dressed and then soon enough it would be time for him to join the ceremony. The last of the girls carried the sapphire blue robe that he would be wearing. It was more ornately decorated than Bern had expected. He was expecting a plain blue robe, something appropriate for a leading religious figure, but what was before him was something he'd expect to see on a king or prince at the very least. There were light blue flowers embroidered around the collar of the robe and running down the length in two straight lines. The cuff had gold embroidery and there was blue lace in places that Bern really didn't think needed any. To go with the robe were blue leggings and subtle blue suede shoes. The shoes and leggings had been made to fit, but the robe was the original and too small for his large build. The robe only just covered his knees and the sleeves only came half way along his forearms. All in all Bern had never felt more ridiculous in his life. He wanted nothing more than to strip off and return to his army leathers.

When he was dressed the serving girls curtsied before leaving the room. Bern couldn't be sure, but he thought he saw them start to giggle. He couldn't really blame them as he looked at himself in one of the many cheval mirrors. He really did look totally ridiculous and there was nothing he could do about it. Obviously the men before him were a lot smaller and he wished they had made him a new robe for the occasion. He would make sure that Linus suffered for his embarrassment.

Suddenly there was a knock on the door that made Bern's heart race. It was still an hour before he had to go and do his duty.

"I'm not ready. Come back when it's time," Bern called out.

The door was then pushed open and Delbert sauntered into the room, followed by Jarwe and Sorrell. Since they had decided to stay for the duration of the ceremony General Jarwe and Captain Sorrell had also taken up residence in the Grand Cathedral. Bern had promoted Delbert and made him his personal advisor. Although he didn't have the experience as most of the other soldiers who were a possibility for the position he had something that they lacked. Bern couldn't put his finger on it, but he knew he had to keep Delbert close. Delbert and his band of former bandits had been given special dispensary to take up residency in one of the inns in the inner city. It was in return for their duty in restoring peace. They were the last people Bern wanted to see.

"I'm sorry my dear, I was looking for General Bern." Delbert did his best to suppress his laugher which was made even harder with Jarwe and Sorrell sniggering behind him.

"Very funny." Bern waved his hand at the intruders. "Believe it or not, but this is supposed to be a robe not a dress." Bern sat down at the small table in the corner of the room.

The comment brought roars of laughter from the three men. They couldn't contain themselves any longer. They all had to admit that they did feel sorry for him. The robe for the coronation looked ridiculous.

"Okay, enough of that. What brings you here?" Bern tried to sound as commanding as he could.

"We just came to wish you luck," Delbert stood a lot straighter now. "So, good luck."

Bern simply shook his head. There was nothing he could say to that. It was good that they had come to show their support, but he really wished no one would see the way he looked. In an hour that would all change anyway.

"I guess we should get moving if we want to get a good spot in the crowd." Jarwe couldn't help but smile.

As the commanders of a visiting army they had been given assigned seats in the circle. The rest of the inner circle would already be filled with people. Those who were lucky to get a place in the crowd would remember this occasion for the rest of their lives. Bern, on the other hand, just wished he could get down to business. If he did survive the final battle and return to his family then he knew it would be a story to tell.

"On your way then. I'll speak to you once it's all over." Bern swatted at the three men.

He had to laugh at himself as he watched his reflection in the mirror.

It had taken him a long time to come to the realisation, but now he had come to terms with the fact that he was in command of the army and all the soldiers were his men. It brought him some kind of peace, but not much. With that thought in his mind he returned to the papers on his desk. It was amazing how much paperwork had arrived in the short time he had been in Castalia. There was a mixture of requests, most minor nobles just wanting a meeting so they could brag to their peers, but there were a good amount of those offering their services and their soldiers to join the army. It was for that reason he had to look through each and every letter. If nothing else it would keep him busy until it was time for the coronation.

The time passed without Bern noticing. Before he knew it there was a knock on the door and it was time for him to present himself to the new High Chancellor. At least it would only be the few servants in the corridors and those with the High Chancellor who would truly see his ridiculous outfit. Those in the crowd would be too far away to truly appreciate it.

The servant walked quickly through the corridors, hurrying Bern along. It was difficult walking in the tight-fitting robe and he stumbled more than once. His heart started to beat faster as they neared the door leading out onto the balcony. He was playing an important part in the coronation of the next High Chancellor, the most powerful man in the Seven Kingdoms, at least in the political world. As much as Bern didn't want to admit it he was the only one to rival the High Chancellor ever since Alaric had disappeared. His oldest friend seemed more content on staying out of the politics and leaving that to Bern. He wished it could be the other way around, except for the fate of the Seven Kingdoms being on his shoulders. He was quite happy for Alaric to carry that burden.

The servant leading him opened the door to the small antechamber which led out to the balcony. Bern was the last of the *Servants of the Seven God Kings* to vouch for the new High Chancellor. There was only one other person in the room. A man dressed in a full white robe with the hood drawn far down over his face, but not obscuring it entirely. He motioned for Bern to sit on one of the cushioned bench seats around the walls. Aside from the benches there were pictures on the walls of all the past High Chancellors and a small side table with flowers in a vase. Bern didn't really take much notice as he sat, his mind was racing. He had known what he needed to say for the last two days, but now his mind seemed to go blank. He had addressed a crowd before, but this was completely different. There was an entire nation who would be hanging on his every word and noticing if he made the slightest mistake.

Suddenly the door opened and a voice boomed from outside. "Bring forth the Witness for Sapphire!"

This was the time that Bern was dreading. He stood slowly and took a step towards the door and then another. It was ceremony to walk, one step at a time and he felt it was just to extend his agony. His heart raced even faster as he stepped out onto the terrace. The crowd cheered when they saw him arrive. The sound was deafening and shook the balcony. It was an amazing feeling as he stepped to the edge of the terrace and looked down. The Inner Circle was completely filled with people. At the front of the balcony seats were set out for the special guests. Then there was a portable barrier separating them from the rest of the crowd. Standing guard was a line of the High Chancellor's Holy Guard, their armour sparkled in the sunlight. Everyone in the crowd was well behaved and no one expected anything different. The Holy Guard was more for appearance than anything else, but they would still act as a deterrent to anyone who thought they might try and cause some mischief.

The terrace was much larger than Bern had imagined. It was at least three paces deep and twenty wide. In the middle there was a small platform with two men standing on it. One was Linus and then other was the Master of Ceremonies. Linus wore a marvellous multicoloured robe, containing all the colours of the *Seven Stones of Power*. The Master of Ceremonies wore white. There was a strange looking tube that protruded up through the podium and stood at head height in-between the two men. To the right of the High Chancellor to be were the six men who had bore witness before Bern. They were all dressed in the colour of the God King they represented. The first thing Bern noticed was that their robes were just as ridiculous as his, although their statures made them look a little better.

"Step to up to the voice amplifier," the MC spoke softly, making sure not to speak into the tube.

Although Bern couldn't be completely sure he assumed that the tube was the voice amplifier. It looked like a common tube, although he knew better than to assume he knew anything. Slowly and carefully he stepped up onto the platform. With the constricting robe the last thing he wanted to do was trip and fall.

When Bern was in place the MC moved the tube so it was in front of his mouth. "Who speaks for the God King Sapphire?"

To Bern's surprise the MC's voice resonated out over the Inner Circle. Bern nearly stumbled backwards in shock. Now he could see why it was called a 'voice amplifier'. At that moment he realised that it was his turn to speak and he should have already started.

"I am Bern il'Fermë, from Arsiliac in Remidia. I speak for the God King Sapphire in his absence. I do not speak knowing his words, but I speak knowing that my heart is true." It took Bern a moment to get used to his words resonating amongst the crowd. Luckily the MC was quietly speaking the words and Bern repeated them into the amplifier. Without the help of the MC Bern doubted he would have remembered all the words and in the correct order. He couldn't understand how the MC could so calmly repeat them. There could be no doubt that he had done so for the other six witnesses. "I speak knowing the heart of the man standing before me. The man who is now a servant to all the God Kings and their servants below them." The speech continued on in much the same matter for almost five minutes before Bern was able to step down. When he did the crowd roared with glee. They knew that the ceremony was coming to an end and a new High Chancellor would be elected.

Bern walked to where the other witnesses were standing. He took his place between them and the High Chancellor. He looked out over the cheering crowd and wondered if any of them knew or even cared what happened to the last one. Rumours had been spread around the city the last few days, but he doubted they would have reached everyone in the Inner Circle. The Master of Ceremonies waited until the cheering died down before he continued the ritual.

"The God Kings have spoken. You are pure of heart and true of mind." The crowd hushed to complete silence when the MC started speaking. "Do you come into the light?"

Linus cleared his throat before taking a step closer to the voice amplifier. "I come into the light with a pure heart and a true mind."

"To become the voice for the God Kings you must give up your past, do you do this willingly?"

"I leave my past behind to walk in the glory of all the God Kings."

The crowd couldn't contain themselves. They had remained silent for the start of the final ritual, but a call out from a young man, brought another round of cheers from the crowd. The MC also had to control himself. He wanted nothing more than to berate the crowd for interrupting the final rite, but that would make things worse. All he could do was wait for the cheering to die down again.

"Your new life needs and new name. What name to do you take?" The crowd went deathly silent again.

"I take the name Tiberius." Linus revealed He was the forth High Chancellor to take the name, but they never used numerals. Instead it was rumoured that each High Chancellor who took the name was in fact the re-incarnation of the previous and therefore the original. As much as Linus didn't like the reasoning he felt that it would make the transition easier. The original Tiberius had a great reputation as being a kind and fair High Chancellor. He also brought a time of prosperity when the Kingdom was suffering.

"Then High Chancellor Tiberius, take this wreath as a token of our servitude." The MC placed a small wreath of desert pea flowers on his head.

The headgear of the High Chancellor was something that was meant to represent his future rule. Most High Chancellors chose intricately designed crowns or coronets. There was something the same about all of them. They were made of gold and always had the jewel relating to the God King he would favour surrounded by a ring of diamonds. Linus, even if there had been time and he was sure the dwarves would have put something together very quickly, would have chosen the wreath of flowers. The only adornment was a sapphire blue rose in the centre. The flower itself was extremely rare and only grew in the grounds of the Grand Cathedral. He thought that was enough grandeur to appease the crowd. It showed that, although he was humble, he had respect for the position.

The crowd roared even louder than before when the coronation was over. Linus, or High Chancellor Tiberius, waved at them. He wanted nothing more than to return inside, but he had to do his duty. There would be a state dinner that evening and the command group of the Alliance would have to act as the foreign dignitaries. Normally the other four ruling kingdoms would send representatives to the coronation. On more than one occasion a king or queen arrived personally.

After what seemed an eternity, the MC motioned for the witnesses to return to the antechamber. Bern couldn't wait to get back inside. As much as the other witnesses tried to be respectful they couldn't help but snigger at his outfit. He wanted to say something but it wasn't the time or the place. All he could think of was returning to his apartment and changing clothes, although he was tempted just to rip the robe off in the antechamber.

"Thankfully that is over!" said the Witness for Ruby, the High Priest of Ruby by the name of Rufus Russo. His fiery red hair matched his Ruby Red robe. Its design would have looked just as ridiculous on Bern as his own, but on the small framed High Priest it didn't look that bad. He collapsed on one of the bench seats. As the Witness for Ruby he was the first to bear witness and had been forced to stand on the balcony for the entire coronation.

"Ain't that the truth," said the Witness for Topaz, the High Priest of Topaz by the name of Simeon Crallo. Again his yellow robes would have looked ridiculous on Bern, but somehow looked appropriate on him, but that didn't make Bern feel any better.

"I'm going to get changed," Bern didn't waste any time.

"I wouldn't act too fast," Simeon suppressed a laugh as he spoke. "You are required to wear the robe at tonight's feast."

No one had mentioned that to Bern and he wasn't sure he liked it. He looked at the others who were all sombrely nodding their heads, but he also noticed that they were trying their hardest not smile. Bern wasn't sure if that was because of the thought of Bern attending an official function dressed as he was or whether they were trying to set him up. Either way he wasn't going to bite. He had played his part and that was enough. He was not going to spend a second longer in the robe. If they wanted him to look the part then they would have to make him a new one.

"I don't think so Simeon. My love for history only goes so far. If that is in fact tradition then it will change tonight." His words were stronger than he intended, but he also didn't want to give them a chance to browbeat him into submission.

"But it's tradition," the chubby Witness for Emerald spoke. Tassos was the only witness not born in Castalia, besides Bern. He was from a small village in Hondin Lel. "You must wear what you are wearing."

Bern shook his head. There was little point in having the conversation. He had made his decision and he wasn't going to change it. He also knew there would be no persuading the other witnesses to change their opinion. Years of history had a lot to answer for, but that still didn't mean it couldn't change.

"As much as I'd love to stay and chat I have more important matters to deal with." He didn't mean to sound rude, but there was no other way to put it.

Tassos was about to protest but Simeon silenced him with a wave of his hand. He wanted to have the last word with Bern, not that he really thought it would make a lot of difference.

"We all want to thank you for restoring peace to the city General Bern," Bern was almost out the door, but he stopped when he heard Simeon's words. "It is a great thing you have done and a great honour that has been bestowed upon you. Don't ever forget that."

Bern nodded, but didn't turn around. He knew exactly what the High Priest was trying to do and it almost worked. The compliment was genuine, he knew that to be true, but the last comment was a jibe. It was designed to make him wear the awful robe to the feast and that was something that just wouldn't happen. He had to chuckle to himself as he made his way back to his quarters. His job had been done and he didn't think he had made too many mistakes. Now it was time to get back to business, at least for the short period of time he had.

When he was back in his rooms the first thing he did was strip out of the robe. He was quite happy to sit in his underclothes. The day was progressing to be particularly warm and he enjoyed the chance to relax. There were papers on his desk and as much as he didn't want to read them it was a job that had to be done. Most of them were minor reports from the army and not all that important. There was also a list of their remaining supplies and requests for more. He was sure the new High Chancellor would grant all his requests. Before he could find anything of any interest there was a knock on the door. Bern was surprised that it didn't open before he granted entrance.

"I am sorry to bother you, Lord Bern." A man of middle age stood a step in from the door. A tape measure hung around his neck and he looked very nervous.

"What can I do for you?" Bern spoke softly. He wanted to try and make the man more comfortable, although he couldn't work out why he was there.

"The High Chancellor sent me," was all he responded. His voice was nervous and his hands were visibly shaking.

As much as Bern could forgive the man his nerves he really didn't have time to be wasting in a pointless discussion. His tact of trying to calm the man had obviously not worked. Now it was time for him to become blunt.

"Spit it out man, I don't have all day. Why has the High Chancellor sent you to me?" Bern snapped.

"He said you might need a tailor?"

Bern sighed and shook his head. On the plus side it looked as though he wasn't going to upset anyone by not wearing the ceremonial robe and he would also get something appropriate to wear.

"Get on with it," Bern stood.

The tailor stepped into the room and moved to where Bern was standing. He quickly used his tape measure to take Bern's measurements. His nervousness made then entire situation very uncomfortable.

When he was done he quickly left the room. Bern had to laugh. There was a time in his life when he was just a simple farmer and no one held him in any high esteem. It was a simple life and one that he wished he could return to. A hard day's work was followed by a hearty meal and time with his family. Now work was followed by more work, or at least that's how he saw it. Most of the city would be celebrating, but Bern didn't have that luxury.

Before he could return to the pages on his desk the door was pushed open and Jarwe, Sorrell and Delbert came into the room. They all held large wooden lidded tankards. Bern could only assume that the drinking had started. Although they didn't look drunk they definitely looked like they had been drinking.

"What have I done to deserve this," he spoke to himself, but was loud enough for the others to hear.

"Now don't be like that." Jarwe sauntered into the room and sat in one of the armchairs before taking a large draught from his tankard. Bern could smell the fruity aroma of the ale and suddenly felt very thirsty. He was grateful they hadn't brought him an ale. He really didn't have time to waste the day drinking, mores the pity.

"We came to see if you wanted to join us?" Delbert sounded hurt, although it wasn't intentional. "The city has already started to celebrate. The streets are filled with people. This is going to be so much fun."

"Don't have too much fun, we have a lot to do before we leave," Bern spoke without thinking.

"Don't be a fun stopper. There's plenty of time to get organised before we leave." Sorrell did his best not to get defensive.

Bern took a deep breath before returning to his seat. He couldn't begrudge the others their fun, even if he couldn't celebrate himself. There would be time for frivolity later in the evening, but he still wasn't sure how much he could participate. He really needed to speak with the dwarves in the morning and that was something he didn't want to be feeling sick for.

"Go and have your fun, but I'll need you in the morning Jarwe. I have to organise a meeting with the dwarves and I want you to be there."

"I'll be there. Just send me a message and tell me where to be." Jarwe smiled as he took another drink.

"I'm assuming you three aren't going to attend the official function this evening?" Bern now wanted to change the subject.

"I really don't think we need to be there. I'm sure you can represent us just as well by yourself and anyway, you're going to be sitting on the head table so you won't even know if we are there or not," Sorrell explained quickly. They couldn't think of anything worse than being stuck having dinner with the priests and other members of the Grand Cathedral when the streets were filled with revellers. Bern would have loved to be anywhere but the official function, but there was no way out. As the Witness for Sapphire he had to be.

"Rumour has it that the women are free and easy during the festivities. I'm not missing out on this opportunity," Sorrell added.

"Just don't go too hard. Remember some of us are still married," Delbert joked.

"Now go and enjoy yourself before I change my mind." Bern wasn't joking. If they stayed much longer then he would find jobs for them to do.

"Remember to send me a message to let me know where you want me to meet you in the morning." Jarwe winked at him as they left the room. As much as Bern was dubious on Jarwe's state he knew the man wouldn't let him down.

"Just make sure none of the soldiers get up to any trouble. Remember to lead from the front." Bern yelled after them.

Bern knew there would be trouble. There would be a lot of alcohol and a lot of men, and whenever that happened there was always trouble. Bern could only hope the soldiers didn't do anything to upset his dealings with the new High Chancellor.

It was with that thought in his mind that he returned to his paperwork. If nothing else it would keep him busy until it was time for him to go to the feast. The thought of sitting on the head table at such an occasion made him nervous. He was sure that everyone would be watching him. That thought made him shiver and he pushed it out of his mind.

The afternoon waned as Bern continued the tedious task of sorting out his paperwork. Soon enough there was a knock on the door and the tailor waited to be admitted. Bern had to admit that he was grateful for the distraction, although he would have preferred it if it was someone else.

The blue robe was much better than the last one he had worn. It was a simple design, as Bern had hoped, made with pure silk. A silk shirt and blue leggings accompanied the robe. All in all Bern was happy with what he had been given.

"I do hope this is too your liking, Lord Bern?" the tailor bowed as he asked the question.

"Yes, thank you, it's very nice" it was time for Bern to change and make his way to the main chapel.

Bern stacked the paperwork on his desk as the tailor bowed again and left the room. In the end he figured the sooner he arrived the sooner he could leave and get back to being busy. At least he hoped that was the case.

Chapter 12: The Party Begins

Bern had to admit that he did look good in his new garb. He only wished that they had made it for him before the ceremony. It was a once in a lifetime opportunity and it was unfortunate that he looked so ridiculous. At least now he could walk into the main chapel with his head held high. He was sure the other witnesses were upset because he wasn't a member of the priesthood. It wasn't that they had been openly rude or offensive to him, but Bern knew they weren't happy. It was a great honour to be a Witness of the God Kings and they felt that he didn't deserve it. Of course none of the other witnesses supported the old High Chancellor, but in the same respect they didn't truly know of his treachery. They had just accepted the fact that it was time for a change.

The Great Chapel had been transformed into a banquet hall. There was no other venue that could hold all the people invited to the High Chancellor's feast and none that were appropriate.

Bern was led to the chapel by two young maidens. They weren't serving girls, but daughters of a merchant from the inner city. It was tradition for the witnesses to be offered virgins, of course Bern declined the offer and there was no offence. The two maidens actually looked relieved. It wasn't uncommon for the witnesses to accept the gift on behalf of the God Kings, but the tradition hadn't been strictly followed for many centuries.

It was customary for the witnesses to be announced to the audience upon arrival. After some closer research Bern had learned that it wasn't completely necessary and no one would be offended if he wasn't. It was bad enough that he had to sit on the right hand side to the High Chancellor. He didn't want everyone to see him enter the room.

The chapel was almost completely filled when Bern finally arrived. He was one of the last to enter the chapel. Everyone else had been too excited to wait and had been lining up outside the doors for up to an hour before they opened. At least he was able to sneak in somewhat unnoticed, at least until he reached the head table. His seat next to the High Chancellor was conspicuously vacant. Everyone would know he was there once he was seated.

"I'm glad you're here." Tiberius stood when Bern reached the table. "Now we can get started."

Bern shook his hand before sitting. He wasn't sure if that was right, but he thought it was appropriate. No one seemed to notice.

At the head table sat the High Chancellor and the seven witnesses. The MC sat on a small table by himself to the left. In front of the table was a large space with a portable parquetry floor. The first table in front of the floor and in line with the head table was filled with the six wizards from the council. All the other tables seated ten people. Bern didn't know if it was the wizards or Tiberius who had decided to seat them by themselves, but they didn't seem unhappy about it.

When the MC saw that Bern had been seated he started the function. He began by introducing the new High Chancellor and then the witnesses. Bern cringed when his name was mentioned. If they didn't know before, now everyone in the room knew who he was and what he was doing there. He had a bad feeling that was going to create more conversations than he wanted.

One conversation he wanted to have was with the council of wizards. He had not really had a chance to speak with them since they arrived and if they were planning on staying with the army then he would need to know. If they weren't, then he also needed to know. There was little time left and it was one thing he needed tick of his list.

As soon as the MC finished the introductions he started the old rites and prayers to all the God Kings. It was the standard format to start all official functions. Once he was done with that it was time for the entree. Bern had to admit that he was ravenous. He had only eaten a light meal and the smell made him salivate.

The head table was the first to receive their food. The entree was a whole quail on a bed of baby carrots and beetroot and a sauce that Bern had never tasted before. He had eaten in a few places in a few different kingdoms, but this was by far the best. He shouldn't have really expected anything less for the occasion. Luckily he only had to wait for everyone else on his table to be served before he could start eating.

When they finished the first course, the entertainment began. A troop of dancers skipped out onto the floor in front of the main table. They were dressed in a multitude of colourful outfits. Bern thought the night might not be as bad as he thought. The female dancers moved seductively whilst the male dancers showed off their strength by doing flips and tossing their partners into the air. The show lasted until everyone had finished their entree. As the dancers left the chapel the servants brought in the main meal.

Many pigs had been roasted over spits for most of the day in preparation. The meat was accompanied with roasted vegetables and another sauce that Bern had never tasted before. The food almost melted in his mouth. Now he was really happy that he had been invited to the High Chancellor's ceremonial function.

"How are you finding the evening?" Tiberius asked as they neared the end of their main meal.

"I have to admit I did think it was going to be a laborious task, but I am thoroughly enjoying myself." Bern had almost forgotten about the business he wanted to conduct. "What is next in the way of entertainment?"

"There is a sword swallower, a fire breather, a number of jugglers and some other entertainers." There was a hint of pride in his voice. "I know what you mean though. There is a lot of work to be done and I really didn't think I could relax, but now it's a different story." Tiberius took a sip of his wine after he spoke. "Tonight is truly a night to celebrate."

Bern had avoided drinking any wine, but after the High Chancellor's speech he figured one goblet wouldn't hurt. He was starting to relax and figured that he should take some time to enjoy himself. The wizards would still be around and he could talk to them over the next day or two. He had not heard back from the Western Dwavern Guild, which meant, for the moment, he had a free day. That was enough for him to start drinking. He raised his goblet and chinked it with Tiberius' before taking a drink. The flavour ran down the back of his throat and settled in his stomach. He had never tasted wine so delicious in his life. That in itself was a dangerous sign.

More entertainment came out when the plates were taken from the head table. Bern had already started his second goblet of wine. The food had been amazing and there was still desert to come. The entertainment made it even easier for him to relax and forget about his problems. He even started a conversation with the other witnesses. It seemed as though they too had been sampling the wine.

It was the early hours of the morning when Bern finally made it back to his apartment. The parties on the streets were still going, but the High Chancellor's function had ended hours before. Once they were done Tiberius had invited the seven witnesses to his private chambers for some more of the wine that they all loved. Bern knew he was going to regret it in the morning, but he couldn't resist.

***

Hulkan sat in the large tavern tent with his father. There were only four other dwarves sitting at the table with them. Not many had decided to enter the inner city to join in the festivities. Although they did accept that the High Chancellor was the ruler they still followed Horinga, the God of the dwarves. The coronation of a new High Chancellor really wasn't something they felt they should be celebrating, but some of the younger dwarves wanted to try their luck in the inner city.

"There is nothing to be celebrating," Ilar barked his agreement with the general consensus with the rest of the table. "It doesn't matter who the High Chancellor is, the sun will rise in the morning and it will set at night. Tomorrow is still another day of work."

"I don't see why you can't just relax for a week and join in with the rest of the city." Hulkan was the only one pushing the point.

"You have been away from your home for too long. You know we don't go in for this ritual. We have our own days that we celebrate," said Baeddan, an older dwarf with tips of grey in his brown hair and beard.

Baeddan was the longest serving member of the guild. He had led the guild for two decades before stepping down. It was better to retire than have someone take the position from him. "I have lived through three coronations, and I don't feel any worse for not joining the city in its celebration."

"This is different." Hulkan wasn't going to be silenced, although he should have known better. "This could be the last time a lot of these dwarves get to see the city. When the celebrations are over the army will be moving and we're going to need every available dwarf." Until Bern was able to speak with Brac, Hulkan had to push their cause. He wished Dorn was with him, but he was keeping a low profile and remained with the Alliance.

"Your brother took all the dwarves we were prepared to send. If he wanted us to commit more then he would have sent word," said Carradoc, another member of the council.

Hulkan had tried to be subtle, if he openly denounced his brother then it would just look like sour grapes. He had already ruled the council until his brother usurped power. Hulkan had already known at that stage that he would have to leave his home, but he had no idea what was in store for him. It was customary to wait five years if Hulkan wanted his position back but that wasn't his intention. What he had to do was convince them that Gilgi was not the trusted leader they thought him to be. He had betrayed them in Avalon and Hulkan knew that something wasn't right. Now he could only hope that the council will vote to move.

"Things have changed since then. Bern will be able to explain it to you all. He has been trying to get a meeting with Brac and the rest of the council. Brac hasn't been returning any of his missives and I haven't been able to get in to see him."

The other dwarves sitting around the table gave each other some sly looks. Hulkan did his best not to show that he noticed. He knew that something wasn't right, but he would have to wait before he made any accusations.

"Brac is a busy dwarf. He doesn't have a lot of time to take meetings of this nature," Carradoc did his best to explain, although it seemed a weak excuse. "There is much for him to take care of since Gilgi left."

The other dwarves suddenly looked uncomfortable.

"What's going on?" Hulkan had to ask.

Carradoc looked at the other council members who, if begrudgingly, nodded their responses. He looked back at Hulkan and then let out a long sigh. The conversation they were about to have was one he wanted to avoid. It was really one that Brac should be having, but he had been his given instructions. At least he wouldn't have to explain it to Bern. That in itself was a saving grace.

"Two days ago we received a letter from Gilgi. It seems as though he has reached Remidel," Carradoc started.

That was old news as far as Hulkan was concerned. Gilgi had betrayed them by taking the army and following Hawthorne. The thought that Hawthorne had also betrayed them hadn't crossed his mind.

"We know that's where they were heading. It's no surprise that's where he is. What does this have to do with things?" Hulkan barked.

"Stay calm son." Ilar tried to relax him. "It will become apparent soon enough."

"Yes, if you wait I will get to the point," Carradoc continued. "It is rumoured that the Alliance is about to march on Remidel."

Hulkan did his best not to look surprised. He had heard that was where they were going once the celebrations were over, but that was only privy to the command group. Bern had instructed them not to inform anyone else until they were ready to march. The rumour that there was a Dark Knight in control of the city now made more sense. There was no other way Gilgi could know what they were planning. That made things even worse. He couldn't fault his brother for being in the thrall of a Dark Knight. He had soon learnt that you didn't need to worship the Evil One to be under his control. He wanted nothing more than to tell the others, but he needed to give Bern the information first. Times had changed if he couldn't completely trust his own kind.

"He has instructed Brac that under no circumstances is he to give anymore dwarves to the Alliance. There is more to the letter, but that is the main part." Carradoc kept it brief.

Hulkan cursed to himself. He should have known things weren't going to be that easy, but he couldn't give up. They needed all the support they could get and although most of the dwarven army were in Remidel there were still plenty of able hands to help.

"Gilgi stole power from me. It is time to get that power back," he said.

"That is impossible. You have to wait five years before you can try to regain control." Baeddan had plenty of experience in the matter and knew the law of the guild better than anyone.

"He has ruled for over a year. That means that someone else can take control of the guild." Hulkan was also still familiar with the laws. It wasn't something easily forgotten.

"But that has never been done before!" Carradoc exclaimed. "He would have to do something extremely wrong to lose power in such a short period of time."

That was something Hulkan was prepared for.

"He has gone against the council. That is grounds for removal," Hulkan returned.

"And just how do propose he did that?" Although there was no real love for Gilgi they didn't share the hatred that Hulkan had. They would be happy to replace him as leader of the guild, but it would have to be done the right way.

"The Council, under Gilgi's instruction, offered the dwarven army to the Alliance. He shouldn't have moved the army without consulting the council." He knew there would be some who agreed with his position, and a lot who wouldn't.

"Gilgi is still in command of our army. It was his decision where the army moved." Gavan had supported Gilgi in his takeover of Hulkan and it seemed as though it would be difficult to sway him otherwise.

It wasn't uncommon for those who fought vigorously for control to start as friends and remain friends afterwards. Ilar had stolen power from Baeddon the last time he had been in control. Hulkan never really had to wrestle control from anyone; his father had already conceded power to him. The political battle was purely for show. Deep down Ilar was proud of his son, Gilgi, for taking power from his brother. He had only hoped that they would have been able to forgive each other by now.

"That is a matter for debate and not for this table," Ilar cut in before Hulkan had a chance to debate the fact.

"That's just the problem. If Brac won't see Bern then this is the only place for the conversation." Hulkan barked.

"Ilar is right. Now is time for ale. Tomorrow is the time for working," Baeddon quoted an ancient dwarven saying.

As much as Hulkan needed to plead his case he knew Baeddon was right. There was limited time for him to spend with his father and his peers. There was a good chance he would never return to Castalia and he needed to make the most of being home. He would have to speak with Bern in the morning. Now it was time to enjoy the night.

***

Jarwe laughed as they made their way through the streets of the inner city. The Inner Circle had been closed once the ceremony was over. The partying would not sully the sanctity of the Inner Circle. The streets were packed with people celebrating the coronation of the new High Chancellor. Delbert and Sorrell had already drained their tankards and now they were looking for somewhere to refill them.

As they walked Sorrell noticed two people disappearing down a narrow laneway. They looked around to see if anyone had noticed them, but little did they know that Sorrell had seen them.

"Hey you two!" he called out to Jarwe and Delbert, trying his best not to draw too much attention. With all the noise one more man yelling wasn't anything of note. "I think something is happening down there." Sorrell indicated with his head so no one saw him pointing. "Let's go and have a look."

Just before they made their way into the alley they saw a shady looking woman sneak out of the crowd. At least that would give them someone to follow. They carefully made their way through the crowd to the entrance of the alley. They stopped for a moment and made a show like they were just resting and waiting for their next move. When they were sure no one was paying them any attention they too disappeared into the alley. The woman was at the end of the alley when they entered and moved through a gap in the fence.

The three men moved quickly without making their presence noticeable to those still on the streets. When they reached the end of the alley they noticed the small hole in the fence. It was something they would have completely missed if they hadn't seen the woman. They would never had thought to sneak through the hole. They would have just turned around and returned to the street.

On the other side of the fence there was another alley, just as small as the one before. The difference was that the buildings which loomed on either side didn't have any doors. Without the hole in the wall it was as if the alley wouldn't have existed. If it was slightly larger they would have assumed it was a courtyard.

"Where did she go?" Jarwe asked. At first he wanted to accuse Sorrell about leading them to a dead end, but he too saw the shady woman enter.

"There has to be a door somewhere around here." Sorrell sounded just as confused.

"Well, my mug is dry, so let's hurry up and find it." Delbert pushed forward. In the army structure he was ranked below the other two men, but for the moment they were all equal.

There were no arguments from Jarwe and Sorrell, men they were just as keen to refill their tankards. They checked the walls on either side of the alley to see if there was anything irregular. It was possible that there was a secret door somewhere, or even a small hole like the one in the fence. There had to be some reason why that woman came down the alley.

It wasn't until they came to the end did they realise where the woman had gone. In the dim light from the building obscuring the sun it was impossible to see the door which had been painted to match the stones of the building. Even from a few paces away it was impossible to see it unless they knew what they were looking for.

"This is very suspicious. I'm not sure if we should really go any further," Delbert sounded concerned. "I don't think we should be looking to get into trouble."

"Ah Delbert, where's your sense of adventure. The city is in party mode, I think we would be hard pressed to find trouble." Jarwe hoped he wasn't going to regret those words. "We've come this far and I really want to see what's on the other side."

There was nothing more to it. There was no turning back. Delbert had a bad feeling that they shouldn't go any further, but he had to admit that he too was curious to see what was on the other side. He had a bad feeling that the old adage about curiosity was about to come true.

Jarwe stepped up to the door, but he paused before opening it. He suddenly remembered that he wasn't wearing his sword. All weapons had been banned from the streets, although he was sure that some people had ignored the edict. He kept a small knife hidden in his left boot, but he really didn't consider that a weapon. Against an unarmed man it would be deadly, but otherwise it would be almost completely useless. He took a deep breath and opened the door.

Surprisingly enough the door wasn't locked. Jarwe had been expecting more resistance, although he didn't know why. With the amount of people Sorrell said he had seen enter the alley he couldn't imagine they'd all have keys.

On the other side was a narrow corridor. With the door open they could hear the sound of people talking. The walls muffled the sound making any words incomprehensible. Whatever was happening was happening behind the door at the other end of the hallway.

"Well, this is our last chance to turn back." Delbert had breathed a sigh of relief when no one was on the other side, but now his heart was racing.

"Nah!" both Sorrell and Jarwe replied before rushing to the end of the hallway.

Delbert shook his head as he followed. They waited for him to reach them before Sorrell opened the door.

What was waiting for them on the other side wasn't at all what they were expecting, although no one really knew what to expect. They seemed to be in the backroom of a tavern. No one stopped what they were doing or even seemed to notice them as they entered. Delbert was quick to shut the door behind them.

The room was packed with people. There was only just enough space left for the three to move closer inside. The room was lit by a number of chandeliers hanging from the ceiling as there were no windows to allow any natural light in.

"Let's get something to drink!" Jarwe said when he was sure no one noticed their arrival.

There was a long bar at the far end of the room. Three busty women in low cut dresses were serving alcohol to the patrons. Delbert was still unsure about being in a back-alley tavern, but Jarwe and Sorrell were already making their way through the crowd. There was nothing for it, but to push forward.

"Can we get some refills please?" Sorrell asked in his best nobleman-like voice.

The bar wench eyed him carefully. Sorrell had already checked to see if there were others in the tavern drinking out of the same tankards and there were enough not to make them look conspicuous. Sorrell simply smiled at her as she poured their drinks. By the decree of the High Chancellor all drinks, food and entertainment for the first night of the festivities was paid for by the Grand Cathedral's treasury. It would by far be the biggest night, but there would still be room for more over the week. Even so the bar wench asked for a copper mark per drink. Delbert wanted to complain, but Sorrell simply paid the fee.

"Something isn't right about this place." The feeling of unrest grew within Delbert as he looked around the tavern.

It was a ragtag bunch in the bar. There were well-dressed ladies and gentlemen mixing with those not so well dressed and some who didn't look like they had bathed for a week or two. It was understandable that the coronation brought those together from all classes, but not in a tavern that seemed only accessible from a hole in a wall. He looked for a front door, but there didn't seem to be any other way in or out. The only other exit was an opening towards the outhouse.

"Relax Delbert. It's time to celebrate. We can worry about the how and why tomorrow," Jarwe tried to calm him.

"Besides I think that bar wench likes me," Sorrell smiled.

Delbert had to shake his head. He didn't think they had been drinking enough for Sorrell to be that delusional. From where he was standing the bar wench didn't seem interested at all. In fact she looked quite suspicious of their presence. That made Delbert feel even more uncomfortable. He wanted to leave, but he wasn't going to leave the other two there. Instead he took a large draft of his ale.

"Does this taste funny to you?" Delbert asked as he checked his palate.

"Relax Delbert. There will be plenty of time for you to stress and this isn't one of them. If it makes you feel any better you can order some troops around in the morning, if you feel up to it," Jarwe winked as he made the jibe.

Delbert took another drink and suddenly felt dizzy. For a moment the room started to spin before he regained his composure. Now he was sure that something was wrong. He was about to speak when he realised that Jarwe and Sorrell were no longer standing next to him. As he looked around the tavern there seemed to be something different in the air.

Before he had time to get his bearings there was a grinding noise from somewhere behind the bar. It was at that moment that he realised the entire tavern had gone quiet. The crowd was starting to back away and Delbert was forced back with the crowd. He had to strain to see what was happening. A false wall behind the bar opened up, in half and the bar wenches slid them back until they were against the wall. A path was now created from the opening to the centre of the room. It was at the moment that Delbert saw there were some ancient runes carved into the floor. There was also what looked to be dried blood. Delbert's heart started to race and he wanted nothing more than to leave the tavern, but there was no way to get through the crowd without making a scene.

What came next almost made Delbert sick, although he wasn't sure if it was an affect of his ale or not. A man dressed in a blood red robe with the collar flared out at the back walked into the room. His hair was long and dark and he had a thinly cut moustache and goatee. In front of him he pushed a naked woman. Scars covered the front of her body and it looked as though she had been repeatedly beaten. Her black hair had been roughly cut as if by a knife. A crude gag covered her mouth and it was clear that she had been crying. Panic covered her face. Delbert wanted nothing more than to rush out and help her, but there was nothing he could do. He was at the back of the crowd and didn't carry a weapon. All he could do was watch.

The man pushed her into the middle of the space left by the retreating crowd. She looked around wildly for a chance to escape, but she soon realised that it was impossible. As she tried to make for the exit the crowd simply pushed her back into the middle, jeering as they did. When she stopped the man grabbed her by her remaining hair, dragging her closer towards him. He pulled her head back causing the crowd to cheer again. When the crowd quietened he pulled the gag from her mouth.

"Please, somebody, help me, please, please," she sobbed. The tears rolling down her cheeks again only brought more noise from the crowd.

The pleas also brought a smile to the man's face making Delbert shiver. He knew there was something wrong about the place as soon as he walked in. He only wished he had listened to his instinct. Again he looked through the crowd to see if he could find Jarwe and Sorrell, but he had no luck. His attention returned to the centre of the room when the man started talking.

"The coronation of the next High Chancellor is almost complete." He paused, but there was no reaction from the crowd. "But there is one more ceremony to take place. He must be anointed. This sacrifice to the Great Lord will seal his rule in tyranny and his birth in blood."

This time when he paused and the crowd cheered in elation. As Delbert looked around he saw for the first time the crazed looks in their eyes. When the cheering subsided the man kept his grip on the woman's hair and kicked her in the back of her knees, knocking her to the ground Delbert realised he had broken out into a sweat. He knew if anyone was paying attention they would have realised that he didn't fit in. Luckily they were all transfixed on the scene in front of them.

Slowly the man pulled a vicious looking blade from inside his robe. Again Delbert wanted to rush to her rescue, but this time he couldn't bring his legs to move. He was trembling in both fear and anticipation. He couldn't watch, but he couldn't bring his eyes from the scene before him.

As the man lowered the knife to the sacrifice's neck there was a sudden crash from the back of the tavern. It sounded like someone had broken down the door. Suddenly hope filled Delbert's heart.

It wasn't long before the door into the tavern was smashed and guards stormed in wearing the crest and armour of the High Chancellor's Holy Guard. The crowd suddenly burst, scrambling to try and get away, but they soon realised there was nowhere to go.

Delbert, the only one in the room who relaxed, was still watching the man and his sacrifice in the middle of the room. Thankfully, when he heard the noise from the back of the tavern he left what he was doing and made a dash for safety. Without a thought for the others in the tavern the man rushed back behind the bar and slid the false wall shut. The naked woman collapsed to the ground and covered her head with her arms. Delbert couldn't imagine what she had just been through and the effect it was having on her.

"Everyone on the ground!" One of the soldiers boomed as they charged into the tavern.

The crowd tried to disperse, but with the false wall completely shut there was nowhere to go. Those who didn't listen to the command and were within reaching distance of the guards were promptly struck to the ground. Those who were silly enough to try and attack the guards were promptly run through. It only took three bodies before the others realised attacking wasn't an option. Even with the extra numbers the guards would easily slaughter them all. Slowly the followers of Nyrra realised they were trapped and there was nowhere to escape.

Delbert remained where he was and just watched the chaos around him. When things started to settle down he approached a nearby guard.

"I am..."

"On the ground scum," the guard barked.

"But I am..." that was all Delbert was able to get out before he felt something hard strike him on the back of his head. Slowly he sunk to the ground as his eyes closed and he lost consciousness.

Chapter 13: A Week of Festivities

Bern woke with a start. He had no idea where he was or what time of day it was. The sun shone in through an open window and he had to shield his eyes. His mouth was dry and his head was ringing. The night before was a blur. He could remember sitting at the head table with the High Chancellor watching the entertainment and enjoying the red wine, but that was it. Everything after dessert was wiped from his memory. It must have been late in the morning because the temperature had risen beyond comfort. He then realised there was someone else in his room.

"Not right now," Bern mumbled. "Come back later."

His half-coherent dribble was met with laughter. The deep rumble could only come from one of two of his companions. He didn't think the Grand Cathedral staff would let random dwarves into his room.

Slowly Bern rolled over and suddenly wished he hadn't. The light shining into his room blinded him and sent another shot of pain through his head. It took a moment before he could see Hulkan standing before him. A moment of hope and terror shot through him which almost made him empty his stomach. Taking a deep breath he settled himself, although he was sure he would need to vomit soon.

"What is it I can do for you?" his voice was hoarse.

"I don't know if you can do anything for me in this state," Hulkan's laughter, which had reduced to a chuckle, boomed throughout the room. "Later I can teach you how to drink, but I think you might need a day or two."

Bern looked around and found a pitcher of water next to his bed. It seemed as though one of the servants knew he would need refreshing. He didn't bother with the crystal hi ball glass, he just lifted the pitcher to his mouth and poured in as much water as he could. When he was done he felt a little better.

"I'm sure you didn't come here to talk about my condition," Bern tried to keep the edge out of his voice, but in his current state that was harder than he thought. "I can only assume you have a good reason for being here?"

The laughter quickly subsided and Hulkan explained his discussion from the night before. He added his suspicion about the Dark Knight in Remidel and his feelings on the matter.

Bern took another deep draught from the pitcher as he let the information sink in.

"Well at least that explains why I haven't heard back from Brac." Bern slowly came up into a seated position and he felt as though his head was going to explode. "I guess I will have to look at other options."

"I don't think there are any other options. I've been racking my brain all night and nothing has come to me. In essence Brac is just a representative for my brother. Now if that letter had not been received then there would be a good chance to convince him and the rest of the council that this is the right course of action, but with Gilgi specifically banning any further action then..." He left the thought open.

The information wasn't how Bern envisaged waking up that morning. He had planned on visiting the dwarves at some stage, but he had hoped he would have one day to himself. It no longer looked as though that was going to happen. Now he needed to formulate a plan to enlist the aid of the dwarves and it looked as though he wasn't going to be able to rest any longer.

"I need to meet with Brac and the other members of the guild council. This must end now. I believe that they don't celebrate the week of coronation?" Bern asked.

"You are right, but that still isn't going to help us. Brac isn't interested in meeting with you. Even without the letter from my brother I don't think he would have spoken with you." Hulkan cursed when he finished.

Bern thought for a moment, his head hurt, but there was not time to feel sorry for himself. A lost day was a day he couldn't get back. As soon as the week of celebrations was over then the army needed to be on the march. There was a chance he could gain a day or two after they left, but he really wanted to be at the head of his army. It would be a long march to Remidel and he needed his soldiers to be ready for battle. Seeing their general at the front of the line would inspire them.

"Well I guess it's time to put my foot down." Bern did his best to smile, but it looked more like a grimace as he stood. "At the very least Brac will have to listen to me."

"He's not going to like it and dwarves can be quite aggressive if they feel threatened," Hulkan warned.

"Then we should..." Bern stopped and suppressed the urge to vomit. "We should take some soldiers with us."

"I don't think you should be going anywhere in your condition. Lucky for you I have just the remedy." Hulkan moved over and pulled on the bellpull.

A servant would be arriving very soon. The High Chancellor had told them that Bern was not to be kept waiting when he needed something. Whilst they were waiting Hulkan wrote down a list. When the servant arrived he instructed her to take the list to the kitchen and have them prepare the remedy exactly as stated in the recipe. She left the room in a hurry.

"I also think you should eat something. That will help with your symptoms." Hulkan smiled as he tugged on the bellpull again.

"I don't feel like eating." Bern suppressed the urge to vomit again before taking another drink. It didn't take long after the liquid filled his stomach for his mouth to become dry again. "I think we should just get moving."

"Trust me, you'll feel much better."

It wasn't long before another servant came to see what Bern wanted. Hulkan instructed that he needed a large plate of greasy bacon, eggs and mushrooms. The servant, recognising the urgency in Hulkan's voice, rushed off. The dwarf knew that Bern would be no good until he had eaten.

It was the food that arrived first as Hulkan had both hoped and expected. The recipe for the elixir was quite involved and he wouldn't be surprised if they needed to find an alchemist. It wasn't a pleasant tasting remedy and it was always a good idea to take on a full stomach.

Even though the servant hadn't been asked he also brought a plate of food for Hulkan. Although he had already eaten a light breakfast he was happy to eat again. He figured he was going to need all his strength if he was going to help Bern fight the council.

"So do we take soldiers or risk going in there by ourselves?" Bern asked.

Hulkan had to think for a moment. Neither option really sounded good to him.

"I think we should bring some soldiers with us, or an armed guard as it might be. I think that would be appropriate for the leader of the Alliance. Let's just hope the council don't see it as a threat." Hulkan decided it was better to be safe than sorry.

There was a knock on the door and the servant entered with Hulkan's remedy. He held the pewter mug out in front him with his face screwed up. Hulkan knew it was from the nasty smell. The sad thing was that it tasted just as bad as it smelt. The only plus was that it would knock the cobwebs out in no time.

"Are you sure about this?" Bern took a quick smell and the urge to vomit was almost overpowering.

"Hold your nose and swallow it down as quickly as possible." Hulkan smiled as he gave the instructions.

Bern grimaced as he reached up and pinched his nostrils. As much as he really didn't want to swallow the vile smelling liquid he also didn't want to feel the way he did. It was going to be a tough day and he needed all his wits about him. Taking a deep breath through his mouth Bern poured the remedy down his throat as fast as he could, making sure he didn't spill any. His stomach automatically churned and it took all his will power to keep it down.

"Let's get you dressed and we can be on our way," Hulkan went to the bellpull again, but Bern stopped him.

"No matter what happens there's never going to be a time when I need someone to dress me." He kept the events of the day before to himself. He didn't think it counted if he was following a deep tradition.

"Very well, but I believe we need to get a message to the army that we need soldiers." Hulkan's voice was sly and Bern knew that wasn't the original reason for him calling the servants again.

Bern nodded as he made his way to his walk-in-robe. He was already starting to feel better. He had no idea what was in the vile concoction, but it seemed to be doing the job.

He was half dressed when a young serving girl entered the room. Instantly she moved to help him dress. Hulkan could have stepped in and stopped her, but it was too entertaining. After a confusing conversation Bern finally convinced the serving girl that she wasn't there to dress him. Hulkan then decided to explain why she was there.

"Let General Jarwe know that we need some guards to meet us at the entrance to the Guild Hall. I should think twelve would be a good number. Not too overpowering, but enough to make them think twice." Bern nodded his agreement. "And send word to my father that he is to assemble the council. The guild has an important matter to vote on." It wasn't exactly a lie, but it would be enough to get most of the members there. There serving girl curtsied and hurried away.

"Okay, then I guess we should get moving," Bern suggested when he finished getting dressed. The servant had a good head start and the soldiers should be waiting for them.

They didn't get more than a dozen steps outside of his room before he was stopped by a young page boy. He couldn't have been more than sixteen years old and he looked very uneasy.

"The High Chancellor has asked for me to fetch you. He needs to see you in his private offices," the page's voice proved he was nervous.

Bern shook his head. This was just what he didn't need. There was no stopping the message getting both to the Alliance and the Guild Council. His only choice was to put off the High Chancellor.

"Tell his holiness that I will meet with him when I am done. At the moment I have business with the guild that can't wait."

The pageboy looked at him with a dumbfounded expression on his face. Bern thought it was the first time anyone had refused a meeting with a High Chancellor. It looked as though the pageboy didn't know how to react. It was not the response that he was expecting and he waited to see what Bern would say next.

"On your way boy. You don't want to keep the High Chancellor waiting, do you?" Hulkan's voice was gruff. He didn't see any point in acting otherwise.

The pageboy quickly hurried away, making sure he didn't run. It was frowned upon for pageboys to be caught running through the hallways. He figured that he would be in enough trouble for delivering the bad news. He only wished that something would strike him down before he reached the High Chancellor. In the end he really didn't know which would be worse.

"I don't envy him," Hulkan chuckled at the thought.

Bern shook his head. He really didn't have time to care for pageboy issues. A year ago he wouldn't have thought of treating anyone like that. He was always very considerate of people's needs, even if he didn't really like them. Now he was a different man. If he had the time it would have worried him, but there were much more important matters on his mind. It was well past time they should be on their way.

It was past midday when they reached the entrance to the guild hall. The city was still crowded with revellers making the trip longer than they expected. The soldiers were already waiting for them and looked like they had been there for some time. Bern recognised their leader, a young corpora from Darshival by the name of Ellard. He had risen quickly in the ranks of the Alliance, which was a testament to him being there. Jarwe wouldn't have left the task of Bern's guard to just anyone, although there was a chance with the festivities that responsible soldiers were in short supply. When he saw Bern and Hulkan arrive he quickly ordered his guards into line.

"General!" he saluted, followed by the others.

"At ease corporal." Bern returned the salute. "Do you know if the council has been assembled?"

"I believe they are waiting for you. A disgruntled dwarf came out at barked at me about fifteen minutes ago. He wanted to know what they were waiting for. He didn't look happy." Ellard spoke very formally.

"That could be any dwarf in any situation." Hulkan's joke was lost on Ellard.

"Let's go." Bern was about to open the door when Hulkan stopped him.

"Best if I go first. The council can be a little touchy about outsiders barging into the guild hall."

Hulkan led the way into the guild hall. From the outside it looked like a simple, yet surprisingly eloquent, sandstone building. Once they were inside the simplicity changed. The foyer had massive marble columns from the floor to the high ceilings. The building was on two levels with the foyer taking up both. Marble stairs with gold flaked rails led up to the second floor. Even with his mind set on the job at hand Bern had to marvel at the design.

They were met in the foyer by two angry looking dwarves. They were both armed with long handled axes and looked as though they were ready to use them.

"Why do you bring these soldiers in here Hulkan?" the red-haired dwarf asked sharply.

"This is the retinue of the General of the Alliance, Cael. There are still agents of the Evil One in the city and it would be folly for him to travel alone." It was a half-truth.

Cael knew that wasn't true, but he wasn't going to push it any further. When it was said and done the council members had agreed to the meeting and that's all that mattered. They had been waiting and Cael didn't want to keep them so on his behalf. He quickly ushered them up the stairs to the second level, leaving the other dwarf in the foyer. They walked down a long corridor that ended in large, mahogany double doors. The handles were made from solid gold.

Cael knocked loudly, using the golden door-knockers. The sound resonated throughout the hallway and suddenly Bern felt nervous. Without waiting for a response he pushed the doors open. Bern turned to his soldiers before entering.

"You wait here. I don't think there'll be any trouble inside." Corporal Ellard didn't look happy, but he saluted nonetheless.

Only Bern and Hulkan entered the meeting room. Again Bern was stunned by the beauty of the room. The walls were solid mahogany with gold skirting and the floor was dark granite. In the middle of the room was a large oval table, again made from mahogany. There were dark stained pots with leafy plants in them scattered around the walls. Paintings of past and present council members adorned the walls, with Gilgi's likeness in pride of place at the far end of the room. Hulkan was quick to notice that his picture had been taken down. It was a little depressing, although he wasn't overly surprised.

Ilar stood when they entered the room. Although he was no longer a member of the council he was allowed to take part in the meeting if he introduced everyone and acted as an impartial chairman. The council figured since he had been a ruling member and his sons were on both sides of the argument that he would be best for the job.

"I assume this is General Bern?" Ilar asked, it was somewhat condescending, but Bern let it slide. He then went around the table and introduced the other dwarves, but it was only Brac's name that Bern was really interested in.

"So tell me why you have ordered us here?" Brac's voice was harsh. It was obvious he didn't want to be there.

"The Alliance needs the support of the guild. There is still much for us to accomplish and we need all the warrior's we can find." Bern suddenly felt flushed.

"We have already given all our warriors, so I'm afraid you've wasted your time." Brac stood. "Now that is over it's time to get back to work."

"Sit down Brac!" Ilar's voice boomed. As the chairman it was the one time he could tell Brac what to do. "We will give General Bern the respect he deserves."

Brac looked as though he was going to explode, but eventually he sat down as instructed. Bern was grateful, but he wasn't sure if it would make him any more malleable. It would be a tough sell, but it was something he had to achieve.

"Very well, go on general." There was no respect in Brac's tone.

"We are nearing the final battle with Nyrra." Although that was their original mission he now knew it was true. The problem he had was trying to explain that to the others.

Before he could continue, Brac interrupted again. "That's what Eldred told us years ago. That is the reason why your brother left with our army and look what happened then."

"Be calm Brac," Ilar spoke again. "Let him finish."

"Thank you Ilar, but that's okay. I understand it is hard to believe, but that doesn't make it any less true." Bern paused as he desperately tried to find the words he needed. Even with the aid of Hulkan's remedy his mind was still hazy. "It is one step at a time. We have solid intelligence that there is now a Dark Knight in control of Remidel. If this is true then we need everyone we can get to free the city and the kingdom."

Brac looked around the table at the other council members. There was a smug grin on his face. Bern had a terrible feeling that he had said the wrong thing. He knew he had just walked into a trap, although what that trap was he didn't know. There was no doubt Brac was going to enjoy revealing it.

"That is exactly what Gilgi warned us you would say. We received a letter from him recently explaining that everything was fine in Remidel. He also said that you would try and convince us that there was a Dark Knight in control of the city." He took a moment to look at the other council members again. "This is exactly what he warned us against. You have been taking your army from kingdom to kingdom taking them by force. I see you managed to take Darshival and Entero, but it seems as though you were a little sneakier when it came to Castalia. I don't know how you managed to depose the previous High Chancellor and put a puppet in his place, but that is a story for another time and one that I'm sure will be lamented for years." Brac couldn't resist the opportunity to make a jibe at Bern. "So you see that is the reason why we will offer no more assistance to your army." The smugness was clear on his face.

Bern sighed. He knew it wasn't going to be easy, but this was not at all what he was expecting. It seemed as though the Dark Knight was one step ahead of him and Gilgi was under his thrall. That only made his job harder, but he wasn't about to give up.

"That is exactly what the Dark Knight wants you to think," There was no doubt in Bern's mind that was the case. "If this was not the case then why wouldn't Gilgi have returned with your warriors?"

The smug expression remained on Brac's face. Bern wanted nothing more than to march down the other end of the table and wipe it from him. It took all his willpower not to return his look with a sneer of disgust. He knew whatever was coming was not going to be good.

"Remidia is having its own problems with the Dark One's evil creatures. Gilgi is staying there until he can rid Faxon's lands of evil."

It seemed as though the Dark Knight had thought of everything. Bern was out of ideas. He had come in expecting a fight, but he didn't foresee the letter from Gilgi. Slowly he turned to Hulkan in hope of aid.

"This isn't what the guild wanted. It was voted that Gilgi lead the army to assist the Alliance." He felt like he had said that a hundred times. "He has betrayed all of us and deserves to have his position revoked."

That removed the smugness from Brac's face. It was a very good point, but one, it seemed, he had not realised. This was what Hulkan had been hoping for. As Gilgi's stand-in, Brac would be next in line for the job and his rightful successor. There would be an opportunity for someone else to nominate themselves for the position, but Hulkan didn't think that would happen. The bloodshed that would follow still wouldn't guarantee the right to lead the guild. It seemed as though Brac saw the potential for his rise sooner than he had anticipated and that would be made even easier without Gilgi there to defend himself.

"What is it you're suggesting?" He kept his gaze on Hulkan even though he knew everyone in the room was now watching him.

Bern suddenly felt a glimmer of hope. He wished Hulkan had explained himself earlier. Knowing that there was a chance to remove Gilgi from power would have been useful information. There would be time to reprimand him later. Now it was just a matter of watching how things played out.

"You could put it to a vote with the council. There are more than enough grounds to have Gilgi removed. You would be his rightful successor. When you're in control you can give the Alliance your full support." Hulkan continued.

"It will take a vote by the entire council." Brac almost licked his lips in anticipation.

"I don't think this is a good idea." A dwarf by the name of Florn spoke his mind. "Gilgi had good reason to take the army to Remidel. That is where the battle is being fought. He has sent word saying he is fighting the Evil One. The battle in Avalon was a ruse to take us away from the real battle. Now the army is where it should be, fighting the Evil One in Remidia."

Bern looked around the table and it seemed that about half of the councillors wanted Brac and half were happy with Gilgi to remain. There were still ten councillors missing from the meeting, but it didn't look good. Even if Brac was to assume power there was still no guarantee he would pledge further support. At least Gilgi would be out and that meant the Dark Knight would no longer have command of the dwarven army.

"I agree. This is madness. Never before has someone tried to wrest power from a leader who is not in the city. It is unheard of." Florn's brother, Jlorn, agreed with him.

"It has not been done before, but it is not out of the question. In extreme circumstances the council can vote in a new leader in the absence of the old one if it is deemed in the greater good of the guild. I think that is exactly what we have here." Hulkan wasn't going to let it go. The idea had been planted and now it just needed time to grow.

"Very well Hulkan. You have made your point. We will organise the council and put it to a vote." Brac stood as he spoke.

"You will do this now?" Hulkan asked. "There is no time to waste on a decision like this."

That was not at all what Brac had in mind. To overthrow the current ruler was something that normally took time. He needed to get in the ear of the other councillors and plead his case. Hulkan knew, given half a chance, Brac would take weeks if not months to get the job done. That wouldn't do them any good. It was time for action.

"Now is not the time for rash action. I will need time to gather the other members." Ilar voiced his concern.

"There is no time. If you want to do this you have to do it now." There was almost a threat in Hulkan's voice.

"What does that mean?" Brac returned to his seat. He didn't like what he was hearing.

"If you don't have what it takes to be decisive I'm sure we can find someone else who is." Hulkan was taking a big risk. There was little chance that someone else would get the required votes to overthrow Gilgi, but he had to put the idea out there. "Now it is up to you do what's right. Are you not going to stand up and take control?" The question was deliberately confusing. Hulkan wanted to keep his mind from the threat.

Brac remained to his seat. That in itself was a win for Hulkan. "What is it exactly you have in mind?" he asked.

"Call the council now. You are still the caretaker of the guild. They will do as you command."

"This isn't right." Florn's voice boomed. "You can't hijack the guild like this. You had your time and now it's your brother's turn. He has made his decision and he has sent his orders. Just let it go."

Hulkan slammed his fist down on the table. He had to admit that he was grateful for Florn's interjection. "My brother betrayed me, but it is not the first time brothers have fought for power and I no longer hold a grudge. This is much larger than me and its much larger that you, Florn," Hulkan had never liked the dwarf. They had grown up together and were the same age. They had been friends once, but that was a long time ago. Hulkan figured that Florn was jealous he had been raised to the council and then leader before him. Florn was the first to stand by Gilgi when he was betrayed. His betrayal was harder to get over than that of his brother. "We are at war with the Evil One. These are trouble times and we need decisive leadership."

"Very well. Call the council to vote." Brac didn't sound completely confident, but it seemed as though Hulkan had pushed him over the line.

"But..." Florn started.

"Enough Florn," Ilar barked. "Brac has spoken. The council will meet now and decided on our future."

With that the meeting was done. Ilar wasn't going to give those opposed to Brac a chance to speak. As much as he remained impartial he had to admit that he had a bad feeling something wasn't right with his youngest son.

"We will meet back here in an hour. Those who can't or refuse to come will have their vote proxied by Brac," Ilar commanded.

That brought murmurs from the other councillors, but no one spoke. There was nothing they could do. As chairman of the meeting it was logical for Brac to take the proxy votes. Those on opposing sides assumed he would vote for the other side, which made no one happy. Hulkan could only hope that his father would make the right decision.

"You will have to wait in the foyer. No one is allowed to sit in when the full council meets, especially on such a matter." Ilar spoke to Bern and his son.

"Of course. We will wait for your decision," Hulkan responded before they stood and left the council chambers.

It wasn't until they were back in the foyer before Bern said anything.

"How long do you think it will take for them to make their decision?" Bern asked.

"It's hard to say. It seems as though some have already made up their mind. That in itself is a good thing, even if they are on the other side. This isn't a decision to be taken lightly. If there is a deadlock this could go on for days." Hulkan was working on the worst case scenario. "Tradition dictates that they take a vote after the first hour. From there they will gauge whether they can get a result today or not."

"So we have to wait at least two hours?" That wasn't exactly what Bern had in mind, but it was worth the wait.

"It does seem that way." Hulkan shrugged his shoulders. He really didn't think they would have a result that day. He couldn't imagine such a decision being taken in such a hurry, but stranger things had happened.

After explaining to his soldiers that they would be required to wait outside for at least another hour the two of them tried to relax as best they could in the foyer. On Ilar's request they were brought food and drink.

As the first hour passed, the council members started to arrive. They didn't seem to take much notice of the two watching them intently. It was hard to gauge a reaction from their expressions. Most of them either seemed annoyed or confused about being called into a meeting. They knew the other council members had met with Bern and Hulkan, but they weren't expecting anything to come from it. What was about to happen would come as quite a shock.

It was a long wait for the first two hours to pass before there was movement from upstairs. Bern couldn't relax no matter how hard he tried. There was much for him to do and the two hours sitting in the guild's foyer seemed such a waste. When the doors finally opened, Bern jumped to his feet.

After what seemed to be an eternity they saw Ilar walk down the stairs. It was impossible to judge what had happened by the look on his face.

"Did the council make a decision?" Hulkan asked before Bern had a chance to speak.

"No, as we expected. It's going to take more than an hour to make such a decision." Ilar shook his head.

Bern's heart sank. The idea was to rush to vote. They didn't think, once the council had time to think, the councillor's would vote Brac into power. There was a still a chance, but the longer the decision took the less likely it would go in their favour.

"There will be no more discussion today. The council will reconvene in the morning,"

"But we need this decision to be made now?" Bern retorted.

"I know, but the council has spoken and there is nothing I can do about it now. You best return to the Grand Cathedral. I'll send word when we have made a decision." Ilar didn't wait for further discussion. He wanted to catch some of the councillors before they left.

Bern was about to speak, but then he stopped. There was nothing he could say and he knew it. It was getting late in the day and they needed to return. The High Chancellor still wanted to speak with Bern and he had delayed him long enough.

The sun was waning when they left the guild hall. The day was later than Bern had thought. The streets were still packed with revellers and if anything there were more people than before. The soldiers did their best to clear a path, but without violence it was hard to get people to move.

The trip back to the Grand Cathedral took much longer than it should and the sun had well and truly set by the time they arrived. Bern was exhausted when he returned to his quarters. There was a light supper waiting for him, the servants didn't know if and when he was going to return, but they weren't going to risk him coming back to no food. It was better they waste the food than risk offending the High Chancellor's special guest. There was also a note waiting for him.

After he had eaten he picked up the letter. He knew it was from the High Chancellor and he knew he really didn't want to read it. As much as Tiberius owed Bern for not only placing him on the throne, but also freeing Castalia from the rule of a Dark Knight, there was still a chance that upsetting him would turn everything around. All he wanted to do was to curl up in bed and go to sleep.

The letter was short and to the point. The High Chancellor forgave Bern for not meeting with him and requested that he join him for breakfast in the morning. That was as good as Bern could have hoped. There was plenty of time for him to rest before his meeting.

Bern promised himself that he would never drink like he did the night before, at least not until the Evil One was dead. He was sure that he had a good time, but he had suffered for it and that was something he couldn't risk in the future. That was the last thought in his mind before he fell asleep just after his head hit the pillow.

Chapter 14: Preparations

There was more food on the table than Bern thought they could eat in a week. Only Tiberius and Bern sat at the banquet table which was filled with a variety of foods including fresh fruit, salted pork, eggs, bacon and everything else you could imagine for breakfast. Bern could only hope that the food would not just be thrown out when they were done. He needed a lot of stores for the army and would hate to see such good food go to waste.

"I'm sorry I couldn't make it yesterday," Bern started the conversation as he loaded his plate with food. "There were matters that had to be dealt with."

"Think nothing of it. I know you are a man in demand," Tiberius spoke after taking a bite of the salted pork. "And if you were feeling as bad as I was you wouldn't have wanted an intense conversation."

If only Tiberius knew the truth. It had been a painful day and he wouldn't have been able to concentrate through another meeting. The dwarves were all he had in him. He felt much better after a good night sleep and he was back, ready to attack the day. The High Chancellor's meeting was going to be a good one to get out of the way early. Although it had been assumed Tiberius would offer all the support he needed nothing had been confirmed.

"What is it you wish to discuss?" Bern asked

"I understand that you are preparing to leave once the celebrations are over?" Bern wasn't sure if it was a question or a statement.

"Yes. It seems as though your kingdom has settled down after the coup and it will be time for us to leave," Bern replied.

"It is getting there. It won't be until the festivities die down that we will know for sure how the people will react. I think that is where the tradition of a week-of-festivities came from. The old High Chancellors figured that people would be more malleable if they could party and relax for a week. Once it is all over and it is time to get back to work they forget the reason behind it all. At least I'm hoping for that to be the case." Tiberius seemed comfortable sharing things with Bern that he wouldn't with others.

"Well, with your plan to filter the information through the city that the old High Chancellor was under the influence of a Dark Knight, that should convince those who would otherwise be set against you. There is always the mine as well, but that might be more detrimental to the Grand Cathedral than what it would be a help," Bern returned.

"Well we are starting by trying to rid the city of all worshippers of the Evil One. We took down three covens in the first day and apparently we got another two yesterday. If you had asked me if there were any of the Evil One's followers in the city before I became the High Chancellor I would have said no. It is quite an eye opener what has been allowed to go on. Now things are changing and they're going to change quickly." Tiberius sounded proud of himself.

Bern had to admit to himself the array of food was very satisfying. The light supper he'd had when he returned had not sated him throughout the night and he had awoken ravenous. He was also glad that Tiberius controlled the topic for the meantime. What Bern needed to discuss had the potential to be unpleasant and he wanted to at least wait until after breakfast.

"So what do you do with them once you have raided their nests?" Bern wanted to keep the conversation going.

"My guards take them to a prison we have in the outer city. It is then they are given a trial and executed. It doesn't take long to put them to death for their crimes." Tiberius almost sounded happy.

That wasn't at all what Bern was expecting, but he couldn't fault him for it. By the sounds of things he didn't think they were going to get a fair trial anyway, but when it was said and done they didn't deserve one. The trials in Jarrat had run in much the same manner. Those who decided to support the Evil One deserved nothing but death.

"Then it seems as though you have things under control here." Bern was now looking for a segue into discussing Castalia's assistance to the Alliance.

"Not even close, but I am trying. I'm in the process now of trying to organise my own house. I have to work out who simply supported Augustus and who followed the Evil One."

"I don't think Augustus himself was a follower of the Evil One," Bern started.

"But his advisor was a Dark Knight. He let a Dark Knight into the most sacred building in the Seven Kingdoms. He must suffer for that." There was a hint of anger in his voice.

Bern sighed. It was a valid point, but he also knew that just because Augustus had been swayed by evil, it didn't mean he was evil himself. His greed had clouded his judgement and he needed to be punished for that. No one should have been sentenced to such conditions as working in the mines. As for his other crime Bern wasn't so sure he was guilty of that. He shouldn't be punished for being the pawn of a Dark Knight. They could turn the mind of even the purest of hearts.

"I think, as the new High Chancellor, you should show mercy to your predecessor. That would be a sign that you will be a benevolent ruler." Bern pushed his plate away before he could put any more food on it. He knew he had already eaten too much.

"Mercy? That is a novel idea, but you might be right. Maybe life in prison instead of a public execution might be the way to go."

"If you have him executed it might anger his supporters to the point of revolution. The last thing we need right now is a civil war."

They let the thought settle in the room for a moment. There was much to think on and Tiberius had to admit that he had been rash. It was a new job for him and one he had not been prepared for. He would make many mistakes in the years to come, but he needed to learn by them. Another key to his rule would be to listen to his advisors. They would be invaluable to him. For the moment, until he knew which ones he could trust, he would listen to the advice Bern gave him.

"You might just be right on that one," Tiberius finally spoke. "There is much that I need to learn. Your advice is very welcome." That made Bern feel a little more comfortable. It seemed as though the High Chancellor trusted his judgement. There was a good chance Tiberius would give him everything he wanted or at least more than he expected. "Are you sure you need to be leaving so soon. I could set you up with a nice job here in the Grand Cathedral. You'd never have to want for anything again. I could have your family brought here in a matter of days."

It was a generous offer and one that Bern could see himself accepting, not that he actually believed that he deserved it. As much as he thought he would always return to his farm when everything was done he wasn't sure that would happen. He dreamed of being with his family again, but that no longer included the small farm in Arsiliac. He had seen so much that he didn't think he could return to the simple life. That made him sad. Before he joined the Alliance he had enjoyed the simple life of a farmer and he wondered if the change had anything to do with the entity that shared his body. Even so he had a long way to go before he could settle down again.

"I could only dream of such a position. Unfortunately my job is not yet done with the Alliance. When it is and if I am still alive, who knows?"

Again the thought was left to float in the air.

"I need your help Tiberius." the High Chancellor had told him from the beginning that Bern wasn't to use his full title, not when they were in private. "Or should I say the Alliance needs your help. We have already fought numerous battles against the Evil One and some of those battles have cost us many lives." Luckily the siege against Castalia didn't last too long. The loss of life was a lot less than it could have been. It was mainly the battle in Jarrat that had cost the most lives, but any loss of life was too much as far as Bern was concerned. "I need all your soldiers." He figured if he started at the top he would get a better result in the end.

"That is a big request," Bern was surprised that Tiberius didn't instantly dismiss the idea. "I knew you were going ask for my support, but I didn't think it would cost me this much." Bern wasn't sure if there was humour in his voice or not. The conversation was not progressing at all like he had planned. Now he had to think quickly.

"You know I wouldn't ask if I didn't need it. I fear we are always one step behind the Evil One. With your army flying under our banner, well, that would shift things in our favour. Nyr..." Bern caught himself before he mentioned Nyrra's name. It was a silly superstition, but he didn't want to offend the High Chancellor.

"It's alright general, you are amongst friends here. I don't fall into the rumour that saying Nyrra's name will somehow summon a great evil." Tiberius grinned as he spoke. "Just don't repeat that in public. It wouldn't look too good for my reputation."

For some reason that made Bern relax, not that he had even noticed that he was tense. Although Tiberius was only new to the position he had been a High Priest for a long time. This was not at all what Bern had expected a High Chancellor to be like. The priest in Arsiliac never spoke out of place. He was a very pious man and had a lot of respect in the community, but Bern could never imagine sitting down and talking like he was now.

"Nyrra knows that the Castalial army is the largest and the strongest in the Seven Kingdoms. That is why he planted his Dark Knight here and I wouldn't be surprised if Za'aroz had been here for years before Nyrra broke free from his prison." Bern opened up. "Now we have an advantage and we have to use it."

It was at that point the servants came to clear the table. Bern was happy for the distraction, it also gave Tiberius time to consider what Bern had told him. Neither of them wanted to speak in front of the servants. They knew one wrong word in front of the wrong servant would mean the entire city would know their business. Of course if anyone was caught divulging information they would be imprisoned, but it was almost impossible to police. It was safer just to be careful what they said in front of others.

"That is a problem I have." Tiberius started, seemingly changing the subject. "I don't know who I can trust. If the Dark Knight was here for that long then there is no doubt that he has followers amongst my staff. I feel as though I have to look over my shoulder every time someone enters the room."

"There is only one solution to your problem. You need to clean your house and start again," Bern suggested.

"That would get rid of those already in my staff, but who's to say more wouldn't come in from the outside. No, I think it's a matter of 'better the devil you know'. But I do have spies on the inside trying to root out those who would betray me." There was an evil grin on his face.

"That is good to hear, but back to the original topic. We need soldiers and as many as we can get," Bern pushed.

"I will give you half the soldiers from my regular army." He continued before Bern had a chance to respond. "Even with that I think there will be some issues within the Grand Cathedral. I don't think those who oppose me will be happy with this decision."

"But it is your decision to make." Bern couldn't believe what he had been told. At best he thought Tiberius would have given him a few thousand soldiers and that would have only happened after much debate. It seemed as though it would be easier than he thought. Half of his regular army would almost double the strength of the Alliance. It was all he could do to keep the broad smile from his face.

"I would offer some of my Holy Guard, but I feel that would lead to a revolution and we definitely don't want that."

"Of course not." A smile appeared on Bern's face. "The soldiers you have offered is more than generous." His smile grew as he spoke.

"Somehow I don't think you were really asking for all of my soldiers?" Tiberius gave him a sly look. He had a feeling he had been duped, although he wasn't completely sure how.

"I didn't expect all of your soldiers, but it wasn't a joke asking for them. What I also didn't expect was half your army, but just because I didn't expect it doesn't mean I don't need it and don't appreciate it."

"Well, when it's said and done, if you fail in your mission it doesn't matter how many soldiers I have hiding behind my walls. If the Evil One prevails then it will be only a matter of time before Castalia falls." There was little humour in his voice. "This is not a decision that I have made lightly and one that has upset many people. I do what I feel is necessary for the survival of the Seven Kingdoms, not just Castalia."

Bern could hardly believe what he was hearing. So far from Jarrat and Kiarome he had been met with resistance when it came to taking soldiers. This was an entirely new situation for him, but that was just the first favour he had to ask, although it was the hardest. He didn't think there would be a huge issue in getting the supplies they needed. Castalia was the most prosperous of the Seven Kingdoms and always had stores of supplies.

"We also need enough supplies to get us to the final battle." That might have been asking too much.

"I would like to agree to that request, but you would need to tell me when the final battle is going to take place. So far as I understand it your next move is to free Remidel from the yolk of the Evil One."

Tiberius knew a lot more than Bern had given him credit for. It was no secret that they were to move on Remidel, but it was also not spoken about lightly. The one thing that Bern didn't want was for the Dark Knight in Remidel and Nyrra himself to know his plans. It was difficult at the best of times, but now it seemed completely pointless. The letter from Gilgi was the most disturbing of all. Either way it was something Bern had to plan around. There was no longer any chance of secrecy, although he wasn't sure there ever was. It always seemed like Nyrra knew what he was doing.

"That is a good question and I only wished I knew the answer. If I had the answer it would make life so much easier." Bern spoke honestly. He knew Tiberius would do well as the High Chancellor. He was very easy to speak to and was a smart man. "All I know is that we need enough food to get us to where we need to go."

"Ha, a very honest answer." Tiberius seemed overly excited. "You don't know how refreshing that is. It seems as though everyone wants to tip-toe around me now that I am the High Chancellor. It has only happened for two days and it is starting to become annoying. I don't know how I'm going to last the rest of my life. Everyone wants to make it seem like everything is okay and I know that is not the case. I know Augustus made some very serious mistakes, but it's like my staff don't trust my judgement. I know they have been in their position longer than I have, but they just need to tell me the truth."

"I guess they are getting used to you as much as you are getting used to them. It's my understanding that generally a new High Chancellor will select new advisors and new staff. I'm sure they are just trying to keep their jobs. It'll take time for you to settle in and for them to trust you. Remember who their last leader was and those who have already been discovered as followers of Nyrra."

"I suppose you're right, but it still doesn't make it any easier. There is a lot to get done before the festivities are over and then the real battle begins."

"Then I am sorry to say that I have to be leaving. I would like to stay and help you mould your kingdom, but I have to go." Bern started feeling somewhat nostalgic. Although he hadn't spent a lot of time with Tiberius there was a kinship that was undeniable. "But back to the issue of supplies. We need food, steel, iron and all sorts of amenities. My administrators are drawing up a list of everything we need."

"Of course I will give what I can, although don't be surprised if it's not everything on your list."

"Anything you can spare will be gratefully received." Bern smiled. The offer was genuine and he knew Tiberius wasn't going to let him down.

"Now, as much as I would love to stay here and talk for the rest of the day I have other issues to attend to. Will you join me for the evening meal? It will be a little more subdued than last time, I promise you."

Bern felt sick as he remembered how he felt when he woke the day before. He couldn't think of anything worse, but he couldn't deny his new friend. It would probably be the last chance they had to socialise before he left. In another day or two he would have to return to the army and make sure everything was ready for their departure. There were a few more things he had to do, but he was hoping to have them done by noon the next day.

"I will be there, but I won't be drinking. You can have that all to yourself." That brought a round of laughter from Tiberius and Bern couldn't help himself.

"Okay, if you say so."

At that point the door was opened and a number of functionaries bundled into the room.

"It seems as though they haven't quite got respect worked out just yet." Tiberius shook his head. "I guess that is it for now. Oh and before you go." He said as Bern stood. "The Council of Wizards has asked you join them. They have set up in a small inn in the Inner City. I will have my Holy Guard escort you. As much as we don't expect trouble we can't be too careful."

Bern smiled and nodded before he left. He was grateful for the escort. It was a lot easier to move through the crowd than for any real protection. Most of the revellers were well behaved, but they still didn't want to get out of the way when someone wanted to get past. Armed guards quickly changed their minds.

There were four Holy Guards waiting for Bern when he left the room. As much as he really didn't want to go to another meeting the wizards were a group he really needed to speak with. He hadn't spoken to them since they arrived. As much as he didn't want to sit down with six wizards he couldn't put it off any longer. The only wizard he really knew was Eldred, but there was something in his memory that told him the council wasn't very accommodating, and the fact that they had asked to see him was even worse.

The guards simply dipped their heads before turning on their heels and leading Bern down the corridor. Bern was quite happy to remain silent. There was a lot going through his head. First and foremost he was trying to recall the memories that he knew weren't his. There were memories of the council somewhere in the back of his mind. The entity which shared his body had put them there, whether by design or by accident they were there, frustratingly just out of reach.

To Bern's surprise the streets were still packed with partygoers. It wasn't even midday and the streets were filling up. Despite the ever growing crowd there was no problem making their way towards the Wizards' residence. The four Holy Guards gained more respect that his soldiers had the day before. It seemed that the crowd was scared of them. Bern wasn't sure if it was the remnants of the last High Chancellor's rule or just the fear that came with the role. As much as he liked to think it was part of both he thought it was more the latter.

When they reached the inn the Holy Guard left Bern at the front door. The leader informed him that he would need to send notice if he wanted them to escort him back to the Grand Cathedral. They estimated about half an hour, but Bern knew it would take longer. It would be just as easy for him to make his own way back. Even without a weapon he was confident he could defend himself if things turned dangerous.

Much to Bern's surprise he found the inn was almost completely empty. He didn't expect to see many at the front, but he expected the bar room at the back be full. Instead the only patrons were the six members of the council. There was a middle-aged man and woman behind the bar polishing goblets and looking quite sour. There was no doubt that this would be the quietest bar in all of Castalia. As much as the innkeeper and his wife were being well compensated they still didn't look happy.

"It's about time!" Brielle was the only one who looked up when Bern entered the room. The wizard, originally from Entero, had a sour expression on her face. Her dark brown hair was tied in its usual bun at the back of her head. Her hair and the subtle wrinkles around her face reminded Bern of a teacher he'd had when he was much younger.

They were all sitting in armchairs at the far end of the room. They sat in two groups of three around a coffee table each. It looked as though they had settled in, sipping tea from fine bone cups and eating shortbread biscuits. Bern had to sigh at Brielle's greeting. He didn't think it was going to be a pleasant meeting. If Tiberius thought his council was being rude then he knew nothing. Bern didn't think the wizards would show anyone outside of their own council any respect, regardless of position. He was sure they would scold a king just as they would a spoilt child. Everything inside of him was telling him to turn and run. If he didn't need information from them then he might have.

"Be calm Brielle," Athena spoke, but didn't look up. She was in the middle of knitting something but Bern couldn't hazard a guess at what. "The general is a busy man, if he wasn't then he wouldn't be worth the position." She had short brown hair and a motherly demeanour that put Bern at ease, at least for a moment.

Brielle crossed her arms across her chest and scowled. She certainly didn't like being berated like that, even though it was just a pleasant reminder of the facts. Bern shook his head. This was going to be a lot harder and a lot more frustrating.

"Please ignore them general," Drake spoke with a deep voice that dripped with power. He was the youngest of the wizards. Despite the strength in his voice he had a soft demeanour. He was clean shaven with shoulder length dark hair that looked as though it had just been brushed. "They start to get a little catty when they don't get their way." He seemed very pleased with himself.

Bern moved closer into the room. He wasn't sure if he should join them. They seemed to be happy in their little group and he really didn't want to spoil it. He really didn't want to be there at all. In the end he dragged an empty lounge chair and sat in the middle of the two groups. The sooner the meeting started the sooner it would be over.

"You summoned me here, so I figured there had to be a reason and not just to insult me." Bern was harsher than he intended and instantly wished that he hadn't been. That attitude was only going to get him into more trouble.

"You would do well to remember your manners Bern. You may be the General of the new Alliance, but we have been around for a lot longer. We have lived many lifetimes and seen many generals come and go. We have earned the respect that has been granted." Brielle was the first to react.

"You hide yourself away on your island. You shroud yourself in mystery and fear. Any ships that happen upon your location are lucky to leave intact. Most are sunk before they reach you. When you walked the Seven Kingdoms you let fear of your craft rule. Respect? I'm not saying that you don't deserve it, but I wonder at how you managed to gain it?" Even as the words came out of his mouth he knew they weren't his own. No matter how hard he tried there was nothing he could do to stop them.

None of the wizards knew how to react. The harsh words were not what any of them were expecting. From what they had been told and what they had seen, they knew he was a strong man. He had taken on a Dark Knight and won. There weren't too many who could claim that. There was something in his words that made them all uncomfortable.

"That is a fair judgement," Gwydion spoke before anyone else could snap. It was obvious that he was the eldest of the wizards with his wispy hair and white beard. Although he could have chosen any facade he enjoyed the aged look. He could see the reactions on their faces and knew what was còming. It would prove nothing to spend their time arguing.

There were much more pressing matters at hand. Time for the final battle, as much as they had all tried to ignore the signs, was getting close. They could deny it no longer and they needed to catch up. "We have been away too long and we have kept ourselves at arms' length for too long, but now is not the time to dwell on the past. We need to look to the future and that is why we have asked you here" It seemed asking and demanding was a fine line, but Bern wasn't going to push the point.

"Very well. You have asked me here and I have come. There's little time left, so let us get to the point." Bern tried to take the edge out of his voice, but it didn't work.

"We need to know what your plans are." Minerva spoke for the first time. She sounded impervious to the arguing and the snide comments.

Bern wished that he had asked the question first. He needed to know what the wizards had planned. There was no denying that their assistance would be invaluable, but it was a matter of whether they could be tamed. If they didn't listen to him and take his command then they could be more trouble than they were worth. Either way, he had been asked first and he needed to respect that. He had already been very disrespectful and he didn't want to push things further. He could only hope that the entity hadn't upset them too much.

"The army is going to move on Remidel. We have reliable information that a Dark Knight is now in control of the kingdom." If nothing else Bern now knew that was true. "When the week-of-celebration is over the army will start marching." Bern kept his explanation brief.

"We were hoping for a little more information." Drake pushed when Bern didn't continue.

"I'm afraid there isn't any more information to give." Bern suddenly felt the eyes of everyone in the room on him. The innkeeper and his wife made him the most uncomfortable. Not that the little information he had given wouldn't soon be common knowledge, he still didn't want too many people to know. "If there was I don't think this would be the right place to discuss things."

"Oh, don't worry about them. They can't hear anything that we don't want them to. As far as they're concerned we're having a friendly conversation about the coronation. They have no idea what is happening," Ulman explained. "It is a subtle spell." Although Ulman was Eldred's brother he looked nothing like him. He had a cleanly shaved head and a strong looking body. Normally he carried a large claymore with him, but with the weapon moratorium he had left it with the army. He was the only wizard who enjoyed physical attributes.

Bern felt a little better, but remained unsure. He was sure it would be easier to just get them to leave the room, but it wasn't worth commenting on. He was just pleased that they couldn't hear what they were discussing.

"If we are safe to talk then I would like to know what your plans are." Bern thought it was a good chance to turn the tide of the conversation.

There was a moment of silence as the wizards looked at each other and something unspoken passed between them. Bern didn't like what he was seeing and it was making the situation even more unsettling. He doubted whatever answer they were about to give him would be the truth. Nevertheless he had to take them on face value and keep his suspicions to himself.

"We are here to see that the job gets done." Minerva was the one who had been chosen to speak. It was decided that she had the most calming voice and most passive demeanour. Her appearance was of a middle-aged woman with shoulder length blonde hair. They figured if the words came out of her mouth they would upset him the least. "Alaric reminded us that we are here to serve as well as advise. For too long have we sat on our island. We have forgotten the land in which we were born, in which we owe our lives." They were not the words the council had agreed upon. The words came to Minerva as she spoke and she knew they were true. "We tried to force the prophecy from our lives. Eldred was the only one who succumbed to its will. We can only hope that it hasn't proved too late for our realisation."

"What are you doing Minerva?" Brielle snapped in shock. "This is not what we discussed."

"Quiet Brielle," Ulman barked. He was a little disturbed by Minerva's change of words, but he was also interested to hear what she would say. He too had noticed the tug and pull of the prophecy and it seemed he wasn't the only one. They had fought it for so long, or maybe it had just ignored them whilst they were on their island, and it would be hard for some of them to accept it now. "We have chosen Minerva to speak and we shall let her speak for us."

"But this is not what we discussed." Brielle wouldn't be silenced. "She cannot make things up now."

"Be calm Brielle," Gwydion spoke. As the oldest and the most revered of the wizards his words were always adhered to. "We must let this play out. I feel the pull of the prophecy and it is time we embraced it."

Bern looked at the each wizard in turn. It seemed as though everyone except for Brielle and Athena agreed with Gwydion. He thought that was very interesting and a good sign. Four of the six was better than he imagined. If they trusted in the prophecy then maybe they might be willing to take orders from him, although he wasn't sure that would ever truly be the case.

"Alaric has asked us to help you in your battle against the Evil One and we can't deny our destiny a minute longer," Minerva continued. "We will be with you until the end. Either we defeat Nyrra or die trying."

"So you will listen to my command?" Bern dared ask the question.

"I don't know if we will go that far," Brielle spoke again. Minerva had said her piece and now they were able to speak for themselves. "We will join your Alliance and we will listen to your advice, but I trust that you will extend us the same courtesy."

"Consider us to be your advisors. We're here to make sure you don't stray off your path," Athena added.

Bern didn't like what he was hearing. The initial offer was amicable, but the changes didn't sound so good. If the wizards weren't under his control then they could be very dangerous. In the end he really didn't think they would be truly under his command anyway. Either way, he needed them on board and there was nothing he could do about it.

"I guess that is a good offer and I doubt I could deny it even if I wanted to." Bern didn't really feel like being gracious. He felt as though he had just walked into a trap. Not only that but it was a trap of his own making. "We will be leaving at the end of the festival. I would appreciate it if you were ready to depart then." Bern stood as he spoke.

"Before you leave," Athena offered him his seat again.

Begrudgingly he did as he was offered. As much as he wanted to leave he felt compelled to stay. That was the first sign that something wasn't right. He suddenly felt hazy in the head and his mind wasn't as sharp as it had been when he entered the inn.

"That isn't a good way to make friends." Bern heard the voice, but it was now far in his mind. As much as it was always disturbing he was happy the entity was taking over. By himself he was no match for the wizards, but with a little aid he would be more trouble than they had expected.

"What are you talking about?" Athena almost sounded hurt at the accusation. "We have been nothing but hospitable towards you. Where are these accusations coming from?"

"It doesn't matter how long you try and stall, I will not let you cloud this mind further. I should never have trusted the six of you to play fair. I should have taken steps when we arrived."

"And who is it that addresses us in such a manner?" Gwydion seemed to be the first to realise they were no longer speaking with Bern. They all moved a little closer and waited for the response.

"Who I am is irrelevant, but let's just say in another life or at least another form I have known all six of you and know all your tricks. I had hoped by you coming here meant you had changed, but it seemed as though I hoped too much."

"We have heard rumours that the general has been possessed by some spirit, but we couldn't believe that it was true." Drake looked at Bern in a new light. It was like he was trying to look right through him.

"This is something that we weren't expecting," Minerva added with just as much awe in her voice.

Heryion had to admit to himself that in all his years he had never known any members of the Council of Wizards to be so amazed. He now wasn't sure if they were caught in his trap or the other way around. Somehow he felt that this was exactly what they were trying to achieve all along.

"I think it is time you put your cards on the table or it is time for Bern to leave." Heryion was comfortable that he was no longer under their spell.

"We need to know what is happening here. It has been a long time since a body has been possessed and the last time it happened things didn't work out well. Both the host and the possessor were dead within a year." Gwydion remained calm.

"This is a little different," Heryion, for the first time in a long time, wasn't completely sure of himself. He had possessed many different bodies, but never one that retained its original host. Besides, he didn't think that Gwydion really knew what he was talking about. That was a good sign. It meant they had no idea who he was. He wanted to keep his identity secret for as long as possible especially when he could still feel that Bern's presence was aware, even if it was somewhere deep in the background. "This isn't the first time I've done this. I've been doing this for longer than you have been alive." He couldn't help the little jibe, not that it would do him any good.

"So at least that narrows it down to who you might be." Athena smiled and Heryion silently cursed to himself. "The next question is what you are doing inside General Bern. Surely you could have found someone a little less prominent."

"He is the closest friend to Alaric. I had no intention of possessing him, but it seems as though I'm not completely void of the prophecy either." Although he had dispersed the spell that would have compelled the information from him he still felt the need to speak. He wouldn't give away too much information, but it seemed to be the best way to get them to relax Hopefully they would let more information slip than they had planned.

Chapter 15: Last Days of Celebration

The rest of the afternoon was like a blur Bern was still in the inn with the wizards, but he was no longer in control of his body. At first he had been glad that the entity had taken over. He could feel the effects of the spell, but there was nothing he could do about it. The entity had promptly put a stop to it, but it didn't end there. The remainder of the time he was with the wizards the entity remained in control. It was a strange feeling. He wasn't sure if he just preferred it when he didn't remember anything. Even being present didn't give him full recall and as he made his way back to the Grand Cathedral he could only remember pieces of the conversation. He remembered the feelings and the emotions that had passed through his body during the time in the inn were still thick in his memory.

Although the crowd was thick Bern seemed to pass through without notice. His head still swam as if he was still possessed. He knew something important had happened between his entity and the wizards, but he just couldn't put his finger on it. He would have to be very careful when he spoke to them. There was no doubt they would push him further once they were on the move again. They would watch him like a hawk and he needed to be prepared for it.

The night passed without incident and Bern kept to his word. Although everyone else in the grand hall partook in the multitude of wines and ales Bern remained sober. The feeling of the other morning was still fresh in his mind, and as much as he would have loved some of the exotic red wines, he abstained. There was too much for him to do to lose any more time in a drunken haze.

When he returned to his apartment he had hoped that there would be word from the guild, but there was nothing. He should have known that it would take longer than a day to get a result. There was little time left and he needed them on board. He could only hope that the morning brought a response.

Bern had every intention of visiting the guild that morning and then return to the army, but he soon realised he wouldn't. During the night a load of requisition forms and other paperwork had been left on his writing desk. He had to admit he thought his conversation with Tiberius was all he had to do, but there seemed to be much more paperwork than there were requests. If there was more time he would take it back to the army and get someone from his staff to go over things, but with the back and forth it would be much quicker if he just did it himself.

At first he thought it was just a plan for Tiberius to keep him around for longer, but when he started reading the request forms he realised that wasn't the case. It seemed as though Tiberius' over officious officials didn't agree with their leader's point-of-view. The paperwork wasn't to delay his departure, but to prevent him from getting what was promised. He didn't see it until he had already signed off on a half dozen proposals and when he did he threw his ink pen against the walls, spraying ink across the room. He had just wasted a full morning and there were still two full stacks of paper waiting for him. He would see that Tiberius would have those responsible punished. There was no time to be wasting with such things.

Before he went to see the High Chancellor he needed to calm down. He was also concerned that he still hadn't heard from the guild council. He knew it could take over a week for them make their decision but that was too long. He needed to go and give them a push and hope for a result.

Just as he was about to leave Bern tugged on the bellpull summoning a servant.

"See that all these documents are promptly burned." Bern's tone was a lot harsher than he meant it to be and the reason he didn't want to speak to Tiberius. He needed time to calm down before he spoke to anyone important. "I'm going into the city, I'll need a guard."

"Ah... There are four Holy Guard waiting outside your room." The young man sounded very nervous.

As much as Bern didn't like berating the servant he had to smile to himself when the servant left his apartment. It seemed Tiberius knew him better than himself. It also showed that the High Chancellor had no idea he had been bombarded with all the paperwork. He shook his head as he left the room, he should have known things wouldn't be so easy. The High Chancellor had agreed to his requests all too quickly. There would be no problems once he had spoken to him, but that would have to wait. Now he needed to get out of the Grand Cathedral.

The same soldiers from the Holy Guard were waiting for him outside.

"General!" The corporal saluted first before the other three followed suit.

Bern sighed, but returned the salute. He had been enjoying not having to salute every five minutes since he had been away from the army, but it seemed that couldn't last forever. If he could he would stop the army from saluting altogether, but that would never happen.

Again the streets of Castalia were filled with revellers. Bern was still surprised, although he really shouldn't have been. It had been the same ever since the High Chancellor's coronation and it would stay the same until the week was over. At least the people respected, or maybe feared, the Holy Guard enough to get out of their way. The journey to the Guild Hall was much quicker than the day before.

The Holy Guard waited as Bern entered the Guild Hall. He was met inside by Hulkan who looked like he was on the way out.

"General Bern!" The use of his title showed his surprise. "I was just coming to get you."

"What's happened Hulkan? And you know you don't have to call me general." He smiled as he spoke, trying to calm his friend.

"The Guild Council has made their decision." Hulkan explained.

"And that answer is?" Bern raised his eyebrow when Hulkan didn't elaborate.

"The Council wouldn't tell me. They said that you had to be present for the announcement." Hulkan shook his head.

Bern wasn't sure if that was a good sign. Either way there was only one way find out. Hulkan led the way to the main meeting room. Inside the table was filled with all the members of the Guild Council. Ilar had to stand at the back of the room. Bern gave him a quick look, to try and gauge a reaction, before turning his attentions to Brac. The temporary leader of the Guild stood.

"The Council of the Western Darvern Guild has made its decision." A rather young looking dwarf, sitting to the right of Brac, spoke. He was the chair of the guild and it was his responsibility to announce the decision. "Due to the nature and time restraints this decision has been made quickly but not in haste. We have given the decision all of the due diligence that it deserves." Bern just wanted him to hurry up and give him their answer, but all he could do was wait for the ceremony to finish. "These are indeed troubled times and it is in these times that it takes strong leadership. Gilgi has been trusted by the Council to lead our army into battle, side but side with the armies of men and elves. He is a strong leader." Bern didn't like what he was hearing. "When no battle was to be had he chose to take the army and assist the land of Remidia. That in itself doesn't constitute to be removed from office." Bern's heart sank. "But the rumours coming from Remidel are quite disturbing. If it is indeed true that there is now a Dark Knight in command of Faxon's kingdom then there is a good chance that he is now in command of the dwarven army as well. This is something that we can't sit idly by and hope for the best." That sounded a little better.

"Enough Arlan. Read the vote and tell us what decision has been made," Brac boomed.

Bern relaxed slightly before tensing again. It seemed he had been reading too much into Arlan's speech. The chairman didn't even know the result. He hoped that there wasn't going to be another speech. Their day was starting to waste away and he wanted to return to the Grand

Cathedral before nightfall. He needed to make sure that the supplies were starting to be sent to the army.

Arlan looked somewhat perturbed by Brac's comment. There was much more he wanted to say. It was the first time he had presided over a vote for the leadership and he wanted to savour the moment. He opened his mouth to speak again, but then thought better of it. The rolled parchment in front of him had the tally of the votes. No one in the room knew the result and the dwarf who counted the votes had no idea what they were voting on.

Slowly Arlan unrolled the parchment. He looked down and read the result. A smile crossed his face when he realised who the winner was.

"By one vote Brac is the new leader of the Western Dwarven Guild." Arlan's smile broadened on his face. He had never liked Gilgi and disliked the fact that he had risen to leader even more.

"Very good!" Bern took the opportunity to speak. "Then you will give us every able bodied Dwarf you have?"

The council didn't look happy that Bern had spoken, but Brac calmed them. It wasn't that he hadn't been expecting the question. In fact he had already prepared for it.

"Unfortunately we won't be sending anymore warriors to join your army," Brac spoke with the confidence of a leader.

"What are you talking about?" Bern was genuinely surprised. He thought with the change of leadership he was about to get what he wanted. "You said you would support the Alliance."

"I didn't say we would offer you anymore dwarves." Brac wouldn't back down, even though Bern looked ready to attack. "I was put in charge to do what it best for the Guild." Bern couldn't believe what he was hearing.

"And what do you believe is the best thing for your dwarves?" Bern snapped.

"I think we can end this meeting," he addressed the other councillors in the room. "We have achieved a lot this day."

Bern held his tongue as the room emptied. He had hoped that by coming to the Guild Hall it would have lifted his spirits, but instead it seemed to make things worse.

It was obvious that not all the council members agreed with the vote. Some of the dwarves looked upset with the decision, but they knew better than to say anything. Gilgi was always going to have strong support. Most of the councillors who had voted him in where still on the council. As much as they wanted to let him know, they would abide by the ruling of secrecy. Brac didn't want Gilgi to know he had been deposed until the right time.

When the room had emptied only Bern, Brac and Hulkan remained.

"The sticking point to the vote was not allowing anymore from the Guild to join your army," Brac finally spoke when they were seated.

"That was the entire point of you taking control," Bern protested. "So what is it that you have in store? I'm assuming this isn't the end of things."

"I can't give you anymore dwarves, but this is what I can do for you. When your army reaches Remidel I am relinquishing Gilgi of his command of our army. Command will fall to Hulkan." Hulkan looked just as surprised with the turn of events as Bern did. It was clear that he had known nothing prior to Brac's statement. "Of course Hulkan will defer to you whilst you are the leader of the Alliance, but when all this business is done then he will be expected to bring the army home."

Even if Hulkan was going to survive the final battle he wasn't sure if he could return home to stay, but that was just semantics, he really didn't expect to survive. Most of those who rode towards such an end wouldn't live to see it through. Hulkan had come to terms with the fact a long time ago. Every day he lived was special and brought him one day closer to his death.

Bern had to agree that it was a good deal in the end. He had wondered, even with Brac in control, how they were going to regain control of the dwarven army. Now, at least, that problem had been solved for him. It wasn't exactly what he wanted, but it would do.

"How do we get to the army if the Dark Knight is controlling them." Hulkan wasn't so sure this was the right plan. "And who's to say that Gilgi will stand by the council's decision?"

"Gilgi wouldn't dare go against an official decision from the council. That would result in treason and his death," Brac replied.

"Hulkan is right. If he is in the thrall of a Dark Knight then he won't know what he's doing." Bern agreed.

That was something that Brac hadn't really thought about. He had just assumed that Gilgi would follow their law.

"I guess you are just going to have to kill the Dark Knight. Isn't that your plan anyway? Once the Dark Knight is dead then Gilgi will listen to what you say?" Brac explained, although it was more of a question than a statement.

That was something Bern had hoped to avoid. He wanted the army of dwarves assimilated into the Alliance before he had to battle with Dargoz. If they had to fight then many lives would be lost. As much as he had managed to kill Za'aroz before things got out of control he wasn't sure the same would happen in Remidel.

"There doesn't seem to be any other choice." Bern resigned to the fact. "I must return to the Grand Cathedral. There is still much to be done and I fear that I am quickly running out of time." Bern paused. "Thank you for all that you have done Brac. I know it can't have been easy for you." Bern turned to Hulkan as he stood. "Be sure that you get all the paperwork in order, we can ill-afford to miss anything. The army moves in four days, we need to have everything in order by then."

"It will only take a day or two to draw up the appropriate documents you'll need." Brac reassured him.

Bern was happy with that. With a little luck he would make it back to the Grand Cathedral before nightfall. He needed to finish everything he needed to do so he could return to the army. The Alliance needed their general back. He was sure the others had things under control, but he still wanted to be there. It would lift the men's morale to see their general amongst them, especially since their week of partying was being cut short.

"I will see that it is done general," Hulkan was a little over-officious for Bern's liking. "I will return to the army as soon as it is complete."

Bern didn't see much point in staying any longer. It was time to be getting back. The Holy Guard was waiting for him outside, standing at attention by the door to Guild Hall. He wondered at how they managed to remain standing so straight in their armour in the heat of the day. It was bad enough in his robes to be out for more than an hour or two. He was very impressed with them.

The Holy Guard managed to get him back to the Grand Cathedral in good time. When Bern had told them he was in a hurry they didn't waste any time. They rushed through the crowds who scattered when they realised who was coming. The last thing people wanted to do was to get in the way of the Holy Guard. There was a good chance they could end up in gaol for the night if they did, not that the guards would have time to arrest anyone.

When he was back in the Grand Cathedral Bern found the High Chancellor in his private meeting room with a number of his staff. He recognised one as the High Priest Simeon, the witness for Topaz during the ceremony, and another two minor priests. He had no idea who the others were. As much as he hated to interrupt Tiberius in the middle of a meeting he didn't have time to wait.

To his surprise Tiberius actually looked pleased when Bern burst into the room and ordered the others to leave. He had thought on it all the way back from the Guild Hall and decided it was the best way to gain the High Chancellor's attention. If he just waited his turn there was no telling how long it would take to gain an audience. The High Priest and the others in the room didn't look at all impressed. The last thing they wanted to do was give up their time with the High Chancellor, but his word was final. When he asked them to leave the room there was no denying him.

"Sorry to do that," Bern apologised when the room was empty.

"Don't be silly. It's good to have a friend to speak with." Tiberius' voice sounded uplifted if albeit a little weary.

"Surely they aren't that bad."

"No," Tiberius sighed and his shoulders drooped "but they all seem to want something. I don't know what my predecessor had been doing in his last few years, but running the kingdom didn't seem to be one of them. I guess I should have spent more time in politics and less time in contemplation."

"You weren't to know what was happening." Bern consoled him.

"That is no excuse, but anyway I'm sure you're not here to listen to me complain about my troubles. What can I do for you?"

Bern explained his problem with the pile of requisition forms that had been left for him the previous night. He now regretted burning the pile. At least if he had the paperwork as proof he could back up his claims.

"I should have known," there was no doubt in Tiberius' tone. "I doubt if I had been in power for a century they would be happy with my decision. The fact that I have only been here for a few days has only made things worse. I am sorry you had to waste your time. I will make sure that everything I have promised is delivered to the Alliance in good time."

Again things seemed to be moving easier than they should. Sure he hadn't achieved the result he had originally wanted from the Guild, but the result was much better. He had been so concerned with gaining more soldiers he had not thought about the long term. He also wondered why Tiberius was being so accommodating. It was at the point he had a suspicion that the entity might have been involved, although he couldn't remember a time he had lost himself around Tiberius.

"Be that as it may you are doing the right thing," Bern offered when he realised he hadn't spoken.

"Given half a chance I'd ride with you Bern," Tiberius continued. "It has been a long time since I picked up the sword, something I fear I will never do again. At least in battle you can look your opponent square in the eyes. In politics your enemies are hidden in the corners, striking only when you are at your weakest."

Bern had seen enough politics to know that his words were true. As much as he didn't like being in command of the army he knew it would be much worse to be a nobleman in charge of a city, or a king or queen in charge of a kingdom. Politics was something he was happy to stay far away from. The little he had taken part in had already been too much.

"Sometimes I think it would be easier just to be one of the soldiers and not the general. The politics aren't quite as bad as what you're facing, but there is enough to spin my head."

"Well you play the game well," Tiberius offered. "And it certainly doesn't hurt having the power of an army behind you. People generally listen when they feel threatened."

"But I haven't threatened anyone!" Bern suddenly felt defensive. He wondered if that's how Tiberius felt, although he couldn't imagine why. An army would still struggle to break down the walls of Castalia.

"Of course you haven't, or at least not deliberately. An army of your size is very overbearing regardless of how of accommodating you try to be. No, that is one thing that you will have to carry around with you until this is all over," Tiberius explained.

"When it's said and done I don't really care how I get assistance, just as long as I get it." Bern spoke the truth.

"That is a good way to be general. I wish I could be as ruthless as that." It was meant as a joke, but Bern wasn't sure it was. Either way he let the jibe pass over him.

"When do you think you will have the supplies ready for the army?" Bern thought it was a good chance to change the subject. He needed to tie off all his loose ends if he was going to try and return to the Alliance in the morning.

Tiberius waited and thought before responding. He hoped that he had not offended Bern. The man was the only real friend he had left. Now that he was the High Chancellor even his old childhood friends would treat him differently. There was no one else he could speak openly with. Everyone else watched their words carefully around him.

"As I'm sure you can appreciate it is quite difficult to get anything done at the moment. Those who aren't celebrating are pushing for advantage. The Holy Guard are the only soldiers on duty. We can have some supplies brought to you over the next few days, but not much will happen until the festivities have finished."

That was something Bern hadn't taken into account. Just because he needed to leave when the festivities were over didn't mean that the rest of the kingdom would work around his schedule. That wasn't going to stop him. In fact he didn't think he had any choice in the matter. The tug of the prophecy was getting stronger each day and when it was time to leave they would be leaving.

"I'm assuming then the soldier situation isn't going to be any different?" Bern asked, although he already knew the answer.

"You're right. We can't even muster the men before the week is up. It will be at least another week before they are ready to march. Again there is nothing I can do about it. How would I be remembered if I was the High Chancellor who put an end to the celebrations?"

"You are the High Chancellor. The people will listen to you." Bern was more hopeful than anything else. Deep down he really didn't want to forgo the celebrations. There was a good chance that most of his soldiers would never return. This would be their last chance to celebrate and he couldn't begrudge them that.

"I don't think I would remain long in power if I did that. I'm sure there are many High Priests who would love to usurp my power." Tiberius had to smile, which in turn forced Bern to.

Bern had faith that Tiberius was going to be a great leader. He would be tough but fair and would return Castalia to its former glory. The only benefit about Augustus' rule was that the coffers were full. Tiberius was going to compensate those who had been forced to work in the mines, and that would still leave plenty of gold and diamonds for other things.

"Well I guess that's about it then," Bern stood as he spoke. "I shall return to the army in the morning. There is still much to organise to make sure we are on the move when the festivities are over."

"How long do you expect it will take for the army to be on the march?" it seemed as though Tiberius hadn't finished and he offered Bern his seat again. "I have organised some food to be brought here for the evening meal. I won't be joining in the celebrating tonight. I need to have a peaceful night's sleep. I'm not as young as I once was. The week of celebration is for those who are a lot younger than I."

One day had been enough for Bern, so he could sympathise with Tiberius. He couldn't think of anything worse than another night of drinking. Although he had well and truly recovered from the first night of the festivities the feeling of sickness was still thick in his mind. He had no problems in remaining with Tiberius for the evening meal, as long as he wasn't asked to leave.

"Most of the soldiers should be on the move the first day. It will take much longer to pack down all the tents and transport all the camp equipment. I would expect that it will take three days for the camp to be completely broken down." Bern explained what he had received in a report the day before. It was good to see there were still those in his army still working.

"Then the Castalial army won't be too far behind you. If they march hard they should catch up before you reach Remidel." Tiberius sounded pleased.

Bern wanted to make sure the Castalial army reached Remidel with them. The extra soldiers might just be enough to avoid a battle, not that he really believed it.

Suddenly there was a knock on the door to break the conversation. Bern was happy to see a servant enter with a platter of food. Since it was the last night he would be staying in the Grand Cathedral he was hoping for some lighter conversation. The meal gave him a good opportunity to change the subject.

The two spoke long into the night before Bern finally decided to retire. He had hoped to get an early night to make the most of the soft mattress, but he couldn't get away. In the end the conversation with Tiberius was much more preferable. He didn't know when he would have a chance for light conversation again.

Chapter 16: A Missing Corporal

Bern left the Grand Cathedral at first light. Tiberius had left him the same four Holy Guards as the previous day. As much as he would like to believe the streets would be empty at such an early hour, he knew they wouldn't be. The streets weren't as busy as they became later in the day, but there were still plenty of people around. Bern couldn't fathom how they could keep going for so long.

A messenger had been sent on ahead to let the command group know that Bern was returning. They were waiting for him in the command tent when he arrived. Bern had to admit it was good to see them again, although he had to admit there was a strange feeling in the air. The entire group looked nervous.

"Where are Orric, Pernian and Kilean?" Bern asked.

The question seemed to make those in the tent relax slightly. It wasn't the reaction Bern had been expecting which made him believe it wasn't the missing elves that was causing the tension.

"The elves were uncomfortable being out in the open for so long," Jarwe started to explain. "They have travelled to a small wood to the north of the city."

"Why didn't they go into the city and join in the celebrations?" As soon as they words came out of his mouth he realised what he had said. Now he was going to have to sit through the answer.

"I don't think that would have been a good idea. Elves don't have much of a reputation in Castalia. They have never had any affiliation with the religious way of men. Alcohol and ignorance would lead to a disastrous situation."

"The elves wouldn't cause any trouble." Bern didn't know why he continued.

"It's not the elves we would be concerned with. The men of Castalia can be quite aggressive when they want to be, not to mention the undeniable rivalry between the dwarves and the elves. Even if we could trust the men of Castalia there is no way we could trust the dwarves."

Dorn didn't even bother to deny the fact. He had grown used to travelling with elves, but he knew well the animosity between the two races. He wished that he could explain to every dwarf what he had learned on his journey, but he didn't think anyone would really believe him and some wouldn't even contemplate the truth.

"Of course. It's safer for them to be where they are most comfortable. There's no point in them making sacrifices whilst the rest of the army is having fun." Bern repressed the urge to smile. It would to be a token gesture anyway. "Now why is it you are so glum?"

Jarwe and Sorrell gave each other worried glances. It seemed neither of them wanted to speak. In the end it was Wojtek who spoke on behalf of his leader.

"We haven't seen Delbert since the night of the coronation." He didn't sound happy about having to give the news.

"We went to a secret tavern down a back alley in the Inner City." Jarwe felt he should be the one to explain. "We left in the wee hours of the morning, but Delbert insisted that he wanted to stay. He looked like he was having fun so we didn't think anything of it."

"Have you checked the tavern to see if anyone knows where he went? I'm sure someone must have seen him leave." With all the people in the city, especially on the first night of celebrations, there was a good chance that no one would have noticed him.

Sorrell and Jarwe looked at each other with worried expressions. It was clear that neither of them wanted to speak. Bern knew he wasn't going to like what he was about to hear. He felt like snapping at them, but decided to just wait for one of them to respond.

"We tried," Sorrell finally spoke. "When we realised he had not returned in over a day Jarwe and I both scoured the city. No matter where we looked we couldn't find the alley or the tavern. We asked everyone we saw and no one knew of a secret tavern down a back alley."

"Well he has to be somewhere. He can't have just disappeared." Bern kept his voice calm. He couldn't believe that Delbert had deserted, but what other explanation could there be? A day or two's absence was understandable, but it had been four. "What are you doing to find him now?"

"We have soldiers looking throughout the city. They have a drawing of him that they are showing people." Sorrell sounded very nervous.

"Then I am sure he will turn up somewhere." Bern tried to sound as confident as possible, although deep down he was worried. Delbert had played a vital role in the Alliance since joining the army. Bern looked for and respected his opinion and he also considered him to be a friend. Something wasn't right, but there were more important matters for him to attend to. "Now we need to prepare to leave. We head to Remidel as soon as the festivities are over. That gives us another three days, including this one." There was no question, but the others knew what he was asking.

"The soldiers have all returned from the city, at least those who aren't going to end up in the brig for a couple of days." Wojtek read from a report in front of him. "The soldiers were all told they could go and have a good time, but they must have returned by now. We estimate that some will remain in the city, even after we have gone. Those who have drunk too much and return in the next couple of days will be punished,"

Wojtek almost whispered the last comment with the thought of Delbert still fresh in their minds.

"Our supplies are starting to get low." Duke Hadar also read from a report. "It is estimated that we only have another week of food, we can maybe stretch another couple of days if we ration out tighter portions." They hadn't been stingy with their food since arriving at Castalia, but they also hadn't been wasteful. Bern had said that whilst they had been able to relax they should enjoy themselves. The final battle was coming soon.

"I have made a deal for supplies with the High Chancellor. Food and other rations will be arriving when the Week of Celebration is over," Bern explained.

"We will already be on the move before our supplies are replenished," Wojtek spoke as if Bern hadn't already realised the fact.

"It will take more than a day for the entire army to be on the move," Bern spoke as if he was speaking to a child. It was petty, but he needed to reinforce to the others that he knew what he was doing. It seemed that some of them were beginning to doubt his ability to lead. "When the celebrations are over the High Chancellor has promised to start restocking our supplies straight away. We will get what we need before we run out." Bern reassured them. "He has also pledged soldiers to join our cause. They will also start mobilizing when the celebrations are over."

Bern thought the news would have been taken well amongst the other commanders.

"That is too late general," Jarwe spoke first before his sentiments were echoed throughout the tent. "We need the soldiers now so they are ready to move with us."

"There will be time." Bern tried to reassure them. "They will reach us before we reach Remidel."

"That is not the only point. They need time to assimilate themselves into the army before we go to war. If, and I pray to the God Kings that we don't have to, but if we have to go to war against the soldiers of Remidia then we are going to need them to be able to work with the rest of the army. I know how difficult it can be joining a new army," Jarwe explained. "And the Remidel army is very good at defending their walls." Jarwe was the General of the Remidian Army, a position he had held for almost a decade, and no one doubted him.

"Then what would you suggest?" Bern asked.

"We hold the army back for a couple of days until we have more supplies and some of the soldiers to arrive," Jarwe retorted.

It seemed simple enough to those in the room. Even Bern couldn't deny the logic, but that didn't change the fact that they would be leaving at dawn in two day's time. There was nothing else he could do. He could feel the roar of the prophecy all over his body. Even the mention of staying longer intensified the feeling. They would be leaving as planned and there was nothing he could do about it.

"That would make sense, but we can't stay any longer. We have already stayed too long." "The final battle is looming and we have to be on our way."

"This is what I don't understand." Everyone looked to Hadar, who had so far remained quiet. "If we are heading for the battle that we thought we were going to have in Avalon, then why don't we just return. Surely Nyrra will have his army meet us there?" It was a legitimate question. Bern only hoped he could explain.

"Now we know that the original battle was a ruse. It was a trick to give the Evil One more time to plan his attack. Now we have to follow the prophecy, and that is leading us to Remidel." That wasn't the only reason, but it seemed like the best place to start. "Besides that we can't leave Remidel to rot. It is in the control of a Dark Knight and that isn't a pleasant thought. I'm sure if you speak to half the soldiers in the Enteroite army they will tell you how hard it is." Bern continued.

"Bern is right," Jarwe spoke. "We can't leave Remidel to rot. We have rescued Kiarome, Jarrat and Castalia, taking us on a journey further and further away from Avalon. My land is now in danger and we need to free it from the Evil One's yolk."

"What about Hondin Lel?" Duke Hadar snapped.

"We've had no intelligence from Lel Dinion telling us there is a Dark Knight in command. It makes sense to stick with what we know," Jarwe returned.

Hadar wasn't going to be simply brushed aside. He knew what Jarwe said made sense, but that didn't change the feeling deep in his stomach. Something was far from right in his homeland and he wanted to find out what it was. The Evil One had encroached on his land, Count Kerwin had been a prime example of that. He was sure there were more of his kind scattered around Hondin Lel just waiting for an opportunity to strike. Now was that time. The Alliance was pretty much as far away as it could be and was heading in a different direction. If the Evil One was ever planning an attack on his homeland then now would be his perfect opportunity.

"Remember King Lisle was sending his army towards Avalon to assist the Alliance and they never arrived. The reports we have received have been all over the place, but it seemed they made it half way from Lel Dinion before they turned around and returned home. Something is not right. There was no reason for Lisle to have his army return unless the Evil One was involved."

That did make sense, but it still did nothing to change Bern's mind. He knew their path had to lead them towards Remidel. Once they had freed the capital he had no idea where they were going. If Lel Dinion was indeed under the control of a Dark Knight then he was sure that would be their next destination. If that was not the case then it would be off to Avalon for the real battle with Nyrra. As much as it was inevitable it was something that Bern would be quite happy to put off for the rest of his life.

"The reports from Lel Dinion have been sketchy at best." Bern knew he had to put a stop to Hadar's objections. Even though most of the Hondin Lel soldiers weren't in the Alliance there were still a good portion who were loyal to the duke. The last thing he needed was rumours reaching them that Hondin Lel was being ignored. "If there is a Dark Knight in the capital then they have yet to make their move." Bern knew his reasoning was thin at best. "Right now we need to fight the battle in front of us. We know that there is a Dark Knight in command of Remidel and that is the direction we need to take."

"How do we know for sure?" Hadar wasn't going to be appeased so easily. "There are just as many reports out of Remidel saying that everything is fine. Why should we treat Remidel with preference over Lel Dinion?"

"Why should we treat Lel Dinion with preference over Remidel?" Jarwe boomed. He could understand Duke Hadar's concern for his homeland, but he wasn't going to listen to him badmouth his own. "It makes sense for us to travel to Remidel."

"Why? Why doesn't it make sense?" Hadar interrupted, his voice rising with each word.

Bern let out a sigh. "Enough!" he boomed as Jarwe was about to continue. "This is getting us nowhere. For those who don't already feel the pull of the prophecy..." He paused and looked around the table. As much as he had not wanted to mention the prophecy he knew he had little choice. "You must know that it is calling us to Remidel. There is no other course we can take. This is the direction we must go and this is the direction I will lead the army."

The tent went suddenly very quiet when Bern finished his little tirade. They had not been expecting such a response. His face had turned a lighter shade of red when he had finished.

It was clear that there was no arguing with him. The decision had been made and that was final.

"Very well general, it is your army to lead. We are just here to advise you," Hadar spoke formally, although there was a hint of sarcasm in his voice.

Bern let the comment slide. He didn't feel the need to put Hadar back in his place. It seemed as though the situation had been resolved and that was enough for him. Now it was time to get organised. The army had to be ready to march.

The command group spent the rest of the morning and into the early afternoon discussing the best way to distribute the incoming supplies. They also discussed the best way to get the army on the move.

The next two days were spent in much the same manner. As much as there was a lot of paperwork to shuffle he was glad for the company. His accommodation wasn't as nice as his apartment in the Grand Cathedral, but he wouldn't trade it for the world. It seemed that everyone had accepted Bern's decision on face value and didn't read any more into it. He was glad about that. It would have been much more uncomfortable if Hadar was still sulking.

On the morning of the last day of the festival the army was finally ready to march. The first line left at daybreak and it would take another three days before the army was completely on the move. This was a deliberate tactic to allow the Castalial army time to catch up.

The supplies promised by the High Chancellor had slowly started to arrive and there was now enough to keep them going until they reached Remidel. Once the celebrations were finally over the supplies would start arriving much quicker. It would take a little longer for the soldiers to be mobilised and then it would take a few days to get them ready to move. At best it would be another week before the Castalial army started following them, but he doubted it would happen that quickly.

The problem of timing weighed heavily on Bern when he had a moment to himself. In the end he realised that stressing about things wasn't going to help. For the moment he had done all that he could.

"The army is on the move." Sorrell read the report as they ate their breakfast in the command tent.

"Very good," Bern replied. "Things are starting to move forward. We need to be leaving ourselves by midday. With that in mind has anyone heard from Delbert?"

There was a moment of silence. It seemed as though everyone was suddenly busy eating. Bern scowled as he looked around the table. It wasn't a great sign that no one wanted to speak. Before Jarwe finally said something he already knew the answer.

"Those who were out looking for him were told to return before nightfall of the last night of celebration. I hate to say it, but if he hasn't returned by now then I don't think he will. He's not the only soldier to be swept up in the majesty of the kingdom. I know it's disappointing, but we just have to accept the fact he's no longer with us." Jarwe spoke quickly, trying to get the words out as fast as he could.

"He will need to found for a court marshal. Desertion is a serious offense." Wojtek wasn't so diplomatic.

Bern couldn't accept that. Although he had not known Delbert for too long, he knew he wouldn't desert. He was loyal to Bern and the Alliance, that was something he was sure of. No matter what the others said he wasn't going to give up on a man he considered to be his friend as well as a valued member of the army.

"Call in his little group of soldiers." The bandits were now soldiers under Delbert's command. They had also played a pivotal role in liberating the city and Bern wasn't going to easily forget that. "We're not going to just leave him here. If he hasn't returned from the city then he is in trouble. All I can hope is that it isn't too late."

The others looked at each other. No one wanted to be the one to tell him that there was little point in continuing the search. But if he didn't want to let it go then there was nothing they could do about it. No one wanted to give up on Delbert, but they had to accept the facts. If Delbert had not returned on his own by now he wasn't coming back. They'd had soldiers scouring the city ever since they realised he was missing and there was no sign of him. Wherever he was he was keeping well hidden.

"Private Horst, reporting for duty," the ex-bandit saluted when he entered the tent. With the absence of Delbert he was the highest ranked in their little group.

"Corporal Delbert still hasn't returned from the city?" It was as much a statement as it was a question.

"No sir!" Horst paused. "To be honest general we are concerned for his safety. It's not like Delbert just to disappear and not say anything. I knew him when he was living in king's Rest and he would never go anywhere without telling someone. Normally it would be his wife, but when she wasn't around he would tell a neighbour," Horst explained, hoping that he wasn't overstepping his mark.

"That's exactly what I thought." Bern looked accusingly around the table when he paused. "Until he returns you are corporal of your small battalion." Bern quickly offered the promotion.

"Thank you, general, but I can't accept. Delbert is the leader of our group, it wouldn't be right for me to take command." Horst tried his best not to sound ungrateful.

"I appreciate your concern, but you need a leader and for the meantime that is you. If you don't want to be in command then that should give you all the extra motivation you need to find Delbert. No one in the army knows him better than you and the other ex-bandits, so I am going to leave you behind to find him, and when you do hurry back to join the Alliance. I have a feeling we are going to need you before this is all over." Bern spoke with leadership in his voice. No one could doubt his plan, even if they didn't believe it was going to be of any use.

Horst saluted proudly. He couldn't deny the general. He wanted Delbert back as much as anyone, but until that time he would be proud to fill the role. All he could do was hope that it wouldn't be for long.

"Very well," Bern started. "Now that is put to bed what is the next issue?"

"I think we are all good now general. Your horse is being prepared and I'm sure it will lift the soldiers' spirits if they see their leader riding at the front of the line," Wojtek suggested.

Bern knew he was right. It was time for them to start the journey towards Remidel. For better or for worse, before long he would have to face another of the Dark Knights. This time he would be much more prepared.

***

Delbert slowly woke. It was dark and he was lying on a cold, stone surface. Trying to stand he realised that his arms and legs were bound. He struggled for a moment before giving up. His bonds were too tight and no amount of struggling was going to free him. Panic filled his body as he tried to remember what had happened. His mind felt like it was covered with a thick fog. The back of his head was aching, but he knew that wasn't the cause of his disorientation. He tried to call out before he realised that a thick gag was stuffed into his mouth and the darkness was due to a blindfold. He could neither see nor speak. All he could do was listen and try and gauge his surroundings.

There was little doubt that he was in a cell of some description. As he concentrated he could hear that he wasn't alone. There were others trying to speak, but all he could hear was muffled noises. It was clear that the others had also been gagged. It was a strange situation. Why was he in a prison cell and why was he bound and gagged? It didn't make any sense to him. He could hear the others struggling with their own bonds. He wanted to tell them to relax, but they wouldn't understand him through his gag.

Slowly the events of the previous night returned to him. He knew something wasn't right. He knew it from the moment they followed that woman down the alley. The others wouldn't listen to him and now it was he who was paying the price. Once the initial panic wore off he was able to think a little clearer. He had been swept up in a sting to capture the Evil One's worshippers. It was an easy mistake to make. He was in the wrong place at the wrong time. When he had a chance to defend himself they would see that he was not a traitor and was in fact doing all he could to defeat the enemy.

That last thought brought him a moment of peace. It would only be a matter of time before he was back with the army. He would learn from his mistakes. Next time he didn't trust a situation he would not be led astray.

Before long he heard a door open and a number of men enter the room. There were more than one set of footsteps, but he couldn't work out how many.

"That one!" a gruff voice barked. "And that one!" With each call Delbert could hear a body being lifted from the ground. He remained perfectly still and listened intently to try and work out what was happening.

The voice picked out five people before they left the room. It seemed as though those who had been struggling for freedom were the ones taken first. That was a good sign. It seemed they were looking for those who had clearly regained consciousness. He would know for next time to make some movement and it would be his time to be freed.

It could have been five minutes or five days before someone entered the cell again. In his limited sensory state Delbert had lost all track of time. All he could do was listen and wait. Slowly he heard others wake in the cell and like everyone before them they struggled to break free. The only way he could tell that pastime had passed was by the feeling of hunger in his stomach. When he woke he had felt sick, but not hungry.

When he heard the guards return and the cell door open Delbert started struggling. If they were only taking five at a time then he wanted to be one of them.

"Take that one!" said the same voice as before. "And what do we have here?" the voice moved closer and Delbert felt as though it was coming from directly above him. "Looks like this one can't wait to hang from the gibbet." That comment brought silence to the cell, apart from Delbert who continued to struggle. He knew he was safe, so the threat meant nothing to him. "Well let's not keep him waiting a moment longer."

Delbert felt two strong pair of hands grab him by the arms and lift him to his feet. Even in the upright position there was no way for him to move, his legs were bound too tightly together even to shuffle forward. The men continued to drag him from the cell.

They passed through a number of doors before Delbert felt a hot breath of air hit his face. A small amount of light made its way through his blindfold and he knew he was now outside. The air was strangely still and wherever he was now was unsettlingly quiet. If he was standing trial with others from the tavern then he figured there would be noises around him.

Surely they would be trying people as quickly as they could. Suddenly a bad feeling entered his body and he felt as though he would empty his stomach.

The floor felt dusty underneath. He didn't know why, but he felt as though he was in a courtyard. It might have been the excessive heat and lack of wind. The air around him felt stale and stagnate, then the bad feeling turned to dread. Something wasn't right. The situation wasn't at all what he had been expecting.

The two men dragged him up a small flight of stairs and onto a small platform. Delbert hoped it was where he could plead his case. That thought completely left his mind when he felt a noose being placed around his neck. Now he knew for sure that things weren't right. It was customary for a trial to be held before being led to the gibbet.

When he was in place the two men let him go. The panic that filled his body was almost overwhelming. He tried to calm himself through controlled breathing, but in the heat and with the gag it was almost impossible. He had to get control of himself. The situation was much worse than he had originally thought and he needed all his wits to get out if it. That thought made him suddenly feel very calm. He felt like he was on the edge of a storm; the calm cool breeze right before all hell broke loose.

As he senses returned he realised there was a man to his left. He could hear the whimpering through his gag. The man had obviously lost all hope and was preparing for his death. Then he heard another man being dragged onto the gibbet. He realised that there were only two more to go. Whatever he was going to do he needed to do it before that happened.

With the bonds still securely tied around his arms and legs there were nothing he could do, no matter how hard he tried. Even if he did manage to free himself there was no guarantee that he would have enough time to convince his captors that he was innocent.

The last two men came into place quicker than he had hoped. His heart was racing and he was out of ideas. Until he was unbound, if he was unbound, there was nothing he could do.

When all the men were in place a guard walked behind them a pulled the blindfolds from their heads. At first Delbert had to shut his eyes and the sunlight seared them. After blinking a few times he was able to look at his surroundings. As he had guessed there were four other men on the giblet with him. Their eyes were wide with fear and Delbert doubted they saw what he saw.

They were in a small courtyard surrounded by high stone walls. At the far end a balcony was cut into the wall about half way up. Three men dressed in the armour of the Holy Guard stood, watching the men below. Although it was hard to see it looked to Delbert that they all wore evil grins. He didn't think that was a good sign at all.

"You stand accused of High Treason. You were caught worshipping the Evil One, he who is a scourge on the Seven Kingdoms, and performing illicit acts. How do you plead?" one of the guards boomed. His voice resonated around the courtyard.

Delbert struggled to be heard through his gag, as with the four other men. All that could be heard was muffled groans. No one could make any words pass through their thick gags. Delbert could now feel all hope of survival slip away. It seemed as though the trial was just for show. They had all been convicted before the trial even began.

Realising that trying to plead his case was fruitless Delbert stopped thrashing around. Instead he stared hard at the man who was accusing him. He could only hope that would convince the guard that Delbert wasn't like the rest of them. Suddenly his mind went blank. He had one thought and that was reaching the guard. There was a lot more he had to do to defeat the Evil One and he wasn't going to die in such a manner.

Unfortunately the Holy Guard wasn't paying any attention to him. He was more focused on the other four who were writhing, trying in vain to break their bonds, and trying to scream through their gags. He didn't even notice that Delbert had stopped straining and remained calm. If he had then he might have questioned his next order.

"It seems no one wants to defend themselves!" his voice boomed which brought a round of laughter from his two companions. "Very well. For the crime of high treason I sentence you to death." Those words brought the dread back to Delbert's heart.

The Holy Guard raised his arm, waited for a couple of seconds, and then lowered it. Suddenly the floor disappeared from beneath Delbert and he dropped two feet. The last thing he heard was a loud snap followed by darkness.

Chapter 17: An Army on the Move

Bern had to admit he was grateful to be back in the saddle. It had been too long since he had been on the back of his stallion. He felt more in control than he had in a long time. Court politics had never been something he had been good at, that was one of the reasons he was just a simple farmer back home. He had never got himself involved in the local council, even when their decision directly related to him. All he could do was trust that they would do the right thing in the long run. Despite his aversion he had managed quite well, although he wasn't sure how much of it had been him and how much had been the entity and the prophecy working on his behalf.

It wasn't until the midday sun was high in the sky before Bern was able to leave the campsite. He rode out with Hulkan, who had returned to the group late in the morning; Dorn and Sorrell. Jarwe, Sorrell's advisor Wojtek and Duke Hadar remained behind to make sure everything went to plan. At first Bern was dubious about leaving Jarwe and Hadar behind after their argument, but they assured him they had reconciled. Bern's decision was final and fighting over the fact would achieve nothing.

As usual the two dwarves looked very uncomfortable on horseback. As much as they would prefer to be on foot it was customary for the leaders to ride, not run, at the head of the army. Bern didn't really care, but the others had insisted. Sorrell looked just as pleased as Bern to be on the road again. He sat proudly on his horse, if nothing else, leading an example for the soldiers behind him.

It wasn't long before they passed the forest where the elves had been staying. As they approached the edge of the forest there were no clues that it contained an army of elves, in fact two armies. That made Bern nervous. He knew they were on the same side, but he suddenly felt uncomfortable.

"Those trees don't look very friendly, do they?" Hulkan kept his voice low.

Hulkan and Dorn rode with Bern to meet the elves, leaving Sorrell at the head of the army.

"Let's just get this over and done with." Bern wasn't in the mood for small talk. He felt very nervous as he passed under the first of the trees.

There was something very unsettling about the closeness of the forest. He wondered if it was the elves or the forest itself that made them all feel so uncomfortable. Even the horses didn't seem happy. The forest itself seemed still, as if it was holding its breath, waiting to see what was about to happen.

"You can lower your arrows." Bern knew there were elves in the trees. "We are friends and mean you know harm."

Bern continued to ride as he called out to the forest. Dorn and Hulkan looked around frantically trying to find who he was taking to, but to no avail. The fact that Bern didn't seem troubled did nothing to ease their nerves.

"Who are you?" a voice called.

"And what are you doing here?" another voice called out.

Bern sighed loudly. Both Orric and Kilean knew that Bern would we arriving that day. He couldn't work out why the scouts in the trees didn't know who he was.

"I am General Bern and I am here to see Orric." Bern announced at the top of his voice. He made a point to sound very disconcerted.

His response was met by silence. He assumed that meant they were on the right path. As much as he never saw the elves he knew they were still there, watching and waiting for them to make a mistake. Bern didn't know if it was his presence or the dwarves that had them riled. Maybe it was just the fact that they would have to leave the forest again that had upset them.

It wasn't long before they came across the main camp of the elves. Bern was surprised that they had put so much together. Instead of the tents they used in the Alliance the elves had small huts. In the small amount of time they had been there they had built a makeshift village. Bern had to wonder if they had built it or if in fact it had already been built in the past. Either way it was an impressive set up.

"It's time to move Orric!" Bern dismounted before he spoke to the leader of the elves. Lord Orric was the eldest elf still alive and the most respected. Even the Northern Elves had a great respect for him, even if they didn't necessarily agree with him.

"I know. We have packed up what we need and we are ready to go," there were no peasantries. It was straight down to business.

"How are the Southern Elves fitting in with your elves?" Bern figured there was some time for discussion as he watched the elves rush around them making their final preparations.

Orric looked around, as if checking to see if anyone was listening. "The assimilation has been painless. It was only a matter of time before the lost ones returned home." He sounded sad.

Bern, himself, never knew the story of the elves, but the memories of the entity crept into his reality. Although the details were sketchy he knew that those now known as the Southern Elves, or the Lost Ones, had once been part of the Northern Elves. Without having the memory in his head he knew that the prophecy was somehow involved, many years before it really became apparent.

"But it is good to have those who were once lost to us return." Orric added on a brighter note.

"I wish I could give you longer to catch up on lost times, but we need to be on the move." Bern cut to the chase. "The Evil One is nearly ready to strike. One of his Dark Knights is now in command of Remidel."

"Yes, that is indeed disturbing news." Orric looked like he was deep in thought. "So that means there is only one more to go."

Although Bern wasn't exactly sure what he meant he nodded his agreement anyway. There was little time for small talk. The army was still on the march and he didn't want the elves to get too far behind. The army was going to be segregated enough as it was.

"How long until you think you will be ready to join the army?" Bern asked, changing the subject.

"We were prepared for your arrival today, but we figured it would be later. I think another two hours should see us packed and ready to leave."

That wasn't exactly what Bern had in mind, but he guessed it could have been worse. It would take the army a good hour or two to pass the wood anyway, so the elves wouldn't be too far behind. With a little luck they would join the tail end of the first group of soldiers. Either way there was nothing he could do about it.

"Let's get back to the army," Hulkan suggested nervously.

Bern had to admit that he wasn't completely comfortable in the trees. It was as if something was watching him, with hatred in its mind. There was nothing left for them to do and he was looking forward to being back in the open air.

"Would you like to have something to eat whilst you wait?" Orric asked. "It would be good to catch up on what I've missed since being separated from the army."

Bern's shoulders dropped slightly before he realised what he was doing. The last thing he wanted to do was offend Orric. He was sure that he was just being silly and there was nothing wrong with the forest. The elves had been residing under the trees for the last week and nothing had happened to them. He looked at Hulkan and Dorn and the two dwarves didn't look happy with the prospect. They hoped Bern would refuse. There would be plenty of time to discuss matters at the end of the day.

"Of course." Bern finally said.

Orric led them to a small clearing with a fire smouldering in the middle. The elf stoked the fire and the sat on the ground. He offered the others to sit as they were still standing. Bern sat down straight away, but the dwarves took their time. It was obvious that they were still very uncomfortable.

"Don't be afraid of the trees. They will behave themselves whilst we are here?" Orric explained. "Please, be seated."

The two dwarves weren't sure what that meant and it did little to ease their nerves. If it wasn't rude then they would have remained standing. Inevitably they sat and hoped they didn't need to linger too long.

Bern explained as best and as briefly as he could what had been happening in Castalia since the elves had left. Orric simply sat and listened, showing no sign of emotion at all. At one point Bern wasn't even sure if he was still listening, but he continued on with his story nevertheless.

"It's good hear that Castalia has an honourable leader at long last," Orric replied when Bern had finished. "It has been a long time since that has happened. Maybe when this is all over the elves and Castalia can trade again."

"I wouldn't hold your breath on that one," Hulkan said. "Although some have forgiven the crimes of the past there is still a bad feeling amongst the Guild towards the elves. No matter how honourable the new High Chancellor is he can't go against the will of the Guild."

"Don't be too surprised if his does." Orric took the bait. "The Guild puts too much emphasis on the job they do. When it's said and done there are many more that could take its place if they decided to leave. As I'm sure your companion will tell you. I have no doubt those dwarves who mine in the southern mountains of the Cloumid Mountain range would fall over themselves to take over the contract in Castalia."

Hulkan didn't even bother looking at Dorn, there was no need. Dorn couldn't deny that there was some truth in Orric's words. Mining for ore in the mountain gave a good return, but that seemed to pale in comparison to the mining of sand for glass and sandstone. The gems they found in the mountains, rubies, sapphires, emeralds and many others couldn't gain the same price as the diamonds found in the mines of Castalia. Those dwarves made a decent trade, but there was little doubt they would trade it in for a better life.

"You have been hidden in your forest for a long time Orric. The life blood of the kingdom is in the work the dwarves do. There is a big difference between the Western Guild and the Mountain Guild. I don't think the transition would be quite as simple as you think," Hulkan returned.

Dorn really wanted to say something, but he also didn't want to get in the middle of the two. Orric remained calm, but Hulkan looked like he was ready to snatch up his axe and start fighting.

"This is getting us nowhere," Bern finally spoke before Orric had another chance to continue. "For the moment the entire conversation is irrelevant. We have many miles to travel and many battles to win before we can discuss who does what. I'm sure by the time this is all over the feuds of the past will be forgotten." Bern couldn't help himself. He continued quickly so nobody had a chance to voice their opinion. "I'm sure it is time we all got moving."

As if to confirm Bern's statement Pernian suddenly appeared at the back of the clearing. His appearance brought a sense of relief to everyone. No one really liked where the conversation was heading. Although Orric had remained the picture of calmness, he was starting to lose his temper with Hulkan.

"We're all ready to leave Lord Orric!" As there seemed to be a sufficient break in the conversation he didn't feel the need to wait for permission to speak. "Your horse is waiting for you."

"Let's be on our way then," Orric stood as he spoke.

There were no objections from the others sitting around the campfire. Everyone was keen to get out of the forest and back on the road. It was going to be a long journey to Remidel and sitting around wasn't going to get them there any faster. As much as no one wanted to rush headlong into another battle there were people in the capital suffering and the Alliance was their only hope.

Only a small proportion of the elven army were visible as they left the forest. Even when they knew who was there they still preferred to remain hidden. Bern thought it was odd, but he didn't want to question them. It was obvious they enjoyed the sanctity of the trees and he wasn't going to try and change that.

When they reached the edge of the forest they could see the back of the first group of the Alliance on the horizon. They had moved further than Bern had expected. If he had planned ahead he would have had more soldiers leave in the first wave. Thankfully it wouldn't take long for them to catch up. It was only two hours before dusk and the army would soon stop to make camp.

"The second wave will be on the move before dawn," Sorrell explained when they camped for the night. "We made good distance today, but it won't be long before the rest of the army reaches us."

Bern felt a little better. He and the other members of the command group had quickly ridden to the front of the army once they were out of the forest. It would still take another hour for the elves to reach the back of the army. They reached the front just as they were starting to set camp for the night making the effort somewhat pointless.

"Each wave of the army will break camp and be on the move before dawn. That way we should all be together when we reach Remidel," Sorrell continued.

"Very good. We need to be all together when we reach our target. I fear the Dark Knight will not let us linger long. We'll need to strike fast if we're going to be successful," Bern added.

"You don't think there'll be a chance to parley?" Even as the words came out of Dorn's mouth he knew the answer.

"Dark Knights will never parley," Orric was the first one to speak. "They will see the city burn to the ground before they surrender. A swift attack is the right course of action."

"General Jarwe might disagree with you when you start bombarding his city," Hulkan added. "We were able to take Castalia with limited damage."

"We also had to throw buildings at Kiarome and destroyed a good portion of its outer wall," Sorell said. "We were fortunate that the Chosen One was able to destroy the Dark Knight before we had to enter into battle."

That was something that they had all forgotten about. Kiarome seemed like a lifetime away, but it was now very pertinent. If it wasn't for Alaric then there was no telling how things would have ended up. Bern knew, even though the entity was a part of him, he still wasn't strong enough to defeat a Dark Knight by himself. Even though his strength had grown with the strength of the entity it still wouldn't be enough. He had six of the seven wizards, but he had to admit that Hulkan and Sorrell were right. There was little chance of getting away without destroying the city, one way or the other. If they waited then the Dark Knight would send the Remidel army out to battle, if not they would have to destroy the walls and raid the city. Bern didn't know which was the better option.

"We will do what we must to defeat the enemy. If we can avoid hurting Remidel and its people than all the better. Remember this is my kingdom, my people. I don't want to see anyone getting hurt, but this is war. Cities are destroyed in war and people die. There is nothing we can do about that. The best we can hope for is victory and a better life for the future." Although Bern wasn't sure the speech was necessary it did seem appropriate.

That was enough to change the conversation. No one really wanted to think about the task ahead of them. There would be plenty of time for planning in the days ahead. It was going to be a long march to the capital.

The army was slow to start in the morning, and once they were on the road they weren't travelling as quickly as they had the day before.

This upset Bern. Every hour or so he looked behind to see the army half a mile behind them.

"You can't have it both ways general," Pernian said when they stopped for the midday meal.

"I know, I know. It's just at this pace it's going to take us over a month to reach the city." Bern sighed.

"We can get the soldiers moving quicker if you like?" Sorrell half told half asked.

"That would defeat the purpose of moving the army slowly out of Castalia and waiting for the Castalial army to join us." Bern knew he was between a rock and a hard place. There was nothing he could do to speed things along.

"Then what would you like from us?" Orric asked the impossible question.

Bern didn't respond. He was in a foul enough mood and he didn't need to be told the obvious. There was nothing they could do to appease him and he knew it. He ate the rest of his meal in silence only vaguely listening to the reports of the supplies coming in from Castalia.

As soon as he finished eating he ordered them to be on the move. If they were going to march slowly then they could march early. He knew it was silly, but it did appease him slightly. The sooner they started the sooner they could camp for the night. Bern wanted nothing more than the day to be over.

It took another five days for the last wave of the soldiers to catch up with the first. Bern was a lot happier when the army was together. Now it was just a matter of waiting for the rest of the Castalial army to join them. Nearly half the army had joined the Alliance and it was estimated that it would take another five days for the rest of them and supplies to arrive. It was longer than Bern had hoped, but it was still satisfactory.

Captain Elyas and Corporal Horace joined the command group from the Castalial army. The first night they arrived they just sat and listened, but on the second night they had more to say.

Elyas was coming to the end of his military life with the forced retirement age in Castalia being fifty. His strong physique and black hair belied his true age. There was nothing that would tell anyone he should be retiring any time soon.

Horace was Elyas' second in command and had grown up through the army under his command. Only just forty years of age he held the same strength as his mentor. There was no doubt the two were well seasoned soldiers and would be an asset to the command group.

"I don't think an assault on Remidel is such a good idea," Elyas stated as they discussed their plan on reaching the capital. Horace nodded his agreement.

"I don't see how we have any other option." Surprisingly it was Jarwe who spoke. He had joined the front of the line late in the morning of the fifth day. "If we wait then we risk an open skirmish with the forces of Remidel."

"I have to agree with Jarwe," Sorrell spoke next. "We need to breach the outer walls and make a rush for the palace. If we can kill the Dark Knight then we can avoid a lot of pointless death."

There was a moment of uncomfortable silence.

"And once we breech the outer wall how are we supposed to get into the palace. The palace walls might not be as strong as the outer walls, but we can't just walk through them." Elyas would not be dissuaded.

"That will be a little trickier, but we have a plan for that." Jarwe looked towards the six wizards who were sitting on their own table.

The Council of Wizards had kept to themselves since leaving Castalia. Much to the chagrin of the command group they had accosted a rather large tent to make their base, as well as a number of servants to erect and dismantle it and tend to their needs. As long as they stayed away, Bern could let those things slide. Now they turned up to their evening meeting without much of an explanation. All Minerva said was they wanted to make sure the command group didn't do anything to condemn the Seven Kingdoms.

"And by that look I assume you need our assistance with something?" Drake asked drolly.

Suddenly Jarwe felt very nervous. The arrival of the council had made everyone uncomfortable, but since they hadn't spoken they had almost been forgotten. Now Jarwe wasn't so sure he wanted to speak the words they had gone over the past few nights. It had been planned that Bern would speak to the council once they had figured out the finer details. Now it seemed that Jarwe had put his foot in his mouth. He looked at Bern who seemed to be busy looking over a number of documents, although Jarwe was sure he was still listening intently.

"We haven't figured everything out yet, but we were hoping if we were able to breech the outer wall then you would be able to get us into the palace." Jarwe spoke slowly, making sure of every word.

"And exactly how do you propose we get you into the palace?" Brielle sneered as she spoke. "It has been a long time since I have been to Remidel, but from memory those walls are made out of solid stone."

The question was met with silence again. Jarwe had already said too much and wasn't about to continue. Bern made a show of casually sorting the paperwork in front of him. He knew that everyone was waiting for him to speak.

"The Council of Wizards is renowned for its knowledge and power. I believe that the Chosen One petitioned you to our aid?" He paused, not expecting an answer to his rhetorical question. "If this is the case then we implore you to share your knowledge and assist us in taking Remidel and freeing it from the grasp of the Dark Knight who oppresses it."

Again there was silence in the tent as Bern finished speaking. None of the wizards had been expecting such words. In the end it was Gwydion who spoke.

"You speak true General Bern. We were sent here to help and help we shall, but there are rules we abide by and we shall not be breaking them." It was a start, but his words seemed twisted. Bern wished he could just get a straight answer from them. There were times for riddles, but this wasn't one of them. "We have sworn not to do damage to the cities of the kingdoms of men. It is these rules that have allowed us to walk freely in these kingdoms."

"You have not walked in the kingdoms of men for over a century. Times have changed and with them so must the rules you have lived by. Evil has taken this kingdom and you must break your rules in order to save it." Bern wasn't going to be put off.

"Who are you to speak to us in such manner?" Althea snapped. "You will show us respect or else I will turn you into a toad. Let's see how you like that."

"Be calm Althea, this is no time for threats," Gwydion said.

"And idle threats at that," Bern's voice changed. "You will learn your place wizard." The tension in the room was palpable. "The plan has not been set, but if you are asked to help then you will."

Althea looked as though she was going to explode. No one had ever spoken to her such a manner. They had accepted Alaric for what he was, a man of power, power they had never seen before. She could understand their subservience to him, but to give that same respect to a simple man. Well, that was not acceptable.

"I think we have said enough this evening," Gwydion spoke again before Althea had a chance to burst. "We shall convene and discuss the matter amongst ourselves. There is much to think about."

With that the six wizards took their leave. Everyone remained silent until they left the tent.

"Are you sure that was wise general?" Sorrell asked.

"There is little time to pander to their sensitive egos." His voice returned to normal. "Given a chance they could spend a thousand years making their decision. They needed a push and that's exactly what I gave them. The sooner they realise who is in command of this army the better."

No one could dispute his words. Everyone was glad that the Wizards had left the tent. If nothing else they had pre-empted a conversation that they needed to have.

"Do you think they are going to help us?" Hulkan asked.

"They will do what is required," Bern replied.

"Don't be so sure," Orric warned. "I have known these wizards for a long time. They don't do anything by force. If they don't come up with the solution on their own there is a good chance they won't agree."

"That is a moot point at this stage. The wheels are in motion and speculation won't get us anywhere. I suggest that we adjourn for the evening and see what the morning brings," Jarwe suggested.

No one argued with that sentiment. No one really wanted to remain in the tent when there was little chance for any further discussion. The comments of Bern and the wizards were thick in their minds.

***

"Something has changed in him," Minerva spoke when they returned to their own tent.

"Don't be silly. He is a simple man and his arrogance is clear," Brielle disputed.

Even though they all knew there was someone or something residing inside Bern it seemed as though some of them had forgotten.

"He needs to be taken over my knee and shown proper respect. That is the best way to get naughty generals to behave." Althea added.

"Minerva is right. There is more to this general than meets the eye." Gwydion ignored their comments. "We need to be careful. I could also sense something in him." He paused in mid thought. "I don't know if it's this so called entity or something else..."

The others waited to see if he was going to finish his thought. They knew there was more, but he wasn't going to offer up the information lightly.

"You recognised something?" Ulman asked in his gruff voice.

"I don't know. When he snapped at Althea I thought I felt something familiar. It was only there for a fleeting moment and it wasn't strong enough for me to grasp." He paused again. "There is power in him. A great power. More than there should be."

"What does that mean?" Brielle snapped.

"I know we like to talk in riddles around other people in case they read too much into our words, but you can drop the pretence here." Althea didn't sound happy.

"Read between the lines Althea. Have you locked yourself up for so long that you have lost your wits?" Drake snapped at her. When she responded with a blank expression he continued. "There is something inside of Bern. Something has possessed his soul, something that shouldn't be there. That is where he is getting his power. This is indeed disturbing and unexpected news."

They all thought back to the meeting, trying to figure out what it was. Although not everyone agreed with Gwydion if what he was saying was true then it was very disturbing. It was bad enough that Alaric seemed to be stronger than they were, now there was a chance there was someone else. It seemed that they had shut themselves away from the rest of the Seven Kingdoms for too long.

"So what are we going to do about it?" Minerva asked the impossible question.

The question hung in the air as they all pondered it. It was time they made a decision. They had been sitting on the fence for too long. The Seven Kingdoms had moved on without them and not for the better. If they were going to succeed then they needed to take action.

"We need to impart ourselves on this little army," Drake started.

"We can no longer sit back and watch. Things have gone too far off track," Brielle added.

"The Seven Kingdoms is lost without our wisdom. We have to act quickly."

Gwydion couldn't believe what he was hearing. They truly had been on their Island for too long. He wished that Eldred was with them. He was the only one who had not forsaken the Seven Kingdoms. He would know the best course of action.

"I don't think we can leave General Bern alone anymore. We need to watch him carefully if we are going to figure out this conundrum." Drake quickly changed the subject.

That was something they all could all agree upon. They needed to figure out what was happening inside the general. The only way they could do that was to watch and listen.

"At the end of the day it should be easy enough." Gwydion decided it was time to speak. "But I don't think we should go to these meetings as a group. One at a time will make them more relaxed. If we all go then there is a good chance they will hold things back. Until they are comfortable with our presence I think that we need to tread lightly."

"That is ridiculous." Brielle snapped. "They need our help and we should make them see this."

"Be calm Brielle," Ulman's gruff voice commanded attention. "We can no longer force our will upon nations. We can't bully these people. We need to work together if we are going to succeed." Ulman's words brought a smile to Gwydion's face. Brielle had always been too full of her own power. She really needed to be taken down a peg. "I will ride with the general at the front of the army. I don't think that will look too out of place." In truth Ulman had been looking for an excuse to join the soldiers. In a previous life he had ridden into battle with his kingdom. It was more than one lifetime ago, but it was still in his blood.

"That is a very good idea. Until we have more information I think we should tread very lightly." Gwydion ended the conversation.

Not everyone in the tent was happy with their decision and Gwydion knew it. He would have to keep a close eye on both the army and the council. There was a good chance that things could turn ugly if he wasn't careful.

Chapter 18: Crossroads

The further they travelled towards Remidel the worse the weather became. Slowly clouds rolled in to cover the sky and the temperature gradually dropped. At first Bern liked the change. The heat of Castalia was unpleasant at best, but now things had turned around too much. On the morning of the tenth day, drops of rain started to fall. It wasn't a good sign of things to come and the army plodded on as best it could. As much as it never snowed so far south in the Kingdom of Remidia, Bern had a bad feeling there might be some to come. He knew Nyrra himself could affect the weather, but he was unsure of the Dark Knight's power. There were memories in his head, memories that weren't his, and they were sketchy at best. If someone was tampering with the weather then that meant they had already been discovered.

There had been many rumours floating around about the Evil One. None of them were confirmed, but Bern had to listen to them anyway. He knew Nyrra was wandering freely throughout the Seven Kingdoms. He also knew that he was searching for the Ruby Stone. That was the only thing that had his attention elsewhere and Bern was thankful for that. Some of the rumours stated that he had already found the stone and was roaming around laying waste to city after city. Bern was sure that wasn't true. If Nyrra had already found the Ruby Stone then they would already be destroyed. Some stated that it was in fact the Evil One who ruled in Remidel and not a Dark Knight. As much as that was plausible, Bern still doubted its validity. Wherever the Evil One was, Bern had to keep a wary eye out for signs of him. The last thing he wanted to do was to be too focused on the mission ahead of him to forget the big picture.

They had moved off the main highway once they started to reach the outskirts of civilization. It was decided that the small villages and towns wouldn't be able to handle the army the size of the Alliance passing through. As much as it would be hard to keep their movements a secret it was best to stay as far away from wandering eyes as they could. If they were spotted, it wouldn't be long before the rumours reached the capital..

Although the bulk of the army travelled around the towns a few scouts were sent out to gather information. There was little chance of getting any solid intelligence, but Bern wasn't going to waste the opportunity. Every now and then some small town gossip could hold useful information. He could also find out if the townsfolk knew of the army moving around them.

Bern sat alone in the command tent at the end of another eventless day. He had a pile of reports in front of him. At least the administration reports he could leave for one of his functionaries. There were more important matters for him to deal with than the running of the army. Two reports had come in from nearby towns early that afternoon. As much as he didn't think they would amount to anything he wanted to read them before the other commanders arrived. It was one of the few times he had to himself, outside of when he slept. It seemed like whenever he turned around one of the wizards was there. At first he thought nothing of it when Ulman joined them at the front of the line. He looked like he was built for war and suited to the role. He made a few little comments but seemed happy just to be there. At night Althea, then Brielle and then Drake joined them; always one at a time. They did little to disrupt the meeting so no one really took any notice. Now Bern was starting to become suspicious.

As he thought there was little pertinent information in the reports. There was one that Nyrra was hiding out in a farmhouse just out of town. Another said he was somewhere in the forests of Entero readying an attack on the capital. That one might have been true, but Bern doubted it. There was a rumour that a massive army was on the march towards the capital, but that was from a town drunk who none of the other residents believed it. At least that was something.

By the time he had finished shuffling the reports and filing them away the rest of the command group started to arrive. This time it was Minerva who joined them from the council. Given a chance Bern needed to get to the bottom of what they were up to, but that would have to wait for the meantime.

"By midday tomorrow we are going to reach the Remi River. There is no chance of the army passing, especially with all the rain we've had. Reports say the river is flowing at its peak. We have two options. There is a bridge ten leagues to the west or we can risk returning to the highway to cross it." Sorrell explained.

That was something the Bern had been thinking about all day. Travelling to the west would add at least a week to their journey, but with the current weather it could be much more. It would only take a day to return to the highway. It was a matter of risk verses reward. He didn't think they could afford the delay. They had managed to get so far without being discovered and he only hoped they could make it further.

"We have to use the highway. We can ill-afford to lose more time." Bern didn't sound overly confident.

"We have a plan to stop being discovered," by the way Jarwe spoke it sounded as though they had already come to the conclusion. "The reports we have received state the highway is relatively free of merchants these days. Apparently it's to do with new regulations coming from the capital. Anyway, we are going to send troops to both sides of the river and shut down the road."

"Can we do that given that it will take us almost a week to get the entire army over the river?" Bern didn't sound overly confident. "Won't the few merchants and travellers on the road be somewhat suspicious?"

"Apparently there have been some storms pass through this way in the last week. We block the highway under the premise that the bridge crossing the river has been destroyed due to the wild weather. That should give us the time to get the army across." Jarwe sounded rather proud of himself.

That sounded like a much better plan. Now Bern could see it working. If the bridge was down then no one would complain about the road block. They would have to find an alternative route if they were going to cross the river.

"Very well, it sounds like you have everything planned." Bern did his best not to sound upset. "We shall head for the highway in the morning and then across the bridge."

"If it makes you feel better I could destroy the bridge once we are all across." Minerva spoke for the first time.

"Thanks, but no. I don't think that would serve any purpose," Jarwe replied. "The week or so it'll take to get everyone across should be enough time to fix what would have needed fixing." It wasn't strictly true, but with enough men it would be possible and that's all that mattered.

Minerva seemed put out by Jarwe's comment, but thankfully she didn't say anything. She just sat and listened and waited for the next conversation.

"So once we cross the bridge we need the army to cut due west and follow the river for another two leagues before we head north again." Sorrell was looking over a map as he spoke. It seems to be the best course away from the highway once we cross the river."

That was something at least. Bern had a bad feeling that they were falling behind. Time was of the essence and it seemed as though it was slipping away. There was something else. Bern could feel a subtle tug in the back of his mind. He couldn't imagine what the prophecy was trying to tell him. He figured nothing would happen until they reached Remidel.

The rest of the evening was spent going over reports and discussing the distribution of supplies. The functionaries in charge of such things were called in to listen and very occasionally give their opinion. Now that the rest of the Castalial army and their supplies had arrived there was a lot more administration work. It was also vital that it was done properly. There would be no chance to restock their supplies until they had overcome the Dark Knight. If they ran out of food then they would be in grave trouble.

They left at first light for the bridge. The command group rode out ahead the make sure the road was clear. Again Ulman joined them for the day. Bern had hoped to be without his wizard chaperone, but it seemed that wouldn't be the case.

Bern kept a brisk pace on their horses, leaving the army behind. For some reason he felt as though he needed to reach the highway in a hurry. He could feel the tug of the prophecy growing stronger with each passing minute. It was all he could do to refrain from whipping his horse into a gallop.

It only took them two hours to reach the highway and then it was a only a short ride to the bridge crossing the Remi river.

"It looks as though the road is clear," Sorrell stated after they had been waiting for half an hour. "I think we can send word back to the army that it's safe to proceed.

Bern looked around nervously. Something wasn't right, but he couldn't figure out what it was. He had an uncontrollable urge to cross the river.

"Let's see what's on the other side," Bern suggested.

Jarwe and Wojtek left the group to return to the army leaving the rest of the command group and Ulman to follow Bern.

As soon as Bern's horse placed a hoof on the narrow stone and cobblestone bridge the back of his neck started to tingle. He instantly reined in his horse and signalled for the others to stay back.

"What's wrong?" Hadar asked.

"There is something wrong with the bridge. I think it's a trap." Bern could sense the nervousness from his horse underneath him. The last thing he needed was for it to bolt across the bridge. Gently stroking its mane, Bern tried to calm it. "Ulman! Can you sense anything?"

Ulman rode onto the bridge and stopped next to Bern. As much as Bern didn't think it was a good idea he didn't want to tell the wizard how to do his job.

"You're right. There is something strange with the bridge, but I don't think it's a trap. If it was then I'm sure those soldiers who moved on ahead to block the road would have been trapped. I know there are some spells that will be specific to people, but it takes a lot of skill and are extremely hard to maintain. Whatever it is it wasn't placed here specifically for us," Ulman explained.

"That's good to know," there was no sarcasm in his voice. "But what is it?"

"Give me a moment." There was a tense wait as Ulman tried to work out the spell in front of them. "To put it simply it's a counting spell."

"What does that mean?" Bern asked before he had a chance to continue.

"Whoever placed the spell wanted to know how many people were crossing the bridge," Ulman explained.

"It seems as though the Dark Knight is expecting us," Bern mused. "Is there anything you can do about it?" Bern asked.

"It is simple enough. I could unravel it quite easily."

"No, that would be just the same. He would know we were on the way. Is there any way you can block the spell long enough for us to get the army past?" Bern suggested.

Ulman though for a while and probed the spell. The tension was building again.

"It is not something that I am familiar with. I would need to speak with the others. I'm sure there is a way to get it done."

"We need to send for the other wizards," Bern called back to the command group.

"I'll go." Pernian was the fastest by horse. He rode a white elven stallion. There were few left and Pernian's status gave him preference.

"I don't think we should stay here any longer," Bern suggested. "Should we proceed forward or backwards?"

"There shouldn't be a problem with us stepping off. The spell shouldn't be affected," Ulman reassured him.

The feeling to move forward was still compelling. Bern wasn't sure if it was the prophecy or the spell. Even his horse didn't seem to want to turn around and step off the bridge. There was a battle of wills for a moment before Bern finally won.

The sun was high in the sky before Pernian returned with the other five wizards. They didn't look to be in any hurry and that annoyed Bern. No matter how hard Pernian tried to urge them forward they didn't give up their gentle pace.

"Why is it we have been summoned?" Brielle sounded exasperated.

"Oh pipe down Brielle," Ulman was in no mood for her attitude. "There is a spell on the bridge. We believe it was set by the Dark Knight who had taken over Remidel."

"Then why don't you just unravel it?" She snapped.

Ulman went on to explain briefly what their problem was and how they needed it fixed. The conundrum was met with silence as the five wizards delved for the spell. Suddenly Minerva burst out laughing. The others quickly stopped what they were doing and stared at her.

"Well, come on! What's so funny?" Ulman barked.

"I'm sorry," Minerva apologised as the laughter subsided. "That spell wasn't left there by a Dark Knight."

"What are you talking about? Who else would leave such a spell?" Bern asked, somewhat confused.

"It's not a very complicated spell. I would say it was cast by a lesser wizard or even a sorcerer. It was created a long time ago for a census keeper in the capital. The king at the time, and I can't for the life of me remember which one, wanted to know who was using his highway. The only way he could successfully know was to mark this bridge."

"Why would he want to do that?" it still didn't make sense.

"I guess so he could make sure he was getting all the taxes for people using his highway. He was a little paranoid about such things. He always believed that people were trying to steal from him. I guess the Kings after him never felt the need to remove it."

"So does anyone still check the records?" Duke Hadar spoke, intrigued by the conversation. He had to admit it was an ingenious idea to keep track of movements around the kingdom. If ever he was able to return home he would seriously consider asking a wizard to do the same for him.

"I have no idea." Minerva responded regrettably. "I couldn't even say if anyone knows the spell is still active."

"In my experience, census takers aren't ones to forget such things." Lord Hadar added. "I am sure there is someone still recording the data."

"Then we are back to square one. If someone is watching the count they will go straight to the king when they notice the pure numbers crossing the bridge and if we simply disable the spell they will do the same. Once the king is informed then the Dark Knight will surely know," Bern sounded despondent.

"It shouldn't be too hard to disable the spell for a short period of time. Unless the census keepers are adept in the art of magic they won't notice a thing. To be on the safe side I think half a dozen of us should travel over the bridge. At least that way it will give them some information to calculate," Minerva explained.

"That is all well and good, but that doesn't explain the urge to cross. Once you step onto the bridge there is an almost uncontrollable urge to cross." Bern wasn't convinced.

"That is simple. Back in the past people came to fish off the bridge. That would upset the census count. The compulsion forces those who step onto the bridge to cross. The locals soon realised that they could no longer use the bridge for fishing and other entertainment and simply stopped trying."

That seemed logical enough and Bern was happy with the explanation. After a quick nod Hulkan, Dorn, Orric, Hadar, Sorrell and Horace rode across the bridge. When they were safely across the other side Minerva started the spell. It took longer than Bern thought it would, but when she was done they were all safe to cross.

This time there was nothing compelling him to cross as his horse stepped onto the bridge. As soon as he crossed to the other side the prophecy started irritating him again. The compulsion wasn't as bad as the spell, but it was still annoying.

"So what do we do now?" Elyas asked. "Do we wait here for the army or continue on?"

Bern thought for a moment. It would still be a long time before the army caught up to them and he didn't think he could remain stationary for much longer. Although their path was to lead along the river he knew he had to follow the highway further. He knew there was something waiting for him, he only wished he knew what it was.

"You can wait here. I need to see what is further along the highway." Bern was about to kick his roan into action, but he was stopped.

"I will come with you," Lord Hadar spoke. "You can't go on alone."

Bern was quite surprised with the response. He was sure that someone was going to question his motives. They all knew it was off their given path and yet no one protested.

"Well I'm going too. I'm not about to be left behind now," Hulkan barked as he moved his horse forward.

In the end Hulkan, Dorn, Hadar, Elyas and Ulman decided to join him. Bern had to admit he was happy with his small crew. Even the addition of Ulman was welcome. Beside the fact that he was part of the council, Bern was actually starting to like him. He seemed to be able to relate better to him than any of the other wizards.

They rode for half an hour at a brisk pace before they came across the Royal Crossroad. Suddenly the tug from the prophecy disappeared and Bern reined them to a stop. He looked at the signpost, not that he really needed to. Pointing the North-West was Remidel. To the North was Zenza City. To the East was Jarrat and the South was Castalia. As he looked at the sign post a sudden feeling of dread came over him.

He knew he was only a three day ride from Arsiliac and his family. As that thought struck his mind he felt the tug of the prophecy again. It was pulling him toward the road to Zenza City. Coupled with the feeling of dread Bern was suddenly concerned for the safety of his family.

"I need to go home!" Bern suddenly said, as if in deep thought.

"What was that?" Hadar asked.

"I need to go to Arsiliac," he replied.

"We can't take the army that way. It will add days if not weeks to our journey and it will alert the Dark Knight that we are coming," Hadar explained.

"I don't plan on taking the army with me. They need to continue on to the capital. I will meet you all there." Bern started his horse in the direction of Zenza City.

"Stop Bern!" Hulkan called and reluctantly Bern reined in. "You can't go on alone. You've read the reports. They all say that there are orglin roaming around the countryside in Remidia. They can't all be wrong. You must take some soldiers with you."

Bern's shoulders dropped and he sighed. He knew Hulkan was right. If he ran into trouble he doubted even the entity would be able to save him. Now he would have to wait for more soldiers to catch up. It seemed that he was spending his life waiting for others.

"We may as well return to the others and let them know what we are doing. It's going to take a while before the soldiers reach us," Ulman suggested.

It did make sense, but Bern wasn't overly happy that it was Ulman who made the suggestion. He still didn't completely trust the wizard. He was sure there was an ulterior motive involved with his suggestion. There was little doubt in his mind the Ulman was going back to report to his five associates. In the end there was little he could do about it. There was no point remaining at the crossroad.

"I really don't think this is a good idea," Drake was the first one to speak when they returned. It seemed as though the wizards were giving up their silent vigil. "There is no telling what dangers are out there. You should remain with the army."

"If you want to know how you're family are doing why don't you send a scout to check on them? You don't need to go yourself," Minerva added.

Bern sighed again. In the end it might have been better if he had just remained at the crossroad. He didn't have to explain himself to the wizards and that's exactly what he was going to do. Until he knew exactly where their loyalties lay they weren't going to get any unnecessary information from him.

"Send for the small group of former bandits. They will come with me." Bern knew he was doing the right thing. "They have served me well in the past and they will serve me well again."

"Are you sure that is enough?" Hadar rebuked. "There is only about fifty men in that group. Surely it would be safer with four or five hundred soldiers?"

"That number will be too conspicuous. I'm not expecting to get into any trouble. We will be fine." Bern wouldn't be persuaded.

Pernian left again in a hurry. He had been instructed to see that all the soldiers were given horses. There was no way Bern was going to be delayed by foot soldiers. The army could spare more than enough to see them all in the saddle.

Those remaining made small talk until Pernian returned with the bandits. Bern had dismounted and was pacing away from them. He wanted to avoid the questions they would ask and the ones he really couldn't answer.

It was late in the day when Pernian returned with the soldiers in tow. Bern was surprised to see so many men with him. He was sure the bandits were fifty at best, but there looked to be at least eighty if not a hundred men following behind the elven lord. He looked for Delbert, but there was no sign of the corporal.

"Good to see you again Private Horst. I don't see Corporal Delbert with you."

"I have some bad news," Horst started after saluting.

"That can wait. We need to be on the move. You can tell me in the saddle."

Along with the bandits, Hadar, Dorn, Elyas and Ulman travelled with Bern. It seemed there was nothing he could do get away from the wizards. At least it was Ulman coming with him and not any of the others. Ulman, in his gruff way, was pleasant enough company and he didn't ask too many questions.

General Jarwe had been left in charge of the army. Bern had assured him that they would return before they were ready to attack the city. Besides the length of the journey the army also had to make siege engines to breech the outer walls. It was impossible to transport such large weapons from Castalia.

It was an hour before nightfall when they reached the crossroad again. Bern had kept a brisk pace without breaking into a canter. There had been little time for conversation. As much as he wanted to know about Delbert he knew there would be time to talk when they camped for the night.

Bern paused again at the crossroad. He wanted to make sure he was doing the right thing. It was a big risk moving away from the army. That had never been part of the plan. He knew that his path would lead him close to his home village, but he had never planned on visiting. It would be too hard to see his family and friends just to have to leave again. Until he was finished he didn't know what to say to them, but it seemed that the prophecy had other plans for him.

"We ride hard until nightfall." Bern didn't wait for a response. He kicked the flanks of his roan and soon enough he was at a gallop. The others quickly followed suit when they realised he wasn't going to stop.

As dusk settled Bern pulled his horse back to a walk. The others soon realised that he wasn't planning on camping any time soon. The clouds from earlier in the day that threatened to burst, but never did, had passed allowing the moon to give them some gentle light. It was enough to guide them comfortably along the highway.

Eventually the others, due to hunger pains, convinced him to stop for the night. They set up camp off the highway in a small grove of elm trees. As much as they didn't think anyone would be along during the night they didn't want to risk being seen.

"So what happened to Delbert?" Everyone waited for Bern to speak as they ate a light meal around the campfire.

As much as Horst had wanted to avoid the conversation he knew it was coming. They had looked long and hard for Delbert and had failed to find him.

"We found the tavern they had been drinking in. There was a sign on the door stating that it had been purged for Nyrra worship. It was from there we realised he must have been taken prisoner." Horst paused as he recalled the events and steadied himself for what came next. "We found the prison where they were taken. The guards didn't really remember anyone enough to make descriptions. Eventually we found one who seemed to recognise Delbert, although he wasn't completely sure."

"So if you found him then why isn't he with you and why did you say that you didn't find him?" Bern interrupted. He was trying his best to follow the conversation.

"We didn't find him as such, but we know what happened to him. He was put to death by the guards." Horst's voice started to croak.

"What!" Bern exclaimed louder than he had wanted. "How could he have been put to death? Surely when he went to trial he would have explained his innocence?" Bern couldn't believe what he was hearing.

No one noticed that Elyas had moved slightly into the shadows. There was an uncomfortable expression on his face. He knew all too well the sort of trial Delbert would have received. Until that moment he had agreed with the process, but now he wasn't so sure. He wondered on how many other innocent people had been put to death because they were in the wrong place at the wrong time.

"They said he was given a fair trial and he confessed his sins, but I don't believe it. There was no way he was a follower of the Evil One he would rather kill himself than do that. We couldn't believe that it was Delbert they had captured, but then they showed us his wedding ring. It seemed once they executed the prisoners they would create a large pyre and burn them all. Anything of value on the body would have been taken. I am assuming this would have ended up being melted down if we hadn't recovered it." Horst pulled a golden ring out of his pocket. He looked at it with remorse in his eyes before tossing it across to Bern.

Bern caught the ring in his right hand before moving closer to the fire. Looking at the outside of the ring he didn't notice anything special before something on the inside caught his eye. He read the inscription aloud. "My Darling Delbert." There could be no doubt who the ring belonged to.

"How could this happen?" Bern shook his head.

"Well..." Elyas spoke softly. "The trials aren't exactly what they seem." At first he had decided to remain quiet, but as he watched their reactions he knew he needed to explain. "It is already assumed that the people who attended these rituals are guilty. The trial is only a show. The defendants are bound and gagged so they can't respond to the accusations. Then they are promptly executed." Elyas sounded ashamed as he spoke.

Bern felt like crossing the camp and striking Elyas, but he knew that would do no good. They had given a fair trial to those accused in Jarrat, but this was a different story. If he had caught those in the middle of an evil ritual then he probably would have done the same thing. There was no point in wasting time on those who were clearly guilty. He wished he could have done something, but there was little point in trying to blame someone now.

That pretty much ended the conversation for the night. No one wanted to say anymore. It was a sad night that ended early. Bern would have them all up and back on the road before daylight. He wanted to be in Arsiliac as quickly as possible.

It took another two and a half days for them to reach the road leading off the highway to his home village. Bern had pushed them hard. He would have pushed them harder, but he didn't want to wear out the horses. There was still a long way for them to travel before they were done.

Bern slowed the pace slightly; it was only a short ride to Arsiliac once they were off the highway. He had rushed them towards their destination for three days, but now he wasn't so sure of himself. Pushing forward had given him little time to think. When they eventually camped for the night he was too tired to really ponder anything significant. Now he knew he had to think of what he was going to say to his family.

The tug of the prophecy couldn't have been much stronger the next morning. Each time he tried to slow his horse the prophecy pulled him forward. It seemed whatever it was that was waiting for him needed to be done soon. Although he tried to slow their travelling it only took them an hour to reach the outskirts of the village. Even pushing hard it should have taken them longer. Bern looked towards the sky, but there was no denying it.

As soon as they reached the village Bern's heart suddenly sank. The stone buildings had been reduced to rubble and those made from timber had been burned to the ground. Bern could hardly recognise the village he had grown up in and spent most of his life.

"Mary!" he cried out as he kicked the flanks of his roan.

Bern rushed off before anyone could stop him. Some of the buildings that had been burnt were still smouldering. That could only mean that the destruction of Arsiliac had been a recent event. Bern could well be racing into a trap.

"Set up a perimeter around the village." Elyas instantly took command. "Go in groups of ten. If you see any indication of the enemy then make as much noise as you can. The rest of you come with me." Elyas didn't wait for anyone to respond. His voice was filled with command and if anyone had a better idea they didn't voice it. Everyone moved swiftly into action. Those chasing after Bern had a difficult time. He had already bolted into the distance and made no sign of slowing down. The others did their best not to lose sight of him as they raced out towards his farm.

When they arrived they found Bern on his knees with his head down. His farmhouse, like the other buildings, had been burnt to the ground. Tears ran down his face. There was no point trying to hide his emotions. He wept not for the building, even though it had been the only home he had ever known, it was his family he cried for.

Elyas and the rest of the soldiers looked through the rubble whilst the others stayed with Bern. They did their best to comfort him, not that they really knew what to do. There were little words could do to comfort someone who had lost their entire family.

"It doesn't look like they are here," Elyas announced when he returned. "There are no bodies anywhere to be found."

That brought Bern out of his weeping. He wiped his face and returned to his feet, suddenly feeling very foolish. As general he needed to be strong for his men, not that anyone thought bad of him for showing emotion. Hope filled his heart. At the very least his family could have been taken prisoner. He hoped beyond hope that they had in fact escaped. Now all he had to do was figure out where they would have gone.

In the end there could only be one solution to his problem. The safest place to travel would be Zenza City. If anyone was able to escape then that's where they would be travelling.

"We need to get moving. If they escaped the attack they would have gone to Zenza City," Bern commanded.

The others weren't so sure that was the right move. They could understand his need to find his family, but there was no telling where they went or if they were even still alive. As much as they were ahead of the army it wouldn't take long for them to fall behind, especially if they were to chase ghosts around Remidia.

"I can find out if they escaped and which direction they travelled, if they left within the last week, which it looks like they have," Ulman offered.

Bern simply nodded. Ulman was a little taken aback at his lack of respect, but he was willing to let it pass. At first he closed his eyes and muttered a few words under his breath. The air around them seemed to shimmer. Suddenly the temperature dropped and a fog settled in. Ulman's eyes started to flicker and the horses became skittish.

Time seemed to stand still while Ulman continued his spell. There was a stillness to the air that wasn't there before. It was as if they were no longer part of the outside world.

Suddenly his eyes popped open and he gasped for breath. As he did the fog completely dissipated and the world returned to normal. The horses settled down and everyone calmed themselves. It was a most disturbing experience and they were glad it was over.

"Well, what happened?" Bern asked when he didn't offer up any information.

Ulman refrained from the urge to berate Bern. The man would need to learn some respect eventually, but now wasn't the time.

"It was a day or two ago, I can't be completely sure which. A great evil passed through here. I don't think it was the Evil One himself or even one of his Dark Knights, but it was evil nonetheless. Whoever or whatever it was is blocking a lot of my vision. I could see your wife and children. They managed to escape before your house was destroyed. Someone from the village ran out and warned them. They left in the back of a wagon. They left in that direction." Ulman pointed towards the road to Zenza City. "Whether they reach their destination is impossible to tell."

That was something. At least they got away before trouble came. With a little luck they would be safe and sound in the duchy capital. That thought would keep Bern going. If he thought his family were dead then he didn't think he could continue, regardless of the entity inside of him. His will was much stronger now, but he would have been quite happy to slip away into obscurity. In fact he would be more than happy to lose his consciousness altogether.

"Let's rally the rest of the soldiers and get on the move." Bern mounted as he spoke.

"I think we should camp here for the night!" Hadar suggested. "My Remidian geography is a little sketchy, but from memory there is a large forest between here and Zenza City. We don't want to be caught there in the middle of the night. If there are orglin around that's where they'll be hiding during the day."

"We can at least travel to Quinaliac. We can camp there the night." Bern sounded desperate.

"Think about it general. If they did this to Arsiliac then they would have done the same to Quinaliac." Hadar continued. "If we leave at first light then we can be at Zenza City well before nightfall. It gives us time if we run into any trouble."

There was still plenty of light left in the day and the last thing Bern wanted to do was sit around and wait. Any time lost was time he could be saving his family. He couldn't feel the tug of the prophecy anymore and that wasn't a good sign. Why was it that no one seemed to want to help him when he really needed it? He knew that wasn't necessarily true, but it felt like it more often than not.

"What you say does makes sense, but there is too much daylight for us to remain here. We make for Quinaliac and then Zenza City in the morning. With a little luck there will be someone in Quinaliac that can explain what happened here.

Chapter 19: Running into Trouble

As they thought, there were no survivors left in Arsiliac. The streets were littered with charred, dead bodies. Bern felt even worse as he looked at them. Although he couldn't tell who anyone was he knew that he would have known some of them. The sadness could only stay for so long before it was replaced with anger. A cold, steeling anger crept into him and that was exactly what he needed. The morose feelings would have brought down the morale of the entire group and they needed to be strong if they were going to succeed.

It took almost another hour for the soldiers to return from their posts. Some of them had gone to scout the area around the village to see if there were any sign of survivors or their attackers. When they finally returned Bern was well and truly ready to go.

"Let's move out. There's not a lot of day left and we need to be in Quinaliac before nightfall. I have a feeling there is evil in the forest and we don't want to be caught there after dark." Bern tried to remain calm as he spoke to his troops.

There was a quick salute and acknowledgement of his words before they started back towards the highway. It wasn't long before Bern had them riding at a gallop. There would be time to slow down once they entered the forest, until then Bern was going to push them as hard as he could. Time was against him and he wasn't going to waste it.

When they entered the forest Bern slowed them down to a canter. At the best of times the forest was a dangerous place to be and the highway leading towards Zenza City was renowned for being the most dangerous stretch of road in the Seven Kingdoms, outside of Nostiria anyway.

"Is it strange that this reminds me of home?" Horst asked as they rode. The newly appointed corporal rode at the front of the line with Bern, Ulman and Hadar.

"There are no forests like this in Darshival!" Hadar returned. "I don't understand what you mean?"

Bern wanted to tell them to be quiet. Ever since they had entered the forest he had been trying to listen intently through the trees. He had felt the tug of the prophecy again and he didn't think that was a great sign. There was something watching and waiting for them, hidden in the trees and Bern had to stay prepared. In the end he wasn't going to be the one to end the conversation. He could feel the tension mounting amongst the others and figured a little light conversation couldn't hurt.

"It's not the trees per say, it's the closeness of the forest. It reminds me of our home in Darshival. Living amongst the trees gives you an affiliation with the forests of the world." Horst explained.

Hadar could accept that response. It did make sense even if he really couldn't understand it. Then he realised he felt the same when he was in a large city.

"I'm looking forward to reaching Zenza City, a nice warm bath and a smoky tavern with cold ale and busty wenches. That's my kind of paradise." Hadar laughed loudly which made Bern cringe. Their movements weren't exactly stealthy, but they were trying their best not to be noticeable. That had now quickly ended for anyone who was within earshot.

Hadar suddenly realised what he was doing and the conversation abruptly ended. They rode for the rest of the afternoon in silence, but everyone felt nervous. There seemed to be hidden eyes, watching them, deep in the forest.

The sun was starting to set when they were still a league away from Quinaliac. The dark shadows increased everyone's nerves and the horses also became skittish. There was a feeling of dread in the air. It was only a matter of time before Bern kicked his roan into a gallop. With the dimming light and the random branches hanging over the road he was unsure which was more dangerous. Galloping towards Quinaliac or travelling through the forest after dark.

Luckily they arrived without incident just before the sun had set. The sight before them, though, didn't fill them with any confidence. No lanterns had been lit to light the streets. There were no lights in any windows and no smoke came from the chimneys. Even on dusk it was cold and the night was only going to get colder.

"I don't think anyone is here?" Hadar stated the obvious.

Bern remained silent. He didn't know how to respond. The soldiers had lit torches so they could see around them, but they had refrained from lighting any lanterns. If there were enemies nearby then they didn't want to create a beacon for them.

"Check the houses. Let's see if anyone is hiding inside. I think we should camp in the village hall tonight. It's large enough for us all to sleep on the floor. I think we should all stay together," Bern spoke finally.

There were no arguments. Although it would have been nice to sleep in a bed, the risks were too great. Bern had a bad feeling that the enemy was close. There was no reason why Arsiliac would have been burned to the ground and Quinaliac left unscathed. The only thought that ran through his mind was that the Evil One's raiders had yet to reach this village.

Despite the risk they decided that they should light a fire in the large fireplace. It was going to the get very cold during the night and they didn't want to risk freezing to death.

Slowly, as the others prepared a light meal, the soldiers started to return. Each time they shook their heads and explained that they hadn't found anyone. It wasn't until Horst returned with an elderly looking man did hope return to Bern. Bern didn't recognise the man, although he had never spent much time in Quinaliac.

"I found this man hiding in one of the taverns," Horst explained as he half dragged the man forward. "He seems to be the only one left in the village."

"Oh thank you general," the man prostrated himself in front of Bern after Horst let go of him. "I have been waiting for you to arrive."

That didn't at all sound promising. "Who told you I was coming?" That was the first thing Bern wanted answered.

"Ah, no one sir." He sounded very nervous. "I didn't know it was you specifically. It came to me in a dream, but I knew it was true. My family thought I was crazy, but I knew I had to wait for you."

If Bern hadn't been in stranger situations he would have thought the man was crazy. Now he was grateful that it was a dream and nothing more sinister. There was much more information that he needed.

"What is your name and where did everyone go?" Bern asked.

"My name is Fayne and I am the innkeeper of the Horse's Head. Two days ago people started arriving from Arsiliac. They said they were attacked by some strange looking creatures. At first we didn't believe them. It sounded like such an unbelievable story. Of course we had heard rumours from other parts of Remidia, but there are always tall tales from passing merchants. It wasn't until they showed us one of the men they had killed that we believed them."

"That is a great story, but what happened to all the people? And what happened to those who came from Arsiliac?" Bern desperately wanted to know where his family was.

"They stayed the night in town and then moved on to the capital. They figured it would be safe in Zenza City. I was the only one who stayed and I wasn't looking forward to another night by myself. Although nothing happened last night I could hear things that I have never heard before. The village was deathly quiet, but I could swear that I could hear noises in the forest."

Bern knew that Fayne was starting to drift away. He couldn't imagine how hard it would be living by yourself with the risk of evil creatures coming to kill you. But it had only been one day and already his mind seemed to be slipping.

"So they are safe?" Bern pushed.

"I have no idea. I can only assume that they made it safely, but until we get there we won't truly know."

Bern had to admit that he had not really planned their next move. He had thought that he would have found the survivors in Quinaliac, although he really didn't know why. Although the town was at least twice the size of Arsiliac it had no real defences. There was a small town guard to keep the peace, but that would do nothing against a rampaging horde of orglin.

"You are safe now Fayne." Bern wasn't sure if that statement was true. He doubted that any of them were. "You can stay with us." Bern thought for a moment. "You look hungry. My men will see that you are well fed."

Fayne looked to where Bern was pointing and saw the soldiers finishing off their meal. "Oh no, this won't do." Fayne suddenly sounded happier, he had a purpose again. "If you would escort me back to my tavern I have plenty of food there. We could have a proper feast." Bern had to admit he was still hungry. "In fact why don't we all move to my tavern? The accommodation is much for comfortable than this floor." As much as that was a tempting idea Bern had to pass. If there was trouble then they needed to be ready for action.

"Thank you, but the food will be enough. Move quickly. You don't want to be outside longer than you need to be."

Fayne nodded his agreement.

"What is our next plan of attack?" Elyas asked when Fayne left with a small group of soldiers.

"I guess we go to Zenza City and see if they made it alright and everyone is safe. I don't think we would be doing our job if we did it any other way." Bern was sure that was the right thing to do.

"Do we have the time?" Dorn asked.

That was a question Bern hoped wouldn't be asked and one that he couldn't rightly answer. All he could hope for was that the prophecy allowed him enough time to do what he needed to do.

"We have to make sure they are safe. If we don't then what are we fighting for?"

"We are fighting for everyone." It seemed Elyas wasn't going to let it slide. "We can't keep going off course for one family if it sacrifices everyone else's."

Bern dropped his head as he thought for a moment. Elyas was new to their group and didn't understand Bern's connection with the prophecy, not that anyone really did, least of all himself. It seemed the right time to give Elyas a lesson.

"There was a reason we had to come here." He held up his hand to stop him from asking the obvious question. "I don't know what it was.

It may or may not become clear in time. All I know is there was no other path for me to take." Bern struggled with his words.

"That doesn't make any sense. We can't just wander around on a feeling," Elyas barked.

Bern looked around for support.

"That's exactly what we do," Hadar returned. He had left on a feeling. He knew that he had to leave and which direction he had to travel, but why? He couldn't answer that question and didn't think he ever could. "We have all been caught up in this whirlwind and it will take us wherever it wants. Is it right? Who knows the answer to that? All we know is that no matter what we do the prophecy will lead us in the direction it wants us to go." Hadar explained as best he could.

Elyas shook his head. He couldn't believe what he was hearing. When the High Chancellor had commanded that he lead the Castalial Army and then pass command to General Bern, he had been expecting much more. Ever since he arrived it seemed as though he had no idea what he was doing. This was not going to be easy, but on the plus side it wouldn't be long before he ended up dead. Someone in command with such little idea would always die early. When that happened he would have his chance to take command. Until then he would just have to accept what was happening.

"I know it doesn't sound like much, but that's the way it is. We have all come to accept it and you will have to as well," Dorn tried to help, but it had little effect.

Elyas was about to speak, but Bern stopped him.

"Whether you feel to tug of the prophecy or not, whether you believe in the prophecy or not, that is beside the point. There is nothing we can do to avoid it and trust me when I say we have tried."

"I don't understand. How can you travel around with no real purpose?" Elyas sounded resigned.

That was a valid question, although it was poorly worded. As much as Bern really didn't like discussing what he didn't know there was no way around it. Elyas deserved answers if he was going to help lead the Alliance. Although he couldn't leave with the Castalial army, the High Chancellor had seen to that, he could cause trouble. Until the soldiers had completely assimilated they would take their lead from their commanding officer.

"We travel with purpose. We travel with the highest purpose of all, saving the Seven Kingdoms. The prophecy makes sure we stay on the right course. What we do when we get there is completely up to us." Bern didn't like what he was hearing. His own words made him cringe.

"Well it doesn't make sense to me, but I guess there is nothing I can do about it." Elyas sounded somewhat hopeful.

There was only a short moment of silence before Fayne returned with the soldiers and the food. There were sides of beef and lamb as well as a whole pig. As well as all the meat there was a wide variety of vegetables, breads and cheeses. It looked as though it was going to be a mighty feast.

Bern had to admit that he was getting sick of the rations they had been given. Although it was quite common for the commanders of an army to eat well, Bern had decided that they would eat the same rations as the rest of the army, much to the chagrin of the wizards.

Seeing all the food being set up to be cooked made Bern regret not taking greater advantage of the situation when he was in the Grand Cathedral. There had been many opportunities to indulge himself that he had passed on. At least for one night he would be able to fill his stomach without thought for anyone who would miss out.

Soon enough the town hall was filled with the smell of roasting meat. It was enough to take everyone's minds from the potential danger. Fayne had also suggested some barrels of ale, but Bern had declined. The last thing he wanted was his men getting drunk. As much as it had been quiet since they arrived Bern highly doubted it was going to remain that way.

When the meal was served there had still been no sign of the enemy. The soldiers had kept the chatter to a minimum, but the tension was palpable. When the meal was finished they started to relax. The conversation became louder, which made Bern very nervous.

The guards came to swap the watch and Bern was keen to find out what they had to report.

"Nothing of any significance." One of the soldiers started.

"What is it?" Bern noticed the other guard didn't seem to agree.

"It is still outside. Unnaturally still," the second soldier spoke.

"You're just being superstitious Corbin," the first soldier snapped. "There is nothing wrong outside. It is just a normal calm night."

"What do you mean by 'unnaturally still'?" Bern ignored the jibe.

"There are no animal noises, no wind rustling the leaves. It is definitely too quiet for my liking," Corbin explained.

Bern knew something was wrong. He didn't need Corbin to tell him to know that. There was a sense of evil in the air and he couldn't believe that no one else felt it. He was sure that Ulman could sense the same thing, but he seemed too relaxed.

As if on cue there was a loud screech from somewhere outside. The sound was enough to send shivers down their spines. Before anyone could react the door opened and one of the new sentries rushed in.

"The orglin are storming the village." The soldier puffed in fear as he spoke. It was only a short trip from the lookout point on top of the hall and he shouldn't have been out of breath.

"How many are there?" Bern asked as the soldiers suddenly moved into action. He was glad that he didn't have to push them.

"It's impossible to tell. We could only tell by the noise. It's pitch black outside. The moon is completely covered." The soldier's breathing was slowly returning to normal.

"We need to get out of here?" Elyas cut in. "If we get trapped in here then we're as good as dead."

"That will be the same if we can't see our enemy," Bern retorted.

"I can help with that!" Ulman's voice seemed to resonate throughout the hall. He had his large sword in his right hand and looked ready for battle. "I'll be able to create enough light for us to see and I might be able to fry a few orglin as well." There was a slight evil tone to his voice.

"Ready your weapons!" Bern boomed. "Let's kill some orglin!"

There was a loud cheer from the soldiers. If the orglin didn't know where they were before then there was no denying it now. Ulman led the charge outside with Bern following closely behind. At first it was completely dark as the guard had informed them. Bern almost fell over as he tried to adjust to the sudden darkness. Instantly he knew something was wrong. The night had not been so dark in a long time.

Ulman had already started casting the spell before he left the hall and he quickly released it once he was outside. A bright globe of light two paces in diameter hung in the air above them. Bern wasn't sure if he really wanted the light when he realised the scene before him. The entire village was crawling with orglin. They looked like they were hunting for something. Until the light appeared they didn't know where they were, which meant their numbers were scattered. That wouldn't last for long, but at least it gave them a chance to prepare themselves.

The orglin shied away from the light as the soldiers filled the area outside the hall. They didn't look as though they were keen to attack when suddenly the light started to fade.

"What's happening Ulman?" Bern asked.

"There is someone out there trying to block my spell." There was a strain to his voice.

"A Dark Knight?" Bern didn't want to think of the repercussions of that.

"No, this is something different. We can talk about it later. Go and kill those orglin."

The same invisible force that drained the light also pushed the orglin forward. As much as they didn't like the light there was nothing they could do. They had to attack and it came hard and fast. The soldiers formed a circle around Ulman. They needed to protect him at all cost. If the light faded then they would all die.

A wave of orglin smashed against the soldiers as the others rushed to join the battle. A sinking feeling hit Bern's stomach, there was no way they would be able to defeat so many of the evil creatures. When one was slain another three were there to take its place. Once their line was broken it would be a short battle, even shorter if Ulman was taken.

The men fought bravely but eventually they started to fall. At first there were enough for some to stand behind the others and rest a moment without compromising the line, but that didn't last for long.

"Ulman!" Bern called out as he slashed another orglin across the throat. "I need you to do something amazing."

"If I do that then we will lose the light. I won't be able to keep both going." Ulman's voice still sounded strained.

"It doesn't matter now anyway. All light will do is show us our deaths. We need something..." Bern's voice trailed off as there was a sudden trumpet call in the distance.

It was an oddly familiar sound, but at first Bern couldn't place it. Then, as he cut aside another orglin, he remembered. It was the same sound he had heard when they had been fighting orglin outside of Jarrat. The elves had arrived.

Suddenly a barrage of arrows shot down in the mass of orglin. Each arrow was a precision death shot. Now the orglin ran around in confusion, they didn't know what to do. The attack was now strongest from their rear. The soldiers in the ring were able to take a step back creating a small space for some of the soldiers to rest. It seemed that they weren't going to die after all.

After the arrows stopped falling the elven warriors attacked. That was it for the orglin. Whoever it was that had been controlling them had now lost that control. Panic overcame the bloodlust and the orglin started to scatter. As they did the light globe suddenly glowed brighter.

"We need to move," Ulman called. "The magic weaver is out there and we need to know who we are up against."

Bern and Elyas followed the wizard whilst the other soldiers chased after the orglin. They were given specific instructions not to follow them into the forest. That would be a job for the elves. Trying to track orglin in the dark, was a recipe for disaster for the soldiers.

They had been expecting a chase through the forest to find the mysterious magic weaver, but instead they found him waiting for them at the edge of the village. Ulman pulled up and held the other two back. Something wasn't right. The battle had been lost and the man should have been fleeing for his life.

"You are not the chosen one," there was a hiss to his voice which Bern instantly recognised as a serpentant. The only question was which one. "That is very disappointing."

"Who are you?" Bern asked.

"I am Sidewinder. You'll do well to remember that name."

"What are you doing working for the Evil One?" Ulman accused. "He who betrayed and enslaved your Goddess."

"Lies." Sidewinder took a menacing step forward before thinking better of it. "When your kind is eradicated from this place the Great Lord will finally rescue the Goddess from the cage you have enslaved her in." There was something fanatical about the way he spoke.

"What do you want?" Bern asked.

"To see you all die."

"Get down!" Ulman cried.

Just as everyone dived out of the way a burst of bright white light shot towards them. Anyone caught in that blast would have disintegrated instantly. When they returned to their feet Sidewinder was gone. It seemed that he was just looking for a chance to escape.

"Let's get back to hall," Ulman suggested. "There's no point in chasing him further."

Bern waited a moment, staring into the forest. He had not seen that coming and that was a concern. It seemed more and more serpentants were coming out of the woodwork. He needed to know more about them, but there was little point chasing him through the darkness. For the moment he had to keep to the plan and he really needed to thank the elves who had saved their lives.

When they returned to the hall they found Lord Pernian waiting for them. The light still shone brightly showing a large smile on the elf's face. Bern couldn't help but to return the smile.

"You are indeed a sight for sore eyes," Bern shook his hand vigorously. "But what are you doing here?"

"You're not the only one who has a connection to the prophecy. As soon as you left for Arsiliac I knew I had to follow. The prophecy led me to this village and just in the nick of time. A few more moments and I think the orglin would have overpowered you."

That was true and something Bern didn't want to dwell on. There was no telling how close he had come to dying that night. That thought made him shiver. It was time to change the subject.

"Come inside Lord Pernian. There is a fire burning and food a plenty. I'm sure your elves would be hungry by now?" Bern offered.

"Thank you general, but we are better suited to the forest." Pernian paused for a moment. "What is your plan for the morrow?"

"We leave for Zenza City. I need to know what happened here?"
That was only part of the reason, but it was true enough.

"Very well. I think our part is done. We will look to rejoin the
army." Pernian saluted before taking his leave.

Another guard had been posted and the rest of the soldiers had
returned to the hall. Bern looked up at the sky before returning himself.
The darkness which had blinded them before had gone even though
Ulman's sphere had almost completely dispersed.

When he stepped inside he was greeted by Elyas, Dorn and
Ulman. They all had concerned expressions on their faces. Bern didn't
think he was going to like what they were going to say.

"We couldn't help but overhear your conversation with Lord
Pernian," Elyas started. He seemed to be the most confident in speaking
with Bern. Bern wondered if the fact they couldn't help overhearing was
because they were pressed up against the door. "I thought we would be
looking at rejoining the army by now. Time is slipping away and if we
delay too much longer the Alliance will arrive in Remidel before us."

It was a valid concern, but Bern couldn't stop until he knew what
had happened to his family. More than that he needed reports on what
had been happening in his home kingdom. That would give him an idea
of what they were marching towards.

"We will arrive when we have to." Bern left no room for
argument. "If you didn't believe in the prophecy before I think Pernian's
timely arrival should prove it to you." Bern waved his hand to silence the
inevitable objection. "It is something that you need to come to terms
with, captain, whether you like it or not. Our path leads us to Zenza City
and that is exactly where I am going to lead us."

There was something in his voice, a commanding tone that
silenced the others. Elyas looked towards Ulman and Dorn for support,
but he didn't receive any. It was at that moment that Hadar joined them.

"Bern is right. Our path is towards Zenza City. All that we need
to do now is get some rest so we can be on the road again at first light.
The sooner we leave the sooner we can reach our destination."

With that everyone went to sleep. For the moment they were
safe. There would be a new challenge for them in the morning.

Chapter 20: Answers

Alaric stumbled as he landed in an open field. He had jumped so many times he had no idea where or when he was. He was sure he had been everywhere on the world that was home to the Seven Kingdoms. He was sure he had visited other planets and even other dimensions. Each time he thought he had found what he was looking for it was just out of his reach. As the days wore on he started to question what he was doing. He couldn't even be sure how much time had passed. It could have been days, weeks, years or just mere seconds since he had left his friend in Castalia.

The frantic journey had taken its toll on him. Even with his new found power he was starting to become exhausted. He thought he had found a way to live without sleeping, but that wasn't the case. Sooner or later he would need to recuperate and he had a feeling it was going to be a long sleep. Until he found what he was looking for he couldn't stop, he had promised himself that. Time was against him and he needed answers if he was going to be able to stop Nyrra.

The air was thin where he was. It was as if he was standing on top of a mountain. It was similar to when he was atop Mount Scorpio. As he looked around he couldn't see an edge, as if he was on a cliff. He doubted he was anywhere close to home, but he hoped he was. Like with all his other jumps he felt he was getting closer. He really didn't think he could to handle another one.

A cool breeze brushed across his face. It was the first thing he had felt in a long time. It was a sign that his power was fading. He had survived in places that his body wasn't designed for. On one jump he had let his guard down and he nearly suffocated in the planets dense atmosphere. He had not made that mistake again. Now his defences were failing of their own accord, but that wasn't such a bad thing. The scent of salt water and tropical flowers filled his nose, although there was no sign of a beach or flowers. The scent pleased him. Of all the places he had landed in, this one felt the most like home. That in itself was a good sign that he had final reached his destination.

Without thinking he started to walk forward. The meadow seemed to go on forever. Although he didn't look behind, he knew the meadow continued on past the horizon in all directions. It was like he was walking in a dream. That idea wasn't completely out of the question, as much as he believed he was in reality he knew not to take anything for granted. Just because he might be in a dream it didn't necessarily mean he was in his own. He had learnt that the hard way.

The further he walked the more relaxed and open he became until he realised the power he had been holding was now completely gone. That should have brought panic to him, but nothing could disturb the calm that washed over him. For the first time in his life he was truly at peace.

"It has taken you a long time to find me!"

All of a sudden Alaric was sitting at an oak table with an old man sitting across from him. He had no idea how he got there. The last thing he could remember was walking through the meadow. The man had wispy white hair and a short, cropped beard. He wore a white robe that almost seemed to glisten in the sunlight. There was something pleasant about his face and his presence. That instantly sent alarm bells ringing inside Alaric's head, but he wasn't going to do anything about them until he needed to.

"Who are you?" That wasn't the first question on his mind, but it was the first that came out.

The man chuckled to himself before he spoke. "I never get tired of that question. It always seems to be the first one asked and the last one I can answer."

Alaric scratched his head. The name Mesula came to mind and then disappeared almost as quickly. All his thoughts were clouded and he didn't think it was from fatigue. There was something strange about the place. Alaric tried to draw in the power around him.

"Save yourself the bother. You can't do that here." The man sounded jovial, as if it had been something he was expecting.

"Where am I?" Alaric asked, forgetting his original question.

"You are in a place between places." He paused for a moment. "This is always a tough question. It is a bridge of sorts. Between worlds."

"What do you mean between worlds?" Alaric tried to shake the cobwebs. But he was still hazy. "I have travelled to a lot of different places, different worlds, but there is something different about this place."

"I wish I had time to explain it to you, but that would take many lifetimes and I believe that you are somewhat in a hurry?" his voice sounded serious.

Alaric had to concentrate. This was the man he had been looking for. This was the place he had been looking for. Now he needed to get the answers he was looking for. The journey would all be for nothing if he didn't ask them and couldn't remember them.

"What is it you came here to ask me?" the old man continued when Alaric didn't speak. "Not many have the power to undertake such a task and normally most give up long before they find me. I couldn't tell you how long it's been since someone has visited me, but then again time really has no meaning here."

It seemed as long as Alaric kept talking the man, although Alaric was sure he wasn't a man, would offer information. Even if it wasn't the information he was after it would give him a better idea of his situation. If this wasn't who he was looking for then he needed all the information he could get. There was a very good chance this was in fact a trap. He needed to be careful.

"I can assure you this isn't a trap. If I wanted you dead then you would be dead already. If I wanted to imprison you then that's exactly where you would be. I'm a patient man, but my patience only lasts for so long."

That put an end to Alaric's plan.

"Who are you?" again that wasn't the question he planned on asking, but it was the one that came out. "Are you a god?"

That brought a round of laughter.

"Would you believe that is the first time I've been called that?" Alaric was pretty sure he didn't call him a god, but just asked the question. "No, I'm not a god. At least I don't think I am. I've never created anything as such."

"What are you then?" Alaric pushed.

"That is a very good question. For all intents and purposes you can call me The Watcher. I think that's a good name for me." He thought for the moment. "Or you could call me the Prophet, or even the Prophecy. That's what you like to refer to me as."

Suddenly it all became clear, or at least things started to become clearer. In fact Alaric wasn't really sure he was any better off, but at least he had an idea of who he was talking to and that he was in the right place. What he didn't know was why he had been drawn there.

"Why have you brought me here?" that was the question he needed to ask.

"Ah, you are smarter than I gave you credit for. Normally it takes years for that question to be asked and that is the question that needed to be asked." That brought a smile to Alaric's face. "I brought you here because you needed to come. The wheels are in motion and I needed you away from the Seven Kingdoms."

That didn't make any sense. He was needed on the Seven Kingdoms. He needed to find the Ruby Stone before Nyrra did. There were only two stones left for him to find and then the prize would be his. He would be able to save all of them. Everyone!

"That is not true." The Prophet was plucking the thoughts out of his head. "You were, or should I say are, I guess that is still the right tense for this situation." Alaric wasn't sure he liked what he was hearing. "Anyway, that's just semantics. You have progressed faster than I could have imagined. Even with me... tweaking things."

"What does that even mean?" Alaric almost bit his tongue for interrupting.

"It means that you are not supposed to find the Ruby Stone. You were never supposed to have it in the first place. I have no idea how it came into your possession. That has never happened before, but it seems that things are back on track. It seems that my counterpart isn't doing his job properly."

"Your... counterpart?" Alaric spoke when the Prophet paused.

"Oh yes, Nyrra is it?" He didn't wait for a response. "He has a Prophet as well. Someone to watch over him and make sure he stays on the right path, just like you." He paused and thought for a moment. "I don't envy him. Nyrra is head strong, well stronger than you. I guess he has been around for a few more years, so he has learnt to push aside that nagging feeling that you so openly follow." Alaric didn't know if he should be offended or not. "But that is beside the point. Now... Where was I?"

"The Ruby Stone?" Alaric was trying his best to focus.

"Indeed! The Ruby Stone was never supposed to come into your possession."

"That doesn't make any sense." Alaric couldn't help himself. "I had the stone from when I was a child. I didn't even know what it was before Eldred came for me."

The Prophet had to think for a moment and scratched his beard as he did. The cobwebs were starting to fade and Alaric was regaining his composure. That was a good sign. He needed all his wits if he was going to succeed.

"That is a mystery to me. There is someone else in play. Someone I have not come across before. That is disturbing. Whoever it is they are messing with things they don't understand. It could have easily been the end of your world if you had fought Nyrra when you did. Luckily my counterpart was taking care of his side of things. I'm sure that will come back to haunt me one of these days."

The Prophet wasn't making any sense. Just when Alaric thought he was going to gain the information he needed he went off on a tangent. It was almost as hard to piece things together as the prophecy. That brought another question to his mind.

"But we were led by the *Prophecy of the Stone*. It told us to take the stone to the Cauldron Mountain and destroy it. I'm assuming you are involved in some way or another?" Alaric pushed.

"Are you sure that's what was written? From what I remember the *Prophecy of the Stone* is very difficult to decipher."

Alaric had to think again. He couldn't actually remember reading the passage. He had just always gone along with what he had been told.

"I'm not sure, and for that matter why is the prophecy so hard to read? If you want to tell us something why not just make it plain?" Alaric decided to get off the point. What had been done had already been done and there was no changing that.

"Anything I can affect so to can my counterpart. Just as I can't let him lead his puppet around he can't let me do the same with mine." Alaric let the jibe pass over him. "Both sides can't win, so we have to make it harder for the other side."

"I still don't understand." Alaric scratched his head.

"Don't be surprised. There is no time to explain everything to you properly. If you understand one thing from your visit here you will be doing well. Some have left more confused than when they arrived." Alaric could easily see how that could happen.

"So there is no point in keeping the *Prophecy of the Stone*?" Alaric thought it was a logical enough premise. "I should just throw it away or burn it?"

A look of horror passed over the Prophet's face. It was the first real sign of emotion he had shown, besides the odd amusement.

"That would be the worst thing you could do. If the enemy got their hands on that book then it would all be over." Alaric's heart raced as he remembered the time when Na'garoz had stolen the prophecy. He didn't want to think of the repercussions if Nyrra had got his hands on it, although he was sure the Prophet was about to tell him. "My counterpart and I distort the instructions we send. If the enemy has the *Prophecy of the Stone* then there is no reason for him to block my messages." Alaric now understood the importance of the prophecy. It wasn't to lead him, it was to stop Nyrra finding out what he was supposed to do.

"So why don't I just burn it and be done with it?" That seemed the most logical choice.

"You can certainly try, but I think you'll find that it will be completely futile." There was an evil smile on his face. "It is indestructible and therefore you must guard it with your life."

"Don't worry it's in safe hands." It was as safe as it could be without being in his own possession. He hoped that Eldred was looking after it.

"That is comforting to know." Alaric wasn't sure if he was being sarcastic or not.

"So what do I do now?"

"You already know what you have to do."

That wasn't what Alaric was looking for. He needed answers, but something else came out of his mouth.

"Then why did I have to come all the way here? I have wasted so much time jumping from place to place and world to world."

"It was a journey you had to take. You will take away what you need from our encounter." The Prophet smiled. "And now it is time for you to get back to your own space and time. To remain here too long is very dangerous for your kind. Regardless of how strong you are, eventually your mind will turn to pulp."

Alaric was sure there was something he was missing. The conversation had not gone anywhere. Sure he had found out a few insignificant facts, but he could have survived without knowing them. There had to be something he was missing. As he tried hard to think a wave of fatigue set over him. All he wanted to do was lie down and sleep.

"By the looks of things I don't think you have the strength to return." There was a concerned expression on the Prophet's face.

"I'm sure I'll be fine after a short rest. A quick nap and then I'll be out of here."

"Hmmm. I guess you have stayed longer than you should have." He thought for a moment as Alaric struggled to keep his eyes open. "I have never done this before, but I guess it's not against the rules." He thought again. "You might want to close your eyes. This is going to be quite a trip."

Alaric only just heard the words as his eyes closed. He didn't know if it was a voluntary reaction or not. Suddenly he felt the air rushing around him. He wanted to open his eyes to see what was happening, but they were too heavy. Time passed as if it had no meaning. He didn't know if seconds had passed or years.

Without warning Alaric crashed onto the ground. Instantly the smell of salt water filled his nose and he wondered if he had gone anywhere, then he felt the soft sand under his face. He knew he wasn't in the Seven Kingdoms. There was no sand that felt so soft to the touch. There was something very familiar about it though. He felt as though he had been there before.

Alaric lifted himself onto his hands and knees before he was finally able to open his eyes again. The Prophet had sent him to Čarolija Island. He had to admit that this was the place he felt most at home, even though he had not spent much time there. There was an aura about the island that brought him peace. Despite that, he still felt exhausted. He knew he could mask that fatigue, but that wasn't what he needed to do. Rest was the only cure. He still had a long way to go and he would need all his strength if he was going to succeed.

Slowly he lifted himself to his feet. They felt weak underneath his weight, but he was sure they would get him to where he needed to go. It was a short trip to the Council of Wizards' village from where he landed. As quick as he could Alaric made his way to the house he had stayed in before.

The bedroom looked just the way he had left it and he truly felt at home. Before his head hit the pillow he was fast asleep. His body wouldn't wake until it had fully recovered. There was no telling how long that would take.

***

It was close. He could feel it. It was all coming together.

Nyrra sat in a small cave somewhere in the middle of Remidia. He knew he was close to finding the Ruby Stone. He could feel it somewhere in the back of his mind. There was an itch in-between his shoulder blades. At first he had ignored it as he had for most of his life, but now he couldn't. It had been roaring in his mind so loud that he couldn't even think. Now he had succumbed, it was back to a slight itch. Now he knew he was close to achieving his goal. Once he had the Ruby Stone in his possession then he would be able to take over the entire Seven Kingdoms. He would be like a God and the worms would have to bow down and grovel before him.

Suddenly a crack of thunder burst outside the cave, shortly followed by a downpour of rain. Not five minutes ago the night sky was clear and a half moon was high in the sky. Nyrra couldn't stand calm weather. It took a lot of power to control it, but sometimes it was worth it just to hear the chaos brewing around him.

Although there was no light in the cave Nyrra had no problems seeing. The cave was familiar to him, but he couldn't work out why, not that it was important anyway. It could have been a cave he used to torment the lesser creatures in the past. Whenever that had happened it wasn't pleasant for those involved and that made him happy.

Things were coming to a head. He nearly had the stone, all his knights were almost dead. Victory would soon be his. In the start he had to admit that he didn't believe in prophecies, but now he wasn't so sure. Regardless of that it was his own strength and power that had got him to this point and that was all that mattered. Soon it would all be over. In the meantime he needed to find his precious stone.

Chapter 21: Into Hondin Lel

No one really felt safe again until they reached the other side of the mountain range. Even Viper seemed unsure of himself. Something had changed in him after their meeting with Kahn. The dragon's threat still rang throughout their ears. The last thing they wanted was another encounter with the Great Dragon. As much as they didn't secure his help from the impending battle with the Evil One he also didn't deny them.

The serpentant had fallen into a malaise. None of them knew why. He had been given his strength back by Kahn, but it was as if something was now missing. Although everyone noticed it no one spoke about it, they were all too busy. They had to concentrate to make it quickly down the other side of the mountain without killing themselves. In reality they were waiting for one of the others to broach the subject. It wasn't until they made camp at the base of the mountain range did Alena finally ask the question.

"What is wrong with you Viper? You've been moping around ever since we left Kahn. I thought you would have been happy that you've got your strength back?"

Viper looked at the fire, but didn't answer.

"Alena asked you a question. The polite thing to do is to answer!" Richmond snapped when there was no response. He had also wanted to know what was wrong and since Alena had broached the subject he didn't see any point in remaining silent.

Viper sharply turned his head to face Richmond. As he did his forked tongue flicked out in a menacing manner.

"Why the sudden interest in my wellbeing? It wasn't that long ago you would have been happy to leave me to die." There was venom in his words.

"We could have left you to die, but we didn't. That should tell you something." Richmond didn't back down, although his heart was starting to race.

Viper returned his gaze to the fire. It was not a conversation he wanted to have, but it seemed as though they weren't about to give up. That was something. It now seemed as though he had been accepted into their group. That was a victory in itself and should have been enough to brighten his spirits, but there was still something weighing on his mind.

"It saddens me that Kahn is the last of the Great Dragons. The Dragon Clans had once been a force to be reckoned with. The Dragon Lords once ruled the Seven Kingdoms, but that time is long past. The glory of the dragons is over." Viper's voice was thick with regret. "I don't know why, but I always thought when we rescued the Goddess there would be a magnificent display of flight by the dragons to welcome her home. Now whatever decision Kahn makes I doubt he'll be around to see her return."

No one had really thought of Viper as a creature having feelings. As much as no one had trusted him at the start they had to admit he had assimilated well into their little group.

"Don't worry Viper. We will see Nyrra dead and your Goddess set free," Richmond offered.

Eldred listened but didn't comment. He doubted that the queen of the Serpentants would ever be free. He doubted that she was even still alive. As much as he didn't have proof he believed that Nyrra had killed her. There would be little point in keeping her alive, especially if he was lying. Eldred couldn't believe that Nyrra would actually let her go. If he did, the queen would be angry and want vengeance. The last thing he needed was another enemy. Despite all the facts he wasn't going to tell Viper his suspicions. As long as he thought she was alive then there was a good chance he would remain on their side and Eldred had to admit he was starting to come in handy.

Richmond's comment didn't do anything to lift Viper's spirits. He still stared wistfully into the fire. It seemed that there was nothing they could say to make him feel better. That was enough to make them all fall into a malaise.

"I think we need to get some sleep. We have ridden hard the past few days, but we still have a long way to travel and at the end of it we have to fight a Dark Knight." Eldred finally spoke. It seemed to be the only way to break the mood.

No one replied, they just slowly made their way to their bedrolls. Eldred could only hope that their mood turned around in the morning. It was going to be a long ride if everyone was feeling morose.

In the morning Viper seemed to be in better spirits, which in turn lifted those in the rest of the group. It seemed as though Richmond's words might have had their effect. Either way Eldred wasn't going to ask any questions.

A light drizzle plagued their morning ride, but that didn't dampen their spirits. The thick tree foliage gave them some protection, but they were just happy to be out of the mountains. The temperature was also considerably warmer.

Eldred kept a brisk pace. He wanted to try and be at the edge of the forest by nightfall. Once they were out of the forest he figured they could be in Lel Dinion in a couple of days. He didn't want to race towards danger, but he figured there was little point in wasting time. There was no telling what trouble Argoz was causing. The sooner they removed him the better, although that would be easier said than done.

There was a narrow trail when they reached the foot of the mountain range, but that soon disappeared. Although the undergrowth wasn't too thick it still hindered their journey. That set Eldred's nerves off and by the time they stopped for the night he was in a bad mood.

"This is getting us nowhere. We shouldn't be stopping now!" Eldred burst out as the others started to make camp.

There was little light left in the sky and it was almost completely dark. Travelling any further would be more trouble than it was worth and they all knew it. Both Eldred and Viper could create light, but they had decided it would be safer not to be a moving beacon.

"Be still Eldred," Alena cooed as she piled twigs in the middle of a small clearing. "Nothing is going to be gained by breaking one of the horses legs stumbling through the undergrowth." Her words made sense, but did little to calm his nerves.

"I know, it's just..."

"You wanted to be out of the forest before nightfall. I know. We all did." Alena finished his sentence. "And if the Prophecy wanted us out of the forest then that's exactly where we would be."

Eldred had to admit she was right. They had been led by the prophecy so many times there was no point trying to think otherwise. He didn't even know why he wanted to be out of the forest.

Regardless of Alena's words Eldred had a restless night sleep. There was something wrong, but he just couldn't put his finger on it. There had to be a reason why they should have been out of the forest. He only wished he knew what it was.

The morning came around without incident. Eldred was relieved, although it didn't change the nagging feeling that something was wrong.

"What is our direction once we leave the forest?" Viper asked.

"We make straight for Lel Dinion," Eldred spoke with a mouthful of food.

"I'm not sure that is a great idea," Alena returned. "I think we should try and get some information on what is ahead of us. I'm sure we still have friends in these parts."

"I guess we could stop by Duke Hadar's estate. I'm sure he still has friends there."

"Aren't we too far north to detour that far?" Richmond asked.

"Yes and no. Alena is right. We need to get some information of what is happening in the kingdom. It might take us an extra week or so, but the last thing we want to do is rush into a trap."

That did make sense. It wasn't like they had an army behind them for support. They were trying to take on a Dark Knight in command of a kingdom with a wizard, a man, an elf and a serpentant. That in itself was crazy, but to rush in half cocked was even more insane. If they indeed still had friends in the kingdom then they would need their assistance.

"It is settled. We make for Duke Hadar's estate. It would have been nice if he was travelling with us. That would make things a lot easier." It sounded as if there was something Richmond wasn't telling them.

Alena was about to ask the question, but she was silenced by a slight hand movement from Eldred. There was time for questions, but for the moment it was time to let things stand. Eldred needed time to think. Things had taken a turn from his plan and he wasn't sure if it was a good idea. He needed to work things out before the next problem arose.

When they stopped for the midday meal Richmond offered the information that had been left hanging in the morning.

"A few years back the duke's sons stopped in Bellarome on their way to Kiarome and I offered them the full services of my city. Hadar's youngest son, Garag, took that a little too far. To keep the story short he drank too much at one of the local taverns, refused to pay the discounted rates and then roughed up a working girl. She had to go to the infirmary and stayed there for a week."

"That is terrible," Alena gasped. She had met Garag and he seemed like a nice enough man. She would have never guessed that he could have been violent and caused trouble.

"Needless to say I had to lock him in my cells for a number of days while he sobered up. Hadar understood, but I don't think Garag really appreciated it. As a favour I said that I wouldn't involve his father, but that did nothing to appease him. He vowed vengeance against me. I just took it as an idle threat from an over exuberant youth, but now it might just come back to haunt me."

"That could be an issue," Eldred sighed.

Eldred had heard of the incident. Just because Richmond had remained silent it didn't mean that Hagar had not told his father. To avoid an incident between the two kingdoms Hadar had agreed to keep the matter quiet.

"Hadar sent Hagar to join the army. The Gods only know where they are now. Garag was left in charge of his Duchy. If he holds a grudge then this could go bad," Eldred continued.

"Would he hold a grudge this long? How long ago was it?" Alena asked.

"It was six years ago. Let's hope that he doesn't," Richmond added.

"There is more than one way to get things done. I'm sure we can persuade him to help us," Viper hissed.

"We will do nothing to harm him, no matter what bad blood there is," Richmond snapped.

"Let's cross that bridge when we reach it. There's no point debating something that might not even happen. I am sure that Garag knows his father supports us and will not do anything to dishonour him." Eldred didn't sound completely confident, but it was enough to end the conversation.

They were quickly back in the saddle. It was still a long way to Hadar's estate and as much as they weren't looking forward to the confrontation there was no time to waste.

The midday sun was high in the sky, albeit obscured by thick foliage, and they were still in the forest. Now Eldred knew something wasn't right. With the way they had pushed hard the previous day they were unlucky not to be out by nightfall. Eldred called them to a halt and looked around. The forest looked much the same as it had all morning. When his eyes couldn't see anything wrong he pushed out with his other senses, but there was nothing there.

"What is it?" Viper finally asked. He too was searching for something.

"I don't know. We seem to be going around in circles. We should have been out of the forest early this morning. Now it doesn't even look like we're close." Eldred explained.

"Do you think someone has cast a spell on us?" Viper returned. It seemed like there was concern in his voice, but it was hard to decipher.

"Not sure. I can't sense anything of the sort, although there is a strange feeling in the air," Eldred explained.

"Should we press on?" Richmond asked.

"If we are being led around by our nose there doesn't seem to be much point. All we're going to achieve is tiring our horses." Alena looked around nervously. Something was wrong with the forest. Even she could feel it now, but like the others she couldn't work out what it was.

"If we stay here then we are sitting ducks for whoever it is that is out there. I think that is a far worse decision." Richmond's nerves were showing. He had no idea what was happening and that made him feel a lot worse than the others.

"Richmond is right. We can't stay here. Let's move on, but keep our wits about us." Eldred gently tapped the flanks of his horse and moved off at a walk.

Another hour passed and there was still no sign of the forest ending. Each time Eldred looked around the forest seemed to be the same. There had to be magic at work, but he should have been able to feel a spell that strong. He could understand not feeling the initial trap, but warning bells should be sounding in his mind. Eventually Eldred reined them in again.

"This is pointless. We're best just to wait and see who it is who has trapped us." Alena smiled to herself, although it was a hollow victory.

"What do you want from us?" Richmond called out in frustration. The others looked at him. "Sorry, but I don't know what else to do. I can't sense things like you can." Richmond shrugged his shoulders.

That made sense, although no one else could sense what was happening around them either. All they knew was that they were trapped and there was nothing they could do about it.

"This is my forest and you are not welcome here!" a sweet, but harsh voice resonated around them.

The sudden voice sent all the horses on edge, as well as their riders. Even Adelanta seemed uncomfortable. That in itself was a bad sign.

"Then let us go. We want nothing more than to leave your forest," Richmond called out to the trees.

In answer to his statement a thick fog rolled in around them. At first it swirled around the horses hooves, unsettling them even further, before creating a wall around the group. There was nothing natural about the fog and even Richmond could sense it. Even if they could move the horses forward they wouldn't be able to cross the threshold. They were completely trapped. Now it was just a matter of waiting for their judgement.

"I have been gone for too long. Evil has crept into my forest and I plan on fixing that." The voice lost none of its venom.

"We are not evil," Richmond spoke again. "We are fighting evil. You have..." Eldred finally silenced him. There was no point in rambling at the fog.

"Who are you? Give us the courtesy of a name." Eldred kept his voice strong.

"Such confidence for the fly caught in the spider's web. Nevertheless the spider shall have her feast." She was not rattled by Eldred's confidence.

"What is it that you want from us?" Eldred sounded resigned as he called into the fog. It seemed they were at her mercy, whoever she was.

The identity of their captor had Eldred baffled. Besides the three on the Council of Wizards he knew of no other females with such power. Even those on the council couldn't create such a spell, at least not without him knowing first.

"I want to rid the forest of evil, starting with the four of you." It seemed as though the spider wanted to play with her food.

"There is no evil here. I am an elf and a friend to the forest." Alena felt it was her turn to speak. "I am the daughter of Orric. If you are a friend of the forest then you will know that name."

Alena's words brought an air of confusion and the fog start to swirl wildly. It seemed as though it was about to break before it settled again. There was a small glimmer of hope, but only for a moment.

"I don't know that name, but I have been away for a long time. Your kind is familiar to me and I believe that you are a friend, but that doesn't change the fact that you travel with evil." It seemed as though Viper was a hindrance again.

"Viper is a serpentant and our travelling companion. He is bound to us and there is nothing we can do to change it," Alena floundered.

"Be that as it may he is evil and by association you can't be trusted. None of you will leave my forest alive, I can promise you that." Suddenly the small area they were trapped in grew dark and a feeling of dread passed over them.

"This is a mistake," Viper tried his best not to hiss, but it was impossible. "My kind is not evil. It is a stigma we have been stuck with from the start of time. We are hunters, predators, but so are many beasts. Are they evil? Is it because we have a higher intelligence that makes us evil?" There was clear anger in Viper's voice. No one had even questioned whether that they believed Viper was evil or not. Just because they had accepted him as a companion didn't mean they completely trusted him. "Sure, some of my kind have been convinced to follow the Evil One, but that still doesn't make us evil. If you are as old as you seem then surely you would know that aggression and passion doesn't equal evil?"

There was another pause and the darkness started to fade. There was a glimmer of hope that they weren't about to be killed. It seemed that they might actually survive the experience.

"I have to admit that you have me in a conundrum. It has been a long time since serpentants have walked in my woods. I can sense your evil now, but was that always the case?" It seemed as though the voice was speaking to herself and not asking the question.

"It is neither true now, nor was it true then. We just want our Goddess back. She has been trapped by Nyrra and only in his death will she be free. Unfortunately not all of my brothers believe the same. Some have been taken up by his lies and..."

"Keep your mindless chatter to yourself, I am trying to think." Viper looked confused if that was possible. He was sure she asked him a question.

"Please tell us who you are and why you have entrapped us?" Eldred finally asked after a minute of silence. "Maybe if we knew your name we could help you understand our plight."

There was another moment silence and the darkness faded even more. It seemed that they were starting to succeed in changing their captors mind.

"You are a wizard, a powerful man?" The question hung on the air. Eldred didn't want to respond. "Yes, I believe that you are. That makes things very interesting for me. Wizards can be evil, but I don't sense that in you."

"Who are you? What is your name?" Eldred pushed.

"Alright. I guess you deserve that much. My name is Cai."

Eldred knew that name, but it had been a long time since he had heard it and he couldn't place it. Then it came to him and hope filled his body.

"You are a Wood Sprite?" It was half a question and half a statement.

The darkness completely disappeared. It was obvious Cai had not been expecting such a response. The mist swirled wildly again before it settled.

"Yes, you are right. I am a Wood Sprite. You are indeed wise. How is it you know of my kind?" Cai asked, her voice a little softer.

"We met one of your kind recently. He was wary of us too.. Gaius is his name and he saw it in his power to let us leave." Eldred spoke carefully. He hoped that the relationship between the Wood Sprites was at least amicable, otherwise he might have just signed their death warrant.

Suddenly the fog vanished and a young girl stepped into the clearing. She wore a leafy green dress with yellow flowers around the edge of her skirts. Her blonde hair fell in ringlets around her shoulders. Although she wore no shoes her feet, she showed no sign of stains from the forest floor. Although she looked to be about ten years old there was a timelessness to her face that was unmistakable. Despite her innocent facade it did nothing to ease their nerves.

"Gaius is a wise one. He was smart enough not to get captured, so I suppose that means something." Cai pondered.

As much as Eldred wanted to be out of the forest he had a feeling that he needed more information. There was something he needed from Cai and he couldn't leave until he received it.

"Who trapped you?" Eldred asked as they all relaxed a little.

"I don't know his name, or even if he had one. He never told us. All he did was keep us prisoner and fed off us. I have no idea how long I was there. I know I was one of the first." Cai looked as though she was starting to become translucent as she spoke. It was a disturbing story made worse by her sudden transformation.

"Who rescued you?"

"A man, Alaric his name was I think." She solidified again at the mention of his name. The reaction on all their faces wasn't lost on her. "Do you know him?"

"How long ago did you see him?" Eldred couldn't hide his excitement.

"An hour, a day, a week. When you have lived as long as I have time has no meaning. It seems like yesterday, but then again, so does the beginning of time." She paused for a moment. "If you are a friend of this Alaric as you seem to be then I owe you a favour. Or at least I shall pass on a favour that I owe him. He saved me and others of my kind and we promised to return to help his cause."

Now things were becoming promising, although Eldred wasn't really sure what she could do to help. Outside of their forests the Wood Sprites had no real power and there didn't seem to be any immediate threat.

"Did he say where he was going when he left you?" Eldred needed more information before he worried about a favour.

"He just said he had a long way to go. He was searching for something or someone, I don't really know," Cai replied.

That really didn't give Eldred any answers, but at least he knew that Alaric was still alive. He had left them in such a strange manner that Eldred wasn't sure what he was doing. Something had changed in him, Eldred was sure of that, and he wasn't sure it was such a good thing.

"So what is it that you are doing?" Richmond asked, changing the subject when Eldred didn't respond.

"I am to clear my forest of evil, not that it's much of a task. It was the first thing on my list if I was ever to escape. There is no telling what evil has crept into my forest in my absence."

"I don't think there is much evil in this forest, but I know where there is," Richmond replied.

"You'd be surprised where evil is lurking!"

"The *Tree of Life* is under attack!" Eldred blurted out suddenly. "That is where you should focus your energy."

"That is Arawn's territory. He is the most powerful there. My power is only substantial in my own forest," Cai explained as if it was rudimentary knowledge.

"Be that as it may, you can still help. If the *Tree of Life* falls then every tree, flower and plant will die. You won't have a forest to protect," Eldred explained in much the same tone.

There was a moment of silence and suddenly a shadow passed over them. A morose feeling settled over the group. No one could explain it, but they all felt it. There was a sorrow that was unmistakable and a tear appeared in the corner of Richmond's eye.

"Yes, I know the battle at the *Tree of Life* is important, but I'm sure Arawn's got it under control. It is his responsibility and it is up to him. If the tree falls then we all fall. I have my own job to do and I will see it done." The shadow passed and everyone felt better again. They were now more confident that the *Tree of Life* would survive.

"It sounds like you have it all planned." Eldred didn't sound too sure of his words. "If you have finished with us we really need to be on our way."

"Oh, of course. I believe that you're not evil and your intentions are clear. Be warned though serpentant, you're kind are not welcome here. If you are travelling alone then you will not be as fortunate." There was venom on her words. Before he had a chance to respond she disappeared.

They all suddenly felt very light headed. No one could be completely sure what had actually happened. They all had vague memories of the meeting with the Wood Sprite, but nothing substantial.

"Let's not try to over think it." Eldred was the first to speak. "We need to get out of this forest as quickly as possible. We don't want to be spending another night under the trees."

They rode as quickly as they could and it wasn't long before they came out at the edge of the forest. They reined in the horses as soon as they were out in the open. The sun was already starting to set and Eldred was sure they hadn't been travelling very long. Even the vague memory he had of their meeting with Cai couldn't have lasted that long.

"We should make camp for the night," Richmond suggested. "We don't know what we are riding into and I think it would be foolish to do so in the dark."

Eldred was still trying to gather his thoughts. He looked around and the landscape wasn't at all what he was expecting. They were too far north. Although he couldn't see the mountain range over the trees he knew they should have been parallel with its northernmost point. Something very strange had happened. It was as if they had lost half a day.

"I think you're right. We need to get a fresh perspective on things in the morning," Eldred said, still deeply confused as he looked around at the land before him.

The feeling of disorientation wasn't lost on the others, but hunger and fatigue took the better of them. They wanted nothing more than to fill their stomach and sleep.

As they checked their packs for food they noticed that there was more than there should have been. There were fresh mushrooms, wild berries and what looked to be cured deer. No one had any memory of hunting, let alone having time to cure the meat. It was another mystery, but one they were grateful for.

Chapter 22: Brothers in Arms?

They were all up at the break of dawn. It was the best night's sleep they'd had in a long time and they all felt well rested. It was a feeling that none of them had been expecting. There was still definitely something strange in the air, but it wasn't anything uncomfortable, if anything it made them feel safe.

"Do you have any idea what is going on?" Richmond asked Eldred.

"I can only imagine that Cai had something to do with it." The mention of the Wood Sprite brought recognition from the others.

"That was a strange meeting," Alena responded.

"Although it was only yesterday it seems like it happened a lifetime ago." Viper rubbed his head as if that would unlock something.

"It seems she created a spell to cloud our memories, although I can't for the life of me work out how or why for that matter. It also seems she put us off our course. We are leagues further to the north than we should be," Eldred explained as he looked around again, hoping that the landscape might have changed, but it was the same as the night before.

"I'm sure she has her reasons." Alena looked around and saw for the first time how far off course they were. "Maybe Alaric instructed her to do so."

That was a promising thought. It seemed that Alaric now knew things that others didn't. If Alaric had set their path then they were confident they were on the right one. Regardless they really didn't have any choice.

"So should we change our course? It seems silly to go so far out of our way now," Richmond started when they finished breakfast.

"I don't think so. It will add a lot of time to our journey. There has to be a reason why we are so far north and the only thing I can think of is that we don't reach Lel Dinion too early," Eldred mused. "I don't know what happened last night, but I'm sure it was for a reason. I will consult the prophecy when we camp for the night and see if there are any clues. For now a think we should start moving. All of a sudden I've got a bad feeling and I don't think we should linger any longer."

The feeling of dread also passed over the others and no one wanted to remain for a moment longer. They quickly packed their things and were soon in the saddle. Being on the move lifted their spirits a little, although they were all still concerned with the time they had lost. No one had any memory of what had happened since they left Cai and they only had sketchy memories of their time with her.

The weather on the eastern side of the mountain was much warmer than that on the west. The northern parts of the kingdom generally had higher temperatures. Eventually there would be snow to the south, but not for another month or two. There were clouds in the sky, but they didn't look like they carried rain. All in all it was a pleasant day.

It took them five more days before they reached the first signs of civilization. They arrived at the castle that had been owned by Count Kerwin and Alena cringed at the sight as she remembered the first time she had been imprisoned. Of course it was nothing compared to her captivity in Jarrat. Compared to that, Kerwin had been a walk in the park.

As they came closer it seemed as though the repairs from Hadar's siege had been completed. With a little luck Garag would be inside. Although Hadar's estate was much nicer than Kerwin's castle the title would passed down to Hadar's eldest, Hagar. It made sense for Garag to try and gain his own title and count was a fine one, not to mention readily available.

"Should we go and see who is inside?" Alena asked. "Or just push on to Hadar's estate."

Eldred reined in the horses and thought for a moment. The plan had been to ride straight through to the estate. At best they would stay there for one night before heading to Lel Dinion. Their planned course shouldn't have brought them anywhere near the castle. Eldred had been very conscious of its location and had planned to avoid it. Now it seemed it was right in the middle of their path. Something had led them there, Eldred was sure of it. He had kept a watchful eye on their journey and he was sure they hadn't deviated.

"I think we should go and see what's happening inside," Eldred suggested. "If nothing else we can bathe and have a hot meal. I for one wouldn't mind washing and getting into some clean clothes." It was a weak excuse, but no one complained. The thought was promising for all of them, even Viper.

Viper had spent months living in the castle when he was keeping a watch on Kerwin. That was his first chance to meet Alaric and Eldred and it gave him the opportunity to interpose himself on the group. He had to admit he was looking forward to returning.

The northern gate was shut, which didn't seem right to Eldred. There had been no sign of any danger since they had entered Hondin Lel. He had to admit that they had been away from society, but he still didn't think there was any need for the castle to be locked up in the middle of the day.

"Approach with care. I have a feeling that something isn't right," Eldred warned as they came within bow range.

The land had started to recover from the disease that Kerwin had brought with him. The boulders and rocks that had strewn the land had been removed. What was just dust and dirt now showed patches of grass and even some flowers grew here and there. The open area did nothing the ease their nerves, especially after Eldred's dire warning.

There was no sign of anyone as they neared the northern gate. It wasn't until they stopped out the front did a small slot open on the guard house. All they could see was a set of eyes looking out at them and they did not look pleased.

"Who are you?" the voice barked. "Speak truly. There are a hundred archers all aiming their arrows at you. One sharp peel on my horn and you will all be dead."

Eldred doubted that was true, but at the same time he didn't look around to confirm it. Despite the lie he knew that they were in danger.

"I am Eldred the Wizard. I helped to liberate this castle from Kerwin and the Evil One. I seek shelter and an audience with the new count." Eldred felt it was better if he didn't introduce his companions. If it was Garag who was in command of the castle then he didn't want to do anything to hinder their entrance.

"Your name is familiar to me, but I'm not sure if I believe your intentions. It is rumoured that you tricked our lord into servitude. It is also rumoured that you work for the Evil One and you had Duke Hadar murdered." The guard's voice still held its command, but there was an edge of something else. "Who else is it that you bring to our gates?"

Eldred had hoped to avoid introducing the others, but there seemed to be no other choice. He wished he had thought up a good excuse for Viper, although he was completely covered and there was no way of telling he was a serpentant.

"This is the Lady Alena, daughter of Lord Orric and heir to the Seat of the Elves." He pointed his hand towards Alena as he spoke. "And this is Lord Richmond of Bellarome." He introduced Richmond and ignored Viper altogether.

"That is very good, but there is also another with you. What is his or her name and why are they completely covered from head to toe?" his voice dripped with suspicion.

"This is Lord Richmond's retainer. He has taken ill on our journey and is covered to stop his disease from spreading." Viper made a show of coughing to play his part.

"If he is that sick then I don't believe we want him inside the castle. These are dangerous times and the last thing we want is an epidemic." Eldred knew the guard wasn't going to let them in. Now it was time to try a different tact.

"Who is in command of the castle now? Since we helped remove the old count I think we deserve to know who his replacement is." Eldred had started creating a spell as he spoke. If the guard wasn't going to just let him in then a little manipulation was in order.

"Wait here! I need to speak with my commanding officer." The guard suddenly didn't sound so sure of himself.

Eldred then realised Viper had created a spell first. It wasn't quite the same as the one Eldred was going to use and it didn't seem to have the desired effect. He was about to berate him when Richmond spoke.

"Maybe we should just leave. I'm sure we'll have a better response at Hadar's estate."

"I don't think that's a good idea. For whatever reason we are here now and I think we should see how it plays out." Eldred whispered. "But what were you thinking?" Eldred kept his voice low as he scolded Viper. "I had the spell covered and we would have been in the castle by now."

"There is something..." Viper was cut off as the slit reopened.

"Count Garag has agreed to see you. Your weapons will be forfeited at the gate and returned to you once you leave."

"We are not going to surrender our weapons. They are vital to our quest and not a danger to you. We are here in peace and nothing is going to change that." Richmond couldn't believe what he was hearing. "I am Lord Richmond of Bellarome and I won't be subjected to such an insult."

"Calm down Richmond. It's not the end of the world." Eldred tried to soothe him. He wasn't happy about giving up his sword, but there was more than one way they could defend themselves. He was sure that between Viper and himself they would be safe enough. "We will surrender our weapons."

There was a moment of silence. Viper was about speak, but then the gate started to squeak open.

"There is something you need to know," Viper started.

"Not now Viper. This can wait," Eldred barked as the commander and half a dozen guards marched out. "We need to see the count and find out what is happening. I have a bad feeling something isn't right."

"Present your weapons." The commander barked before Viper had a chance to respond.

Reluctantly they all gave up their weapons. Even the knives they used for cooking and eating were surrendered. It seemed a little excessive, but that was the instruction the guards had been given. The feeling of unrest only increased inside Eldred. This kind of security was too much, even for such troubled times.

"Is that the last of it?" the commander asked.

The guards nodded their response when they were satisfied with the search. Eldred was glad he had placed the spell on the chest containing the stones. He cringed at what would happen if they had been discovered, especially the Jade dagger. There was no chance Eldred would let them take the chest, even if they did have every intention of returning it.

Viper was about to speak again as they rode through the gates but the commander cut in.

"You would do well to remain quiet until you reach the throne room. Strangers aren't taken too well here and your words might insight the locals." The commander kept his voice low, but it lost none of its power.

Once they were inside the castle they were told to dismount as the stable hands came to take away the horses. No one really wanted to leave them, but there was no other choice. There could be no doubt that something was amiss. They felt, more than ever, that they were walking into a trap. Viper looked more nervous than the others and he wanted nothing more than to speak with Eldred, but it didn't look like he was going to get a chance.

It was obvious that the walls had been patched up since Hadar's army had destroyed them. All the rubble had been cleared from the castle forecourt and despite the man power needed to undertake the repairs; the castle seemed to be relatively empty. Apart from the group heading up the main stairs there was no one else outside. It was eerily quiet, which only added to their discomfort.

Inside the castle was a different story. The halls were filled with functionaries rushing around on an errand or two. They looked too busy to care about visitors. There was a sense of fear about them.

"What is happening here?" Eldred asked the commander. "It seems as though things aren't any better than when we were here last." The comment was fair, but he was never going to get a great response.

"I said keep quiet and I mean keep quiet." He spoke in a hushed tone. There was an edge of fear in his voice.

Eldred didn't push any further. It was clear that the commander of the guard was only doing what he was told. It was a strange situation and only patience was going to give him the answers that he required. Viper still needed to speak with Eldred, but he didn't want to say anything in front of the others. He too realised that Eldred would have to wait to hear what he had to say.

The commander paused when they reached the throne room door. It was clear that not only did he not want to open it, but he also didn't want to knock. Eventually he turned to Eldred.

"You can go on in. I believe you are expected." The commander didn't wait for a response. He just turned and hurried back down the corridor. He wanted to be as far away from the throne room as he could.

Eldred didn't wait. It was the perfect opportunity for Viper to speak, but there was nothing he could do. The wizard pushed the door open with confidence and stepped into the room. The scene before him wasn't at all what he had been expecting.

At the far end the new count, Garag, sat alone. There were no signs of the last count anywhere. All the paintings and tapestries had been stripped from the walls. There were rugs and cushions scattered on the floor with a number of half naked women sprawled out across them. At first a rage built up inside of Eldred and he had to push it down before he continued. He then realised there was someone standing behind the throne. They were dressed in a black robe with the hood drawn, obscuring them completely from view. Whoever it was Eldred knew they weren't a friend.

"Count Garag, I am surprised to see you here," Eldred took a number of steps into the room as he spoke. "I thought your father had left you charge of his estates?" He tried to get straight to the point and get Garag on the back foot.

"That is a fine way to present oneself to the new count. I know you have deceived my father into believing you were his friend, but I know that is not true. You will not pull the wool over my eyes like you did him." His words seemed off, but Eldred pushed that to the side.

"I have known you since you were a child. You know that I have done nothing to deceive your family. I have always been a friend to your father, and his father and his before him and I have always done what I could to assist them in their time of need. Why do you question my character?" Eldred tried to delve into Garag's mind but realised someone had blocked him.

"Oh you see, I came prepared for this meeting." An evil smile crossed his face as he saw the change in Eldred's expression. "I will not have my mind twisted by your magic. I have my own protection." The grin remained on his face. "You were right. You knew exactly what he was going to do." He spoke to the hooded figure lurking behind the throne.

As if he had just been noticed the figure walked out from behind the throne. There was a presence about him that made Richmond's skin crawl and yet it was somewhat familiar. He wasn't the only one who was surprised when a scaled hand pulled back the hood of his robe revealing a reptilian face. Viper was the only one who was prepared for the revelation. For the moment he was prepared to remain anonymously behind the others, but he knew that wouldn't last long. He was surprised that his brother had not already named him. For the moment he seemed to be focused on Eldred. That would be his downfall. When the time was right he would strike, but until then he would remain silent.

The others resisted the urge to turn around and look at Viper, as much as they wanted to. They didn't know that he had cast a small spell keeping them facing forward, even Eldred hadn't noticed.

"What is this treachery?" Eldred didn't know what else to say. He pulled himself short as he remembered that Viper was still in the room.

"The treachery is on your behalf Eldred. My advisor has been very instructive," Garag snarled.

"At least give me the name of he who would besmirch my name."

"I am surprised you don't know me wizard." The serpentant sounded insulted. "I am Taipan. I would have thought you would have known that, but it seems that I might have given you too much credit."

Now Eldred could see the resemblance, although when Eldred had seen him last his scaly skin had been a lot darker. Now it was a dull yellow, with only specks of brown. They would have to tread lightly. Taipan could be as dangerous as a Dark Knight and if Viper was also cut from the power around them they were completely helpless.

"I do apologise Taipan. I didn't recognise you." Eldred felt it was wise to placate him.

"Don't patronise me Eldred, we know of your scheming and it comes to an end here. You will never see the light of day again," Taipan hissed.

Now it all became clear. There would be no real discussion. Anything they would talk about would just be wasting time. They were trapped. Without magic and without their weapons they were completely defenceless. There was only one way Eldred could see them getting out alive and that was something he didn't want to do. He still had his pack which contained the five *Stones of Power*, but there was no telling what would happen if he tried to use one.

"What is this treachery brother?" Viper asked as he stepped forward, revealing his face.

"Ah, I should have known you would be here!" If Taipan was startled by Viper's appearance he didn't show it. Garag on the other hand looked shocked that there was another serpentant in his throne room. "It is your fault that I am forced to be here in the first place, I have to take over from where you failed."

Eldred was suddenly very confused. He wanted to ask the question that was on all their minds, but he didn't want to interrupt them. He hoped his question might be answered in their discussion.

"But this isn't the time for that conversation. We shall speak of this later, if you survive." There was no emotion to his voice. Taipan could have been taking about the weather.

"We have all been betrayed by the Evil One." Viper tried to appease his brother. Taipan was renowned for being the most powerful of the serpentants and it was obvious that he had recently shed his skin. Depending on the time frame he would either still be weak or he would be more powerful than ever. Viper hadn't tested his own skills since their meeting with Kahn, but he knew he would be stronger.

Although Taipan was working for Nyrra he was still a serpentant and Viper would see the world destroyed before killing one of his own. If Taipan was the first to strike then there was nothing he could do. As much as he didn't think his brother would fight him, it was against the law of the Goddess, there was no telling how deep Nyrra's betrayal had sunk in. "You shouldn't be doing this brother. This is not what the Goddess wants."

"How dare you speak for the Goddess?" Taipan's voice rose. "You gave up that right when you betrayed her. We are all lucky that Nyrra hasn't already killed her for your betrayal."

"Wake up to yourself Taipan. You were once considered our leader. Surely you can see through his ruse. Nyrra has imprisoned the Goddess and only with his death will she be free."

"Enough of this talk?" Garag didn't sound so sure of himself. All the talk of the Evil One and the Goddess had him confused. He had been confused a lot lately. He thought they were doing the right thing, but now he wasn't so sure. It was the wizard and his motley crew that worshipped the Evil One. For the first time that thought didn't seem right to him, but it quickly passed. "You will spend the rest of your days in my dungeons, where traitors belong." Some of the confidence returned to his voice.

"That isn't going to happen," Eldred's voice was firm.

"And just how are you going to stop us?" There was an evil sneer on his face. "I have your weapons and my friend here has blocked you from the power you so desperately need." The sneer grew broader. "Soldiers! Arrest them."

Three soldiers to their left and three to their right drew their swords and slowly started to approach. As much as they would listen to what the new count ordered, they also weren't sure they were doing the right thing. There was also something about Garag and Taipan's nonchalant stances that made them nervous. Although they were the only ones with weapons they didn't feel as though they held the advantage.

Eldred dropped his pack to the ground. Although using the stone wasn't something he wanted to do he didn't seem to have a choice. The power of one of the stones should be enough to break Taipan's spell, although he wasn't confident he would survive to see the results.

Before Eldred had a chance to move any further Viper stepped forward again. He raised his hands out to his side with his palms out. Before the soldiers could get within striking distance they were lifted from the ground. The sound of chinking steel on stone was heard as some of them dropped their swords in surprise. It was not at all what they were expecting.

"Do something!" Garag boomed to Taipan.

"What?" Taipan gasped when he realised he couldn't cast a spell.

"Do as I command!" Panic filled Garag's voice when nothing happened.

There was little Taipan could do. The spell keeping Eldred from the power was gone. He had no idea how it had happened, there should have been no way Viper could break his spell and block him.

"I have the power of the dragons within me. When I met Khan he breathed his life force into me."

A flick of his fingers was the only indication he had adjusted the spell before the soldiers flew against the nearest wall. Although it didn't seem as though they struck the wall very hard, all six slumped to the ground unconscious.

A sudden look of fear appeared on the Counts face. He wanted to flee in terror, but his legs wouldn't move. Somewhere, deep in the back of his mind, a voice was telling him to stay. He wasn't sure why, but he knew he had to listen to it. Although the spell Taipan had cast on him was gone his mind was still hazy.

Viper took another step forward and hissed, just loud enough for everyone to hear. "Forgive me Goddess for what I must do!" The words sent a shot of fear into Taipan's heart.

Before anyone had a chance to react Viper swung his arms around in front of him. The air shimmered from his palms towards Taipan. When it struck, he was flung back against the far wall.

"What is going on here?" Garag's voice sounded hoarse and confused.

"You will regret this. This is just another sign that you have betrayed the Goddess and all your brothers. The next time we meet you will you not live to see us part, that I promise you." Taipan flicked his tongue at the group before disappearing through a door behind the thrones.

"Should we go after him?" Richmond asked, not really keen to follow.

"I have already done too much. I couldn't forgive myself if we killed him, if that's even an option." Viper, for the first time since they had known him, sounded regretful.

"Viper is right. I don't think it would prove favourable to follow Taipan. There is no telling what he would do if he was cornered and I for one don't want to find out," Eldred agreed. He was just relieved he didn't have to use one of the *Stones of Power*. "What do you have to say for yourself count?" Eldred's words were firm.

"I...I'm sorry Eldred." He rubbed his head before he spoke again. "I don't know what came over me. One day I was at home and then... What did you call me?" There was genuine confusion in his voice.

There was a pause. No one had been expecting that question. It was Richmond who was first to come up with an answer.

"You are now Count Garag. You have taken command from Count Kerwin and it seems as though you have carried on from where he left off." Richmond didn't go easy on him.

"I think... someone... is going to... have to explain..." was all Garag managed to sat before he collapsed to the floor.

Again a shocked silence fell around the room. No one had expected him to have such a reaction and no one knew what to do. As far as the rest of the castle was concerned they were prisoners and the scene before them did nothing to help their cause. The count and his six guards were all unconscious. There would be little chance of explaining the situation, but on the other hand they couldn't just leave the men where they were.

"What should we do?" Richmond asked in panic.

"We can't just leave them here," Alena sounded shocked at what Richmond was implying.

"I don't particularly want to spend the night in a gaol cell either," Richmond replied sharply.

"It won't come to that. I saw the look on the faces of those in the halls. It didn't look like they were happy with the situation. Even the guard at the gate didn't seem quite right, despite his staunch attitude." Alena explained. "I'm sure the soldiers will just be glad that their new count is no longer under the thrall of a serpentant."

That seemed to make sense to everyone. The soldiers Viper attacked would have only a vague memory of what had happened and it already seemed that Garag had no idea. That would prove in their favour.

"Guards, the count is in trouble!" Richmond suddenly called out at the top of his voice.

Before long the door was pushed open and a dozen soldiers rushed into the room with their swords drawn. They were all instantly confused. It wasn't until their eyes reached the count lying on the ground did one of the soldiers move into action. He took a tentative step forward before he spoke.

"You are under arrest?" he didn't sound at all sure of himself. "For attacking the count and his guards?"

"Don't be ridiculous," Richmond snapped before the soldier could continued. "We saved the count from a rather nasty creature." Richmond hoped that he wouldn't offend Viper. He was relieved to see that he had covered himself again. "A serpentant had Count Garag in his thrall. If we hadn't intervened when we did there is no telling what would have happened. Unfortunately these brave men were caught in the crossfire. But that is a story for another time. I think it would be a good idea to take the count to his rooms where he'll be a little more comfortable and someone should probably find the count's physician. I'm sure he'll make a full recovery, but it's better to be safe than sorry."

There was no time for the soldiers to question Richmond's story, he made sure of that. It was not the first time he had spoken to soldiers in such a manner. When he was commanding his soldiers in Bellarome he found it best not to give them time to think, especially if you wanted them to undertake a potentially fatal mission. It seemed as though his plan had worked. The soldiers quickly moved into action.

After the unconscious guards and the count were removed from the throne room, Richmond called over one of the soldiers.

"Have the count's steward come and see us. We are going to need rooms for the night and some food would be nice." As the soldier was about to leave another thought crossed his mind. "Oh, and see that our weapons are returned to us."

"I'm sorry my lord, but we were instructed to take your weapons." The soldier sounded embarrassed.

"And who do you think made that command? If we still had our weapons maybe this wouldn't have happened," he showed the mess that was still scattered around the throne room. "Now I think you would be wise to follow my instructions."

The soldier bowed before leaving. He wasn't sure he trusted Richmond's words, but he knew it was better to agree than argue with a nobleman.

It wasn't long before they were soaking in hot baths and relaxing for the night. They were confident that Taipan was long gone and the threat was over. This was the first real opportunity they had to spoil themselves since they had left the Wizards Isle and they were going to take it. There was nothing else they could do until Count Garag had recovered anyway and that wasn't going to happen that night. There would be plenty of time to worry after a good feed and a good night's sleep.

Chapter 23: The Truth

In the morning Eldred requested to see the count. Initially his request was denied as the count still had not woken from his coma, but when Eldred explained he could help the soldiers quickly changed their minds. Richmond's presence, with an evil scowl on his face, certainly helped persuade them.

The physician was pacing around when they reached the count's bedroom. There were two young ladies sitting on either side of the bed, alternately dabbing Garag's face with wet towels. Their clothes were too nice to be serving women. Richmond guessed that they were suitors hoping to one day be the Countess. If it wasn't for the severity of the situation he would have found it quite humorous.

"Please, give me some room." Eldred stood at the end of the bed when he spoke to the two ladies. He didn't want to move to either side because he knew the other lady would remain and assume he had chosen her for the role.

When they left, he walked calmly to the side of the bed. Slowly he delved into Garag's mind in an effort to see what was wrong. Luckily he didn't find anything residual that Taipan had left behind; whatever the spell the serpentant had used it didn't seem to be very strong. Eldred concentrated for a moment before releasing a subtle spell. Instantly Garag opened his eyes and gasped for air. The sudden movement made everyone in the room jump.

At first the count seemed dazed and confused, but slowly he regained his senses. When he did he looked around the room. At first he didn't recognise the newcomers, until he saw Eldred.

"Great Wizard! You are a sight for sore eyes. What brings you here? Is there word of my father?" the questions rushed out of his mouth.

Eldred laughed out loudly. "It seems your recovery is fast, young count."

"Why do you call me count?" A sudden realisation came over him. "Duke would be my title if my father and brother were dead. Tell me Eldred. Are they dead?" panic filled his voice.

"Calm yourself Garag. Your father is fine. I haven't heard word from your brother, but I have to assume the same. You have assumed the role of Count of Lel Keldon," Eldred explained.

"What? When did this happen? Why is my memory so sketchy?"

"One question at a time Garag." Eldred kept a warm, comforting smile on his face. "From what I hear it was about two weeks back. It seems the repairs were all but done and the people needed a count."

"I shouldn't have been that person." Garag protested. "My life is at home looking after my father's estates while he's away."

"What's done is done." Eldred tried his best to get Garag to relax. He had been through quite an ordeal and the extra tension would do him no good. "You are now the count and there is nothing you can do about it."

"I can renounce my position!"

"That wouldn't prove anything. The people need a leader and from what I gather they are happy with you. Kerwin was a pox on this land and a strong leader is what it needs to recover," Eldred explained.

"But how did I become the count? That's what doesn't make sense. The last thing I really remember is sitting in court with mother. There was a visitor in town that said he had news on father. Everything else from there on is hazy."

Eldred had hoped to wait a while before explaining what really happened, but it seemed Garag wasn't going to let it go.

"That visitor was a serpentant by the name of Taipan," Eldred explained. "He placed a spell on you and convinced you that you were the rightful replacement for Kerwin. Truth-be-told I don't think he was far wrong, but I doubt that was his true intention." Eldred paused and looked over at Viper. There was something the serpentant was keeping secret. He knew more about the situation than he was letting on. That was a conversation they were going to have to have sooner rather than later. "Now I think you should get some rest. There will be time for revelations later." With that Eldred ushered everyone out of the room before Garag had a chance to argue.

They didn't speak until they were back in Richmond's guest room. As a visiting noble he had been given the largest room available. It was much more comfortable to have their discussion there.

"It's time to tell me what's going on here Viper. It's no coincidence that you were here when we first met and now Taipan. What is the significance of this place?" Eldred cut to the chase.

"What do you mean?" Viper tried to act innocent.

"Don't do that Viper!" Eldred boomed. "You know exactly what I'm talking about. You knew we were walking into a trap and you could have prevented it."

"That's not exactly true, although I should have realised that Nyrra would have found someone to replace me," Viper confessed. "I don't know what it is about this castle, but it seems to have some significance. Nyrra knew that you would be travelling this way, at least once, and he told me that I had to kidnap Alena and bring her to him." There was an awkward silence. "I was never going to do it!" he spoke defensively, but the others didn't look convinced. "I came here to make sure that Kerwin didn't succeed. The Evil One put a lot of effort into controlling this place. He bestowed some great power on the former count. If I wasn't here then there is no telling what might have happened. He might have even succeeded first time around."

"So what about Taipan? When Nyrra failed with you, he put your brother in your place?" Eldred still didn't like what he was hearing.

"That does seem to be the case, but I wasn't to know. I thought when I let you leave last time that was the end of it. I should have known better. I apologise, but things have worked out for the best and I believe that I have suffered enough," Viper replied.

"Suffered? How have you suffered?" Alena didn't like what she was hearing. "You put me out like bait and then claim you have suffered. How could you have..."

"It's okay Alena." Eldred tried to calm her. "Attacking another serpentant is a crime unpunishable to his kind. It has never been done before. What Viper did today could very well see him ostracised from his brothers." That was enough to quieten her harsh words.

"Not only that, but I may have sealed the Goddess's fate. I don't think Taipan or anyone of my brothers will believe me now. Even those who were on my side will surely change their minds once Taipan speaks to them." Despite his sorrowful words there was no regret in his voice.

"Then why did you do it?" Alena asked. "Surely we could have found another solution?"

"I did it because I believe the only way to save the Goddess is to destroy Nyrra and the best way to do that is to make sure you all make your final destination," Viper spoke honestly.

If there were any doubts of Viper's loyalty before, they were now gone. He had risked everything to save them from his brother and although his motives were different, the end result was the same. Now he was bound to them and everyone accepted it.

It was mid-afternoon when Garag finally surfaced and he called for the others to join him in the throne room. They had all decided, and there were no complaints, that Viper should remain in the room prepared for him. As much as he was covered they didn't want to take the risk of anyone realising who or more importantly what he was. They would simply explain that Viper was exhausted from their travelling and the excitement of the previous day's events.

The throne room had been cleaned and tables and chairs were being brought in for the evening meal. The first thing Garag had done when he recovered was ask his chief steward to organise a banquet for his new guests.

"My friends, thank you for joining me. I'd prefer to get business out of the way before the feast tonight." Garag greeted them.

"That is very generous, but you didn't need to go to all this trouble on our account." Eldred said. Although there didn't seem to be any animosity between Garag and Richmond he didn't want to give the new count any reason to remember the past.

"As my steward explained to me there was no real celebration when I became count. As much as it was an unorthodox rising to power, the people of Lel Keldon seem happy enough with me as their leader. I think that is reason enough for a celebration. The people deserve it considering what they have been through over the last few years. Kerwin's subjugation wasn't pleasant and although I didn't do anything untoward, the people were concerned with my rise to power," Garag explained.

"Well that does sound like a good excuse to celebrate. We will enjoy some respite tonight and then ride to see your mother in the morning. We need information about what is happening in the capital," Eldred explained.

"Then you'd be best to speak with my brother. I believe that Hagar has not long returned from the capital," Garag explained. "I'm sure he'll be able to answer any of your questions."

"That was one of the questions I needed answered." They moved to a more comfortable position as the conversation continued. A table and chairs had been set for them along with a decanter of wine as well as a pot of tea. "We were wondering why Hagar never made it to the Alliance. Duke Hadar promised the army to the Alliance and Hagar was supposed to lead them there."

There was a moment of silence as Garag thought. His memory was still sketchy, but he knew the answer was there somewhere. Everyone sipped their drinks as they waited for a response.

"The command came from the king himself, that I can remember. That is all I can remember. I know there is more to the story, but you will have to ask my brother." Garag spoke honestly.

That was clearly the end of the conversation. Eldred wasn't so sure Garag's memory was as cloudy as he made out, but he wasn't going to push any further. Whatever the reason for the army being turned around he preferred to hear it from Hagar himself.

"So what do you know of the capital?" Eldred changed the subject.

"I don't have any information. I'm sorry Eldred, but my memory is still hazy. I'm afraid that I'm not going to be much use to you."

"That's alright. Any information you have could be vital to us. Is there anything you can remember?" Eldred wasn't going to let it go. If they were going to waste a day staying for the feast then he needed to make it somewhat worthwhile.

Garag paused as he thought, taking a sip of his wine. Alena shook her head. She was the only one who was drinking tea. It seemed as though it was going to be a big night and she wouldn't be surprised if there were some sore heads in the morning.

"I do remember hearing something about the king having a new advisor." Slowly some of his memories were starting to return. "In fact I believe it was the new advisor who sent the serpentant to place me in power here." He paused and thought again. "I'm not sure if that is true or not." He didn't sound confident.

There was no doubt in Eldred's mind that the new advisor was the Dark Knight Argoz. At least he now had confirmation, if there was ever any real doubt. He didn't think there was going to be much more useful information from Garag. Now they really needed to be on their way, but they were obliged the stay for the feast. There was nothing wrong with having a good meal and another good night's sleep before they hit the road again.

Before Garag could continue with his thought he was called away by his steward.

"I'm sorry, but there seems to be some business I need to take care of," Garag apologised. "All my resources are at your disposal whilst you are in my castle. If you need anything you need just call for one of my staff." And with that Garag left them.

When they were alone, Alena spoke. "I think we should keep moving. We have gained all the information we are going to get from here. I don't see any advantage in remaining for the feast tonight."

Richmond was about to protest her statement, but Eldred silenced him with a wave of his hand. If it was definitely time to leave then he was sure he would feel the tug of the prophecy. There was nothing urging him forward and that generally meant it was time to remain where they were.

"I don't think another day of rest is going to hurt us. We should stay until morning and make sure that Garag is comfortable to run this land." It was a weak excuse, but it was enough to silence Alena. Even as she spoke she knew they weren't going anywhere.

They all took the opportunity to bathe and relax for the rest of the afternoon. The sun had almost completely set when they were finally summoned to the throne room.

An armed guard escorted them through the corridors and around the back of the throne room. The front entrance was filled with those waiting to join in the feast. Garag had ordered that no one be admitted until his guests of honour had arrived. Eldred though that was very foolish, them being guests of honour, but he didn't complain. At such short notice there were no visiting lords or ladies, so it did make sense that they be treated as special.

Richmond had to admit that he was impressed when he stepped into the room. It seemed as though the inhabitants of the castle had been waiting for such an occasion. He knew whenever he planned such festivities it took at the very least a week to get everything prepared, but it seemed as though they had put everything together in less than a day. Richmond could only think that they had everything in the wings ready to go once their new count had regained his senses.

The entertainment started with a fire breather and a juggling duo. They started as soon as the guests of honour were seated and the main doors were opened.

"This is very impressive," Richmond complimented.

"It seems as though we didn't have a real celebration for my new position. The people have been ready ever since I became count. It was just a matter of moving it all into the throne room." Garag returned, but he couldn't keep the smile from his face. "This is going to be a good night," he added before bursting into laughter.

The food and wine flowed around the room and there were plenty of both. Alena again declined the offer of wine, unlike the other two. She could forgive Richmond. He was a man and subject to overindulgences, but Eldred was a different story. He was a wizard and should know better. They would need to be on the road early in the morning and the last thing they needed was to be delayed by a pair of sore heads. Despite her feeling she wasn't going to ruin their fun.

"I can't begin to thank you for what you have done for me," Garag addressed Eldred as the main course was being cleared. "My steward gave me a brief rundown of what has happened since I came into power. The hold the serpentant had over me made me do some things that I'm not proud of. I'm grateful you came along when you did. Apparently I had created some laws that would see good people end up in my prisons. I hate to think what would have happened to them."

That was a thought that wasn't worth thinking about. Both Eldred and Alena had been imprisoned by one of Nyrra's agents and they knew it wasn't fun. As much as they had received special treatment that also heard the cries of others being tortured.

"Let's hope that this is the last time Nyrra tries to take control of Lel Keldon." Eldred offered. "I don't think that our paths will cross here again, at least not until this is all over. There should be no reason for him to try again."

"I hope you are right Eldred," despite the drink his voice was sober. "But I'm not going to take that for granted. I have sent word to the king that I need more soldiers to defend this castle."

Eldred was about to take a sip of wine, but he stopped before the goblet reached his lips. That was not at all what he had hoped to hear. In fact he didn't think he could have heard anything much worse.

"When did you send your messenger?" Eldred asked, returning the goblet to the table.

"Shortly after we met this afternoon. With a little luck he should be halfway to the capital by now." Garag seemed surprised at the question.

"Then it's not too late to send someone after him. I'd imagine he would have stopped somewhere for the night. If you send someone after him now he should be able to catch him before morning," Eldred returned.

"I don't understand your request Eldred. Do you want to leave me at risk of attack? I know you don't believe there is a threat, but after Kerwin we are well undermanned."

"Not at all." Eldred afforded himself a light chuckle. He hoped it would ease the tension. "We believe there is a Dark Knight now in control of the kingdom." Eldred's voice became stern. There was no time for humour now. "I don't think it would be a good idea to let the Dark Knight know that Nyrra has lost control of this castle. The last thing we want is to give him an excuse to return and attack," Eldred explained.

It took a moment for the information to register, but when it did Garag quickly stood and motioned for his steward to approach. As much as he didn't want to believe there was a Dark Knight in the capital it wasn't a risk he was prepared to make.

"I think I might call it a night!" Alena exclaimed suddenly once the steward had left. "We need to be up early in the morning to be on the road again." She wasn't sure if the other two received the hint.

The festivities were still in full swing as Alena made her way out the back door. Two guards escorted her back to her room. Although she knew her way and felt that it was completely ridiculous the new count insisted. They wanted to walk her into her room, but she promptly denied them.

Alena waited at her door for her escorts to leave her view. She was not sure why she insisted on turning them away or why she waited so long to open her door, but as soon as she walked into her room she wished she hadn't. Even as the door slowly opened she could sense the presence in her room. Instantly she reached for her sword before she realised that she wasn't wearing one. The flowing silk dress, which the count had provided her for the feast, was not suitable for fighting. All the odds were already stacked against her.

It wasn't until she stepped into the room did she realise who she was up against. Even though Viper was bent over, looking through her packs and clothes, she recognised him. At first he didn't seem to notice that she had entered the room and as she closed the door he suddenly froze, stood upright and turned around. The hood of his robe was down and it looked like he no longer cared to keep his identity secret. There was something else though, something more disturbing. A crazed expression sat on his face. It was hard to tell his expressions at the best of times, but Alena was sure that was it.

"What are you doing?" Alena snapped, the sudden fear replaced with anger.

"Where is it? Where are they?" he turned around and started pulling clothes out of her packs. Alena just watched in shock. She had no idea what he was looking for. "I know you know where they are. Now tell me or face the consequences." He kept rummaging through her possessions as he voice rose.

"I have no idea what you're talking about Viper. Now get out of my things." Alena took a step forward, but went no further as Viper suddenly rose again.

"Don't lie to me, elf." It was his turn to take a step forward as Alena retreated back towards the door.

Before Alena could put a hand on the doorknob Viper cast his spell. All her muscles froze from her neck down. There was nothing she could do. She was trapped.

"See, there is nothing you can do." He started to pace back and forth. "I can rip you to shreds if I want to." There was no denying his threat. Alena knew that she was completely at his mercy. "Tell me where it is."

"I still don't know what you're talking about." The words were hard to say. The pressure on her chest made it very hard to speak.

Her words enraged the serpentant further and he increased the grip on her chest. Alena gasped for breath as it felt like her chest was going to explode.

"I can't help you if you don't tell me what you are looking for." The words struggled out of her mouth.

Viper barged forward until he was standing face to face with Alena. "The stones, elf. I want the stones. I know they are in a box. Now tell me where they are."

Alena was in shocked at his words and his motivation. There had been plenty of opportunities for him to steal the stones. She couldn't work out why he was trying to now.

"I don't know where they are," she squeaked as the pressure tightened again. "Only Eldred knows where they are. I promise. If I knew I'd tell you."

Viper suddenly looked unsure of himself, but the fanaticism was still there. Something wasn't right and Alena needed to figure it out before it was too late. Viper returned to the middle of the room, but he was not going to stop his interrogation.

"The Great Lord told me that you knew where they were." Viper didn't sound so confident as the words came out of his mouth.

Before he had a chance to continue or Alena had a chance to question him, the door burst open. First into the room was Eldred, followed by Richmond and two guards. There were more soldiers outside, but there was no room for them to enter.

Viper launched a small ball of flame at Eldred, but it didn't make it half way across the room before fizzling out. Eldred was prepared for an attack and had one of his own ready. He had expected the return of Taipan and it was the sight of Viper that had stayed his hand. Viper didn't waste a moment. He turned and shot a larger ball of fire at the back wall which exploded once it struck. A large hole appeared in the wall and before anyone had a chance to react Viper disappeared through it to the other side.

"Go after him!" Richmond wanted to, but had better sense. Eldred was the only one equipped to handle the serpentant, but he didn't seem to be in any hurry. "What are you waiting for?"

Viper had left the spell that had restricted Alena and Eldred was carefully unravelling it. The serpentant had left a dangerous little twist to it. With every passing moment the constriction continued. If Eldred had chased after Viper then Alena would be dead before his return. That wasn't the only reason, but it was certainly the most important.

"Guards, go after him!" Richmond commanded. "I don't want him leaving the castle."

"Save it Richmond." Eldred let himself be distracted. "Those men will only get themselves killed if they approach Viper. He's gone now."

The soldiers listened to Eldred. As much as they would have done as they were ordered they would rather not. They knew how dangerous a serpentant could be and they didn't think they would survive the encounter.

"Now make yourself useful." Eldred motioned him towards Alena who was starting to waver.

Unfortunately Richmond was too slow to react and Alena collapsed to her knees. As soon as she was released from the spell she sucked in as much air as she could, causing her to cough violently. Richmond quickly moved to her side, but she promptly pushed him away. She remained on her knees for a full minute as she tried to regain her breath. Eventually her breathing calmed down and she returned to her feet.

"Are you alright?" Richmond asked, still standing by her side.

"I will be," she still sounded weak. "Viper took me by surprise." The excuse was weak, but no one mentioned it.

"Let Count Garag know that everything is okay," Eldred commanded one of the guards. "I don't want him to cancel his celebrations on our behalf." That was as good an excuse as any to clear the room. Despite the large hole in the wall opening to the next room Eldred was comfortable with their privacy. "What happened here?"

Alena moved to her bed and looked at the hole in the wall as she tried to collect her thoughts. She didn't know what to make of her encounter with Viper. It certainly didn't make any sense. They all trusted him and as much as his motives seemed to be legitimate now she now wasn't so sure. There was something that didn't sit right with her. As much as she couldn't be completely sure of what happened she had to share what she saw.

"He was looking for the stones." Alena finally blurted out.

"What?" Eldred wasn't completely sure he heard correctly.

"He was looking for the *Stones of Power*," she repeated.

"Why would he be in here?" Eldred was still trying to comprehend the statement. "He knows that I have the chest."

"This doesn't make any sense," Richmond added. "Why would he choose now to try and steal the stones?"

"Richmond is right. There were many other opportunities for him to try and take the stones. He could have used Kahn to try and get them. Are you sure that's what he was doing?" Eldred still couldn't get his head around things.

Even Alena had to think back on her experience. She knew that it didn't make sense, but she was also sure that it had happened.

"Are you sure Taipan didn't return?" Richmond asked.

That thought had crossed her mind, but there was no doubt it was Viper. The two serpentants, as much as they looked alike, were clearly different.

"I know it wasn't him. As much as I couldn't tell between the other six I know what Viper looks like. It was definitely him, but there was also something different about him. It's hard to explain, but I guess the easiest way is that he seemed crazed. It was almost like he was possessed. He was babbling about the Great Lord and he needed the stones. Is it possible that Nyrra got to him?"

Eldred pondered on the idea. He didn't think that was the case. As much power as Nyrra had Eldred was sure he would feel his presence if he was that close.

Before Eldred had a chance to answer there was a knock on the door and the count promptly entered without waiting for permission. He looked a little unsteady on his feet, but there was nothing but determination on his face.

"I came as soon as I heard," the count slightly slurred his speech before catching himself. "My soldiers are sweeping the palace for the serpentant. I can't believe he returned after you defeated him."

Richmond was about to speak, but Eldred silenced him. The count didn't need to know there was another serpentant in the castle. He was sure that Viper was now long gone.

"I'm sure he's gone for good this time. He tried to steal something from us, but to no avail. We will leave at first light and if his business is unfinished then it will be with us. I have no doubt that he will leave us alone tonight," Eldred explained. "Now if your soldiers are covering the castle I think we would all like to get some sleep."

The count wasn't overly happy with being dismissed, but there was nothing he was prepared to do about it. It was getting late and his guests wanted to sleep. All he could do was to be a gracious host and accommodate him.

**

"It is done!" Taipan had an evil grin on his face.

"Then you don't need to keep me here any longer." Viper sat, bound, by the campfire. The ropes were magically sealed, preventing him from simply breaking free.

Taipan never left the castle after the attack from his brother. Instead he found a small, secret nook to hide himself until the festival started. He knew that they wouldn't let Viper take part. From there it was easy enough to capture his brother and leave the castle undetected.

"What of the stones?" Viper asked. "Wasn't that the reason for your return?"

"They weren't there. Not where you said they would be."

Viper had had his little revenge. He had told his brother that Eldred kept the stones in Alena's room.

"I cannot help you there." Viper replied. "I was assured that was where they were keeping them, but then again I'm not sure they really trusted me." It was hard for him to keep a straight face, especially when he saw a look of understanding on his brother's face.

"I guess you are right." Taipan paced around the fire. "Oh well, I never really thought I would succeed anyway. I'm sure that wizard would have many nice little traps set."

"But your Great Lord would be able to diffuse all of them." Viper almost spat the words.

Taipan wanted nothing more than to strike his brother, but he had already gone further than he wanted. It was purely retaliation to Viper's attack, but that didn't excuse him. Regardless he was sure the Goddess would forgive him once she was free.

"He is not my Great Lord and you know that. I do what I do, as we all do, to save the Goddess. Only Nyrra can save her now, you know that and you should accept it. All you're going to do is to get her killed." Viper had heard it all before. Taipan's rhetoric was frustrating him.

"You were once considered our leader. Our most revered of brothers." Viper knew he was on dangerous ground. "Our Goddess is the prisoner of the most evil creature in the Seven Kingdoms. Nyrra doesn't care about her or us. He is only using you and the others to do his bidding. When it is all over and he sits on his throne he will kill the Goddess and all her followers with her."

Suddenly Viper was struck across the face by a bolt of air. The blow was so violent that it dislocated his jaw. Luckily, like most snakes, that was something he could do on his own. With a little effort he was able to move it back into place. It was more the fact that Taipan was willing to strike him that caused him concern. Things were starting to fall apart and he knew that it was all his fault. He had been the first one to strike out, he had attacked Taipan. At the time he thought it was necessary, but now he wasn't so sure.

"I am still the strongest and if you want to call me your leader, well, that's just fine. What you need to do is understand that you risk the life of the Goddess with what you are doing and I can no longer sit by and let you." Taipan hissed uncontrollably when he finished speaking.

There was no telling if that was a good sign or a bad sign. Viper was starting to get to him and now he was in a very dangerous position. As much as he didn't believe that Taipan would go so far as to kill him he couldn't be completely sure. Either way he couldn't go back on his principals. He knew that he was right and regardless what his brothers did it was only his success that would see her free.

"You must see what you are doing is killing her. Nyrra is evil and nothing will change that. Our only way to save the Goddess is by destroying him." Viper continued his speech.

Taipan raised his hand and Viper was again struck by a blast of air. He paced around the campfire as Viper put his jaw back into place. As much as Viper wanted to continue he knew he had to wait for a response from Taipan.

"It seems we are at an impasse. I should have known if anyone was going to betray the Goddess it would be you." Viper was about to protest again, but again he was struck before he could speak. "You have no idea what a dangerous game you are playing. I only wish I could end your life now, but the Goddess would never forgive me. Instead I'm going to give you a fighting chance. I will leave you here, bound and let's see if you can survive the hungry animals." With that Taipan simply turned his back on his brother and walked away from the campsite.

Viper tried to wriggle out of his bonds, but to no avail. With Taipan gone, the spell would eventually wear away, but for the moment there was nothing he could do. All he could hope for was enough time to catch the others. There was little chance they would believe his story, but he had to try. He knew his job wasn't over. There was still something he had to do before the Goddess could be freed. He could only imagine it had something to do with the Dark Knight in Hondin Lel. If that was the case it didn't give him much time at all.

Chapter 24: What's a Friend For?

The three were up with the sun and were quickly on their way to Bordertown. They were sure that the castle was safe and the new count would keep it that way. They were the ones in danger. Now there were two serpentants nearby, and there was little doubt they would be after them. There seemed to be no other explanation for Viper's strange behaviour, it could only be that Nyrra had finally got to him. If he was ever an ally before, that had quickly changed. Now he was an enemy again and one who could never be trusted.

They rode in silence. No one wanted to discuss the events from the night before. Instead they pushed their horses hard, they wanted to be at Duke Hadar's villa before nightfall. Eldred was sure that's where he would find Hagar. There was little doubt that he would want to be close to his mother at such a time. There was little point in him being elsewhere.

It wasn't until the sun was high in the sky before Eldred finally called them to a halt. Richmond's horse was covered in sweat and the pack animals looked like they were ready to drop. Eldred had wanted to leave the pack animals behind, but to keep the pace it meant Adelanta would have to allow Richmond on his back and Eldred wasn't sure that would happen.

"Do we think Viper is after us now?" Richmond asked as they ate their midday meal. "I can only assume that's why we have kept up such a brisk pace." It was a tongue-in-cheek comment.

Eldred had ridden fast to cease the chance of conversation was only a crutch for his concern for Viper chasing them. It wasn't until Richmond asked the question did he realise it was just a crutch for his concern about Viper chasing them.

"I don't know what his motives are now." Eldred admitted.

"I think he made his true motives clear last night." Given time to think Alena had decided that Viper was indeed showing his true intentions. "He wants the stones and he serves his Dark Lord. We should have killed him when we had the chance, or at least let him die."

"Are you sure Alena? Last night you weren't that confident in his motives. As you said yourself there was a crazed look about him. I'm not so sure that Viper was in his right mind last night. If that is the case then he isn't truly our enemy, but a friend in need of assistance." Richmond replied.

Eldred sat and listened. He had to admit that both sides made sense. There was no reason why Viper should just suddenly change his feelings. When it was said and done he was only fighting for the survival of his own kind and the freedom of his walking deity.

"What if Nyrra got to him?" Alena offered. "Then even if you are right Richmond and Viper hasn't betrayed us he still can't be trusted. Regardless of what has happened in the past he is now our enemy."

Eldred had to agree, although there was something in the back of his mind telling him otherwise. He just couldn't get past the events of the previous night.

"Alena is right. Whatever happened before last night is in the past. Viper showed his true colours and there's nothing we can do about it. I should have seen it coming. Taipan wasn't going to let things slide. Whether it was Nyrra or his brother, Viper has changed sides. I have little doubt that he will try and chase us down. All we need to do now is stay ahead of him."

"But he knows where we are going. It won't take him too long to catch us. We still need information and that will take time," Alena added.

"That is true and that means we have already lingered here too long," Eldred stood as he spoke.

"Be calm Eldred," Richmond motioned for him to sit again. "We have not yet finished eating and the horses still need rest."

"There will be time to eat and recover once we reach Hadar's estates." Eldred retorted.

Richmond stuffed a slice of salted meat in his mouth before tossing away a half eaten piece of bread and a slice of cheese he had yet to touch. As much as he hated wasting food he wasn't going to risk an upset stomach from rushing it.

It was just on dusk when they reached Duke Hadar's Villa. Smoke billowed from the many chimneys as the cold started to set in. It was a promising sign that Hagar was indeed home. The kitchens were working hard and it seemed as though there was more than just the family for so much activity. Eldred could only hope they received a friendly welcome

As expected the gates leading into the villa where shut. It was common practice these days and Eldred didn't expect anyone to leave themopen when not required. He wondered if they ever would again, even if they were successful.

"We are here to see Hagar, duke of these lands in his father's absence." It wasn't technically true, but he thought his words might coax him access.

"And who are you to request entry to his private villa?" the captain-of-the-guard boomed from atop the gate.

"I am Lord Eldred and friend to these lands. I have known the duke for many years and ask for a bed and lodging for me and my friends."

There was no response from the gate. Eldred didn't think that was a good sign until the gate slowly started to open. Considering all the troubles they normally had gaining entrance he was surprised that this time it was so easy. Eldred remembered back to the last time they had been at the villa and they had been welcomed in a similar fashion. It was good to know that he had at least one friend left in the Seven Kingdoms. When the gate was opened two armed soldiers walked out to greet them.

"It is an honour to see you again Lord Eldred," The captain-of-the-guard had been in the duke's service for almost forty years. His once black hair was now completely grey and his face was home to many wrinkles. Despite his aged look he had lost none of his strength.

"Captain Gavril, I am glad to see you, although I must admit that I thought you had retired?" Eldred instantly wished he hadn't asked the question.

"Well that is a story for another time. Needless to say when the duke offered his soldiers to the Alliance some of us... more senior officers needed to come out of retirement." Gavril laughed as he spoke.

Eldred was glad he didn't offend the captain.

"Is Hagar here?" Eldred quickly changed the subject.

"He is in a meeting at the moment, but I'm sure he'll be keen to see you." Gavril smiled as he spoke.

They were quickly ushered into the villa as the stable boys cared for the horses. All the animals looked grateful for the rest.

"Wait here. I'll ask if Hagar will see you." Although Gavril knew the answer he still had to ask.

It seemed as though the captain had just shut the door when it was opened again and Gavril ushered them into the room. Eldred found it odd that he didn't introduce them, but then again he was a soldier, not a functionary. As much as Eldred always complained about the formalities he had to admit he had grown used to the grandeur.

The way Gavril had spoken Eldred assumed the conference room would have been filled with people, but there were only three sitting around the large mahogany table. At the head of the table was a large man with dark hair and a dark beard. He was the spitting image of his father and could be no doubt he was Hagar. Sitting on the seat to his right was his mother. The Duchess was a portly woman, but that hadn't always been the case. Her once youthful beauty and figure was now wearing with age. Despite that she was still an attractive lady.

The man sitting to Hagar's left was not at all who Eldred expected to see. It was a familiar face, although he wasn't sure if it was a good sign or not. Lorio, the court magician from Lel Dinion had a concerned expression on his face. He was the quintessential magician with a long grey beard and grey hat. He wore a dark grey robe and a staff rested against the back of his chair. That was one of the things that got to Eldred. There was no need for such theatrics and it only proved to cover his inability in the art. There was no denying the animosity between Eldred and Lorio, but he wasn't sure that's what the look was for. He was sure there was something a lot deeper in his expression and that wasn't a good sign.

"Thank you for seeing us in such short notice..." Eldred started his formal speech, but Hagar cut him short with a wave of his hand.

"You have been long known to be a friend of my family. Of course you are welcome at my table," Hagar motioned for them all to be seated. "Not to mention the fact that my brother sent word of your arrival." There was a moment of silence before Hagar burst out laughing. His deep rumble of laughter caused everyone else in the room, except Lorio, to follow suit. "I'm sorry. Where are my manners? Would you like something to eat and drink, or maybe you would like to change into something more relaxing. I know you must have ridden hard to get here in one day."

"Thank you, food and drink would be nice. The other will have to wait. We are in desperate need of information," Eldred replied.

Hagar quickly organised the food and some wine to be brought in. Before Eldred had a chance to continue Hagar had some questions of his own.

"The messenger told me that a serpentant had taken control of my brother's mind?"

"That is true, but he is gone now. I don't think Garag is going to have any more trouble. I believe the serpentant was after us." Eldred offered.

"Regardless, my family will forever be in your debt. When I heard what Garag had done I thought I was going to have to take my father's soldiers against him. He had no right to assume the position." Hagar was starting to get angry. It was obvious the events of the past few days had been a concern.

"Well it seems to have worked out for the best. The people of Lel Keldon are pleased with their new count. I don't think you need to do anything now." Eldred did his best to reassure him.

"That is pleasing. I hope that he does well. It is a relief to know there is a good man to the north. It'll be one less thing I have to worry about when I finally take over from my father."

Eldred waited a moment before taking his chance to change the subject.

"We have heard some disturbing news from the capital. Maybe Lorio will be in a better position to answer our questions," Eldred started.

"Ask your questions Eldred and if we can answer them we certainly will." Hagar shot Lorio a stern look. If the court magician had thoughts of withholding information they were promptly extinguished.

"We have heard a rumour that the king has a new advisor, is that correct?" Eldred thought he better tread lightly before revealing the nature of said advisor.

"That is one way of putting it," Lorio scoffed.

"What did I say Lorio?" Hagar's voice was stern, but levelled. "You're not in the king's court now. He may put up with such nonsense, but I won't." He paused and let the threat sink in. "It is funny you should mention that Eldred. We were just discussing the same matter. Now Lorio, if you are prepared to be civil, I think you should continue with what you were telling me."

"Very well." Lorio still didn't sound at all happy, but he wasn't going to push Hagar any further. "A while ago a man came with the Princess Marina. He claimed to be her servant and that was confirmed by the princess herself. Instantly I knew there was something wrong with the man, but I didn't have any proof, and King Lisle seemed happy enough for him to stay." Lorio paused and took a drink from his tankard.

"What name does this man go by?" Eldred took the opportunity to ask a question. He didn't really know why he needed to know the pseudonym Argoz was using, but it felt pertinent.

"He calls himself Lord Argian." Lorio didn't like being interrupted by Eldred, but he remained calm. The last thing he wanted was to spend a night in the cells.

"Lord Argian?" Hagar asked. "I thought you said he was princess Marina's servant?"

A look came across the magician's face as if it was the first time he had come across the realisation. Those two facts were in direct opposition to each other. He quickly calmed himself in the hope that no one noticed his reaction.

"Yes, that is indeed a disturbing fact. My recollection is somewhat hazy, but when they first arrived he went just by the name Argian. It wasn't until later that we started calling him lord. It was clear at that point he was no longer Marina's servant. In fact at that point it was considered that Marina was his servant. It's odd, but looking back that didn't seem at all strange."

If there was any doubt that Argian was indeed Argoz it was now gone. He had left the common trails that a Dark Knight did when assimilating into a new place. Memories of those he had touched would be faded and things that should have been obviously wrong didn't seem out of place at all.

"Go on Lorio, what else did he do." Eldred urged him gently.

"For some reason it is very hard to remember exactly. It is like a shroud has been placed across my mind," he spoke honestly without thinking. It wasn't like him to show any weakness. "He then started advising the king on all sorts of strange matters. Any soldiers who were out in the field were returned to the garrisons inside the city. The gates were ordered to be shut and only opened on Lord Argian's say so."

"And what was Lisle doing about this?" Hagar boomed, frustrated with what he was hearing.

"Simply going along with whatever his new advisor told him. It was like he was in a trance. It was like we were all in a trance. Nothing seemed to be out of place. Everything Argian told us seemed to make sense."

"Then how did you manage to get out of the city?" Richmond asked, senseing something was missing from the story.

"I was just getting to that Lord Richmond." Again he seemed put out by the interruption, but he remained calm. "Once a month I drink a tonic of my own invention. It helps to keep my mind invigorated. When I took my monthly dose I could finally see through the fog. I thought of speaking with the king, but when I went to see him Lord Argian was sitting on the throne and Lisle was kneeling next to him. There was a look on Lisle's face, like he had no idea what was happening around him. I knew then that I needed to get out."

"If Argian had the gates shut then how were you able to leave the city?" Richmond asked.

"I am still the court magician and that means something in the capital, if not in the outer kingdom." That was a direct jibe at the treatment he was currently receiving. "When I tell the soldiers to open the gates then the gates get opened."

"You don't command more respect than the king himself." Hagar didn't like what he was hearing. Something didn't add up. "If Lisle commanded the gates not to be opened then they will remain shut."

Eldred also had to admit that his story didn't add up. It was worrying that he was lying, and his reasons behind it. If Argoz still had control of him then they were in grave danger. Their best chance of success was the fact that Argoz didn't know they were coming, but that could all be a moot point if Viper had truly betrayed them.

"Let's just leave it at 'they opened the gate for me'. It's not imperative to the story." Lorio brushed it under the table. "I came straight here in hope that Hagar could help. Most of the other nobles will do whatever the king tells them. I know in the past that Duke Hadar has had no problems standing up to the king when he doesn't agree with him. I was hoping that his son would share his father's bravado." No one was sure if it was a compliment or an insult.

"And that pretty much brings us up to date." Hagar added.

If Eldred really needed confirmation he just got it, but that wasn't the information they required. He thought for a moment. He wasn't sure how the others would take the knowledge that Argian was in fact the Dark Knight Argoz. In the end he thought it was better they knew.

"Argian is a Dark Knight." Eldred just hit them with the revelation. "He is using typical mind control tactics to take control of the kingdom." It was all too common now. There wasn't a kingdom's ruler that the Dark Knights hadn't controlled at one point in time.

"That can't be true!" The comment was more from denial than disbelief.

"I sorry, but it's true," Richmond confirmed. "The two left the Alliance when we were outside of Jarrat. At that stage he was under the guise of Captain Aimon."

"And why didn't you root him out earlier?" Lorio interrupted Eldred before he could finish. "Surely a wizard of your standing could recognise a Dark Knight hiding amongst you. If you had caught him then none of this mess would have happened in the first place."

Richmond suddenly slammed his fist on the table. The impact rattled the goblets and silenced everyone.

"Be still you old fool," Richmond shouted, unable to control his anger. "When the Dark Knight was parading around as Aimon, Eldred and Alena were prisoners in Jarrat and you don't know what they had to endure whilst they were there." Richmond was starting to go red in the face with rage.

"I am sorry Lord Richmond, I meant no offence." His apology was more out of fear of what Richmond would do to him than any real remorse. "Please continue and forgive my outburst. These are troubled times in Hondin Lel and sometimes my passion takes me away from my senses." In Lel Dinion no one would dare speak to him like that, for fear he would turn them into a toad. Here he knew that Eldred could do much worse and he needed to be careful. In Lel Dinion he had the backing of the king. In Bordertown Hagar was impartial. If anything he leaned on the side of the wizard.

"Be calm Richmond, he wasn't to know." Eldred tried his best to diffuse the situation. "Now as Richmond has explained I wasn't there to see what actually happened. It is my understanding that not only does he have control of Princess Marina, but through her he commands the Sapphire *Stone of Power*. Do you know if the princess is wearing a ring with a sapphire inset in it?"

Lorio thought for a moment. He had to admit that he had marvelled at her beauty a number of times, but he had never really taken any notice of her hands. He racked his memory, but nothing came to him.

"I'm sorry, but I can't recall seeing a ring," Lorio replied.

"That's alright. I'm sure Argoz would want to keep that a secret." Eldred explained.

"Are you sure?" Richmond asked. "I would have thought he would want everyone to know he was in control of the Sapphire stone? It seems that it would put him in a position of power."

"Don't forget that he is still masquerading as someone else. Now he is Lord Argian. If he wanted everyone to know who he is and what he has I'm sure he'd go by his real name. No, he is still trying to take control by subversion," Eldred explained.

"So what does that mean?" Hagar asked, a little confused at the conversation.

"It means we need to be very careful. If he does indeed have control of the Sapphire stone then he is twice as dangerous." Eldred continued.

"Then it seems it would be folly for you to continue on to Lel Dinion," Hagar offered. "Maybe you should choose a different route or even stay here for a while until you work out what to do?"

That was the most sensible suggestion they had heard in a long time and yet it was impossible to make true. None of them wanted to race headlong towards a Dark Knight, let alone one with a *Stone of Power*. It was only now that the severity of the situation was starting to sink in. Despite their fears there was nothing they could do about it. They had to go to Lel Dinion and they had to free its people.

Staying in Bordertown, as much as it was a pleasant idea, was also fraught with danger. Now that Viper had shown his true colours there was no chance for them to rest. At least until they had finished in Lel Dinion the serpentant knew where they were going. If they lingered too long in any one place he would surely catch them. Viper by himself wasn't a real problem. Although he was very dangerous, Eldred was confident he could best him in a battle. It was the addition of Taipan that made it worse. Eldred knew he would have no chance of defeating two serpentants and the others would be no use in a battle of magic, even Lorio.

"Thank you for your offer Hagar, but unfortunately that's not going to be any use to us. We have enemies both at our rear and our front. Remaining here would only delay the inevitable for a short period of time. Maybe for a day or two at most and then our road will still lead us to Lel Dinion," Eldred said.

"Well if you are going to rescue the king then I am coming with you," the words didn't seem right coming from Lorio.

"Are you sure Lorio? It is going to be a dangerous mission and there is no guarantee you will survive or any of us for that matter." Eldred was in two minds. On one side Lorio's knowledge of the city and an extra man would be invaluable. On the other Eldred wasn't so sure he could trust him.

"I know we have had our differences in the past Eldred, but I can put that behind me if you can save the kingdom from a Dark Knight. From the sounds of things you will need my help."

Eldred had to admit Lorio was right. Although he was just a magician anyone with even a little power would be a vital asset. That was one of the reasons why he was willing to take a risk on Viper. If he had not betrayed them then he would have been vital in the battle with Argoz. Now they needed anyone they could get. Eldred really wished Alaric would return from wherever he was.

"Very well Lorio, you may join us. We will need everyone willing and able."

"Well I'm not completely useless," Hagar stood suddenly. "And I have a small army with me."

"Thank you for the offer Hagar, but you need to remain here and protect your father's estate," Eldred returned.

"That is not true," Duchess Pelagia spoke for the first time. The others had almost forgotten she was there. "I am more than capable of looking after things."

"Mother, you know that father left me in command in his absence." Hagar protested. "Eldred is right. I have a commitment to uphold here."

"That is just ridiculous. You need to go with Eldred to help save the king, that is your commitment. I have lived here for longer than you and I have run the Duchy in Hadar's absence more than once and I am more than capable of doing it again." Pelagia's voice was surprisingly firm.

If it was just a matter of Hagar leaving with them and Pelagia managing the estate then Eldred wouldn't have an issue, but there was much more to the story than they knew.

"Good then it's settled. I will have my soldiers ready to march in two days. Then we can leave for the capital." Hagar stood as if the conversation was over.

Eldred sighed, more noticeably than he had originally intended.

"Please, sit Hagar, there is more you need to know." Eldred resigned himself to the fact that he was going to have to explain further about the serpentants. "For starters I don't think leading your soldiers against the capital is a good move. From what I understand Argoz has made Lisle bring the bulk of his army back within the city gates. It would be like throwing a stone against a tower. No, if we are going to succeed then we need to get into the palace without anyone knowing we are there."

"That makes sense," Hagar begrudgingly sat back down. "What else?"

"There is more to the serpentant story than we let on," Eldred started. "One of our companions was the serpentant Viper. He was with us for the last couple of months or so. Over that time he built up a level of trust with us. It seemed as though that was a mistake. When we were with your brother he tried to steal something from us. When we caught him he attacked us before fleeing. Now we can only assume that he's following us and that means he'll be coming here next. One thing you don't want to do is leave this Villa defenceless against him. He is very dangerous."

"Then it looks like my obligations are going to keep me at home." Hagar didn't sound happy.

"Don't be so melodramatic son. You will go with them to Lel Dinion." Pelagia spoke as if Hagar was still a child.

That was not the response anyone was expecting.

"What are you talking about mother?" Hagar sounded both surprised and hopeful.

"Your father left you in charge not only because you are his first son, but because you were the most suitable. What do you think Hadar would do if he was in your position?" The question hung in the air. "He would do what needs to be done to save his king. As much as he loves his family and his people he knows that king and kingdom comes first. That is why he has so much respect from his people."

That might not have been completely correct, but it was enough to sway his decision. Little did he know it was the tug of the prophecy that he could feel and there was nothing he could do to avoid it.

"You are right mother. I serve my people best by serving the kingdom. It is my duty to help save the king from the clutches of the Dark Knight." It sounded all well and good, but Eldred doubted that Hagar understood the severity of their task.

"You should get ready. We'll be on the road at first light," Eldred spoke to Hagar and Lorio.

Lorio stood, but Hagar remained where he was.

"I will make sure my affairs are in order and I am ready to leave first thing in the morning. You should go and get ready Lorio. I have a few more questions for these three."

As much as Lorio didn't like being dismissed he did have some things do before leaving. Although he had only arrived at the villa that morning he had already unpacked some of his things whilst he was waiting to see Hagar.

"What is it you want to know?" Eldred asked.

"How is my husband?" Pegalia asked before Hagar had a chance. "It's been months since we had word from him. We have had a few sketchy reports, but we don't even know where the army is at the moment. You would think with an army the size of the Alliance it would be easy to find where they are and what they're doing."

"The last information we had from the Alliance was that they were moving on Castalia." Pegalia gasped with fear.

"What are they thinking? No army has ever been able to breach the walls of Castalia. Surely they are all dead now?" Tears welled in Pagalia's eyes.

"I don't think that is the case. I'm sure if the Alliance had been destroyed then we would know about it. That I know to be true." Eldred did his best to reassure her.

He could certainly understand her point-of-view. Those who had tried to invade in the past had never succeeded in breaching the walls. The fortress of Castalia was impregnable, but that didn't change the fact that Eldred didn't believe they had been destroyed. He didn't know what had happened, but he knew Bern and the Alliance would have succeeded. He only wished he knew their next move. If they were on the way to Lel Dinion then they were potentially running into danger for no real reason. He quickly wiped that thought from his mind.

"Do you really think so?" Pagalia sounded hopeful.

"I'm sure of it. There is still more to be done and the army cannot falter yet," Eldred reassured. "But more information on their location would be nice."

"We could send scouts to try and find them?" Hagar returned to the conversation.

"We'll be long gone before they even come close to returning." Eldred reminded him that they were leaving in the morning. "But even though I don't think it would be a bad idea to find out what is happening."

"Where should we send them?" Pagalia sounded excited at the prospect. She really wanted to find out what her husband was doing and if he was still alive.

That was a good question. Castalia would be the best place to start. At least if the army wasn't still there, which Eldred doubted that it would, someone would know where they were headed.

"I would send them straight to Castalia. Otherwise they could be chasing ghosts around the Seven Kingdoms for the next ten years."

That made sense to everyone. Now there was nothing left to talk about. Eldred had received some information, but not everything he needed to know. At least if he was leading them into a trap they would be prepared for it, as much as they could be. As much as he hated to admit it he would have much preferred to have Viper with them. The serpentant, given that he was on their side, would have been very handy against the Dark Knight.

"So what's the plan when we get to Lel Dinion?" Hagar quickly changed the subject.

That was a question Eldred didn't want to be asked. In truth he had no idea what he was going to do if they managed to get into the castle. It was bad enough that they had to face Argoz, but if he controlled Marina and by all accounts the Sapphire stone, then things were going to be twice as dangerous.

"We need to get into the castle and we need to destroy the Dark Knight as quickly as we can. The last thing we need is for him to know we are there," Eldred explained.

Hagar paused for a moment. He wasn't sure if he should push any further as Eldred didn't seem to be overly forthcoming with the information, but he decided that if he was going to put his life in danger then he needed to know what they were getting into.

"That is all well and good, but how do you plan on killing the Dark Knight?" Hagar asked.

"There will time for that later. For now I think it might be time to get some rest. We have ridden hard and will have to do the same tomorrow." Eldred promptly put an end to the conversation.

There was no chance for Hagar to argue with the old wizard. They did look somewhat exhausted from the day's ride and he would be an ungracious host to keep them any longer.

"I will have some relaxation baths run for you. That should rest your weary bones. When you have finished, your rooms will be ready," Hagar offered and no one complained.

As much as Eldred wanted to read through the prophecy he knew that he had to rest. There were more long days in the saddle and he would need all of his strength if he was going to defeat Argoz.

Chapter 25: A Fearful Night

As the sun started to creep over the horizon the group met at the main gates after eating a quick breakfast. Hagar had arranged a fresh horse for Richmond. The elven horses showed no signs of fatigue and actually looked excited to be on the road again.

Hagar was the last to arrive and was accompanied by his mother. Palagia had a stern expression on her face.

"Take care of yourself Hagar. I want you back here soon. Hopefully I will have word from your father by then." She kissed Hagar on the check before he mounted his chestnut mare.

With Hagar in the saddle they were ready to go. Along with the new horse for Richmond there were half a dozen pack animals for their possessions. As much as it would slow down their journey Eldred had to agree it was better for them not to put any extra strain on their horses. It could have taken them two days with just the horses, but it was going to be at least four with the pack animals. In the end he was in no real hurry to reach Lel Dinion. As long as they stayed ahead of the serpentants that was all he really cared about. Rushing towards his doom was not something he was keen to do.

At least the sun was shining as they left the Villa. The clouds that had threatened to break the day before were all gone. Small fluffy white clouds scattered across the sky and it looked as though it was going to be a pleasant day. At least that was one thing going in their favour.

As expected, with the pack animals weighed down with their possessions, the journey was slow. Eldred couldn't tell if time was acting as it should or whether they were in fact making better time. Either way they stopped by a small brook for their midday meal.

"Lovely morning for a ride!" Hagar spoke jovially when they stopped.

No one really felt the need to be enjoying themselves. They all knew what they were riding towards and there was nothing pleasant about it. His attitude was quite baffling for the others. They remained sombre and only when no one commented did Lorio finally speak.

"We have been fortunate with the weather. Nothing worse than riding in the rain."

Instantly they all wished Lorio had not spoken. Although there was no correlation between the two events, they had to blame someone for the dark clouds starting to roll in from the west. They all knew it wouldn't be long before the clouds opened and by the looks of them the rain was going to be heavy.

With the clouds looming overhead they started out again. No one wanted to be sitting around when the rain came. With a little luck they could make it to Lel Caminon before it began and they started to push the pack animals as hard as they could.

Despite their increased pace it didn't help them. It was only an hour after they had left the brook before the skies opened. Eldred remembered the weather being very similar to the last time he travelled to Lel Dinion. The last storm wasn't natural and he could only hope that this one was and it didn't strengthen throughout the afternoon.

His hopes were shattered shortly after as a great bolt of lightning flashed across the sky. A moment later a great boom of thunder followed and with it the rain started to pour. What had been just a light shower was now nearing torrential.

Memories of the last time they had travelled the road to Lel Dinion returned to Eldred. Although that rain had not been natural the current downpour was just as debilitating. The hard packed road became slippery and they had to slow their horses.

"Now this is some lovely Hondin Lel weather!" Hagar yelled into the storm. There was humour in his words that no one else found funny.

"You have a strange sense of humour Hagar," Lorio didn't sound impressed.

"Come on Lorio. It has been a long time since we have had a storm like this. I remember as a child falling asleep to the sound of rain. It is a very pleasant memory for me. I can only hope this rain lasts through the night," Hagar shouted back.

His words made Eldred think that maybe he was wrong that the storm was in fact natural. With Viper behind them and Argoz in the front there was no telling what was real. He felt he would feel if anyone was tampering with the weather. It was a powerful spell and almost impossible to hide. On the other hand the Sapphire stone had power over water. Eldred quickly wiped that thought from his mind. The ramifications weren't worth thinking about. He knew the chance of them reaching the castle without Argoz knowing was slim, but he had to hold onto that idea.

The sun had not set, but it may as well have, by the time they reached the gate at Lel Camion. The dark storm clouds obscured any light the sun was trying to shine through. No lamps were lit over the gate, which wasn't a good sign.

"I am Hagar, son of Duke Hadar and we require entrance to Lel Camion." Hagar did his best to yell over the storm, but there was no response from inside the guard house.

"What are we going to do?" Hagar asked Eldred when it was clear no one was there.

"I guess we could try the door into the guard house?" Eldred wasn't sure why, but it felt like the most logical response.

Hagar dismounted, handed the reins to Richmond and walked towards the guardhouse door. He didn't really know why he was doing it, if the gate was down then the guardhouse door would be securely locked. To everyone's surprise Hagar simply pushed the door and it swung open. He paused for a moment before walking inside. Something was definitely wrong.

The others remained outside in the storm while they waited for Hagar. They would have followed, but the horses and the pack animals wouldn't fit through the door. The rain beat down on them for what seemed like an eternity until one of the gate doors slid open. No one moved until they saw Hagar and he motioned for them to enter. Once they were through he shut the gate and replaced the large plank of wood barring it from the inside.

There were no lanterns lit inside the town walls. Even in the pouring rain there should have been lights. Eldred looked around as best he could, but there was no sign of life. There were no lights in the houses around the gate either and in the end he decided that he had to do something about it. Without warning the others he created a small ball of light, which floated a pace above their heads.

The sight before them sent chills down their spines and not just from the cold rain trickling down their backs. The buildings were charcoal husks. It looked like they had been burnt out for at least a week. The streets were lined with mutilated bodies. Flesh had been ripped from their bones. The rain had washed away most of the blood, but there were still stains on the cobblestones.

"What in the God's names happened here?" no one could hear Hagar over the raging storm. "What happened here?" he repeated, much louder.

Eldred rode a little further into the town before he dismounted. There was a dead body on the side of the street with its left arm missing and half its head gone. Instantly he was able to recognise the scratches and bite marks. He really didn't need to investigate the mangled body to confirm his fear. It was obvious it had been an orglin attack. By the look of the body the attack had been three or four days prior. Eldred doubted that the orglin would still be in the area. He hoped, at least, they were safe for the moment.

When Eldred was satisfied he remounted and returned to the others. They were still close to gate, not really wanting to move too far. There was something very unsettling about the sight before them.

"It seems as though this was an orglin attack," Eldred called over the storm. "We should try and see if there is a building that hasn't been destroyed. We need to get out of this rain and hopefully get some relief for the night."

As if on cue the rain and wind suddenly stopped. It was now eerily quiet. Eldred's heart started to pound, he was the first one to realise that it wasn't natural. He wasn't sure if it was the storm or the fact that it ended so suddenly, but he knew there was magic involved. Not only that but powerful magic. Whoever had caused it was strong, maybe even stronger than Eldred himself and that wasn't a pleasant thought.

The floating light grew brighter now that it didn't have to fight with the rain. Suddenly shadows started to appear where there had been none before. Everyone grew more nervous with each passing moment.

"What's happening?" Lorio finally asked, fear evident in his voice.

Eldred didn't answer, partly because he didn't know and partly because if he was right it meant that Nyrra was close and that wasn't worth thinking about. Eldred would be a formidable opponent for a Dark Knight, but he was no match for the Evil One himself. He doubted even if he dared use one of the *Stones of Power* he would stand a chance.

"I don't know, but I have a very bad feeling," Hagar replied when Eldred didn't.

As soon as the words came out of his mouth there was movement in the street ahead of them. At first they thought it was the just the globe of light shimmering off the pools of water, but soon enough they knew they were wrong. Horror filled their souls as the body in front of Eldred slowly started to rise. Even with one arm and a half eaten head it had little problems getting to its feet.

The horses reared and whinnied in fear. Even the elven horses couldn't contain themselves. The pack horses tried to back away, but only got as far as the gate. If the fear wasn't so powerful they might have tried to bolt past the walking corpse, but all they could do was shake. The riders struggled to stay in the saddle, eventually opting to dismount. Alena was the only one who remained mounted as she was able to calm Lluvia. Once they were riderless the non-elven horses bolted past the walking corpse in terror. Adelanta and Tormenta followed to make sure they were alright. Alena could feel that Lluvia wanted to go after them, but refrained from moving. She wouldn't leave until her mistress commanded her. After a moment Alena figured it was better for all the horses to remain together. Before dismounting she told Lluvia to lead the pack animals to join the others and keep them safe.

"Do something about that!" Lorio barked at Eldred, his fear even more evident.

Eldred felt like saying the same thing to Lorio. The court magician had always acted superior to Eldred, although his abilities we only just a step up from an illusionist. It was all well and good in the safety of his castle, but in practice it was a completely different story.

As much as the spell to reanimate a dead body was complex it was surprisingly easy, depending on the body, to unravel. It seemed that most dead bodies didn't appreciate moving again and were quite happy to be laid to rest. Eldred reached for the energy around him. There was a feeling of evil in the air, but he did want he had to. When he was comfortable he went to release the spell, but nothing happened. The body continued to slowly move towards them. His spell had not been blocked, it had never been created. It was as if the spell had been completely wiped from his mind.

Without thought he reached out with his hands together, palms facing outwards. A ball of fire shot out and hit the walking dead in the chest and burst into flame. The body didn't seem to notice and all the attack seemed to do was increase the danger.

"That didn't seem to do anything!" Lorio responded.

"Thanks for the update Lorio," Eldred snapped.

The only saving grace was the slow movement of the dead body. Even on fire it didn't seem to pose much of a real threat. All they had to do is give it a wide berth and they would be able to move past it. Eventually the fire would scold the flesh and hopefully burn the bones, or at least make them brittle enough to break.

"I've had enough of this!" Hagar barked as he drew his large broadsword. The weapon seemed to be the most appropriate for the occasion. He also wore a rapier, but that would be almost useless.

He took two steps forward before swinging the sword as hard as he could. The blade swept through the body's neck completely severing its head. The blow still did nothing to stop its advance.

"Take out its legs," Alena suggested.

That seemed to be the most logical approach. Hagar took a step backwards before swinging his sword again. This time he severed the body's right leg, just above the knee. The dead body stumbled and fell to the ground, still aflame. Hagar took a step back, thinking that was end of it, but the dead body still crawled forward. Although it was now next to useless it was still disturbing.

"What do we do now?" Richmond asked.

"I think we just leave it and move on," Alena suggested.

"I think not!" Hagar wasn't finished.

The puddles of water had extinguished the flames making the attack less perilous, but Hagar brought his sword down again and again until the body was severed into many pieces. Each part twitched for a moment before it laid to rest.

"Well it looks like we're safe now?" Even as the words came out of his mouth he wished they hadn't.

As they looked out towards the town they could see a number of other dead bodies slowly coming to life. Some were missing limbs, but they all slowly came to their feet and started moving towards them. Some of the bodies moaned, adding to the horror they all felt. Those without any legs scratched their way along the ground. It was like something from a scary story, told to children to keep them in at night.

"What do we do now?" Lorio asked in terror as more and more bodies came to life.

"We take them down!" Hagar boomed. "Don't stop cutting until they stop moving."

Hagar didn't wait for the others to respond. He moved forward, but slowly and deliberately. He was in no hurry to rush into danger. The dead moved at a slow pace and rushing into battle would certainly see him dead and probably soon enough, joining those he was trying to kill.

Richmond, Alena and Eldred all drew their swords. Lorio, who didn't carry one, retreated as far as he could. His staff wasn't going to be much use and he figured it was better to stay out of the way.

Hagar stopped when he reached the first intersection. The bodies in front of him were still a good twenty paces away, but down the other streets more dead bodies started moving towards him and others were slowly coming to life. He could only hope the horses had found somewhere safe to hide.

"What is it?" Richmond asked when they reached him, but looking down the streets he answered his own question.

"Are you sure there is nothing you can do Eldred?" Alena asked, trying to remain calm.

The only chance he had was to use one of the stones, but he didn't even know if that was going to help. It wasn't an option worth considering. He had a bad feeling that was what someone wanted him to do and he wasn't going to give in to fear.

"No, we have to fight. I'll take the front, you take the left Hagar and Richmond you take the right. Alena you give us a cover of arrows until you run out, then help take whoever looks like they need it the most," Eldred commanded.

As much as Alena didn't want to be left behind, she was the best shot and the only one with a bow and quiver. It made sense for her to assume the role. As the others moved into position she fired an arrow at one of the bodies. It stuck in its head and as soon as it did the body dropped to the ground. It twitched and then lay still.

"How many arrows do you have?" Hagar asked.

"Only another dozen on me," Alena replied.

"Well you shoot and we'll collect."

The bodies were moving so slowly that the idea might work. Either way Alena wasn't going to die wondering. She sent another arrow down the street before turning to another.

Hagar was the first to reach the body. Regaining the arrows was more difficult than he had first imagined. The dead bodies didn't seem to notice or care that there were some falling around them. They would simply walk over those that lay on the ground. They didn't even try to walk around.

"I'm out of arrows," Alena called to all three.

Eldred seemed to be having the most difficulty. There were almost twice as many dead bodies moving down his street than the other two combined. Each time Alena dropped one with her arrows another was there to push forward. In the end Eldred decided it would just be easier to cut them down.

Richmond was having a much better time of things. As soon as Alena fired an arrow he was there to pluck it from its corpse. Once he had the arrow he ran back to return it to Alena. He slashed at the bodies, in a vain effort to stop their advance, but they didn't seem to care about the weapon that would slice them apart, nor did they really seem to take much notice of him. Alena had just shot another body and as Richmond bent over to retrieve it he didn't notice a body moving up beside him. Before he had a chance to react the body simply brushed past him and kept moving.

The move was so startling that Richmond lowered his sword as he stood. It was as if he wasn't even there. More and more bodies just ignored him and kept dragging themselves forward. Suddenly the realisation came to him. They weren't after him, they were after Alena.

"Pull back to the gate!" he called over the ruckus.

"What are you talking about?" Hagar called back as he hacked at another dead body.

"I'll explain when we get there." Richmond made his way back to Alena and then motioned for her to follow.

Eventually Eldred and Hagar made their way back, sweat pouring from their brows. They didn't look happy. Surprisingly, enough after all the carnage, there wasn't a drop of blood on them.

"This better be good Richmond. There are a lot more to kill and now they have us trapped." Eldred barked.

Little did they realise, but Lorio was now hiding in the guard house. No one really seemed to take any notice.

"The bodies, they just ignored me. They seem to be after Alena. Did anyone else notice that?" Richmond offered.

"I have to admit they didn't really seem interested in fighting back. If anything they do seem to be focused on moving forward," Hagar replied.

The bodies had converged on the intersection and were now moving towards the gate. There was no chance of getting past them. There looked as though there were hundreds of them.

"So what does that mean?" Alena asked, her voice surprisingly calm.

"Well, we should be able to cut them down easily enough if they're not going to fight back." There was an evil grin on Hagar's face.

"We can't stop them all. There has to be another way?" Richmond asked.

"I say we open the gates and leave. That has to be our only option," Eldred replied.

Richmond looked over his shoulder at the bar on the gate.

"What about the horses?" Alena asked. "We can't leave them here."

"Adelanta will look after them and it doesn't look like the dead bodies are interested in anyone or anything else. I think Eldred is right. Our best move is to put distance between us and them."

"When they are all out of the town we can double back around them and shut them out. I think it's a good plan," Hagar agreed.

Without further discussion Hagar sheathed his large broadsword on his back and turned to the gate. Taking a deep breath Hagar tried to lift the bar, but it wouldn't budge. It had taken an effort, but he had removed it and then replaced it when they arrived. Now, no matter how hard he tried, he couldn't move it.

"What's taking so long?" Richmond asked as he watched the wave of dead bodies slowly moving ever closer.

"It won't move. It's stuck," Hagar shouted back.

Richmond sheathed his sword and moved to help. Even with Richmond on the other end there was still nothing they could do.

"Well it looks like that idea is gone," Richmond sighed.

"I hate to break it too you, but those dead bodies are getting closer," Alena's voice now wasn't so calm.

"I guess we should start taking them down then," there was a hint of pleasure in Hagar's voice.

"Wait!" Eldred exclaimed. "Something isn't right here."

"What are we waiting for?" Richmond returned. "They're nearly upon us."

"I don't know, but something isn't right."

"You just figured that out?" Richmond returned.

"Just wait."

As the bodies crept ever closer their hearts started to pound. Either way there was little chance that they could stop them all. There seemed to be even more filling the streets and it looked like there were more than just the population of the town. Just as they came within two paces they suddenly stopped. The air shimmered around them before they dropped to the ground, twitched once and then lay completely still.

"What was that all about?" Hagar asked aghast.

Eldred didn't answer.

"I'm not sure, but I think we're about to find out," Alena explained as the air started to shimmer in front of them again.

They stood and waited. There was nowhere for them to go. The gate was barred and they weren't about to try and cross the sea of dead bodies.

As the air continued to shimmer, so too did the bodies. Suddenly they started to fade and before long the streets were clear again.

"Well, it looks like we're free to go," Hagar smiled.

"Not yet," Richmond held out an arm to restrain him as the air continued to shimmer.

A body slowly started to coalesce in front of them. At first a pair of legs appeared, wearing a pair of black leather boots. Next came the body, wearing a black steel breastplate with a flowing cape at the back. Last came his head and arms. Shoulder length blonde hair framed a face that was beyond beautiful. Deep blue eyes stared at Alena with an intensity that made her blush.

"Thank you for helping..." Hagar started.

"Be quiet Hagar, he is not here to help us," there was a mixture of fear and anger in Eldred's voice.

"Who is he?" Alena asked, knowing that her heart flutter was misplaced, but she couldn't help feeling drawn to him.

"That is Nyrra!" there was doom in Eldred's revelation. "What do you want?" He was almost too afraid to ask the question.

The stones were safely stored on the back of one of the pack horses. Now Eldred was thankful for Lorio's cowardice. If nothing else he needed to make sure that Nyrra didn't get the stones. Even if they didn't make it out alive he knew Alaric would find them. That was all that really mattered.

"Where is the one you call Alaric?" Even his voice was sickly sweet.

The man standing before them wasn't at all what they were expecting from the Evil One. He was too attractive. They, except for Eldred, had been expecting someone much more hideous.

"Are you sure that is Nyrra?" Hagar asked. "Something doesn't add up."

"Be quiet Hagar. Do not talk again," Eldred spoke through clenched teeth, trying not to let Nyrra see him. "Alaric is close by. He should be here soon if you dare to meet him." The threat was weak, but Eldred didn't know what else to say.

"I doubt that very much, but I had to be sure. I knew that he wouldn't let the elf die like this. He would have destroyed those corpses long before they got within striking distance. No he is still gone." Nyrra sneered as he spoke and for a second his facade changed. It was so subtle that no one was even sure it really happened or whether it was a trick of Eldred's ball of light.

"What are you talking about?" There was something very disturbing about Nyrra's comment and Eldred hoped he could pry some information from him.

"Well this is indeed interesting. So your Chosen One has gone off and left you and didn't tell you where he was going. Maybe it seems he doesn't trust you anymore?" Nyrra's grin was positively evil.

"I know exactly where he is and I don't need you to tell me," Eldred bluffed.

"I doubt that very much, but if you want to believe your own lies that is up to you." Now he now didn't seem as sure of himself and that was Eldred's chance to strike.

"Well if you think you know better?" He let the question float on the air for a moment. "I didn't think you did. Now I assume there is a reason for you to be here."

"You forget yourself Eldred. I am much stronger than you and could kill you with a simple thought."

"So why don't you enlighten me," he pushed.

"Very well. Alaric is no longer on our plain of existence." His smirk grew at the look of confusion on Eldred's face.

"How could you possibly know that?" Eldred lost himself in the confusion.

Nyrra shook his head. "I can't believe you are one of the most revered wizards of your kind. You really don't seem to know much at all. I can sense Alaric. I've been able to since his birth. Oh, don't look so surprised. We have been linked in one way or another since the beginning of time." He responded to the look of shock on all their faces. "I don't know exactly where he is, I just have a feeling of his general direction." It seemed Eldred's plan was working. It seemed as though Nyrra was revealing more than he should.

"So where is he now?" Eldred let slip.

"So you don't know where he is. I appreciate the confirmation." It seemed as though Nyrra was also playing Eldred for information.

"I've had enough of this," Hagar drew his large broadsword as he spoke. Without thinking he charged towards the Evil One. "I will finish you now and end this!"

Before he came within three paces he was lifted off the ground by a magical force. There was no sign that Nyrra had cast the spell, even Eldred couldn't feel any magic being used. Then, with just subtle flick of the wrist, which was all completely for show, Hagar was launched into a nearby burnt out building. He crashed through the ashen framework and came to rest on the floor. He lifted his head slowly before losing consciousness.

Nyrra burst into a fit of laughter. As he did his facade suddenly changed. His once fair skin now turned purple and leathery. His nose grew to a point and boils and warts sprouted all over his face. The blonde hair remained, which made him look somewhat ridiculous. If it wasn't for the terror they felt they would have laughed.

"Now I would love to stay and kill you all, but there is more pressing matters that I have to deal with," there was no humour in his threat.

Before anyone had a chance to react Nyrra promptly disappeared. Even after he had left, their hearts still pounded with fear. An encounter with Nyrra at the best of times was a harrowing experience. Theirs was one they would not forget for the rest of their lives.

"Get Lorio," Eldred spoke to Richmond. "Alena you find the horses, I'll see to Hagar. I think we should put some distance between us and Lel Camion before we rest for the night."

As much as they were all tired from the ordeal no one could think of anything better. No one wanted to spend a second longer in Lel Camion than they had to.

Chapter 26: More Trouble

They finally came to rest in a small grove of trees about four leagues from Lel Camion. They wanted to travel as far away from the dead town as they could before they rested. If they weren't all beginning to fall asleep in the saddle they would have continued.

In the morning a frost had covered the ground. The sun had risen through the clouds, but it gave very little heat. It wasn't until a small fire was burning brightly that they felt normal again. It looked as though it was going to be a cold day, but at least there was no rain in the clouds. It seemed the storm was Nyrra's concoction and not a sign of poor weather to come.

Besides a sore head Hagar had suffered no major side effects of his crashing through the building, that and a battered ego. He wasn't really sure what he was expecting by attacking Nyrra, but he thought he might have a least stood a chance. His head was still ringing in the morning as a reminder not to do anything so stupid again.

They rode as hard as they could for the next three days. It was mid-morning on the fourth day out of Lel Camion when the walls of Lel Dinion loomed on the horizon. Eldred reined them to a halt before they were within sight of the towers. He reached out with his senses before he spoke.

"It seems the gate is still locked tight." Eldred started. "Now Lorio you managed to escape the city, so I'm assuming that you know how to get back in?"

Lorio was silent for a moment. He really didn't want to answer the question, but everyone was waiting.

"I'm not sure if I remember how?" There was little confidence in the lie but no one believed him.

"Cut the act Lorio." Eldred wasn't in the mood. "You know how to get in and out of the city undiscovered. Now you need to get us in or do you want to leave the Dark Knight in charge?" It was a cheap shot, but he made his point.

"Very well, but be sure that you don't take advantage of this knowledge once everything is done," Lorio warned.

They all agreed, although they were more concerned about their present predicament, not the future. Even though they weren't in view from the tower Eldred could see, or sense might have been more accurate, guards in the towers and patrolling the wall. There was no chance for them to approach and then enter the city unseen.

"We'll have to wait until nightfall," Eldred explained.

"Can't you just hide us Eldred?" Lorio scoffed. "I've heard it's quite a simple spell." He sounded keen to enter the city.

"I could ask you the same question Lorio?" Eldred didn't like what he was insinuating. There was no response. "In short, yes I could, but it would be better for us to wait until nightfall. I will need all my strength to battle Argoz."

No one could deny that. Eldred was the only one who could contend with the Dark Knight. Even at full strength he didn't think he could contend with one who commands a *Stone of Power*, but for the moment there was no other option. The only chance would be to use one of his own and that was something he didn't want to do. His biggest fear was that the stone would consume him.

"I guess we should set up camp. We may as well try and get some sleep. By the sounds of things it's going to be a long night," Richmond suggested.

Although no one was tired there was little else to do. They moved down the other side of a small hill so there was no chance of being seen from the parapet. A campfire was out of the question. The smoke would easily be seen rising from behind the hill and although there was no way to tell it was them, they didn't want to risk anything.

The day seemed to pass painfully slowly. As the others tried to sleep Eldred opened the great tome to try and get some insight on what they were about to get themselves into. As usual there was no useful information. Eldred was beginning to wonder if there was any use in reading the prophecy anymore. It had been a long time since he had been able to glean anything helpful.

As the sun started to set they ate a light meal. It was going to be a long night and they needed some sustenance. A nervous silence settled over the group. They all knew what lay before them and they all knew their chance of survival was slim. It now seemed such a futile exercise. They were going up against a Dark Knight in command of a city and possibly a kingdom. Eldred was strong, but he wasn't that strong.

"Are you sure this is the right thing to do?" Richmond finally asked the question that was on all their minds.

"No." Was all he said as he started to pack up the camp. There was nothing he could say to make the others feel better, so he felt it was better to say very little. It wasn't a conversation he wanted to have. He wanted nothing more than to turn and run away. If he had to dwell on the fact then he was afraid he would.

"What are we going to do with the animals?" Hagar asked.

"We'll have to leave them behind," Lorio spoke first. "The way into the city is too small for the horses. Whatever we need to take with us we need to carry ourselves." He didn't sound overly excited about his last revelation.

Richmond and Hagar unloaded the packs from the animals whilst Alena and Eldred worked out what they needed to take. There seemed little point in taking any of the food. Whatever they needed to eat they would find inside the city. Besides a change of clothes each and their weapons they only brought the chest with the stones and the prophecy. There was no way Eldred was going to leave them behind.

Alena spoke softly to Lluvia telling the mare to keep the other animals safe. When she was finished speaking Lluvia gently nuzzled her neck before turning to the task in front of he.

"I guess we should get this done," Eldred spoke when no one made a move to leave.

The night was dark as they set off and thick storm clouds covered any light the moon would have given them. Without being able to create any light the going was slow.

They travelled around to the north of the city. Although there were no lights on in the outer city they made sure they kept a decent distance. It seemed as though the outer city was deserted, but they didn't want to risk being seen.

The further they travelled to the north the houses became sparser and sparser. It wasn't until they reached a small stream did Lorio stop them. The banks of the stream sloped down a pace on either side. If it wasn't for Lorio they would have walked straight into the ditch. There was an odd smell coming from the stream.

"This is one of the waste conduits leading away from the city," Lorio explained as he carefully lowered himself down.

Now the smell made sense to everyone and they weren't keen to follow the court magician. The last thing they wanted to do was stink like waste when they entered the city. It would be very hard to remain anonymous like that.

"It's alright," Lorio spoke once he was on the stream bed. "This is one of the least used conduits. The stream is at a trickle."

"But all the sewers have iron bars blocking anyone from sneaking into the city," Eldred protested.

"You can stand there and argue all night or you can trust that I know what I'm doing." Lorio didn't appreciate what Eldred was insinuating.

Eldred had to admit he was right. There was no other way into the city and Lorio had escaped somehow. He couldn't imagine he would lead them through a waste outlet for no reason. Eldred was the first to follow Lorio then Alena, Hagar and Richmond.

Lorio only waited for Eldred to join him before making his way towards the city. Even though the walls of the stream gave them some protection they still didn't create any light. Every now and again a squish could be heard from underfoot as someone stepped in something soft. No one really wanted to know what it was and they could only hope it was mud.

They could soon see the torches burning on the parapets and knew they were approaching the city walls. Occasionally a light was passed between the guards. There was no way they could see into the ditch, but they still had to be careful.

"I need some light," Lorio whispered when they reached the wall.

"Impossible. The guards will see us," Eldred replied.

"Isn't there some way you can shield the light from the men above us?" Lorio asked.

"I can but we run the risk of the Dark Knight knowing we are here," Eldred snapped.

"Fine!" Lorio didn't sound impressed. Before anyone could respond he mumbled a few words under his breath. "There you go. I might not be as powerful as you are Eldred, but there are things that I can do."

Eldred cursed silently to himself as a small ball of light appeared. The spell Lorio conjured was very simple. So simple that he had completely forgotten about it. Being able to do things with pure thought and power made it easy to forget the simple word spells a wizard learnt as an apprentice. It was now time for him to do something that Lorio couldn't.

Although the light spell was very simple it was not one that could be done by word only. Of course there were light spells Lorio could create, but he didn't have the same control that Eldred had and the last thing they needed was to be caught.

When Eldred had finished a small ball of light replaced the one Lorio had created and floated above their heads. With the new light they could all see a blanket of darkness above it. No light was able to pass through and now they could see what was before them.

As Eldred had already told them, there were iron bars crisscrossing the tunnel barring any entrance into the sewers. The sight made everyone's heart sink, except for Lorio. Eldred was about to say something, but he paused as Lorio moved towards the grill.

Before he touched the iron Lorio inspected the bars closely. Eldred seriously believed that Lorio didn't know what he was doing. He was about to speak when Lorio stood upright and gripped the middle cross bar. With little effort he twisted the bars to the left and the entire grill moved a fraction. The movement was so small the others weren't completely sure they weren't seeing things.

When Lorio was sure he had the grill in the correct place he gently pushed it forward. A moment later there was a grinding noise and to everyone's surprise the grill rolled into the wall.

"Quickly, it's on a timer." Lorio said as he moved inside the sewer.

The others followed without thinking, their feet splashing in the shallow water. As much as they had tried to avoid the filth along the ditch there was nothing they could do about the sewers. Hagar just made it inside before the grill rolled back into place.

"That is very impressive," Hagar had to voice his opinion.

"It was built by a group of ingenious smugglers a long time ago. Purely mechanical, no magic involved at all." He looked at Eldred as he made the revelation.

"How did you come across it?" Eldred asked, ignoring the jibe.

"A court magician has access to certain documents that no one else does. One of them has the location of this secret entrance into the city," Lorio sounded very smug.

The water in the sewers splashed over their ankles as they walked. The subtle odour that had hit them when they entered the ditch had increased. The small light globe followed them inside and lit the way, although they weren't sure they wanted to see what they were walking in.

Before long they reached a crosspath in the sewers. On either side the paths elevated out of the sewer system. They all wanted to be out of the filth. Once they were above the flow of waste they could work out their next plan.

"Do you know where we have to go now?" Eldred asked.

Lorio looked to the left and the right, but there was nothing that gave him any indication of which way to go. He put his pack down and rifled through it. The further he looked the more his heart sank. He realised he had forgotten to pack the map with directions through the sewer system. After all his good work he was now going to look like the foolish court magician they all thought he was.

"It seems as though I left the map behind." Lorio couldn't believe the words as they came out of his mouth.

"So what do we do now?" Eldred kept his voice calm.

"I guess we have to choose a path and work our way out. I'm sure there are many exits we can take," Alena added.

"I was down here last time we were in Lel Dinion. There are many exits into the city. I guess one is as good as another." Eldred added.

Lorio was surprised that no one berated him for making such a stupid mistake. He wouldn't have let the others off so easily. It made him relax and feel more comfortable.

"Let's get moving. We aren't going to find the way out standing here," Hagar sounded excited.

They moved off along the left side passage. They had a purpose and that seemed to improve their spirits. Even Lorio seemed excited to be on the move.

Eldred increased the size of the ball of light so they could all easily see their way. With the added light they could see footprints in the dust on the passage floor. There was only one set of footprints and they soon identified them as Lorio's. Once they realised they stopped again.

"So if we can keep following your footprints where are we going to exit the sewers?" Eldred asked.

"I entered the sewers from within the palace grounds, but I doubt we'll be able to follow my footprints that far. These tunnels do get used every now and again," Lorio added.

His words made sense. Every now and then the city watch would patrol the sewers in search of criminals.

Despite knowing the dangers of the sewers they didn't seem to care. If they had then they might have been more careful as they made their way towards the palace. Before they knew what was happening they were surrounded by a group of bandits.

"And what do we have here?" the lead bandit spoke as he approached the group with his sword drawn.

Each of the bandits held a torch, and as soon as Eldred realised he let his ball of light fade out. No one seemed to notice, or at least if they did they didn't comment on it.

"We are just passing through. We're not here for any trouble." Eldred replied, ignoring the imminent threat.

"No one just 'passes through' the sewers. There are only two reasons for someone to be here. They're either up to no good or trying to catch someone who is up to no good. Now which one are you?"

Eldred didn't know what he could say to get them out of their situation, at least without knowing who he was speaking with.

"We are just looking for a way out," Eldred spoke after a moment of thought.

"If you are looking for a way out then we are just the people to help you." The leader paused for a moment. "First I think you should give my men your weapons. I'd hate to give anyone the wrong idea."

Eldred thought for a moment. In the end he decided they didn't have a choice. The last thing he wanted was to fight in the sewers and if they didn't comply that's exactly what would happen. He only hoped in the end he could talk his way out of their current predicament. He had a feeling that he could trust the bandit regardless of their lot in life and he might be able to get some more information on what was happening inside the palace.

"Very well. Give them your weapons," Eldred commanded.

The others were about to protest, but they knew it would do no good. If Eldred thought it was safe to relinquish them then they would have to trust his judgement.

"Now if you would be so kind as to follow me I think it would be better if we spoke in a more comfortable setting." The leader offered.

"Certainly, but it would be nice to know the name of our captor before we go any further." Eldred stood firm.

"My name is Vasil and you are not our captives, you are our guests. We just don't want any mistakes to happen. That's why I've requested your weapons."

Although Eldred knew that Vasil wasn't telling the whole story he was happy enough that, for the moment, they weren't in danger. If anything they might have just found someone to guide them through the sewers. It was going to be much better for them if they could surface inside the palace grounds than the city.

Once they were disarmed Vasil led them through the sewers. They walked down many tunnels, taking many different turns. Eldred had no idea how the man was able to find his way. He looked to see if there were markings on the walls or the floor, but he couldn't see any. That was exactly how the marks were designed. If anyone could see them then it wouldn't be long before the soldiers knew where to go. The markings were so subtle only those who knew where to find them could find their way.

Eventually they came across an iron door. In the dim torch light it would have been easy to walk straight past it. The door was inset into the think stone walls. Vasil knocked and then waited. The sound resonated throughout the sewers. Eldred wasn't sure if that was the best way to keep the place secret, but he had to trust Vasil knew what he was doing.

"What is the password." A voice came from the other side.

"It's Vasil, I have people with me. Just open the door Bogdan!" Vasil tried to keep his anger in check.

The sound of muffled voices could be heard on the other side before the door was unlocked and pulled open. Vasil went in first followed by Eldred and the others and lastly the remaining bandits.

They entered into a large basement. It reminded Eldred of the last time he was in sewers, although that basement had been a lot smaller.

He wondered how many basements there were. He put that thought out of his mind and concentrated on the sight before him.

The basement was lit by a number of torches in wall sconces. The bandits placed the torches they had in the empty places, the others were extinguished and left against the wall. A number of chairs sat around the outside of the basement with a large table and chairs in the middle. It looked as though it had been set up as some kind of meeting room. On the far side a set of stairs led up to a trapdoor that had a large padlock keeping it safely shut.

"Please, have a seat. And then we can work out what we're going to do with you," there was little humour in Vasil's voice.

They were outnumbered three to one. Since they were disarmed the only way they could survive an attack was with the use of magic. Eldred wasn't sure if he could take them all out, so he needed to tread very carefully.

"As I told you before, we are just trying to get out of the sewers. It looks like you have saved us that problem. Now if you would just unlock the trapdoor we can be on our way." Eldred knew that wasn't an option and it wasn't really what he wanted, but he had to play the game. He sat when he finished speaking and was followed by Alena, Hagar, Lorio and Richmond.

"All in good time. If you answer my questions honestly then you might just live to see the sun again." The malice didn't match his playful tone, but there was no doubt that the threat was genuine.

Vasil sat at the head of the table. The other bandits stood around the edge of the room. None of them sat as they wanted to watch the reaction of their prisoners. He waited a moment before speaking again, watching their faces closely. He was trying to gauge a response before he even started asking the questions.

It was a strange looking group. The old man in the lead didn't look as frail as his age would suggest. The second old man looked somewhat familiar, but he couldn't place from where. The woman, although he wasn't completely sure, he thought was an elf. The two men were the only ones who looked normal, but in that they still looked the most out of place in the strange little group. Vasil knew there was more to them than he first thought.

"Now, you might be telling me the truth that you're trying to find your way out of the sewers, but that doesn't explain what you're doing here in the first place?"

As much as Eldred knew the question was coming he hoped that it wouldn't. He had no lie to tell and he couldn't tell them the truth.

"We stumbled into the sewers by mistake. We were..." Hagar started to speak when Eldred didn't. "Well let's just say we were looking for something."

Vasil thought for a moment. He didn't believe a word that Hagar told him, but he had to tread softly if he wanted to get the truth.

"And what was it you were looking for?" Vasil followed up.

"That is something that we're not at liberty to divulge. Let's just say that we didn't find what we were looking for and now we just want to leave. We're not here to cause any trouble for anyone."

Eldred was glad that Hagar was taking the initiative, but he thought the lie was too thin. There was no way that Vasil was going to fall for it, but at least it gave him time to think up a better excuse. He only hoped that Hagar didn't give away any real information.

"Well if you can't tell me then I guess we have a problem. I don't believe that is why you are here and now that you know where we are we can't let you leave." Vasil almost snarled as he spoke. It didn't seem that the gentle approach was going to work, so he decided to push harder.

Hagar looked at Eldred with an apologetic look on his face. It was a sign that he was out of ideas. Now it was up to Eldred to speak, but just before he could Lorio jumped in.

"I am Lorio, court magician to the king." Eldred could have hit the man for speaking. "We are here on important business and delaying us could cause the downfall of the kingdom."

Lorio's words caused Vasil to start laughing, which in turn brought a round of laughter from the other bandits. The sudden mirth enraged Lorio and before Eldred could silence him he spoke again.

"And what do you think is so funny?" Lorio barked.

His words instantly silenced the laughter.

"I would be very careful if I was you, court magician." Venom dripped from his words. "We might not look like much, but I can assure you that you would be dead before you can do much damage." He paused to let the words sink in. When Lorio didn't retort he continued. "Why would you think we care what happens? If you hadn't noticed we are the scum of the kingdom. Kings come and Kings go, but we will remain here, in the sewers, doing our best to survive. So you see if you work for the king you are no friends of ours."

Lorio was about to speak again, but Eldred silenced him with a stern look. This time it was Alena who spoke before Eldred had a chance.

"This is bigger than just the king. This is something that even you can't hide from," Alena spoke passionately.

That brought Vasil's attention. There was something in her tone that made him listen.

"And what does an elf have to do with all of this?"

"Enough of this!" Eldred jumped in before Alena had a chance to respond. Suddenly the lights started to fade. The spell was subtle and wouldn't attract the attention of the Dark Knight, but he hoped it would be enough to have an effect on the bandits.

At first no one seemed to notice, but as time passed the room became darker and darker. As it did Eldred seemed to grow bigger. He could see that his little ruse was having its affect.

"This is no laughing matter. There is one of the Evil One's Dark Knights in control of the king. He has worked his way into the palace and the Gods only know what mischief he is up to. We need to get in to stop him." Eldred figured the time for lies were over. When he finished talking he let the room return to normal.

"And who are you to take on a Dark Knight?" Vasil was no longer confident.

"I am Eldred, one of the Council of Wizards. Lorio has already introduced himself. This is Hagar, son of Duke Hadar, this is Lord Richmond of Bellarome and this is Alena daughter of Orric." The flood gates were opened and the information came pouring out.

Vasil didn't know what to say. With the exception of Alena he recognised the other names. His confidence was now completely gone. He thought they could take Lorio, but with the addition of Eldred he figured they had lost the advantage. Now he realised why they had given up their weapons so easily. Little did Vasil know that Eldred was prepared to create powerful spells.

"So, that still doesn't explain why you are lurking through the sewers." Vasil didn't know what to day.

"I would have thought that was obvious," Eldred spoke quickly before the others could. "We are trying to work our way into the palace without being seen."

Vasil thought for a moment. Finally things were starting to make sense. Although he still wasn't sure he was getting the full story.

"There is something else. Something you're not telling us." Vasil wasn't about to give up, even though he knew he had been defeated.

Eldred raised a hand to silence Lorio. He knew why the magician wanted to speak. He wanted to make sure Eldred didn't reveal their entrance into the sewers but that was not something he was prepared to do.

"We believe that the Dark Knight is in control of one of the *Stones of Power*." Eldred wasn't sure he should reveal that information, but he figured he had to tell them something.

That piece of information brought gasps and hushed murmurs from the other bandits. Vasil wasn't sure exactly what to make of it, but he knew it wasn't good.

"Do you really think you can defeat this Dark Knight?" he asked.

"I don't know." Eldred spoke honestly. "But we have to try. We can't leave Lel Dinion in the thrall of a Dark Knight; for right or for wrong we have to do something." The prophecy was leading them towards the palace, that was something that Eldred did know and he knew he couldn't go against it.

"Very well. Wait here. I'll be back shortly." Vasil had all the information he needed.

Vasil produced a key and walked up the stairs. He unlocked the padlock before pushing the trapdoor open. He was followed by half a dozen of the bandits. The rest remained around the outside of the basement, not wanting to get close to the group. Eldred's spell had done the job. The tension was thick as everyone waited for Vasil to return.

It was a tense fifteen minutes before the trapdoor was opened again. Vasil was the last through and he returned the padlock before walking down the stairs. Eldred watched him closely and didn't think it was a good sign. He had a bad feeling Vasil wasn't going to give them good news.

"It seems that the rumours are true," Vasil started the conversation in a manner that Eldred didn't expect. "We have been hearing some disturbing rumours from within the palace over the last few weeks. Not only that, but we have been seeing some changes in the city. Now normally a change in power wouldn't make any difference to our lives, but this is different. Anyway, to cut a long story short, we believe your reasons for being in the sewers."

"What does all that mean?" Eldred couldn't wait.

"It means that we have decided to help you. We might be the filthy underworld of the city, but we do have honour. We have no love for the king and his rules, but we have even less love for the Evil One."

Eldred knew there was more to the story. As much as he wanted to get into the palace he knew he should hold out for more information.

"There has been an influx of people in the sewers over the last few weeks. They are not part of the city guard, we know that for sure. Unfortunately that is all the information we have. A couple of times we tried to capture them, but each time our men ended up floating in the waste. You were the first group who came without a fight," Vasil explained.

"So it seems that the Evil One's agents are moving about the city, using the sewers to remain hidden," Eldred mused.

"That doesn't make any sense," Alena added. "If the Dark Knight is in control of the city then why would his agents need to be skulking through the sewers?"

They all had to admit that Alena made sense. If the Evil One was in control of the city there was no need for skulduggery. There had to be another reason.

"So what does that mean?" Vasil didn't sound happy.

"I have no idea," Eldred replied. "That is why we need to get into the palace. It seems as though things are not at all what they seem."

"I don't like where this is going," Hagar had lost his confidence. "We shouldn't be rushing into the palace without more information. We have no idea what we are going to be walking into."

"And where do you propose we get that information?" Lorio snapped. "It's not like we can just walk up and ask anyone on the street."

"We are not without our influences." There was a broad smile on Vasil's face.

"What are you talking about?" Eldred didn't sound happy.

"We have our spies all over the city. You don't become a successful gang of thieves without information. If you want to know what is happening in the palace then we have the men for you."

"Let's go and see them then." Eldred replied.

"Relax Eldred. It's not quite that easy. Our informers don't just hang out waiting on the off chance we need them. It's a little more technical than that," Vasil explained.

Eldred had to admit that made sense, but that didn't change his concerns. They needed to enter the palace as soon as possible. They didn't have time to waste, but on the other hand they didn't need to rush into a trap. Something wasn't sitting right. He knew they needed more information and if it took another day then so be it.

"Very well. What do we need to do?" Eldred asked.

"We will go to the surface. There are a few taverns where people from the palace like to come and drink. With a little luck one of our contacts might be there."

Without waiting for confirmation Vasil stood from the table. The others looked to Eldred to see what he was going to do. There was nothing for it but to trust the bandit. It was the only way they were going to get the results they needed.

Chapter 27: Searching for Information

Vasil lead them out of the basement and into what looked like an abandoned storefront. It looked as though the basement was larger than the building itself. Eldred wondered if it had ever been used as a shop or whether it was built specifically to cover its true use. He was going to ask the question, but then thought better of it. He didn't think the bandits would be overly open about their headquarters. It was surprising enough that they weren't blindfolded. Lorio was the king's magician and really shouldn't now about bandits' hideouts, so Eldred thought he should let his curiosity pass.

The small alley they came out in was dark. There were no lanterns to light the way and the only light they had was from the torch Vasil carried. As they left the alley Eldred knew why they hadn't been blindfolded. There was a lantern lit at the end of another small alley giving them a point to walk towards. It was at the point that Vasil extinguished his torch and left it at the entrance. Eldred figured it would only be by pure luck that he could find the abandoned shop again.

At the end of the second alley they came out into a larger street. The buildings didn't look well maintained and Eldred realised they were in the poor quarter. He was glad that Vasil had returned their weapons. The poor quarter could be very dangerous at night and he wasn't sure the small group of bandits would be enough to save them if any trouble happened.

Besides Vasil there were three other bandits with them. One was the man named Bogdan who had admitted them into the basement. The other two were introduced as Bion and Korinna. Eldred's first impression of Korinna was that she was a lady of the night. She also was dressed in a tight fitting leather shirt and short skirt. Her stockings had a number of rips and her light brown hair was tattered. She also had a number of dirt stains on her face. Eldred thought she might have been quite pretty once, but the years of living on or under the streets had taken its toll. He wondered why she was going with them, but it wasn't his place to question it.

Bion was a strong looking man. His short cut brown hair had dirt through it and his stern face had similar dirt streaks. He looked like he could use the sword that hung by his side. All in all it was a strange little group that walked through the streets of Lel Dinion. Eldred didn't think they would run into any trouble.

There were a few shady looking characters on the street as they walked by. They looked ready to strike until they recognised the man who was leading them. No one was going to attack Vasil, all the thieves and urchins knew better than to attack him. If they did they wouldn't be alive long enough to celebrate their spoils.

It wasn't long before they came across a rough looking tavern. The sign hung loosely on one chain above the door. Eldred just made out the name as the Drunken Mule. The timber door had seen better days. There were sword marks from the brawls that had gotten out of hand. Some of the scars looked very recent. Eldred wasn't sure if they were walking into the best of places. He only hoped that Vasil knew what he was doing.

The sight inside wasn't much better. Eldred had been in some seedy looking taverns in his time, but nothing came close to the Drunken Mule. Sawdust was strewn across the floor to cover the remnants of emptied stomachs and even though it was still early in the night, there didn't seem to be many sober patrons. Clouds of smoke filled the air and the smell of stale alcohol was thick. Eldred wondered if anyone had come within a hundred paces of the palace. He didn't think he would gain any useful information.

Vasil ignored the drunks around him and walked to the bar. A young serving wench stood serving drinks to the many patrons. As much as it was more than a one woman job she seemed to be coping well.

"Evening Vasil," she sounded nervous.

"Evening Siny!" Vasil did his best to sound jovial. "A round of ales for me and my friends."

"Are you sure this is a good idea?" Eldred whispered into Vasil's ear as Siny poured their drinks.

Vasil listened to his words but didn't respond. He knew exactly what he was doing. It would be all too suspicious if they didn't drink. They were conspicuous enough as it was and he didn't want them to stand out even more. At least the time walking through the sewers made his new friends smell like they belonged ther.

"What brings you out tonight?" Siny asked as she handed over the first of the drinks. "I haven't seen you here for a long time."

Vasil passed the ales behind him before returning his attention to Siny. "I'm looking for Thales. Has he been in tonight?" He came straight to the point.

"Sorry darling, I haven't seen him all week." Siny started to relax.

Vasil nodded his appreciation and then led the group away from the bar. As they moved towards the back of the tavern a large man stumbled into Vasil. Vasil brushed him aside without taking any notice, he was more concerned about speaking with the others.

"Don't you think you should apologise?" the man slurred.

"I'm sorry," Vasil dismissed him without really acknowledging him. That made the drunk man even angrier.

The man stumbled his way to the back of the tavern and pushed Vasil in the back. Not expecting the attack Vasil wasn't able to brace himself and he stumbled forward until he hit the wall. As he turned around the large man swung his right fist at his head. At the last moment Vasil ducked and the man's fist hit the wall. Before he was able to recover Vasil struck out. His open hand hit the man square in the throat. Vasil didn't wait; as the man gasped for breath he punched him in the stomach and then the face. The last blow was enough to knock him to the ground.

"I think we should get out of here before things get out of control." Vasil casually stepped over the drunken man and made his way to the exit.

The fight had gained the attention of everyone in the tavern. Normally a fight would start a brawl, but no one wanted to risk a fight with Vasil. Those who knew him knew exactly what he was capable of and those who didn't weren't about to find out.

"Was that part of your plan?" Eldred asked once they were outside again.

Vasil ignored the jibe.

"Is that a normal night?" Hagar asked.

"Normally it's much worse." Korinna replied. "But people are normally smart enough not to start trouble with Vasil." She added as an afterthought.

"What do we do now?" Alena asked.

"We move on to the next tavern. It's the only way you will get the information you need." Vasil didn't sound happy. "Remember we are doing you a favour, don't forget that."

Eldred was about to retort, but he was silenced by a look from Alena. There was nothing to be gained by annoying Vasil. As much as they were working towards a common goal they needed Vasil more than he needed them.

It was getting late into the night when they finally found the man they were looking for. Eldred had lost count of how many taverns they had been to and in each one they had to have a tankard of ale. By the time they reached the last tavern they were starting to feel the effects. Vasil was the only one who didn't show any signs of being drunk. Luckily there were no more fights, at least none that they were involved in.

"You are a hard man to find." Vasil greeted Thales.

"What are you doing here?" Thales kept his voice low.

They had made their way to the Princely Drop. It was one of the better taverns and was close to the palace. The group looked completely out of place. It was definitely not a hangout for the criminal element of the city. Vasil had hoped Thales would be at another tavern, but it was not the case. Now they stuck out more than ever. The tavern was almost empty and there was no missing the newcomers.

"We need to talk. I think we should go somewhere a little more private." Vasil got straight to the point.

"It's getting late and I have to work in the morning. I was just going to finish this drink and then call it a night." Thales seemed very nervous.

"This can't wait. Is there somewhere a little more private we can talk?" Vasil was also becoming nervous. He could see the eyes in the tavern moving towards them.

"There are a few rooms out the back. I'll see if we can borrow one."

Thales moved quickly to the bar and spoke to the serving lady. When he finished she nodded her head and then signalled to a young man standing by the door. Thales signalled to the others to follow him.

"What's this all about?" Thales did not sound happy.

"Remember who you're talking to Thales." Vasil wasn't in the mood for his attitude. "You wouldn't be where you are today if it wasn't for us."

The words put Thales back in his place.

"I'm sorry Vasil. What can I do for you?"

"We need information on what's happening in the palace."

"I don't know what you mean?" Thales looked genuinely confused.

"We understand there have been some new visitors arrive recently."

Thales thought for a moment. When he realised what Vasil was talking about it became clear on his face.

"Ah you mean Princess Marina." Thales missed the plural in the question. "She has recently been betrothed to Prince Rives. When King Lisle XII, pray the day never comes, dies he will be king and she will be queen. The wedding will be a..."

"And does the king have a new advisor." Eldred had to interrupt.

Thales shot Vasil a questioning look, but the bandit leader simply nodded his agreement.

"Not that I know of. There hasn't been anyone else arrive." Thales wasn't sure what Eldred was getting at.

"So you're saying no one arrived with the princess?" Eldred pushed.

"Oh, no, the princess did have an escort when she arrived. I believe it was Captain Aimon from Entero."

"And what has the captain been doing since he entered the city?" Vasil jumped in before Eldred had a chance. He figured it was better if he did the questioning.

"He didn't stay long, maybe a day or two. You understand that I'm not privy to all the palace news," Thales sounded somewhat defensive.

"So where did he go?" Vasil asked.

"I don't know. He was here one day and gone the next. I can only assume he was here to escort the princess and then he returned to the Alliance. I believe that is where he was from?"

"That doesn't make sense." Eldred mused aloud and then silently cursed himself for speaking his thoughts.

"What doesn't make sense?" Thales suddenly looked very nervous. "Who are these people Vasil?" He looked around nervously for a way to escape. There was only one door and there was no way he could make that. The window on the far wall was his best chance.

"Relax Thales. I can vouch for these people and that should be enough for you."

As Vasil spoke Hagar moved between Thales and the window blocking his chance for a quick escape.

"Is there any other information you can tell us on the running of the palace?" Vasil continued the questioning.

The expression on Thales face changed. It was obvious he just remembered something important.

"I was going to elaborate earlier before I was interrupted." He sneered at Eldred before continuing. "The king and queen became ill two days ago. From what I've heard the physicians don't know what's wrong with them. That is why the marriage announcement has come at such an opportune time."

"But Prince Rives is the youngest son. He shouldn't be the heir," Vasil sounded confused.

"King Lisle made the announcement after Prince Lisle was killed in a tragic riding accident. The king decided that Princess Romana would not be his heir and made Rives the heir apparent. Prince Rives is now in command until Lisle recovers from his illness. Now honestly that is all the information I have. I'd like to return to the palace now."

Eldred motioned for Vasil to follow him to the far side of the room. Something wasn't sitting right with him and he didn't want Thales to leave with confirming something with Vasil.

"I don't think it's a good move letting Thales back into the palace. He has too much information. If he mentions our presence, even in passing, then we could be walking into a trap." Eldred whispered.

"I think you're right. He seems a little too keen to get back," Vasil agreed.

"I'm afraid that isn't an option," Vasil spoke as he walked back towards Thales. "We have another job for you and that means you have to come with us."

"No, Vasil. I can't do that. If I get caught then I'll lose my position," Thales whined.

"We got you that position and don't you forget it. Now it's time for you to pay that debt." Vasil wasn't going to back down.

"I paid you for your services. I paid in gold." Thales sounded shocked.

"Sometimes debts are more than gold can pay and this is one of those times. I'm sure people would love to hear how you managed to get your position in the palace." The threat was real.

In the end Thales knew he had no choice. He was between a rock and hard place and the only chance he had was to follow Vasil.

They made their way out through the tavern, trying to remain as inconspicuous as possible. That was not an easy task considering there were only half a dozen people left inside. They hoped that people would soon forget their presence and not start any rumours.

They moved quickly through the streets back towards the poor quarter. The clouds that had covered the moon earlier in the night had passed and the extra light made their journey easier.

When they were back in the poor quarter they all relaxed a little. There was less chance they would run into the city watch and soon enough they would be back indoors. They had taken a big risk walking through the city, but it seemed as though they were going to remain anonymous for the moment.

Vasil didn't lead them back to the shopfront, instead he took them down a different alley to an abandoned warehouse. Eldred wasn't sure where they were going, but a thought suddenly came into his head. The stones were in his pack back at the shop. He couldn't leave them there. He needed to take them into the palace on the chance he would need to use them.

"Where are we going?" Eldred asked as Vasil led them into the warehouse.

Inside, the warehouse had been set up like a bunk house. It was one of the many locations that thieves used as accommodation. It was in better condition than expected. It wasn't the most luxurious of residences and there was some discarded rubbish on the floor, but all in all it would be a suitable place to sleep.

"This is the best place to get some rest. There is nothing more that we can do for the night. I will make sure someone is posted on the door to keep Thales from trying to leave," Vasil made a point of not looking at Thales as he spoke.

"What about our packs?" Eldred cut straight to the point.

"Don't worry. We shall all need fresh clothes if we are going to infiltrate the palace. If we go in as we are we will stick out. I will have fresh clothes brought in for us before morning." Vasil explained.

"That isn't what I'm talking about. There is something in my pack that I need."

"Very well. I will have your packs brought here, but I wouldn't be surprised if your gold is missing."

Hagar was about to protest, but Eldred silenced him with a wave of his hand. He figured that Vasil and his band of thieves will have earned the gold by the time they were finished. Regardless of the result the coins they carried wouldn't be required. Either they killed the Dark Knight, freed the kingdom, and received a nice reward or they failed and they would all be dead.

They were shown to a slightly more private area of the warehouse. There was a temporary wall built around five bunk beds. It was as much privacy as they were going to get.

"This doesn't make any sense." Eldred mused, more to himself than the others.

"What doesn't make sense?" Lorio asked.

"Why would the Dark Knight bring Marina to the palace only to leave again? He couldn't be so strong that he could control her from outside the palace. Maybe he could do it for a few days, but eventually he'd lose control. Not only that, but I'd be able to feel the power needed for such a spell."

"Then he has to still be in the palace," Richmond spoke the only obvious answer.

"But Thales said he left," Eldred retorted.

"Not exactly," Alena spoke softly. "He said that Aimon was there one day and gone the next. He didn't actually say Aimon had left the palace. There is a good chance he is still there."

They all stopped and thought on Alena's words. They made sense, but they still didn't explain everything.

"That could be true, but Thales said there was no one new in the palace." Lorio wasn't convinced.

"Then he has to be someone else." Hagar thought it was obvious enough.

"Again, it would take too much power for Argoz to change facades and keep control of Marina," Eldred explained.

Again they stopped to think on the problem. It was getting late in the night and the alcohol was clouding their judgement.

"There has to be another explanation." Eldred dropped his head. He was trying his best to think, but the answers weren't coming to him.

"Maybe we should get some sleep. This will be clearer in the morning." Alena suggested.

The others agreed. It was late and as much as they had slept during the day they felt exhausted. It was going to be another long day and they needed their wits about them. Eldred was the only one who didn't retire. He wasn't going to sleep until the *Stones of Power* were back in his possession. He had a bad feeling they would be key to their success. If there was something more frightening than facing a Dark Knight it was having to use one of the stones. It was something that he never wanted to do. There was no telling what would happen if he tried.

***

Marina stood out on the balcony of her royal apartment. The night sky had cleared and it was turning out to be a pleasant night. She stood in a blue silk nightgown and a cool breeze lapped at her naked ankles. She took a drink of wine from her golden goblet.

Life had taken a rather sharp turn in last few days. When she had first arrived at the palace she had not felt well. She had felt hazy. That all changed when she put the Sapphire ring on. All of a sudden her mind cleared.

The last few weeks had been a blur. Only now was she starting to recover fragments of her memory. The Dark Knight Argoz, who had been parading around as Captain Aimon, had drugged her in the camp outside of Jarrat and stolen the Sapphire ring. She had ridden hard to catch him, but he had secured the ring and hidden its power from her and it was only pure luck that she came across him.

Slowly she remembered the conversation she had with the Dark Knight, but she had no idea how close she had been to losing her life.

"The stone is mine!" Her anger overwhelmed her senses.

Argoz laughed. There was nothing she could do to take the stone back from him. His first instinct was to kill her. He could have done so easily, but something stopped him. There was something about the woman that intrigued him. For the moment he would stay his hand.

"You cannot have the stone, but if you like, you can travel with me for a while."

Marina didn't know what to say. It wasn't the response she was expecting. She knew it wasn't right, but all she could say was thank you. Not only that she was grateful for the offer.

Argoz thought for a moment. He didn't know why he had made the offer. He didn't need a travelling companion and she would only be trouble, and yet the offer came unbidden from his lips.

As they travelled he realised that a princess would make it easier for him to gain entrance to the palace. He knew there was a reason why he had brought her along. Not only that but she was very attractive. He had not enjoyed the touch of flesh like some of his brothers. It was not something that interested him, but there was something different about the woman before him. Something stirred inside him, but for the moment he would let it pass. When the time was right he would make his move.

The rest of the journey was still clouded. Her next memory was reaching the palace. Argoz used her to gain entrance. Of course the king would admit someone as important as Princess Marina. For someone who didn't know it would simply seem that Aimon was her escort.

Suddenly she heard something stir from inside her apartment. For a moment she thought that her betrothed had woken, but that wasn't the case. It was a simple sleeping potion she had put in his wine, but it would be enough to keep him unconscious until morning.

His advance on her had become too much. She had no intention of sleeping with the prince. Their marriage was simply a means to an end. With the king and queen dying it would not be long before she would rule her own kingdom. Then when her father died she would rule two. She had always known she was born into greatness, she just never realised how much.

She drained her goblet and then refilled it with the decanter sitting on the table beside her. This was the life she was born to live. She wasn't born to ride the countryside fawning over a mere man. She was a princess and needed to be treated like one. Her life was of luxury not the hardships of fruitless travel.

As she thought on her life the Sapphire gem started to glow softly. It was as if the stone could read her emotions. It always seemed more content when she was happy. It was as if they were joined by some mystical force. A gentle voice cooed inside her head and she felt at peace.

For a moment she turned around and looked back inside the apartment. The prince was still sound asleep on one of the many couches. It wasn't uncommon for a royal couple to share an apartment before getting married. Marina figured it would be easier to keep an eye on the prince if they lived together, but there was no way they would share a bed.

It wouldn't be too long before she could be rid of him. The king and queen would not last the week. Their sudden illness couldn't have come at a better time. Of course Prince Rives would have to mourn for the loss of his parents. That was the reason she needed to rush the wedding. It would have to happen in the next few days. No one would be happy that the king and queen wouldn't be able to make it, but they would have to live with it. They would be even less impressed when their new king died suddenly.

That thought made Marina smile. She had grown up with court intrigues and she knew how to play the game very well. With the death of her new husband that would allow her to marry again. The people would demand that their queen should have a king. Alaric would be returning to her soon. She could feel him. He was far away, but getting ever closer. They would be married and, as the children's stories tell, live happily ever after.

As she returned her gaze to the city she felt a sudden shift in the atmosphere. Something had changed and it was so sudden that, for a moment, she was short of breath. The Sapphire stone glowed brightly for a second before going dark again. The new development upset her and she returned inside. It was time for her to retire for the night. She would have to deal with whatever it was in the morning. She was so close to getting what she wanted and she wasn't about to lose it all.

Chapter 28: Intrigue

Their new clothes were waiting for them when they woke in the morning. They were all surprised with the quality of the apparel. There was a red silk dress for Alena with a small ruby gemmed silver necklace. The others had silk shirts and linen pants to wear in a variety of colours. They would certainly not look out of place in the palace.

The morning gave no new revelations to their dilemma. Eldred was tempted to start reading the prophecy when his pack arrived, but decided against it. The alcohol still clouded his mind and the prophecy was hard enough to decipher at the best of times.

"What's the plan?" Hagar asked as they ate a miserly breakfast.

"I guess we wait for Vasil to return and then we head into the palace," Eldred offered.

As if on cue Vasil entered the warehouse followed by Bogdan, Bion and Korinna. They were dressed in similar finery to the others. It was amazing the contrast from the night before. If they didn't already know they were a group of criminals then they could easily be mistaken for nobles. Eldred didn't like what he saw, it would be hard enough for the four of them to remain anonymous. It would be much harder with eight.

"Good morning Vasil," Eldred kept his voice level. He didn't want to jump to any conclusions.

"Are we ready to go into the palace?" Vasil asked.

"I don't think it's a good idea you coming along with us. This is going to be dangerous and we are more likely to reach our location with a smaller group." Eldred already had his speech prepared.

"We know the palace very well. I think you'd be surprised at how useful we're going to be." Vasil retorted.

"With all due respect I think I know the palace a little better than all of you." Lorio tried not to sound arrogant, but it didn't work.

"I'm sure you think you do. But there are places that you wouldn't even think of. How many times have you seen me in the palace?" Vasil asked.

"None, don't be silly. You have never been in the palace."

"Exactly. I have been in the palace more times than you'd believe. I have passed you in the corridors on many occasions. I guess I was never important enough for you to notice." A smirk appeared on Vasil's face and Lorio's turned a lighter shade of red.

"And what would you be doing in the palace?" Lorio asked when composed himself. His left eyebrow raised as he spoke.

"That isn't important." Eldred could see things going downhill fast. "What's important is getting us into the palace. The Dark Knight has to be in there somewhere and we need to find him. We need to rescue Marina, Lel Dinion and the Seven Kingdoms." It was overkill, but it had its effect.

"There's a small culvert that opens into the kitchens, to be more precise, into a storage room." Vasil knew that revealing its location he would no longer be able to use it. Luckily there were many other ways into the palace. "We'll have to take to the sewers again, but that is the only way in, short of knocking on the front door, but I guess that would defeat the purpose." He waited for a response. When none came he continued. "Bogdan, if you would be so kind as to find Thales for us, I think it's time we should be leaving."

Bogdan nodded his agreement before leaving and they all waited in an uncomfortable silence until the two returned. Thales looked as though he didn't sleep at all. There was no doubt if he could be anywhere else in the Seven Kingdoms then he would be. He knew that he had asked the impossible to get his position within the palace, but he never knew his debt would cost so much. If he was caught sneaking a band of criminals into the palace then not only would he lose his job, he could also lose his life.

"Please Vasil. You don't need me anymore. Let me go back to the palace. I will be berated for being late, but I won't lose my job," Thales pleaded.

"It'll be alright Thales. If we don't need you then you will be free to go, but until then you'll be coming with us." Vasil stood his ground. He wasn't exactly sure what Thales was going to do for them, but he knew he couldn't let him go.

Before Thales could voice his protest Vasil lead them towards the back of the warehouse. They reached a door with a thick padlock and Vasil produced a key and opened it. He waited for the group to pass through before entering himself. The bandit guard nodded at Vasil before locking the door behind them. Even if they wanted to there was no going back.

They entered an empty small room with a flight of stairs leading down. Vasil took the lead again and led them into another small room. They came to padlocked, iron door and Vasil used the same key to open it.

The stench of the sewers hit them as soon as the door was opened, it was even less pleasant when they entered. Vasil and Bogdan took the lead with Korinna and Bion taking the rear. Each of the thieves carried torches to light the way. The last thing they needed was someone taking a wrong step and falling.

Hagar made his way to front of the group. He had questions for Vasil, although he wasn't sure they would be answered.

"I don't understand your setup Vasil. It seems as though you have enough gold to give up your life of crime. These outfits could not have been cheap?" He let the question sink in.

"I was born into this life. It's all we've ever known." It was a simple response.

"That's not what I mean. I've never known thieves to be so well organised in a city. Normally it is every man for themselves and once they have stolen enough they look for a different lifestyle before they end up on the hangman's gibbet." Hagar pushed.

"Yes, I see what you mean. The guild was set up many years ago, before then the city was a rabble of criminals, everyone was stealing from everyone. King Lisle X sent his soldiers to clean up the streets. Anyone caught stealing would be sentenced to death. He was hard on crime and there were no grey areas. That's why a group of thieves got together to form the first Thieves Guild. By working together and regulating the trade they were able to reduce the risk of death. When King Lisle X finally died the new king changed the laws. Thievery wasn't a death sentence anymore, but by that stage the guild was already set up and working well."

"So how do you all work together? I would have thought stealing was a solitary profession." Hagar was enjoying the conversation. One day he would be a duke and the information would come in quite handy.

"We have an administration group that keeps a tally of who has taken what from where. We make sure that no one get's robbed too many times. We also supply protection to those shops that need it. There are some thieves in the city who aren't part of the guild. We make sure that they don't steal from those who pay us for protection." Vasil explained. "It's a little more complicated than that, but you get the general idea."

"So what do you do if someone steps out of line

"We have our own system of punishment. The most severe is being exiled from the guild. For those who have lived on the streets before, that is enough of a threat to keep everyone on the straight and narrow so to speak."

Hagar was about to ask another question, but Vasil silenced him with a wave of his hand. "We are getting close to our destination. It's best if we remain quiet now." Although silence wasn't completely necessary Vasil didn't want Hagar to ask any more questions.

Again Eldred was astonished at how easily Vasil could navigate the sewers. After the first turn Eldred would have been completely lost. There was no way he would be able to make it back the way they had come. Luckily they wouldn't have to. Whatever happened in the palace they wouldn't be going back into the sewers anytime soon.

Eventually Vasil stopped them at a small tunnel leading into the wall. It was just large enough for them to walk through if they crouched down low. It was not going to be an easy journey as the tunnel sloped upwards.

"Originally this was a waste chute for the kitchens, but over the years it has been taken out of use. The room that it opens into is now a storeroom," Vasil explained.

At least they weren't going to be walking through filth. That was something Eldred had been worried about. If they had to walk through waste then they would stink. Now it seemed as though he had worried for nothing.

"Thales. You go first and make sure the coast is clear," Vasil ordered. "Oh, and I wouldn't think about running away once you are on the other side." It was a threat as much as a warning.

Thales started up the chute whilst the others waited at the bottom. It wasn't long before he returned.

"This part of the kitchen is currently vacant. I suggest we hurry." He said before turning around and making his way back up to the kitchen.

Vasil quickly ducked into the chute followed, one by one, by the others. It was a difficult journey for the short distance. Once they were all through they had to move out into the kitchen. There was not enough space in the storeroom for them all to stand comfortably. Luckily Thales was telling the truth and the kitchen they were in was vacant. There were a number of kitchens in the palace. Some, and all, could be used at any given time. It was pure luck that the one they were in was empty.

"Now what do we do?" Hagar asked.

"I guess we need to make our way to the throne room?" Lorio surmised.

"I don't think we should rush in there just yet," Eldred responded. "Let's have a walk around and see if we can gather more information."

Lorio didn't like the idea of skulking around the palace. It would only be a matter of time before he was recognised, but he couldn't argue with Eldred.

"Can I go now?" There was a hint of hope in Thales voice.

"Not just yet. We may need someone to explain our presence and for the moment we need to keep Lorio's identity a secret. At least we need to try for as long as possible," Eldred replied.

"You don't need me. You can talk your way out of any situation." He spoke to Vasil. "Please, let me go." Thales was shaking with fear.

"Eldred is right. For now, you come with us." Vasil wasn't sure it was completely necessary, but he wasn't going to dispute Eldred.

Thales led the way out of the kitchen. He wanted nothing more than to make a break for it, but to run would be just as bad as getting caught with the group. There was a lot of movement in the corridors outside the kitchen. Thales had hoped since the kitchen was empty the corridors would be too. It was still a few hours before the midday meal, so the level of activity didn't seem right.

"So what else would you like to see?" Thales tried to make it seem that he was showing some new guests. If anyone really paid any attention they would see through the ruse. The city, more so the palace had been in lock down for the past week. Fortunately everyone was too busy with their own business to care about the small group.

"Let's have a look around the apartments," Eldred said, keeping up the ruse.

Thales led them through the kitchens to a flight of stairs leading to the ground floor of the palace. When he reached the top his heart jumped, both with fear and hope. Standing there was a group of soldiers with their swords drawn. It was as if they were waiting for them and that's exactly what the others thought.

"What have you done Thales?" Vasil was the first to make the accusation.

"Nothing, I promise. I had nothing to do with this."

"Put your hands up and don't even think about going for you weapons." The lead soldier commanded.

There were only a dozen guards and Eldred knew they could easily take them, but in the confines of the corridor there was a chance someone could lose their life. Not only that, but the soldiers were only doing their job and didn't deserve to die. There was more to the situation.

"It's okay, Vasil." Eldred stopped forward, then addressed the soldiers. "We'll come along quietly, but we won't be relinquishing our weapons."

That was not the response the soldiers had been expecting. Their weapons would be useless against the Dark Knight, but Eldred wanted to try and assert some authority. In the end he really didn't think it was going to work.

"Well... I don't know." The soldier sounded flustered. "The princess didn't say anything about your weapons. She only said that we were to escort you to the throne room as soon as you entered the palace."

The words brought a feeling of dread. If Thales didn't betray them then no one should have known about their arrival. As much as Eldred didn't know the man he didn't think he had betrayed them. On the positive side it seemed they were able to keep their weapons.

"I think you two should stay here," Eldred said to Vasil and Thales and they nodded their agreement.

"Very well. Let's be on our way then," Eldred tried sound as casual as possible.

The soldier nodded before turning around and making his way towards the throne room. The soldiers seemed happy enough to leave with the group. They didn't seem to worried about the two left behind.

At any point they could have drawn their weapons and killed the soldiers before they even knew what was happening. Eldred struggled to work out their current situation. Nothing made sense. Either way they were going to find out soon enough.

Everyone scattered in the hallways as they saw the soldiers marching through. They knew not to get in the way of the palace guards. There had been many rumours of people disappearing mysteriously in the corridors after crossing the soldiers. Nothing had happened in the past few days, but no one wanted to risk it.

The throne room was all but empty when they arrived. They entered through a set of large oak doors with a multitude of ornate patterns on them. They entered into the side of the room. On their left were a number of large arches. Each arch was open allowing the sunlight to stream through. On the other side was a large terrace. Normally the arches were kept closed, except on special occasions when the terrace was needed to house guests. It was an interesting sign. No one was completely sure if it was good or bad.

The far wall was covered with large tapestries. Some just a multitude of colours; others depicted famous figures from Hondin Lel's past. The wall behind them also had tapestries. There was one for each member of the royal family.

Their attention was drawn to the front of the room. There were four golden thrones on a small stone dais. One throne was larger than the other three, the one reserved for the king. To everyone's surprise it was Princess Marina who sat on that throne. To her left sat Prince Rives and as he looked at them, Eldred suddenly realised what had happened to the Dark Knight. He could sense the energy around the prince and knew that he had changed from the facade of Lord Argian.

Marina was dressed in her usual sapphire blue. When she had regained her senses she had all the palace's seamstresses make her new dresses. All were to be made from the same blue material. More than one seamstress had been sent to the dungeons for not getting the right colour. Her black hair hung loosely around her shoulders with small blue forget-me-not flowers tied in. Still the most prominent feature was the sapphire ring on her left ring finger.

Prince Rives was dressed to match the blue that his betrothed wore. He wore a blue silk shirt, with blue stockings and blue shoes. He seemed disinterested in the arrival of the group. He didn't even look like he realised they were there.

The soldiers left as soon as the group was inside. They seemed nervous and didn't want to wait around in case there was another order. It was all very disturbing for Eldred. Something was wrong with the situation, he knew that, he just didn't know what.

"Welcome Eldred. We are happy you have decided to grace us with your presence. And it seems that you have brought with you some prominent guests." It was at that moment that the princess' eyes fell on Lorio. "And our court magician, you have been sorely lost these past few days. Our king and queen are in poor health and I'm sure you would be of great assistance to our physicians."

When she stopped speaking no one knew what to say. They all remained quiet until she spoke again.

"I'm assuming you didn't come here just to stand in my presence. What is it I can do for you?"

Eldred still didn't have a response. He didn't want to speak in front of the Dark Knight, but it seemed he didn't have a choice. He would have to be very careful with his words, but before he could speak Lorio stepped forward.

"I would dearly love to visit the king and queen, if you permit." He bowed as he spoke.

Eldred could have struck out at him. It seemed his cowardice had finally overcome him. There was nothing he could do. He couldn't make a scene in front of the Dark Knight. For the moment it didn't seem as though their lives were in danger and he wanted to keep it that way.

"Of course Lorio, I wouldn't expect anything less." Marina didn't seem too worried about the magician.

After he was given permission for his request Lorio didn't know what to do. It was never his plan to run out, but now there was no other option. There was silence as he stood still before finally leaving the throne room.

"Don't worry Eldred. He is self-important and really doesn't need to be here. I will speak to him later." Marina continued. "Now, if you would be so kind as to tell me what brings you to Lel Dinion?" There was something in the question that didn't sit right with Eldred. It was as if there was something more pertinent she wanted to ask, but she was falling on ceremony.

"Is there somewhere we can speak privately?" Eldred kept his eyes on Argoz, but the Dark Knight didn't seem to be taking any notice.

"We are in private. There is no one within listening distance." Marina sounded confused before Eldred indicated towards Prince Rives with a nod of his head. "Oh, the prince. Don't worry about the prince. He's not going to say anything to anyone."

"What is going on here Marina?" Eldred asked, even more confused with her answer.

"I will do the questioning Lord Eldred. Remember you are in my palace now." Marina's tone changed from playful to stern.

"This is not your palace Marina," Hagar couldn't help himself. "This palace belongs to King Lisle and Queen Mara."

"And who do you think you are, Hagar, son of a duke, to address me in such a manner? My patience for such matters will only stretch so far. Remember that next time you wish to speak." Her tone was now completely hostile.

Hagar stepped backwards after the tirade. He had not been expecting such a response and suddenly felt ashamed. There was no chance of him speaking again without permission.

"We are here to make sure you are alright Marina. We heard a rumour that you were kidnapped by a Dark Knight?" It wasn't a complete lie. He knew there was no way he could lie to her. All he could do was refrain from telling the complete truth.

"I am grateful for your concern Master Wizard, but as you can see I am no one's prisoner. It is sad to say that the king and queen will be dead in the next couple of days, but on a brighter note the prince and I will be married and I shall be Queen of Hondin Lel." There was something in her tone that disturbed Eldred.

"That is good to hear." Eldred was trying his best to piece together the puzzle before him. He knew that Prince Rives was the Dark Knight Argoz. The only thing he could think of was that he was using all his energy to control Marina and that was why he looked so dazed and confused. "But who is it I'm really speaking with?" Eldred decided to run with his theory.

Marina looked genuinely confused for a moment before she realised what he insinuating. When she did she couldn't control her laughter. When she settled there was no sign of joy on her face. She sneered at Eldred just before she spoke.

"I am no one's thrall Eldred. Don't you make the same mistake that Argoz did." As she spoke she stroked his hand. "He is my pet now and I shall use him for a long as he is useful to me."

"This doesn't make any sense Marina." Eldred shook his head. "Please tell me what is going on? What happened to Prince Lisle and Prince Rives?"

Marina thought for a moment. In the end she decided that she could afford the information. There was still time left.

"It wasn't long after we arrived in Lel Dinion before Argoz had disposed of Prince Rives and taken his place. Now you must understand at this stage I was in a daze. I didn't know what was happening. Once he had usurped Rives' body and position his next task was to kill Prince Lisle. It would be easy enough for him to convince everyone that King Lisle had named him successor over Princess Romana, but never over Prince Lisle. No one even questioned them when they rode out of the city with guards. I don't know how he convinced Lisle to ride out with him, but the rest is history. He managed to kill the prince and claim it was a riding accident. From there he was able to twist King Lisle's mind so that he was named heir apparent and that about brings us up to date."

Eldred thought for a moment. There was a piece missing from her story. He wasn't sure if she had deliberately left it out or just didn't think it was pertinent to the conversation, but Eldred wasn't going to let it slide. The initial concern and fear had passed. From all accounts the Dark Knight had been subdued and all he had to do was deal with Marina.

"And how did you become betrothed to the Dark Knight?" Eldred realised that wasn't the question he wanted to ask. "Why would you marry a Dark Knight?"

Marina was about to answer the original question, but paused at the second. It wasn't at all what she was expecting. She thought for a moment before responding.

"Someone needs to take control of the city. There is so much evil around that I need to do something. This is the only way I can gain control."

"What of the king and queen. It can't be coincidence that they are suddenly both deathly ill?" Eldred pushed.

"No, it's not a coincidence, but a necessity. They are both weak minded and need to be removed from power." Her words seemed to echo through his mind.

"You poisoned the king and queen?" Eldred gasped.

"There was no other choice. Argoz had so easily controlled their minds. It was the only option I had." Marina sounded confused with the questioning.

"That's not right Marina. You have to cure them." It was Alena who said what they were all thinking.

Marina looked at Alena as if she was seeing her for the first time. Her face contorted in thought as if she was trying to work out who it was and then the realisation crossed her face.

"The elf, I have heard of you." There was venom in her words. "You are lucky to be alive from what I've heard. I would have thought you would have wanted to stay that way."

Alena was about to retort and then thought better of it. There was something wrong with Marina, she knew that, and she didn't want to provoke her. However she had done it, she had captured a Dark Knight and seemingly controlled him. Anyone who could do that was very dangerous.

"I am in control here and don't any of you forget it. Now you will answer my questions." Marina's anger was showing. "What I'd really like to know is where is Alaric? The last time I saw him was in Jarrat. He was with the Alliance, but I'm guessing that he is now travelling with you?"

Eldred took a step backwards. There was something about the change in her tone that had him concerned. There was an evil glint in her eye. Eldred wasn't sure if he really wanted to answer her question, but in the end he knew he didn't have a choice.

"Alaric was travelling with us for a while. He left us at the Scorpion Mountain and we haven't seen him since." Eldred explained.

"And where was he going?" Marina sounded annoyed.

"I wish I knew," Eldred spoke honestly. "He didn't let us know where he was going or when he'd be back. I really wish he had."

"What about the prophecy?" Marina nodded at Eldred's pack, which now sat on the ground beside him.

Eldred quickly picked it up and slung it over his shoulder in an attempt to hide it. He had no idea how she knew he had it. There was no way she should know.

"How do you..."

"I'll be asking the questions and you'll be answering them. What part of this don't you understand?" Marina interrupted.

"As I'm sure you know, the prophecy is not easy to understand. I've yet to find anything about Alaric's location."

Marina thought for a moment. There was silence in the throne room. No one wanted to speak before Marina did. In the end it was Argoz who broke the silence. For the first time he seemed to realise there was someone else in the throne room.

"What's happening? Who are these people?" His voice was hoarse.

"It's alright my love. These are my friends. Go back to what you were doing." Marina waved her hand in front of his face and he seemed to return to his comatose state.

Eldred had to think. The situation was nothing like he had imagined and that had put him off from the start. He had been expecting to fight a Dark Knight not have a discussion with Princess Marina, one he was apparently losing. Something had gone wrong and he needed to work it out. It seemed Marina was starting to get agitated and as she did the Sapphire stone started to glow. Eldred didn't think that was a good sign.

He didn't know why, but he suddenly felt that they were in danger. Not from the Dark Knight, but from the princess.

"If it is not too much trouble I think we would like some rooms. It would be good to clean up before the midday meal." Eldred was reaching for an excuse.

"You look fine to me Eldred. Is there something you're hiding from me?" She looked at him closely. "What else do you have in that pack of yours? It seems odd to me that you're the only one with possessions. I would have thought all your companions would need packs if they were planning on staying?"

Again Eldred didn't know how to answer. He couldn't tell her about the stones. Although Marina claimed she was in control he couldn't be certain. Although he didn't know her that well he assumed she was acting out of character.

"We travelled lightly as we weren't sure of the reception we were going to receive."

Marina pondered the question. She knew the wizard, as with all wizards, could be very crafty. There was something he was hiding and she wasn't going to let it rest.

"Show me what is in your pack," Marina's voice was forceful.

"I'm sorry Marina, I can't do that." Eldred stood firm.

"You will address me as princess or your highness." Marina stood as she spoke and the sapphire glowed ever brighter. "Now open your pack."

Eldred felt a shift in the energy around him. To his surprise he realised that Marina was preparing for an attack. Eldred was only just able to put up an invisible, magical barrier in front of the group as a line of blue light shot out from the centre of the Sapphire ring. The light hit the shield and spread out, but didn't penetrate it. Marina knew if she continued she could break the barrier, but that wasn't want she wanted. All she wanted to do was assert her dominance and she was satisfied that she had done that.

"I guess you weren't expecting that?" It was a rhetorical question. "That was just a warning. It wouldn't have done any real damage if you hadn't protected yourself."

Eldred wasn't really sure if that was true. Either way it seemed that Marina was a genuine threat. At least with the Dark Knight he knew what they wanted and what they would do to get it. With Marina he had no idea. He didn't know what she wanted and had no idea what she was capable of.

"This isn't necessary Marina. We are no threat to you or your hold on Hondin Lel." Eldred took a step back as Marina took one forward.

Marina opened her mouth to speak when something suddenly caught her attention. She looked around nervously as if she was trying to see something that wasn't there. It was the perfect time for Eldred to strike, but he couldn't bring himself to attack.

The air started to shimmer in one of the arches. Marina was the first to see it. Her look of astonishment brought everyone's attention around as a figure slowly started to coalesce. It wasn't until the air stopped moving that everyone realised it was Alaric. The sun shone through from behind him creating a shadow where he stood. No one could see the expression on his face until he took a step forward.

Alena was the first to react. Without thinking of the consequences she ran towards him and wrapped her arms around him. Alaric's expression suddenly changed, first to surprise and then his face softened. He returned the embrace and for a moment let his head rest on her shoulder before gently pushing her away.

"Alaric?" Marina's voice trembled. This had been the moment she had been waiting for, but it wasn't playing out the way it had in her mind every night. She stumbled backwards until she returned to her throne. "What is this about?"

"I've come for the Sapphire stone Marina." He didn't even seem to notice the Dark Knight sitting next to her. His tone was level as he came straight to the point.

"What?" Marina couldn't believe she had heard correctly.

"It's time Marina. I need the stone. You have to give it to me." The stone's glow started to dim. It was as if it was afraid of the man standing before it.

"I don't think that is going to happen." Marina quickly regained her composure. There had been a tear in her eye that was now gone. "We are joined, Sapphire and I. We are one and there's nothing you can do to tear us apart."

Alaric stepped forward. He was about to continue when he saw Argoz for the first time. Even in the guise of Prince Rives he was easy to recognise. He realised things were not at all what they seemed. There was a change in Marina. She had power, a power that had not been there before. She was still beautiful, but now there was something else.

"Don't test me Alaric. I don't want to kill you." Her voice was level. There was no lie in her threat, or at least she believed what she was saying.

"Be careful Alaric," Eldred warned. "There is something not right here. She attacked us just before you arrived. She has..." Before Eldred could finish he was picked up off the ground by invisible hands and thrown across the room until he struck the wall. He sunk the ground, but remained conscious.

"This is unnecessary Marina," Alaric started.

"I will not be pushed around. This is my throne room and you will show me respect," Marina interrupted.

Alena and Hagar moved to Eldred's side. They wanted to make sure he was alright. The thieves remained where they were. They knew breaking into the palace was going to be a risky job, but they had no idea what that had got involved in. They wanted nothing more than to leave, but they didn't want to risk being noticed.

"No one is pushing you around Marina."

"You will address me as princess or as your highness," Marina snapped.

Alaric shook his head before he continued. "Marina, you will give me the stone. I wish it didn't have to come to this, but I need it if I am going to defeat Nyrra."

Marina thought for a moment. As much as his words made sense there was a voice inside her heard telling her otherwise. The stone didn't want to go and she didn't want to lose it.

"There is another way!" The soft voice spoke inside her mind.

"How?" She mouthed the words she spoke in her head.

"You know what you have to do."

As the words came into her head so did the idea. There was no other option. Alaric must die!

Slowly Argoz stood from his throne. The dazed expression was now gone from his face. He grimaced once before a sneer crossed his face.

"The Cursed One, it seems that our paths have finally crossed. It's a shame this is where your journey ends."

Chapter 29: Power of Water

Alaric prepared himself for the attack from Argoz. He knew he could defeat the Dark Knight. His power had surpassed all of them. Even if there were two or three Dark Knights he knew he could defeat them all. The situation, however, called for a subtle tact. Something had changed inside Marina. He could feel it as soon as he materialised in the throne room. Until he could work out what it was he needed to be careful.

Argoz stepped down from the dais. His movements were slow and deliberate. Alaric knew he was drawing energy from around the room. The attack was going to come soon and it was going to be powerful.

"Do it!" Marina barked, sounding impatient.

Argoz didn't wait any longer. He did as he was instructed. A ball of fire shot from his hands towards Alaric. The flame ball didn't reach half the distance before it disappeared without a trace. Alaric didn't even move. There was a pensive look on Argoz's replica face of Prince Rives. As much as he had not thought his attack was going to kill the Cursed One, he had at least expected to hit him.

The next attack took longer to come. When it was clear that Alaric wasn't going to retaliate Argoz planned his next assault. After what seemed like an eternity the air started to swirl in front of Argoz. The vortex was a pace in diameter and moving at a quick pace. Without warning a bolt of lightning shot out from the vortex towards Alaric. It travelled only slightly further than the ball of flame before it disappeared, but that wasn't the end of it. Alaric could feel the vortex trying to draw him towards it as the lightning bolts continue to shoot outwards. Despite Argoz's effort Alaric remained standing.

"Stop playing with him Argoz and finish him. That is what your Great Lord wants." Marina urged.

Argoz's face started to go red with the strain as he drew in even more power. Alaric already held all the power he needed. Whatever Argoz threw at him he would easily counter. As he waited for the next attack Alaric noticed a flake of skin peel off the side of the Dark Knight's face. That was the sign he was looking for.

Before Argoz was able to attack again Alaric released his own spell. A cylinder of yellow light encircled the Dark Knight. There was little space for him to move and without thinking Argoz reached out and touched it. Instantly his fingers started to smoke as they burned against the magical barrier.

"Very clever Alaric, but not unbreakable." Alaric was surprised to hear Marina speak.

It seemed that she wasn't going to let her thrall be killed so easily. Another line of blue light shot from the Sapphire stone towards the cylinder. When the two lights collided green sparks bounced to the floor. The blue light didn't stop until it had completely vaporised it.

The Dark Knight was ready for his next attack. This time Marina was going to help him. The blue light fired again from the stone. This time it was directed at Alaric. His focus had been on the Dark Knight and he hadn't factored in an attack from Marina. At the last moment Alaric dived forward and rolled out of the way of the blast as Argoz made his attack. With all the power he could muster he created another fire ball and sent it flying towards Alaric. There was no time for Alaric to defend himself and the fire ball stuck the ground before completely engulfing him. The shape of the fire indicated Alaric's movement. He finished his roll and then quickly came to his feet. What was surprising was that he wasn't flailing or screaming in pain. He stood calmly as the fire licked at his body. No one in the room knew what to do, so they all waited to see what would happen.

Alaric deliberately kept the flames burning around him, for effect and to give him time to think. He knew e had to be careful. He had come prepared to face Argoz, but not Marina and the Sapphire stone. The situation had suddenlt become more dangerous.

When the flames suddenly subsided everyone could see that Alaric remained unharmed. The flames had not touched him at all. Now it was the time to counter. He had to destroy Argoz quickly. Things were starting to get out of control.

Argoz didn't know what to do, but Marina was not about to stop. She had lost the advantage of surprise, but she still had strength. The voice inside her head told her so. "Don't let him take me." The soft feminine voice cooed inside her mind. She would kill Alaric if that's what it took to keep Sapphire. They were joined now and she couldn't let her go. She now knew that her life with Alaric was a lie. He loved the elf and there was nothing she could do about it. As she was about to unleash the Sapphire stone on Alaric again she suddenly realised she couldn't move.

"What's happening?" She wanted to ask the question aloud, but her lips wouldn't move. The question remained inside her mind.

"It's him," the voice sounded annoyed. "I told you that you couldn't trust him."

"Help me," Marina's mind-voice whimpered.

"I thought you were stronger than that. I can help you, but I can't do it all for you." The voice was stern.

Alaric had cast the spell to immobilize Marina before he turned his attention to the Dark Knight. He knew he had to move quickly. The hold he had over Marina wouldn't last long, if his assumptions were correct.

"I think that it's time for you to go now." Alaric sneered at Argoz.

The Dark Knight had one more trick left. The words seemed to wash over him as he prepared for one last attack. The energy had all but left him, but that wasn't his idea. He had drawn his sword and was about to charge towards Alaric. It was a long shot, but it was all he had left.

Argoz was never going to be able to kill Alaric without magic. Alaric didn't even seem to notice the sword in his hand. In a physical battle Alaric would have easily killed the Dark Knight. Alaric's skills with a blade far outweighed Argoz's, however they would never find out.

The spell was cast and Argoz froze mid-step. Once he was caught in Alaric's trap there was nothing he could do. It gave Alaric time to try and master his next spell. It was one he hadn't used before and he wasn't sure of the result. He knew if he wasn't careful Argoz wouldn't be the only one to die.

The Dark Knight tried his best to move but his struggle was internal. No matter what he tried he couldn't break Alaric's spell. His only chance for survival was from Marina. As much as he hated to admit it he had no idea what to do. The spell should have been a relatively easy one to break, but there was something different in the way Alaric had created it. He suddenly realised he was completely outmatched. Something had changed in the Cursed One and if he hadn't been subdued by Marina he would have realised it before it was too late. At least that was what he told himself.

Before Marina could free herself Alaric put his plan into action. If the others hadn't been watching the Dark Knight intently they would have missed it. One moment Argoz was frozen in mid-step, the next he disintegrated completely. It was as if he had just been blinked out of existence and in fact that was pretty much what happened. The only reminder of his existence was the missing piece of floor where his right foot had been.

All in all Alaric was happy with the result. A small portion of floor wasn't too bad all things considered. Only Eldred really understood the magnitude of what Alaric had done. If he hadn't seen it himself he wouldn't have thought it was possible.

"What have you done?" Eldred gasped.

"All in good time," Alaric brushed the question aside and faced Marina.

Whatever feelings Alaric had held for the princess were now gone. She was still beautiful, more beautiful than he could ever believe, but his desire was gone. He needed the Sapphire stone, that was the only connection he now had with her. Since their embrace he had put Alena at the back of his mind. There would be time to work out his feeling for her. It seemed as though Marina was the true threat and that was disturbing. Slowly she was starting to get her movement back as the Sapphire stone shone ever brighter.

The last thing Alaric wanted to do was to fight, unarmed, against a *Stone of Power*. His power had grown, but he wasn't sure how much. As that thought ran through his mind something else stirred inside him. He looked over to where Eldred had returned to his pack. Suddenly he realised what it was.

Before Eldred had a chance to do anything his pack opened and the box containing the stones started to levitate. Eldred reached out for it but it flew away before he could reach it. He breathed a sigh of relief when it headed towards Alaric. If Marina got her hands on the other stones there was no telling what would happen.

Marina was slowly breaking through the spell Alaric had placed on her as the lid to the chest snapped open. Whatever spell Eldred had placed on the chest was gone. The old wizard couldn't believe what he was seeing. It wasn't that he didn't think Alaric could break his spell, it was the fact that he could do it without any effort. Eldred couldn't feel any use of magic from him. That thought was both disturbing and exhilarating. It seemed that the Chosen One was finally coming into his full strength. There was now hope again that they could defeat the Evil One.

Alaric kept his gaze on Marina as he reached into the chest. He pulled out a velvet pouch, he didn't need to look to know which stone he had. Just as Marina was about to break through his spell Alaric revealed a gold bracelet with an emerald stone inlaid in the middle. He held it in his right hand with no intention of wearing it. When he placed the velvet cover back in the chest the lid shut and it slowly floated to the floor.

As soon as the stone was freed from its velvet prison Alaric heard a female voice scream inside his head. The noise was more of an annoyance than anything else, but he quickly silenced it nevertheless. He didn't have time to fight with the stone. Marina was at one with the Sapphire stone and Alaric needed to be the same with the Emerald stone.

"You can scream all you like once this is done," Alaric spoke with his mind voice.

The Sapphire stone glowed brighter as Marina finally got her movement back. As it did it seemed as though the Emerald stone paled in comparison. Eldred watched on, unable to move. There was no spell, he just didn't know what he could do to help.

"I am sorry to have to do this Alaric, but I have no choice. I can't let you have her and it seems as though you have left me no other option." Marina's voice remained calm, yet there was an edge to it that didn't seem natural.

Only Alaric truly knew that he was speaking with the Sapphire stone. He knew Marina was still in there somewhere, but until he had the stone she would remain in the background.

"Time for words is over." Alaric sneered.

The Emerald stone started to glow stronger as Alaric pressed his will on it. The stone would not help easily, but Alaric was stronger than he had ever been. There was nothing the stone could do to resist his will. It would be a lot easier if it just helped, but then he risked losing control like Marina had.

It was the Sapphire stone that made the first strike. The stones in the walls and floors started to shake and slowly water started to spurt through the mortar from the pipes below. It was not at all what Alaric was expecting. He stood and watched as the water ran along the floor and pooled in front of Alena.

"I wouldn't wait too long!" the voice whispered inside his mind.

Alaric shook his head and ignored the comment. He needed to wait and see the spell before he could to counter it. It was a spell he had never seen before and that worried him. Slowly the water started to rise from the floor and it didn't take long for him to realise what was happening. At first the water formed a pair of legs. They were thicker and taller than normal legs, but there was no doubting that's what they were.

"Move now before it's too late!" the voice spoke louder as Alaric stood and watched the water monster quickly forming in front of him.

He knew the voice was right, but he didn't know what to do. This was not what he had been prepared for. He thought he would be fighting a Dark Knight and liberating the princess, not fighting her and the Sapphire stone. He fiddled with the bracelet as he pondered what to do.

It wasn't until the water giant was fully formed that Alaric finally moved. With a quick motion he secured the bracelet around his left wrist before drawing his sword. As he did the Emerald stone start to glow even brighter. The water giant had its own sword that shimmered as it slowly started to move.

Alaric took a fighting stance as the water giant lumbered towards him. As quick as a flash Alaric ducked under its first attack and charged forward. It seemed things were going to be easier than he thought until he slashed at the giant. His blade simply passed through the water and when he turned around he saw that he had done no damage at all.

"I am afraid to say that this is your end!" Marina started to laugh. "And don't you think of trying to help." Although she remained looking at Alaric she spoke to the others.

Eldred was the first to realise that they were frozen to the spot. There was nothing they could do to move and he couldn't even touch the energy around him. All they could do was watch and hope that Alaric succeeded. There was little doubt if he didn't they would be next.

Alaric ignored Marina's words as he looked down at his sword. The only sign that he had hit the giant was a droplet of water on the tip. It was obvious that he wasn't going to win physically. He would need to use magic to defeat the giant, only he wasn't sure which spell he could use.

"Let me help you," the voice cooed inside his head as the giant slowly started to turn around.

"You will, but not now," Alaric sounded annoyed with the distraction.

The giant swung his watery sword towards Alaric. All he could do was raise his own sword and hope for the best. The two blades struck with a splash of water. A shot of pain ripped through his arms as he strained to hold back the giant. Before it was too late Alaric lowered his sword and ducked his head allowing for the water sword to harmlessly pass over him.

With Alaric distracted by the water giant it gave Marina the opportunity to attack. She watched carefully as Alaric struggled to hold off the giant. When he finally let the sword pass over him Marina released her own attack. A beam of blue light shot from the Sapphire stone and even if Alaric had seen it he would not have had to time to stop it. The light struck him on the side of his face and sent him flying across the room. The smell of burning flesh filled everyone's nostrils. If the others could have moved they would have retched at the putrid smell, but there was nothing they could do.

A little shaken Alaric lifted himself from the floor. The left side of his face was charred to the bone and Marina cringed for a moment at the sight of his once beautiful face before stealing herself for another attack. The man had betrayed her and now he must die. She didn't know why that thought kept creeping into her mind, but there was nothing she could do to deny it.

Alaric didn't seem to take any notice of his charred face. He was more concerned with the lumbering giant coming to make another attack. Although Marina was the real threat he could only fight one battle at a time and he needed to destroy the water giant.

Unbeknown to anyone else Alaric had already prepared his attack on Marina. Slowly vines started to creep their way in from the balcony. No one noticed the movement, they were all focused on the battle in front of them.

Marina shot another bolt of blue light, but this time he was prepared. The water giant was out of reach and he was able to dive forward and roll away from the attack. Normally he would have used magic to block the light, but he was preparing his own attack. His blade was all but useless and was only good for defence and defence was just going to get him killed, sooner or later.

Suddenly a ring of fire encircled the water giant up to its waist. The magical creature didn't seem to notice the flames until it tried to step through them. A loud sizzle and steam filled the air as the monster tried to pass the barrier. It wasn't enough to kill it, but it was enough to slow it down and distract Marina.

"Do you think that is going to stop my pet?" Marina sounded amused. "I think not."

The air shimmered above the water giant. Slowly dark storm clouds appeared and a flash of lightning shot towards Alaric, but fizzled out before reaching him. Instantly there was a boom of thunder and then rain started to fall. Before long the flames were extinguished and the monster was on the move again.

Alaric, keeping his sword in his right hand, raised his left hand in front of him. Suddenly a burst of flame shot from his palm and struck the water giant on the chest. Water turned to steam as the fire ate into it. Marina wasn't going to just let her monster be destroyed. The Sapphire stone glowed ever brighter as the water giant started to repair itself, all the time moving even closer to Alaric. When it was in striking distance Alaric relinquished his spell.

"Now let me help you!" the voice screamed inside his mind.

Alaric didn't have a choice. Time was running out. The vines were inching closer to Marina and he needed to have the water giant destroyed before she noticed.

As Alaric relaxed his control on the Emerald stone his sword started to glow green. At the same time he felt something scratching at the back of his mind. Instantly he knew what it was and he wasn't happy, although he didn't nothing to block it. He needed all his energy to defeat Marina and her pet monster.

"I wouldn't try that if I was you," there was strain in his mind voice.

"I'm trying to help you."

"No, you're trying to control me. That won't happen and will never happen again. If you don't stop I will make sure you spend the rest of time locked in that prison of yours." Alaric warned. There was no time to mince words.

A moment passed before the scratching stopped. It seemed as though Alaric's threat had hit its mark. That was one less thing he needed to worry about. The most imminent threat was the water giant and now it was within striking distance.

Again the water giant swung high with its attack and again Alaric simply ducked underneath. Without thinking he slashed out with his sword but instead of passing through the water, like it had before, the blade bit into it. The blade slashed across its stomach as if it was cutting through flesh. The water giant roared in pain, the first time it had used its voice.

Marina was shocked as she watched the battle. She had not thought her pet monster could be touched by steel. Despite the cut it fought on, swinging in a downward motion, trying to cleave Alaric in two. Again the powerful blow was too slow and he deftly side-stepped the attack. Before it could recover Alaric slashed out again. This time a chuck of water was cut free and splashed to the ground.

It was time for Marina to change her tact. The Sapphire stone glowed brightly as the water giant started to shrink. In a matter of seconds it had halved in size. Now its stature was much lither and its sword had reduced, it looked much the same as the elven blade that Alaric had.

With its new size came a new speed that caught Alaric off guard. It was all he could do to defend the flurry of attacks. Marina smiled at her new pet monster. Its effectiveness was obvious to all in the room. Its skill with the blade was matched only by Alaric's own.

The battle was frantic as it continued. Sweat dripped from Alaric's brow and occasionally water splashed from the monster, which could only be attested to the strain. Eldred was happy to see that it wasn't just Alaric who was feeling the pressure. If he had taken his eyes from the battle he would have noticed that Marina was also starting to waver.

Alaric needed to finish the battle. The vines had almost reached Marina and his time was nearly up. Alaric clenched his teeth, exposing those on his burnt side, as he forced his will on the Emerald stone. His blade glowed an even brighter green as he prepared for his final attack.

With the extra magic in his sword Alaric prepared to defend another attack from the water monster. The two blades struck and Alaric's passed straight through the water. He didn't wait for the monster to realise what was happening. He slashed left and right, each time reducing the size of the monster and increasing the puddle on the floor. There was nothing Marina could do to repair it, but she wasn't about to give up. Finally releasing the control she had over it she was able to concentrate her attack on Alaric.

Again the blue light shot from the Sapphire stone. This time it struck a green force field before it was able to strike. He had been prepared for the attack even before the water monster collapsed to the floor. It was what he wanted her to do. Before she knew what was happening the vines snapped into action and entangled up her legs before wrapping her arms to her body.

"What is this?" She screamed.

"It's over!" Alaric barked.

A soft green glow surrounded him and suddenly everyone realised that his face had returned to normal. There was no sign of the severe burn that had scarred him. Alena almost cried out in joy when she realised he was going to be alright. It was also then that they were slowly starting to get their movement back. It seemed that Marina's spell was starting to dissipate. She would now need all her power if she was going to break Alaric's spell.

"What has become of you Marina?" Alaric walked forward until he was standing no more than three paces from her. He stood between the princess and the others, so they couldn't see their faces.

"You have forsaken me Alaric. We once shared something special, but it seems as though you prefer your elf." Marina spoke through clenched teeth, so the others couldn't hear her words.

Alaric knew it was Marina who spoke, but it wasn't the princess he wanted to speak with. He knew the Sapphire stone was controlling her. There was no way she would attack him on her own. He needed to get the stone away from her and he hoped that would bring her back to normal.

"Why are you doing this?" Alaric ignored her comments. "You risk destroying us all with this little game that you're playing. Surrender to my will and I will let your thrall live."

No one else in the throne room was able to follow the conversation. Even Eldred, with all his knowledge, had no idea what Alaric was talking about. He allowed himself a sigh of frustration. There was a time when people would come to him for answers and not that long ago. Now he felt like a simple novice begging for scraps of knowledge.

"She wants to be with me and I with her. There is nothing you can do about it. You might have enslaved my brothers and sisters, but you won't enslave me."

The green glow faded as Marina spoke and was only just visible. Alaric shook his head as he heard a whimpering inside his mind. There would be time for reprimands later. Even though he had imprisoned Marina in vines the battle was not over. He could feel the rage brewing inside her and there was little chance he was going to be able to talk her down. But he had to try.

"That can't happen. She's not yours to have." Alaric returned as he put more energy into the vines.

The battle between the two was now invisible to the others. Only Eldred could feel the power moving between them. As Marina tried to break through the vines Alaric used his power to strengthen them. He knew they wouldn't hold much longer, but he still had to try.

"You can take control Marina, but don't let the stone rule you." It was only then that the others understood what was happening.

"Oh you misinterpret the situation Alaric. I want this. We are one and there is nothing you can do to separate us." Marina smiled an evil smile. "Now you have a choice, Alaric. I will let you and your friends leave. The Dark Knight is dead and now you can be on your way."

"And what is it that you want in return?"

"Don't listen to her, it's a trap!" the voice spoke inside his head before Marina had a chance to answer. Although he couldn't be sure he thought there was fear in the voice.

"I'm not going to listen. Steel yourself. There is still time I will need you." A droplet of sweat appeared on Alaric's brow.

"It seems as though the strain is getting to you. I guess you aren't as strong as you thought you were." Marina sniggered. "Now it is time for me to destroy you."

As soon as she finished speaking Marina released the spell she held over the others and they all stumbled forward. As much as she wanted to keep them imprisoned she needed all her energy to defeat Alaric. Once he was dead she could easily dispose of them.

Without thinking Richmond drew his sword. Now that he was free he wasn't going to sit idly by. Fear had rushed through his body since they had arrived, but now it was gone. All he could think of was helping Alaric.

"Be still!" Alaric called to Richmond without taking his eyes from Marina. The last thing he wanted was Richmond getting in the way and getting himself killed. He knew what he was doing and he needed the others to stay out of it. Ideally they'd leave the room, but he knew that wasn't going to happen.

Marina wriggled in her prison and suddenly the vines dropped to the ground. A blue light shot down from the Sapphire stone and the vines burst into blue flames. The flames licked at Marina's skirts, but did nothing to burn her. Alaric simply watched and waited.

"Such a weak spell? I would have expected more from the Chosen One," Marina sneered.

"Now it is time for you to help!" Alaric called inside his mind. He hoped he had chosen the right stone for the job.

The voice inside his head had started whimpering when the vines caught alight. There was no response to his command and his heart sank. He needed to use the stone's power if he was going to survive. A knowing smile crossed her face as she realised what was happening.

"It seems as though you have already failed. My sister will no longer help you. Now it is time for you to die!"

A blue colour came across her face and Alaric knew the Sapphire stone was taking over. It would not be long before Marina was completely gone. This was what Alaric was hoping for. The risk of hurting Marina was not reduced and of course the vessel could be destroyed, but that wasn't Alaric's plan.

"NOW!" Alaric boomed inside his head.

The whimpering suddenly stopped as Alaric forced his will on the Emerald stone. The stone would work for him, not against him. He had learned how to command the stones, which otherwise would push to control him. In the past he had come so close to losing control and if that happened there would be no returning. If he didn't act soon that would be the fate to befall Marina as well.

Alaric used his sword as a conduit for the stone's power. He pointed his blade at Marina and a green light shot towards her. As much as it was a powerful attack he knew that it wasn't going to reach its destination. A blue light shield appeared around her and as the two lights came together sparks of blue and green splashed out over the throne room floor.

Marina stood with a smile on her face. There was nothing Alaric could do to stop her, or at least that was what the voice inside her mind was telling her. Even as the battle raged on she could feel herself slipping away. She felt as though she should be scared, but the feeling of elation washed that away.

The battle lasted for five minutes before Alaric let his green light of power fade away. Marina was left standing with a large grin on her face. He puffed as he tried his best not to look exhausted, but he failed. The trap was set as Marina prepared for her attack.

A beam of blue light again shot from the Sapphire stone. Alaric raised his sword, but made no other sign to defend himself. The blue light struck his chest before completely engulfing him. Richmond, Eldred and Alena gasped as Marina burst out laughing.

No one in the room realised Alaric he had created a fake version of himself. It was the dummy that was struck with the light and was in the process of being consumed. With everyone distracted he wasn't going to waste a second. No one saw him materialise behind Marina and it wasn't until he struck her on the back of her head with the hilt of his sword that they realised he was there. It was too late for Marina. Before she knew what had happened she sunk to the ground, unconscious.

Alaric made no move to catch Marina as she dropped to the floor. As much as he really didn't want to hurt her he was disappointed she had let the Sapphire stone take control. As much as he hoped that was what had happened he knew it wasn't true. Marina had wanted the power as much as the stone wanted to control her. Something had changed in her and Alaric doubted there was any recovery.

When Alaric was sure that Marina was unconscious he removed the bracelet from his wrist. The voice screamed inside his head before it was suddenly silenced. He wasn't in the mood. Slowly the chest lifted from the ground and floated towards him. There was a whimpering voice in the back of his mind, it was more of a subtle annoyance than anything else and soon enough it would be gone.

With the Emerald stone safely returned to the chest Alaric was able to concentrate on the Sapphire stone. He knew this battle was not going to be pleasant, but he was confident he was strong enough.

The stone had not stopped glowing even though Marina lay unconscious. Alaric knew that he had to be careful. Even though its conduit would be of no use, the stone still had its power. Although Alaric was powerful he knew not to take a *Stone of Power*, lightly.

A chill filled his body as he slowly drew the ring from Marina's finger. The others watched on in awe, still unable to bring themselves to speak. The sapphire glowed brighter at his touch and his arm felt as though it was about to freeze.

"Return me!" Spite filled the female voice in his mind. "I am not something to be possessed. You have no right..."

"SILENCE!" Alaric screamed inside his mind and the coldness finally left his body. "You will do as I command and if you do, when I am done, I might consider returning you to her." That was a lie. There was no chance Alaric could return the stone to Marina. She had already proven that she could not be trusted.

Alaric looked at the ring as he rolled it around his palm. The glow had left the stone completely and Alaric hoped that was the end of things, but he knew it would not be. The Sapphire stone would not yield so easily.

"What do you want of me?" the question was subservient. Alaric thought he preferred the supreme arrogance to its change of tone.

"There will be time for that. For now I just want you to behave." Alaric's facade remained blank as the conversation continued inside his mind. It was that blankness that caused everyone else to remain where they were. No one knew what was happening and no one was going to break the stalemate. It would be up to Alaric to rouse them when he was ready. "For now you will need to stay still with the others."

The chest lid opened again and Alaric reached in. Suddenly there was a screaming inside his mind as the stone realised what was about to happen. Ignoring the sound Alaric reached in and pulled out a small velvet pouch. The pouch had not been there before, but Alaric just ignored the fact. He knew when he pulled his hand out it would be there.

Without a second thought Alaric plunged the ring into the pouch and pulled the drawstrings tight. Instantly the screaming stopped. He then dropped it in the chest with the rest of the stones and let the lid close into place. The chest then gently floated to the floor before Alaric turned to face the others.

Alena couldn't contain herself anymore. Ignoring the limp body at his feet she raced towards him. Alaric only just had time to brace himself before she threw herself into his arms and kissed him on the lips. Alaric accepted the embrace for a long time before gently pushing her away.

"There is work to be done."

Chapter 30: Alaric's Return

The thieves had been given their own rooms whilst they were staying the palace. After hearing about the battle between Alaric and Marina, from Eldred, Vasil had wanted to return to the safety of the sewers. Although he didn't know Alaric he knew enough to be afraid. Eldred had called him the Chosen One, but he wasn't so sure.

Alaric had insisted that they all stay in the palace for the meantime, the last thing he wanted was rumours spreading throughout the city. With any luck they would be on their way again before anyone else knew he was there.

There was no time for the others to become reacquainted with Alaric. As much as they all had questions for him, most being the same, he had quietened them all with a wave of his hand simply telling them there would be time later. For the moment he had too much work to do.

"Take Marina to her apartments to rest. I fear I may have struck her too hard." Alaric had checked her pulse and her breathing before he spoke. "She will live, but she will need time to recover." It wasn't only from the blow she needed to recover from, she would need time to get over the effects of the Sapphire stone and that would be much more difficult.

Richmond and Hagar moved into action. Richmond rang the bellpull to summon the servants, who quickly arrived to tend to her.

"What are we going to do now?" Alena asked.

"For now I hear that King Lisle and queen Mara are deathly ill." Alaric's voice was devoid of emotion. "Does anyone know what is wrong with them?"

There was a moment of silence before Eldred answered. "We believed that Argoz did something to them, but it seems as though Marina was pulling his strings all along. As for an answer to your question we don't know. We only arrived shortly before you did."

Alaric had hoped that he would be able to heal the king and queen without the use of the Topaz stone, but it seemed as though that wouldn't be the case. It wouldn't be long before Marina recovered and he didn't want to risk their lives.

"Then we better see what we can do," he said as he walked out of the throne room without waiting for a response. The others looked at each other, not knowing what to say. Eldred simply shrugged his shoulders before following after him.

Alaric moved through the palace on a mission. Although he had only been there once before, he knew exactly where he was going. The others had to hurry their steps to keep up with him. There was no doubting something had changed in him. They had noticed it before he left from Mount Scorpio, but he had changed even more. Alena had felt it when she kissed him. The warmth she had felt in his touch before was gone. He was as cold as steel. She wanted to tell the others, but she couldn't find the words.

Lorio jumped up from where he sat when Alaric stormed into the room. When he realised who it was his face turned red with rage.

"Who do you think you are? Storming into the royal bedchamber like you own the place?"

Alaric ignored the Court Magician and walked to the other side of the bed. The king and queen lay peacefully next to each other. Their breathing was slow and steady and there was still colour in their faces. If Alaric didn't already know they were ill he would have just guessed they were sleeping.

Lorio was about to protest again, but Eldred silenced him with a cough and a stern look. Until he figured out Alaric's new personality he didn't want anyone to enrage him. Eldred had been afraid of the Dark Knight, but it was nothing compared to how he now felt about Alaric. He felt that he could explode at any moment and there was nothing any of them could do about it.

"There is indeed some evil magic at play here." Alaric mused to himself. "There is also something else..." he let the thought trail away.

Eldred couldn't remain silent any longer. "What is it?"

Alaric raised his head at the sound, but he didn't turn around. Eldred held his breath for Alaric's reaction. Slowly he turned around to face the others, a stone cold expression on his face.

"Argoz has had a hand in this, as well as Marina," Alaric explained. He studied the queen carefully without moving. "It seems that Argoz poisoned them and Marina has done something to keep them alive. That spell is waning quickly. Another hour or two and they would be dead."

"I don't understand. Why would Marina want to keep them alive? I thought she wanted them dead to gain power of the kingdom?" Eldred asked.

"It's not as easy as that," Lorio started. "For Marina to marry Argoz and become queen she would need the blessing of Lisle and Mara."

"So what would have happened if they had died? Surely they would not expect the man they thought was their son to live alone."

Richmond was surprised that Hagar didn't understand the laws of his own kingdom. It was something he had learnt as a child. His father had made him study the laws of all the kingdoms, including the ancient laws of Nostiria.

"For the heir apparent to marry a noble from another kingdom they would need permission from the king. It seems that Marina knew this even if Argoz did not. If the king and queen died then she couldn't gain power." Richmond lectured those in the room.

"That makes perfect sense. It seems Marina is craftier than we thought," Hagar added.

"The reasoning is irrelevant. It's the end result that I'm concerned with. Now if you don't mind I need to concentrate." Alaric scolded them.

His words were icy cold and instantly silenced everyone. No one was going to argue with him. If it was silence he wanted it would be silence he would have.

When Alaric was happy with his diagnosis he turned to the chest of stones. The chest had happily floated along behind him from the throne room and had settled itself on the bedside table next to him. Without touching the chest Alaric lifted the lid and a velvet pouch gently floated towards him. Once it was in his hand he opened it and removed the Topaz sceptre. The Topaz stone glowed gently as it was released.

"I'm surprised it's taken you so long. I would have thought you'd have needed me by now." The soft man's voice came inside his mind.

Alaric ignored the words. As much as he was grateful that it wasn't screaming, he wasn't going to respond. The Topaz stone was one of the easier stones for him deal with. He didn't so much as have an affinity with it as much as he had an understanding. The Topaz stone was the healing stone and to be confrontational would be an oxymoron. Despite the fact the stone still could not be trusted. Alaric knew, given half a chance, it would try and gain control of him.

Without waiting, Alaric waved the sceptre over the king's head. Even though the Topaz stone was designed to cure there was a chance it would cause their deaths. If the stone removed the waning spell before the poison then the king and queen would both die. Alaric knew he had to force his will on the stone to get what he wanted. He could feel death in its heart, a strange emotion from the stone.

The stone started to grow brightly as Alaric searched for the Dark Knight's spell. There was simple poison at work, but there was also magic. Finding the spell was not going to be easy. Alaric had been right, without the aid of the Topaz stone he would not have been able to cure the king and queen.

The spell was deep in the king's subconscious, but Alaric was able to find it. As soon as he found the spell it didn't take him long to remove it. With Argoz's spell gone Alaric was then able to cure the poison. The effects of Marina's spell would dissipate on its own and he decided not to waste time with it.

Finding Argoz's spell in the king meant it would not take long to heal the queen. The Dark Knight had placed the spell in the exact same spot.

Alaric didn't waste any time returning the sceptre to the chest when he was done. He breathed a sigh of relief. As much as he was strong enough to control the stones, each time he did it came with its own risks. He was confident that the king and queen would soon recover and that was enough.

"What happens now?" Lorio asked.

"They will recover in time. It might take a day or two, but they will be fine now," Alaric explained.

Lorio looked back to his king. There didn't seem to be any change in his condition. Although his knowledge of the *Stone of Power* wasn't extensive he did know a little. By using the Topaz stone Alaric should have been able to wake the couple, healing them completely.

"That isn't good enough Alaric," For a moment Lorio forgot who he was speaking with. "You heal them completely. We need King Lisle back sitting on the throne."

Alaric had turned his back on the bed and was about to walk away when Lorio continued speaking. He paused for a moment before turning around. As he did the light seemed to shrink away from him. His cold expression now seemed downright viscous. Lorio suddenly remembered who he had just berated and shrunk back into his chair as far as he could go.

"And just who do you think you are speaking to?" Alaric didn't wait for a response. "You don't question my motives. Just be thankful that your rulers will not be dying today and that is due to my abilities. If you wish to try and use the Topaz stone, well, be my guest?" Alaric raised an eyebrow as he asked the question.

"No... Thank you... Alaric." Lorio trembled as he spoke.

Alaric wasn't going to continue. He knew what Lorio's response was going to be and that was enough for him. There was plenty of work to do and little time to do it. There was definitely no time for petty arguments.

"Call your servants, Magician. Have a room prepared for me. There are things I need to do before I leave Lel Dinion."

Lorio didn't like being spoken to in such a manner. If it had been anyone else they would be cooling their heels in the dungeons. He knew all he could do was to obey him. He rang the bellpull by the side of the royal bed and almost instantly the door opened and two young pages entered the room. Lorio barked his orders and they rushed into action.

"Be well Lorio!" Alaric's words sounded strange as he left the royal bedchamber.

Again the otheres didn't know what to say as they followed behind. It still didn't seem like the right time to speak. Eldred was sure that when they reached Alaric's rooms he would explain what had been happening. They all rushed to keep up the pace. The pages, who had initially ambled through the hallways, were now running. They would have to at least reach the apartment before Alaric, even if they couldn't have it set for him.

Although Alaric had not been told which apartment he would be given he walked through the halls knowing exactly where he was heading. Even when the pages were out of sight he didn't break his stride. He didn't look back, although he knew the other two would be close behind. He had hoped to avoid the conversation about where he had been, but he knew he couldn't. It would only be a matter of time before they pressed him and his cold attitude would only get him so far.

The pages were still rushing, trying to set the apartment as best they could, when Alaric stormed through the door. Although it was completely unnecessary he knew the pages would talk and he wanted them to know that he was not someone to be trifled with.

"There will be maids along shortly to make the bed and bring fresh linen for you, my lord." As much as the page tried to remain brave the squeak in his voice gave him away. "I can have them run you a bath if you wish." He braved another speech when Alaric didn't answer.

"You can leave now." Alaric dismissed them when the others arrived.

Alaric paced around his new apartment. He let the chest come to rest on one of the bedside tables. Slowly it started to waver before it disappeared completely. If Eldred had not seen it with his own eyes he would not have believed it. Again there was no sign of magic from Alaric. He couldn't believe he had come so far in such a short space of time.

"So what do we do now?" Alena finally asked when no one else spoke.

"One thing at a time Alena," Alaric said as he gazed out the window. There was a small garden terrace outside his apartment. "There is a more pertinent question that you want to ask."

Alena looked at Eldred who in turn shrugged his shoulders. He knew exactly what Alaric was talking about, but he didn't want to speak. Eldred was still confused at the situation and didn't want to give anything away until he was sure what was happening. In the end it was Richmond who spoke.

"Where have you been?"

Alaric's shoulders slumped when he heard the question. It wasn't the one he was looking for, but it was one he knew he would have to answer. The only problem was that he really didn't know where he had been, but at least he was able to get that conversation out of the way.

"That is an interesting question." Alaric kept staring out at the terrace. "I have literally been here, there and everywhere and even some places in-between." Alaric paused as he thought on what he said. In his mind it was quite clever, but he knew it wouldn't appease anyone. "I have been travelling between worlds, trying to find answers. I didn't know what I was looking for, but I knew I had to find it. In the end I found what I was looking for in a world between worlds. A space and time that doesn't exist like you know it."

No one knew what he was talking about. Although he wasn't watching the others he knew they all looked confused and he couldn't blame them. Even as the words came out of his mouth he knew they wouldn't make sense, but despite that they were the truth. He turned to face the others before he continued.

"Where I have been isn't really the point though." Alaric wasn't going to wait for the question to be asked. He needed to remain detached and he wasn't sure how long he could keep up the facade. "It is what I found, now that is the point." He waited a moment for the revelation to sink in. "It seems that we have all been taken for fools." Alaric continued to recall the story of the old man in the world between worlds between worlds. Once he started he knew he couldn't stop. If he stopped then he didn't think he'd be able start again.

When Alaric finally finished no one knew what to say. The story was so fantastical it had to be true, but if it was then all they thought they had known was false. Alaric wasn't going to speak again until someone commented.

"So what do we do now?" Eldred finally asked, but didn't wait for an answer. "Even when we thought we knew what we were doing it was hard enough." Eldred thought about all the sleepless nights he had spent pouring over the frustrating text.

Alaric knew that was true and he felt the same way. It was nice when they thought that the prophecy would lead them in the right direction. There had been comfort in that knowledge, but that was no longer there.

"What are we going to do about the Ruby stone?" Alena thought she'd narrow the question down. "He really can't be serious that we are to let Nyrra find it?"

It was a question that Alaric had asked himself many times since he had been given the revelation. "I don't think we have any other choice. It is Nyrra's destiny to fight me with the Ruby stone and that's how it's going to be. For now we need to concentrate on finding the Onyx stone.

That is the only one left for me to find and somehow I believe it is the most appropriate."

No one liked what they were hearing. Now that Alaric's coldness had started to melt, Eldred's confidence was returning. "How do we even know this strange old man was telling the truth? There is every chance that he lured you there to give you misinformation."

It was a valid premise, but Alaric knew it wasn't true. Like most things he couldn't explain, he just knew what the man said was fact. He had travelled too long and too far for it to be anything else.

"It's no lie." Was all Alaric could say.

There was little point in arguing. They could tell by the look on his face that there was no explaining his reasoning. All they could do was accept the fact and move on.

"So we find the Onyx stone?" Alena asked.

"What about the others?" Richmond didn't give Alaric a chance to answer. "Do you know what the Alliance is doing?" It was the question he had been dying to ask and couldn't wait a minute longer.

Alaric knew it was coming. He could sense the Alliance, although he couldn't tell exactly where they were. Bern was another story. Before he left he could have appeared right next to him at any time. That in itself had been a comforting thought, but ever since his return something had changed. Now he had no idea where Bern was and that worried him. He knew he wasn't with the Alliance, but that was it.

"The army is moving on Remidel. Whether they are there or not yet I can't be sure. What I do know is that there is a Dark Knight in the palace. Like all the other kingdoms he has managed to weasel his way into control. He now has power over Faxon."

There was a pause as everyone soaked up the information. Even though Richmond had asked the question it was hard to believe that Alaric had an answer.

"So we should travel to Remidel and help them. If there is a Dark Knight they will need our help." Richmond really meant they needed Alaric's help.

Alaric returned to the widow, placed his hands on the frame and shook his head. He should have known the response was coming. In hindsight he should have kept his knowledge to himself. No one would have questioned him if he had just told them he didn't know. Now there was a new problem before him.

"Are you alright?" Alena squeaked and then blushed with embarrassment.

Her tender words brought Alaric around. For the first time he realised he was amongst friends again. He needed to lean on them for support, at least for the short time he could. Before long he would have to do it all on his own.

"Thank you Alena," Alaric's voice softened and the tension in the room suddenly lifted. "No, we won't be travelling to Remidel just yet. Until I know what Bern is doing we must sit tight here."

Although it didn't make any sense no one questioned him. All of them thought they should be travelling to Remidel to help the Alliance, but they also knew there had to be a reason. They all felt the pull of the prophecy and they all knew there was nothing they could do to oppose it. If Alaric said they had to stay then that's what they would have to do. No one felt the pull stronger than him.

"If that's the case I suggest we find something to eat. It's been a long day and I for one am hungry." Eldred suggested.

Alaric wasn't about to argue. Although he wasn't feeling hungry it had been a long time since he had eaten. With his new powers he wasn't sure if he even needed to eat, but he wasn't going to wait to find out.

Time was growing short and Alaric wanted to be on the move again. He knew that he had to find the Onyx stone, it was the only one left, but for the moment he had to stay put. He could feel the prophecy in the back of his mind and it was telling him to remain in Lel Dinion. All he could do was hope he could leave sooner rather than later. There was much to be done and little time to do it.

Chapter 31: Prince Hawthorne

When Galt didn't return with word from the Alliance Hawthorne knew he had failed. As much as he hoped Galt had failed on his return journey he knew that wasn't true. His letter had never reached General Bern. There was also little doubt that if his emissary had been captured then Gilgi would know about it. If that was the case he didn't show it.

Shortly after he had sent Galt to the Alliance, Hawthorne had been banned from his father's council. He couldn't understand why Gilgi had kept him alive if he knew he was plotting against him. At least it was a sign that he didn't have complete control of the kingdom. If he did then he would have sent the crown prince to the dungeons.

The hardest part of his palace imprisonment was the lack of information. No one would tell him anything, if they indeed knew anything. He had also been banned from leaving the palace and entering the city. In the end he may as well have been in the dungeon.

For the past two days Hawthorne had felt the tug of the prophecy at the back on his mind. It had been a long time since he had felt such a tug and initially he tried to ignore it. There was still much he needed to do in the palace, at the very least find a way to remove Gilgi from his father's council. That would not be an easy task.

In the end Hawthorne had to succumb to the prophecy. By the afternoon of the second day the gentle tug became a forceful pull. Wherever the prophecy was leading him he was forced to go.

All the servants kept their heads down as he walked past. It was from fear not deference that kept their eyes on the floor. That in itself broke Hawthorne's heart. There was no reason the palace staff should fear him, but it was obvious that they would be punished if they spoke with him.

Prince Hawthorne had decided he could no longer sit idle. With each passing day the city was slipping into the grasp of the Evil One and that was something he couldn't allow. He needed to leave the city and find the Alliance. Only with the help of the army would he be able to free his kingdom.

The previous day he had his most trusted servant put together a pack for his journey and leave it at an inn by the Southern Gate. He would have done it himself, but it would have been too suspicious for him to walk the palace halls with a pack on his back. He also arranged for his horse to be taken to the inn's stables. It would be obvious with his horse missing that he was gone, but he figured once he was out of the city it really didn't matter. He would much rather have a comfortable journey on a familiar animal than have an extra day or two's head start.

As he left the palace a familiar thought came to him. It wasn't that long ago his father had sent him to Elhjem to see what all the fuss was about. At first he had not believed, as his father did, that there was an evil force coming. He also didn't believe they should have sent part of their army to the east. In the end he was partially right. If they had not gone to Avalon then they would not be in the troubles they were now in.

There was little point in going over the past. What he needed to do was focus on the future. That was the only way he could save his kingdom.

The courtyard at the front of the palace had few people milling around, but much less than usual. At first Hawthorne didn't seem to notice, but the more he moved towards the gate the more he felt that everyone was watching him. Suddenly a cold shiver ran down his spine and he forced himself to stop. Something wasn't right and he didn't want to walk into a trap.

He was standing in the centre of the courtyard watching everyone else was walking around the edge. Hawthorne placed his hand on the hilt of his sword, a precaution more than anything else. Something was definitely wrong and he needed to be prepared.

He didn't have to wait long to find out what was happening. He heard the sound of the palace doors opening behind him and the chinking of armour coming down the stairs.

When he turned around he half expected to see a group of armed dwarves walking towards him, but instead there were a dozen of the Royal Guard. Their armour sparkled in the sunlight and they certainly looked the part. Hawthorne thought he knew all of the soldiers in the Royal guard, but the twelve were unknown to him. At least that would make things easier, he didn't want to kill anyone he knew. With any luck the twelve men before him were just as evil as the dwarf who sent them.

The soldiers stopped when they were five paces from their prince. One solider took a step forward to speak with Hawthorne.

"You have been requested to return to the palace." His voice boomed.

Hawthorne knew it was not a request. His fingers tapped on the hilt of his sword. He didn't want to be the first to draw, but he needed to be ready. There was little doubt that if he was going to leave the palace he would need to kill the twelve men before him. The thought made him sad, but it had to be done. He also knew he wouldn't be able to return, if he did then there was no chance of escape.

"I am the Crown Prince of Remidia and you have no command over me. Lay down your weapons and return inside," Hawthorne's voice was full of command.

The response was not at all what the soldier was expecting. He had been given the instructions from King Faxon himself and he was expecting the order to be followed. It was Gilgi the dwarf who had explained what to do if Hawthorne refused. At first the soldier didn't believe it, but he knew better than to question the order.

"We have been ordered to bring you in one way or another," the soldier didn't sound sure of himself anymore. There was no command to his voice, even though he tried his best.

He really didn't want to kill the men before him, but it looked as though he wasn't going to have any choice. Before he could make another move he was struck on the back of his head. The blow was not enough to make him lose consciousness, but it was enough to drop him to his knees and blur his vision.

As he tried to stand he saw a set of feet in front of him. He tried to lift his head to see who it was, but another blow stuck him and darkness overcame him.

It was dark when Hawthorne finally came to. He rubbed his head before he realised where he was. Instead on resting in a soft bed he was lying on the dirty floor of a prison cell. Slowly the memory came back to him and he jumped to his feet. There was no surprise when he realised his sword was missing. He couldn't believe that his own soldiers had locked him away.

"Guards!" Hawthorne's voice was dry and cracked. It didn't have the commanding presence he wanted.

"Ah, the Great Prince is finally awake." A fat guard waddled over carrying a torch. His voice dripped with contempt.

Hawthorne shook his head. He couldn't imagine what he had done to upset the guard. There was no reason why he should be treated in such a manner. The situation was completely out of place and his head was still ringing.

"What am I doing here?"

"You don't remember me, do you?"

Hawthorne tried to think, but he couldn't form any solid memories. There was something familiar about the man, but he couldn't place from where.

"I didn't think so. I was once the Sergeant-At-Arms in the training yard. You didn't like the way I was training the troops and thought I would be better placed in the dungeons."

Hawthorne thought for a moment and then it came to him.

"Sergeant Benton?" he gasped.

"Dungeon Master Benton now and as you can see the years have not been kind to me."

When he had been the Sergeant-At-Arms he had been a fit muscular man with short cropped, blonde hair. The man standing before him was completely different. Most of his hair was gone and his weight had got away him. It was obvious why Hawthorne didn't recognise him.

"Now it's time for me to get my revenge. I never thought I would get the chance, but the Gods can be kind sometimes." Benton licked his lips.

"I would be very careful if I were you. You can't honestly believe that my father will leave me here?"

"Who do you think gave the order to bring you here?" Benton laughed as the realisation crossed Hawthorne's face.

"Well I'm sure he didn't tell you to kill me by dehydration. Make yourself useful and get me some water." Hawthorne couldn't let Benton get the better of him.

"So it's water you want? I think I can help you with that."

Benton untied his pants and dropped them to his ankles. At first Hawthorne wondered what he was doing and only just managed to jump out of the way as his gaoler relieved himself on the cell floor. Hawthorne couldn't believe the arrogance. He would take great pleasure in killing him once he was freed. He couldn't believe that his father would leave him in the dungeons.

"There you go, enjoy."

"You have just signed your death warrant. You can't honestly believe I will stay here long?"

Benton was suddenly distracted as he heard footsteps approaching. When he saw who it was a large, evil grin appeared on his face.

"I think this should answer your question," Benton laughed as he walked away.

Hawthorne didn't have to wait long before he saw the dwarf appear. His heart sank when he realised it was Gilgi. There was no doubt that he was the one who had him imprisoned.

"I hope you are enjoying your new accommodation?"

"I'm sure you didn't come down here to discuss pleasantries," Hawthorne wasn't going to bite. "What do you want?"

"Straight to the point my prince, I like that." Gilgi paused. "Unfortunately for you that won't do you any good, you see you are my prisoner now and this is my city."

"Who are you?" Hawthorn wanted answers.

"Ah, so you're not as ignorant as I thought." Gilgi thought about what he was going to say next. "I'm the Great Lord's greatest of Knights. I am Dargoz." He seemed very pleased with himself.

The revelation came as no surprise to Hawthorne. It all made sense. Although his decision to leave the Alliance was certainly warranted it was not the right decision. Gilgi had put the idea in his head from the start. It seemed like such a good idea at the time. He wondered if the Dark Knight had manipulated him further.

"What do you want?" Hawthorne asked.

"Ha, I have what I want. I have control of your kingdom and soon enough I will reign with the Great Lord." Dargoz sneered.

"Then why are you here? Did you just come to gloat?" Hawthorne tried to remain in control of the conversation.

He needed to gain as much information as he could. While he was imprisoned he knew the Dark Knight would be more pliable. He could gain a valuable insight to relay to the Alliance once he escaped. There were many guards in the dungeons and he was sure one would still be loyal to the crown.

"I see what you are thinking." Dargoz smiled as Hawthorne quietly scolded himself. "You will not leave here and once the Cursed One's army has been disposed of you will be sentenced to death. Whatever I say here will die with you."

There was little doubt that Dargoz believed what he said, but Hawthorne was still hopeful. He was the crown prince and heir to the kingdom. There was surely someone who would help him escape. The promise of wealth, position and a better life would get him out.

"That is easy to say, but the Alliance will crush you, like it has crushed your brothers before you." Hawthorne sneered.

Dargoz was about to speak, but paused. For a moment Hawthorne thought he was going to take the bait. He thought about pushing further, but decided to wait.

"I know something that they do not," the smile returned to his face as his voice dripped with venom.

When Dargoz didn't elaborate Hawthorne knew he had to push him further.

"That's easy to say, but I'm sure the other Dark Knight's felt the same as you." He should have been frightened, speaking with a Dark Knight, but there was nothing but contempt in his voice and that was what goaded Dargoz the most. "I think you can go now. I'll just stay here peacefully and wait for my rescue."

When he finished speaking Hawthorne turned his back to the Dark Knight and started towards the other side of his cell. The insolence was enough to enrage Dargoz. Hawthorne only managed three steps before he was frozen. Despite that he was prepared for the attack his body filled with fear. Slowly he was turned around and then slid back towards the bars.

"Do you think you can ignore me so easily?" Spittle flew from the dwarf's mouth and settled in his beard. "I am one of the Great Lord's chosen. I could crush you like a bug."

To accentuate his point Hawthorne felt a squeeze on his windpipe. His initial reaction was to reach up and clasp his neck, but his arms were still pinned to his side. With each passing moment it was becoming harder and harder to breathe. All he could do was clench his teeth as his face turned redder and redder. Just before he thought he was going to lose consciousness Dargoz released his grip and Hawthorne sucked in as much air as he could.

"Now you see what I am capable of and that is only a small taste of my power."

"But you cannot defeat an army by yourself," Hawthorne was not about to give up. "If you could then this war would already be over. Even your Great Lord couldn't defeat the Alliance by himself." His words proved to enrage Dargoz even further.

"Be careful of what you say, prince. There are worse things than dying, I can assure you of that." There was no stopping his rage, but he made no further move to hurt Hawthorne. "I will tell you why I will succeed where my brothers have failed." Hawthorne remained frozen where he stood as he listened intently. "I know the Alliance is coming. I know they will be here soon. I will have a little surprise waiting for them." Dargoz took a step back and smiled. It was like a weight had been taken from his shoulders. "You see I have control of your army and I'm not planning on hiding behind your pitiful walls. I'm not even going to wait for the Alliance to arrive. In five days the entire Remidian Army will march through the city gates and go to war with them."

"You can't do that!" Hawthorne finally lost his composure and he silently cursed himself for doing it. The smile returned to Dargoz's face as he realised he had finally rattled the prince. Hawthorne took a deep breath before he continued. "The Remidian soldiers won't stand a chance. You'd just be destroying them." Hawthorne's voice remained level.

"That is true, not that I really care, but there will be another little surprise waiting. When the battle starts there will be something waiting for them at their rear." Dargoz paused and considered if he should divulge any further. "There is a horde of orglin that will attack. Your army will be in disarray and then destroyed."

Hawthorne forced a smile onto his face to hide the horror he was feeling. He had worked so hard, he couldn't lose the upper hand now. There was little chance for him to escape and he needed to do everything he could to get out and warn the Alliance.

"Thank you, that is the information I need," Hawthorn's voice croaked.

Dargoz looked around nervously. He was the one controlling the situation, but Hawthorne's words didn't make any sense. There was no way the prince could escape and yet he seemed too confident. There was one way to wipe the smirk from his face. Slowly he released the spell and let Hawthorne move again.

"Dungeon Master!" he called out. "Now you will suffer for your arrogance. My only regret is I don't have the time to bask in your pain."

Dargoz didn't wait for Benton to return before leaving. Hawthorne didn't waste any time. He turned around and scanned the cell. He needed to find something he could use to help him escape. His heart sank when all he saw was a small pile of straw for a bed and a bucket for his waste. All he could rely upon was his strength.

"Looks like it's time to have some fun," Benton sneered as he spoke.

In his right hand Benton held a nasty looking cudgel and in his left a set of keys on a large iron ring. Hawthorne retreated to back of the cell, trying his best to look afraid, as Benton pushed the key into the lock. If his plan was going to work he couldn't let his gaoler know what he was thinking.

After opening the cell door Benton slapped his cudgel against his leg. Hawthorne couldn't believe his luck and took his opportunity to attack. Lowering his head he charged into Benton and stuck him in the sternum with his shoulder. The sudden movement took Benton off guard. The momentum took the two of them crashing to the ground and Hawthorne quickly rolled off the body and jumped to his feet. He couldn't give Benton a chance to recover.

With the gaoler still down Hawthorne kicked at his stomach. To his surprise Benton reached out quicker than expected and grabbed Hawthorn by the ankle. With a sharp twist he was back on the ground.

Despite his large frame Benton was still surprisingly nimble. Both men came to their feet at the same time. The cudgel remained on the floor in the prison cell. Both men gave it a quick look, but realised neither had time to get it. The battle would be unarmed, at least until Benton was able to get support.

"Guards!" he called at the top of the voice.

Hawthorne didn't wait to move into action. His only chance of escape was to deal with Benton before the other guards arrived.

Again Benton was quicker than Hawthorne expected. Hawthorne struck out with both fists and Benton deftly defended each attack. All he needed to do was wait for support. It had taken him so long, and something he thought he would never achieve, to finally have Prince Hawthorne. He now had him in the position he wanted and he wasn't about to let him escape. He would pay for what he had done.

As the battle continued Hawthorne heard the sound of rushing footsteps behind him. He knew that he had one chance to escape and he had to risk it all. Quickly he feigned another attack with his right fist before striking out with his left leg. He struck Benton just below the knee with all the might he could muster. The blow was enough to knock Benton to his knees and Hawthorne didn't waste any time with raising his knee and hitting Benton on the chin.

The sudden change in attack worked. Benton was unable to continue the fight and Hawthorne had his chance to attack. Before he was able to take another step Hawthorne felt two pairs of hands grip each arm. No matter how hard he tried to struggle there was no escape.

Before Benton knew what was happening he heard a loud cry of pain come from Hawthorne. As he looked up he could see three inches of sword protruding from just below his chest. It wasn't common for prisoners to try and escape, but when they did it was a death sentence. His guards were only trying to do the right thing by Brenton, but they had just given him a death sentence. If the prince died then he soon would follow. The dwarf wouldn't forgive his failure.

Hawthorne couldn't help but smile as he saw the look on Benton's face. There was no doubt that his revenge was now complete. A trickle of blood ran down from the side of his mouth as the smile disappeared. If he died then there was no chance to save his kingdom. That was the last thought in his mind as he lost consciousness.

Chapter 32: A New Challenge

Although everyone was tired from the orglin attack the previous night they all woke with a new purpose. Bern was always surprised at how well the group of bandits from Darshival had assimilated themselves into the Alliance. If he didn't know any better he would have assumed they were hardened soldiers. The orglin attack would have been enough to send anyone running to the hills, but they remained as stalwart as ever.

Pernian met them in the Horse's Head for breakfast as soon as the sun had risen. Fayne made sure all the soldiers were well fed. If it wasn't for them then Quinaliac would have been completely destroyed. The little food they had left was easy to part with.

"I don't know what to say Pernian," Bern began when the elf was seated. "If you hadn't arrived when you did then we would all be dead."

"Think nothing of it general. I could think of many times that you have saved all our lives." Pernian brushed off the compliment as he started eating.

"So what is the plan for today?" Ulman asked.

"We head for Zenza City. We need to get answers," Bern replied.

There was a pause as everyone took in the information. As much as that had been the plan they all wanted to return to the Alliance. The army was marching on Remidel and it would need their assistance. Although they were only a small part of the army the soldiers would need to see their commanders for added morale.

"Are you sure this is the right decision?" Duke Hadar was the first to speak. "If we head straight for Remidel we should make it before the others arrive."

"You really want to go trekking through the forest?" Bern raised an eyebrow. "I didn't think so. There are still orglin there and we have no idea how many more there are. That is the most direct route to the Alliance, but the safest route is via Zenza City."

Hadar's shoulders slumped, he knew Bern was speaking the truth. The safest route would be to take the King's Highway from Zenza City and it was more than likely the quickest. What would slow them down was what Bern had planned for them once they reached the city. There was little doubt he would not return to the Alliance without seeing his family.

"I don't know why the prophecy is leading us towards Zenza City, but there is little chance we could end up anywhere else," Bern looked at his food as he spoke.

There was no arguing. Deep down they all knew he was right. The tug was not as prominent for the others, but they all felt it. Whatever was waiting for them in Zenza City couldn't wait. They all thought on that as they continued to eat.

"What are you going to do with the Fayne?" Hadar broke the uncomfortable silence.

"I think we should take him with us," replied Pernian. "It will not be safe here with the orglin so close."

Fayne edged his way closer to the table as he heard Hadar mention his name, although he remained far enough away to remain unnoticed. He wanted them to speak candidly and they wouldn't if they knew he was there.

"Pernian is right," Hadar agreed. "This village will be destroyed once we leave. We have to take him to Zenza City so he could be with the rest of the residents of Quinaliac."

Bern was about to speak when Fayne walked to the table. There was something about the look in his eye that silenced everyone.

"I won't abandon my village. This is where I grew up and if need be this is where I will die." There was a strange edge to his voice.

"We cannot force you to go, but it is the safest thing for you. If you die with your village then it proves nothing." Hadar remained calm.

"Someone has to clean up these dead orglin. You only assume the orglin will return, but if you leave there will be no need for the evil creatures to attack."

Hadar was about to protest, but Bern silenced him with a wave of his hand. Bern shook his head slowly as he realised it was another time he would have to make a decision that would affect other people's lives. He knew the answer and just hoped no one questioned him on it.

"Fayne will be safe to stay. The orglin won't be coming back." Bern kept his head low. He didn't want to make eye contact with anyone. "For now there is no danger in staying here." For the moment it was true, but he didn't know how long it would remain that way. There seemed to be more and more orglin ravaging through the Seven Kingdoms. That could only mean that the final battle was close and he wondered if it was even the right decision to travel to Zenza City.

Bern was grateful that no one questioned his statement. Ulman watched the others carefully. As much as he wanted to speak he decided it was better to just to watch and listen. He wasn't sure if the others trusted him and he didn't want to do anything to risk his position. It was frustrating for the great wizard, but that was what he needed to do.

"Fayne is right," Pernian finally said. "You go on to the city and the elves will help clean the village. We can't leave it in such disarray."

"That is very noble of you Pernian, but I think you should come with us," Captain Elyas said. "There is no telling what is ahead of us and you have already saved us once."

"We will meet you at Zenza City. I'm sure you'll be safe to reach there without me."

"Pernian is right Elyas," Bern added. "We can't just leave chaos in our midst, but Elyas has a point. You can't stay here too long. When the sun reaches its pinnacle you must leave. We all need to be in the city before nightfall."

With the events of the previous night no one needed him to explain his reasons. The last thing they wanted to do was spend another night outside the safety of the city walls. There was no telling how many more of the creatures infested the surrounding lands. It seemed as though Nyrra had an unlimited supply.

Bern finished his meal before he stood and faced Fayne. "Thank you for your hospitality, but we must be leaving now."

The two men shook hands before Bern led the others outside.

In the light of day the village looked much worse than it had the previous night. Blood and body parts were strewn across the ground. It seemed some of the orglin were caught in a feeding frenzy. As Bern made his way through the slaughter he noticed bite marks on some of the bodies, not just on the men and elves, but the orglin as well. Not too long ago he would have lost his breakfast, but that was in the past. Even the smell of death wasn't enough to make him gag.

The elves had already started the mammoth task of cleaning up the village. There were two piles of bodies being heaped in the village square, one of orglin and one of men. The dead elves were being taken into the forest. The piles were growing large and they had only just started. The bodies would need to be burned at some point to make room for more. At least the pile of orglin was much bigger than that of the villagers; it was a small mercy for Bern.

Things had come too close to home for Bern's liking. His home village had been destroyed and there was a good chance a Dark Knight held the capital. Zenza City was his last hope for his kingdom. He knew the duke would have to come to his aide once he realised what was happening in Remidel.

"Are you excited at the prospect of seeing your family again?" Bern had not noticed the dwarf walk up beside him, but he did his best to hide his surprise.

"I'm not even sure if they will recognise me anymore," Bern said as he stared out in front. "So much has happened since I left home." The entity that resided inside him was no doubt the biggest of the changes, but neither wanted to mention it. "I am now the General of the Alliance. I have sent men to their deaths. Good friends have died and it wasn't that long ago I was just a simple farmer. I rose with the sun and slept in the evening, my life was simple. What am I going to say to them when I meet them?" It was a rhetorical question and Hulkan let it pass. "How do I explain to them what my life has been like?"

"I wish I had an answer for you, but there is none. I think you will just know what to say when you meet them." Hulkan thought back on seeing his father again after so long. It was difficult at first, but it was worth the effort. With the final battle looming he wasn't sure if he would ever see him again. "I think we should focus on the road ahead. There is no telling what is waiting for us once we leave the village." Hulkan wanted to take Bern's mind off his family. The last thing the general needed was to slip into a malaise.

"You're right Hulkan. That's what I like about you, you'll always keep me grounded." Bern smiled.

The rest of the soldiers were waiting for them at the edge of Quinaliac. The horses had been saddled and brought to the front of the line.

Even though the clouds were dark and there was a cold wind in the air, Bern was happy to be in the saddle again. The ride was enough to take his mind from his family. As they left the village the forest loomed up on either side of them creating a gloom that reflected the group's sombre mood. Bern wished he had brought the elves with them. They would have all felt more comfortable with them following them through the forest. There was a feeling of evil that made them all uncomfortable.

"Do you think there are orglin in the forest?" Captain Elyas spoke loudly, to no one in particular.

"It sure does feel like it." Duke Hadar shivered as he looked left and right, trying to find the eyes he felt were looking at him. He found no sign, but it didn't make him feel any better.

"There is no doubt there are orglin in the forest," Bern said from the front of the group. "The question you should be asking is... do you think they are going to attack us during the day?" There was no humour in his voice.

Everyone thought on the question, but no one answered. As much as they all believed the orglin wouldn't attack during the day, at least not since they had been beaten so badly the previous night, no one wanted to risk speaking the words aloud. The thought made everyone even more nervous, and that was not the effect Bern was hoping for.

."I wouldn't worry too much. I doubt they will attack again. I'm sure we'll be safe until we reach the city." Bern reassured them.

His words gave little comfort to the rest of the group. The trees seemed to loom over them and the dark sky did nothing to ease their nerves. He kept his head straight and ignored the urge to look into the forest. He needed to remain stalwart to reassure the others.

No matter what Bern did there was no brushing aside the feeling that there were many eyes watching them. Bern could only hope that it was just the thought of the orglin causing the feeling and not the orglin themselves. Eventually the urge got the better of him and he started to stare into the forest. As he expected there was nothing to see.

Everyone breathed a sigh of relief when the forest suddenly broke and they were out in the open again. Although the tension didn't completely lift it wasn't long before Bern could hear the sounds of laughter coming from the soldiers behind him. He couldn't imagine what would bring their mirth, but he didn't have the heart to stop it.

They had not been out of the forest for more than fifteen minutes before the skies finally opened. The rain was soft at first, but it didn't take long before it was a powerful downfall. Bern had to wonder if it was due to the men's jovial attitude. There was little time for joy in the current situation and it seemed even the heavens were not going to give them any respite.

Bern estimated it was around midday when he found a small grove they could gain some shelter. No one was overly keen to stop, but Bern insisted. The horses were struggling along the road and the rain had turned the hard packed dirt to slippery mud. They would need a break if he was going to push them hard in the afternoon.

"Are you sure we have time to break?" Hadar called over the storm as he tried to shield his face from the rain. "At this pace we won't make the city by nightfall and if this storm persists it's only going to get worse. I really feel that we should keep moving."

Bern made an effort to strain to listen, although he could hear perfectly well. He wanted to try and deflect the question, but there was nothing he could do about it.

"Patience is what is required," Bern called back. "Is there anything you can do about the weather Ulman?"

"I'd love to be able to help, but we do not try and change the weather. The slightest change here can cause complete disaster in other parts of the kingdoms," Ulman explained.

Deep down Bern knew that would be the case, but he still had to ask. He also knew what he had to do. He could feel the entity in the back of his mind and knew it was trying to take control. If they were going to reach the city before nightfall then he would have to let it take over. Slowly he let himself drift away.

"I know the dangers, but we don't have the time to waste," Bern's words took everyone by surprise.

"What are you going to do?" Ulman asked as Bern stood.

He ignored the wizard and walked away from the trees. Ulman was about to rise, but he was stopped by a hand from Hulkan.

"I don't think that is Bern," he warned. "Whatever he is about to do it's for the good of all."

"If he is attempting to divert the storm then he could risk the lives of many. There is no telling the destruction that could cause," Ulman warned.

"It is the risk of a few to save everyone else," Hulkan tried to his best to sound reasonable as he yelled over the storm. "For the time we have known Bern and the entity that shares his body we have learned that sometimes we just have to trust he is doing the right thing."

"Tell me what you know about this entity?"

"I don't think now is the time for casual conversation. Another time." Hulkan returned his attention to his soggy food.

The wind whipped at Bern as he walked out into the open. At first he had thought the storm wasn't natural, but then decided that it was. There was no evil in the air and if the storm had been forced upon them he would be able to feel it.

When he was far enough away from others he stood and looked towards the sky. The rain beat down against his eyes, but he ignored the pain. He could feel the entity scratching again at the back of his mind. The last thing he wanted to do was openly relinquish control of his body, but he really didn't know what else he could do. Only the entity could resolve the situation.

"You have to give me control," the voice cooed inside his mind. "I can't help whilst you are blocking me."

Bern shook his head. He wanted the voice gone, he wanted the entity gone. For a moment he thought that, even with the storm raging around them, they could make it to the city before nightfall. The thought didn't last long and slowly he let himself fade into the background. It was the strangest feeling, letting himself go. Every other time the entity had taken over by force and without him knowing.

"This will be a lot easier if you just relax," coaxed the entity inside his head.

That was not something Bern was going to do. He knew if he relaxed then the entity would take over completely and that wasn't something he could risk. Each time he lost control it was getting harder and harder to regain it. It seemed as though the entity was no longer happy just residing in the background.

Everything grew hazy. Bern only just managed to stay conscious when he suddenly stopped fading away. The entity was in command of his body, but he still remained in control. He was going to see exactly what the entity was going to do. If the entity could use his body then there was no reason why he couldn't use it himself. All he had to do was work out how.

Bern felt a sudden rush of energy and he tried to push it away. He didn't know where it had come from and he felt as though it was going to overwhelm him. His grip on reality was starting to slip.

"You can't stay here Bern. I need complete control if I'm going to do this." The voice sounded strained.

As much as Bern didn't want to, he knew the entity was right. There were more to things than he could possibly imagine and he was only hindering their cause. They didn't have the time to waste.

The next thing Bern knew he was sitting with the others under the trees. The storm was still raging around them, although it did seem to have lightened slightly.

"What was that all about?" asked Hadar, still having to shout over the weather.

"What was what all about?" The last thing Bern could remember was eating a soggy meal.

"You said you were going to fix the storm so we could travel quicker," Ulman sneered. He knew there was nothing he could do. It seemed as though there was more hype than actual truth to the legend.

Bern put two and two together and realised the entity had taken over again. With the realisation also came a feeling of exhaustion. He had to push it behind him and keep going. They needed to ride hard if they were to make the city before nightfall.

"The storm will subside soon." The words came unbidden. "But we need to be on the move again."

Bern didn't want anyone to question him further. As much as they knew he wouldn't be able to answer they would still need to ask. He wished the memory would return to him. He knew something important had happened an in time he hoped he would remember.

As soon as they were back in the saddle the rain started to ease and the wind subsided. The road was still muddy, but they moved quicker than before. It was still going to be a tough journey, but the easing weather lifted their spirits.

"Are you sure this was the right thing to do?" Ulman rode up next to Bern. He noticed there was something strangely powerful about him since his return and that in itself was very disturbing.

"No, but it's not like we had any other choice." Bern didn't like what Ulman was insinuating. At the time he thought it would be a good idea to take a wizard with them, but that was quickly changing. Bern knew Ulman had a secret agenda and until he knew exactly what it was he would have to choose his words carefully.

"There is always another choice. Tampering with the weather is forbidden. If the other wizards find out what you've done then they will want to imprison you," Ulman warned.

Bern shook his head. He couldn't believe what he was hearing. It seemed as though the wizards still didn't truly appreciate their situation. They were stuck in their old ways and would need to change their thinking if they hoped to survive Nyrra's onslaught. The Evil One wouldn't abide by their rules and the sooner they accepted it the better. As much as he wanted to say something to Ulman he knew it would do more harm than good.

"The Seven Kingdoms will be safe, don't you worry about that." Although Bern didn't know what he had done, he knew what he was saying was correct. "I dampened the effects of the storm. I didn't shift anything, so there will be no adverse effect elsewhere."

Bern's words did nothing to settle Ulman's concerns, but he decided not to press any further. Whatever the entity had done it seemed to be working. The storm was starting to subside and their speed had increased. There were more important matters to discuss.

"So what are we going to do once we reach the city?" Ulman asked.

Bern stared ahead and tried to ignore the question, but he knew Ulman would persist. There was something drawing him to the city. At first he thought it was the pull of his family, but the closer they came the more he doubted it. He was sure there was something important he had to do in Zenza City.

"We see the duke. If we're going to get more information then that is the best place to start." It was the best he could do.

"It seems a little perfunctory at this stage with what's going on. Shouldn't we have some sort of plan moving forward?"

There was no answer Bern could give that would appease him. He knew Ulman, as with the other wizards, was not used to being led around. If he could have made up a reason he would have, but he was too interested in the feeling of dread he could feel building.

"I think we should leave the general alone now. There'll be time for conversation later," Duke Hadar rode up alongside them.

Ulman wasn't happy, but he knew he couldn't push any further. Bern took the opportunity to push his mare to the front of the line. He hoped everyone would leave him be, but Hadar pushed on.

"There is something not right with Ulman. I don't fully trust him." He looked over his shoulder to make sure Ulman wasn't listening.

Bern sighed before he spoke. "The wizards have been on their island for a long time. We need to be patient, they need time to adjust."

"I don't think they are trying to adjust to anything. I think they're trying to control things and that worries me." Hadar paused and looked up as the rain splashed on his face. "I wish Eldred was here. He'd know what to do with them."

As much as Bern wished for the same thing he wasn't entirely sure Eldred could do anything about them. None of the other wizards had agreed with his decision to search for the Chosen One and follow the prophecy. He doubted that they would take anything he said seriously.

"I agree, we do need to be careful around them, but we can't be too paranoid. I have a feeling we are going to need their help before too long. I'm sure Ulman will get a chance to prove himself."

As Hadar let his horse move back down the line Hulkan caught up to Bern. He was starting to think that they were deliberately not giving him a chance to be by himself.

"Don't worry about them Bern. We know that this can't be easy for you," Hulkan started and when Bern didn't reply he continued. "Are you excited to see your family again?"

Bern had almost forgotten that his wife and children were in Zenza City. He wondered if they would even recognise him. So much had happened since he had left his farm in Arsiliac and the thought made him suddenly nervous.

"Are you alright Bern?"

"What? Yes, sorry. I was just thinking about my family." A smile appeared on his face. "It has been so long since I saw them last. For a while there I didn't think I was ever going to see them again."

"I know what you mean. It was such a relief to see my father again when we reached Castalia. When I left my home, so many years ago, I never thought I would see my family again." Hulkan returned Bern's smile.

"What about your brother?" Bern changed the subject.

The smile quickly fell from Hulkan's face. They had been having such a nice conversation he didn't know why Bern had to ruin it. His brother had betrayed not only him, but the Alliance as well. If he was ever to meet his brother again then he would kill him, but he couldn't tell Bern that.

"When I see him again I will arrest him for treason and have him sent back to Castalia to be tried by the guild." He thought that was the answer Bern was looking for. "I have no doubt he will be put to death. What he's done is unforgivable."

Bern thought for a moment. He wasn't sure he completely agreed with Hulkan's line of thinking. It had been a confusing time when they were in Avalon and he could see Gilgi's point of view. There was a clear threat to Remidia and Hawthorne needed support, but there was something more to the situation that nagged him.

"You don't think that he deserves a chance to explain himself?" He knew the trial would be quick and his fate would already be written.

"What are you talking about Bern? We all witnessed what he did in Avalon, not to mention what he did to me and the guild. No Bern, he deserves death and one way or another I will make sure that happens."

Bern thought for a moment. There was more to Hulkan's words than he was letting on.

"I'm not sure if all is what it seems with your brother. I know you have history with him, but I believe there is more to the situation than what you think. Don't be so quick to dish out death."

Hulkan let Bern's words echo in his mind and he let his horse drop back to the others. All he wanted to achieve was to lift his leader's spirits, but instead Bern managed to dampen his. The steady drops of rain and the dark clouds mirrored his feelings.

No one else tried to speak with Bern and he managed to move his horse a good ten paces in front of the others. With the storm clouds overhead it was hard to gauge how long they had before nightfall, but Bern knew it couldn't be too long. Although the day had passed without incident he couldn't shrug the feeling that something wasn't right. There had been no sign of the elves, but they weren't expecting to see them until they reached the gates.

As the sky darkened they crested a small hill and the city appeared before them. Bern reined his horse to a stop and looked to the sky. He estimated there was only an hour before nightfall, enough time for them to comfortably reach the city. The sight brought relief to his heart. Throughout the day he had his doubted they would make it.

Zenza City was the second largest city in Remidia, second only to Remidel. A large stone wall encircled it with four main gates allowing entrance from each direction of the compass. From his position on the hill Bern couldn't tell if the Southern Gate was opened or closed. Although the rain and the darkness obscured his view, he still felt something was wrong.

"I don't think we should linger here general. Besides the obvious weather issue, there is an evil feeling on the air," Elyas said when he reached the hill.

Bern knew he was right. There was something evil and the last thing they needed was to be outside the city. Despite his words Bern couldn't bring himself to move his horse. Before he spoke he looked over his shoulder to see if the elves had caught up, but there was no sign of them.

"I don't think we should move until the elves arrive. It's getting late in the day and we shouldn't leave them outside the city." That was not the real reason, Bern didn't want to move.

"We can wait for them at the city gate," Elyas retorted. "We shouldn't stay here any longer."

Bern thought about arguing, but as he looked at the others he knew there was no other excuse for them to remain. Just before Ulman was about to speak Bern urged his horse to a trot. He wanted to increase it to a gallop, but he didn't think that would be an appropriate way to approach the gate. He didn't know what sort of response they would get from the guards and they didn't want to do anything to put them off.

They all looked at each other before following after him. They were all used to him acting strange and knew better than to question him.

As they approached the city they noticed that the highway was completely empty. There was no one else coming or going. Even with the bad weather there should be people moving about. There were no lights in the farmhouses and no smoke from the chimneys. Bern's feeling of dread increased the closer he came to the city gates.

It wasn't until he was within one hundred paces of the gates, did he realise they were shut. Bern knew it wasn't a good sign. There was no reason why they should be closed. His heart sank as their chances of entering the city before nightfall diminished.

As they got closer Bern saw something hanging from the wall. At first he didn't know what it was, but when he did he thought he was going to be sick. Despite the feeling he couldn't bring himself to look away.

Two charred bodies swung in the breeze. They had been burned beyond recognition. One was a woman and the other a man. There was no doubt they had been left there as a warning, but Bern couldn't for the life of him work out what for. By all accounts there had been no attacks on the city and if there had he didn't think the warning would stop the Evil One's agents.

"What do you think that means?" Hadar's voice was thick with disgust.

"I don't know, but it can't be a good sign," Elyas responded, showing just as much distain.

Bern rode to the gate in silence before he dismounted. A rage was building inside him and he had to contain himself. He would have to stay focused before he accused anyone of the atrocity before him.

Taking a deep breath he steeled himself before banging on the gate. He knew it would be futile exercise, but it made him feel better. The guard house was to the right, but it looked vacant. When there was no answer he banged again.

"What are you doing general?" Elyas asked. "No one is going to be able to hear you."

Bern ignored the question. He knew he had made enough noise to raise someone. Before too long a door to an archer's perch opened above one of the hanging bodies. The man who looked out didn't look happy.

"What are you? Stupid? Can't you see that the city is closed?" He didn't give anyone a chance to reply. "Now go away or the rain won't be the only thing coming down on you."

Bern was about to speak, but the guard closed the door and returned to what he was doing. He thought about knocking again, but something stopped him. Instead he turned to the others.

"We're not getting into the city tonight. We need to get out of this rain," Bern mounted as he spoke.

"Wait Bern?" Elyas cut in. "You can't give up so easily. I've dealt with guards like this all my life. If you want I can speak to him. I'm sure once he realises who we are and why we're here he'll be more than happy to open the gate for us."

"Elyas is right Bern," Hadar added. "You said yourself that we needed to be in the city before nightfall. There is no telling what is out here and there is no telling how long it will be before the storm strengthens."

Bern looked towards the sky. There was very little light left in the day. For a moment he thought the rain was falling heavier, but he couldn't be sure. One thing he did know was that they needed to be inside and soon. Although they would not be in the city before nightfall, they still needed to find shelter.

"The time is not right for us to enter the city. We don't want to reveal ourselves yet." Bern's voice changed. "For now we need to find shelter for the night and in the morning we will find our way in, one way or another."

Bern didn't wait for a response as he started away from the others. When he looked up he saw a sight that sent a feeling of relief through his body. The elves were making their way towards them. He felt much better knowing they would all be together.

"Well met Pernian," Bern greeted the elf when they arrived. "Any problems on the way here?"

"The forest was quiet. There were no signs of any orglin," Pernian replied.

"I guess that's a good sign then," Bern paused. "We will be staying outside the city tonight. In the morning we will gain entrance."

Pernian just nodded. When he saw the gate and the others riding towards him he figured that would be the case. He also knew that there was little point in asking Bern what had happened. It was clear the general didn't want to explain any further.

"We need to find some shelter. I don't think this rain is going to ease."

Pernian knew there was more to the statement, but he still refrained from asking. As much as he didn't mind the rain he knew it would be better if they were sheltered for the night; needless conversation was only going to hinder them.

"There are a number of farmhouses just off the highway. By the looks of them they have been abandoned. There is a large one with a large barn attached that should do. We're best to keep everyone close."

Pernian looked over his shoulder. He didn't seem too happy with the prospect, when he returned his gaze to Bern there was a grimace on his face.

"There is a small wood not far from here. I think my elves would much prefer finding shelter there." Pernian was also hoping to spend the night outside, but knew he would need to stay with the rest of the commanders.

"Are you sure you wouldn't rather get out of the rain?" Bern asked.

"The trees will keep us dry. Remember that we have an affinity with the woods. I will get them settled and then meet you at the farmhouse."

Bern nodded his agreement. There was no more time for conversation. The feeling of dread had increased and almost overwhelmed him. They needed to be inside and they needed to do it quickly.

Chapter 33: Zenza City

They reached the farmhouse just before the sun completely disappeared. The soldiers took the horses to the stables before settling down in the barn. The farmhouse was a large double storey, stone building. It was large enough for everyone to spend the night in comfort.

As expected the farmhouse had been vacated. They stumbled around in the dark before Dorn finally found a lantern and was able to light it. His dwarven eyes were best suited to the darkness from his years in the Cloumid Mountains, even better than Hulkan's.

When they were able to look around it was clear that the occupants had left in a hurry. There was still half eaten food, starting to grow mould, on the dining room table. The chair at the head of the table been knocked over. The situation didn't seem right to anyone.

Pernian arrived soon after. As soon as he was happy that his little group of elves was safe he made his way to the farmhouse. There was definitely something evil on the night air. Pernian could feel it as he walked through the darkness. He couldn't relax until he was safely inside.

"What do you think happened here?" Hulkan asked Dorn as they searched the farmhouse.

"I don't know, but it looks like the owners left in a hurry," Dorn replied.

They found three children's bedrooms with the beds a mess. The blankets were thrown back as if someone had grabbed the children in a hurry. The wardrobes were all full of clothes.

"And it looks like they didn't even pack," Hulkan added. "We should tell Bern what we've found. He may want to find us somewhere else to spend the night."

Bern didn't sound overly surprised at the news. He sat on a large two seater lounge chair in the sitting room with Pernian and Hadar. A large fire burned in the hearth as they attempted to dry themselves.

"I think you'll find most of the farmhouses will be the same. Whatever happened here it certainly scared the residents enough to leave all their possessions behind."

"Do you think they were killed?" Hadar asked.

"I doubt it. The mould on the food is only a few days old. If they had been killed then I'm sure we would have seen bodies lying around," Bern replied.

"We could hardly see anything when we arrived. There could have been dead bodies no more than three paces away and we wouldn't have seen them," Elyas disagreed.

"Be that as it may I don't think that were killed. There is no sign of a struggle. Sure, they left in a hurry, but that doesn't mean they were under attack. I don't know why they left, but I'm sure they are still alive."

It was a good enough reason as any. No one was really interested in why the farmhouse was empty. All they cared about was getting warm and dry and having something to eat. It had been a long and tiring day on the road and soon enough they would be able to sleep.

"So what was deal at the city gates?" Hadar changed the subject when it was clear no one was going to speak.

"They were shut!" Bern didn't know how to respond.

Hadar shook his head before he continued. "I know that, and you know that's not what I meant. I have seen you do some strange things, but I have never seen you give up so easily. Why didn't you try harder to get us into the city?"

Bern had been asking himself the same question. For the entire day they had been racing towards Zenza City so they could be inside before nightfall. It should have been an easy task, but with the stormy weather it had been almost impossible. It made no sense to him why he would turn away from the gates without really trying to gain entrance. He knew he could have found some way into the city, but there had been something holding him back and he knew better than to try and ignore those feelings.

"There is something missing, or at least there is something we still have to do before we enter the city," Bern tried his best to explain.

"Do you know what it is?" Hadar asked.

Bern shook his head. No matter how hard he thought, he couldn't work out what they needed to do. He knew that the farmhouse had something to do with it, but that was all. He could only hope in the morning the answer would come to him, otherwise he would have to enter the city.

"We need information, that is what we need," Elyas barked. "Something is very wrong here. I have never known a farmer to leave his farm when they are not under attack. I don't know what's happening around the other side of the city, but as you all can see there is no attack coming from the south."

"You're right." Bern had grown up being a farmer and knew he wouldn't leave unless it was an emergency. "Something is terribly wrong here, but I don't think it's something we can work out tonight." Bern paused for a moment. "We will look around the farms at first light and see if anyone is still here." Bern knew there was someone still outside the wall. He could sense it.

"Then I suppose we should eat something," Elyas spoke with enthusiasm. "There is still some food here. I'll see what I can make without using our supplies."

Bern wasn't overly happy about stealing the famer's food, but their supplies were starting to run low. He had been relying on the fact that the Duke of Zenza would give them more for the journey to the capital. If they couldn't get into the city then they would have to make straight for Remidia.

The thought of food and the smells coming from the kitchen lifted everyone's spirits. For the moment it seemed as though they were safe from the evil that was growing outside. It was a pleasant change to the day to be warm, dry and comfortable. They almost forgot their worries as they sat around the dining table and laughed.

The reality of the situation came back all too quickly when they finished eating. The events of the day had exhausted them and the sound of the storm raging about outside did nothing to help. Whatever Bern had done earlier had finally worn off.

"I'll take the first watch tonight?" Elyas offered, although he was feeling deathly tired.

"I don't think we have to worry about setting a watch tonight. I think we will all appreciate a good night's sleep. I have a bad feeling that tomorrow is going to be a trying day." Bern's words echoed through their minds.

Bern took the main bedroom. Although no one offered it to him, he knew they would insist. He didn't want to have the conversation and figured it was easier for him just to do what they expected. It was a large room with a large four poster bed. The bed was comfortable enough, the mattress was a little too soft for his liking, but that wasn't what kept him awake.

Although he knew they were safe for the night the evil feeling that had been growing throughout the day still bothered him. He thought it would be a relatively simple trip to the city. He would see his family, enlist help from the duke and then be on the move to Remidel. It seemed as though that would not be the case.

It was late in the night and the storm still raged outside when Bern finally fell asleep. His dreams were filled with pain and evil creatures. When he woke in the morning he felt as though he had not slept at all. The last thing he wanted to do was rise and he thought about rolling over and trying to get back to sleep. Before he had a chance to change his mind there was a knock on the door and Hadar entered.

"Good news general," he started. "The storm has abated during the night. There is still a light shower outside, but it is still an hour before dawn. With a little luck it'll be gone by the time we have to move again."

The thought of leaving the farmhouse did nothing to lift Bern's spirits, but if the rain stopped then at least it wouldn't be so bad. The smell of bacon frying in a pan hit his nose and suddenly he was excited.

"We found a nice stash of bacon and eggs. The bread is a little stale, but I think it will be a breakfast to remember." Hadar walked over to the window and peered around the curtains. "It looks as though the rain has eased off again."

Bern slowly lifted himself from the bed. His body ached from his restless dreams. It was as if the pain he had suffered in his dreams had become a reality. The smell of cooking food made his mouth water, and at least they would start the day well regardless of what happened when they left the farmhouse.

Everyone was awake and sitting at the table when Bern arrived. There was more food than Bern had expected. Beside the eggs, bacon and toasted bread there were mushrooms, small sausages and tomatoes.

"This looks like a breakfast fit for a king," Bern laughed as he sat at the table.

"We figured that the food would go to waste if we didn't eat it." It was a weak excuse, but an acceptable one.

"Well, either way, it's too late now," Bern commented as he scooped food onto his plate. If nothing else he would enjoy his breakfast.

"What's the plan for today?" Ulman asked as they started eating.

As much as Bern just wanted to enjoy his food in peace he couldn't blame him for asking. There would be little time after they had eaten to discuss matters. Once the sun had risen they had to start scouring the countryside for answers.

"We need to search for someone who can give us an idea on what is happening inside the city. I'm sure what is happening in there and what is happening out here is closely related. Until we know what we're up against I don't think we should rush into things," Bern explained.

"That's all well and good, but our supplies are running low. We probably have a week's worth of food left if we ration it," Hadar explained.

That was something that Bern had thought about, but he was sure they would find the answers they needed sooner rather than later. There was little doubt in his mind that they would be in the city before nightfall. It was the manner in which they would arrive that had him stumped.

The conversation became light for the rest of the meal. Although Bern's explanation had not really appeased anyone it was enough to keep them going. When there was more information they knew Bern would share it.

There was a knock on the door shortly after the sun had risen. With the dark clouds and the curtains drawn it was hard for the commanders to know it was light outside. Bern had insisted the night before that they close the blinds. He didn't want whatever was outside looking in on them. Despite how silly it sounded the others didn't question him.

"We are ready to leave," Private Horst said.

"Very good," Elyas replied.

"What are the orders, sir?"

Everyone looked at Bern for the answer.

"There is at least one person still in this farming community. There may be more, but that is irrelevant. What we need to do is split up and search the surrounding area. Whenever you find someone bring them back here and have someone posted to watch them before we all return. At the latest we should be back here for midday, sooner would be better. The sooner we get the information the sooner we can be inside the city."

There would be no more explanation, even though his words didn't really make sense. There was no way he should have been able to know there were people in the farmlands, but they didn't even question it. If he said there were then there would be.

Outside the ground was muddy and many puddles were scattered around. The sky was grey and it looked like it could rain at any moment, although Bern was sure it wouldn't. The soldiers had already started to spread out to begin the search.

"Where should we start looking?" Ulman asked Bern.

The wizard was not about to leave Bern on his own. As much as Bern would have preferred it he didn't want to say anything. The others had all paired off, so he figured it was better for him to do the same.

"Let's try to the south." There was nothing drawing him south, there was nothing drawing him in any direction, he just figured it was as good a place as any.

"That's a good idea. We can cross over the highway and see if the gate has been opened," Ulman suggested.

As much as it did make sense, Bern didn't like the fact that Ulman had realised it first. He hoped the gates were still shut. If they were open then the others would want to rush inside. Until he spoke to the person he was looking for they couldn't risk it.

Bern started off without responding. His horse struggled through the mud as they made their way. It would have been more frustrating if he was in any hurry. He didn't know why, but he knew time was something they had plenty of.

It didn't take long for them to reach the highway. Bern almost couldn't bring himself to look at the gate, but when he did he was relieved to see it was still closed. There would be no pressure to enter the city until they were ready.

"So who are we looking for?" Ulman asked after they had passed over the highway.

"There are still people hidden outside the city. We need to get them all together and get some answers as to what is happening. We also need to make sure that they are all safe," Bern had prepared the answer. He knew the question would be asked eventually and it was enough for Ulman.

Soon enough they came across another farmhouse. It was only a single storey and made from wood. There was no comparison compared to the one they had stayed in. After a quick inspection they realised that it too had been abandoned.

They continued to follow the line of the wall as it wrapped its way around the city only diverting to check out the many farmhouses and barns they came across. It wasn't until mid-morning that they reached a dilapidated farmhouse. The windows and doors had been boarded up and it looked like it had not had occupants in over a year.

"I don't think it's worth checking this one. It's obvious this farmhouse hasn't been lived in for a long time," Ulman said as he urged his horse to continue.

Bern wasn't so sure. There was something strange about the situation. Ulman was too quick to dismiss it for Bern's liking. He would have done the same himself, but there was something nagging in the back of his mind.

"Wait Ulman," Bern called out. "I think we should have a look inside."

Ulman was already passed the house and didn't look happy when he was called back. Bern had already dismounted and was waiting at the front door for him.

"I really don't think we should go in there," Ulman warned.

"And that is exactly the reason we should." Bern smiled.

Bern didn't wait for a response as he pulled one of the boards that was blocking the door. The board came away a little too easily for a house that had been abandoned. Seeing the first board come away, Ulman helped with the others.

They both looked at each before Bern slowly pulled the door open. There was no musty smell coming from inside instead there was a fragrant smell in the air.

"Hello!" Ulman cringed as Bern called out into the house. "We're not here to hurt you. We just want to speak with you."

Despite his words Bern's hand rested on the hilt of his sword. As much as he didn't think there was any threat inside, he needed to be sure.

He slowly took one step before he stopped. He thought he could hear muffled voices from somewhere towards the back of the house, but when he tried to listen there was nothing.

"Please, we mean you no harm. We're here to help you," Bern called again, as Ulman waited ouside.

Suddenly Bern saw some movement from the end of the small hallway. To his surprise he saw a young girl. She couldn't have been more than six years old. Her long brown hair was tattered and dirty and there were smears of dirt on her face.

"Who are you?" her voice was croaked.

"My name is Bern," he spoke softly. "Who else is here with you?"

"No one, I'm here alone," Bern could hear subtle movements from behind her and knew she was lying. "Please leave me alone. I don't want to go into the city," she said, sobbing in-between words.

"I'm not here to take you into the city. Who else is with you?" he asked again.

There was a sudden noise from a room behind her and two boys rushed out, each brandishing a pitch fork. They rushed towards Bern, but then stopped when he drew his sword. The boys were no older than thirteen and Bern really didn't want to kill any children.

"You don't look like a soldier from the city," one of the boys said.

"I'm not from the city." As he started he heard Ulman approach from behind and secretly motioned for him to stop. He thought he would have a greater chance of success if the boys thought he was alone. "What are you doing here?"

"Leave us alone," the girl approached as she spoke but then half hid behind one of the boys legs.

"Why don't you start by telling me your names?" Bern lowered his sword, but he didn't sheath it. The boys looked frightened and could attack at any moment. He didn't want to do anything to make them react.

The children looked at each other. It was not at all what they had been expecting. No one knew how to respond. It was the little girl who spoke first.

"My name is Cayley. This is my brother Cayden," she indicated to the boy she was still hiding behind. "And this is Paden."

"Where are your parents?" Bern asked.

No one answered and a tear appeared in the corner of Cayley's eyes. Whatever had happened their parents were gone.

"Is there anyone else here?" Bern continued when it was obvious they weren't going to respond.

"I think it's time you answer some questions," Cayley seemed to get some confidence back. "If you're not from the city what are you doing here? Do you know how dangerous it is to be outside the city walls these days?"

"Everywhere is dangerous at the moment. We want to take you somewhere safe where we can talk." Bern slowly sheathed his sword.

The move seemed to calm the children. It was Cayley who made the first move. Slowly she moved out from behind her brother and walked towards Bern. When she was within two paces she reached out her arms and Bern scooped her up into his. Bern was surprised, but he couldn't think of anything else to do.

Her first move was to sniff his neck. "He smells clean." She paused for a moment. "I like him. Get the others and let's go."

The two boys didn't know what to say. The young girl had obviously made a decision. They looked at each other before Paden disappeared to the back of the house. When he returned there was a trail of children behind him. Bern counted ten in total and estimated their ages to be between four amd ten. It was obvious that Cayden and Paden were the oldest.

"What happened in there?" Ulman asked when Bern stepped outside. If he was surprised to see Cayley in his arms he didn't show it. She had her arms wrapped around his neck and she buried her face in his shoulder when she saw Ulman.

"We have found who we were looking for." It was the only response he was going to give.

He tried to lift Cayley onto his mare, but she kept her arms tightly wrapped around him. Bern had to smile. He remembered how his own daughter used to hold him so tight when there was thunder about. The thought made him both happy and sad.

The boys led the rest of the children from the farmhouse after looking around nervously. At first they didn't look happy to be outside. There was a clear amount of fear on their faces. When they were happy that there was only two of them they motioned for the others to follow.

Ulman was the only one who rode. Despite the young children he wasn't about to walk through the mud. Cayden and Paden still carried their pitchforks and the others carried whatever meagre possessions they had.

"I like you," Cayley whispered in Bern's ear. "You're a nice man." She paused. "I don't like your friend. There is something strange about him."

Bern hid a smile as Ulman glared at him, but he couldn't resist his laughter. Her words reflected Bern's own feelings, although he knew there was nothing evil about Ulman. The wizard had just been too far away from the rest of the Seven Kingdoms.

It was a long trudge through the mud back to the large farmhouse, but they made it back before midday. Those who had returned first had set up some tables in the barn. They had raided the nearby farmhouses and found a few more children, but no adults. Bern figured that would be the case.

"Is there anyone left to return?" Bern asked Elyas when he found him.

"Dorn and Hulkan still haven't returned and Pernian has only just arrived," Elyas explained as he looked around the barn. "We've gathered enough food to feed everyone, but I don't know what we're going to do with the children after that."

Bern had another good look around the room before he answered. "Have we found any adults or just children?"

"It seems as though all the adults have gone. None of the children have offered any information and we figured it was better to wait for you before we started."

Bern nodded his approval. The last thing he wanted was rumours being spread before he was able to gauge the situation. Children were prone to telling wild stories and it was going to be hard enough to get the truth.

"Why don't you go to the others," Bern spoke softly to Cayley.

The girl shook her head, whimpered and held on tighter. It was obvious that she didn't want to be separated from him. He could certainly understand her scepticism, but he would have thought she would prefer to be with the other children. Since he needed to speak with them he figured it would be just as easy to start with her.

"Let's go find a seat and something for you to eat, then we can talk," Bern suggested.

Cayley looked around the barn nervously before nodding her agreement. She remained in Bern's arms until they reached a table at the back of the room. For a moment he thought she was going to fight him, but slowly she eased herself down. She waited for Bern to sit and then climbed onto the seat next to him.

Bern had to smile. There was something about her that melted his heart. He had lived in such a tough environment he had forgotten the pure joy of a child. The thought made him miss his own children even more and almost brought a tear to his eyes. He choked down the urge to cry before he signalled for some food to be brought to the table.

"What would you like us to do with the other children?" Elyas had made a point to bring their food.

"Just see that they are looked after." Bern made sure Cayley was busy with her food before he spoke. "I think I will get all the answers I need."

Bern didn't need to mention Cayley for Elyas to know what he was talking about. Although he hadn't known Bern for long he knew enough not to question him.

"Can you tell me what's been happening here?" Bern started with a vague and innocuous question.

Cayley just shook her head in response.

"Do you know what's happening in the city?" he pushed a little harder.

Cayley didn't look at him when she shook her head again. It seemed as though she didn't want to speak and Bern took a deep breath. He knew she was the one to give him answers, he just had to work out the right questions to ask.

"Where are your parents?"

Cayley stopped what she was doing and looked Bern in the eye, her own started to water. He didn't want to upset the child, but he needed answers.

"Dead!" She paused. "Or gone, like all the other parents," despite her best efforts she started to cry.

Without a second thought Bern scooped her up in his arms and held her close until she stopped crying. Her tears almost forced him to weep, but he remained calm. His stalwartness reassured her and soon enough her crying subsided. She wiped her eyes and her nose on his shirt before looking up at him.

"I'm sorry for my outburst, I just miss my family." There was something strange about her words.

"That's alright dear. Please tell me what you know," Bern cooed, despite his concerns.

"It all started about a month ago," her voice was eerily calm. "At first there was a feeling of dread that filled the night air." She paused for a moment. "That isn't exactly true. It started almost a year ago. There were rumours that the Evil One was planning an attack on the city. The duke had been acting strange, all paranoid, and then he closed the gates and wouldn't allow anyone entrance." Bern remembered when Alaric had tried to enter Zenza City to buy a barn. He had not been able to and subsequently the deal went sour. It seemed like a lifetime ago. "That only worked until the food supplies started to run out and then he was forced to open the gates again. Things seemed to go back to normal. There was no sign of the Evil One or any of his forces. That was until about a month ago. No one really noticed it at first, but then the rumours started to spread. There was something evil in the night air. If you were caught outside after dark there was a good chance you would never be seen again. At least you weren't seen out here."

Bern had felt the evil growing as the light had faded the night before. Pernian had been out in the open after dark, but he had not mentioned seeing anyone. Bern had to wonder how close the elf had come to death, or whatever befell those who were taken.

"Do you have any idea what it was?" He wasn't sure why he had asked the question, but he felt as though she would know the answer. He could feel the entity scratching in the back of his mind, trying to get out. No matter what it wanted Bern wasn't going to submit. He was so close to getting the information that he needed that he wasn't going to risk losing it.

Cayley looked up at Bern with a questioning expression on her face. It was as if she was trying to place where she had seen him before. The look was enough to make Bern feel uncomfortable. There were tears in her eyes that didn't reflect on her face.

"It was evil, that's all I know. I was too scared to leave the house with the others," Cayley whimpered. "One by one, sometimes two or three at a time, the adults would leave their houses and they would never return. Despite the evil feeling it was as if they were drawn to the night air. Luckily none of the children have been drawn out, but I don't know how long it's going to last. The night is getting... hungry. The longer it goes without a victim the stronger the evil becomes. Before long I'm afraid the night will take us all."

That was a disturbing thought. Bern knew they couldn't enter the city until they worked out what was happening outside. They would need to spend at least one more night in the farmhouse. If what Cayley said was true then they would have to be especially careful. If the night wanted adults then they were plenty more for it to take.

"Do you have any idea what is drawing the adults into the night?"

Cayley shook her head and looked down at the table. Whatever confidence she'd had was gone. Slowly she started to scratch at the table, as if any distraction would send Bern away. Bern thought about questioning her further, but he doubted he would get any more information. He stroked her hair softly before he lifted her back onto her own chair.

"I will be back later," he cooed as he stood. "I need to see if the other children know anything."

Cayley didn't look up as he left. He had thought she might have tried to stay with him, but she remained where she was.

"Have you been able to overhear anything the children have been saying?" Bern asked Elyas when he reached the other side of the barn.

"Most of the children don't seem to want to mention what has been happening. It seems that they are just happy there are some adults around again, but there is a story that some of the boys on that table have been telling," Elyas pointed at a table with Cayden and Paden and a group of six other boys. "They're talking about some evil in the night. They haven't mentioned anything specific, but it might be worth speaking to them."

"Very good Elyas, I will. If you and a few others start speaking to the other children hopefully we'll get the answer we need."

Bern made his way to the boys and spoke before he sat. "Everything okay here?"

"Yes sir!" Cayden responded.

Bern wasn't sure if he was being sarcastic or genuine. Either way he didn't have time to worry about it. The day had already started to slip away and time was against them if they wanted to be within the city walls before nightfall. Even as the thought entered his mind he knew they would stay at the farmhouse again.

"So I hear you know what is lurking in the night," he lied.

"No sir." Paden shook his head. "There is something evil in the night, but no one has seen it. No one is stupid enough to risk leaving their homes during the night." Paden thought about mentioning the adults, but decided against it.

"I know the adults have been drawn from their buildings but the children haven't had the same pull, but I wouldn't be so blasé." Bern knew he should have gone easier on the children, but there was something about Paden's arrogance that annoyed him. "We need all the information we can get if we are going to help you."

Paden's mouth dropped open. He had not been expecting Bern to react like.

"No one goes out at night," a young boy with dirty blond hair at the end of the table spoke. "We keep the curtains shut and try not to listen to anything. When my parents left our home I heard a strange wailing noise. I think that's what made them leave and took them away. I always make sure that my ears are covered when I go to sleep." He looked around nervously as if there was something evil listening to him.

Bern thought for a moment. He tried to pull on the memories of the entity, but nothing came to him. Since he left Cayley the entity had returned to its dormant state. He knew that the creature calling the parents out was in his memory somewhere, but without help he wasn't able to reach it.

"Is there anything else you can tell me?" Bern asked.

"I'm scared," the youngest of the group said.

Bern couldn't help himself but smile. "It'll be alright. You're safe now."

The boy spoke again as Bern turned to move away. "I'm not scared for us, I'm scared for you."

Bern stiffened as he heard the words, but he didn't turn around. He couldn't let the children see the concern on his face. There was something very disturbing about the boy's words. Slowly he started to walk away, the confidence returning to his stature.

"It looks like we're going to have to stay here again tonight," Bern found Pernian standing outside the barn. The elves had avoided it as much as they could.

"I don't think that's a wise decision. There is something wrong here and the sooner we are in the city the better," Pernian replied.

"I know, but we don't have a choice. All you need to do is make sure your elves stay in the forest." The decision wasn't up for discussion. "There is more going on here than what we think and we can't go rushing into the city unprepared." As much as he wanted to enter the city he still knew he was making the right decision.

"There is something evil stalking the night," Pernian explained as if Bern didn't already know. "I could feel it when I was returning last night."

"I know Pernian," Bern interrupted.

"I don't think you do," Pernian snapped. "We could all feel the evil in the air as the sun was setting, but after dusk it was completely different. I felt as though something was watching me, but of course I couldn't see anything. As I neared the farmhouse I felt a sudden compulsion. Something was drawing me towards the city. The feeling almost overwhelmed me when I reached the front door. Once I was inside the feeling slowly drifted away."

That concurred with what he had been told. What he didn't understand was what would have made the adults go outside after dark, and after the others had gone missing. He was sure they would have known before it was too late that they shouldn't be out.

"That is good to know," Bern simply said. "That is why it's even more important that the elves remain in the woods. If they step out then there is a good chance they will be taken."

"Taken by whom?" Pernian wanted answers.

"That I don't know," Bern replied. "All we know is that someone is taking the adults after dark. It seems that eventually the pull will be so powerful that they will be drawn out from inside."

Pernian didn't respond. As much as he had hoped Bern had some answers he knew he didn't. There was a mystery surrounding them and there was only one way to find out what it was. It was something that Pernian didn't like.

"You're going outside tonight?" Pernian cringed to ask.

"Yes!" Bern replied.

Chapter 34: Night Terror

The children had been left in the barn with the soldiers when the sun had set, all but Cayley. When it was clear that Bern wasn't going to return, she made her way to the farmhouse. No matter what he said to her she would not leave his side. In the end he decided it was easier to keep her with him. He could only hope that she remained in the farmhouse when he had to leave.

The soldiers had been given strict instructions that by the time the sun had set, the doors and windows were to be boarded shut. No one was to leave until the sun rose in the morning. The children didn't seem as concerned as the soldiers with their new command.

Pernian made sure to tell his fellow elves that they were not to leave the woods no matter what happened during the night. He also made certain he returned to the farmhouse before nightfall. The last thing he wanted was to be left outside in the dark.

"So what is your plan?" Pernian asked as they ate their evening meal.

Bern had spent the rest of the afternoon trying to gather as much information as he could. At best the other children had told the same story and at worst nothing at all. No one had any idea what had drawn the adults away or where they might have ended up. He had decided not to tell anyone what he was planning until they were all together. The later they knew about it the less time they had to talk him out of it.

"I'm going out into the night to see what is taking the adults," Bern said bluntly.

His comment brought silence to the table. With all they had learned during the day they couldn't believe what he was suggesting. No one who had gone out into the night had been seen again.

"I'm going with you!" Cayley blurted.

Everyone looked at the little girl in shock. If Bern's words had come as a surprise no one was prepared for hers. Even Bern didn't know what to say. He had been expecting the others to rebut, but he didn't expect anyone to offer assistance, let alone the little girl. Suddenly he felt the entity scratching at the back of his mind again.

"I don't like the sounds of this," Ulman was the first to respond. Bern wished that it had been anyone except the wizard. "It is too dangerous for you to be walking around in the dark. We came here to speak with the duke and that's what we should be focusing on. In the morning we'll take the children into the city with us where they'll be safe. After we speak with the duke we can work out our best plan of attack." It was a valid argument, but one Bern wasn't interested in.

"We don't know why we came here. We assumed that it was to speak with the duke and I'm sure we will in the end, but for now we have another mission. We need to investigate what is happening out in the farming community before we enter the city. Both scenarios are linked and we need to work this one out first." The entity was fighting even harder to get out, but Bern would not submit.

"So who else do you want to take with you?" Elyas asked, as stalwart as ever, although something in his tone made Bern believe he didn't want to be chosen.

Bern had not thought about taking anyone with him. It was going to be a dangerous mission and he didn't want to risk anyone's lives. It had been such a surprise when Cayley had spoken that he didn't know what to say.

"I will go by myself. If I don't make it back then you will have to tell the duke what happened."

His words didn't fill anyone with confidence. They were already dubious about his decision and it seemed as though he was just sacrificing himself. There was no way they would let him go alone.

"I'll go with you," Dorn barked. "I have spent enough time in the dark not to be afraid."

"You're not the only one," Hulkan added.

Bern had to smile as one-by-one they all offered to join him. To his surprise even Ulman offered to assist and Bern almost took him up on the offer, but he knew he had to go alone. It was too great a risk to bring the others with him and if he got into trouble he doubted any of them could help.

"Thank you all for your offers, but I must do this alone."

"You won't be going anywhere without me," Cayley said.

There was no doubt to the tone in her voice and the glare she shot Bern had everyone perplexed.

"Okay, who is this girl and what does she have to do with everything?" Hadar couldn't help himself.

Bern figured the question would come eventually, but he had no idea how to answer it. As the day continued he could feel something growing between them. There was a connection, but he had no idea what it meant.

"She is a child we found today." Bern did the best he could. The look she gave him didn't help. "She has been very helpful." Even with the compliment her face remained sour.

"That explains nothing." Ulman shook his head. "There is clearly something between the two of you."

Bern had also noticed it, but he had no idea what it was. He thought about letting the entity take over, but decided against it. He was finally getting somwhere on his own and he didn't want to let go.

"There is nothing more to tell." Bern dismissed the accusation.

When it was clear that Bern wasn't going to continue all eyes moved to Cayley. They knew there was more to her than the little girl they saw before them.

"Why are they looking at me like that?" She looked at Bern and almost started to cry.

"Enough," Bern's voice boomed. "There are more important things to discuss."

"It seems as though it's all been said." Hulkan shook his head.

"Not quite. Cayley and I will try and find out what's happening outside, but you all need to be prepared if we don't return." Bern's words were ominous. "If we're not back by dawn you need to make your way into the city. I have a feeling that there is something wrong with the duke and it will be your job to work it out."

Ulman was about to question him, but Hadar silenced him with a wave of his hand.

"Our next move is to join the Alliance at Remidel. It would be great if we could get some more support for the army."

The room went silent as they all thought on what Bern had told them. It seemed as though he didn't expect to return and that was a worrying thought. If it was so dangerous then he should not be going at all. Hadar finally spoke his mind.

"I know this is your homeland, but surely your life isn't worth risking. I will go and see what's happening outside. At least if I don't return then you can continue to the Alliance."

Bern smiled. "Thank you for the offer, but you would be dead for sure if you went out of there. At least Cayley and I will have a chance to get some answers." Bern looked at the young girl. "Now I think we should get out there. I can sense the evil trying to creep in. We don't want anyone leaving by mistake."

Bern stood before lifting Cayley from her chair. He thought about carrying her, but he thought that might look a little strange. Instead he softly placed her on her feet.

"Lead the way," Bern offered.

It seemed odd, but the little girl led Bern towards the front door. The others looked at each other, dumbfounded for a moment, before following after.

Bern removed the boards blocking the doorway before he turned back to the others. "Make sure you return the boards after we're gone."

"And how will you get back in?" Elyas asked.

That was a very good question and one Bern had not thought about. If they didn't board the door then they would risk being tempted outside by the evil. It would be difficult for them to return, but that was the risk he had to take. In the back of his mind he really didn't think they would be.

"We'll work something out. The most important thing is for you all to remain inside."

When he finished speaking Bern slowly pushed the door open. A blast of evil filled the room and everyone except for Cayley backed away. She didn't seem to be affected by it.

"Come on Bern." Cayley strolled out into the darkness without a care for the evil that enveloped her.

"Here, take this with you." Dorn offered Bern a torch he had just lit. "At least you'll be able to see where you're going."

"Thank you, but no. It will only be a beacon to the evil that awaits us," Bern replied.

Dorn was about to speak again, but Hulkan cut in first. "Maybe you should have a secret knock so we know when you return," he suggested.

Bern just smiled and started to walk away. He waited until the he heard the boards being hammered back into place before he followed Cayley into the night. A cold wind blew around the farmhouse making his cloak flap.

"Hurry up Bern," Cayley called over her shoulder. Bern could only just see her ahead of him and it didn't look as though she was planning on waiting.

The mystery behind the little girl only strengthened. She didn't seem worried about the evil that was growing ever stronger around them. They had drawn a bath for her and found some clothes in one of the bedrooms. It seemed that the family before them had a girl around Cayley's age. There were many brightly coloured dresses, but she chose a black pair of trousers and a black shirt. The two items didn't seem to fit the wardrobe, but they were there nonetheless.

Bern quickened his pace until he reached her. For the first time he noticed her brown hair had been platted into a long braid. He wasn't sure which of his commanders had taken the time to do such a thing and it seemed quite odd. Cayley seemed quite happy with it and let it swing back and forth as she walked.

Suddenly the feeling that someone or something was watching them was almost overpowering. Again Cayley didn't seem to notice, but Bern couldn't just push it aside. He gently placed a hand on her shoulder.

"There is something close," Bern whispered.

"I know," she looked at him with a questioning expression on her face. Despite the darkness Bern could see her clearly. "You don't feel it do you?" The question was odd.

"Of course I feel it. I was the one who mentioned it." Bern scowled.

"There's no need to be like that." Cayley pouted. "Come on, we have further to go before we're done."

Bern was finally realising what it was like for the others when the entity took over. It was very frustrating to get little titbits of information. He wondered if Cayley suffered the same affliction as him. Suddenly he felt the entity scratching at the back of his mind again. It would be a lot easier if he just lost control, but he had decided before he left the farmhouse that he wasn't going to. If he was going to see his family again then he needed to remain in control.

Suddenly there was an ear piercing screech coming from behind them. The sound made Bern's heart pound and Cayley snatched his hand. When Bern looked around he couldn't see what had made the noise, but that didn't make him feel any better.

"Let's keep moving," she whispered.

Her words were enough to get him moving again. He didn't know what had made such a terrible noise and he really didn't want to wait around to find out. Deep down he knew that whatever it was it would find them soon enough.

"Where are we going?" Bern asked as they neared the city wall.

Cayley shot Bern a questioning look. He was about to ask her who she really was when another mournful wail came from behind them. This time it sounded much closer, but again when he turned around there was nothing there. Slowly he let out a breath. He had not even realised he was holding it.

When he turned back around his heart nearly jumped from his chest. Floating about a dozen paces in front of him was a ghostly apparition. The female figure glowed white. Her face was shredded, as was the tattered dress she wore. As he looked down her spectral form he saw that she had no legs. He cringed at the thought of how she must have died.

"Be careful Bern," Cayley warned. "That's a wraith."

He already knew what it was. It was said that wraiths had once been people who had died a terrible death. Their spirit had been trapped and they were destined to wail their way through the Seven Kingdoms until they eventually found peace. It didn't look like the one floating before them was going to find peace anytime soon.

Slowly, not wanting to cause a reaction, Bern unsheathed his sword. He didn't know why, but he knew that wraiths were afraid of steel.

It wouldn't kill it, it was already dead, but it would be enough to drive it away. With his left hand he gently pushed Cayley behind him. She made no effort to stop him.

The wraith made no attempt to attack Bern and he made no move forward. She let out another wail and waited for Bern to respond.

"What's it doing?" Bern asked.

"It looks as though it doesn't want to attack us. Maybe it wants something else," Cayley suggested.

"Do you think it wants us to help it?"

As if in answer to his question there was another wail, this time from behind. Bern didn't need to turn around to know there was another wraith floating behind him. He relied on Cayley to make sure it didn't come within striking distance.

"It seems that it was waiting for backup," Cayley offered.

Against his better judgement Bern glanced over his shoulder. As he expected he saw another spectral figure floating towards them. This time it was male. His phantom clothes were tattered like its counterpart and it was missing a left arm. It stopped, but made no move to attack.

"I don't like this!" Bern whispered.

"I think you're right," Cayley replied as another wail came. "It seems as though they're communicating with each other. I think it would be wise if we leave now."

Bern didn't need to be told twice, but as he tried to leave the female looking wraith moved to block their path as the male kept pace behind them. When Bern took a step forward the female floated backwards. They made no move to advance but would not let Bern gain or lose any distance on them.

"I guess that isn't going to work," Bern sighed.

"At least they haven't attacked us. Maybe you were right and they do want help."

"Either that or they are still waiting for the right time to attack." Bern didn't think they were friendly, nor did he think they wanted assistance.

"Do you have anything to fight with?"

"I'll be able to hold my own," it was a cryptic response.

Bern wasn't sure exactly what she meant, but he didn't have time to question her. The two wraiths wailed simultaneously followed by another cry. A third wraith wailed before appearing on their left hand side. This one looked as though it had been a child when it had died. Bern couldn't tell if it had been a boy or a girl. Its face was indistinguishable and there was no hair. Bern guessed the child had died in a fire.

"If we stay here much longer I believe we are going to become surrounded," there was a touch of fear in Cayley's voice.

Bern knew she was right, but there didn't seem to be anything they could do about it. Whenever they moved the group of wraiths moved with them. It was as if they were in complete synchronization.

"If you have any suggestions I would surely like to hear them." Bern did his best to keep the frustration out of his voice.

Cayley thought for a moment, but there was no response. As long as the wraiths were out of reach there was nothing they could do.

"Let's make our way to the gate. There is steel around the it and the wraiths won't be able to back into it."

"Are you sure that's a good idea?" Bern whispered, although he wasn't even sure the wraiths could understand him. "Do we really want to force a battle?"

"Wraiths hate steel and light. The closer we get to the city the more of both we'll have," Cayley spoke normally, not caring if the wraiths could hear her.

"Do you think the city watch will help us?"

"Doubtful," Cayley replied. "But you never know. Either way it has to be better than just waiting for them to attack. We have no idea how many more are out here."

As if to answer, they heard the wraiths wail again and a fourth joined the trio. Bern braced himself for an attack, but they made no move. It seemed they were still happy just to surround them. As much as Bern wasn't sure of Cayley's plan he didn't have any other ideas. He hoped the entity would give him some assistance, but it seemed to have disappeared into the back of his consciousness.

The two started slowly at first, just to make sure the wraiths remained at a distance. When they were comfortable they weren't going to be attacked they picked up the pace. As much as Bern wasn't sure they were doing the right thing he wanted to see the result. His nerves were on edge and he had bad feeling it was exactly what the wraiths wanted.

As they neared the Southern Gate he realised there were no lit torches along the wall. The glow from the wraiths gave enough light to see a few paces all around, but outside of that it was completely dark. That made Bern even more nervous.

Just before they reached the gate, Bern stopped. He had to grab Cayley by the shoulder to stop her from continuing. He noticed the wraiths were focused on him. They didn't waver as Cayley took a step closer. He thought about letting her walk through the gap between them, but he didn't want to risk anything.

"Are you sure this is the right thing to do?" Bern asked.

"No, but what other option do we have." There was something reassuring with her honesty.

Slowly Bern took a step forward and the wraith floated back towards the gate. It seemed as though the spirit didn't know what they were planning. It wasn't until his next step, when it touched a steel strap on the gate, that it realised what was happening. A wisp of smoke drifted from its back as it wailed, this time in pain.

The noise should have been enough to alert the guards on night duty, but there was no movement from the wall. If there was any thought that they would receive assistance from within the city, it was all gone. Whatever they were going to do, they would have to do on their own.

When Bern realised there was not going to be any help, he moved into action. Taking two quick steps forward, he slashed at the wraith. His sword passed straight through, leaving behind a stream of smoke. Not a scratch was left behind, but Bern hadn't expected one.

The wraith screeched in pain, but made no move to attack. Whatever the wraiths had in mind it seemed that killing them wasn't it. The other three wraiths kept their distance as Bern continued to slash at the first. After another three passes the wraith wailed and then disappeared. As much as Bern hoped he had destroyed it he knew he hadn't.

With the first wraith safely gone he turned to face the others. He retreated until his back was against the gate. He felt more comfortable knowing nothing would come from behind. The three wraiths remained at the same distance and didn't seem concerned at the disappearance of their partner.

"What do you want?" Bern asked out of frustration.

The male reached out his arm and pointed to the east. Bern stared for a moment, stunned to have received a response. He looked to the east and the wraith was also pointing out along the wall.

"Should we see what it wants?" Bern asked.

"I don't see that we have any other choice," Cayley replied.

Bern shrugged his shoulders and walked towards the fourth wraith, another indistinguishable child. He cringed to think at who would be callous enough to burn children alive. He knew if they were burnt post-mortem then it would not affect the wraith's appearance. The thought made him angry.

The wraith kept the same distance as Bern approached and it wasn't until they reached their destination, that it stopped moving. Bern almost stumbled into it before he was able to recover.

Bern looked around to see why they had stopped. They were at a fairly nondescript location along the city wall. Bern walked closer to investigate, but before he came close enough the three wraiths wailed. He stopped what he was doing and looked at them. They were pointing to a place away from the wall. The light they gave didn't carry far enough for

Bern to see what it was and a feeling of dread passed over him as he slowly started to walk forward.

After a dozen paces, he came across a sight that made his heart jump. Shallow graves had been dug as far as the eye could see. He stopped before he reached the first grave and the wraiths wailed at him again. They had not reached their destination, but Bern was not willing to walk into the makeshift graveyard. He had a bad feeling that he didn't want to know what was waiting for him.

When it was clear Bern wasn't going to proceed on his own the three wraiths started to edge forward. Bern thought about attacking them with his sword, but decided against it. There was obviously something they wanted to show him and he knew it was important. Slowly he started to follow the male wraith through the graves.

Eventually the child stopped and the other two wraiths moved to float behind other graves. The other childlike wraith floated behind the grave next to the other child. The next grave remained empty with the male wraith floating behind the one beside it. Bern figured that the empty grave must belong to the female.

"What do I do know?" Bern asked Cayley.

"I think they want you to dig up their graves," Cayley replied.

"With what?" Bern sounded shocked.

"There's a spade over there."

Bern had no idea how she knew it was there. The spade was just on the edge of the light and lying on top of a grave. He looked at the wraith and when it was clear it wasn't going to move he collected the spade and started digging.

The rain had softened the dirt and had not allowed it to set, even so, the drenched ground was hard to move. Bern made sure he didn't throw any of the dirt onto the grave next to it. Once he started moving the dirt, it became easier than he expected. Again he felt the entity scratching at the back of his mind, trying to take control. If there was one thing he knew, it was manual labour and he didn't need the entities assistance.

When he moved all the dirt he found a charred body on the ground. He didn't need to take a closer look to recognise that it was the body of the wraith floating before him.

He jumped slightly when he felt Cayley's hand on his arm. She gently pulled him away from the grave. He was about to speak, but the words were caught in his mouth. A tear welled in his eyes as he thought about the child before him.

"Steel yourself Bern," her words were gentle, but they sent a chill down his spine.

Cayley moved forward until she was standing by the child's feet. Bern could hardly bring himself to breathe as he waited to see what she was going to do. The feeling of dread grew in him making his legs start to wobble.

Cayley slowly rubbed her hands together before waving them in a circular motion over the child's feet. To Bern's amazement her hands started to glow, gently at first. Slowly the body started to shimmer and the charred flesh started to flake away and disappear. Within a minute the burnt skin was completely gone and a young girl wearing a floral dress lay on the ground.

Before Bern could grasp what had happened the wraith spoke, drawing his gaze. "Thank you!" When it finished speaking it slowly disappeared.

With the wraith of the girl gone the other two remaining wraiths let out a wail, but this time it was different. The sound had a hint of sorrow and longing. It almost brought tears to Bern's eyes.

What happened next stayed his grief. One after another wraiths started to appear at the head of their graves. Bern recognised the woman wraith taking her place at the head her grave, looking none the worse for his attack.

The graveyard became illuminated by the eerie lights of the wraiths. Bern looked around in awe before he remembered there was a girl in the grave before him. Despite the dread he still felt compelled to look.

The girl had soft brown hair covering her face and her arm rested peacefully against her chest. Bern knelt beside the grave and softly brushed the hair away from her face. This time the tears came unbidden and there was nothing he could to stop them, even if he wanted to. His hand trembled as he lifted his dead daughter to his chest. Without a care for any repercussions he lifted his head and screamed at the top of his voice. His wail was echoed by all the wraiths surrounding him. Cayley used all her willpower not to break down and cry. The sudden revelation was devastating to Bern and he would need her support, especially since there was more to come.

Bern stayed and rocked his daughter back and forth for a minute before he finally let her go. His reaction took Cayley by surprise. After he had laid his daughter back on the ground he grabbed the shovel and jumped to his feet. He moved to the next grave. He didn't need to move the dirt to know it was his son, another burnt corpse. He couldn't even remember putting the spade in the ground before all the dirt had been removed.

Cayley didn't wait for him to speak. Once Bern had taken a step backwards she moved into action. Like the first time she waved her hands over the body making them glow. The charred skin started to flake away and soon enough a young boy's body remained.

At first Bern couldn't bring himself to look, but in the end he knew he had to. Lying before him was the body of his son Jonathan. Slowly he knelt down and cradled him against his chest. The tears flowed and Bern wasn't sure if they were ever going to stop. In his worst nightmares he couldn't think of losing one of his children let alone two. When he started his journey he wasn't sure if he would ever return to his family, but he never thought they would die before him.

When the tears finally subsided, Bern let his son rest upon the cold ground. He could hardly bring himself to stand, knowing what was waiting for him.

Cayley had already moved to the next grave, but she waited for Bern to remove the dirt. He knew his wife was buried beneath the mound and he knew it was his responsibility to unveil her. As he lifted the spade the field of wraiths wailed, reflecting his sorrow. The sound washed over him as he started to dig. Time seemed to stand still as the dirt slowly started to move. Before Bern knew what had happened the body had been uncovered. He couldn't bring himself to look upon her corpse. The memory of the wraith's appearance was thick in his mind and he didn't want the image of his wife replacing it.

Realising what Bern was doing moved Cayley into action. The slashed body was a lot easier to heal than that of the charred ones. It wasn't until Cayley touched his arm did Bern bring himself to look upon his wife's corpse. For a moment he couldn't bring himself to move, but eventually he knelt down beside her.

As Bern cradled his dead wife he felt the entity scratching at the back of his mind. If only he had let go earlier he wouldn't be suffering the loss he felt. Slowly Bern started to let go. He didn't have the energy to fight anymore. The entity could take control for all he cared, it could take control forever. With his family gone he had nothing to live for. With each passing second he could feel himself slipping away. He knew that this time he wasn't coming back and he didn't care. As the darkness crept over him he welcomed the sweetness of death. Soon he would be united with his family and that was all he cared about.

"Are you going to be alright Bern?" Cayley finally asked when he came to his feet.

"Bern is gone," Heryion had returned, although Cayley knew him by his true name.

"You're finally back!" Cayley wrapped her arms around him in joy. Despite the tragedy that lay before them she was happy.

"There will be time for that later," Heryion said as he gently pushed her away. "We need to set these poor souls free before sunrise."

In response to his words the wraiths wailed. There was no fear in their screams. There was something peaceful about their cries. There was no malice and no fear in them.

Chapter 35: Asgard and Esgard

The sun was starting the rise as the two made their way back to the farmhouse. They quickened their pace as they knew it wouldn't be long before the soldiers started to rise. Bern had told them to enter the city if they hadn't returned, but that had been a mistake. Something was terribly wrong in the city and they didn't think the army would be of any use.

With Bern gone the entity referred to itself as Heryion. It was how he had known himself for many years. That would soon change now that he had found his partner.

Heryion and Cayley were able to clean the graveyard and free the wraiths. It had been a tough job and they both felt exhausted, but there was no time for rest. There was too much work to do and little time to do it.

When they returned to the farmhouse they found the soldiers and elves assembled out the front. It looked as though they were ready to march.

"Looks like we made it just in time," Heryion whispered.

"Thank the God Kings that you've returned," Elyas greeted them.

"When the sun rose we feared for the worst," Duke Hadar added.

"What happened?" Ulman couldn't wait to ask the question.

As much as Heryion knew the question was coming he had hoped it wouldn't. There was little time for explanation, but they needed to know. Slowly Heryion started to recall the previous night's events and they all listened intently.

"So that's what was taking the adults?" Lord Pernian asked. The elf seemed the most concerned with what had occurred.

Heryion had to think for a moment. As much as he didn't really think that was the case he decided not to share his fears. "I believe so. It would seem that the wraiths didn't want to be alone."

Cayley shot him a strange look, but didn't say anything. She knew the wraiths weren't involved in the intrigue, but she had to trust he knew what he was doing.

"So now we need to get into the city. I'm sure the duke will want to know what's been happening," Elyas suggested.

"Cayley and I will see the duke. I have another task for you. There are a lot of bodies that need a decent burial."

"Surely you will need our help inside the city, general. We don't know what things are like in there. It could be dangerous," Hadar protested.

"That's why it will be better if it's just Cayley and I. We can move around unnoticed. A group of soldiers and elves would be too conspicuous." That wasn't the real reason, but it seemed to appease the group. "And we can't leave these bodies out to rot. It won't be long before the crows start circling and that's no way for these good people to end up."

It was clear there would be no arguing with him and his words did make sense. As much as the soldiers would prefer an open battle they would follow their orders. Heryion was hoping that the task would keep them busy until it was time to leave.

"Shall we join you in the city when we're done?" Hulkan asked.

"Not yet. When you are done return to the farmhouse. We will meet you back here."

There was a moment of silence before Ulman finally spoke. "How long should we wait for you?"

Heryion hadn't considered how long it would take them to achieve their goal. He didn't really know what they were trying to achieve.

"If we're not back in two days then you need to move on Remidia. The army will be arriving soon and they will need your help."

No one looked happy, but it was clear that their general had made his decision. They would have to do the work of labourers whilst Bern and a child did the work of trained soldiers.

"What shall we do with all the children? What should we tell them?" Dorn asked before they dispersed.

It was another question that Heryion didn't want to answer. There was a good chance that all their parents were somewhere in the grave site and he couldn't trust anyone in the city to take care of them. For the moment they would have to remain in the farming community. He just hoped there was enough food for them to survive until he could sort things out in the city.

"They will have to remain here for now," Heryion was relieved when Cayley spoke. She had spent time with the other children and would have a better idea what to do with them. "Their parents are all dead and I don't think we want to tell them yet."

"They will start to ask questions soon," Hadar protested.

"Just tell them that we're looking into the disappearance of their parents and will let them know when we have more information. The dangers in the night have gone, but for now they will all need to stay in the barn."

Despite the confidence in Cayley's words everyone looked to Bern for a definitive answer. It seemed like as good an idea as any so Heryion nodded his head. All he wanted was for the soldiers to leave so he could speak with Cayley. It had been a long time since they had been together.

When it was clear the nod was all the response they were going to get, the group broke off. Heryion led Cayley into the farmhouse, the night's work had been exhausting and they both needed something to eat. As much as he wasn't hungry he knew the body he inhabited needed sustenance. With Bern finally gone it would take a while for his body to adjust, but soon enough he wouldn't need to sleep or eat as much. Until then he would need to keep the body strong. Sleep would be useful, but there was no time.

Inside the farmhouse the two busied themselves finding something to eat. The command group had almost cleared the cupboards, but they found enough for a meagre breakfast. It wasn't until they were seated around the dining table did they speak.

"Where have you been all this time Asgard?" Cayley used his true name for the first time.

"I could ask you the same question, Esgard?" Asgard smiled as he spoke.

"How long has it been? One century, two?" she returned with a similar smile.

"What is time to the likes of us? One century or one millennium, the main point is that we've found each other just in time."

"True. I was worried when I lost my last body that I wouldn't see you again and this has all been for nothing. I was a washer woman for a long time in Oldtown in Entero. It was a fairly innocuous lifestyle. I figured that's where I would finally meet you after all these years, but then my body failed suddenly and I was sent adrift. My spirit drifted towards Remidel and the sensation of that's where I belonged grew even stronger. I knew then that's where I needed to be, but as I was passing by Zenza City I was suddenly sucked into this body, the body of a child. I had a terrible feeling that I had been taken off my true course and I would never find you. Despite being a child her mind was strong and no matter what I tried I couldn't take control of her. I tried to leave, but there was nothing I could do to escape. When things started to go wrong in the city I figured that I couldn't abandon the other children and here we are. It wasn't until you arrived that I was able to control her and now she's gone."

Asgard knew there was much more to the story, as there was with his, but there was no time to dwell on the past. He would need to share his story with her and then they had to gain access to the city.

"I found myself the body of a jester travelling the Seven Kingdoms with a group of entertainers. His life was aloof and it was the perfect guise for me to take. His mind was weak and it didn't take me long to gain control. I don't think anyone missed me when I left the troupe on our way between Remidel and Lel Dinion. I was drawn to the Cloumid Mountains where I thought I would find the Chosen One. Instead I found a follower of the Evil One. He was a dark wizard with more power than I expected. At this stage I thought I was drawn there to destroy him, but that wasn't the case. He caught me by surprise and trapped me in a magic box. It was there I waited for... I have no idea how long. Time had no meaning in that box. No matter what I tried I couldn't break free. It wasn't until the Chosen One and his group travelled through the mountain that I was freed."

"So the time has finally come," Esgard interrupted in awe. "As the years slipped away I didn't think we'd ever get a chance to fulfil our destiny."

When he was sure she was finished Asgard continued his story. "I was surprised to learn that Alaric had already gained the Ruby stone. Things had progressed further than I thought and the fact that we hadn't found each other by then had me greatly concerned." Asgard paused to finish his breakfast. "I travelled with him for a short while before I had to leave on a different task, knowing that I would return when I was needed."

"Surely you would have needed to travel with him when you found him? That is one of the tasks that was assigned to us." Esgard interrupted again.

It was an annoying habit of hers, Asgard recalled, but with all that had happened he couldn't blame her.

"I knew I was doing what was right. There was a group travelling with Alaric and they would be able to get him to his destination, or at least as far as he could go without me. I met him outside the City of Night and helped him to the top of *Crenallous*. It was there that Nyrra was able to separate me from my body. I underestimated his power and even though he was only in spectral form he was able to defeat me, but I had achieved what I needed to so it didn't really matter. It was from there that I made my way into Bern. I should have realised when I met the group that he was who I needed to be, but I was too focused on the task in front of me. It would seem that my task wasn't to stay with the Chosen One, but to assist Bern in becoming the General of the Alliance. His will was strong, but at the start it was easy to take control of him when I needed to. Eventually, as my memories merged with his, he was able to work some things out for himself and eventually he was able to block me from taking control. Now that his family is dead he has let go. His spirit is no longer in this body."

Asgard had been concerned when Bern had found Cayley and not let him take control. No matter what he tried he could do nothing, but watch. As much as he was sad for Bern's loss he was glad to now have complete control. He still had a lot of work to do but things would now be much easier.

"For now I think it would be best if you call me Bern and I call you Cayley. If we use our real names then it will raise too many questions. With the Council of Wizards now travelling with the army I'm sure at least one of them will recognise who we are," Asgard explained.

Esgard nodded her head in agreement. Their next problem was trying to explain why a young girl was travelling at the head of an army. Asgard had yet to think up a good excuse and Esgard hadn't mentioned anything. There was still time to work that out, but for now there was a greater task at hand.

"Now I think we should see what is happening inside the city," Asgard suggested. "I think with our current guises that I should be the father and you should be my daughter."

"You've been waiting for this for a long time, haven't you?" She couldn't keep the smile from her face as she spoke. "But I'm not sure I really look like your daughter."

"I'm sure no one will take too much notice. With all the refugees through the city I doubt anyone will really care about us."

"But it doesn't seem like they've been letting any of the refugees in. At a guess most, if not all, are in those shallow graves."

Asgard knew that she had a good point. There was a chance that there were no other refugees in the city.

"Maybe we could be merchants or even nobles?" Esgard suggested.

Asgard looked at the clothes he was wearing and really didn't think he would pass as either, although it was a much better idea. They would be less conspicuous if they could blend in with the others in the city. Suddenly he remembered that Bern did have some finery in his pack. As much as Bern never liked wearing fine clothes the others insisted that he always brought some with him.

He quickly changed into a deep purple doublet with black trousers and a black coat. Although the sun had met them first thing in the morning, clouds had now moved in and it had become cool outside.

Esgard changed out of the clothes she wore the night before and found herself a dress of matching purple. There was also a small silver necklace she found on the dresser. She thought if she was going to look the part then she should wear some jewellery. Asgard wasn't overly impressed when he saw her, but he kept his comments to himself.

"I don't think that sword will be appropriate," Esgard pointed at Bern's large broadsword.

"I won't need a weapon, you know that." Asgard had no intention of wearing it.

"But if we're going to keep up appearances you should wear something," she retorted.

Asgard sighed before returning to the room where all their possessions were on the floor. He rifled through them all until he came across a rapier that looked like it would do the job. He wasn't sure whose it was and hoped it wouldn't be missed. Either way he knew they had to return before they left for Remidel. Despite what he had thought his original task was, he was still the General of the Alliance and that's where he needed to be. He was sure he would also meet up with Alaric again before it was all over.

"Okay, how does that look?"

"You look like a merchant." She paused and thought. "One that has been out on the road anyway, that beard of yours is starting to look messy."

It had been a long time since Bern had the chance to shave properly and his facial hair had grown into something that resembled a beard.

"I don't have time to shave, they'll just have to deal with it," Asgard sounded offended.

"Then it's a good thing I'm here," Esgard grinned as she spoke.

She climbed onto a chair so she could stand face to face with him. He shot her questioning look that she brushed aside. Slowly she waved her hands over his face. Asgard felt a warm sensation and when she had finished his facial hair was completely gone.

"I'm not sure that was a great idea. We expended a lot of energy last night and I have a bad feeling we're going to need a lot more later today," Asgard scolded her.

Esgard simply smiled and kissed him on the cheek. "Now that's much better," she said as she jumped down before he could swat her.

"Okay, playtime is over. Let's get ourselves into the city. Remember from here on we should refer to each other as Bern and Cayley."

"Yes sir!" she saluted.

Bern shook his head. He should have known better. Instead of a retort he just started for the door. They had already spent too much time in the farmhouse, it was time to find out what was happening in the city.

It was late in the morning when they reached the gate. It was shut tight and it looked as though no one was around.

"So how do you want to do this?" Cayley asked.

"I guess we should try and get in the old fashioned way first. We don't want to expend any more energy than we need to." Bern walked to the gate and banged three times before stepping back.

The same archers door opened as before, but it was a different man who poked his head out. He looked at the two and studied them carefully before he spoke. "The city is closed. You need to leave." He paused and looked back inside before speaking again. "Things aren't safe here. You're better to head for the capital."

He was about to close the door again, but something made him pause. The guard looked back inside to make sure he was still alone before he returned his attention to the two below.

"What is it you want?"

"We need access to the city," Bern spoke slowly. "There is something important we need to do inside."

The guard simply stared down and didn't respond. It seemed as though Bern's words were not having their affect, but at least the guard was willing to listen to them.

"My father and I have important business in the city," Cayley used her best little girl's voice. "It is cold and scary outside the city walls. Last night we heard terrible wails and I couldn't sleep. I was ever so frightened. Please, kind sir, let us into the city."

The guard thought for a moment before he spoke. "I have heard tales of the wails in the night, but I am yet to hear them myself. From what I've been told they are enough to scare the strongest of men, but I still think it is safer for you to continue your journey. My captain will be here soon and if he sees the two of you then he is likely to kill you." To accentuate his point he looked over his shoulder again.

"We know of your troubles and we have come to help you." Bern thought he would give it a try. "We can't leave until we have solved your situation."

The guard looked perplexed. It was not the response he was looking for. There was something very strange about the pair. At first he thought they were father and daughter, but the more they spoke the less sure he was. The entire situation didn't seem right, but he couldn't bring himself to leave. It made no sense how two people could be at the gate without horses to carry them. It also seemed strange that two people who looked like merchants would try and enter the city without any cargo.

"Please, it is cold and frightening out here. Let us in the city," Cayley was almost whimpering.

"Of course. I will have the gate opened at once for you." The guard quickly shut the door and moved into action.

"I really wished you hadn't done that," Bern scolded her. "We have no idea what is ahead of us, but I know we'll need all our strength."

"It was either that or we stay out here. There was no way he was going to let us into the city without a little tampering. It's taken much less energy than if we were to pass through the wall or worse, make a hole."

Although she had a valid point Bern was still not happy. He was sure there was a tough test ahead of them. Ever since they had reached the gate he'd had a bad feeling there was someone powerful inside.

"You have been alone too long. You forget that we are two again and our power is strong. Whatever is waiting for us we will be victorious."

Bern had to admit that she was right. Ever since he had been defeated by Nyrra he had been having doubts about his own power. Now that he had been united with Cayley there was much more he would be able to achieve, maybe even destroy the Evil One.

The first sign that they had achieved their goal was the grinding sound of the portcullis. Time seemed to stand still until the right hand gate was finally pushed open. The guard only opened it enough for the two to squeeze through. He poked his head around the corner before returning inside.

"Hurry up. If anyone sees me letting you in then I will lose my job, at best. At worst I will be flogged," fear was thick in his voice.

Bern and Cayley hurried through the gate and under the small gap in the portcullis. Bern had to duck slightly to avoid scraping his head against the spiked ends. When they were through the gate the guard moved quickly to close it, but when he moved to the wheel to lower the portcullis a gruff voice barked from behind them.

"Private Radclyffe! What do you think you're doing?" his voice boomed. "You know the duke has forbidden the gates to be opened. No one is allowed into the city." He drew his short sword as he spoke.

Radclyffe looked at the two, as if for the first time, and a confused expression fell on his face. He knew he had opened the gate for them, but he had no idea why. He looked from the captain back to Bern, hoping one of them would give him answers.

"Well Private? I'm waiting."

"I... They were outside and they needed to come in. They have important business in the city," was all he could say.

"I don't know how you convinced the private to open the gate for you, but now you have to convince me. If I don't like the story you tell you will be hanging from the gates to warn the next couple who try."

Cayley took a step forward, but Bern restrained her by placing a hand on her shoulder. She wasn't happy with what the captain was insinuating and he didn't want her causing any problems. There was chance they would need to fight, but if he could avoid it then he would. The last thing he wanted was to announce their arrival by fighting.

"We are here on very important business. We must see the duke straight away," Bern's voice was full of confidence.

"That's funny. I'm sure the duke would have sent word if he was expecting visitors."

It was a common response and one that Bern was prepared for. He thought it would be great if one day they were welcomed with open arms, but he doubted that would happen anytime soon. They were only drawn to cities controlled by the Evil One's agents.

"Of course if the duke knew we were coming then he wouldn't need to hear the news we bring. That is why we must see him immediately."

The captain didn't know how to respond. He knew the words made sense, but he also knew what waited for him if he was wrong. They had been told that under no circumstances was anyone to be admitted into the city, by punishment of death. If the two were false then his life was over and even if they weren't his life was not guaranteed.

"Then why don't you tell me your news and I'll decide on whether the duke will want to hear it." The captain was pleased with himself.

"The information I have is for the duke himself. If the wrong people hear it then it could be disastrous," Bern continued his ruse.

The captain snarled and took a menacing step forward. Bern's hand went to the hilt of his rapier, not that he thought it would be much use against the short sword.

"I'll give you one more chance and then I'll be forced to kill you."

"Very well, but it'll be your life on the line if the information get's out." Bern paused, hoping his words might change the captain's mind, but when it was clear they didn't he continued. "There is a hostile army approaching the capital. King Faxon has sent us here to gain help from the duke. The army will be on them any day now and time is of the essence. The king has demanded that the duke send his entire army to help defend his city." It wasn't a complete lie and with a little luck they would have heard of the Alliance's approach on Remidel.

The captain didn't know what to think. The answer was not at all what he was expecting. With all the turmoil in the Seven Kingdoms it was plausible that Remidel was under a potential attack. On the other hand the duke had been quite specific about not letting anyone in the city.

"What do you think, Private?" he asked when he realised Radclyffe had remained silent for too long.

"I don't know captain," Radclyffe was surprised at the question. "I think you should take them to see the duke. We can't ignore a command from the king.'

The captain thought for a moment. The last thing he wanted to do was see the duke. Then an idea came to him. "You're right Private. You should take them to the palace immediately and let them explain why you let them into the city." All responsibility would now fall on Radclyffe.

The captain would avoid all reprisals; at least that was what he was hoping. "Why are you still standing there? Move!"

"Yes... yes captain." Radclyffe saluted before motioning Bern and Cayley to follow him.

The Southern Quarter was strangely empty. Being the poorest part of the city it was normally filled with beggars and thieves pestering those going about their business. The only people on the streets were soldiers dressed in Ducal Guard uniforms.

"Aren't there normally more people in the streets at this time of day?" Bern thought the journey would be more pleasant if they made conversation.

"There used to be and then the duke decided to clear out the streets in the Southern Quarter. Since the gates were shut to the outside there seemed little point in allowing people through this area of the city. Without the trade passing through it is now mainly just criminals and paupers."

Before they could travel too far they were stopped by a group of bored looking soldiers. Bern was sure they were just looking for something to do, but it did nothing to ease his nerves. Ever since they had left the gate he had a feeling that something bad was about to happen.

"Where do you think you're going?" the soldier's voice was dripping with arrogance.

"I am taking these two to see the duke. They have important information from..."

"We have important information for the duke's ears only," Bern interrupted before Radclyffe could give away too much information. Until he knew exactly who was in charge of the city he didn't want the information to get out.

"Well then, let's hear this important information and we'll decide if it's worth you bothering the duke." As he spoke the other soldiers encircled the group.

"Do you really think that we would let these two through the gates if the information wasn't important?" Radclyffe thought he was doing the right thing, but he was mistaken.

Hearing that they had been allowed into the city made all the soldiers draw their swords and level them at Bern and Cayley. No one made any move to attack, but they were ready to strike at any moment.

"No one is allowed through the gates. You have just signed your own death warrant, along with theirs," despite his words the soldier made no move forward.

Bern wanted to see what Cayley was doing, but he didn't want to lose eye contact with the soldier. He had a bad feeling if he did then they would attack. Even with their powers he doubted they would be able to stop all the soldiers at such a short distance, at least not unless they struck first.

"You don't think I know that," Radclyffe's voice was strangely powerful. "Of course we wouldn't have opened the gates unless it was of the utmost importance. These two bring a message directly from King Faxon and have been instructed only to tell the duke."

"And how do you know this is true?" the soldier didn't sound appeased.

"To gain entrance into the city we insisted that they tell me what the information is, do you honestly think we would let them into the city without knowing what it was? I deemed the information to be worthy of seeing the duke."

The soldier took a step backwards, but wasn't completely convinced. "That still doesn't explain why you let them into the city. Surely you could have just sent them on their way and relayed the information yourself. No, something isn't right here."

Both Radclyffe and Cayley sighed at the same time. Bern knew that she was manipulating the Private again, but there was no other option. The soldiers wouldn't believe their tale and only through Radclyffe could they gain entrance to the see the duke.

"Do you really think the duke would believe me if I came knocking on his door?" Radclyffe paused and then let his question sink in. "Of course not. Now I don't think the duke will be overly pleased if he finds out you have delayed the king's messenger. How do you think he'll react?"

The threat hit its mark and it clearly showed on the soldier's face. The others didn't look so confident anymore either. The confidence in the Private's voice had them taken aback. The duke's guards didn't have any respect for the soldiers who guarded the gates. Normally the Gate Watch deferred all decisions to the duke's guards, but there was something different about the Private before them. He had a confidence that didn't match his position. The last thing the soldiers wanted to do was to lose face and the longer they remained in conversation, the greater that chance was.

"Very well. We have more important things to do." The soldier scoffed before he indicated to the others to leave them.

"Like guard an empty street?" Cayley grumbled when they were out of earshot. She didn't appreciate their arrogant attitude. Any other time she would have given them a lesson in humility, but she knew Bern would get angry with her.

"What just happened?" Radclyffe asked.

"We just had a run in with some of the duke's guards, but they decided that we were right to continue," Bern explained quickly.

Radclyffe seemed to accept the answer without question. He just wanted to get them to the duke and then leave. His life was on the line and he didn't want to wait any longer than he had to figure out his fate. There was something very strange about the two messengers and he just wanted to get as far away from them as he could.

Suddenly the buildings around them changed as they entered the Merchants Quarter. The shabby single storey buildings became two storey stone houses and the streets became much wider and cleaner.

As they walked through the streets they noticed few people outside. Like the Southern Quarter the duke's guard patrolled the streets. The citizens looked very nervous and they moved at a quick pace, keeping their heads down.

"What is happening here?" Cayley asked finally.

"The streets are not safe to be walked these days. The duke has proclaimed that anyone loitering is to be arrested on the spot. It's a move to avoid any further conflict in the city," Radclyffe explained as if it was a perfectly reasonable order.

Cayley and Bern looked at each other. If there was any doubt before there was no question that something was seriously wrong with the duke. The only question was what.

The duke's estate was situated on the border of the Merchants, or Eastern, Quarter and the Northern Quarter. The Northern Quarter housed the city's elite. Only the richest of families could afford houses there. A red brick wall encircled the duke's estate. It was more for decoration than keeping the anyone out. An ornamental iron gate on the northern side was the only entrance and a dozen guards stood blocking it.

"Go away!" was all the lead soldier said.

Bern had had enough of the negative responses they were receiving. The day was starting to slip away and he had no time for another useless conversation. He would allow Radclyffe to attempt to gain entrance whilst he worked out his next plan of action.

"We are here on important business to see the duke. Let us pass now or you will be in serious trouble." Radclyffe stood tall as he spoke.

"I said go away and I mean go away. The duke has given us specific instructions that no one is to be admitted today."

Bern had a bad feeling that the duke knew they were coming. That changed everything. He had hoped to be able to gauge the situation before revealing himself, but it looked like he wouldn't get the chance. If the duke did know who they were then there was no point in hiding their abilities.

Radclyffe was about to speak again, but Bern stepped forward. "I'll take care of this."

"I don't want to tell you..." the solider started, but didn't get to finish his statement.

"You go to sleep now," Bern said and then the soldiers all dropped to the ground.

"What have you done?" Radclyffe asked in horror.

"We have no time for this. They are simply asleep. They will wake up shortly and have no recollection of our visit."

Cayley gave Bern a stern look. He had chided her for using her abilities to gain entrance into the city and get past the first group of soldiers. What she had expended was nothing compared to what Bern had just done. Her power was just as great as his, but it seemed as though he was taking their current facades to heart. He was acting the parental figure a little too much for her liking. Despite the fact that she had tried to leave the body of the little girl, there was nothing she could do. It seemed the Prophecy wanted them to remain as they were.

"Let's go!" Bern exclaimed.

As they stepped through the gates a feeling of dread filled Bern; it was almost enough to make him turn around and run. He had a bad feeling they were about to walk into a trap, but there was nothing they could do, and way they could turn back.

Chapter 36: An Old Enemy

Unlike the rest of the city, the duke's estate was a hive of activity, yet it was not at all what they expected. Young men and woman lazed around the fore-garden with their shirts off. Bern's initial reaction was the cover Cayley's eyes, but he refrained. She would not appreciate being treated like a child and the things she had seen over the years would put their current situation to shame. Radclyffe was the only one who seemed concerned with what they saw.

Along with the topless men and women there were naked children playing amongst the many fruit trees. There were apple, orange and peach trees. Despite the time of year the trees were full of fruit. Not only that, but the temperature was considerably warmer inside the grounds of the estate. The entire situation was disturbing.

The three walked towards the main building. Although not as impressive as some of the palaces in the Seven Kingdoms the house was unique in its own right. Sandstone had been shipped up from Castalia, at a great expense to the Duchy. The two storey building spanned the width of the estate and the roof was lined with archer's perches in case of an attack.

On any other occasion they would have marvelled at such a building in the middle of Remidia, but all they could think about was the task at hand. Radclyffe lead them towards the main double doors, leaving Bern and Cayley walking behind. Although there didn't seem to be any guards around they didn't want to risk it. It would be much more plausible with the Private in the lead.

No one seemed to take any notice of the three as they made their way towards the house. As Bern looked around he thought they all looked like they were in a trance. The feeling of dread increased as they neared the entrance.

The double doors leading into the estate were normally protected by at least two guards, but this time they weren't.

"Something isn't right here," Radclyffe stated when they reached the doors.

"You're only just figuring that out?" Cayley's tone was dripping with sarcasm.

Radclyffe looked at Bern who just shook his head before he replied. "You need to be prepared for danger."

The private nodded before he opened the left hand door. Despite his concerns when they started their journey he was prepared to see things through to the end. He could sense that the pair was good at heart and he felt compelled to help them, no matter what awaited them inside.

On the other side of the door they were met by an empty foyer. Large marble columns ostentatiously held up the ceiling. A vast expanse, which was normally filled up by various dignitaries and servants, was completely empty. At the other end of the foyer was a large set of stairs and on either side were sets of doors.

"Which way should we go?" asked Cayley.

"I've never been in the duke's estate before. I have no idea where he'd be at this time of day." Bern replied.

As if in answer to the question a man appeared at the top of the stairs. He was dressed entirely in black, unlike the duke's normal retinue, with a black tunic, black stockings and black velvet slippers. When he saw the three he slowly and deliberately descended the stairs. The group waited at the door for him to approach.

The first thing Bern noticed was the glazed look in his eyes and the blank expression on his face. There was also something about the way he moved that was very rigid. There didn't seem to be any real life to him.

"The duke has been waiting for you, follow me!" his voice was monotone.

Bern and Cayley knew there was no point in trying to speak with him. Radclyffe, on the other hand, didn't fully appreciate the situation.

"What's happening here?" Radclyffe asked.

The functionary didn't even flinch at the question. He didn't seem to notice that Radclyffe had spoken at all. The Private was about to re-ask the question, but Bern told him not to bother. There would be no response and to continue the questioning would be fruitless.

They were lead up the stairs and then taken to the right. At the end of the landing was a single, ornate, oak door. For some reason Bern didn't think they were being led towards the duke.

On the other side of the door was a long corridor with many doors on either side. The man in black led them almost half way along before opening a door on their left. Inside was a small sitting room with a coffee table in the centre and four armchairs around it.

"Wait here. The duke will be ready for you shortly," was all he said before leaving and closing the door behind him.

"What do you make of this?" Cayley asked Bern.

"There is definitely someone of power here. Who it is though I have no idea," Bern replied.

Radclyffe was listening intently although the other two didn't seem to notice he was there. It had been such a strange day that he hadn't had a chance to stop and think about who they really were. They had managed to gain entrance into the city, which had been impossible and then they managed to gain entrance to the duke's estate, which should have been even harder. Not only that, but it seemed as though they were expected. He was about ask the question, but then thought it would be better just to listen.

"Do you think it's one of Nyrra's Dark Knights?" Cayley asked.

The sound of the Evil One's name made Radclyffe choke, but he stopped himself before the others seemed to notice.

"I don't think so. There is only one Dark Knight left alive and by all account's he's in Remidia controlling King Faxon. With what's happening there I would take it as fact. No, this has to be someone or something else. It could be a serpentant. They have been coming out of the woodwork lately. We came across Sidewinder in Quinaliac. He may have made his way to the city and taken control of the duke."

"The timeline doesn't fit. I feel that whoever is in control here has been in the city for at least a month. It wouldn't make any sense for him to risk losing control to come and find you."

Cayley's words made sense and Bern didn't really think it was a serpentant. He recalled their meeting with Count Kerwin and Viper in Hondin Lel and it didn't really seem as though the serpentant was in control. As much as Bern didn't want to voice his remaining option he couldn't keep it to himself.

"It couldn't be the Evil One himself, could it?"

"What!" Radclyffe couldn't help himself. Cayley simply ignored his outburst.

"Nothing is impossible, but I highly doubt it. I'm sure he would have more important matters to deal with than trying to hold a minor city in Remidia. That and I think we'd notice his presence. Even he couldn't hide all his power from us."

Bern was about to refute her statement but thought better of it. He didn't really think Nyrra was controlling the duke and it wasn't worth the argument. That still left them with the conundrum of who was.

"You never know. The duke might just be an agent of the Evil One and no one is controlling him," Cayley suggested.

"I won't hear you speak of the duke like that!" Radclyffe jumped to his feet. "I have lived in Zenza City all my life and the duke is loved by all his citizens. If there is evil at play then it is not the duke's doing."

Cayley shook her head at the interruption and was about to scold him when Bern cut in. The Private had just taken in a lot of information and Bern felt compelled to ease his mind. The man had helped them gain access, not only into the city but into the estate and he deserved more than being left in the dark, especially since it might cost him his life.

"The Evil One is very powerful. The duke might not even realise he is under his thrall. I'm sure the duke is a good man, but there can be no doubt that something is wrong," Bern did his best to calm him.

As much as Radclyffe didn't want to believe his words there was little he could do. He knew he was no match for the pair before him and there was little to be gained from getting himself killed. If he stayed close then there was a chance he would survive and he would be able to see what was happening with the duke before he chose any sides.

"Do you think it's strange that we have been sent in here, even though the duke was expecting us?" Cayley asked as the situation started to get to her.

"I'm sure it's common for guests to have to wait for the duke," Bern replied, not really believing his own words.

"But we're not really guests now, are we?" Cayley paused for the rhetorical question to sink in. "I think we should leave. The longer we stay here the easier it will be for them to trap us."

Bern had to admit she was right. The longer they stayed the more it felt like a trap. The fact that the duke knew they were coming was bad enough. Everything was just too suspicious. It was time for them to go on the offensive again. Asgard wished he had taken control of Bern's body sooner. If he had then a Dark Knight or any agents of the Evil One wouldn't have been a problem, now it would take time before he was at full strength again.

"You can stay here if you like Radclyffe, things are about to get dangerous," Bern offered.

"Thank you, but I want to see this out to the end. You never know, I might come in handy," although he didn't really believe his words, he offered anyway.

Although the door was locked it didn't stop Bern from simply opening it. It would take more than a simple lock to keep them inside. He had half expected a spell to be blocking their path, but there was none. There was seemingly nothing to stop them from wandering freely around the estate.

"Where do you think the duke will be?" Bern asked.

"I guess we could start checking room by room," Radclyffe suggested.

"That would waste too much time. We need to start at the most logical place and that would be the large double doors at the top of the stairs. If I was to hazard a guess I would say that's the main entrance to his private chambers," Cayley replied.

It was a good place to start. It would make sense for the duke to be waiting there for them. Before they reached the end of the corridor the door opened and the servant appeared. They froze, but it seemed as though the servant didn't notice them. It wasn't until he was standing directly in front of them did he realise they were there.

"The duke is ready to see you now and apologises for keeping you waiting." He used the same monotone voice as before.

There was nothing for it but to follow him. Since they had decided to move they had hoped to catch the duke unawares, but it seemed that wouldn't be the case. The servant didn't wait for a response before turning and leading them back the way he had come. The three simply followed without speaking. Since they were heading for the same result they didn't see any point in asking any questions.

Despite their guess to go through the double doors at the top of the stairs they were led back down to the ground floor. The strange man in black took them through the door to the right side of the stairs. Instead of another hallway or a small room, they were led into a large library. Books sat on shelves along the walls, and tables and chairs were in the centre of the room. At the far end sat a man that they assumed was the duke, even Radclyffe wasn't completely sure.

That man was older than Bern had been expecting. His once chestnut hair was streaked with grey and his face was lined with fine wrinkles. He body still held all the strength from his youth and the only sign he was losing it was a small pot belly. He was dressed completely in black. Over his tunic he wore a black leather jerkin and despite the warmth of the estate he wore a long black coat.

"Duke of Zenza I presume?" Bern started, wanting to break the silence.

The duke looked up from his reading for the first time since they had entered. There seemed to be a confused expression on his face until he realised who was standing before him. When he did a smile crossed his face.

"Ah, so you must be the general I have been hearing so much about. You do look different from the last time we met."

The words were confusing to Asgard. He was sure that when Bern was in control of his own body he had never met the Duke of Zenza. He didn't even know the duke's real name. Although Bern's memories were starting to fade he knew they had never met him, which meant they had to be very careful. Whoever was behind the duke knew who he was, but he was unsure if he knew his facade or his true self.

"So I hear that you have an important message for me. I would dearly love to know what it is." An evil grin crossed his face. Clearly he knew they had nothing for him.

"There is news from the capital," Radclyffe cut in before he could stop himself.

"Oh really? I've had some interesting news from the capital myself. I would really be interested to see if yours is the same," he seemed rather pleased with himself.

Bern was still trying to figure out what was happening with the duke. There was something very familiar about the situation and it was disturbing him. It wasn't often a situation got the better of him and he would have to be extremely careful until he figured things out.

"I wouldn't think about lying to me. With one word I can have this room swarming with soldiers. No matter how good a general you are I doubt you'd be able to kill all my guards."

That was the answer to his first question. It seemed as though the duke recognised Bern, not Asgard. That gave him a subtle advantage, but it still didn't answer how he knew him. He was sure the farmer had never been to Zenza City. There had never been a memory that he could recall.

"Why have you closed off the city?" Your people are dying and you do nothing!" Bern hoped that he could avoid the original question.

The duke burst out laughing, but that only lasted for a moment. When he finished he shot Bern a pensive expression as if he was trying to work something out. Suddenly a realisation crossed his face.

"You don't know who I am, do you?" the question made him smile. "Well for now you can call me Duke Hamnet. Now I think you should answer my question."

Bern had hoped that he would gain more information, but it seemed as though his opponent was also being cautious. At least for the moment he didn't seem to notice Cayley. That was one advantage they had. If he was focused on Bern then Cayley could plan her own attack. He only hoped that she waited until he gained the information they required. Despite the feeling of dread there was also a feeling that something very important was about to happen.

Bern had to make a decision on whether the duke was just being played or whether he was indeed an agent of evil. Whatever he decided would affect the story he was about to tell. Either way he knew he couldn't lie. If he did have information from the capital then there would be no chance of duping him.

"There is an evil that is infecting Remidia and it seems that your land is no different. Not three nights ago we battled, and defeated, a horde of orglin outside of Quinaliac." Bern paused, but there was no reaction from the duke. "Arsiliac has been wiped out altogether. Your farming community outside these walls have all but been destroyed. The men and woman were turned into wraiths." Still there was no reaction, and Bern still couldn't gauge the situation. "But fear not duke, we were able to release all the wraiths last night and they will no longer haunt your city."

His last statement finally brought a reaction from the duke. A sneer crossed his face at the mention of the wraiths. It was clear that it wasn't the first time he had heard about them. Bern hoped that he could force some answers out of him, but when the duke didn't respond he knew he would have to poke a little harder.

"Oh, were they your pets? I'm so sorry. If we had known then we might not have done it." His tone was full of mockery.

"You think you're so smart don't you?" The duke stood as he yelled. "It didn't take me as long as you think to create all those wraiths. In fact once I got started they took care of themselves. It seems the citizens of this city aren't overly happy with their lives and that has nothing to do with me."

That was the answer Bern needed. The duke was gone and something else had taken control of his body. Now he had to work out who or what it was. He was sure the last remaining Dark Knight was in Remidel and a serpentant wouldn't change his appearance. No matter how hard he thought, nothing came to him. He needed to get the duke to reveal himself.

"Now I believe you have information from the capital and I would love to hear what you have to say."

Bern paused and thought how he was going to answer.

"There is a Dark Knight in the palace and he has control of the king. We figured that we would come here for help, but it seems that ship has already sailed." Bern kept his story short.

"That is very good to know. I'm sure Dargoz will be pleased to hear that his ruse is up. So I guess your next move is to send your army in against him? Speaking of which I would have thought your army would be camped outside my city with you inside. Would you care to tell me where it is? I have been looking forward to an open battle and would love to send my soldiers out to die." The smile didn't leave his face as he spoke.

Whoever had control of the duke was indeed powerful to know the real name of the remaining Dark Knight and it only proved to increase Bern's frustration. He had no idea who he was up against.

"Let's cut to the chase," Bern tried a different approach. "I'm not going to give you the location of the Alliance. Now why don't you tell me what you are doing here? This doesn't seem to be a location of much design for your master."

"You say that and yet here you are. There was a reason for me being here and I would say you have just shown me what it is. Now unless you would like to spend some time in my dungeons I think you should tell me where the Alliance is and what it is planning," Duke Hamnet ordered.

Bern couldn't shake the feeling that there was something very familiar the duke. It was really starting to irritate him. He wanted to ask Cayley if she knew anything, but he didn't want to draw any attention to her.

As much as Bern didn't want to admit it he knew the duke had a point. There was a reason why they had all been drawn together, and he needed to be the first to work it out.

"The Alliance is set to destroy the Evil One's army and that is all you need to know."

"That is a very obtuse answer, but irrelevant. We know the Alliance is marching on Remidel and that is exactly what we want it to do. Now that I have its general it will be all the weaker."

Suddenly Bern felt a tugging on his shirt sleeve. As much as he didn't want to acknowledge Cayley he couldn't ignore her.

"What?" he said, his tone harsher than he meant.

"I think we should get out of here. This is getting us nowhere."

The duke looked at Cayley, seeing her for the first time. He suddenly realised that the situation wasn't at all as it should be. The general of an army shouldn't be marching into a hostile city with a young girl.

"And what do we have here? A little girl? What game are you playing at general?"

"I think you're right. Take Radclyffe and get out of here. I can't leave until I know who we are dealing with," Bern offered.

"Don't think that I'm going anywhere without you," Cayley sounded offended.

"So there is more to this little trio than meets the eye. It seems as though I might have been led into a trap if I hadn't been so careful."

"You seem to know much about us, but we know little about you. Why don't you regale us with your tale?" Bern tried to provoke him.

The duke wasn't about to fall for such a simple ruse. He needed to know more about the strange man before him before he gave anything away.

"I think I might leave you to it," Radclyffe spoke. He could sense the tension and didn't want to remain any longer. He was a simple gate guard and he had already seen too much.

After making his statement he quickly made his way to the door, but before his hand touched the doorknob he was stopped. No matter what he tried, he couldn't move. Panic crossed his face as he was stopped by an invisible barrier. Although he didn't know what was happening the other two did and they were thankful he had just revealed another secret about the duke.

"I don't think anyone is going anywhere," the duke snarled.

Since the duke had made the first move Cayley thought she would make one of her own. The spell surrounding Radclyffe wasn't a great one and she easily broke it. When she did a grimace passed over the duke's face. Radclyffe stumbled forward, but made no further move to leave. His heart was pounding with fear and he just wanted to run and hide, but his legs wouldn't move.

"So there is more to you than meets the eye. It seems that I might have to step things up," Hamnet said.

A swirl of energy whirled around the duke. Bern and Cayley could tell there was little power in what he was planning, but they still needed to be prepared. Neither of them thought it was a sign of their opponent's strength, it seemed as though he was going to test them first.

The air wavered in front of them and slowly they were pushed backwards, without thinking Bern swatted the spell away and they were left standing still.

"It seems you have some skill," Hamnet mused. "Let's see what else you can do."

Bern prepared himself for the next attack, but Cayley wasn't going to be so passive. She was still feeling the effects of the previous night's work and the spells she had cast to get them in to the see the duke. The last thing she wanted was for her energy to be drained blocking silly little tricks.

Before Hamnet could cast his next spell he was caught in Cayley's trap. He started raising his arms when they were suddenly stopped. Cayley used a similar spell to the one Hamnet had used on Radclyffe, only much more powerful. Only his head and face could move, but there was no change to his expression.

"This has gone on for long enough. Now it is time for you to tell us who you really are!" Cayley's voice was full of command.

"I see your little kitty has claws general. Now I can understand why you brought her with you." There was no fear in Hamnet's voice. It remained as confident as ever. "I must admit that you have me perplexed though. I have never known one of your kind to be so powerful so young. It's a shame you have underestimated me."

The rhetoric was just a ruse to keep them distracted whilst he worked on removing the spell. Cayley cursed herself when he freed his arms. She felt his power and it was filled with evil. It was something she hadn't felt in a long time, but it was unmistakable.

"Something is very wrong here," she gasped.

Thunderous laughter came from the duke when he heard her words. "You are starting to see, but it's a shame your general isn't as intuitive."

"What is he talking about?" Bern asked.

"This can't be right. From what you've told me all the other Dark Knight's have been killed?" Cayley sounded confused.

"Dargoz is the only one left, why?" Bern didn't like what she was insinuating.

As much as Hamnet wanted to give him the answer he wanted to see what Cayley was going to come up with.

"This is a Dark Knight. I know it's been a long time since I have faced one, but his power is unmistakable." Cayley couldn't believe what she was saying.

With the new revelation Bern suddenly realised why Hamnet seemed so familiar. He could have kicked himself for not seeing it in the first place. He was relieved that the Dark Knight hadn't taken advantage of his oversight. Even with the upper hand Bern wasn't sure they would have been able to defend a full attack. As he thought, he quickly prepared himself for the next one.

When nothing came and it was clear that Hamnet was waiting for Bern to speak and he relaxed slightly.

"So Morgoz, you have returned."

The room fell silent as everyone soaked in Bern's statement. Only Radclyffe didn't truly appreciate what had been said. Bern had killed Morgoz himself in the Cauldron Mountain, there could be no doubt in his mind. Something very bad was happening and he didn't know what he should do.

"You are finally seeing the truth, general," Morgoz sounded smug. "Now you know where we have met before?"

"Yes and I know where I defeated you before." The confused expression on the Dark Knight's face showed Bern that he had said too much. With the realisation of who Morgoz was he had forgotten that the Dark Knight didn't really know his true identity.

Morgoz looked at him closely. He had been so focused on the general that he hadn't bothered looking any deeper. Morgoz still remembered his death, although the memory was fading. It had been when he faced off with the Cursed One. He remembered there had been someone else in the chamber, but he was sure it wasn't Bern. The man was smaller and had less of a physical presence. That was why he was able to kill him. Morgoz had not taken him as any real threat, but he wouldn't make the same mistake again. Until he could work out exactly who Bern was he would have to remain cautious.

"I have all the information I need from you. I think it's time for you to leave," Morgoz's tone became softer.

His change of tact surprised everyone. Radclyffe thought about making a run for it, but he still couldn't bring himself to move. Bern knew they had just gained the upper hand, but he didn't know how long he could keep it.

The information that Morgoz had returned, and therefore the other Dark Knights might also have returned, was of vital importance. On the other hand he couldn't leave Zenza City in control of a Dark Knight.

"I don't think we'll be the ones leaving. You have been a pox on this land and it's time you left." Bern took a menacing step forward.

"Very well, I've done all that I can do here and now I have some very interesting information for the Great Lord. I'm sure he'll be interested to know the two of you have returned." It seemed as though Morgoz had finally realised who Bern and Cayley really were.

There was a small window of opportunity and Bern needed to take it. He raised his hands and two flames shot out at the Dark Knight. The fire consumed the table he had been sitting at, but he knew Morgoz was already gone. The Dark Knight had disappeared just before the fire struck its target.

"Is it over?" asked Radclyffe.

"No it's only just begun!" Bern's words were ominous.

Epilogue: A Long Time Coming

They sat in horror as the scouts told them what they had seen. After the previous report they had been expecting the *Tree of Life* to be in danger, but they had no idea things had progressed so far. Palen looked around at the others and sighed.

The scouts had been sent out at dawn to gauge the situation before they attacked. It wasn't that he didn't believe what Eldred had told him, he just wanted to make sure. What he heard did nothing to ease his mind. He now knew he had made the right decision to liberate the *Tree of Life* instead of joining the Alliance. From the information he had received from the scouts. it didn't seem like the tree had much life left. Another day or two at best they guessed.

Kyrene looked at her husband. As the last two remaining members of the council it fell on them to decide what to do. There was no doubting they would need to attack, but it was how that mattered. From all accounts there were thousands, if not tens of thousands of orglin attacking the *Tree of Life*. It would take more than a frenzied attack to destroy them all. Even at their peak the Northern Elves would have struggled for numbers. With the current atrocities she doubted they would have five hundred strong warriors left.

The truth of the matter was that their numbers were closer to two hundred and that included those capable of wielding a spear. The task ahead of them was almost impossible, but not one they could turn away from. If the tree fell then life wouldn't be worth living.

"So what do we do now?" asked Torrin. As the magistrate he was second in command to the council members, but he still shouldn't have been privy to their discussions.

"We need to attack and we need to do it before nightfall. At night they will gain more power," Kyrene suggested.

"Their numbers will overwhelm us if we openly attack them," Palen pondered. "We need a different tactic." He knew that was true, but he had no idea how they were going to achieve their goal. It had been a long time since he had prepared tactics for battle.

"There is plenty of cover in the trees surrounding the orglin. We could sneak some archers high above them. The orglin will be too busy trying to destroy the *Tree of Life* to notice. The archers could thin their numbers down a little before they realise what is happening," Torrin suggested.

It seemed like a good enough idea, but Palen wasn't convinced. "That is taking a big risk. Not all the orglin are attacking the tree at once. There simply isn't enough room with their numbers. Surely those who are in the background will be looking for attacks. I'm not sure we can take that risk."

Kyrene placed a calming hand on Palen's. There was a chance what she was about to say might upset him and she wanted to be prepared.

"Everything we do is a risk. There is no easy path for us to take and many elves will die here today. All we can hope to achieve is to save of the *Tree of Life.*"

Palen knew she was right and he knew there was no other way. He had just hoped if he disagreed with Torrin's plan then someone would come up with a better one. There weren't enough council members left and tradition dictated that no one else was allowed into their meeting. Even having the magistrate present was bad enough.

"Very well. Gather as many archers as we have left and all the arrows. Let's hope we have enough to put a dent in their horde." Although his words were hopeful Palen knew that wasn't true. They did have a lot of arrows, but there were many more orglin.

Most of the elves were proficient with the bow, but only the masters were chosen for the task. They would need many elves on the ground to attack when the orglin realised what was happening. The master archers could continue to hit their targets when the battle was being fought on the forest floor.

"I think you should give them a speech before we leave. The elves have been despondent since we left our home and they've received little information," Torrin suggested.

Palen knew he was right, but he didn't know what to say. He could hardly tell them they were marching to their doom and he couldn't lie to them and tell them everything was going to be alright. The truth of the matter was that most of the elves would never be returning home and there was a good chance none of them would.

"My fellow elves!" Palen started when they were all gathered. "The *Tree of Life* is under attack by the Evil One's most evil of creatures. If the tree dies then all plant life will die along with it. Our home will be destroyed and all that we love. Now I will not lie to you. What is ahead of us is the hardest thing we will ever have to do, but also the most important. Stay strong in the heat of battle and we will be victorious."

His words brought a round of cheers from the elves. It wasn't a bad speech and it seemed to have roused them from their malaise. When he was finished Torrin took over. He needed to explain to everyone what the scouts had told them. They would need to be prepared for the chaos that awaited them. If he didn't warn them, there was a chance some of the elves would break and run with fear.

The archers left at a silent run when Torrin finished his speech. They would need to be in place well before the rest of the elves reached the battleground. Palen decided to lead those on foot. As much as everyone wanted him to remain, being one of the last two council members, he insisted that he march with the other warriors. If he was to send his elves to their doom then he would share their fate.

When they reached the forest surrounding the *Tree of Life* they couldn't believe the sight before them. The archers had successfully made their way into the trees and the ground was scattered with dead orglin. It seemed that they had been able to take them by surprise, but it was clear that the surprise was now over.

They were still too far away from the *Tree of Life* to see what was happening, but there was no time to think. After realising that they couldn't climb the trees to get the elves the orglin started setting them on fire. It was a tactic that no one had thought possible. Charred trees and bodies scattered the scenery, but all was not lost. There were still elves remaining in trees, trying their best to kill the orglin before the fire got to them.

"Our brethren are in trouble. Let's go and help them!" Palen yelled at the top of his voice. At first they had wanted to try a surprise attack, but with the change of circumstance he thought it best to try and divert their attention as quickly as possible. "Drive a path to the *Tree of Life*. From there we will be able to defend her."

They had hoped the archers would have been able to make their way closer to the tree, but that had not been the case. Once the warriors made their way through the orglin hoard the archers would need to follow. They were too far away to be able to help once they reached the *Tree of Life*.

The elves rushed the through the orglin. The skilled warriors were too much for the frenzied creatures. If they had been in an open field then the orglin would have overwhelmed them, but the elves were able to move in and out of the trees, negating their superior numbers. The archers shot down from above making sure none of the other elves were taken by surprise.

When they reached the *Tree of Life* the scene was more horrifying than they could ever have imagined. Around the base of the tree lay piles of burnt bodies. Orglin circled around the charred corpses hurling sticks of fire at the tree. There were many scars at the base of the tree where they had tried to scratch their way into it. It seemed that they had realised it was a fruitless exercise and the tree was able to strike back. Throwing fire seemed to have more of an impact. Black scars ran up the trunk with the lower branches burnt to a crisp. The tree still held its canopy, but it didn't look like it would survive for much longer.

"I can't believe it!" Torrin gasped in horror.

"You don't have to believe it, just attack!" Palen led his elves into the fray.

Their sole objective was to save the tree and if that meant putting their own lives at risk then that was what they had to do. The orglin surrounding the tree were not prepared for the attack and it didn't take long for the elves to dispose of them without casualty, but that was where their luck ran out. When the clearing was empty of live orglin those waiting in the forest rushed in to attack.

As the swarm was about to overwhelm the elves there was a shimmer in the air and suddenly everything froze. Neither the orglin nor the elves could move an inch. The only thing moving were the leaves on the *Tree of Life* even though there was no wind. A great fear ripped through the elves. The orglin were too stupid to feel any fear.

Suddenly a figure appeared through the trees. A glow surrounded the silhouette making it impossible to know if it was male or female, friend or foe. Those who were in a position to see, which included Palen, didn't know if it was a good sign or a bad one. They could only hope that the figure had come to help them.

Before anything happened the light slowly started to fade. When it was gone a man stood before them. He had a presence about him that was unmistakable, even more than his physical appearance. He had long dark hair which fell around his square set face and shoulders. He wore light brown trousers, but no shirt and nothing on his feet. There was something about the new arrival that calmed Palen. Hope filled his heart as the man walked through the crowd.

The man didn't seem to care about the orglin or the elves. He moved through them with as much disregard for both kinds. Carefully he picked his way through until he reached the tree itself. Then he looked up at the carnage the orglin had created.

"What have they done to you, Mother?" he asked, sorrow thick in his voice. Although Palen couldn't see him anymore he guessed there was a tear in his eye.

Slowly he placed his hands on the tree, just above two nasty scars. His hands started to glow and Palen could feel a sudden heat radiating from behind him. Although he had no idea what was happening he wanted nothing more than to be able to turn around to watch. Something wonderful was happening and he wanted to experience it completely.

The light from his hand enveloped the tree and as it did the *Tree of Life* suddenly began to heal. The charred wood and scratches slowly disappeared. The lower branches, that had either been burnt or ripped off, sprung back to life and were slowly filled with leaves.

"Tell me who has done this to you?" anger now filled his voice.

Palen wanted to speak out, but there was still nothing he could do to move. Like the others, all he could do was stare straight ahead and listen to what was happening. He envied the orglin that were facing the tree.

"Who did this to you?" his voice was now ice cold. There was a moment of silence before he spoke again. "So be it."

Palen felt a sudden surge of energy around him. The power was like nothing he had ever felt before. When the elves held rituals around the *Tree of Life* it emitted a great amount of energy, but nothing like this. Something was about to happen and he could only hope it was good.

Slowly at first, one by one, the orglin burst into flame. Although the creatures couldn't move they could feel the fire searing into their leathery flesh. Each orglin died in great pain, as was the want of the *Tree of Life*. None of the evil creatures would remain alive.

"What about these others?" Palen's heart sunk when he heard the words. "Are you sure? Very well then."

Slowly the elves were released from their invisible bonds. Palen stumbled forward as he continued his last motion. Without caring who was watching him he turned around to face the man.

"Please don't kill us!" was the first thing to come out.

"Don't worry Palen, I'm not here to kill you. I know I have been gone for a long time, but the tree has brought me up to date," his voice was calm as he walked towards him.

"I'm sorry, but this entire situation has me confused," as Palen spoke the other elves came to see what was happening. "Who are you?"

The question brought a round of laughter from the man. It was the first sign of glee he had shown. The noise filled the elves with happiness, although they didn't know why. All Palen's doubts of the man faded away and now he wasn't even sure if it was a man standing before him. He knew that he wasn't an elf, which made for another interesting question.

"I guess I shouldn't be surprised that you don't remember me, as I had forgotten you. It has been too long since I have been home," he spoke mysteriously. "This is my forest and I am Arawn."

Palen thought for a moment. He knew he had heard the name before, but he couldn't place where. After a couple of minutes passed, a look of knowing crossed his face. "You are a Wood Sprite?" he asked in awe.

"That is correct," Arawn smiled.

"Where have you been? It has been a long time since we have seen or heard of you and your kind," Palen continued.

"That is a long story and one for another time. Now that the evil little creatures are gone I think it is time for a celebration. I know the tree would love if you would dance and sing around her."

***

Jarwe sat on his horse a top a small hill and looked down at the sight before him. On the horizon was the city of Remidel, but that wasn't what caught his attention. It was the army assembled before them that gained his thoughts. There had been no word from the city that they were preparing for attack. Even the scouts had noted nothing of the soldier's movements. The night before there had been nothing in the field below them, now there was a full army ready for battle.

Another thing that baffled Jarwe was the location. The Remidian army was too far away from the safety of the city walls. Any advantage the archers would have had was gone.

"What do you think?" Sorrell asked after he rode up next to him.

"I don't know what to think. It doesn't make any sense. If the Dark Knight knew we were coming then why wouldn't he fortify behind his walls?" Jarwe replied.

They had all thought the same thing when they saw the army at first light. They had all been prepared to march the last few leagues to the city when they were met with the scene before them. The opposing army made no move to advance and it seemed as though they were happy with their position.

"It doesn't make any sense, but then again it didn't make any sense when Za'aroz sent his soldiers out to fight us in Castalia. They don't care if they lose soldiers. All they care about is destruction and that is what this will bring," Sorrell explained.

The two sat alone on the hill. The rest of the command group were rallying the soldiers for battle. As much as no one wanted to fight the Remidian army it seemed as though they wouldn't have a choice. If there was going to be a battle then they needed to be ready. Either way they were not going to make the first move. Jarwe had commanded that they wait. He had hoped they would have sent an emissary, but that had not been the case.

"If that was the case then I'm sure we would have been thick in battle by now," Jarwe paused as a thought entered his mind. "No, there is something else. Something isn't right," he mused.

Sorrell didn't like what he was hearing, but he knew it was true. If he was going to lead an army outside the safety of a city's walls then he would want to attack as soon as possible. With the cover of night they could have got the jump on the Alliance. Something was definitely wrong.

"Should we try and entreat with them?" Sorrell finally asked.

"I don't think that would prove anything. If they wanted to speak with us then they would have sent someone already. It almost seems like they are waiting for something."

Sorrell didn't think they were waiting for the Alliance to attack. They outnumbered the Remidian army by at least ten to one, at least that's what Sorrell estimated. As much as he didn't think the Dark Knight cared how many of his men got slaughtered he didn't think it was a suicide mission. There would be more dead bodies if the Alliance had to siege the capital. There had to be another reason why they were assembled where they were.

"What should we tell the troops? It won't be long before they are ready to march," Sorrell asked.

"Bring the rest of the command group here," Jarwe seemed to ignore the question. "And bring the Council of Wizards."

Sorrell stopped when he heard the mention of the wizards. They had tried to avoid them as much as possible. It seemed that Bern didn't trust them and they had done nothing to prove him wrong. Although he didn't know what Jarwe had in mind, he didn't think the wizards were right choice.

"That's right," Jarwe didn't have to turn around to know that Sorrell had stopped. "It's time we took advantage of their knowledge. We have nothing to fear from them."

"I know, but..."

"There are no buts, we need the wizards!" Jarwe snapped.

There was something strange in his voice. Ever since Bern had left there had been a change in the general. He was more pensive than before and constantly had a concerned expression on his face. Although it was annoying, Sorrell was just happy that he hadn't slipped back into the malaise that had taken him in Avalon.

Jarwe remained where he was until Sorrell returned with the others. As he stared out over the field there was no further movement from the opposing army. Jarwe was beginning to wonder if there was in fact an army before them. That was the main reason he wanted the wizards summoned. Only they would be able to tell if it was just a magic trick.

It was midday by the time Sorrell returned with all the commanders and the council. It had taken a lot longer than Jarwe had hoped. The army would be more than ready to attack and they would have to make a decision soon.

"What is this all about?" Brielle did not sound impressed at being summoned in such a manner.

"You have been brought from your home to help and it's about time you started," the other commanders were shocked to hear such stern words. No one had spoken to the wizards in such a manner since Bern had left and Jarwe was in no mood to deal with their petty mannerisms.

"I think you forget who you are speaking with," Drake spoke in defence of Brielle. "You will..."

"I forget nothing," Jarwe spoke between clenched teeth. "You forget who I am. I am the general of this army, at least until General Bern returns. You too are now part of the army and you will listen to my command."

His words brought a number of coughs and grunts, but it was Gwydion who spoke. "Of course general. It has been a long journey and some of us miss the comforts of our island." He didn't look at anyone in particular. "What is it you need of us?"

"The army before us. Is it real or is it just a magic trick?" Jarwe came straight to the point.

The wizards looked out at the army, as if seeing them for the first time. No one had even thought the army could be a ruse.

"There is definitely no magic out there. That is indeed the Remidian army."

One by one the other wizards confirmed what Althea said. That was not the answer Jarwe had been looking for. If it had been magic then it would have made sense, but now he would need advice from the other commanders as to their best course of action. Without doubt he wished that Bern was back, or more the entity that always seemed to know what they should do.

"So their army just sits there, waiting for something," Jarwe mused.

"Maybe that is a good thing," Corporal Horace spoke. "The rest of the Castalial army has yet to join our rear. This will give us time for them to catch up."

That was something that also bothered Jarwe. The Castalial soldiers should have caught up with the Alliance two days ago. They had been instructed to march hard whilst the Alliance was taking their time. Each time they had sent word, the response had been nothing out of the ordinary.

"That isn't going to help us," Jarwe replied. "We already have more soldiers than the Remidian army. If we attack it will be a bloodbath."

"Then why has the Dark Knight assembled them before us. It would make more sense for him to defend behind the walls of Remidel," Wojtek voiced the obvious. "There has to be another reason why they are here."

"That is why I've asked you all to join me. Does anyone have any idea what is happening?"

"I would say it's a trap," Orric, the eldest of the elves, spoke slowly. "What sort of trap though, I cannot say."

"We are going around in circles," Wojtek blurted and Sorrell could have cursed at his advisor. "This is getting us nowhere. Our soldiers are prepared for battle. We need to make a decision."

"Wojtek is right," Jarwe conceded. "If the Dark Knight doesn't want us to attack then that is exactly what we must do." Jarwe could hardly believe the words as they came out of his mouth. Before him were his countrymen. He would know a lot of the soldiers and he was about to order their deaths. Some would even have been his friends, a long time ago. "Have the soldiers assemble below this hill. We will march on the army within the hour."

There was a moment of silence as everyone thought on his words.

"Are you sure this is a good idea?" Horace asked.

"Of course I don't think it's a good idea, but it's the only idea we have. If we wait then we are playing into the Dark Knight's hands. We can't march around them and we can't just leave. The last thing we want is a hostile army to our rear. All that's left is attack." As much as Jarwe had hoped someone would come up with a better plan he knew it wasn't going to happen.

"Very well general," Sorrell said. "Let's get this army on the march."

Everyone left the hill except for Jarwe. He wanted to remain behind and keep an eye on the opposing army. There was something mesmerising about the soldiers lined up before him. He felt if he was to leave then something bad would happen. He knew it was silly, but he couldn't brush it aside. The rest of the command group was more than capable of getting the Alliance ready for battle.

It wasn't long before Jarwe could hear the clang of armour as the soldiers started to march up the hill behind him. As much as he wanted to turn around he still could not take his eyes from the Remidian army. Even as the soldiers started to make their way past him his eyes didn't move. It wasn't until the rest of the command group returned did he turn his attention away.

"It's not too late to change your mind," Sorrell offered.

"I wish that was the case."

As the swarm of soldiers made their way over the hill, a horn blast could be heard. A second, and louder blast, came in response. The sounds sent a shiver down Jarwe's spine. He didn't know what it meant, but he knew it couldn't be good. The soldiers continued on, although some looked up at their commanders to see if there had been any change. They all knew better than to linger and kept moving.

"What is that all about?" Jarwe asked as he moved his horse around.

"I think we're about to find out," Sorrell said as a rider approached.

The scout was dressed in a leather tunic, not armour like the rest of the army. His horse had a lather of sweat and it was clear that he had ridden hard. It seemed the horn blast was not good news.

"General!" the soldier saluted when he arrived.

"Spit it out man," Jarwe snapped when he didn't continue.

"We are under attack at the rear of our camp!" He burst out.

"What? How can that be? We've had no word of soldier's movements." Jarwe looked back over his shoulder. "The Dark Knight doesn't have enough soldiers to make a decent attack."

"It's not soldiers," the scout didn't wait. "It's orglin!"

The words took everyone by shock. Finally things were starting to make sense. No one had thought there would be orglin nearby and it seemed that's exactly what the Dark Knight was counting on. Sorrell was the first to recover.

"How many are there? Do we need to turn these soldiers around?"

"I don't know. As soon as we were attacked I was sent to give you the message. That's all I know."

"Halt!" Jarwe cried at the top of his voice. The command penetrated the field and the soldiers stopped their march. "Where are our horsemen and archers?" Jarwe looked around, but could only see infantry.

"We were not prepared for battle when we set camp last night. The horses are picketed in the middle and I'm not entirely sure where the archers are," the soldier had lost all his confidence.

"Damn!" Jarwe swore. "We've certainly been caught short."

"What do you want to do with the soldiers?" Sorrell asked.

"The main threat is to the rear. Have half the horseman and archers go defend it, and have the rest brought up here. If there is an attack we want every advantage we can get," Jarwe ordered.

Before anyone could move to give the commands there was a great yell from the field below. That was the only warning they received as the Remidian army moved into action. The Alliance soldiers didn't know what to do. It was not what they expected and they needed orders from their leaders.

"Charge!" Sorrell was the first to react.

Hearing the command forced the soldiers into action. Given a choice they would have chosen a different tact, but they had been trained to follow orders and that's what they would do. They had no idea what was happening at the rear.

Jarwe couldn't believe he had walked straight into a trap. They were fighting a battle on two fronts and that was never a good sign. He was sure the Dark Knight didn't care about the deaths on either side of the battlefield. For a moment Jarwe thought that it might be the final battle that was supposed to take place in Avalon, but he quickly put that thought out of his mind. The battle before him had to be won and he was the general.

"See that not too many die here today," Jarwe commanded Sorrell. "I'm going to the other side of the battle."

"Are you sure that's a good idea?" Sorrell asked as Jarwe rode away.

"There are orglin to be killed!" Jarwe called back as he kicked his horse to a gallop, as best he could through the moving soldiers.

***

The sky was red and lightning flashed in the distance. The dark clouds looked as though they carried rain, but if they burst it was brimstone that would rain down. The desolate land was a fitting backdrop for what lay before him.

A beast sat on a throne, on a ledge, a hundred feet up the side of the largest mountain in the Northern Wasteland. His torso was thick with muscles and covered with a purple and red leathery skin. Black pants covered its legs which were similar in design. Its head was large and pointed with two spiral horns on either side. Although it had been the site of his prison, the wasteland seemed more like his home than Nostiria. In a different time and place Nyrra could have been happy to remain, but it was neither the time nor the place. The time for the final battle was drawing near and this time he would be victorious.

Below him gathered a crowd of evil creatures. This was his true army, not the pitiful creatures called the orglin. They were just a distraction to his enemy. They were stupid creatures, but they were vicious and easy to control. They would fight until they were dead and never surrender. That was their role and he had to admit they played it well.

He smiled as he looked at all the monsters assembled before him. There were great trolls, standing eight feet tall, some with tusks and some without. Their arms were as thick as small tree trunks and their legs were even thicker. Tufts of hair spotted their bodies in no particular order. They could easily rip a man's head off, but the problem was that they would try and eat the body instead of moving onto their next victim. They were inevitably hard to control in battle, and even in peace. Normally they were solitary creatures and it took a lot of power to bring them all together. When the frenzy came over them, nothing could sate their anger but death itself.

Next he saw his band of ogres, much taller than the trolls standing an average of ten feet, but much fewer in numbers. Their bodies were completely void of hair and their muscles grew in strange clumps. They were inherently smarter than the trolls and easier to control. The ogres looked least at home in the group. Like trolls they liked to live alone or in pairs. They didn't like the clutter of groups and they looked very nervous. It was Nyrra's promise of lands for their very own kind that kept them in check, not his immense power.

The minotaurs made him smile. They had the bodies of mighty brown bears and the head of a bull. They were simple but powerful creatures. Unlike the other two creatures the minotaurs were not born evil. They were peaceful and spent their lives deep in the mountains. It was the dwarves who gave them their fearful reputation as many of them were taken in the depths of the mountains, although it was only their nature to feed. It was their weakness of mind that made it easy for Nyrra to twist their gentle spirits and add them to his army of evil.

There were many other creatures in the valley below him, stretching out as far as he could see. It was almost time for them to start moving. There was no time for him to make a run for the City of Night, he would have to settle for the ordained battleground of Avalon. Deep down he knew there could be no other place.

Nyrra stood from his throne and walked to the end of the ledge so all below could see him. He spoke in a voice that echoed throughout the crowd. His words were in a language long forgotten to the Seven Kingdoms, but even those creatures who only communicated in grunts and moans could understand him.

"The time is neigh. We move on the weak creatures that would enslave you or wipe you out altogether. They imprisoned us in this wasteland, but now it is time to make their world a wasteland." A roar came over the crowd. "It is time for us to destroy them all. We will take their land for our own and they will suffer for eternity."

Nyrra sat back down and basked in the glory of the frenzy he had caused. There would be some death and that would make it all the more glorious. There were plenty of creatures before him and there were still more to come. The stupid creatures called men and elves, wizards and dwarves, would have no idea what hit them. There was no way they could be prepared for what was coming. His servants had successfully kept them busy and with a little luck had depleted their numbers.

He smiled at the thought of his servants. 'Dark Knights', that's what they liked to be called, or 'The Chosen'. They were stupid titles for those who were just above worms in comparison to the Great Lord. It was something the enemy wouldn't be expecting. They had been so busy trying to kill them that they didn't think for a moment that was exactly what he wanted.

It was finally time. When there was only one of the seven left he could start bringing them back. It was in the prophecy all along, he had just not been able to decipher it. There was also something else, something much more important. It was the key to everything and it had been missing for too long.

Slowly Nyrra placed his hand in his trouser pocket and pulled something out. It had been too long since he had pushed it aside. He couldn't go more than an hour without touching it. It felt warm and comfortable in his hand. He had almost forgotten the pure elation he felt.

He held it tight for a full minute before he slowly relaxed his fingers, closing his eyes as he did. He almost couldn't bring himself to look upon its beauty. From his palm a deep red glowed, even deeper than the red around him. The Ruby Stone was finally back in his possession. When he had made it disappear from the Cursed One on *Crenallous* he wasn't sure if he would ever see it again. Now that last piece had fallen into the puzzle.

For a full hour he sat and watched the stone whilst the creatures raged below him. Finally he put the stone back in his pocket and stood from his throne. The time had come. It was time he unleashed his army of horror on the Seven Kingdoms.

www.ingramcontent.com/pod-product-compliance
Lightning Source LLC
Chambersburg PA
CBHW030750030726
47497CB00001B/217